"Christ's

Holy

Square"

By

David T Craggs

 **New Generation Publishing**

Christ's Holy Square

When Leonardo da Vinci painted his *Last Supper* he did not know that on the table in front of Jesus Christ was a shallow wooden tray, not quite square in shape and measuring about the span of a hand across. Laid out in the tray in a special pattern were thirteen pieces of pot, varying in both colour and shape, and each one with a Greek letter engraved into it. During the proceedings Jesus gave out the pieces to his disciples, keeping one for himself. Over the next half century the pieces travelled far and wide with their owners, then became lost to the world.

A chance finding of a Dead Sea Scroll almost two thousand years later revealed an account of the Last Supper. It also revealed that if mankind did not 'mend its ways' God would destroy the Earth and all that lived upon it. But he did give mankind a get-out.

All thirteen pieces of pot had first to be located then re-assembled in their origin positions within a wooden square by the leaders of the thirteen most powerful nations in the World to show their commitment to making the world a better place.

The task of locating the pieces fell to a professor of archaeology at an English University. Once done 'Christ's Holy Square', as he called it, was re-assembled at the UN. But that wasn't the end of the story for mankind did not keep its promise. God was about to wreak his revenge when he discovered a threat from far beyond the Sun's boundaries.

Dear Reader

Most books that people read either have a narrator who tells the story throughout the book, or a principal character who does so. 'Christ's Holy Square' is different. Its characters are the narrators, telling their own parts of the story as they occur.

The Author

The Narrators

The Author
Marcus Tullius - a cavalry officer in the Roman Army
Professor Peter Robertshaw - Head of Archaeology at South
Riding University, Doncaster,
England
David Rogers - a teacher friend of Peter Robertshaw
Jesus Nazarene - the Son of God
Chuck Oldfield - security guard, United Nations Headquarters, New York
Cecil Gee - reporter, New York Herald
Milad Mansouri - cabbie, New York City
Henrietta Percival - pathologist at Bethesda Hospital, New York City
God

***

'Christ's Holy Square'
Prologue

Narrator – the Author
66AD

Maximus, the impressive white stallion of Marcus Tullius, a cavalry officer in the army of the glorious Roman Empire, suddenly stopped dead in his tracks, refusing to move one step further. He instinctively knew that something wasn't quite right, but didn't know what.

Marcus first looked around him, worried that someone hidden in the long grass was about to attack him. A Roman soldier occupying someone's precious land was always a target. But the area as far as the eye could see was clear.

Marcus looked down. Was the ground, covered with small stones, making the footing of Maximus uncertain? Because of the long grass it was impossible to see if that was the problem. Marcus urged him to move forward, squeezing his legs against the horse's sides. Reluctantly Maximus did so, trusting his master's judgement.

Then, without the slightest warning, the ground collapsed underneath both horse and rider, revealing what looked like a bog. As Maximus kicked out his front legs, searching for some sort of purchase, his whole body moved forward again. His rear legs were now no longer on solid ground, and they also kicked out only making matters worse.

Maximus was now sinking fast, with Marcus still in the saddle. As the water level rose above the horse's mouth and nose, making it impossible for him to breathe, Marcus realised that there was nothing he could do to help his trusty steed. He struggled to free his feet from the stirrups, but found that his boot straps were somehow entangled in them.

Maximus's whole body was now under water and the downward suction formed by his huge body was dragging Marcus down with it. His heavy military attire only made his predicament worse. The water was soon up to his mouth, then over his nose. As he held his last breath his eyes tried to pierce the black water. He started to see flashing lights and realised that his whole body was beginning to shut down. He was in the process of dying.

Finally his whole life seemed to flash across his closed eyes in an instant. Then blackness…Permanent blackness.

Chapter One

Narrator – Marcus Tullius, a cavalry officer in the Roman Army
64AD

My name is Marcus Tullius, the Officer-in-Charge of the Cavalry Division in the Roman garrison town of Danum, sitting on the banks of the River Don, one of northern Britannia's great rivers. It is my role to start off the story of 'Christ's Holy Square'. This part will end with my unfortunate and untimely death by drowning whilst out on patrol with my horse, Maximus. As a Roman soldier I always wanted to die in battle, but it was not to be. What I now know is that my death was to play an important, indeed essential, part in God's great plan to save the World he'd created from total destruction.

I remember very little about my childhood other than that I was born and raised on a farm just outside the village of Grotto San Stefano, to the north of Roma, the capital of Italia. I now know that the year of my birth was 16 Anno Domini, although at the time my family and I did not know that. Future happenings that I will describe later determined that year.

When I was old enough I was expected to pull my weight on the farm. When I could barely walk I helped my elder brother, Agricula, to collect the eggs from the hen coupes. At six years I was milking cows and goats, and by the age of twelve I was assisting my father in the ploughing of our small fields using our faithful donkey Julia. The work was hard, but I'd been brought up to think that this was to be my role in life. I soon developed other ideas, however.

The farm on which I'd been raised lay close to the road from Roma to the north, and almost daily I saw soldiers moving in that direction. Although uneducated and unable to read I knew through word-of-mouth that Roma was at the centre of a huge Empire covering, as I thought all the World. This Empire was expanding day by day and this was the reason why so many soldiers were required.

As I watched the soldiers passing close by our farm I realised that a life working the land was not for me. I'd seen my father work his fingers to the bone for little reward. Agricula was following suit and seemed happy to do so, but such a life was definitely not what I envisaged for myself. Being a soldier seemed to me to be a worthy career. Although I say it myself, I was a bright lad and felt that I would be able to work my way up the ranks. But the biggest attraction of all was the opportunity I would get to travel, maybe to the end of the known world, where ever that was. Word-of-mouth couldn't of course tell me that, other than that it was a very long way away.

I finally made my decision when I saw a soldier of obviously high rank leading his men along the road. He was mounted on the biggest horse I'd ever seen, white in colour and totally under the soldier's control. I said to myself there and then - that's going to be me in a few years' time.

And so at the age of eighteen I left my home to join the army. My parents wished me well, feeling proud that their son was going to serve the 'Empire'. My brother thought me quite mad, pointing out that soldiers were frequently killed because they were fighting barbarians who fought like animals. He had already lost two friends, brothers, who'd lived on a farm up the road, and who had joined up. They'd been fighting in a god forsaken place called Gallia, a long distance away to the north, where it snowed throughout the winter. They'd been ambushed while patrolling a gorge, the barbarians showering stones on them from the cliff tops. As they lay dying their assailants moved in and castrated them - their way of showing that they could remove the great Roman soldiers' manhood. News eventually filtered back to the brothers' parents of their fates, but in the case of the mother, not the gruesome way they had taken their last breath.

As I left my home my brother couldn't resist shouting to me: "Beware the barbarians, Marcus…And watch your bollocks." Fortunately both my parents were out of ear shot, tending to the sheep at the end of the paddock.

From a camp just outside Roma, where we did our initial training, we were quickly moved south to what I now know to be Sicilia, a large island surrounded by a sea known as Mare Internum. The long walk south was gruelling and to some extent took the glamour out of being a soldier. My legs had ached and my feet had bled, the result of ill fitting sandals.

During further training in Sicilia we were informed of our first mission abroad, not to that god forsaken place called Gallia where they did unmentionable things to your 'unmentionables'. We were going by ship to a place called Palestina, where we were told trouble was brewing.

Our task would be to sort it out, whatever that meant.

Before making the crossing to the island of Sicilia I had never seen the sea before. This sea, I was informed, surrounded most of Italia, with just a bit of the country to the extreme north not having a coast line. As the blue sea sparkled in the bright sunlight we were given time off to relax and cool off in the warm waters. Much to my surprise the sea tasted salty, something I'd never even thought of and certainly couldn't explain. Also much to my surprise, few of my comrades could swim, not apparently ever having had the opportunity to learn. I'd been lucky. Close to our farm was a large lake called Lago di Vico that all the youngsters in the area played in throughout the hot summer months. My brother Agricula was an excellent swimmer. And it wasn't long before he had me in the deeper water, paddling my little heart out in order to keep afloat. Needless to say, in a matter of weeks I'd become almost as good a swimmer as he.

Sicilia was a training post in preparation for the conflicts to come. Here we fought each other incessantly with swords, often drawing blood. We had to be able to attack, but also be able to defend ourselves, often when outnumbered. This, we were told, was where the incessant training would come in. If you could draw the blood of a comrade, think how easier it would be when faced with an enemy.

Spear throwing came next. We had to be able to engage the enemy from a distance. This was done by showering them with lethal spears, raining from the sky. I, although I say it myself, was particularly good at throwing a spear. From an early age we'd learned how to make them from a straight branch cut from a willow tree. The skill was then to be able to launch them true so that they always flew point first and hit their target that way. There was of course a very good reason for acquiring the skill. Wolves, wild cats and boar roamed the edges of our farmland where we kept our cows, sheep and goats. The spear was our only defence against them.

The day finally came when we left our homeland for distant shores. We boarded the ship and set sail, being at the same time informed that we would be calling at another large island, further east - that of Cyprus. Evidently trouble was always brewing there. We were just calling in to show our faces in order to impress on those Cypriots just who was boss.

The journey from the Sicilian port of Syracusae to Paphos in Cyprus took us sixteen days, but every single minute was horrendous. The sea was mountainous, and combined with the forces of a strong westerly wind, almost capsized us on several occasions. But worst of all I discovered, much to my cost, that I was prone to seasickness - that most horrible of ailments when all you feel like doing is crawl into a dark corner and slowly die. It didn't make me feel any better to discover that most of my comrades were equally suffering.

At long last we landed at the port of Paphos, on the island's south west corner. Early impressions were that it wasn't a particularly attractive port, both in its shabby appearance and the way those Cypriots who were working on the quayside stared at us, hatred in their eyes - better not be caught alone in some dark alley. It was not difficult to imagine your fate if they managed to get hold of you...Maybe they were also in the habit of removing the manhood of Roman soldiers. No, I decided that I definitely did not like Paphos.

Fortunately for all of us our stay in Cyprus was short. The situation in Palestina was rapidly deteriorating and there was talk of some sort of uprising, with some man professing that he was King of the Jews. During Roman occupation there could be no place for such a person. It would be our job to stamp down hard on such subversive talk, and if need be sort out this so-called King of the Jews once and for all.

Our journey, the relatively short distance to the port of Caesarea, on the coast of Palestina, taking just over two days, could not have been more different from our earlier one. The sea was calm, just like our lake at home, and a gentle breeze took our ship along with it at a leisurely pace. On reaching the port of Caesarea, an attractive one compared with Paphos, we found the locals by comparison friendly and willing to help us unload our ship. Within a matter of hours we were encamped just outside the port in the Roman Legion Headquarters of Judea, awaiting further instructions. This was the first time we'd seen a countryside that was almost totally barren, with only small patches of vegetation. This was so different to the countryside of Italia, with its vast green fields and forests. Even Cyprus was green and its mountains covered in trees. We were now in a different world, and those who had served on the land across the Mare Internum to the south had spoken of sand stretching as far as the eye could see, and beyond. How did one possibly survive in such conditions? And why would anyone want to rule over such land?

Those instructions came two days later. We were instructed to march south as quickly as we could, to the towns beside a stretch of water known as the Sea of Galilee. We were told that the area was a centre of potential trouble, but little more about it, other than it was all being stirred up by one man. Was he a great warrior, a good general, a leader of men? Well, according to reports he definitely wasn't the first two, but definitely was the third. In fact as he walked along, thousands followed him. Why, we soldiers couldn't understand.

We were told that we'd nothing to fear from this man. He was only a carpenter, but had taught himself to read, and could communicate, not only in Hebrew, but also in Greek and Latin. Only scholars were supposed to be able to do that, not workers in wood. I could recognise Greek words but had no idea of their meaning, and I could barely read Latin. This was something I had to master if I intended to move through the ranks. This man-of-the-people never carried a sword or spear and, we were told, spoke incessantly about loving one's neighbour and laying one's life down for a friend.

This special man apparently had several names – The Nazarene, Jesus, The Christ, The Son of God, the Son of Man, The Messiah, King of the Jews. And it was this last name or title that worried the leaders of the Roman Occupying Force. Even some holy Jewish men, who we were told were called Pharisees and Sadducees hated the man for what he apparently stood for. But we were told not to trust them. Evidently they'd betray their own grandmothers for a piece of silver. I quickly formed my own opinion on this group of hypocrites. Envy was, we were told, one of the seven deadly sins, but who would not be envious of a man who could command the attention of thousands when you yourself found it difficult to get a handful of people to listen to you? Yes…the Pharisees and Sadducees were envious of this Jesus character.

So, what was the problem with this rather special man? Well, it appeared that our Roman masters saw him as a threat to stability in the country. If he professed to be The King of the Jews, would this be a rallying call to take up arms and rebel against the occupying force? What if the huge crowds that followed him suddenly appeared one day with swords, spears and shields, all secretly made by artisans in the towns' numerous cellars? Then the Romans would have a problem. And that was the reason why we were heading south to prevent such a problem developing.

I found the various small towns in the area of Galilee fascinating places. To the casual observer, as we raw soldiers were, life appeared to go on in a normal civilised way. People went about their business unhindered by us, unless an incident took place where we had to act, theft being a common crime, especially from we Romans. The markets were always full of both people and produce, the people buying their requirements from the traders, farmers and fishermen. Even the people were freely allowed to worship their God in special buildings called temples, again unhindered by we Romans who didn't believe in that sort of thing. The towns were indeed very strange places, but friendly. As members of the occupying force, we were more than happy to patrol them.

It wasn't long before we heard on the grapevine, a system where a Jewish informer fed us information for a couple of pieces of silver, that this man known as Jesus was going to address a gathering of people by the shores of the Sea of Galilee. Our commanding officer instructed us to pair up and mingle with the throng, not only to show a military presence, ready to act if things got out of hand, but also try to understand what was behind Jesus's message to the people. Was it subversive, a threat to the Empire, or simply a code for a better way for people to live their lives?

One immediate problem was the language barrier. The local people spoke Hebrew, we obviously only spoke Latin, but were already picking up the odd word of the local tongue. To get round this we recruited interpreters, and there were plenty available to do the job for a few pieces of silver. At first the locals didn't like the idea, looking upon the interpreters as traitors who were helping the occupying force. But soon they realised that when trouble flared up, as it sometimes did, and neither soldiers nor locals could communicate, the situation got nasty, often leading to local people being arrested, and very occasionally even killed. The interpreters were essential in such situations, and for this reason they were tolerated.

I had been paired up with a colleague called Maximus, or Max as he was known to all of us. Our interpreter, only a bit of a lad, but very good, was called Jacob. He had worked on a market stall, selling fruit and vegetables. His stall had been a popular one with the Romans because of his ability to speak their language.

Soon we found a large gathering of people on a piece of high ground overlooking the Sea of Galilee. This man called Jesus was already addressing the gathering, numbering many hundreds of people.

It wasn't long before they were eating out of his hand, soaking up his words like a sponge. He spoke, using stories that involved real people so that those listening could place themselves in their position. And that included us too, for Max and I were sitting amongst the people, listening intently to Jacob, as he rattled off what Jesus was saying, but in Latin. At first the people around us were suspicious of our presence, glancing at us out of the corner of their eyes. If we smiled at them they simply lowered their eyes and stared at the ground. If they spoke, it was in whispers, with minimum mouth movement, frightened that Jacob could lip read what they were saying.

Then, completely unexpected, Jesus shouted across, and in Latin too: "Good to see our Roman friends are with us today…Welcome, both of you…How do you call yourselves?"

This really put us on the spot. No one had ever told us whether or not we should reveal our names to the enemy, if indeed Jesus was our 'enemy'. But somehow it didn't matter. I yelled out: "Marcus." My colleague shouted with equal enthusiasm: "Maximus."

"Welcome Marcus…Maximus to our gathering…And to you too, Jacob…Make sure you translate my words correctly."

As if a magic wand had been waved, those around us lifted their heads and smiled. Some even shouted: "Welcome Marcus…Welcome Maximus," mimicking Jesus. Soon Jacob was picking up the conversations around us, with people speculating what Jesus would say or do next. The word 'miracle' was frequently mentioned, but not having heard the word before, we had no idea what it meant. And although Jacob had heard the word before he did not know its true meaning.

The closest followers of Jesus were called disciples. Jacob informed us that he'd heard that there were twelve of them, who followed Jesus wherever he went. They were also the link between their master and the people, as was shown by what they did next.

Sitting in front of Jesus were several people who appeared to be in some way disabled. The disciples asked for all of them to be moved closer to their master. All did so, helped by others who appeared to be looking after them. Some had to be led - obviously blind. Some had people shouting loudly at them. Were they deaf? Were they dumb? There were also several lame people, some walking with crutches, others having to be carried. All were placed before Jesus.

Everybody waited in anticipation. Most had heard that Jesus had on occasions healed the sick - even on one occasion bringing a child back from the dead. What would he do today?

The multitude of observers hadn't long to wait. Jesus rose from his sitting position and moved amongst the group of sick people, placing his hands on their heads, closing his eyes and saying a prayer.

10

Max and I looked on, first with interest, then with utter amazement, as we saw the blind take their first independent steps, obviously able to see, at least something. The helpers of the deaf stopped shouting at them, and the dumb started to speak to each other. But what amazed us the most was the way the lame threw away their crutches and started walking, then running, even jumping up and down in obvious excitement. Had it all been one big trick? Had these people been specially recruited to act as if they'd been in some way physically disabled? At first this passed through our minds, but when those around us started to rejoice, saying that they'd known the healed people for many years, some of the blind and deaf having been that way since birth, and some of the lame having had accidents many years ago, we realised that there had been no trickery. Miracles had definitely taken place.

Max and I felt like rejoicing with the rest of the multitude of people, but we had to be careful. It was considered an act of treason if a Roman soldier supported any member of the 'enemy', and this Jesus man was considered a member of the enemy by the occupying force. Even the high priests, Pharisees and Sadducees, hated him and would do anything in their power to get rid of him. Some soldiers had already been seduced by his charisma and had paid the penalty for it…that penalty being their removal back to Caesaria and imprisonment there.

During the following weeks Max and I, accompanied by Jacob, followed Jesus around, as instructed to do so by our superior officer. We were therefore in our military uniforms. Jesus always made a point of acknowledging our presence, but this time only with the slightest of nods.

On one such occasion, again having picked up the information on the grapevine, we found him in an area just north of the Sea of Galilee, where he was addressing the largest crowd we'd seen so far. After speaking for several hours to them he realised that they would be hungry, some having travelled from distant towns and villages in order to see and hear him.

At that point two small children were brought to him by his disciples and, thinking he would be hungry, they presented him with what looked like food - loaves of bread and fish. Jesus first placed his hands on their heads and blessed them. He then looked up and appeared to pray. The people sitting in front of us stood up in anticipation and to get a better view. Past experience told them that when Jesus lifted his head to the heavens and prayed, 'strange' things happened. For several seconds we were unable to see what was going on.

Then Jesus shouted to the assembled mass: "Please be seated and I will feed you…There is enough for everybody."

The people did as he commanded, such was his charisma. Soon several children gathered round him and appeared to collect something from the disciples. They then moved outwards, distributing what they'd collected. To everybody's amazement it was food - bread and fish. One of the children, not a bit afraid of two military men in Roman uniforms, came across and presented the two of us plus Jacob with chunks of newly baked bread and small pieces of boneless fish. Not having eaten since early morning, we soon consumed the food…and good it tasted too.

That word 'miracle' was soon being whispered amongst the mass of followers. I had already formed my own opinion as to what had happened. Nevertheless I, with Jacob's help, asked a young woman who was sitting close by. She cautiously replied, aware that those around were watching and listening: "It was a miracle…He took five loaves and two fishes from the children and turned them into enough food to feed us all…You have witnessed this yourselves."

Both Max and I had seen various types of magic shows as we'd moved around the country. Travelling entertainers were common place in military camps and the tricks they played on we soldiers were only too familiar to us…gold coins being produced from behind the ears of members of the audience; young girls climbing up ropes and vanishing; even lions in cages disappearing, then reappearing. All those who saw such acts knew that there was some form of trickery taking place, but not how the tricks were done. But that didn't matter. What they'd seen had been entertaining, enjoyable…and that's all that did matter.

But where was the trickery here? How could five loaves and two fishes be multiplied hundreds, maybe even thousands of times in order to feed a multitude of people? I had my own explanation…Large amounts of bread and fish had earlier been brought in and somehow hidden from view, ready to be distributed later. But wouldn't someone have seen this and spread the word around?

Or had it been a miracle after all…Some sort of act by the Son of a God that Max and I refused to accept the existence of? At that precise moment we had no idea. But what we did realise was that something very strange was taking place within our minds. We were slowly but surely being converted, but to what, we also had no idea.

In order not to reveal the slow conversion that was taking place within us, Max and I accompanied by Jacob, started to join the multitudes following Jesus, but in garments that enabled us to mix, unnoticed, with his followers. We even managed to get close to him, mingling with his disciples. Jesus always spotted us and could have greeted us by name, but in his wisdom decided not to. He, only too aware of the risk we were taking, simply nodded across, showing his recognition of us.

At one such gathering we heard that something referred to as the 'pass-over' was approaching, and would be celebrated. Being a word we'd never heard before I decided to ask the young woman who was seated on the ground a short distance away from us: "Woman...What is the Passover?"

She at first looked at us suspiciously. Surely all Jews knew about the Passover. Nevertheless she explained: "Many years ago the children of Israel were imprisoned in Egypt and Pharaoh would not let them go...The Lord therefore hit the Egyptian people with many plagues."

Her explanation so far, puzzled me: "Why were only the children imprisoned?...And what do you mean by plagues?"

She smiled: "All the people were called children because that's how our Lord referred to them... Now let me describe the plagues to you...Each one was meant to persuade Pharaoh to release our people, but he refused time and again...First the rods of all Pharaoh's wisemen and sourcerers were turned into serpents...The second was to turn the rivers, streams and lakes into blood, killing all the fish...The third was a plague of frogs...The fourth plague killed the Egyptians' cattle...The fifth rained hail of such intensity that animals and men in the fields were killed...The sixth was a plague of locusts...In the seventh, darkness covered Egypt for three days, and during this time Pharaoh was finally persuade to let our people go because the Lord killed the first born of the Egyptian men and their animals...Even then, when our people reached the Red Sea on their way to the Promised Land, and Moses, with the help of our Lord, parted the waves to allow them to cross to the other side, Pharaoh ordered his horsemen and chariots to chase after them and bring them back...This was against the Lord's will and he released the waves after our people had crossed, drowning the Egyptian soldiers...That's how our people escaped from Egypt to the Promised Land."

Max and I looked at her in disbelief. I asked: "How do you know all this?"

Her answer was simple: "I know this because it is written in the scriptures and I have studied them at length."

During her account there was one word that she hadn't mentioned - Passover, so I asked: " But you still haven't explained what the Passover is..."

"Ah, yes...I will do so now...The Lord told his people to kill a lamb and celebrate...He also told them to mark their front doors with the blood...When he moved across the country, killing the first born of the Egyptians, he passed over all those houses that were marked with blood...And from that day on we have celebrated the Passover with a feast."

Max and I exchanged glances, feeling that we now knew the importance of the word 'passover' and why there was indeed a reason for the Jewish people to celebrate. But how would Jesus celebrate the Passover? Would he do so with talk that he, the King of the Jews, would free the Jewish people from Roman oppression, as the Lord his Father had done all those years ago in Egypt? Would he follow this with 'plagues' of such magnitude that the Roman occupiers would take fright and leave the Holy Land forever? Or would he simply carry out more miracles, showing a power that the Roman healers could only dream of? Max and I therefore decided to get as close to Jesus as we could over the period of the Passover. But we would need a bit of local help.

***

Chapter Two

During our following of Jesus, Max and I got to know many of his close friends very well. One was called Zachariah, a potter, living and plying his trade in Bethany, a small town to the east of Jerusalem and only a short distance away. We had seen him on many previous occasions because he delivered his pots to the small Bethany garrison where we were stationed, but had never spoken to him. Now we looked upon him as a friend, one who was prepared to keep us informed about the whereabouts of Jesus.

Zachariah told us that he had been a follower of Jesus for just over a year, after hearing a man of the law ask him how he could inherit eternal life. Jesus told the lawman to love his neighbour as himself. This confused the man and he asked Jesus who his neighbour was. Jesus gave him an example by tell a story of a Good Samaritan, a man from another part of the country, who went to the aid of a person who had been attacked by thieves and left badly injured. Jesus described how others, including a priest, walked by on the other side, refusing to help. The Samaritan even took the injured man to an inn and paid for his care. Jesus asked the lawman who was the injured man's neighbour. The man answered, the Samaritan, to which Jesus replied, go and do likewise. This story had so impressed Zachariah that he had decided to become a follower.

Soon Jesus and his disciples started to frequent Zachariah's home, calling for supper after spending a long day out in the country, preaching to the multitude of followers. His home and workshop were on the outskirts of the town, where he turned out pots of outstanding beauty and quality. Not surprising, his goods were in great demand by those in high position, both Jew and Roman.

His home's grandeur showed that he was a wealthy man. It had a bath and a complicated heating system that had been built in by Roman workmen who had come from Italy to build the garrisons now dotted across the Holy Land. Some of the locals envied his wealth, but Jesus told him not to worry about their petty jealousy, because those who worked hard were entitled to keep their earnings and do whatever they wanted with them. This jealousy hurt Zachariah because he was also known in the area where he lived as a generous person, helping those who were old, poor or suffered some disability.

The house had a long upstairs room looking east over vineyards as far as the eye could see, that allowed Jesus and his twelve disciples to meet, unseen and unhindered. Jesus always sat at the centre of a long narrow table, with his disciples taking up their seats, six either side of him. Zachariah then provided the group with a wholesome meal which he insisted on serving himself, allowing him to take note of the proceedings. These meetings took place regularly, and it followed that the group would celebrate the Passover there.

But one thing puzzled Zachariah, at the same time causing him great concern. He tried to explain to me: "When Jesus spoke to me about celebrating the Passover at my home he also added that this would be his last supper...He also asked me to make some small mementoes that he wished to give out to his disciples at this last supper."

Thinking that such items would probably be in the form of a special drinking vessel or plate, items often bought in the local market as souvenirs by we Romans, I did not pursue the issue. I did however ask Zachariah if he knew why Jesus would not be attending any more suppers at his home. His reply not only puzzled me, but caused me great concern.

"He told me that it was written in the scriptures that he, the Son of God, would be betrayed by one of his own disciples, arrested, tried and found guilty...He would be sentenced to death and would be crucified...This had to take place before his resurrection and ascension could follow so that he could join his Father in Heaven."

Both Max and I were taken aback by Zachariah's revelation. How could this possibly happen to such a harmless person, who preached the qualities of goodness and kindness as the only way to live one's life? What was most worrying from our point of view was that this could only take place if the occupying force were to allow it...and that would inevitably involve Max and I, whether we liked it or not.

What we now needed to know was, when would all this take place? Zachariah's answer shocked Max and I: "Within the next few days...In fact Jesus's betrayal and arrest will take place tonight...This is the reason why his meeting with the disciples at this, his last supper, will be very special...He did tell me that he would be showing them a way of remembering him that he hoped would last forever, but he did not elaborate...He did say, however, that his betrayer's identity would be revealed this very evening."

What Max and I later discovered from some of our soldier colleagues was that the high priests and elders were plotting to have Jesus killed because he'd blasphemed by pronouncing that he was the King of the Jews…At least this was the official line. No doubt jealousy played a big part, the priests and elders not being able to abide the idea of Jesus being so popular with the people.

We were also told that one of the disciples, by the name of Judas Iscariot, had become possessed by Satan and offered to betray Jesus to the priests for a fee of thirty pieces of silver. This would take place after the last supper, when Jesus would probably retire to a quiet area called Gethsemane to pray. Judas would identify him to the soldiers who would be present, with a kiss. His arrest would then take place.

After the last supper Zachariah met up with us so that he could inform us on what had taken place during the Passover celebration. Knowing that Max and I were soldiers, members of the occupying force, he wondered if there would be any way in which we would be able to help Jesus. Before we could consider this it was essential that we knew exactly what had already happened…and what was planned for our charismatic friend.

Zachariah explained what he'd seen and heard as he'd set out the food and drink for the last supper. He also explained how he'd earlier presented Jesus with the small pot mementoes he'd made for him, and how Jesus had brought them to the supper on some sort of wooden tray.

Zachariah had then moved to leave the proceedings, but Jesus invited him to stay. Since there was no room at the long table itself Zachariah had sat at the serving table just beside the closed door.

During the supper Jesus stopped the proceedings. He then took bread, broke it up into pieces and distributed it amongst the twelve disciples, saying: "Take…Eat…This is my body which I give to you…Do this in remembrance of me." His disciples did so.

He followed this act by taking a small silver chalice, misshaped and scratched with age, filling it with red wine then passing it round, at the same time saying: "Take…Drink…This is my blood which I shed for you…Do this also in remembrance of me." His disciples did so.

It was at this point that Jesus gave out the mementoes that Zachariah had made, to his disciples, keeping one for himself. Zachariah didn't elaborate on what the mementoes were, and I didn't consider it important to ask. I assumed as I had before that they would be decorative mugs or plates. Jesus then told the disciples that one of them would betray him, the betrayer being the one who dipped his hand into the bread bowl at the same time as he.

Minutes later both Jesus and Judas the Iscariot dipped into the dish, revealing to the other disciples that he was indeed the betrayer. Knowing that he was no longer welcome at the supper, Judas left. Zachariah said that he probably went to let the high priests know that Jesus would soon be moving to a quiet area in order to pray.

Zachariah had been correct in his thinking, for Jesus and his disciples moved first to the Mount of Olives and then into the Garden of Gethsemane where he asked them to stay awake and be vigilant while he prayed to his Father in Heaven. Sadly, as Max and I observed, having been earlier informed that Jesus would move into the Garden, and were therefore already waiting, the disciples fell asleep.

As nightfall approached we mixed with the disciples, giving them our moral support. Under our garments we had our swords, just in case Jesus wanted our help. Shortly afterwards Judas arrived with several men, armed also with swords. They were not soldiers, however, but had probably been specially recruited by the high priests and elders to arrest Jesus. At a prearranged signal Judas kissed Jesus in order to identify him to the men.

As the men moved in on Jesus, two grabbing him roughly by the arms, I reacted violently, drawing my sword from beneath my garments. My first blow, aimed at one of the men's head, cleanly sliced off his ear, which fell to the ground.

I was ready to strike again, this time to kill the man, but Jesus stopped me, rebuking me with the words: "Put your sword away, Marcus...Don't you think that if I wanted an army to protect me, my Father in Heaven would provide me with one?...But if I did that the scriptures would not be fulfilled...And they must be." He then bent down, picked up the ear and held it in place at the side of the man's head, at the same time saying a prayer. When Jesus removes his hand the ear had healed itself. There wasn't even the slightest trace of blood. His disciples, Max and I marvelled at the way that Jesus, even at the time of his arrest, was still prepared to perform a miracle to the benefit of one of his arresters.

At this point Roman soldiers appeared on the scene, having been sent for by the arresting party, fearing trouble from the disciples. When Max and I saw them approaching, carrying lanterns, we fled and hid behind a clump of trees. As we looked on we immediately recognised colleagues in the group, colleagues who could, and probably would identify Max and I if ordered to do so by a superior officer. All we could do now was to helplessly observe from behind the trees.

As Jesus was being led away the disciples followed, but at a distance. As they passed a woman, who had observed the arrest she confronted them, shouting out at Peter: "You were a follower of Jesus of Galilee…Were you not?"

Peter angrily replied: "No…I know not the man." He then broke down and cried, for Jesus had predicted that his most faithful disciple would deny that he knew him, on three separate occasions before the cock crowed three times to herald the start of a new day. All Max and I could do was to comfort him, knowing that had our commanding officer confronted us with the same question we too would have denied knowing Jesus, such was the weakness and lack of conviction of man.

The following day Zachariah searched the streets of Jerusalem looking for Judas Iscariot, finding him outside the temple and in an obvious state of distress. Zachariah speculated to himself as to why. Could he have had a restless night during which Satan had praised him for what he'd done, and God had despised him? Judas was no doubt having a fit of conscience.

As Zachariah pretended to pray in the temple he observed Judas arguing with the high priests, at the same time handing them something. There was a clink on the floor and Zachariah realised that Judas was attempting to hand the silver coins back to the priests, who were obviously refusing to accept them, one dropping on the floor. Judas, not knowing what else to do, threw the rest of the coins across the floor of the temple. He then hurriedly left.

Still overwhelmed with guilt Judas went to a nearby woodland and, using a length of rope tying up a donkey grazing in an adjoining field, hanged himself from a tree. Zachariah, following some distance behind, arrived at the scene too late to help, as Jesus would have expected him to do. Judas was already dead.

When the priests heard of Judas's suicide from Zachariah, and being embarrassed by the scene in the temple that many people had witnessed, they asked two young boys to collect up the silver coins. The coins were then used to buy a piece of land close by the wood, known locally as the Potter's Field because in years gone by a thriving pottery had extracted

19

clay from it. It was in this field that Judas Iscariot, the betrayer of Jesus Christ the Son of God was interred. After witnessing all of this Zachariah rushed to the garrison where Max and I were stationed hoping to inform us of all he had witnessed.

Max and I had already been detailed for duty because news of Jesus's arrest was already widespread. If a large number of his followers were to congregate in Jerusalem it could spell big trouble for the occupying force.

As we moved out on patrol in full combat uniform, including shields and spears, Zachariah attracted our attention from across the square by pretending to be drunk, shouting out obscenities about Roman rule at the top of his voice.

Before our Commanding Officer could detail someone to sort Zachariah out, Max and I quickly moved across the square in order to reprimand him. As we wrestled with him, keeping him on his feet as he staggered around, he was just able to relay to us as much as he knew, before we sent him on his way with a severe warning about his future behaviour. As we joined our colleagues the Officer nodded approvingly. The last thing he wanted was a confrontation situation so early in the day. From our point of view the other soldiers hadn't the slightest idea that we were close friends of Zachariah. They simply knew him to be a follower of Jesus.

The high priests wanted to see Jesus tried, convicted and sentenced to die, as quickly as possible. They feared that when the news of his arrest reached the multitude of people who supported him they could easily storm Jerusalem in their masses. If this were to happen the Romans would blame the priests for not having control over their own people. The priests therefore brought Jesus before Pontius Pilate, the Roman Governor.

Pilate was procurator of the area of Judea. His main residence in the Holy Land was in Caesarea, on the coast, where the Roman garrison numbered about three thousand soldiers. As the time approached when the Jews celebrated their Passover, Pilate and many of the soldiers moved to Jerusalem, anticipating trouble.

Pilate was known to be a fair, but weak man, wanting an easy and uncomplicated life. He was therefore always ready to appease the high priests by bending to their wishes if it meant peace, how ever fragile that peace was. When Jesus was brought before him by the soldiers Pilate asked the high priests what the charge was. One replied: "He has blasphemed by pronouncing to the world that he is the Christ...The Son of God... The King of the Jews."

Pilate had already heard from his confidants that Jesus was a harmless preacher, and certainly his preachings were no threat to law and order in the country. In fact since Jesus had started to preach about neighbours treating each other with civility, kindness and understanding, the degree of unrest had noticeably fallen.

But not wanting any trouble from the priests, he questioned Jesus, saying: "How answer you the charge?"

Jesus stood silent.

Pilate asked him again, but still Jesus refused to answer him.

Max and I looked on from a distance, willing Jesus to defend himself with words and actions so powerful that Pilate would have no alternative but to release him. Alas, we were to be disappointed.

Frustrated and at a loss what to do next, Pilate took the easy way out, as he had done on previous occasions when the priests had insisted on him restricting the number of followers who were allowed to congregate in the centre of Jerusalem when Jesus was preaching.

At the feast of the Passover Pilate had for some years pleased the masses by releasing a prisoner of their choice. Previously the prisoner chosen had been one who had been wrongfully imprisoned, usually on a trumped-up charge of plotting against the state, but on this occasion, and persuaded by the priests, they chose a murderer by the name of Barabbas.

When Pilate shouted to them: "Who shall I release to you...Barabbas or Jesus, who is known as the Christ?"

They yelled at the top of their voices: "Barabbas...Barabbas."

As Pilate sat on his seat of judgement, ready to pronounce sentence, his wife, Percula, sent one of her maids with a message. I was standing to the right of him and Max to the left. The maid had no alternative but to speak loudly to her master because of the chanting of the assembled mass: "Husband...Have nothing to do with this man called Jesus...I have had terrible dreams about him during the night...Dreams so bad that I refuse to describe them to you."

Both Max and I heard the message and this gave us hope, for it was a well known fact that Pilate was dominated by his wife. But we were immediately disappointed because, pressured by the priests, he again asked the crowd what they wanted him to do.

"Release Barabbas," they shouted.

"And what shall I do with Jesus?"

"Crucify him...Crucify him."

Pilate, realising that he had lost all control of the situation, and being influenced by his wife's message, called for a bowl of water from one of his attendants. He then washed his hands, at the same time saying to the assembly: "I am innocent of the blood of this just person...If you want to see the deed done, then you do it yourselves...I wash my hands of it...But remember, this man's blood will be on all our hands today."

As Barabbas was released to the masses amid shouts of: "Barabbas...Barabbas...Barabbas," some of our colleagues moved in and took hold of the arms of Jesus. Max and I looked on, powerless to influence events. First he was whipped into submission, then his outer garments were removed, to be replaced by a scarlet robe. A long reed was placed in his right hand and a crown of thorns was placed forcibly on his head. Blood started to stream down his forehead as the thorns stuck into his flesh.

It was at this point that I spotted a strange shaped object round Jesus's neck, hanging from a thin black thong probably made of leather. Jesus saw me staring at it, and as the soldiers were waiting for Pilate's next instruction, beckoned me across. He then lifted the thong over his head and gave me the object, at the same time whispering: "Look after this, Marcus...And it will look after you."

I quickly secreted the object within my clothing, intending to study it in greater detail later.

To humiliate Jesus further the gathered multitude, following the lead taken by the chief priests, knelt before him and started chanting: "Hail, King of the Jews...We worship thee...We worship thee."

The robe was removed, to be replaced by Jesus's garments. He was then marched away, passing through the masses. As the soldiers forced a way through several of the assembly spat at him and attempted to strike him with what ever they had in their hands.

Almost to order a large wooden cross was produced. Jesus was instructed to carry it, but before very long he was struggling with its weight. I was about to rush forward and help, when Max pulled me back: "No Marcus...Already we are under suspicion from some of our colleagues...Don't do anything to reinforce that suspicion...I will get help."

Max then shouted across to a large, strong-looking man: "You

22

there…Your name?"

"They call me Simon of Cyrene."

"Well, Simon of Cyrene, help this man called the Christ by sharing the load."

There was no objection because Simon had been a follower of Jesus since the day he had appeared the area.

By this time the group making its way along the road had dwindled to a handful, mainly soldiers, although I did observe Jesus's disciples following some distance to the rear. The rest of the masses, a cowardly lot in my opinion, had dwindled to nothing, no doubt not wanting to witness the act that was now about to take place…an act that they had pressured Pilate into enforcing. Maybe they thought that Jesus would wreak vengeance on them all for what they had done. If they weren't there at the final act he would be unable to do that. My mind went back to the day a follower of Jesus explained to me the meaning of the word 'Passover', when the Lord above had selectively picked on the Egyptian first-born to kill. It would serve all of them right if he did the same again, but selecting all those who had chanted: "Crucify him…Crucify him." But I knew that Jesus, a lover of all people regardless of their beliefs, would not want that to happen.

Eventually we reached a place unfamiliar to me, a slight hill, overlooking the surrounding countryside. There was an eerie silence about the place and a smell of decay. As I looked down I could see holes in the ground. The whole area smelt of death, making me feel uneasy. I whispered to a colleague: "What is this place?"

"Golgotha…The locals call it the place of the skull…This is where people are put to death."

I then realised that the holes were where crosses had previously been let into the ground.

Only being able to guess what was coming next, for neither Max nor I had witnessed a crucifixion before, and not wanting to witness that of Jesus, we moved away, pretending to form a barrier against the disciples with our spears held parallel to the ground. Our commanding officer again looked on approvingly, not wanting any trouble from the followers of Jesus. This also gave Max and I the opportunity, for the first time that day, to speak to them.

Peter surprised both of us by saying that what was taking place had been prophesied in Jewish scriptures written a long time ago and had to be fulfilled. When we asked him how that could be he had no reply, but added that this was the reason why Jesus insisted on the prophecy being followed to the letter.

Andrew added that the same prophecy also stated that Jesus would be resurrected from the dead in three days' time and would ascend into Heaven to join his Father. We already knew about the miracles he'd performed, but could this really be how his life on Earth would end? This final act would certainly push our faith and belief to the limit.

As Max and I spoke to the disciples, our backs to what was going on, we heard the first of the three nails being hammered in. The second and third followed. Jesus cried out in agony, but we were powerless to ease his pain.

We then heard the hammering repeated twice because a decision had been taken to crucify two robbers at the same time. I felt sad at the way Roman law, supposedly the most just anywhere in the known world, had been so badly enforced. How could a known murderer be released to the people just as two robbers, whose only crime may have been to steal a few silver coins from some rich merchant, were being crucified? Where was the justice there?

As the ropes were being attached in order to pull the three crosses upright into their deep holes a soldier who I'd always hated because of the brutality he showed when controlling the followers of Jesus, took a long thin plank of wood, nailed it to the top of Jesus's cross and scribbled across it using a piece of charcoal extracted from a fire close by:

THIS IS JESUS THE KING OF THE JEWS

The three crosses were then raised into position. The two robbers screamed out in pain as their bodies pressed down on the three nails. Jesus silently accepted the pain not wanting the soldiers to hear his agony. Some onlookers, having followed some distance behind, hesitant to witness the result of their earlier actions, now arrived at the heart rending scene.

One called out to Jesus, mocking him: "Thou destroyed the temple and built it in three days…Save thyself."

Another one shouted: "If thou be the Son of God come down from the cross."

I whispered to Max: "Why doesn't he?"

Max shrugged his shoulders, not having an answer.

It was then the turn of the chief priests, scribes and elders to mock

24

him, speaking to those assembled at the foot of the cross: "He saveth others...Himself he cannot save...If he be the Son of God come down from the cross...If God be his Father why doesn't he save his Son?"

Even the two robbers mocked him, realising that Jesus was not going to do anything for himself, or for them: "Help thyself, and us as well...Or hast thou no power?...Tell us."

As all this mockery was going on I could see soldiers, colleagues of mine, casting lots for the clothes of Jesus. One then soaked a sponge in vinegar, placed it on the end of his spear and forced it against Jesus's mouth. I wanted to take the spear from the soldier and force it through his heart...But realised that I couldn't.

As darkness spread over all the land Jesus suddenly called out: "Eli...Eli...lama sabachthani."

Puzzled, I asked Peter to translate, which he did: "He called to his Father in Heaven, saying: 'Father...Father...Why hast thou forsaken me?' But his Father hasn't, because the scriptures have to be fulfilled."

This puzzled me even further. How could words written hundreds of years before dictate what was happening at this very moment? They couldn't...And yet they were.

It was after his plea to his Father that Jesus dropped his head and gave up the ghost. What happened next terrified all present. A giant earthquake hit the land shaking the rocks free from the side of the hill where we were standing, sending them hurtling into the valley below. Even the three crosses swayed violently with the tremor. And we were told later that the veil in the temple had been torn down its full length with deafening force. Some even said that the graves in nearby yards opened up, their bodies coming to life and walking into nearby streets.

As he looked on, not only in disbelief, but also in fear, our commanding officer spoke, just loud enough for all of us to hear: "Truly this was the Son of God." He then moved away in order to be on his own so that he could mourn without feeling embarrassed in front of his men. As my colleagues stared up at the pitiless sight I moved across and joined him, trying not to attract the attention of the others. I pulled him towards me in a hug. As our eyes met he realised for the first time that I, one of his trusted soldiers, had been a follower of Christ for some time. I realised that on seeing the death of Jesus my commanding officer had become a convert himself...One of us.

Jesus had always had his women followers. They were always present, but in the background when he spoke to the multitudes that

25

gathered when news spread that he was going to address them. On that terrible day the women were also present, having followed the procession from afar. One was called Mary Magdalene, another, also called Mary, was the mother of Jesus. There was also Joses, the mother of the disciples John and James. And there were many others who had also followed. As they approached the top of the hill they collapsed to the ground in grief at the sight.

Mary, Jesus's mother, cried out at the top of her voice so that all present could hear: "Lord…Why hast thou allowed this to happen to thy, and my, Son?"

Mary Magdalene with equal passion, yelled out: "What sort of God would allow this to happen…Thou are't no God I recognise. "

The other women, realising that nothing could now be done for Jesus, started to make preparations for his burial. After returning to Jerusalem they sought out a rich man who went by the name of Joseph of Arimathaea.Although also a local councillor, the man had been present at many of Jesus's gatherings and he had often provided refreshments for the followers in the form of wine and bread. The women needed his help.

First they had to ask Pontius Pilate to release Jesus's body for burial. Not seeing any problem with the request, he willingly agreed, for he saw it as the final chapter in a story he wanted to forget. Only within the last twenty four hours his wife had come out in terrible boils that covered her face. Both were convinced that they were a plague put on her by Jesus or his Father, for both were familiar with the 'Passover' story.

***

Chapter Three

Putting the three crosses in position had been a difficult enough job, but getting them down appeared impossible, without taking an axe and cutting them down as one would a tree. And this is what we had to do. Max and I took it in turns hacking Jesus's cross as close to the ground as we could. As we did so we were conscious of his lifeless body shaking violently above us at ever blow of the axe.

As Max was about to make the final cut I and my colleagues manned the ropes that had been earlier attached in order to raise the cross. This enabled us to control it, preventing it crashing to the ground with Jesus's body still nailed to it. The same method was then used on the crosses of the two robbers.

Since the nails had been hammered home there was no way of removing them. We therefore had no alternative but to force the hands and feet of Jesus through them, and this is what we did. As we did so I had to fight back the nausea that welled up inside me. I wondered why the most civilised Empire in the known world, or so we'd always been led to believe, resorted to such a barbaric act of punishment.

Once the body was free it was washed, wrapped in clean lengths of linen and placed in a cave that had been hewed out of the rock in readiness for a friend of Joseph who was close to death. The cave or sepulchre as it had now become, even had a large stone that was rolled into place in order to seal it off. Both Mary Magdalene and Mary, mother of Jesus, kept vigil by the stone to prevent anyone interfering with the sepulchre.

Since Max and I had been on duty from early that morning, along with the other soldiers, our commanding officer marched us back the garrison for sustenance and rest. Crowd trouble was anticipated the day after Jesus's crucifixion so we would again be on the scene early.

As I lay on my bunk, going through all that had taken place on that fateful day and not being able to get the sound of hammering of nails out of my mind, I suddenly remembered the object that Jesus had given me just before his crucifixion. After carefully removing it from the leather purse on my body belt I turned up the oil lamp on the wall above me in order to study it.

The object was made of white glazed pot, in the shape of a six sided figure, small and thin enough to fit in the palm of my hand with my fingers closed over it. Just below the top edge was a tiny hole through which was threaded the thin black thong. But what fascinated me most were the two Greek letters that were engraved into one side of it. Although my knowledge of Greek was limited I did recognise them. The top one was theta - θ, the eighth letter of the alphabet, and underneath it was pi - π, a letter I knew was used in mathematics - something to do with circles. Did the two letters in some way represent the life of Jesus? If so, I had no idea what it was. Unfortunately I would not now get the opportunity to ask him about the significance of the two letters.

But what I did remember were the words he spoke to me when he gave the piece of pot to me: "Look after this and it will look after you." Did it have special powers? Again I had no idea. Jesus had worn it round his neck. I decided to do likewise, but first I would need a longer leather thong so that the piece fell low upon my chest, hidden from view beneath my uniform or any garment I happened to be wearing. Thin leather thongs were used to hold our body armour in position so I had one immediately available. I decided there and then that whatever the circumstances I would never, ever remove the piece from my person.

The following day Pilate, who thought that his dealings with Jesus were now at an end, found that he was sadly mistaken. When he heard that the priests, scribes and elders wanted an audience with him he anticipated further trouble and asked for soldiers to be present. Max and I were standing at the side of him when the chief priest spoke: "As you are aware, Pilate, the scriptures say that Christ the Son of God will rise from the dead, pass amongst us before ascending into Heaven to join his Father...Jesus has also preached this message...I do not trust his disciples...They may remove the body and tell the people that he has already risen from the dead and ascended to his Father...It is important that this is not allowed to happen...Otherwise it will cause great unrest throughout the Land."

I winked at Max and whispered: "It certainly would do...Think what would happen if those who had seen Jesus on the cross, then saw him walking amongst them, preaching as if nothing had happened to him...Even the minds of our Roman colleagues would be in total turmoil."

Pilate, envisaging how trouble could quickly escalate, but not wanting a military force to be seen by the sepulchre, suggested to the priests that they too should stand vigil in order to ensure that Jesus did not leave it...dead or alive. And this is what the priests did, standing close to the followers of Jesus, who had already taken up their vigil.

Max and I, along with our colleagues, were sent back to the garrison, but we quickly changed and returned to where the sepulchre was. When we arrived we saw two groups of people - to the left the followers of Jesus, but all women, to the right the priests, scribes and elders. Both groups were fast asleep.

We were about to move in and wake the followers when suddenly two men in shining garments appeared, so dazzling that we had to move behind a tree to protect our eyes. Silently they rolled back the stone, as if it was made of light wood, and entered the sepulchre. As we looked on from a distance three men came out of the opening in the rock, the two who had entered and another - Jesus, full clothed in a garment that also dazzled us.

Max opened his mouth to shout across, but I clamped my hand across it: "No, Max...We don't want to wake the priests and elders...Let Jesus move away...Then we'll wake them."

But we didn't have to shout, for Jesus glanced across to where we were hiding behind a tree and acknowledged our presence with a nod of the head. Both Max and I lifted our hands and waved.

As Jesus disappeared down the road that led back to Jerusalem the two men in shining garments moved the stone backwards and forwards, this time noisily in order to wake those who were asleep. Immediately Mary Magdalene and Mary, the mother of Jesus, moved into the sepulchre, only to discover that the body wasn't there. As they puzzled at what had happened, one of the men in shining garments spoke: "Why seek you the living amongst the dead?...He is not here, but risen...Go now, assemble all the disciples together and tell them what you have seen and heard."

The priests, full of suspicion, accused the women of pushing the stone back and removing the body, but the women ridiculed them, shouting: "How could we, mere women, move such a heavy stone?"

Since Jesus was no longer there the priests, scribes and elders left the scene, also heading for Jerusalem.

Max and I, worried that the chief priest would recognise us as soldiers and tell Pilate, we waited until it was safe to join the women. When we did so we told them that we had witnessed all that had taken place, including seeing Jesus come out of the sepulchre and leaving on the road to Jerusalem. On hearing our news the group hastily set out on the same road, Max and I tagging on behind them.

Just before entering Jerusalem we met Peter and told him the news: "Jesus is risen…Jesus is risen," we shouted loudly. But he would not believe us. He had to see for himself, and returned to the sepulchre to seek confirmation.

As he entered the sepulchre he was greeted with the same question that the two men in shining garments had asked the two Marys: "Why seek you the living amongst the dead?…He is not here, but is risen…Go now and tell the others."

Peter, now convinced, ran as fast as he could to find the other disciples, but we had already located them in various parts of the city. When Peter arrived the disciples were already waiting for him. As he told them of his findings at the sepulchre, which Max and I confirmed, a stranger joined our group. We, who had seen Jesus leaving the sepulchre, knew that the stranger was he, but his disciples did not recognise him even when he spoke to them in the same way he had done on so many previous occasions: "Peace be with you."

They could of course see him, but still didn't believe their own eyes, thinking they were seeing his spirit after death. It was only when he invited them to place their fingers into the holes in his hands and feet that they realised that they were feeling flesh and bone, not possible with a spirit. He was in fact their living master.

Jesus then asked them to sit down before him. Max and I joined them, having been invited to do so by Peter. At first we hesitated, aware that others were watching from a distance. Was one of them a soldier not in uniform who could recognise us? But somehow we didn't care.

Jesus addressed us, but only briefly. He appeared to be in a hurry, as if he had to keep an appointment elsewhere: "I want you now to go and preach the word of the Lord to all the nations of the World…Start here in Jerusalem then move out in all directions…My Father in Heaven will be with you at all times, giving you the strength to fulfil your mission…His mission…There will be no limit to how far you can go."

He then slowly walked out of Jerusalem, taking the road to Bethany. We followed like sheep following their shepherd. At a point on the outskirts of the town, where the ground rose slightly, he took up his position. After turning to face us he invited us to kneel, which we did. He held his right hand high in the air and made the sign of the cross as he spoke: "May the Lord bless you and keep you...May the Lord make his face shine upon you and give you his peace...In the name of the Father, and of the Son, and of the Holy Ghost...Amen."

Jesus's final act was to turn to the east. As he did so the cloud, that had been thick all day, suddenly opened up, allowing the narrowest beam of sunlight to fall upon him. Slowly, and before our very eyes, he rose, moving up the beam, finally disappearing through the hole in the cloud.

All of us fell prostrate on the ground at the sight. Peter was the only one to speak, the rest of us lost for words: "Our master has now joined his Father in Heaven...It is our task to go forth and preach his word...Let us start this day."

"But Peter...Where will we go?...We know nothing of countries outside the Holy Land." These were the words of Andrew, and all the others nodded in agreement.

Peter looked directly at me: "Help us Marcus...You have come to our land from afar...Tell us what is beyond our boundaries."

With the help of Max I told them all I knew. Max picked up a twig from the ground and drew in the sandy ground a map of the world he knew, remembering one he'd seen during his training as a soldier. I then spoke to the disciples, pointing with the twig as I did so: "We are here in Jerusalem...To the north is Damascus in Syria and above that Mesopotamia and Armenia...To the east is Arabia Magna and further still the great rivers named Tigris and Euphrates...Even further east is a country we call India...To the south is Sinai and into Egypt, where the children of Israel were kept in captivity...Here on the coast is the great city of Alexandria...To the west is the port of Caesarea, then a large sea known as Mare Internum that will take you to the islands of Cyprus and Creta...North of them are the countries of Asia and Macedonia. Here lie the great cities of Constantinople and Ephesus...Further west is Sicilia, the largest island in the Mare Internum and north of that is Italia, with its capital Roma, the centre of our great Empire...That is where Max and I come from...North of Italia is Gallia and finally Britannia, but they are far, far away."

"But how will we survive on such long journeys?" This was Thomas, one of the younger disciples and the least confident.

Peter reassured him: "We will work our way, seeking help, food and shelter from local people...Remember what our Lord said to us...His Father in Heaven will be with us at all times...We may meet again on our journeys, but if we don't we will all meet in Heaven when we take up our places at the side of our Lord…Never lose faith…Now go on your way."

Max and I watched as the eleven disciples slowly made their way back to Jerusalem, before setting off on their epic journeys. Up to that point they had been mere disciples - followers of Jesus. Now they were Apostles - their role to preach the word of Jesus abroad.

Reluctant to leave the safety and familiarity of their surroundings, for the next few weeks all of them preached mostly in small groups to those within the boundaries they knew. There was no trouble, as the priests, scribes and elders had predicted (even hoped), and this allowed Pilate to return to Caesarea.

But just before he did so, and unknown to him, his wife, Percula, asked Peter to meet her in her private apartment. The boils she'd suffered during Jesus's trial had slowly spread and now covered most of her body. She knew that Jesus had performed miracles, even bringing people back from the dead, but had that power been given to his disciples?

Their meeting took place in her private chambers while her husband toured Jerusalem for the last time. In Peter's presence she unashamedly took off all her clothes so that he could witness her unsightly body. Every area was covered with boils ouzing yellow pus. Peter had never seen anything like it before and felt sorry for the poor woman.

She then spoke to him: "I know your master was able to perform miracles…But can you?…If so I command you to heal my body." Immediately she regretted her choice of words: "Er…I apologise for my use of the word 'command'…Please take pity on me and help me…I will do anything…Give you anything…A few gold coins?" Again she regretted her choice of words, knowing that the services of a disciple of Jesus could never be bought. Falling to her knees she burst into tears and made her plea: "Please…Please help me."

As Jesus had taught his disciples to do, Peter showed compassion on her. Placing both his hands gently on her head he prayed out loud: "Dear Lord, please may it be thy will that the plague consuming this woman leaves her…Through Jesus Christ our Lord…Amen."

Pilate's wife loudly repeated the word: "Amen."

Peter then asked her to immerse herself in a bath of water as hot as she could bear. A maid quickly provided this by filling a bath in the corner of the room with hot water collected by pitcher from an adjoining room which housed some sort of central heating system. As Pilate's wife soaked herself she screamed out in agony as the hot water washed the pus out of the boils. This left a mass of red sores with holes at their centres. These slowly closed and the redness faded to nothing. Within the space of just an hour all signs of the boils had completely disappeared.

On climbing out of the bath both she and Peter observed that her skin was as unblemished as a baby's. Unashamedly, still naked and her body dripping wet, she hugged the disciple. As she dressed she asked him how she could repay him: "Tell me what I can do, and I will do it."

Peter's request was simple and to the point: "Ask your husband to stop his soldiers brutalising my people...And never again allow them to crucify an innocent man...In fact no man at all."

Pilate's wife assured him that her husband would take such action.

Not surprising, for Pilate did everything his wife asked him, or rather told him to do, before he left for Caesarea with her he first reduced the size of the garrison at Jerusalem, then issued those officers who would be staying, with the following orders: "There will be no more ill-treatment of local people from this day on...Neither will there be any more crucifixions...If I hear different, the salt mines at home await the culprits...Now see to it."

Because of Pilate's decision to reduce the Jerusalem garrison Max and I had to also leave the area. There was talk of many soldiers returning to Italia, before moving on to Gallia, where there was increasing unrest threatening the Empire itself. Both of us were homesick and this would give us chance to see our families again. On the day I'd left the farm my mother had been far from well. Would she be alive when I eventually arrived home? I had no idea.

That evening, as I removed my clothing in order to get washed before retiring to bed, my eyes fell upon the piece of pot around my neck...the only item I had to remind me of who I now knew to be Jesus Christ the Son of God. As I turned it over and over with my fingers I got to thinking. My mind went back to the Last Supper, when Jesus gave out mementoes to his disciples, mementoes that had been made by the potter, Zachariah. I had assumed at the time that Zachariah had probably made some highly decorative cups or plates for Jesus to distribute.

But had he? Or had he in fact made thirteen pieces of pottery, identical in shape and colour to the piece I held in my fingers, only differing in the Greek letters that were engraved into them? Had Jesus given these out to his twelve disciples, keeping one for himself? And if so, what letters had he chosen? Twelve at random, keeping two more for himself? Or had he for his own good reason chosen fourteen special letters, and if so, what possibly could that reason have been? At that point I had no way of knowing the answers to any of my questions.

But if Jesus had distributed such pieces why hadn't I seen them round the necks of the disciples when I'd talked to them earlier? Then it occurred to me. They may have been frightened of being associated with Jesus, so they would have made sure that the pieces of pot were well hidden from view. Of course, if I could have seen all twelve pieces of pot that I suspected the disciples were wearing around their necks I may well have been able to answer all but my final question. Only Jesus himself would have been able to tell me how he had chosen the fourteen letters, and for what reason.

But alas, that was not now possible. I also had it on good authority that all the disciples except one, Judas Iscariot, were now acting as apostles of Jesus and had already left the area, moving north in order to carry out the task that he had set them. Even Zachariah, who could have answered all my questions, apart from the one asking how Jesus may have chosen the Greek letters to be engraved into the pieces, had joined Simon Peter and was also heading north. He had informed his wife that he would be away for a few months.

There was just one glimmer of hope. If one or more of the apostles intended to travel west they would first head for the port of Caesarea in order to take a ship. I was also heading in that direction. With a great deal of luck I could meet up with one of them - maybe two, even more.

***

Chapter Four

Caesarea Maritima, to give it its full name, was a large and busy port with a deep water harbour constructed on Herod the Great's instructions, as were large warehouses to store goods to be exported, or had been imported. There was a flourishing market there, attracting masses of people from the surrounding area. The town had impressive buildings, even temples and a theatre overlooking the sea, where plays were regularly performed by both local actors and those who came from afar to promote their abilities.

But the one building that had the most attraction for the younger soldiers was the one housing the Baths that Herod had had built. After a hot day patrolling the streets of the town a plunge into the cold clear waters, followed by a massage if required, were always welcome.

Herod, also a keen sportsman, decided to hold a major sporting competition every year in a specially designed arena on the edge of town. The event soon gained popularity, and when he introduced huge purses filled with gold as prizes the event attracted athletes not only from Judaea itself, both Jews and Romans, but also from across the sea - Cypriots, Cretians, Macedonians, even Sicilians.

Because of all this activity, designed to encourage the people of all backgrounds to socialise, there was little trouble in the town, everybody appearing to get on well together, going about their business peacefully. Even the Romans soldiers whose task it was to keep order were friendly and tolerant to those who had a faith, even though they had little or no faith themselves. If trouble of an aggressive nature, likely to threaten the peace, did break out it was usually the result of over-indulgence in the local and cheap red wine that was far too freely available. A night in a cold uncomfortable cell to sober up was usually sufficient punishment.

When Max and I, along with the rest of our battalion arrived in Caesarea in the evening after a long three day march from Jerusalem we expected to sail to Sicilia the following morning. What we didn't known was that the day after our arrival coincided with the last day of 'SPORTSFEST', Herod's annual event, of which he'd been the proud benefactor. Now Herod the Great's successor, Herod Antipas, was in control of affairs. We would sail two days later on the noon tide.

The final day of the great sporting event was always a fun day, the serious competing having taken place earlier in the week. Most of the competitors had in fact already left along with their prize money, not wanting to risk losing it, drinking, gambling and accepting the favours of the many women ready to take it from them.

On the final day there were four events, designed not only to show skill, but also to entertain the public. There was however serious prize money to be had. After hearing what would be involved, Max and I, along with some of our colleagues decided to enter. I would enter the first event - throwing the spear. Let me explain: "The thrower, using an infantryman's spear (all being made to a standard length and weight), throws at five target circles set out on the ground...These vary in both diameter and distance away, and are numbered according to the degree of difficulty hitting them - five being the highest score, one being the lowest...Each one has a slightly raised white disk in the centre. This allowed the target to be seen from a distance...The thrower gaining the highest score with five throws is declared the winner. In the event of a tie there is a throw-off until a winner is found."

Max, always a good bowman, decided to enter the second event - shooting the arrow. He describes this event to you.

"Five circular targets are set out in a straight line along a wall roughly ten paces apart...Each target has five circular zones painted on it - the outer zone is white and scores one point, the next one in is green and scores two points, the next black, scoring three, the next red and scoring four...The inner zone is gold and scores five...Shooting at the targets would be easy to a good marksman, but there is an added difficulty...the marksman has to shoot five arrows, one at each target as he stands on a chariot, being driven at speed past them at a distance of about twenty paces."

My good friend Cassius was always game for anything, so we decided to enter him in the third event - catching the rope. He too describes the event.

"A specially made stage has been set up in the centre of the arena...It is made of wood, ten paces long and the height of a man...Set up about two paces in front of it is a tall square wooden frame with a thick knotted rope hanging from it with a heavy stone weight attached to its end...Beneath it is a narrow stretch of muddy water, and beyond this a deep pit of sand...A steward, standing on the edge of the staging, pulls the rope towards him using a long stick with a hook on the end...He then allows it to swing outwards…As it swings back, the competitor, timing his run along the staging, grabs the rope and swings outwards…He now swings back as far as he can before again swinging outwards and releasing the rope…If he gets the timing right he lands in the sandpit…If he gets it wrong he lands in the muddy water…Each competitor has five swings…The winner is the one to jump the greatest distance into the sand pit."

The fourth and final event was the Relay. Let me describe it to you: "Ten members form a team, each member running the length of the arena…But there is an added complication - each runner has his legs tied together with a rope half a pace in length, allowing him to only take short steps…Five runners position themselves at one end of the track, five at the other end… The first runner hands over a short length of rounded wood called a baton, to the second runner, and so on…The change-overs are watched closely by stewards to ensure fair play…The team coming first is the winner."

Our full team, made up of myself, Max, Cassius and Brutus along with others of our battalion, was like a military force, but not in uniform. The crowd did however have a good idea who we were.

My event not only required the strength to launch the spear a great distance, pin point accuracy was also important, and this is where I was able to score better than the other competitors. As a child I first learned to walk then throw a spear, or rather a short thin length of twig at the dog, not hurting him of course. As I got older the twigs became longer, heavier and sharper, until they were no longer twigs, but spears.

As a farming family rearing livestock we had to be able to defend our animals against wild boar, wolves, even rustlers. This we did by arming ourselves with spears as we patrolled our land. It was inevitable that during our patrols my brothers and I organised competitions to hone our skills. These always involved throwing at targets of various sorts - thin trees, circular cow pats on the ground, even fastening a small bale of straw to the dog with a long string and getting him to run across the field. This gave us a moving target - the bale, not the dog. Once the throwing skill had been acquired, one did not lose the technique, and I came to the competition in Caesarea with that technique well groved into my brain.

I was drawn to go last of the ten competitors. This enabled me to study not only their physique, but also their technique. All had muscular upper bodies and appeared to be capable of throwing the spear out of the stadium if they wanted to, and all decided, probably out of sheer bravado, to go for the target the greatest distance away.

Although distance wasn't a problem accuracy was, and only three of the nine registered the maximum score of five points. I decided to be less ambitious and easily pinpointed the target scoring three points.

So, after round one I was fourth in the competition. Those in front of me strode around, sticking their chests out, filled with self confidence. Those without a score looked upon me with suspicion, wondering why I'd chosen the easier option. They'd also noticed that my spear had entered the ground in the centre of the small white circle, such was the accuracy.

In the next three rounds the other competitors still continued to throw at the highest scoring target, sometimes spearing it, but more often missing it, while I continued aiming at the third target, hitting it on all three occasions. As the rounds progressed the lead changed several times, but I kept my fourth place throughout the competition.

All was to play for, or throw for, in the final round. After the others had thrown, the top three scores were 16, 15, and 14, all three throwers missing their final target. My score was 12, but with my final throw to come. To win I needed to spear the five target, to take my score to 17. Since I hadn't thrown that far before, the leader looked on as I prepared my run-up, confident that he'd already won.

I launched the spear in the direction of the most distant target, confident that the ability to throw the distance and accuracy to hit the target were still programmed into my brain from childhood. As I knew it would, the spear slowly arced over in flight and descended point first towards the ground. At first I thought I may have given the spear a bit too much height that would cause it to dip early and fall several paces short of the target, but I was wrong. It fell perfectly, spearing the white disk in the target's centre. My score of five pulled me one point ahead of the rest of the field, but that was enough. The first prize, a purse of a hundred silver denarii, was presented to me by Herod Antipas himself, who insisted on presenting all the prize money. I had earned myself with five throws of a spear the same amount as I earned as a soldier in four months. Most of my competitors congratulated me, but those who I'd overtaken walked off in digust, one shouting: "Luck bastard."

It was now the turn of Max to repeat my success. He too would be relying on a skill learned as a child. I asked him to explain to me.

"During my childhood my family lived on an estate owned by a rich Roman Senator…His palatial villa was on the edge of a huge forest in

Lombardy...My father, with ten men under him, looked after the forest for the Senator....As part of his pay he was provided with a small cottage for he and his family to live in...From an early age I accompanied him when he went hunting in the forest...The senator was a lover of venison so our prey was usually deer, and the occasional wild boar...I soon had my own bow, specially made for me by my father, and my own special arrows... As I became older it was evident to him that I had a flair for the sport, often out-shooting him, especially when the deer were running at high speed...I had the knack of judging their speed so that deer and arrow arrived at the same point at the same time...It was this skill that I would be putting to the test today, although in this case I would be moving while the target remained stationary."

There were also ten entries in this competition, including Max. As a result of the draw he was first to shoot. I've asked him to describe the event as it progressed.

"After choosing my bow and five arrows from a selection that were available I stepped up onto the chariot...After widening my stance to give me maximum balance I positioned my first arrow in the bow...I then indicated to the driver that I was ready...He initially set of at a slow pace, but quickly accelerated...As the chariot swayed from side to side on the rough uneven surface of the arena I realised just how difficult my task would be...My first arrow hit the gold, probably because I had time to line up my shot, but the next two arrows missed their targets completely...This was not surprising because I had to extract each arrow from the quiver on my back, position it in the bow, line up and shoot in the space of less than three seconds...Having managed to establish some sort of technique I succeeded in hitting the red zone with each of my remaining two arrows, giving me a final score of thirteen points...To say that I was disappointed is an understatement."

Some of the other competitors openly laughed at what they considered to be a pathetic performance. Max however assumed a philosophical approach - if you think you can do better, show me.

As the competition progressed it became clear that the abilities of the opposition varied considerably. After eight competitors had taken their shots Max, with a total score of thirteen, was lying in first place and feeling confident. Alas, the last two competitors were slightly better, the ninth to shoot scoring five, one, four, four and two to give a total of sixteen. The tenth did even better, scoring four, two, five, three and four giving him a total of eighteen. Max ended up in third place, but that wasn't too bad, for the prize money was twenty-five silver denarii, equivalent to a month's pay as a soldier.

The third event was also the funniest, at least from the spectators' point of view. I asked Cassius to describe the event as it progressed.

"Since the event appeared not to require any real skill, unlike the throwing and shooting events, there were twelve entrants willing to have a go...Like me they intended to treat it as one big laugh...I was drawn third, so I had a chance to see the techniques adopted by the first two as they got the first round started...The first to go got it just right, timing his run to allow him to catch the rope just as it started its outward journey...This gave him a good swing, followed by an even better return, before leaping off at the end of the second outward swing and dropping into the sand pit...A wooden peg was placed at the side of the pit where the last part of his body made a mark in the sand...The rest of us were so impressed, we clapped to show our appreciation...The spectators were less enthusiastic, probably because the competitor hadn't dropped into the muddy water...The second competitor got it all wrong, almost from the word go...He commenced his run-up a little too late and found himself diving for the rope as it was halfway along its forward swing...Sadly, at least for him, but not for those watching, he failed to grab the rope and belly flopped into the water, sending a column of mud high into the air...All credit due to him, he emerged with a big grin on his face, and it was this that brought the cheers from the spectators...One thing the first two attempts had shown me was how essential it was to time my run-up exactly right. You then at least had a chance of using your body to swing out and back on the rope before timing your leap into the sand pit.And this is exactly what I did, passing the first competitor's wooden peg by a good half pace...I was now in the lead, but it was early days."

Like the previous events the lead continued to change as the event progressed, and at the start of the final round Cassius was in fourth place. It was now his fifth and final go. He described how it went.

"By this time the staging, and indeed the rope itself, were covered in slimy mud, the result of those who'd dropped into the water being determined to have another go and at least get an imprint in the sandpit...As the first competitor commenced his run-up he lost his footing at the final moment, missing the rope completely and crashing into the muddy water... The second moved more cautiously, but hadn't the speed when he made his jump for the rope...His swing was almost non-existent and he too dropped into the mud...It was now my turn, could I use a different technique? I decided that I could...I commenced my run as far back as I could, using the still dry part of the staging. This gave me a good turn of speed...As I hit the slippery section I decided to go into a slide, moving across the staging at frightening speed...Instead of jumping for the rope from the treacherous edge I simply slid off the end...My timing couldn't have been better, the rope just beginning to move outwards. I grabbed it, swung my legs as far forward as I could, then backward in order to maximise the swing...At the end of my second forward swing I stretched my legs out in front of me as far as I could and as I hit the sand my momentum rolled me forward, resulting in me falling out of the pit at the far end altogether...I knew I'd jumped well, and was pleased to see the steward move my wooden peg at least half a pace ahead of the one that had been in the lead."

The other competitors, some begrudgingly, clapped at the sheer skill of Cassius's performance. The stadium erupted with noise as the spectators also appreciated what he had achieved. Of course, Cassius thought that he'd already won, confident that the remaining jumpers wouldn't reach his peg. Sadly he was wrong. The remaining competitors tried his sliding technique and one, the last to jump, managed to master it.

Whether the extra mud that had been deposited on the staging after Cassius's excellent jump had made it even more slippery, I don't know, but the speed the jumper attained on his run-up. or slide-up, was quite unbelievable. The transfer to the rope was done to perfection as were the swing and jump following Cassius's technique. As a result he hit the sandpit almost at its end He too tumbled over, landing heavily on the hard ground outside the pit. At first all watching thought he'd badly hurt himself, and a deathly hush filled the stadium. But when he got up, dusted himself down and waved his arms, both fellow competitors and the spectators enthusiastically applauded. Cassius's attempt had been good... but this one had been better.

Cassius received his second prize, a purse of fifty silver denarii from Herod Antipas, equivalent to two months' pay in his role as a soldier of the Roman Empire.

The final event was the Relay Race - ten teams of ten runners - a hundred in the arena at the same time...Quite a spectacle. Since I assumed the captaincy of our team I will describe the event as it progressed. There was no advantage to running in a particular lane therefore there was no need for a lane draw, but each team had to sort out its running order. After some discussion it was decided that Max would start the race off, followed by Cassius. I would run the final leg. This made our team - Max, Cassius, Brutus, Flavian, Hadrian, Maximilian, Scipio, Tacitus, Virgil and myself.

Suddenly, just like a magician pulling rabbits out of a centurion's helmet, as we soldiers had seen on many occasions when the troops were being entertained by a travelling group, the head steward extracted numerous lengths of rope out of a sack. All were identical in length, just over half a pace long, and each team would require ten lengths. The knack was to use as little of the end of the rope as possible to tie round each ankle. And it would be fair to say that those with thin ankles were at a slight advantage over those with thick ones. The whole idea of loosely tying the ankles together was to limit the length of stride so that during the race those with long legs were not at an advantage over those with short ones.

Herod Antipas started off the final event with the drop of his oversized scarlet handkerchief, following a tradition established by his father who had, up to his death, started the final event at every competition since he'd inaugurated the SPORTSFEST several years ago.

Max set off as fast as he could, but soon realised as he crashed to the ground that running fast was far from easy. And he wasn't alone for out of the ten starters eight fell before the finish.

As Max handed over to Cassius he looked to be in about fifth or sixth place. More tumbling took place as the race progressed, but one thing soon became apparent - team members who had short legs seemed to cope better with their ankles being tied together than the taller members with the longer legs…And over half our team were of the short leg variety.

By the halfway point we were well in the lead, probably a good ten paces, and when Tacitus handed the baton over to me the lead had increased further. I set off, confident that I would be the first to cross the line…maybe too confidently. I had seen enough of the other competitors to know that some sort of rhythm was essential in order to stay on ones feet, but somehow I couldn't master the technique. After crashing to the floor twice my lead had all but disappeared. After stumbling within sight of the finishing tape two competitors came storming past me. I had thrown away an unassailable lead in the last few paces of the race. My team mates gathered round, consoling me, but I knew that my over

42

confidence had lost us, or rather me, the race.

Because there were ten members in each team Herod Antipas had decreed that the prize money was ten times that for the individual events This meant that our team received a purse of two hundred and fifty denarii, which wasn't to be sniffed at.

Once I'd got over my disappointment Max, Cassius and I totalled up our winnings. My first in the spear throwing plus my third in the relay gave me one hundred and twenty five denarii. Max's second in the arrow shooting and third in the relay gave him seventy five denarii. And finally Cassius, with his second in the rope jumping and third in the relay also gave him seventy five denarii. Between us we had won no less than two hundred and seventy five shiny silver denarii in little over five hours...Not a bad rate of pay. It was going to be a good night in the drinking houses of Caesarea.

But first the three of us had to clean ourselves up. After sweating profusely in the hot sun for most of the day we must have stunk to high heaven, although funnily enough we didn't notice it. Fortunately Cassius hadn't fallen in the mud bath so he didn't look any different to Max and I. We did however get some funny looks from the local women as we walked past them on our way back to the garrison. Some held the sleeves of their garments to their noses and gave us a look of disgust. But there was nothing we could do until we reached the communal baths. These were only a stone's throw away from the garrison. We therefore gathered a newly washed set of clothes from our rooms before entering the baths.

There were in fact two Baths, the smaller East one for men of senior position - senators, bankers, businessmen and members of the military above the rank of commanding officer, and the larger West one for the rest, that obviously included we three.

The East Bath showed that no expense had been spared on its construction, the marble used having been imported all the way from Italia. Although open to the air the bath was surrounded by a narrow roof supported by elaborately carved marble pillars. Between these were seats, also made of marble, where those of importance sat putting the world to right as they dried off before entering the massage room. The water, clean and slightly heated, entered the bath from the mouths of two huge carved marble lion heads.

The whole surround was patrolled by young, muscular, handsome men, wearing only the briefest of loin cloths. Their role was two fold, to cater for the needs of their clients, including acting as masseurs, and also to ensure that only those men of sufficient status were allowed to enter the bath area. But one had only to observe for a few seconds to realise that some of them had more than a passing relationship with their masters. Longing glances were made. Help was given to those who required it as they entered and left the pool by the slippery marble steps. Whispered messages were passed, as were coins, usually gold in colour. And occasionally a young and hugely attractive young man would leave with an often ugly and grotesquely fat old man. One could only guess at the reason.

By contrast the West Bath, for the plebs that included us, had been intentionally designed differently to emphasise who it was intended for. The main structure was of local sandstone. The canopy above the sides was of interwoven reeds and supported by rough timber uprights. The seats were also of rough timber, and it was wise to put down a towel before sitting down to avoid getting spells in the sensitive parts of your anatomy. There were massage tables, but these were set out so that all could see. There were masseurs too, but these were old, rough and ready, markedly contrasting with the young and handsome men who patrolled the bath for the 'superiors'.

The water entered the West Bath via a large square lead pipe withsome sort of white deposit round its edge. Although crystal clear the water was intensely cold having travelled via a system of aqueducts from the distant hills. Heating it was considered an extravagance for the plebs.

The three of us undressed, aware that the eyes of the 'ugly mob' were on us waiting to assess how well we were endowed. As I was about to lift my tunic above my head I suddenly realised that the piece of pot around my neck, on its thin leather thong, would become immediately visible. One of the onlookers was bound to see it and take an immediate interest. Although it wasn't an attractive object, nor did it have any obvious value, if indeed you could say that about an object that Jesus Christ the Son of God had once owned, it could be worth stealing. Maybe the owner would pay a couple of dinarii for its return. I therefore lifted the thong over my head at the same time as my tunic, rolled the tunic up with the object concealed within its folds. I then placed it on one of the seats. Who in their right mind would steal a dirty, smelly tunic? As for money, we purposely only had a few bronze sestertii in our waist bags, having left our prize money back at the garrison. There was no point in tempting providence.

The three of us slowly immersed ourselves in the clear water. Initially the coldness took our breath away, but we soon became used to the temperature. As we lay on the bottom in the shallow end, just our faces above the surface, the soreness in our muscles, the result of a strenuous day in the sports arena, slowly dissipated as we relaxed. The effect was almost soporific, and at one point I slowly sank below the surface, only to inhale a quantity of water. I shot up onto my feet coughing and spluttering, much to the amusement of my colleagues.

After climbing the rough steps out of the bath, drying ourselves off and declining offers of a massage from the ugly mob, we dressed into our clean tunics. At this point I located the pot pendant in the folds of my dirty garment, carefully extracted it and placed the looped thong, unnoticed by the other two, over my head, making sure that it was again concealed.

The three of us then headed for the exit, passing an opening that allowed us a view of the bath for the privileged few as we did so. Cassius and I looked through, fascinated at the sight, observing the longing glances of the old and unattractive, and the returned contemptuous looks of the young and handsome, until a purse of coins was jingled. I glanced at Max, wondering what he made of it all, and immediately detected that same longing look in his eyes. Max had already focussed on the young man nearest to where he was standing. It was at that point that it all made sense to me

Max was three years younger than me and I'd been aware for some time that he idolised me as one would an elder brother who seemed to know all the answers and could do almost anything. This appeared to have started when the two of us had taken an interest in a very special person who preached to the people who followed him how they could lead a better and more rewarding life…that special person being Jesus Christ.

Being young and inexperienced Max wasn't aware of the dangerous game that we were playing. On the one hand we were Roman soldiers, there to keep the peace. On the other we had already become passive members of Jesus's ever increasing group, slowly passing through some form of spiritual conversion. This had to be done using all my guile to avoid raising the slightest suspicion of our commanding officer and the other soldiers. Max had been quite happy to follow my lead.

It was during our many hours together that I often caught him simply staring into my eyes, almost longingly. But I always interpreted those looks as some form of adulation. Never having before experienced or even witnessed the physical attraction between two men it had not registered with me that that was what I was now witnessing. Max was a lover of men, not of women. But I was definitely not the answer to his prayers for there was nothing that excited me more than a young attractive maiden. We had to find someone with similar inclinations, maybe one of those young men who patrolled the baths. There was only one problem - we were due to sail on the morrow's noon tide,

After a wholesome final dinner of stewed goat, chunks of warm bread and fresh fruit at the garrison, Max and I dressed for a night on the town. Cassius would have accompanied us, but had taken a turn for the worse having, we think, possibly strained his heart during the rope jumping contest. He had complained to us of pains in his chest for some weeks, but we thought it was over-indulgence in food, and had had little sympathy. An examination by the garrison's physician revealed that such pain was far from normal and that a period of complete rest was required, Cassius would not even be allowed to sail with us tomorrow.

**

Chapter Five

Our first port of call was the *Herod-the-Great*, the most popular communal drinking house in Caesarea. Like the baths the house was also divided into two different areas - the Best Room where those who frequented the East Bath were also found, and the Common Room where the rest of us were expected to do our drinking.

Never having been in the drinking house before I found the place fascinating. Across one end of the room where we were was a high counter behind which stood four young and attractive women of, we found out later, Cypriot origin. They served their customers with their drinking requirements - local wine made in a well established winery just across the way. It was rolled across in earthenware vessels, suitably corked. Behind the counter a man uncorked them and poured the potent red liquid into large jugs, ready for serving. Ale was also available, having been brewed in house. This was stored in wood barrels which the man tipped on their sides before hammering in a brass tap. The women simply filled up their jugs in order to serve those who preferred a longer, less alcoholic drink, although, as we found out later, the ale was also pretty potent.

The first observation I made was that the young and handsome men who we'd seen earlier at the Baths tended to prefer the Common Room, mixing with their own kind when relaxing rather than socialising with the 'money' men. The second observation I found most interesting. The young and often attractive women also preferred the Common Room. Even those who sold themselves for sex appeared to prefer to be with those men who were less wealthy, yet young and handsome, in preference to the obscenely rich, mostly ugly and always foulmouthed who frequented the East Bath. I'd have thought that money was the overwhelming driving force of such women of easy virtue, but evidently I was wrong.

These women weren't foolish of course, for they knew that in the evening of the final day of SPORTSFEST there would be those present in the Common Room who had prize money burning a hole in their money pouches. There was nothing better than drink to light the flame of desire, and the women knew it.

But Max had no interest in them. His eyes were elsewhere and it wasn't long before he and a handsome young man, propping up the counter, made eye contact. Max, a handsome young man himself, ambled across. Words passed between them then Max returned: "I'll see you in the morning back at the garrison."

My warning reply could have been lengthy, pointing out the dangers of going off with strangers who would fleece you. Maybe even hurt you. Maybe even kill you. It had happened before. On the day we'd arrived in Caesarea some months ago the body of one of our kind had been pulled out of the harbour, dead. An examination had revealed that he'd had his throat cut. An investigation had also revealed that on that very day he'd been paid and had last been seen, worse for wear, in the *Herod the Great*.Our commanding officer had warned us of this, advising that we should never be out on our own at night. But I knew that Max wouldn't heed my warning. I therefore simply said: "Don't forget…We sail at noon tomorrow." Minutes later Max and his newly acquired friend left holding hands. I found it very strange. I also knew that I had a lot to learn about life.

It wasn't long before a group of us, all having competed in the day's sporting activities, started laughing and joking about our various performances. One, a giant of a man who seemed incapable of throwing a spear only a short distance, had launched one completely out of the stadium. On its flight it had picked up some washed women's underwear on a clothes line before sticking into a nearby tree. The incident could of course have ended in disaster, yet somehow it sounded funny, especially after a tankard or two of strong ale.

Others had fallen off the chariot before even firing a shot, in the arrow shooting event. But the accounts bringing the greatest laughs were from those who had ended up in the mud bath. Some had apparently nearly drowned. Others had taken in mouthfuls of the evil smelling liquid. But the loudest laugh, causing all those present in the Common Room to stop their conversations and look across to see what was happening, came when a slightly overweight comrade called Antony described one of his attempts: "I set off along the staging and, following your technique, Cassius, I went into a slide on the slippery surface…I grabbed the rope but seemed unable to swing forwards or backwards on it…Slowly, as my arms weakened, I slid down the rope…Equally slowly, the cold mud crept up my body as I became immersed in it…Although I managed to just keep my head above the surface I couldn't help tasting it…I was convinced that the others had earlier pissed in it. "

As midnight approached, the Common Room thinned out as drinkers, many worse for wear, started to make their way home, home for the soldiers being the garrison. Like me, several were sailing at noon the following day.

Throughout the evening I'd laughed and joked with one of the young women behind the counter every time I'd got my round in. She seemed to be attracted to me, and I certainly to her, so when she indicated to the others that she was leaving I took my leave and followed her out. As we walked down the street she linked arms with me and our light hearted conversation continued, and in Latin too, her job having given her a good command of the language. She already knew my name, having heard my colleagues use it on several occasions during the evening. She was called Martha and worked at the winery during the day. She lived with her eight year old son called Aaron, in a small house at the end of town that had once belonged to her parents, who were now dead. Her husband, a builder, had evidently lost his life in an accident whilst working on one of the town's ambitious projects.

Not knowing Caesarea at all, having only spent a matter of hours there, and only in daylight, I was soon lost. We weaved our way through the narrow streets, the only light being from a full moon. But charged up with strong ale and excited at the prospect of what I hoped would follow, the last thing on my mind was being lost, nor did it occur to me that in the morning I would have to somehow find my way back to the garrison in time for roll call.

We entered a house through an unlocked door and Martha, feeling her way, managed to light an oil lamp in the centre of the room. She then took the lamp in one hand, my hand in the other and led me to a staircase. As we ascended she placed her finger to her lips indicating that we had to be quiet. At the top she pointed at a closed door and whispered: "My son, Aaron is asleep in there…We must not wake him."

I nodded, fully agreeing with her. The last thing I wanted was for the young boy to wake then spoil the fun that I hoped was soon to follow.

Martha first extinguished the lamp then, by the moonlight streaming through the window, undressed. I hesitantly did the same, never having been in this position before. We then laid on the bed, side by side, neither feeling confident to take the initiative. She then whispered: "You're only the second one I've laid with since the death of my husband."

Feeling the need to be honest, knowing that she would soon realise that I was inexperienced, I replied: "And I've never done this before."

"Don't worry…I will show you what I want you to do."

When she opened her legs I took the hint and moved on top of her, my knees pushing her legs open even further. Thinking that all I'd to do now was to push my erection home I thrust forward. Martha winced at the pain and realised I needed a little help. She therefore guided me in. As I thrust backwards and forwards above her I was aware that the pendant around my neck was dangling onto her face. She reached up with her hands, took hold of the leather thong and eased it over my head. She then dropped it on the rug at the side of the bed. Our love making could now continue, unhindered by any distractions.

When I woke the following morning the sun was already streaming through the window. Martha was moving about downstairs and I also heard a young boy's voice. After quickly dressing I descended the stairs, to be greeted by a pleasant smile from her and a puzzled look from the boy who didn't speak. Being at a loss what to say neither did I.

The angle of the sun told me that the time must be about ten o'clock. Roll call back at the garrison would take place at eleven in preparation for our embarkation at noon. I had to get back as soon as possible.

There was no time for something to eat although Martha tried to persuade me to at least share a warm bread roll that she'd just purchased at the bakers across the street, and a thick slice of goat's cheese. But I did not have the time. I had to take my leave.

As I did so I thanked her for the wonderful evening I'd had. I then reached into my purse and extracted ten silver denarii. I did not want to give her the impression that I was paying for her favours so I whispered: "Get something for the boy."

She accepted the money gratefully then called her son to her: "Aaron, I want you to take my friend back to where the soldiers live…We'll then go to the market and see if we can get something you'd like…You're always saying you'd like a dog…Well, lets see if there are any puppies for sale."

The boy's eyes lit up at the word 'dog' and I assumed that he had been pestering his mother a while for one.

With a nod of Aaron's head in the direction of the door I made my move, again thanking Martha for a lovely, and from my point of view, very educational evening. It had been my first experience with a woman and I wouldn't be forgetting it in a hurry.

Aaron set off at a quick pace, knowing that the sooner he was back the sooner he and his mother would get to the market. Maybe there would be just one or two puppies for sale, and maybe there would be one or two other children also looking for them. He'd heard adults say that the early bird gets the worm, and he wanted to be the early boy getting the puppy.

As we weaved our way through the maze of narrow streets of Old Caesarea I realised that on my own I'd have never been able to make my way back to the garrison. As we rounded a corner the boy pointed, but didn't speak. There in front of us were the open garrison gates, with a soldier in full uniform on duty. I thanked the boy for his help, not knowing if he understood me or not. I also felt that he himself needed rewarding, even though I had given his mother a few denarii, I therefore reached into my purse, extracted another coin and gave it to him. For the first time he smiled and for the first time spoke, and in Latin too: "Thank you…And God go with you." He then shot off. The market was calling him.

Once in the garrison I quickly collected my worldly belongings together, which amounted to very little, changed into my uniform and headed for the parade ground for roll call. Max was already there, but seemed reluctant to speak. He certainly didn't want to turn his face towards me…and I soon realised why. He'd obviously been beaten up sometime between leaving the ale house and arriving back at the garrison.

I whispered to him: "What happened, then?"

His reply was what I expected from a colleague with immense pride: "I don't want to talk about it now, Marcus…Maybe later."

I cursed myself for not having warned him before he'd left with his 'friend'. But would he have heeded my warning? I doubted it. It didn't occur to me that what had happened to him could quite easily have happened to me after leaving the alehouse with Martha.

As we stood there at ease on the parade ground, waiting for roll call followed by our commanding officer marching us down to the harbour, I felt uncomfortable in a new set of leather body armour that was far too small for me. As I eased my fingers into the neck band to release the pressure on my throat I suddenly realised that the pot pendant was missing. I remembered having it when I left the ale house so I must have somehow lost it between then and now…but where?

Then it came to me. Martha had taken it off me whilst we'd been making love and had dropped it onto the rug at the side of the bed.

51

I now had to somehow retrieve it, and had only minutes to do so. I dug Max in the ribs: "Quick…Follow me." I hadn't time to explain. Like the good friend he was he followed as I ran towards the garrison gates. On arriving there I looked at the junction at the top of the road, not having any idea which road Aaron and I had come down. The task was hopeless. I would probably need the whole day to somehow reverse the route the boy had brought me.

Max, totally puzzled, asked: "What the hell's going on?"

"I went back home with a woman last night and lost something."

"What was it?"

"Haven't got time to explain…Sufficient to say that it was very precious to me."

Max guessed, wrongly as it happened: "You mean your prize money?"

"No…Far more important than that."

Max looked even more puzzled. What could be more important than a purse full of silver coins?

Initially I was furious with myself for being so careless with something so valuable. I was even annoyed with Martha for not reminding me about it. But quickly that fury and annoyance turned to sadness. I had lost one of the most precious items in the world, one given to me by Jesus Christ the Son of God just before his crucifixion. How could I have been so careless and thoughtless?

Reluctantly accepting that my situation was hopeless I turned and headed back towards the garrison gates.

Then I heard a distant shout…the shout of a child. I turned, to see Aaron running down the road towards me, holding something high in the air. Gasping for breath, he stuttered: "M-my mother says this is y-yours." He then passed the pot pendant to me. Understandably, I gratefully accepted it and thanked the boy profusely, at the same time giving him a hug.

Max nodded his head in amazement: "All this fuss over a funny shaped piece of pot, dangling from a black leather thong…Quite mad."

It was then that I realised that I had never taken Max into my confidence over the piece. I now had some explaining to do, but not just now.

Aaron then surprised me again, and in a way I couldn't have predicted in my wildest dreams. He reached under his spotlessly white tunic, opened some sort of purse on a leather belt and pulled out another piece of pot, also hanging from a black leather thong. As he passed it across to me he again spoke: "A man called Matthew left it with my mother two weeks ago...She wondered if you wanted it?"

I examined it closely, particularly looking at its colour, shape and for any sort of inscription on it. The colour was pea green, the shape a perfect triangle, all three angles looking identical in size, and one side had the Greek letter τ, tau, engraved into it. The thong passed through a tiny hole at one of the triangle's points. I always assumed that Jesus had given out twelve identically shaped pieces of pot to his disciples, the pieces maybe differing in their colour and the letter engraved into them, but I was obviously wrong. Was it even possible that all thirteen pieces, including his own, had their own unique shape and colour? I suppose it was.

I decided to hold the piece against the piece that Jesus had given to me. The side of the triangular piece was identical in length to one side of my piece. This immediately got me thinking - six triangular pieces of pot would fit round my piece, making a pattern of seven pieces in all. But Zachariah the potter had made thirteen pieces altogether. So, assuming that they did form a new pattern, how did the remaining six pieces fit in to make it? When I later had time on the ship to do so I would sit down with charcoal and paper, and work out how the pattern could look.

So, Jesus had given this piece to Matthew during the Last Supper. But why had Matthew then left it with Martha? Was he worried about losing it and felt that it would be safer with her? Or was it a form of payment for services rendered? My mind flashed back to what she'd said to me before we'd made love - since her husband had died she'd only slept with one other man before me. Was this other man in fact Matthew himself? I suddenly felt jealous.

Max and I heard a lot of shouting coming from the parade ground. The roll call had started. We had to get back to our positions in time to shout out our names at the required time, otherwise we would be declared absent without good reason, one of the most serious charges in the Roman Army, and in a battle theatre punishable by death.

I therefore quickly gave Aaron another silver coin, at the same time telling him to thank his mother for two items that she couldn't possibly have known the value of. As he ran off up the road I shouted: "I Hope you get your puppy."

As he reached the corner at the road junction and disappeared round it I just managed to pick up the words: "So do I."

Max and I ran across the parade ground to take up our positions in the line. As we did so I managed to slip both leather loops over my head and tucked the two pieces of pot beneath the top of my body armour. I had already decided to give Max the newly acquired one. Jesus said that the piece he gave me would look after me, whatever that meant. Maybe the piece I passed on to Max would look after him too.

Did all the pieces that Jesus gave out at the Last Supper have some sort of mystical powers? The one he gave to me just before his crucifixion presumably had, so why not the others?

***

Chapter Six

At noon on the high tide, although the sea level hadn't increased very much to me, our ship sailed out of Caesarea harbour, three others following us. Our commander-in-chief informed us that each ship was carrying fifty men, a total of two hundred in all. We would call at the port of Limassol in Cyprus just to see if the natives again wanted putting in their places. We would then head for Syracusae, in Sicilia. The total journey would take about twenty days, four days more than the inward journey, but of course we would be sailing against the Mare Internum's prevailing wind from the west. Our captain looked at the sky and assured us that at least the three day journey to Cyprus would be a calm one.

That evening, while the sun was still above the western horizon, I found a quiet place on the deck as near to the stern as I could get. I was therefore well away from the other soldiers who were enjoying themselves throwing large leather bags over the side attached to ropes, filling them with seawater and hoisting them aboard. They then threw the water at each other. The practice kept them cool, kept them clean, but above all from my point of view, kept them well away from me.

With me I had a large sheet of paper and a thin length of charcoal, both items having been purchased from one of the numerous market stalls down by the harbour. I first spread the paper on the flat deck then pulled out the white piece of pot from beneath the tunic I was wearing, lifting the black thong over my head as I did so.

I placed the pot on the paper and carefully drew round its six sides with the charcoal. This gave me my starting point. After lifting the second piece, triangular in shape, over my head, I place it on the paper so that one of its sides was positioned exactly against the top side of the first piece. I then also drew round it.

At that point Max came across to invite me to join in the fun, but soon realised by my serious look that what I was doing was important to me. He backed off when I assured him that I would reveal all that evening.

Having drawn the two shapes I wanted I quickly looped both thongs back over my head, again hiding both pieces of pot beneath my tunic. It was essential that the other soldiers, apart from Max, who had already seen the two pieces, didn't set eyes on one or both of them. There were soldiers on board who had seen the disciples of Jesus with similar objects round their necks at the time of his crucifixion. They would wonder how the devil one of their own also had one, even two.

I stared at my drawing so far. It didn't tell me very much. I therefore decided to expand it by simply adding identical triangular shapes against the remaining five sides of the six sided shape. This immediately gave me a six pointed star. I counted the number of shapes - seven in number. But Jesus had given out twelve pieces of pot at the Last Supper. Including his own piece that made thirteen in all. So how did the other six pieces fit into the pattern?

It took me only a few seconds to work it out. By drawing a square round the star the positions of the six pieces were revealed - four at the corners and one down either side - thirteen in all. Jesus's design had been unbelievably simple. Within a square about the size of the span between one's little finger and thumb he had produced a pattern that could represent himself and his twelve disciples. Sadly the square had now been broken up into its thirteen individual pieces, and each piece was on a journey into the unknown, including the two in my possession. Never again would they be re-assembled to form Jesus's square.

That evening, after a hearty meal of roasted goat, the roasting process carried out on deck, and at one point was in danger of setting the main sail on fire, much to the captain's annoyance, I asked Max to accompany me to the stern where we were able to find peace and quiet. It was time to put him in the picture.

I commenced by taking him back to earlier in the day when I grabbed him off the parade ground and led him to the garrison gates where we met the young boy called Aaron: "Can you remember the boy handing me two pieces of pot, one white the other a sort of pea green colour, both attached to thin leather thongs?"

"Yes…But what's so special about two pieces of coloured pot?…You can see something similar on any rubbish dump…Pot is easily smashed, you know." Max couldn't see what all the fuss was about.

I lifted the two pieces of pot over my head and before speaking pulled out the drawing I'd made earlier from beneath my tunic, but kept it folded: "Well now…Take my word for it, for every word is true…At the Last Supper, you know, when Jesus told his disciples that one of them would betray him, leading to his trial, a guilty verdict, his crucifixion, resurrection and ascension into heaven…" I paused not only to allow Max to take it all in, but also to allow me to get my breath back.

He nodded, indicating that so far he was following all that I was saying.

So far, so good...I continued: "Well...At that supper he gave each of his disciples a small piece of coloured pot attached to a thin leather thong, each with a different Greek letter engraved into it...He also had a piece for himself... His instruction to them was to tie the ends of the thong together then place the loop over their heads so that the pieces of pot could be worn round their necks." (I assumed that something along those lines must have been said by Jesus, but of course I had no evidence to support that opinion).

Max spoke: "So...The white piece in your hand belonged to Jesus, and he gave it to you...What about the green piece?"

"Ah...This belonged to Matthew, he having received it from Jesus."

"How do you know that?"

"Remember what the boy said?...A man called Matthew had stayed at his mother's house and had left the piece of pot with her...Presumably for safe keeping...But she must have thought that it would be safer with me."

Max appeared to accept my story, but still couldn't see what all the fuss was about.

I decided to show him the drawing I'd made earlier, at the same time describing how I'd constructed it. This seemed to arouse Max's interest: "Crafty...Who'd have thought that a star surrounded by a square would give exactly thirteen shapes...The same number as he and his twelve disciples?...Very clever indeed." He paused for a second, then continued: "But you've only got two of the thirteen pieces...You're not hoping to make a collection of them all, are you?"

"No...nothing like that...It would be an impossible task any way...No, I just intend to do what Jesus asked me to do - wear it round my neck at all times."

"But why is it so important to do that?"

"Well...When he gave it to me his words were - Look after this and it will look after you...I have no idea what he meant by that, unless it's like some sort of lucky charm...I suppose only time will tell."

"And what about the other piece?"

"I want you to wear it in the same way...Maybe it will also act as a lucky charm for you too...You've nothing to lose, have you?"

"Well, no...But it was originally given to Matthew...Won't that make any difference?"

"I don't know…Presumably only time will tell," was my unhelpful repeated reply.

Max placed the loop with the piece of pot on it round his neck, tucking it under his tunic to hide it. Hopefully any mystical powers it possessed would rub off on him.

As we approached the Cypriot port of Limassol, intent on 'showing the flag' for the Roman Empire, we observed a small rowing boat edging towards us. When it was a ship's length away it abruptly stopped. This surprised us for we expected the two men rowing it to come aboard.

Just as the captain was about to issue an invitation one of the men shouted across the water: "Typhus…Typhus in Limassol…Do not land."

We had all heard of typhus. Some of us had even been infected by it in the past. It was a disease that was caused by a bite from a mite that lived on rats. And the port of Limassol had more than its fair share of the rodents. The disease could spread like wild fire, and had we landed it would have been through us all in a matter of days.

But not landing had its disadvantages. A call at the Cypriot port would have been our last opportunity to replenish our stock of fresh water and food before commencing the long journey to the port of Syracusae on the south east tip of Sicilia. Alas we could not afford to take the risk.

As we entered the waters to the south west of the island of Creta the weather and hence the sea conditions dramatically changed as the cold northerly wind blowing down the Mare Adriaticum from the Alps met the warm westerly wind sweeping along the length of the Mare Internum. Rain came down incessantly like a shower of spears from the sky. The conflicting wind patterns whipped up the sea into a maelstrom of chaos. All sail had been taken in in order to avoid the ship capsizing, as it surely would have done.

It was now a case of riding out the storm until it blew itself out. Most of us spent most of the time hanging over the side being violently sick and wanting to die. Of course there was no sympathy from the captain who, he informed us, had never been seasick in his entire life. All he did was rant and rave about the vomit that was being projected along the side of his precious ship. Fortunately each breaking wave washed it away.

The storm persisted on and off for several days. All the time we were drifting, but the captain assured us that we were not in any danger, being well away from any land. But he was wrong. The wave pattern suddenly changed, becoming more mountainous, with waves now breaking over the entire length of the ship. We were being swamped. The captain had seen such a change in wave pattern many times before. He rushed to the side and scoured the horizon for land because he knew that the depth of water beneath his ship was decreasing. But the continuous rain reduced visibility to almost zero.

Suddenly we all heard a chilling grinding sound, followed by the ship rising, then crashing down on something very solid. We had in fact run aground, but still could not see any land. As the ship was pounded on the unseen rocks it slowly started to break up. First the mast crashed down, trapping men under all the rigging. As those still free worked frantically to help those who were trapped a loud cracking sound told us that the ship's back had broken. Realising that all was lost the captain shouted: "Abandon ship...Every man for himself."

Those who were in a position to save themselves were now torn between continuing to help their colleagues or somehow getting themselves safely overboard and swimming towards the sound of the pounding surf. A huge wave then hit the crippled ship, sweeping the mast, the rigging and many of the men trapped beneath, overboard and into the boiling sea. Some were lucky enough to come to the surface, free, but others were lost in the utter chaos.

I grabbed Max by the arm and pulled him towards the ship's stern. For a few seconds I'd watched the wave pattern and observed that waves were hitting the prow of the ship, running the full length of it and then washing over the stern. To me it seemed to be the safest point to get off the ship. As the next wave, by far the biggest I'd seen so far, rushed along the deck towards the stern I shouted to Max: "Jump...Now." Trusting me he did so, and I followed him. As we did so the wave hit us with great force carrying us well away from the ship and the floating debris that was all around it, debris in which we could so easily have become entangled.

I surfaced and, riding the waves, looked around for Max. There was no sign of him. As the waves carried me away from the wreck I spotted his blonde head bobbing up and down in the water some distance away. I shouted across, but the noise of the storm drowned out my voice. I therefore had no alternative but to swim towards him. For a brief moment I thought how lucky I'd been to have lived as a child close to a lake where I'd learnt to swim, even managing the lake's full length of almost a league at the tender age of eight.

I felt confident in the mountainous waves, experiencing no fear as I set out towards Max. As I got nearer he spotted me and waved. He'd managed to grab hold of a piece of decking as it had floated past him. When I reached him I also grabbed it. There was little point in expending energy, swimming to keep afloat.

As I knew it would be, the decking was carried on the waves towards the unseen shore. The sound of the pounding surf was now deafening, but both of us knew that we had to go through it in order to survive.

Then a huge breaking wave hit the decking, tearing it from our grasp. The next wave hit us carrying us after it. Were we heading for a deadly rocky shore where we would be beaten to a pulp, or a sandy beach? I could only pray that it was the latter.

My pray was answered. The next wave dropped me heavily on something solid, but not sharp. I reached down to it and found that I could grab a handful. It was sand, lovely soft sand. I now found that I could stand, although each incoming wave attempted to knock me over. Slowly I staggered out of the water, still uncertain on my feet. But I had made it. I had survived.

I looked around me, but could not see Max. He'd been holding onto the decking with me so he could only be a short distance away, assuming that he too had been washed towards the beach. As the next wave broke I spotted his body in the water, head down and making no movement. In a state of panic I rush in and grabbed him, pulling him above the breaking waterline. He was obviously not breathing so, not knowing what else to do, I turned him over onto his back and pummelled him viciously on the chest.

This brutal act, for a reason that I couldn't explain, did the trick, for Max coughed and spluttered, at the same time shooting water out of his mouth. Within a matter of seconds he was breathing quite normally. As we laid there on the warm sand, for during our ordeal the sun had decided to show its face, we realised just how lucky we were to have survived. But had it been luck? I suddenly panicked. In the total chaos of the last half hour had I lost the piece of pot that had originally been round my neck? I felt for it, and to my delight I felt its unusual shape through my saturated tunic. Was Max's piece also still around his neck? I felt for that too, and sure enough it was there.

I scanned the beach in both directions, looking for other survivors like ourselves. There had been fifty soldiers on our ship. Surely some of them had made it to the shore, but I saw no bodies, alive or dead. All I could see were bits of debris - parts of the deck, lengths of rope, ripped pieces of sail, even the full length of the mast. Since the beach appeared to have small headlands at both ends, with coves probably beyond them, I could only hope that there were at least one or two survivors on the beaches there.

But what if there weren't? What if we were the only survivors, not only out of the fifty men on our ship, but also out of the full complement of two hundred men on the four ships that had been making the journey to Sicilia

My mind flashed back to those very words that Jesus Christ had spoken to me minutes before his crucifixion: "Look after this and it will look after you."

Had he also said the exact same words to his disciples during the Last Supper, and that included Matthew the original owner of the piece of pottery that was now around Max's neck? Was it just possible that these two insignificant pieces, pieces that most people wouldn't have looked twice at, had indeed been responsible for our survival due to some sort of power that they possessed, when all others had been lost in the chaos of the storm? If not, our survival must have been sheer luck.

But luck hadn't come into it, I was confident of that. Those two simple pieces of pot, through the power bestowed into them by Jesus, his Father or both, had indeed protected us against the evils of the storm, ensuring our survival. We had in fact been protected by a force that came from above. Since witnessing the crucifixion of Jesus my faith had hardened. After this event it was now rock solid. There was indeed a Heaven, with a God looking down on us, offering protection to those who believed. And the reason why none of the others had survived, if indeed they hadn't? They were non-believers. It was as simple as that.

As we lay on the beach, slowly drying out and recovering our energy, we became aware that a group of men, four in number, were walking towards us along the beach. Outnumbered and without any sort of weapons, we had to hope that they were friendly.

When they reached us one, apparently their leader, spoke. At first he spoke in what I recognised as Greek, although my knowledge of the language was almost non-existent. Realising this, he spoke again, but in Latin: "My name is Andreas, these are Menelaus, Artemas and Ulysses...Who are you, and where are you from?"

I studied the man. He looked about forty years of age, with a

61

sculptured face that seemed to show great character and an experience of life. And yet it oozed kindness and understanding. This gave me the confidence to answer him freely. In our possibly precarious position there was little point in staying silent or lying. One thing was certain, although I didn't know if it carried any weight in this place, the sand beneath us was part of the Roman Empire, as all land was along the northern coast of the Mare Internum, and we were Roman citizens. But I wasn't naïve enough to think that there weren't pockets of resistance throughout the Empire: "I am Marcus…This is Maximus, but I call him Max…We are Roman soldiers and we're en route to Sicilia from Palestina, but our ship was wrecked in the storm…We're lucky to have made it to the shore."

Andreas asked two simple questions, requiring two simple answers: "How many ships?…And how many men?"

I immediately realised why he wanted to know this information. Wrecked ships meant useful, even valuable, items being washed ashore. Any survivors could create problems, especially if they were prepared to fight and had the energy to do so. But I felt that being honest was our best means of being well treated. Anyway, why should we care if they retrieved items, valuable or not, from the sea or beach? Such items would be of no use to us: "We were four ships, each carrying fifty men…Two hundred in all."

Andreas replied: "We saw you from the headland to the east, but saw no one else…Very few survive when wrecked along this coast…Most bodies aren't even washed up here…Some have even ended up on the beaches of Zakinthos, and that's all of thirty six leagues away…You have indeed been very luck."

I smiled at him, then at Max, at the same time checking that the piece of pot beneath my already drying tunic, was still there: "Yes…Lucky indeed…But can you tell us where we are?"

Andeas, obviously knowledgeable about the local weather conditions, maybe even a fisherman, smiled as he answered: "Your captain, just south west of Creta, would have changed to a north westerly course to head for Sicilia, probably the port of Syracusae…But the storm, as it would do at this time of year, drove your ship northwards…You ran aground on the south-west tip of Achaia…near the fishing village of Pilos…Heard of it?"

I shook my head, at the same time trying to hide my surprise at the question. How would a simple Roman soldier recognise the name of a fishing village in Achaia? I was almost tempted to ask if he had heard of the Italia village Grotto san Stefano where I came from, but in our precarious situation, decided it wouldn't be sensible to put him on the spot.

His next words, however, at first frightened us then gave us hope, making us feel that our situation wasn't as precarious as we'd originally thought: "There are pirates in the area who prey on the Roman ships that trade throughout the Mare Internum...But the ships are now protected by your navy and as a result many pirates have been killed...If they discover you they will kill you...But don't worry, we will help you...We hate the pirates because they steal our fish."

As we made our way to the village, all the time watching out for pirates who may have come ashore to shelter from the storm, our newly acquired friend explained the help he and his colleagues could, and would give us: "First we must disguise you as sailors...This will allow you to pass through the village to the harbour, where we will put you on a ship that will take you to the port of Tarantum...Have you heard of it, it's a Roman port?"

He asked his question as if he expected us to know every port on Italia's mainland, when in fact, as country boys, we knew barely two - Neapolis and Rhegium, the port from which we'd sailed to Messina, on Sicilia earlier that year.

I wanted to know more about Tarantum so I asked: "So, where is this port of Tarentum, and how far away is it?"

"You'll sail north west for about four days, covering a good two hundred and forty leagues...The port is on the Gulf of Tarantum, almost the most southerly point of Italia...The local farmers who keep many sheep in the area send us their wool...Our women wash, dye, spin and weave it and return it as cloth...The trade has gone on for many years - you have better wool, we have better weavers...The route is known by us all as the Wool Route."

On the outskirts of Pilos we observed in the distance a group of men sitting outside what was probably an ale house, or whatever they drank in these parts. Andreas grabbed Max and I, pulling us behind a wall: "Pirates...Follow me." He and his colleagues led us through the narrow backstreets, finally stopping at a whitewashed cottage standing on its own. He knocked on the newly painted blue door and without waiting for a response, entered. The rest of us quickly followed him through.

63

As we entered what appeared to be a dining room, linked to a kitchen, a woman came down a flight of well worn stone steps from a room above. She smiled at us and spoke to Andreas: "Right, husband, who have we here, then?…They look as if they could do with a good meal."

Andreas answered her: "Two young Roman soldiers, Helena, washed up on the beach, just off the Point…As far as we know the only two survivors out of over two hundred sailing west to Sicilia."

At first Helena appeared saddened at the news, then smiled and, by the wave of her hand, invited us to sit down at a huge table surrounded by six heavy wooden chairs. We did so and the four men joined us. It only then struck me that three had not said a word, leaving all the talking to Andreas. Although his Latin was only minimal we could at least understand him. Max and I had picked up a smattering of Greek whilst in Judaea, and we used that when we could. As a result the two of us were able to communicate adequately with the others.

In a matter of minutes Helena was dishing out goat stew from a huge iron pot that was resting on a grill above the glowing embers of a wood burning fire. Large loaves of bread were placed on the table, ready to be broken into chunks in order to soak up the gravy.

The stew was unbelievably tasty and no doubt Helena had used all her culinary skills whilst producing it. The household obviously ate well. The effect on Max and I was immediate, for although it was warm and sunny outside, and our tunics had already dried, we had both been shivering when we'd entered Andreas's house, probably the after-effects of our ordeal. Now we were revived, but incredibly tired, as shown to our hosts by our eyes slowly opening and closing after our sustenance.

At this point Andreas made a suggestion: "Helena, take our guests upstairs to rest…We will go down to the market place and buy the sort of clothes that sailors wear…They'll have to look the part if they are to be taken on as crew on board a ship heading for Tarantum…They'll certainly be expected to work their passage."

Andreas could see panic in my eyes and sought to reassure me: "Don't worry…You can pull a rope, climb a mast, scrub a deck, can't you?…And don't worry about the language…The captain will almost certainly be Roman…But to get in his good books, tell him who you are and what has happened to you…Above all tell him that you are soldiers with combat experience…Pirates are known to operate in the waters between Pilos and Tarantum…Your fighting skills could come in handy."

After a couple of hours of much needed sleep we were awakened bymuch laughter coming from the room immediately below us. As we descended the stairs some sort of clothes show was on the go. Two of the men, Artemas and Ulysses, were dressed and parading across the room in canvas shoes, dark blue trousers made of what looked like sail cloth, and white short sleeved shirts, obviously made of cotton, as our tunics were. We assumed, as it happened quite rightly, that the clothes had been purchased in the market and were the latest fashion in sailors' dress. Since the clothes looked new, meaning that Max and I would stand out in them in any ship's crew, Menelaus suggested giving them a worn appearance: "Come...let me teach you some Grecian wrestling in the yard outside...It's a bit muddy after the storm but that won't matter."

Although we'd heard of the sport we'd never learned the art. It was time for our first and only lesson.

As I changed into my new clothes I removed the white piece of pot from around my neck and passed it to Maximus for safekeeping, at the same time jokingly pointing out to our hosts that it was a lucky charm, purchased from a market stall in Cyprus. I was now ready for action. Menelaus showed me where to grip him, before taking a powerful grip of me himself. He then explained the rules: "You must keep your grip at all times...Using the strength in your arms and your legs you have to throw me to the ground on my back, holding me down while the referee counts up to five...Let's give it a go, shall we?"

Within five seconds I'd been thrown to the ground, with Menelaus landing heavily on top of me...Artemas, acting as referee, counted to five. The same happened again, and again, but on the fourth attempt, after the two of us, had danced round the yard several times, much to the others' amusement, I succeeded in tripping up Menelaus. This time he crashed to the ground with me on top of him. Artemas quickly counted to five. As we stood up he patted me on the back: "Well done...You are a good wrestler."

It was now Max's turn to learn the art of Grecian wrestling, but first he passed to me my and his piece of pots for safe keeping, also joking about their 'lucky charm' qualities. His opponent was Ulysses. Max's contest followed much the same pattern as mine, with him also winning on the fourth attempt. I was convinced that both our experienced opponents had decided beforehand how both contests would go.

The result of all this was that our trousers and shirts were now covered in dirt from the muddy ground. Our shirts were also torn round the shoulders. When Helena saw them she took a needle and thread, intentionally dark in colour, and stitched up the tears as roughly as she possibly could. It was essential that the stitching looked as if an incompetent man had done it. Our clothes were now ready to be tested at the recruiting office on the quayside at the port of Pilos where we hoped to be taken on to work our passage to Tarantum. But that would take place tomorrow.

The following morning, before sunrise, and after a night on a straw palliasse on the floor of Menelaus's home, Max and I sat down in the tunics we'd originally sailed in, to a hearty breakfast prepared by Helena. It appeared that there was no shortage of goat's cheese, warm bread and fresh fruit in the household. We then changed into our mudded clothes. As we did so we both ensured that our precious pieces of pot were securely round our necks and well hidden from view under our shirts.

Menelaus was shortly joined by Ulysses and the two of them escorted us to the recruiting office. Recruitment was, we were told, usually carried out by the first officer of the ship looking for crew. But Menelaus spotted someone he knew. As he walked across to have word, Ulysses put us in the picture: "The captain of the *Julius Caesar*, the premier ship on the Wool Route…It will be loaded up to the deck with its valuable cargo of the best quality woollen cloth, intended for the elite in Roma, Neapolis and Pisae…He always does his own recruiting."

Menelaus rejoined us: "You're in luck…The captain was only looking for one crew member, but when I told him that both of you were Roman soldiers who had been shipwrecked only yesterday en route to Sicilia, he offered both of you a berth to Tarantum…Just pull your weight and be on the look out for pirates…They know the ship and know its valuable cargo."

***

Chapter Seven

The *Julius Caesar* set sail at noon and as it did so we shouted our thanks to Menelaus and Ulysses who were on the quayside. The sea was calm, so different from the last time Max and I had been on the water. The wind was also light, little more than a breeze, and uncharacteristically warm for the time of year, when the usual wind was cold, coming down from the north, straight from the distant northern Alps. The warm breeze had probably originated from the huge expanses of desert to the south.

The captain informed us that if pirates were to strike it would be at night and within a few days of leaving Pilos. They did not like to get too near the coast of Italia, where the waters were patrolled by the Roman Navy, sailing out of Tarantum. He also showed us his weaponry that consisted of five shields, ten spears, two swords and eight bows, with a good supply of arrows. Max and I checked over the weapons, finding that the shields were little more than cowhide stretched across a square wooden frame, not what we were used to. All but two of the spears were badly warped, restricting their true flight to barely five paces, but that may be enough. The swords were rusty and lacked any sort of balance, so essential in a good fighting weapon. Four of the bows had no strings at all, but the remaining four looked in good condition, as were most of the arrows. The arsenal was unbelievably poor to guard a ship with such a valuable cargo.

During the remainder of daylight Max and I carried out remedial work on the weapons, much to the annoyance of the other crew members, who were sweating in the heat as they put on maximum sail to catch the lightest of breezes. In their eyes we were already shirking.

There was little we could do about the shields other than fasten two of them back to back. The two layers of hide may just stop a spear or sword blade passing through, but not an arrow shot at close range. Of course the shield was heavier, but it would only have to be carried a few paces. As Max was choosing the best of the spears, selecting only four, I studied the two swords. The hilts of both were down to the base metal. After hunting around the deck I found a long length of thin cord, ideal for what I wanted. As I loosely coiled it up, one of the crew shouted something in Greek that I didn't understand. He then grabbed hold of the coil, but I held on tight and pushed him away.

The other members of the crew stopped what they were doing and came across. A fight could be quite entertaining. Max, having ample experience of patrolling areas in the Holy Land, when confrontations of this sort often got quickly out of hand, rushed across to offer me support if I required it.

The man came back at me and, suspecting that I'd no idea how to wrestle, grabbed my shirt and tried to throw me to the deck. But he got a shock, for in those four rounds I'd earlier had with Menelaus I'd learnt a thing or two. First I momentarily relaxed, almost into submission, then when my opponent thought he was getting on top I retaliated at lightning speed and, to my surprise the tactic worked. My opponent's feet lifted off the deck as I pulled his body over my protruding hip. He appeared to twist in the air then crash to the deck with me falling on top of him.

Thinking that that was the end of the matter I got to my feet and walked away, picking up the coil of cord as I did so. But my opponent had different ideas. He extracted a knife from a scabbard attached to the back of his belt and rushed at me.

Max shouted a warning: "Marcus…Behind you."

I spun round and immediately put into operation many of the unarmed combat skills I'd learnt during the numerous sessions I'd undergone at my basic training school. I stepped to one side, allowing my assailant to comealongside me. Like lightning I tightly grabbed the hand holding the knife, with my left hand, at the same time swiftly chopping down on the wrist with the side of my right hand. The effect of this swift action was to make my assailant drop the knife. As he moved away in obvious pain, I added insult to injury by picking up the knife and throwing it overboard. The others cheered me. Being new crewmen they didn't know my assailant, nor me for that matter. All they were interested in was congratulating the victor. Had it been him they'd have congratulated him instead.

After this small altercation I got down to tightly binding the sword hilts with the cord. The binding was far from ideal, but at least each sword now felt comfortable in the hand.

That night, while all but two of the crew slept below deck, the captain at the helm, the first officer at his side using the stars to navigate, Max and I took up our positions, he at the stern, me on the prow. Both of us had earlier changed into black longsleeved shirts and trousers conjured up from somewhere by the First Officer, and our faces and hands had been rubbed with lampblack. It was essential that when the full moon broke through, its light didn't reveal our positions.

Earlier all the crew, on my recommendation, had been instructed to stay below deck during the hours of darkness. If pirates were to get on board Max and I needed to know that if we shot or speared a shadow moving across the deck it was one of them and not a member of the crew.

During our basic training we had been taught to communicate by a series of whistles, imitating as best we could the call of some local animal or bird. This was especially useful at night. We therefore decided to use this method as a warning of imminent danger, for the distance between us was all of thirty paces.

Both of us armed ourselves according to our preferences. Both chose a shield, but whereas I preferred the bow and a handful of arrows, Max chose the four good spears. We had at hand the two swords, but hoped not to have to use them because that would mean hand-to-hand combat, and in the dark, too. Once settled, hiding behind the stout timbers surrounding the deck, we waited, hoping that it would be an uneventful night.

Unfortunately we didn't have to wait long. The moon, that was intermittently breaking through the thick cloud was, on the one hand, a godsend, allowing Max and I to see an approaching enemy, but on the other allowing the enemy to see us, if only as dark shapes, if they managed to get on board. They expected to use the element of surprise. So did we, and I felt that we had the advantage.

The night was remarkably quiet. There was little or no wind to flap the sails, nor were there any large waves to crash against the ship's prow as it cut through the water. The first I heard was the faintest splashing of water, the sound one hears as a rowing boat slowly approaches you. However quietly one tries to row, grease even being added to the rowlocks to prevent squeaking, it is nigh impossible to prevent the sound of the oars entering and leaving the water.

The sound, appearing to indicate an approach from the front of the ship, suddenly stopped, telling me that a boat of some sort was gliding into position just below the prow. I made a screeching sound. hopefully resembling the noise made by a seagull who was resting on the top of the mast, as Max and I had arranged to signal an imminent attack from the front. Max replied with a similar screech. He'd picked up my warning.

I picked up the bow, my choice of weapon, and positioned an arrow into it. I was ready. A round black shape suddenly appeared above the side, having probably looped a rope around the anchor and pulled himself up. I bided my time. The shape was undoubtedly the head, a relatively small target in the dark. I would probably only get one arrow off before other pirates showed themselves. My first arrow had to be a 'kill'. But two things were in my favour - the pirate had to use both his hands to pull himself over the side and therefore couldn't at that precise moment use any sort of weapon. And more importantly, he didn't know that I was there.

The black shape of the head was followed by the broad outline of the chest, a much easier target. I took careful aim at its centre and released the string from my finger tips. I immediately heard a slight thud. The arrow had hit its target. The pirate gasped and disappeared from view as he lost his grip. I fully expected to hear a splash as his body hit the water, but instead heard a dull thud. He had obviously fallen back into the boat, probably on top of the others, and probably no bad thing for it told them what to expect if they poked their heads above the 'parapet'. But I did hear a splash, and quite a large one too. I suspected that their dead colleague had been dumped over the side of the boat. There was obviously no room for sentiment in the world of being a pirate.

I then heard action taking place towards the stern. Max was under attack. I rushed along the deck to the rear, to find him fending off two assailants who were attacking him with swords. There was no time to work out how they'd managed to get on board…they were there. If, on seeing them, Max had managed to launch one of his spears he'd obviously missed, with no time to get another off.

Max slipped, lost his grip on his sword and fell on his back. He was now at the mercy of the pirates. As one kicked the sword out of Max's reach the other lifted his sword with the intention of plunging it into Max's chest. As the sword descended he managed to twist to one side to see it plunge deeply but harmlessly into the deck.

"With you Max," I shouted, to let him know that the new person joining the fray wasn't another pirate. The effect of my arrival was to divert the attention of the pirates to me, allowing Max to retrieve his sword. It was now a case of two against two, but only for a second, for another pirate approached from the front of the ship, probably also having climbed up the anchor.

It quickly became obvious to me that our three opponents weren't competent swordsmen. They'd always succeeded against unarmed crew or those worse than themselves, but not against two soldiers who had undergone hours of rigorous training in a Roman army camp. We'd been taught to fight back-to-back and this is what we did. Max took on one of the pirates, I the other two. As the five blades flashed as the moonlight fell on them I felt mine strike home on a pirate's arm. He yelled out in pain and retreated. I could have followed to push home my advantage, but instead stay close to Max.

The injured pirate, losing blood profusely, had no heart to return to the fray. This allowed me to now concentrate all my energy on the other one. He was older and more skilful, and put up a good fight, but when I showered attack after attack on him he backed away and climbed up onto the edge of the deck, presumable to give him the advantage. But that allowed me to slash at his legs and this is what I did, cutting deep just above the knee. At that point he lost his balance and fell overboard. The welcome splash told me that we wouldn't be seeing him again.

Max, too, was doing well, driving his opponent back across the deck with a series of lunges. As the pirate tried to defend himself he appeared to ease his grip on his sword. Max's next lunge saw the sword shoot across the deck. Its owner, deciding that he'd had enough, ran to the side, climbed up and jumped. The welcome splash told me that we'd also seen the last of him.

This left the pirate with the slashed arm. As I approached him, sword at the ready, he raised his arms in submission. Maybe I should have killed him there and then. But, following the code that had been instilled into all of us during our training, I accepted his surrender. While I checked his bleeding wound Max disappeared, to return with a long thin length of cloth which he first thoroughly soaked in seawater before binding it tightly round the pirate's arm. It was important not only to staunch the bleeding, but also to cleanse the wound. The pirate let out a cry as the salt water hit the raw flesh, but it had to be done, otherwise he would be in danger of losing his arm through infection.

And what about the two who had fled overboard? Had a rough sea been running, their rowing boat that had probably been rowed from a mother ship, would have drifted beyond their reach. Drowning would therefore have been their fate. But on that particular night, with a calm sea, little wind and a full moon they may well have been able to reach the boat and live to continue their piracy.

At that point the captain joined us on the deck, having kept well away during the fray. He now exercised his over riding power: "This renegade will be locked up in a cell we have on board to imprison mutineers…He will be fed a basic diet of bread and water, and when we arrive at Tarantum he will be handed to the authorities to stand trial for piracy." He also added that as far as he was aware this was the first time a pirate had been captured alive. Usually their missions were successful, the ship's crew often being slaughtered and the ship taken to one of the many uninhabited islands in the Mare Adriaticum where the valuable cargo was unloaded. The ship was then usually scuttled in order to hide all the evidence. After a period of time the cargo was then sold to the highest bidder on what was known throughout the Mare Internum as 'The Black Market'.

As Max and I were getting over our ordeal, first washing ourselves down, at the same time checking that we had come through unscathed, we then rested on some blankets that had been put down for us by members of the thankful crew. It was at this point that I got to thinking - why had Max ended up facing two assailants? Didn't he manage to get a spear off at one of them? I decided to ask him: "Did you miss with your spear, Max?…Must have been difficult in the dark, seeing your target."

"Er, no…I saw both of them come over the side, but rather than launch a spear at one of them I picked up my sword and faced them both…I felt really confident."

I immediately had my suspicions. Spearing one of the assailants would have placed Max in an advantageous position, but he decided against that course of action. Why? Suddenly I knew what had gone through his mind. It was all to do with the piece of pot round his neck. He genuinely thought that it was some sort of lucky charm that would protect him against all evils, and that included being attacked by pirates. The stupid boy. I had to tackle him about it: "Max…Just tell me why you decided to take on the two pirates with only a battered old sword in your hand…A bit foolish wasn't it?"

Max appeared not to pick up what I was getting at: "As I told you…I felt really confident…In fact I'd never felt so confident in all my life…It was a weird feeling…I felt invincible…Could have taken on a whole army."

My suspicions were confirmed. He had indeed felt invincible. But I had to remind him of one indisputable fact: "So what happened when you lost your sword and your assailant almost pinned you to the deck with his sword?"

"Oh…That was nothing…I just moved away and he missed."

God…the stupidity of the man. He didn't realise just how lucky he'd been.

But had it been luck? Or had some guardian angel been looking over him at that precise moment? And had it all to do with a small piece of pot, hanging from a thin leather thong around his neck? Quite honestly I didn't know. Even I was now confused.

But if that 'power to protect' was real, were there any limits to that power? My mind flashed back to a warm summer afternoon in Judaea. Max and I had followed the masses who were themselves following Jesus in a hilly area by the Sea of Galilee. Jesus sat down in the shade provided by a high cliff and addressed them.

But it wasn't long before the hecklers, who were always present and consisted mainly of supposedly holy men such as priests, shouted to Jesus: "If you are the Son of God climb to the top of the cliff and throw yourself off…He will protect you from the fall…We will then believe you."

Whether Jesus could have actually survived the fall, unhurt, I didn't know, but he decided not to be tested in that way. Or did he know that his survival would have been beyond the limits set by his Father?

This was the problem with Max's attitude. Maybe the piece of pot did offer some protection for the wearer, but it was essential that he didn't think that the protection was there regardless of how foolish he was acting. Could he jump off a high building and somehow survive unhurt? Of course not. He needed telling.

"Er, Max…You worry me…I think that you believe that the piece of pot around your neck will protect you whatever the circumstances…It will not…When Jesus gave them out he expected the wearers to act sensibly at all times and not take unnecessary risks…On this occasion you did exactly that."

He looked sheepishly at me, knowing that I was right. He had been incredibly foolish not having first attacked with his spear. Maybe God above had saved him from certain death, but he had been wrong to place God in that position in the first place. He decided to answer me honestly: "You're right, Marcus…I did have a feeling of supreme confidence, but I also had in the back of mind the power that I thought the piece of pot may have…I even pulled it from beneath my shirt and kissed it, just as the two pirates came over the side…I was wrong…It won't happen again…Sorry."

The rest of the journey was thankfully uneventful, but one thing both Max and I had noticed was the respect that both of us were shown by the other members of the crew, even the one I'd had the confrontation with on our first day as crewmen. This was undoubtedly due to the way we'd fended off the four pirates. The crewmen, especially of ships carrying valuable cargo, had heard all the tales of being boarded at night by pirates, who had ruthlessly killed all the crew but the captain, who was forced to sail the ship to its secret destination, before he too was killed. Bodies were far too often picked up at sea, often in fishermen's nets. Badly decomposed ones were put back in the water for the fish to finish off, but those in better condition were sometimes taken back to port for a decent burial. It must have always been a difficult decision to make by the fishermen. I didn't envy them their task.

The weather was kind, with a gentle south easterly breeze driving us slowly to Tarantum, our destination. Above all there were no sightings of boats on the horizon that could have been pirate crafts, shadowing us. Maybe the two pirates that we'd driven back overboard had somehow made it back to their base and spread the message: "Don't attack the *Julius Caesar*…It's too well defended."We could only hope that that had happened.

After three boring days at sea where there was little to do but idle our time away because the ship more-or-less sailed herself, we heard the lookout enthusiastically shout: "Land on the horizon…Dead ahead."

The rest of us cheered at the news. Back to civilisation at last. Several hours later, during which time we sailed across the huge Gulf of Tarantum, there was much activity on deck. Every square yard of sail had to be taken in and stored, all but a small mizzen that was used to manoeuvre the ship into the harbour and into position by the quayside. Ropes were then thrown to waiting men who tied the ship's prow and stern to large stone bollards projecting upwards from the quay. When all was secure the captain instructed his crew to stay put until he'd been ashore to register his ship's arrival. He also had another important task to carry out, one that was definitely in their interests, but said nothing about it.

Since there was little point in Max and I staying on board, preferring to seek out the Tarantum garrison to register our arrival and to inform our superiors of the total loss of four ships and just short of two hundred men in a storm that had raged just to the south west of the island of Creta, we decided to leave with the captain.

His first port-of-call was the harbour master's office. Here he registered the arrival of the *Julius Caesar* and gave details of the ship's manifest. But equally important he gave a detailed report of the pirates' unsuccessful attack, particularly where exactly the attack had taken place. This was essential so that ships returning to Pilos or sailing beyond to the many destinations in the eastern Mare Internum, could be warned of the very real danger.

The captain, with Max and I still by his side, then called at the office of the owners of the *Julius Caesar*. Here he also registered his safe arrival, with his manifest intact. He also repeated his account of the pirates' unsuccessful attack, at the same time saying: "If it hadn't been for these two, (he nodded in our direction), we would have lost the ship and its valuable cargo... Although they were outnumbered two-to-one they fought off the the pirates, definitely killing one of the four assailants, injuring two others before they managed to escape overboard...The other was captured...He's locked up on board my ship."

The young clerk recording the information left his seat and knocked on the closed door of an adjoining office. A shout of: "Enter," was heard and the young boy did as instructed, closing the door behind him. Seconds later he opened it accompanied by a large old man with a mass of white hair and wearing what looked like a very expensive purple toga. Around his neck was a thick gold chain with a huge gold medallion hanging from it. He reeked of wealth.

The captain whispered to us: "Lucius Severus, the ship's owner...He has a fleet of twenty altogether...Very wealthy...Very wealthy indeed, but doesn't hide away in some villa up in Tuscany, preferring to be down here keeping an eye on things...A good man...It's rumoured that he's related to Emperor Tiberius himself."

That was all very interesting and Max and I were undoubtedly impressed. But we couldn't see the point of lingering in the office. We wanted to seek out the garrison, which was probably some distance away, on the outskirts of Tarantum. But as we edged towards the open door that would take us back onto the quay, at the same time thanking the captain for having accepted us as crewmen and bringing us back to 'home' soil, Lucius spoke: "Not so fast, good men of the Empire...Let me first thank you for your brave act that undoubtedly saved both my ship and its crew from this menace of piracy, which we face daily on the

75

high seas…Only last week I lost three ships…Disappeared without trace, and almost certainly by the hands of pirates…If only they'd had such brave men as you on board to fight off the assailants, they would now be safely in their ports and their crews home with their loved one…We can only guess what has happened to them…But the omens aren't good."

Lucius Severus then disappeared into his office, returning five minutes later carrying two identical black leather purses. He passed one to Max and one to me: "Please will you accept these as a token of my thanks for saving my ship, it's crew and it's valuable cargo."

I gratefully thanked him on both our behalves, at the same time feeling the coins inside my purse. How many there were was anybody's guess, but it felt a considerable number. I saw Max doing the same. As it happened, this little windfall was very welcome, for both of us had lost everything in the storm, including all the money we'd won during the Sportsfest in Caesarea several days earlier.

And our luck continued, if indeed it was luck, or was it simply our just deserts? We'd just taken our leave and were now outside in the bright sunshine, when the captain joined us, at the same time handing each of us another purse: "Your wages for the trip…As crewmen you worked your passage…This is your pay." He then held up a large leather bag and shook it. It too was full of coins: "I must now get back to the ship and pay my crew, or there'll be a mutiny on board."

As we went our separate ways I shouted to him: "By the way…Where's the garrison in Tarantum?"

"Go to the end of the quay, then climb the hill…At the top you'll see it straight ahead…It's the huge building with lots of flags flying above it …Can't miss it."

He was right, too, for when we reached the brow of the hill there in front of us was a very impressive building, more like the villa of a wealthy man, (the name Lucius Severus sprang to mind), than a base for the roughest of the rough, as we soldiers were often described as.

As we approached the main gate, open but with two guards on duty, we were abruptly stopped, which wasn't surprising since we were still scruffily dressed as crewmen of a merchant ship. What right had we to simply stroll into the garrison? None what ever, dressed the way we were.

One of the guards challenged us: "You can't come in here…Military personnel only….State your business or clear off."

I didn't like his manner and told him so: "Careful, soldier…You're in

76

danger of being put on a charge for insubordination...We are military personnel...From Palestina...Both of officer rank, (which of course we weren't)...Dressed like this because we've been working under cover...It's a long story which we prefer to tell to your superior officer...Take us to him."

The guard was now in a bit of a quandary. Should he continue his bombastic attitude towards us, taking the risk of addressing disrespectfully someone of a rank superior to himself? Or should he tread cautiously and refer us to a higher authority? Wisely he chose the latter: "Wait here and I will seek advice." As he moved away he nodded to his fellow guard, a signal to him to keep a beady eye on us.

Minutes later he returned, accompanied by someone presumably of senior rank. The centurion, if indeed that was his rank, spoke quietly, asking us to identify ourselves and to explain why we were there.

"My name is Marcus Tullius and my fellow soldier is Maximus Gregorius...We were sailing from Caesarea to Syracusae when a great storm struck us just south west of the island of Creta...Our fleet was of four ships, carrying in total two hundred and infantrymen...All were lost...We two are the only survivors...We were driven onto the shore at Pilos where local fishermen found us... With their help we managed to get on a merchant ship that was sailing to Tarantum...That's how we come to be here." There seemed little point in mentioning that during the journey we had also saved the ship from pirates. "Braggers" weren't much liked nor tolerated in the Roman Army.

The senior officer listened intently to what I'd said then suggested that I repeated my story, more fully if possible, to a scribe who would record all the details. He led Max and I to a room where several scribes were at work, writing away on huge desks. Some were copying documents, others were taking down details from interviewees, and others were sat there apparently seeking inspiration before putting their ink loaded quills to paper. Were they the 'thinkers', I wondered?

At this point the officer left us in the capable hands of the scribe. This enabled Max and I to relax and speak freely about our ordeal, commencing at the point when we sailed out of the port of Caesarea after several weeks of patrol duty throughout the state of Judaea. At the mention of the name Judaea the scribe stopped writing and lifted his eyes: "Were you there when this Jesus Christ man was crucified...It was quite a moving occasion, I understand?"

His revelation puzzled me. How could he possibly know details of that event? It was doubtful that anybody who knew about it, maybe even witnessed it, could possibly have got to Tarantum before us and told the tale to anyone who was prepared to listen, for example the scribe. Admittedly we'd been shipwrecked, but we'd also been quickly found by the fishermen of Pilos, who got us on a ship to Tarantum the following day. Nobody could have got here faster than Max and I. And yet the scribe appeared to know about the event. I had to know how.

"Er, scribe…In answer to your question…Yes, we were there at that man's crucifixion…In fact my colleague and I were on patrol duty at the event and witnessed the whole thing…But how do you know about it?"

He proceeded to explain: "A few days ago I was drinking in one of the alehouses down by the harbour when a scruffy individual entered. He too had come from Caesarea, having called at Cyprus and Creta, where he joined a ship bound for Tarantum as a member of the crew."

It then occurred to me. Several days, I'd lost track of time how many, had elapsed between the day that Jesus had been crucified, and today. If someone had witnessed the event and then for his own good reasons, immediately headed for Caesarea, picking up a ship to Cyprus, then to Creta, and finally on to Tarantum, he could have arrived before us. That could be the only explanation.

It was at that point that a thought flashed through my mind. It was a chance in a million, maybe even more, but I had to know the man's name if at all possible: "Please tell me more about the man and what he told you…Did he give you his name, for instance?"

"As a matter of fact he did…He called himself Simon Peter…Said he was an apostle of this Jesus man…Not knowing what an apostle was, I asked him to explain, which he did…I must say that he was quite convincing."

I looked directly at Max and we both gasped. My million-to-one chance had been in fact correct. The last time we'd seen Simon was when Max and I had addressed the disciples, telling them how and where they could spread the word of Jesus. I distinctly remembered Max drawing a huge map in the sandy soil, allowing me to show them where places like Italia, Achaia, even Armenia, were, and how they could travel to such places. Simon must have headed for Caesarea almost straight away, with the intention of picking up a ship and heading west, hence his arrival at Tarantum a day or two before us.

I was prepared to commence my description of the sequence of events on arriving at Caesarea, including our success at the Sportsfest, when the scribe continued: "That evening, after a few beers, during which time others had joined Simon and I, we started to play a game of dice...At first we played for a few sestertii, but soon the stakes went up...It wasn't long before Simon had lost all his money and in his final game he lifted a funny shaped object that he'd been wearing round his neck, over his head and placed it on the table...Said it was special because Jesus himself had given it to him...Seeing that it was only a piece of coloured pot attached to a black leather thong, worth maybe a couple of sestertii, certainly no more, I was reluctant to accept it as his stake...But I did so because I liked the man and didn't want to fall out with him....Besides we were all having an enjoyable evening."

I couldn't wait to ask my next question: "So...What happened to the piece of pot?"

The scribe, using his fingers, pulled the object from beneath the neck band of his tunic and lifted it over his head. He then passed it across to me, at the same time saying: "I put it around my neck because I was afraid of losing it...I half expected Simon to seek me out the following morning in order to make me an offer for it...In fact I'd already decided that if I met up with him I'd give it back to him...But of course I didn't see him again."

"Did he say where he was heading?"

"Yes...To Roma...He said he wanted to preach the word of Jesus at the very heart of the Empire...I told him that it would be risky doing so, but he wouldn't heed my warning."

I studied the peculiar shaped piece of pot that I now held in the palm of my hand. Its shape was difficult to describe...a sort of rectangle, cut across its breadth at an angle. Its colour was a rich purple that immediately reminded me of the colour of Lucius Severus's toga. But what caught my eye most of all was what was inscribed on it - the Greek letter ν, the fourteenth letter in the Greek alphabet and possibly the last one Jesus used.

Since it made sense that I should become custodian of the second piece of pot to make its sudden appearance, the first having been given to me by Martha in Caesarea, I made a suggestion to the scribe: "Since Max and I are heading for Roma let me take the piece with me...There is just a possibility that we will run into Simon there."

The scribe, feeling uneasy about having in his possession something that had been handled by a man called Jesus, who had said he was the Son of God and had been crucified for it, was only too willing to allow me to take possession of it: "That makes sense to me...Besides, I have no faith like you people seem to have...To me it's just a piece of pot on a loop of thin black leather...Could be some sort of souvenir bought in a Greek bazaar as far as I'm concerned."

I thanked him, and he continued recording our story up to the point where Max and I tried to gain entry to the garrison a few minutes earlier.

That night, having first been attached to one of the garrison's cohorts and later having consumed an excellent communal meal of roast lamb, followed by a variety of fruit and washed down by a good quality red wine (the soldiers at this garrison certainly lived well), Max and I settled down for a well earned rest in our new accommodation.

As I lay there, thinking about my newly acquired piece of pot, my mind went back to the day we both left Caesarea. I distinctly remembered whilst on the ship drawing out on a piece of paper, (unfortunately lost in the storm), the various shapes that I thought all thirteen pieces of pot could have had. I had now seen three and so far I'd been correct. It was also my guess that I knew the shapes of the other ten pieces. What I didn't know was their colour and the Greek letter Jesus had used for each piece. He hadn't simply chosen the first fourteen letters of the alphabet otherwise π and τ would not have been on his list. Had he therefore simply chosen his letters at random across the whole alphabet? Or, had he chosen fourteen special letters?

There was of course no way of knowing the answer to these two questions, neither was there any way of finding them out without seeing all thirteen pieces - something impossible. I personally suspected that Jesus had in fact chosen fourteen special letters, possibly spelling out a very special word that would have great significance to the world, maybe even some sort of message to mankind. It seemed to me the obvious thing for him to do.

There was only one weakness in my reasoning – all thirteen pieces had to be together in order for that message to be revealed, and at that very moment ten of the pieces were probably spread across the countries at the eastern end of the Mare Internum.

One thing I did know was that the four letters I already knew - θ, π, τ and v told me absolutely nothing.

The garrison at Tarantum was huge and housed two cohorts of soldiers, totalling almost one thousand legionaries in all. Because of its strategic position it was the starting point, along with Syracusae in Sicilia for all missions going east - to Achaia, Phrygia, Palestina, Aegyptus. It was also the finishing point for missions returning from those areas. consequently there was much activity at the garrison, with many tales to tell...and to listen to.

It wasn't long before Max and I were telling our story of the crucifixion of a man called Jesus Christ, a story that fascinated the other soldiers, who couldn't understand how such a person, with no power or status, could have commanded the attention of multitudes of people, often numbering thousands. Neither could they understand how he'd been looked upon as a threat to Roman rule in the country, to the point of him being tried, found guilty and executed. Max and I had to be cautious how we described events. It was essential not to give the slightest hint that we had followed Jesus around during his preachings as part of our military duties and had eventually become 'believers' ourselves. Of course we tried to keep the small pieces of coloured pot around our necks, hidden from view below the necklines of our tunics, but on occasions they were seen. On such occasions we simply explained them as mere lucky charms purchased in the market place in the Cypriot port of Limassol.

Although other soldiers told vivid stories of battles, mass killings, gruesome crucifixions, even described huge pointed stone structures reaching up to the sky called pyramids. These had been seen in a country called Aegyptus in the south-east corner of the Mare Internum. But it was our story of Jesus Christ that all of them found to be the most fascinating.

Max and I had been granted seven days' leave in order to get over our shipwreck ordeal. Of course we had nowhere to go to take it, our homes being hundreds of miles away to the north, with no chance of getting there. We therefore had no alternative but to take our leave in the garrison itself. This enabled us to see what was going on in other parts, and it wasn't long before we met up with the cavalrymen, for the Tarantum garrison was also a training school for the Roman Army's cavalry.

Although having been brought up on a farm I'd never been on a horse since my father thought one a luxury that we could ill-afford. I'd thereforenever had the thrill of riding one at speed. We did have an old donkey, but it could hardly walk and was looked upon as a pet. Max on the other hand had. From an early age he had patrolled the local area where he lived with his father, and horses were used to cover the huge distances involved.

As both of us looked on as the cavalrymen were being put through their paces the instructor in charge, mounted on a huge white horse, approached us: "Interested?...I'm always on the lookout for suitable legionaries to become cavalrymen...As our great Roman Empire expands, being able to cover great distances as quickly as is practically possible is essential...Cavalry men are the answer...Come, meet some of our horses."

He then led us to a building that was obviously the stables, and a huge building too with, we were informed, a hundred horses in their stalls. As Max and I walked along, stroking the heads of the horses as we did so, I became fascinated, almost mesmerised, by the majestic beasts. All their eyes where bright and their ears erect showing their alertness. Above all they appeared to like the physical contact with humans. One horse in particular caught my eye, a stallion black as coal. He immediately responded to my touch and as I moved away from him to look at the next horse he stretched his head as far as he could in an effort to follow me. On seeing this I returned to him, again stroking him with increased vigour.

"He likes you," said the instructor, smiling: "Would you like me to have him brought out?"

I couldn't resist the offer: "Please do...But I'll warn you, I've never had anything to do with horses before...We had an old donkey on the farm at home, but I was never allowed to ride him."

"Well...There's always a first time," replied the instructor, who then asked a young legionary, who couldn't have been more that eighteen years old, to place a halter over the horse's head and lead him out into the training arena.

"This is Brutus," continued the instructor: "All our horses have names and once paired with a cavalryman they stay together until either man or horse dies or is killed, which in the theatre of battle often takes place at the same time." The instructor's message was blunt and to the point as indeed it had to be in a military situation, but it made us acutely aware that these huge majestic creatures were as vulnerable in battle as their riders.

The instructor took the reins from the young legionary and promptly handed them to me: "Here...Now I want you to walk round the full perimeter of the training arena, talking to Brutus as you go...He will simply walk at the side of you on the rein."

I was just about to set off on my long walk, for the area of the training arena was huge, when the instructor stopped me: "Before you set off let me get Max a horse. He can then accompany you."

Max, knowledgeable on all things to do with horses, especially how they were ridden, said to the instructor: "Mind if I ride rather than walk?"

The instructor's eye lit up. Here was a legionary who could already ride: "Yes, by all means...I'll have Julius saddled up for you...He's a young stallion...Still a bit frisky, but I'm sure you'll manage him."

Five minutes later the young legionary led out a grey horse, equal in height to Brutus. As he did so it was immediately obvious that Julius was indeed lively, and Max initially had difficulty getting his foot into the stirrup. Eventually he did so with the help of the instructor, who held the horse's head steady. Once in the saddle and reins in hand, Max confidently squeezed the horse with his knees and it moved forward. I quickly followed, Brutus alongside me. Our cavalry training had begun, albeit in an elementary sort of way.

That did it for both Max and I - we were hooked. We wanted to be part of the Roman Army's cavalry section. During the next month we both underwent our training, which in my case soon included the exhilarating experience of riding Brutus at a full gallop. We learned how to charge with spears outstretched, and to shoot arrows from a bow, something I initially found difficult because I had to allow Brutus to control himself rather than me controlling him. But he seemed to instinctively know what I wanted him to do.

Of course there had to be a down side to the otherwise enjoyable training. We were entirely responsible for our animals. We fed and watered them, groomed them and also mucked them out. The instructor believed implicitly in 'bonding' between man and beast, hence his insistence on our spending every minute of the working day with our horses. It was even said, jokingly of course, that if he'd had his way he would have had his cavalrymen sleeping in the stables with their steeds.

Now a fully fledged cavalryman with a horse of my choosing, I took a momentous decision, not one taken lightly. I decided to tightly tie the purple piece of pot that the scribe had passed to me in Tarantum, and had been given to Simon Peter by Jesus, onto Brutus's bridle. If indeed the piece had any protective powers, maybe it would protect him too. The other cavalrymen, who had already seen the pieces of pot that Max and I wore around our necks, and who believed our story that they were simply lucky charms, purchased in Limassol market, smiled at my gesture. Surely nothing so simple could protect a horse in a skirmish with the enemy.

***

Chapter Eight

It was now time to move. News had come through from returning soldiers that all was not well in central Gallia. The garrison at Lugdunum, the provincial capital some eight hundred miles to the north, left under strength by the movement further north of a thousand soldiers, had been routed by the rebels. Reinforcements, having earlier been assembled in Genua, had been ambushed and wiped out as they'd moved through the northern edge of the Alpes Maritimae, reputed to be the most dangerous area in the whole of Gallia.

The military force in Tarantum was divided into two groups. The cavalrymen, a hundred in number and led by a cavalry centurion, would go overland up the whole of the country, calling at villages on the way to rest and pick up provisions. After a two day stay in Roma, where tactics for the future mission would be discussed, a task force would be assembled in Genua. It was anticipated that the five hundred miles to be covered would take in the region of fifteen days.

The foot soldiers, a full cohort of five hundred, would travel to Genua by sea, a much longer journey than going overland because it would initially take the ships south to Sicilia before heading north to the huge naval base of Neapolis. A call would then be made at Ostia, where the soldiers could stretch their legs in the town for the day. This call would enable the centurions to travel the few miles inland to Roma where they would meet up with the cavalry leaders for the tactical talks. The ships would then continue their journey to Genua, covering in total a distance of some eight hundred miles. Given good favourable conditions on both land and sea it was anticipated that both groups would arrive in Genua at roughly the same time, give or take a day or two.

When our cavalry group reached Roma for its short stay I asked my centurion if I could call at my parents' farm, only a short distance away, near the village of Grotto San Stefano. He gave me permission and asked Max to keep me company. Our instructions were to be back in camp by sunset the following day.

As we approached the farm I could see that little had changed, at least on the outside - same old farmhouse and barn. But one thing had changed, and a big change too. As Max and I entered the farmhouse one important person was missing - my mother. As my father explained she had died of some sort of chest disease a month earlier. She hadn't been well when I'd left so it didn't come as a big surprise to me. Even then it had a devastating effect. I enquired where my elder brother, Max was, funny how he shared the same name as my closest friend. Father informed me that he had taken some sheep to market and would be back before nightfall.

That night, over a tasty and wholesome meal of chicken, home grown vegetables and copious supplies of wine - good wine, not the poor quality stuff that we'd been having to drink during our journey north, we chattered late into the night. Both my father and brother found our accounts of the life and death of a man called Jesus Christ most fascinating, finding it hard to believe, as indeed most people did who we told.

The following morning, before we returned to Roma, both father and Max took us to the village of Grotto San Stefano, where mother was buried in the local graveyard. This did at least enable me to wish her a belated farewell. We then said our reluctant goodbyes before heading back to Roma. At least I was pleased to see that father was well and that brother Max had no intentions of leaving the farm to make his future elsewhere. I couldn't help feeling a tinge of guilt for having taken that decision to do so myself.

During our stay in Roma we were allowed 'relaxation' time in preparation for our trek north to Genua. This enabled Max and I to search for Simon Peter, but it was like looking for the proverbial needle in a haystack. We of course had to be careful. What if he'd been arrested for trying to preach the word of Jesus Christ? Could our enquiries as to his whereabouts indicate some sort of association? As it happened, there was no sign of Simon, nor had anyone heard of him. Maybe he hadn't got as far as Roma. Maybe he'd been ambushed by robbers. Not having his piece of pot to protect him, maybe he'd even been killed.

After a two day stay in Genua, to allow we cavalrymen to recuperate after our forced ride from Roma, and those who'd travelled by sea to get their 'land legs', the task force was assembled.

The following morning, at sunrise, the force moved off in a north-west direction, heading first for Torino then the northern edge of the Alpes Maritimae. The mountain range of snow covered peaks had few passes suitable for horses to easily traverse through, some heavily weighed down with provisions and equipment, one pass was always used - the one linking the villages of Modane to the east and St Michel to the west, before heading for Chambery and onto Lugdunum.

In places the pass was more like a narrow gorge, known locally as the Modane Gorge, with steep precipitous sides reaching almost to the clouds. On the one hand this provided protection from the blizzards that often swept across the whole area, but on the other a notorious place for an ambush. On more than one occasion the Gallia rebels, sometimes only a handful in number, had attacked from above, showering huge rocks onto the relatively unprotected Roman soldiers in the gorge. All they could do was hold their shields above their heads and pray that they didn't get a direct hit. Unfortunately the horses in the group had no protection at all, resulting in many being killed outright by rocks smashing onto their vulnerable skulls. Those soldiers and riders who could retreat did so. Those who were too badly injured to do so could only put up what fight they could, before being ruthlessly slain by the rebels, who would have entered the gorge from the north. After weapons and clothes had been removed the lifeless bodies were thrown into the fast flowing river that roared through sections of the gorge. The horses, now dead, were butchered for meat, for horse meat was a rare delicacy of the Gallia rebels.

But on this occasion we were lucky. Scouts, travelling light and with rock climbing skills, had gone on ahead. They'd managed to climb above the gorge and surveyed the ledges that the rebels used to launch their aerial attacks, and had reported back that the whole area was deserted. Not even a shepherd tending his flock was seen. This allowed our full party of both foot soldiers and cavalrymen to pass through the length of the gorge unhindered. Once safely through and on a flat plain where any approaching enemy would be easily seen, we made camp for the night. This allowed our leaders to discuss the absence of the enemy, which was most unusual. They came to the conclusion that since the garrison just outside the provincial city of Lugdunum, some hundred miles to the north, had been routed and taken over by the rebels, those who would normally have waited for us above the gorge had withdrawn to the garrison to strengthen its defences. This did of course mean that we would have a big battle in front of us - the recapture of it, an unenviable task. At least we would be able to see our enemy, and not have huge rocks showered down on us.

And luck shone on us for a second time. As we approached the garrison at Lugdunum, but well out of sight of its lookouts, we observed four horsemen approaching us at speed. At first it was impossible to see whether they were friend or foe. Our cavalry centurion, sensing some sort of trickery or a ploy to distract us, bravely rode out to meet them, spear at the ready. Still some distance away they met, appeared to have a friendly conversation, and the centurion led them into our camp. As they conferred with our senior officers the message flashed through the ranks that they were scouts who had ridden from Augustodonum, some hundred miles to the north. They had ridden as fast as they could with valuable news.

The garrison at Lugdonum had been built on the western outskirts of the city for what seemed a sensible reason, at least to the city's Roman elders, who did not want it and its uncouth rowdy soldiers in the centre of their beautiful and well run city. This made it vulnerable to attack, and this in fact was what had happened, the garrison being attacked at night and overrun. Fortunately several soldiers had managed to make their escape northwards and had ended up at Augustodonum after an arduous march taking several days.

On hearing the disturbing news the military experts of Augustodonum planned the re-taking of the important garrison. They knew that if reinforcements were to arrive at all they would come from the south, in fact from Italia itself. They also knew that if their army, moving down from the north, could join up with the reinforcements approaching from the south, the attack on the garrison would have maximum effect. It had therefore been the four horsemen's task to find that approaching force, and by sheer good luck they had done so. To ensure that they weren't observed by the rebels at Lugdonum they had bypassed the city well to the east.

The horsemen put forward their plans to our military strategists, and a plan of attack was drawn up. In five days' time, at sunrise, the garrison on the outskirts of Lugdonum would be attacked first by our force from the south, then shortly afterwards by the force from Augustodonum, approaching from the north. Of course the force to the north needed to know that we to the south had in fact already arrived on the scene and were ready for the battle to commence. The four horsemen therefore returned north in order to report back, but before doing so they were given the simplest of instructions on how the two armies would communicate and hence coordinate their joint attack.

And so, at sunrise, after five days of planning and preparation we took up our position, unseen, on the edge of the forest to the south-west of Lugdunum. Not having seen the garrison and not knowing anything about it, a local farmer had been persuaded to describe it to us in exchange for our pledge that we would not slaughter and eat his cattle, sheep and goats. It was a huge square wooden building surrounded by a circular wooden wall three times the height of a man. The wall had two large sturdy gates to the north and south. The walls had internal walkways that enabled the garrison to be defended by archers from above. It always had a good supply of food, but did not have its own well. This meant that all the water had to be brought in using large bags made of animal skins. The farmer had heard that since it tended to have an unpleasant taste, the drinking of wine was preferred. He also said that on the night the garrison had been overrun by the rebels the Roman soldiers, celebrating the birthday of their commander-in-chief, had had too much and had been ill-prepared for the attack. In fact there had been no guards on duty at all that night.

The plan of attack was simple, if indeed any could be described in that sort of frivolous way. We would commence it as the sun came above the distant eastern horizon. Initially our force would attempt to storm the walls, using ladders that had been earlier made from sturdy branches cut from the trees in the forest. If our foot soldiers could gain access and open the gates we, the cavalry, would storm in at speed, spears at the ready. I felt both excited and frightened at the thought, for it would be my first experience of fighting whilst riding a horse. As the battle was raging on the south of the garrison, hopefully fully occupying the enemy, a message would be sent to the northern force instructing them to attack.

Our attack began. As our foot soldiers moved across the open ground they were showered with arrows from the garrison's high wall, but they were well protected by the metal shields that they held over their heads as they advanced like a blanket creeping across the ground. Unfortunately some arrows, possibly new ones with sharp metallic points, did manage to pierce the shields and hit the soldiers. Their metal helmets provided an additional layer of protection, but their shoulders were vulnerable to the penetrating arrows. In some cases a soldier's shield was actually pinned to his shoulder. Obviously in great pain he stopped his advance and tried to retreat causing chaos in the ranks.

But our soldiers did eventually reach the foot of the wall and made their preparations to scale it. Fearing that their defences were about to be penetrated the rebels massed on the ramparts, swords at the ready. At this precise moment the northern force was instructed to attack, and this was done by a simple but well tried method of signalling. Acting on an instruction from the cavalry centurion I rode to a point on the edge of the forest west of the garrison, holding a shiny copper disc about the size of the palm, in my hand. The cavalry centurion had an identical disc. Using the rays of the sun he sent a signal, two flashes, to me using the disc. I in turn sent the same signal in a northerly direction, to where I guessed the northern force was assembled. And I guessed correctly, for seconds later I observed the returning two flashes. I in turn flashed back to my centurion, who now knew that the attack from the north would commence in a matter of minutes.

Too late, the rebels realised what was happening and some vacated their positions on the southern ramparts in order to move to the north of the garrison and defend the ramparts there. In the rebels' confusion both our south and north attacks succeeded, with our foot soldiers ascending the ladders meeting little resistance. There was some hand-to-hand fighting on the ramparts, but our well trained soldiers soon overwhelmed the opposition, hacking the rebels down and kicking their lifeless bodies over the side, as they progressed. Although we didn't know, we assumed that something similar was taking place on the northern ramparts. In no time at all the southern gates were thrown open and we charged in on our horses, chasing the rebels down as we did so. Unhindered by the bulky shields that we had earlier decided to leave behind, we were able to reach down and hack at the rebels with our swords as we passed them at speed.

The rebels, now in total disarray, had no alternative but to retreat to the garrison's main building. Those who managed to make it quickly shut the substantial doors, leaving many of their comrades on the outside. All they could do, with their backs to the wall, was fight to the death, and this they bravely did. They had no intentions of surrendering, and we were in no mood to take any prisoners. In no time at all the area between outer wall and inner building was awash with blood. But that was how battles usually ended up - one big bloody mess.

Things suddenly went quiet. All the killing outside the building had been completed. Any moaning rebel had been quickly dispatched and our injured had been taken onto the plain outside the garrison in order to receive attention.

As I looked around me I suddenly became disgusted with myself for what had happened and the part I had played in it. I felt the strong urge to pray to my God, Jesus's father, asking for forgiveness. This I did by first dismounting, then placing my head against the piece of pot that I had attached to Brutus's head. At the same time I extracted from beneath my body armour the piece that Jesus had given to me, and held it tightly in the palm of my hand. An onlooker would think that I was whispering into Brutus's ear, but I was fervently praying. Probably misguided, I thought that being in contact with two of the pieces of pot that Jesus had owned would double God's forgiveness.

But would he forgive me at all? I didn't know. And if he did, or didn't, how would I know? I had to trust that he would, for as Jesus had told us on many occasions: "Confess your sins and ask for God's forgiveness, and he will do so." That is exactly what I did, and funnily enough, I felt strangely tranquil after doing so.

For the next five days we had a stalemate situation, with the rebels prepared to 'sit it out' until their food and water supply ran out. On our part we were prepared to play the waiting game, for ample provisions were brought in from Lugdunum a short distance away. But waiting for what? If we attacked, breaking down the massive doors, we would lose more men in the hand-to-hand fighting that would inevitably follow. And what would we do with the prisoners if the rebels surrendered? Were we prepared to put defenceless men to the sword? The answer to this question was probably yes. It would weaken the rebel numbers in the area and also set an example that we, the occupying force, were not prepared to tolerate subversive action.

It wasn't long before rumours spread through our ranks that the rebels were holding hostage soldiers who had survived the overrunning of the garrison, but had not managed to make their escape to the north. How many we had no idea, but what we did know was that if we broke into the building and engaged the rebels in battle, they would kill the soldiers before we could save them. This knowledge therefore placed our officers in a dilemma. Should they attack, knowing for certain that an unknown number of hostages would be killed? Or should they, showing apparent weakness, continue to hold back?

As it happened they did not have to take action either way, the dilemma being solved for them. On the sixth day, just before sunrise, one of the foot soldiers, just about to end his night patrol outside the building wall heard a short sharp crack a short distance away. Cautiously, he went to investigate, aware that he would be an easy target for a rebel archer shooting from the top of the wall.

He soon found what had made the sound. A stone the size of a fist had obviously been drop from the top of the wall, the soldier hearing its impact with the ground. But more importantly something appeared to be wrapped round the stone - some sort of paper. The soldier carefully removed the paper, slightly damaged by the impact, and immediately observed that there was some writing on it. Although he recognised it as Latin, not being able to read his native language meant that he had no idea what it said. Quickly he took it to his centurion who, being a man with some basic education, immediately read the message out. Since it was unlikely that any of the rebels could read or write Latin, the note had probably been written by one of the more educated hostages.

The message simply stated:

We have twenty hostages - all Roman soldiers. Allow us to leave with our lives and we will release them unharmed. Otherwise we will kill them all. We are not afraid to die.

The centurion immediately sought out his commanding officer, a man named Maximilian, who quickly assembled the six other centurions so that a discussion could take place, followed, hopefully, by a decision on the action to be taken.

One centurion by the name of Virgil, a cold heartless brute of a man, known as 'the butcher' because of the ruthless way he killed his opponents, plunging his sword into their lifeless bodies several times even though the first plunge had probably killed the opponents outright, didn't see a problem: "We attack the garrison building from front and rear, and once inside we kill all the rebels…No prisoners, except one, their leader…We'll crucify him on the plain outside the garrison as a message to the others that we're not prepared to be mucked around."

"And what about the hostages?" enquired the centurion who went by the name of Tacitus, and obviously cared about the hostages' welfare.

"They'll just have to take their chances…If they're real men they'll fight to the death, for the glory of Roma," was Virgil's unsympathetic reply.

"Some glory," murmured the centurion, Cassius: "There's nothing glorious about being slaughtered like dogs for no good reason."

Cassius then gave his opinion: "Let's go along with the rebels' request, and once the hostages have been released our cavalrymen can then charge in and finish the rebels off."

Fully supporting Cassius and half supporting Virgil, the centurion who went by the name of Julius, added his input: "Let's get the hostages free first, then we can run down the rebels as they make their escape…We can capture their leader, alive, and crucify him as Virgil suggested…It will send out a clear message to the others."

Having listened to his seven centurions, and being a believer in some sort of democracy, Maximilian put the issue to the vote: "Say 'Aye' if you think that we should allow the rebels to escape in exchange for the hostages being released unharmed."

Six centurions responded: "Aye", but with varying degrees of enthusiasm. Tacitus had no doubts, but Cassius could also appreciate Virgil's point of view.

"And who thinks that we should storm the building and let the hostages take their chances?"

Virgil roared a defiant 'Aye', then, reluctantly accepting defeat, added: "But we shouldn't let the rebels escape into the countryside to fight another day…Once the hostages are released, our cavalry could still chase after them before they reached the cover of the forest, and finish them off."

Maximilian, being an honourable man, didn't agree: "If the rebels release the hostages unharmed they will be allowed to make their escape to the forest and the villages beyond, where most of them probably live."

Virgil was far from pleased with the decision, but kept his silence. He'd had his say. Time would now tell if he'd been correct in his assessment of the situation.

A reply was quickly scribbled out and the paper was then folded round the stone that had originally been used. The reply was brief and to the point:

We accept your terms. Release the hostages unharmed and you will be allowed to leave, also unharmed.

The soldier who had found the stone now had the task of returning it. This he did with great enthusiasm, just managing to clear the top of the wall with his upward throw. Secretly he hoped that it would hit one of the rebels on the head as it descended.

Minutes later, as our foot soldiers looked on in anticipation, with us on our trusty steeds standing behind them, the huge double door slowly creaked open. As the hostages emerged, twenty in number, we could immediately see that each one had a rope round his neck, tightly held be a rebel walking behind, who was also seen to be pushing a sword into the hostage's back. This was no doubt done to stop them making a sudden dash for freedom.

The looks on the hostages' faces said it all. They were terrified, and the obvious bruising round their eyes indicated beyond a shadow of a doubt that they had been mistreated.

I glanced across to where Virgil was standing and observed him tighten his grip on the hilt of his sword. He was agitated and looked like a caged lion raring to be released.

The procession of both rebels and hostages slowly made its way across the paved area between the central building and the outer wall of the garrison. It then passed through the open gate before heading across the half mile or so of grassland between the garrison and the edge of the forest. As it did so Virgil and Maximilian entered the building to see who or what was left. As they descended the steps to an area that was obviously used as a prison, divided into ten individual cells, to their horror they found soldiers hanging from the ceiling, obviously dead, and had been so for some days.

Both charged back outside, Virgil in the lead, determined to take action - bloody action. But Maximilian managed to restrain him: "Wait until the hostages are released...Then we move in at speed...And with a vengeance."

Midway across the grassland the rebels thought that it was safe to release the hostages, and did so. Both groups then ran as fast as they could in opposite directions - the rebels towards the cover of the forest, the hostages back to the safety of their fellow soldiers.

Maximilian, accepting that the rebels had in part broken their side of the agreement by earlier murdering the helpless soldiers by hanging, gave the order to attack. And since the rebels could not be caught by the foot soldiers before they reached the safety of the forest it was up to us, the cavalry to do so. Virgil stood at the side of him, smugness written across his face. As the cavalry prepared to set off, he shouted: "And bring their leader back alive…I'll deal with him."

Max and I, along with the others charged across the grassland at great speed. The feeling was exhilarating. We were going into battle, admittedly only into a small skirmish, but it felt great. This was what all the earlier training had been about.

As we passed the hostages I slowed down and shouted: "Which is the leader?"

"The one with long red hair, dressed in black leather…You can't miss him," several replied.

In total confusion the rebels scattered in all directions, but had no chance as we sped towards them, swords at the ready. I caught up with one, and with one swing of my sword decapitated him. At that precise moment any thoughts of God disapproving my actions were nonexistent. Max caught up with another and plunged his sword into his back, almost pinning him to the ground.

Then I spotted the rebel with the long red flowing hair and dressed in black leather - the leader. He'd almost made it to the trees when I caught up with him. He turned, sword and spear at the ready, prepared to put up a fight. It was the first time I'd faced the enemy, one to one. As I sped towards him he launched his spear. At first I thought it was going to strike home just below Brutus's neck, but it fell short, harmlessly hitting the ground just in front of him.

The leader and I were now in contact. As we slashed at each other, hoping for a hit, I reached down further, still trying to use the advantage of my height above him. But I lost my balance and felt out of the saddle, hitting the ground with sufficient force to wind me. Unfortunately for me the impact also dislodged the sword from my grip.

Not immediately realising his good fortune the leader hesitated to press home his advantage, and this gave me just enough time to get to my feet. I went for my sword, but my opponent was too quick and promptly kicked it well away from my reach. All I could now do was to try and avoid the slashing of his sword as he charged towards me, by retreating.

All the time Brutus was becoming more and more agitated, instinctively knowing that his master was in great danger. Equally instinctively he reared up on his hind legs to his full height then dropped his fore legs onto the leader's head and shoulders, crashing him to the ground. This time it was he who lost his sword.

Quick as a flash I retrieved mine and pressed it hard into the leader's chest, but not sufficiently hard to do any real damage. He had to be taken alive. The other cavalrymen, having caught up with the other rebels, putting them to the sword as they did so, came across and formed a circle round the leader, who I now had on his feet.

Max jumped down from his saddle, tied the leader's hands in front of him with a long length of rope, then handed me the remainder. I was to have the privilege of leading him into our camp. Minutes later, amid cheering from my fellow soldiers, both foot and cavalry, I handed the rope to Virgil. He was now in charge of the leader's fate.

As we settled down for the evening, still outside the garrison and well away from the carnage inside it, we heard sawing and hammering coming from the edge of our camp. Virgil and his men were in the process of making a huge cross from some timbers extracted earlier from the forest.

Roughly an hour later we again heard hammering, this time accompanied by screams of pain. The leader was being nailed to the cross.

In a matter of minutes the cross had been raised to its upright position, the leader hanging from it. The crucifixion had been completed.

Both foot soldiers and cavalrymen couldn't resist having a look. Some jeered at the leader, who was still alive, just. Others, who had never witnessed a crucifixion before, stood there in silence. No doubt some considered it a just penalty, but others were obviously moved by the event. What a humiliating way to die. Far better to be cut down in battle fighting to the end.

Of course Max and I had seen it all before. We'd already witnessed a crucifixion - that of Jesus Christ, the Son of God. It had been hard to take in then. It was equally hard to take in now. How could man inflict such a horrific way to die on a fellow human being? We were supposed to be God's ultimate creation. But without doubt when it came to inflicting pain and death on our own kind we had no equal in the whole of the animal kingdom. Was this how God had wanted us to ultimately develop? Surely not.

Later that evening, as I lay on my bedroll on top of the thick grass, I went over the brief skirmish I'd had with the rebel leader. There was no doubt that I'd been incredibly lucky. If it hadn't been for my trusty steed, Brutus, sensing my precarious position and taking the only action he could to help his master, the leader would have plunged his sword through my chest, instantly killing me. This made me think, yet again, about the protective powers of the two pieces of pot that Brutus and I shared between us. Had the one attached to the side of his head protected him against the leader's spear attack? I didn't know. But what I did remember was seeing a spear heading straight for him suddenly dipping in flight and dropping short. Had the one around my neck also protected me from the leader's sword by getting Brutus to take action to defend me? I didn't know that either. All I could do was to think back to Jesus's words, when he gave his piece of pot to me: "Look after this and it will look after you."

And since Brutus was in effect looking after the other piece, the one originally belonging to Matthew, presumably it was looking after him too.

But still all the killing disturbed me. Then I remembered a few words that I'd heard on more than one occasion when in the Holy Land - words not ever spoken by Jesus, who's message from his Father in Heaven to his followers was: "love thy neighbour...And if your enemy smites you across the face - turn the other cheek." But words spoken by the priests and scribes of Israel, quoting from the old holy scriptures, supposedly also being the words of God: "An eye for an eye...A tooth for a tooth." In other words inflict on your enemy the same treatment that he had inflicted on you. My dilemma was deciding which of the two codes of living to follow - forgiveness or revenge. Could a soldier in the Roman Army live by both codes at the same time, depending on the circumstances? I somehow doubted it, but felt that I had to try.

Now that the garrison at Lugdunum was again in Roman hands, Maximilian decided to leave a cohort, numbering two hundred and fifty foot soldiers with their three centurions, at the garrison in order to avoid another repeat of the rebels' successful attack on it. The second cohort of foot soldiers would head north, first to Augustodonum, then Lutetia, and finally to the northern coast and onto Britannia. Since the Lugdunum garrison was not a cavalry base we would accompany the foot soldiers on their journey north. We were heading for the northern border of the Roman Empire.

***

Chapter Nine

Since the garrison at Augustodonum was well defended with a couple of cohorts of foot soldiers plus fifty cavalrymen, Maximilian decided to lead us north to the provincial capital Lutetia. We were told that the whole area round the town, known locally as Parisii, was now quiet and there was no trouble from the local people. Earlier the various tribes had regularly fallen out with one another, and the Romans had taken advantage of this, doing deals with some tribes against the others. It had been a classic case of 'divide and rule'.

In fact that part of Gallia was now a civilised, wealthy area where trading with Roman merchants was widespread. Latin had been adopted as the official language and the administration of the area was based on Roman lines. The inhabitants had even been given Roman citizenship.

There was however still a threat from the east, where the Germani and Helvetii tribes occasionally attacked local villages, raping and pillaging when they did so. For this reason a strong military force was kept at Lutetia.

The town itself had been developed on this particular site many years ago because of its special position. At this point there was the confluence of the River Seine and two smaller rivers. As a result a large marshy area had developed that had to be crossed by those heading north to the coast, were the port of Portus Itius, used by Julius Caesar and his invasion force some eighty years earlier, provided the crossing point to the island known as Britannia. An island in the River Seine at that point allowed relatively easy crossing.

Lutetia was an 'oppidum' town, so called because it was a main settlement and administrative centre. It was walled and entry and exit were through huge gates. Its open aspect as a result of its position on a slight rise in the ground ensured that it couldn't be approached by an enemy without the enemy being seen. Because of its strategic importance it was also a garrison town with a cavalry section.

As our military force of both foot soldiers and cavalrymen approached the town it was obvious to us that it was a hive of activity. As we passed through the large open gates we could immediately see the development that was taking place, the most obvious being the extensive paving that was being laid down to produce a roadway through the town. And it wasn't long before we were informed that the extensive building that was taking place was for a new Forum, Theatre and Baths. There was already a huge amphitheatre and a spectacular aqueduct that brought fresh water to the town from the surrounding hills. We were surprised to find such a well developed town so close to the northern boundary of the Roman Empire.

The day following our arrival in Lutetia was designated a 'rest' day by Maximilian. Our foot soldiers had force marched from Lugdunum, passing through Augustodunum without stopping, and had covered the two hundred and fifty miles in only ten days. We cavalrymen had obviously travelled the same distance in the same time, but of course not on foot. We therefore felt a little guilty at having been given the same rest period as our foot soldier colleagues.

But the following day the apparent unfairness was corrected when the Commander-in-Chief at the Lutetia garrison summoned Maximilan and informed him that a small village a few miles to the east of Lutetia had been invaded by a drunken mob of men who lived in a close by village. Evidently this falling out between local villages was common place and keeping the peace appeared to take up much of the time of the soldiers at the garrison.

But on this occasion the situation had evidently got completely out of hand. One or two men villagers had been killed trying to defend their woman folk, and there had apparently been some raping of the women, although on this point the young boy, no more than ten years old, who had ridden the few miles as if his life had depended on it in order to bring news of the troubles, had only been able to say with any degree of certainty that he had seen his mother and sister being dragged into a barn.

The Commander-in-Chief decided that the quickest way to take effective action was to send a small company of cavalrymen, ten in number, to restore the peace. Maximilian chose his men, that included Max and myself. We quickly mounted up and set off. Not being burdened with any heavy armour, only having our swords and helmets for protection, we were able to make good speed.

When we arrived at the village we were immediately faced with a problem that we hadn't anticipated - who was a genuine resident in the village and who was an invader? All the men looked the same. Fortunately the young boy, a bright lad, was able to help us identify the interlopers.

Everything seemed to be going well as we rounded up the villains-of-the-peace, when suddenly two drunken individuals emerged from what appeared to be a cowshed some twenty paces away. Both were swaying from side to side, no doubt the result of too much of the local wine. Far more worryingly, they had bows in hand, with arrows pointing in all directions, including directly at us, as they swayed, waving their bows in the air.

Hesitantly, Max and I slowly approached them, talking as we did so, trying to calm the situation down. The men could barely stand, and both Max and I knew that if the arrows were released it was anybody's guess where they would find their mark - that mark possibly being us.

The trouble with a bow with its arrow in place is that it only takes the slightest relaxation of the fingers to release it, and this is what happened on this occasion. I'm sure quite unintentionally, one of the men did exactly that. The arrow sped towards me at lightning speed and almost struck home before I could take any form of evasive action. I say almost struck home because by sheer good luck it struck the hilt of my sword. This had the effect of deflecting the arrow harmlessly away and it stuck in the ground a couple of paces to my left. Had its course been just one inch to the right or left it would have found its mark just below my ribs, no doubt doing untold damage.

This involuntary action caused the other man, almost in a panic, to release his arrow, but in the direction of Max. He too had no time to take evasive action and the arrow glanced the top of his helmet before sticking in the trunk of a tree just behind him.. Had that arrow been an inch lower it would have penetrated Max's forehead or one of his eyes.

The two men, now unarmed and therefore presenting no danger to us, allowed Max and I to rush them, quickly overpower them and tie their hands behind their backs.

With the interlopers now grouped together, surrounded by Roman cavalrymen, swords at the ready, just in case, Maximilian asked the villagers to assemble before him. He wanted them to identify those guilty of two unlawful killings that had earlier taken place. This was quickly done, the villagers immediately pointing out two scruffy individuals who had tried to evade recognition by crouching down behind their equally scruffy colleagues. These two were separated from the rest, tied loosely together and led away in the direction of Lutetia where their case would be heard by the local magistrate before the passing of sentence. They would no doubt use as their defence the fact that they'd been senselessly drunk and couldn't remember anything about the incident, but their defence would fall on stony ground. Roman justice usually applied the 'eye for an eye - tooth for a tooth' principle, funnily enough the same principle as the old Jews of the Holy Land advocated, but a principle that was at odds with the teachings of Jesus Christ.

Maximilian then asked the women of the village the most embarrassing of questions, but it had to be asked if justice was to be done: "Were any of you raped by these men?"

No hands went up and the women remained silent, but their inaction may not have told the true story. With their men folk standing beside them it would have been a brave woman who would have admitted being a victim.

Maximilian had no alternative but to accept their word. He therefore read the riot act to the other interlopers, stressing that the Roman authorities would not tolerate such behaviour and that if need be, some harsh punishments would be handed out, those probably taking the form of a good flogging.

All this had the effect of sobering up the men a little. He then sent them on their way. At first they walked slowly, eyes looking down, not wanting to make visual contact with the womenfolk nor the soldiers. They then burst into a trot which soon became a speedy run. As they sped away they realised that they'd managed to escape, all but two, unpunished. When they reached the brow of a small hill, a point where they would immediately disappear over the top, I saw two of them place their arms across each other's shoulders, laughing and joking as they did so. Had I been a betting man I'd have backed money on them having been involved in some sort of sexual assault of one or more of the women. They had had their wicked way and this time had got away with it.

But I knew that if those women had been brave enough to admit to their men folk that they'd been raped, two courses of action would then have followed - their men folk would have shunned them as being 'unclean', and this would have been followed by the rapists been found with their throats cut, lying in some ditch.

As Max and I lay on our bunks that night we both got to thinking about the day's happenings. How incredibly lucky we had been, yet again. The slightest twist of my body would have resulted in the arrow piecing my rib cage, with dire consequences for me, even my slow painful death. The slightest lifting of Max's head would have resulted in the arrow piercing his brain. In his case death would have followed instantaneously.

I reached beneath the neck band of my tunic and pulled out the piece of pot on its thin leather loop. As I held it in the palm of my hand I felt a weird tingling effect. Was it imagined, or real? I had no idea. I gently squeezed it, saying a silent prayer at the same time. I was convinced that it had saved my life, yet again, as Jesus said it would do. I then thought how foolish Max and I had been to approach the two drunken men, bows and arrows at the ready. Surely there must be a limit to the protection the pieces of pot would be able to offer. Equally surely, if we were blatantly stupid in our acts, a time would come when our apparent invincibility would be tested to the full and found wanting.

Typical of Max, his comment was short, unemotional and to the point: "God…We were lucky today…Must be these lucky charms we're wearing."

I'd thought on more than one occasion that he didn't appreciate just how lucky he'd been since wearing the piece around his neck. It was almost as if he took the luck for granted, something I'd never done. I'd been tempted on more that one occasion to ask him for the return of the piece, but realised that if he then were to have an accident, possibly fatal, I would never be able to forgive myself. All I could do was to ask him to take greater care of his personal safety in future.

"As a reward for all your hard work and dedication", as Maximilian had put it to his foot soldiers and cavalrymen, we were given permission to attend a play at the huge Lutetian Amphitheatre.

The play, put on by a group calling themselves the GalliRoma Theatre Company that consisted of both local people, mainly women, and those Roman men who were interested in acting, was the Greek play *Lysistrata*, written some four hundred years earlier by a writer named Aristophanes. It was evidently one of the favourites of Roman soldiers who were a long way from home and therefore beyond the influence of their female loved ones.

When Max and I arrived at the semicircular amphitheatre we found it already almost full of people, seated and looking forward to their entertainment. The organisers had purposely arranged the audience so that the men and women were segregated either side of the central aisle. The reason for this became apparent as the play progressed.

First, a bit about the play itself. It is the story of a Greek woman called Lysistrata who decides to try and stop the Peloponnesian Wars between Athens and Sparta by unusual means. She persuades the young women of Greece to withhold their sexual favours from their men folk until they agreed to end the wars. This inevitably leads to a battle between the sexes because the men think that war 'matters' are nothing to do with mere women. Initially all the women agree on the course of action, but soon the younger ones, desperate for sex start breaking ranks and have to be pulled back into line by their elders.

The old women, in support of their younger sex decide to take over the Acropolis where the country's treasury is kept, locking the wooden gates behind them. Starved of money the men could not now conduct the wars.

The old men also in support of their younger sex decide to try to get into the Acropolis by setting fire to the gates. More old women come along and pour pitchers of water on the fire to dowse it, soaking the old men in the process.

The situation is now getting completely out of hand so a magistrate is called to make a decision. Lysistrata explains why the young women have taken the action, pointing out that they grow old, childless, while their men folk are away fighting. As they become older they become less desirable to men. The magistrate states that the men also grow old, but Lysistrata points out that as they do so they still are able to keep their desirability to the younger women.

The magistrate arranges peace talks between the two groups. After much discussion the men reluctantly give up their warring. The women, pleased with the result, immediately reinstate their sexual favours. The play ends with both men and women singing and dancing, and disappearing in pairs behind a screen in order to renew their relationships. At this point one is expected to use one's imagination.

During the play there was plenty of chorus singing where the women appealed to the female part of the audience for support, and the men singers did likewise, appealing to the men in the audience. It wasn't long before the two sexes in the audience started to jeer in a light-hearted way at each other across the central aisle, as the organisers had intended.

At the end of the play, as the players took their bows, we in the audience rose from our seats and enthusiastically applauded. This went on for some time, as we refused to let the players leave the stage. Eventually things died down and we slowly filed out of the amphitheatre.

As we did so many men and women paired up and left together, most laughing and joking at what they'd seen and heard. Others appeared to be seriously discussing the theme of the play and one wondered if the women were laying down their terms for the future relationship with their menfolk who were probablymembers of the Roman army based at Lutetia.

During the early part of the play I'd been too busy watching, listening and taking an active part in the audience participation to have kept an eye on Max. Why should I have anyway? But had I done so I'd have spotted him eyeing up a pretty little thing just across the aisle from where we were sitting. He had realised after all that he was more attracted to a member of the opposite sex rather than one his own.

But as the play progressed and the point was reached where the magistrate became involved, things went very quiet as he and the audience listened to the cases put forward by both women and men. It was then that I became aware of Max's antics. Out of the corner of my eye I could see him gazing longingly across the aisle as the girl teased him by concentrating on what was being said, thus avoiding eye contact. When she did eventually look across and smile, Max's face beamed, and it wasn't long before both were mouthing words to each another. Whether they were able to make out what was being said, I don't know. I tried to work out what the girl was saying, but failed miserably to do so.

Initially I was puzzled. Back in Caesarea Max had given the impression that he wasn't interested in the opposite sex, his longing gazes towards me and his night out with one of the handsome bath attendants apparently showing his true feelings.

But, equally apparently, his inner sexual feelings had changed. Had it all come about with increasing maturity, I wondered? I could only assume that it had, but I was certainly no expert on the subject.

What happened at the end of the play reinforced this view. Max apologised for abandoning me, said goodbye, at the same time promising to see me later back at the garrison. He then disappeared into the night hand in hand with the girl. I didn't of course mind because I'd already decided to spend the rest of the evening at the ale house, just round the corner from the amphitheatre. I knew I would find there some of my fellow cavalrymen who had been on our little excursion to sort out some drunken rebels the previous day. Max's company would have been welcome, but certainly not essential.

As our conversation progressed it was inevitable that it would get onto the events of the previous day, with comments showing how the incident involving Max and I and the two drunken rebels had been viewed by our colleagues. Some admired our bravery. Others expressed how foolish we'd been to approach the rebels.

I jokingly put it all down to the lucky charms around our necks which all our colleagues now knew about, having seen them on numerous occasions and believing our explanation that they'd been purchased from a market stall on the waterfront of the Cypriot capital of Limassol.

One colleague commented: "The gods certainly smiled on both of you yesterday, Marcus." Little did he realise how close to the truth he'd been.

It was now getting late, and knowing that we all had to be on parade the following morning we drank up and rose to make our way towards the open door. Suddenly one of our younger colleagues who had left five minutes earlier, burst his way back into the alehouse: "Quick, Marcus...Max has climbed to the top of the amphitheatre and is walking along the narrow parapet...He's obviously drunk and shouting down to some girl on the pavement below."

I rushed out in a panic not quite knowing what action I could take, other than appeal to his stupidity and tell him to get himself back down to ground level. I turned to the girl: "What the hell's happened?"

Tears streaming down her cheeks she tried to explain: "We went back to my place, had a few drinks and started discussing the play...Then, obviously worse for drink, he tried to make love to me...I jokingly pushed him away at the same time telling him he could if he promised to leave the army...As I said, I was only joking...He went outside to be sick, but did not return, so I went looking for him...This is where I found him, at the top of the amphitheatre."

As the young girl was giving me her account of events Max was shouting down to the girl: "Make love to me, Flavia...Make love to me."

I whispered to her: "Tell him that you will, if he comes down...Tell him."

Realising that this little lie could hopefully solve the problem, she shouted up to him: "Yes...Yes, Max, I will, but only if you come down, now."

"I don't believe you...You're only saying that to get me down...I bet Marcus told you to say it."

I was now getting both annoyed and frustrated: "Get down here, Max, right now, or I'll come up there and drag you down."

He appeared not to hear me, or preferred not to, for he continued to appeal to Flavia: " I'll leave the army...Honest I will."

At this point he decided to sit down on the parapet, but lost his footing and slipped over the side, just managing to grasp the edge as he did so.

Knowing that he had no chance of hanging on for any length of time I rushed up the central aisle of the inside of the amphitheatre, taking me to the top. I quickly found him and reached down, grabbing both his arms as I did so. Max was a heavy muscular man. I knew I'd no chance of pulling him up. He had to try to help himself: "Try to climb back up, Max...Use your feet. "

"Can't Marcus...No shoes."

I looked down, and he was right. At some point he'd lost them, or intentionally taken them off. He tried to get some purchase with his bare feet, but to no avail."

He then lost his footing altogether and this left me holding onto the entire weight of his body. He was incapable of helping himself, and I was slowly, but surely, becoming incapable of holding him.

Slowly his arms slipped from my grasp as my fingers lost their strength, and Max plunged to the ground, hitting it with a thud, the sickening sound I remember to this day. I rushed back down the aisle and headed for the point where I knew he'd hit the ground. The girl was holding him in her arms, tears streaming down her cheeks. Max wasn't dead, but life was quickly ebbing from him.

I forced my way through the crowd that had formed and knelt at Max's side, at the same time gently easing him out of the girl's arms and into mine. Max had been my constant companion since the time we'd both joined the army. At the time of his passing I felt that his place should be as close to me as possible, not in the arms of a girl he'd just met and who was probably in part responsible for his impending death.

In almost his last gasp he managed to whisper to me, so quiet that I had difficulty in hearing it: "Why didn't Jesus save me, Marcus?"

Knowing I'd little time I searched for an answer, but of course I knew deep down that there wasn't one. I'd told him on numerous occasions that there was probably a limit to the protective powers that the piece of pot around his neck, possessed. Well, on this occasion that limit had been surpassed. Had we both had the time I could have also reminded him how Jesus had resisted the taunts of the Pharisees who had told him to jump off a high cliff so that his Father in Heaven could save him, thus proving that he was the Son of God. But as Max took his last gurgling breath, blood streaming from his mouth, there was little point in reminding him of my cautionary words.

After gently kissing him on the forehead I reached under the neckline of his blood soaked white tunic and gently eased out the piece of pot that I'd given to him way back during our time in Tarantum, taking possession of it. Those who witnessed this and who knew both of us well didn't find my action at all strange, for to them we were as close as brothers could be. I heard one of our colleagues whisper to his mate: "Looks as if his lucky charm ran out of luck." And he was right, too.

Since we were only a stone's throw away from the garrison news of Max's death quickly arrived there and a party of soldiers, carrying a stretcher, was soon on its way to the scene of the accident to pick up his lifeless body.

Later the following day Max was buried in a simple ceremony, with only a few friends, including the young girl, present. Had he died in battle the ceremony would have been conducted with full military honours. I hoped that when my time came, my death the result of fighting the enemy and not the result of some stupid, self inflicted accident, my funeral would be of the latter type. Max, being an excellent soldier, had deserved better.

As the soil was being dropped onto his lifeless body I was tempted to throw the piece of pot that had been round his neck for several months, into the hole in the ground, It seemed the rightful place for it. But had I done so it would again have been lost, something that I felt Jesus would not have wanted. I therefore placed the thin black loop of leather holding the piece, still slightly damp with Max's blood, around my neck. I now had three such pieces, one piece still attached to the bridle of my horse, Brutus. I hoped that I wouldn't be foolish enough to think that two pieces around my neck instead of one would give me twice the protection.

Within a week the decision had been taken to move some foot soldiers and cavalrymen northwards to the coast, then across the sea to a country we were told was called Britannia. This was good for me because the move took my mind off Max's death. I'd also been promoted to the rank of cavalry officer, with responsibility for some fifty horsemen. Their needs had now to be uppermost in my mind.

But one thing I did do, just so that Max would always be with me if only in spirit, was to ask my Second-in-Command, a young man called Hadrian, to ride alongside Brutus and I on Max's horse, Julius. Both horses had come into our possession at the same time in Tarantum, when we'd both been recruited to the cavalry section of the Roman army, so my action seemed entirely appropriate.

***

Chapter Ten

I was just settling into the Britannia way of life in Londinium when I received what turned out to be my final posting. Just south-west of Eboracum, in the north of the country, was the garrison town of Danum, sitting on the banks of the River Don. My position there was to be Commander-in-Chief of the Cavalry Division, a position I'd worked hard to achieve after commencing my cavalry training in Tarantum. Since then I'd patrolled on horseback the full length of Gallia before ultimately crossing into Britannia.

I'd only been in Danum two months, but already I felt at home there. The conditions were good - plenty of food and drink, and the friendly local women were always willing, especially for the odd silver coin, or so my younger officers informed me. Above all, the natives weren't too hostile, trouble only brewing up when they were caught stealing - usually food, salt, weapons and the occasional horse if it had been left unattended, a crime punishable by imprisonment for both stealer and the soldier who had left it tied up, usually outside one of the many ale houses.

Although I was a long way from home, home being the tiny village of Grotto San Stefano, just north of Roma itself, life was pretty good in Danum. Of course it was summer, the most pleasant time of the year. Not intensely hot like it was at home.

Having heard from the other soldiers, who had already served a couple of years in northern Britannia, the weather would soon become cold, wet and generally unpleasant as winter approached. But the season would soon pass and the vines, just south of the town would again produce their sweet full bodied fruit in abundance. The local wine could not compare with those produced on the sunny slopes of Tuscany and Lombardy, but it wasn't too bad. One thing was certain, the more you drank, the better it tasted. And the local women apparently liked it too. It lowered their inhibitions and made them even more willing. On a good night, with wine in abundance, it was possible to get what one wanted without even one silver coin changing hands...or so my young officers informed me.

But my womanising days were long over. And besides, I'd met Beth within a matter of days of arriving at Danum. I'd met her in the market place where she was selling the produce - fruit, vegetables, eggs, milk and poultry, from her father's smallholding just off the road to Eboracum, the north's major town.

It had been love at first sight for both of us. In no time at all I had been introduced to Beth's family. Her parents immediately took to me, even though I was some five years older than her, and of course a Roman soldier. Beth had never married and her parents felt that she was beginning to think that her sole duty in life was to look after them. That was the last thing they wanted, so when a Roman officer of some standing showed an unusual interest in their daughter they actively encouraged the relationship.

I immediately started to teach her Latin for I wanted her to take up her rightful place at the side of me when I attended the various functions I had to attend as Commander-in-Chief of the Cavalry Division. Some of her friends, who had mastered the language, were already working as assistants to bankers and accountants in Danum, so it was essential that she could hold her own with them. The last thing her parents wanted was for her to languish on the smallholding for the rest of her life, feeling duty-bound to them.

Beth's two brothers didn't at first take too kindly to her newly acquired man friend. I was a member of the occupying force, in other words, the enemy. But over time they started to warm to me. I made their sister very happy, but more importantly from their point of view I taught them a working understanding of Latin. This helped them immensely when negotiating prices for their produce in the market place. The Roman soldiers tended to make their purchases from those locals who could communicate with them…and Beth's brothers could. In fact they became the envy of the other traders, and this occasionally led to friction between them, especially when the brothers had sold up by midday, and the others were struggling, wondering whether they'd either have to sell their produce off at rock bottom prices, or take the produce home to be sold another day. But most of the food was perishable, milk barely lasting a day, fruit and vegetables looking unappetising within a matter of hours. This friction was considered a price worth paying by the brothers as they returned home, hands empty and pockets full of jingling Roman coins.

Within a matter of a few months I was accepted as one of the family. There was even talk of us setting up home together within the garrison, married of course. Before Beth decided to tie the knot she did have one reservation, one acceptable to me. She would not accompany me if a future posting sent me out of the country, say back to Gallia, or even back to Roma.

My pride and joy was without doubt a horse that Beth's father had given to me for my birthday. Sadly, Max's horse, Julius, had died, apparently of heart failure during a strenuous cross country training run. This of course left my Second-in-Command, Hadrian, without a horse. So my birthday present was timely. I gave Brutus to Hadrian, and my new horse became my trusty steed. He would need some intensive training and that's what I gave him.

The stallion, that I named Maximus, after the close friend I'd so tragically lost some months earlier in Gallia, was truly a majestic animal, white in colour and so big that I had great difficulty in mounting him. In fact Beth's father made me some special elongated stirrups of intricate design to enable me to lift myself up. Initially the horse was a bit frisky, suspicious of his new owner, but soon both man and beast became a common sight throughout the garrison town.

When I arrived in Danum I had around my neck, hanging from loops of thin black leather, two pieces of pot that had first made their appearance at the Last Supper, when Jesus met his twelve disciples for the last time. As Max died in my arms I removed the piece of pot from around his neck not wanting it to become lost. There was also a piece on the side of Brutus's head, attached tightly to his bridle. This I removed when I passed the horse on to Hadrian.

Although I'd always thought that the rightful place for all three pieces was around my neck, they were uncomfortable, pressing painfully into my skin every time I put on my protective metal breast plate, as I did every time I went out on duty. Not wanting to hide the pieces away in the wooden box under my bed where I kept my other personal belongings, I decided to continue wearing the piece that Jesus had given to me, and to tie the other two pieces tightly to the bridle either side of Maximus's head. Maybe if they had any mystic powers, not likely judging from the way Max had so easily lost his life, they may just protect Maximus in some way or other, not that he would need it, being so big and strong.

Those who saw the pieces of pot on the side of Maximus's head showed mild interest and asked how I had acquired them. Since telling the full story would have taken the best part of a day and probably not believed anyway, I decided to show a little dishonesty, simply replying:

"Oh, from a bazaar down by the harbour in Limassol, the main port of Cyprus…There were all sorts of different shapes and colours, and each one had a different Greek letter engraved into it…Those who bartered for them liked to choose one with the first letter of their name on it." I then realised I'd chosen my words badly, for the three pieces I had in my possession had the letters ν, τ, θ and π engraved into them. The letter μ□(mu) for Marcus, was nowhere to be seen. One or two observant individuals who knew my name and also had a smattering of Greek, pointed this out, but since none of the local people had heard of Cyprus, let alone its main port, they quickly lost interest.

Even though Officer-in-Chief of the cavalry section at Danum garrison I still insisted on 'being seen', doing my fair share of duties, usually patrolling the outer edges of the town. If there was to be any trouble from the local youths it was usually after a drinking or betting session, and usually took place on the strip of heathland that separated the town from the adjoining woods, or down by the river.

When on duty all cavalry soldiers were expected to be prepared for any sort of trouble. This meant wearing full combat attire. Metal or padded guards were placed over shins to protect against the local women who had the habit of kicking out if they were being restrained for any reason…the usual reason being an excess of red wine. The upper body was either protected by a thick leather sleeveless top (lower ranks) or a metal breast plate (upper ranks). Finally he wore a helmet, made of thick leather (lower ranks) or of metal (higher ranks). Just how elaborate the helmet was depended on the rank, with some high ranking officers having colourful plumes projecting from their helmets. It was all very much a status thing.

All the soldiers on duty carried a sword, slipped through a ring in their leather waist belts. Occasionally a shield and a spear were also carried, but only when trouble was expected, which was very rare in Danum.

It was a warm evening in early September. The sun had just dipped below the distant Pennine Hills and dusk was fast approaching. I found it fascinating that the hills I could see to the west had almost the same name as the mountains at home. Were the names Pennines and Appenines in some way related, I wondered?

In full uniform befitting my rank, I proceeded to carrying out my patrol duty on my trusty steed, Maximus. I loved to patrol alone and felt confident when doing so. This was for two main reasons - one, I was no doubt an impressive figure mounted so high up and in full combat attire. Who in their right mind would want to tackle me? And two, I had, over my first few weeks at Danum built up a good relationship with the local population, if indeed that was possible, I being a member of the occupying force. I was always helpful, especially to the elderly, and always fair when sorting out disputes. Of course my relationship with Beth and her brothers helped. But above all, I had slowly gained the trust of local people.

My route took me down towards the bank of the River Don, where I'd heard that some local youths had set the ferry boat adrift, much to the annoyance of the ferryman who, although well into his seventies, had had to swim out to retrieve it. Evidently it had happened before, and he'd complained to the Officer-in-Charge of the garrison. I had been asked to investigate. Rather than give the task to one of my underlings I decided to investigate the issue myself.

Taking a route that was unfamiliar to me, Maximus and I ended up on the river bank itself some four hundred paces from the crossing point. As we approached some thick long grass Maximus stopped dead in his tracks, refusing to go a step further. His instincts told him that something wasn't quite right. I, staring downwards, couldn't see anything unusual. Maximus had ploughed through long grass many times before without any problem. In fact most of the grass on the river bank was long, having grown to that length during the summer months. It was just beginning to show signs of dying off. I urged him forward, with a gentle squeezing of my knees. He reluctantly did so, trusting me.

Suddenly the ground below Maximus's front feet collapsed, almost throwing me out of the saddle. The long grass parted, revealing that he with me on his back had walked into a bog that had been concealed by the thick long grass growing in a floating crust of vegetation. He kicked out with his front legs, trying to find some sort of purchase, but to no avail. His body simply moved further into the bog.

In a matter of seconds the water was up to my feet. Maximus was struggling, trying to find solid ground beneath him, but this only made matters worse, and the sinking continued at an alarming rate. Soon the water was up to his mouth and nose. He was fighting for his life.

I, realising that I could no longer help him in any way, fought for my own survival. I tried desperately to free my feet from the stirrups, but to no avail. The straps of my boots had somehow become entangled in them.

Then I broke free, only to find that my heavy combat gear was weighing me down. As Maximus, now almost certainly dead, sank deeper, his huge body created a suction that stopped me from trying to somehow paddle my way upwards. Soon my mouth then my nose were below the surface. I could no longer breathe.

As death approached I couldn't help but ask the question - why hadn't the piece of pot around my neck, the one that Jesus had personally given to me, with the words – look after this for me and it will look after you - protected me from this deadly circumstance? And why hadn't the two pieces attached either side of Maximus's head, a sort of double guarantee, similarly protected him? I could only come to one conclusion. God above had decided that my and Maximus's time had 'come'. It was time to meet our Maker.

My life started flashing before my very eyes. Although only from a simple background, my life had nevertheless been a momentous one, with one particular incident standing out way above the rest - the crucifixion of Jesus Christ. As the peaty water slowly filled my lungs I forced out one last gasp. Then everything went black.

Although it didn't take place instantly, I was confident that I would ascend into Heaven and meet up with all those who I knew would have made the journey before me, in particular my mother, my faithful friend Max and of course the most charismatic man I'd had the privilege of meeting - Jesus Christ himself.

Narrator – the author

Had a passer-by approached the spot a minute later all they would have seen was a large pool of stagnant peaty water with the odd bubble rising to the surface. There was no indication whatever that seconds earlier a majestic Roman officer, fully clothed in combat uniform befitting his rank and on an equally majestic white horse, had been standing just in front of it.

Of course a huge search was organised by both the Roman Authorities and Beth's family. Had Marcus been ambushed by dissidents who had killed him and thrown his lifeless body in the river? Had Maximus been spirited away to be slaughtered and eventually eaten? But there was no evidence of foul play. Marcus and Maximus had simply disappeared from the face of the earth. It would take almost two thousand years before the truth of this most unfortunate accident was revealed to the world.

***

Chapter Eleven

*Narrator – Professor Peter Robertshaw, Head of Archaeology at
South Riding University, Doncaster, England*

My story commences in the year 2011 with two significant
archaeological discoveries, made over 2300 miles (or if you prefer -
3700 kilometres) apart, apparently not in any way related. But as time
would tell they certainly were, and in the strangest and most unlikely of
ways.

By the way, my name is Peter Robertshaw and I'm Professor of
Archaeology at the South Riding University, based just outside
theYorkshire town of Doncaster. The university was founded in 1851 by
Lord Percy Braithwaite, who owned a huge property with many acres of
land just to the north of Sheffield. The family residence, known as
Eastfield Manor, was a huge stately home, certainly on a par with
Chatsworth House to the south and Nostell Priory to the north.

Lord Braithwaite had lost his wife several years earlier, and since he
had no heir, he left his whole estate to the nation on one condition, that it
became a university with the name 'University of the South Riding'.

Although he was fully aware that the word 'Riding' was from an old
Viking word meaning 'a third', and that if there were already a North,
West and East Riding, as indeed there were, there couldn't be a fourth, he
insisted on sticking to his guns. Lord Braithwaite hated his property
being in the West Riding, a huge expanse of land stretching north as far
as the County of Cumberland and no more than a few miles from the
Irish Sea.

Feeling that the exact meaning of the word 'Riding' was of little
significance in that day and age he tried to persuade several
Governments to create a South Riding, to encompass the city of
Sheffield and the towns of Doncaster, Rotherham and Barnsley, but to no
avail. It is interesting to note that his wish did eventually come to pass in
1974, when a Local Government Act created another Metropolitan
District known as South Yorkshire, along with West, North and East
Yorkshire. Although it is likely that Lord Percy would have approved of
the change he would have hated the name 'South Yorkshire'.

Eastfield Manor still stands today and forms the administrative centre
of the university, with the various modern departmental blocks built

around it on the many acres of land, one of which is my Department of Archaeology.

Now, back to those TWO significant discoveries I mentioned earlier. The first took place only a stone's throw away from the university, on the banks of the River Don, where the foundations of a call centre were being excavated as part of a new Don Valley Industrial Development.

Details of the discovery came in the form of a call to my department office from Doncaster Council's officer responsible for cultural affairs, a John Pemberton, who I happened to know very well.

"Hi, Pete, it's John - cultural affairs...Just had an interesting phone call from the new Don Valley Industrial site...Evidently the JCB driver has unearthed some sort of object."

"What do you mean...Object?" was my puzzled reply.

"Well...I know it sounds daft, but it looks like a Roman soldier mounted on a horse....They've managed to reveal a helmet with what looks like a head inside it, the shoulders and what looks like the top of a horse's head...It appears to be in remarkable condition, probably due to the boggy ground acting as a preserver."

This was staggering news. Almost lost for words, I managed to splutter out:"Tell them to stop digging...Immediately."

"I've done that already, Pete...Are you able to get down there for a look-see?"

"Yes...I'll be at the site in ten minutes."

Driving like an idiot in the heavy traffic and in the process scaring the living daylights out of an old dear who was crossing the road with her shopping trolley, much to my eternal shame, I arrived at the Don Valley site. Quickly pulling on my 'excavating' gear - muddy wellington boots, waterproof golfing trousers, a high visibility yellow jacket and of course the obligatory hard hat, I joined the site foreman who with the driver of the JCB, were staring into the shallow hole. John Pemberton had already joined them.

I made a superficial examination of the helmet - Roman, no doubt about it, which wasn't surprising since Doncaster, or 'Danum' as it was known to the Romans, had been a garrison town, positioned on the important route between Lincoln to the south and York to the north. I could also see on the unfortunate man's shoulders, leather straps, possibly supporting an as yet unearthed breast plate. All I could see of the horse's head was the top of the skull, with two protruding tufts of hair - probably the ears.

John spoke first: "Well...Obviously Roman...But as far as I'm aware, the Romans weren't in the habit of burying their officer ranks on horseback when they died...Any ideas, Pete?"

As it happened I had, but first I pointed out to him that although the Romans hadn't made a practice of it as far as I was aware, there were some good examples in history: "Many prominent people idolised their equine companions...Alexander-the-Great, with his horse Bucephalus, and Napoleon Bonaparte with Merengo spring to mind...But although the idea may have appealed to them, neither had their horses buried with them...But I do know of a very prominent person who did...Ghengis Khan...If the historians are correct he had some forty horses buried with him when he died, just in case he needed them in the after life...But in the case facing us I think that the gentleman and his horse were most unfortunate."

John, the site foreman and the JCB driver looked at me, puzzled. I therefore explained my theory: "I suspect that the Roman soldier was riding alone close by the river when the horse walked unsuspectingly into a bog, where it and its rider sank rapidly, disappearing without trace...What he was wearing weighing him down."

"Such as?" asked the foreman, wondering what the soldier's dress could have consisted of.

"Well...He may have had metal shin shields, a metal breast plate and of course the helmet...A sword...Maybe even a shield...There would have been some suction, too, preventing him getting out...However it happened it must have been a rapid and horrible death for both rider and horse."

Assuming that the horse was of a height anything up to two metres, maybe even more, I asked the JCB driver to manoeuvre his bucket so that he could dig down to that depth, but a good metre to one side. As he did so the saturated soil broke away revealing one side of the horse and rider, almost perfectly preserved.

As the foreman look on, agog, John offered an explanation for the excellent condition: "It's something to do with the acidity of the boggy ground and the absence of oxygen...I believe well preserved bodies have been found in the bogs of Ireland."

The foreman nodded, but now other things were on his mind. He'd already been on sites in the Doncaster area where Roman artefacts had been found, and the whole job has come to an abrupt halt, much to the annoyance of all concerned...all except the archaeologists like myself. And here was yet another example. At this point conflicting hopes applied. The foreman's hope was that the find would be a 'one off'. The site could be quickly excavated and the job again put on track. My hope was that this find would be one of many on the site, all to be plotted and carefully excavated. It could even be a Roman grave yard, maybe the best to be revealed in England...even Europe.

Sadly, it did turn out to be that 'one-off', but what a find it was. My team and I, working an eight hour shift system round the clock, both for security reasons and to get the job done as quickly as possible, were able to wash away the soil using a low pressure water spray down one side without the horse and its rider collapsing on us. The water spray also helped to preserve the whole structure by preventing it drying out. This was a method we'd seen used to good effect to preserve the timbers of Henry VIII's ship the *Mary Rose* when they were brought to the surface.

After taking numerous photographs of all the steps so far taken, a large strong wooden board was placed vertically against the side that had already been washed down. This was held in place by the JCB's bucket. A second JCB then dug a deep trench half a metre away from the other side. A second verticle board was postioned in this trench, pressing against both horse and rider.

With both JCB buckets pressing against the two boards, in effect sandwiching the horse and rider between them, the drivers carried out the most intricate of manoeuvres. Slowly, exercising great coordination, they tilted both boards, with the horse and rider trapped between them, until the sandwich was horizontal. The uppermost board, now unnecessary, was carefully lifted away. This allowed us to wash down the newly exposed side.

A large crane with its hook connected to four cables attached to the lower board's four corners then lifted it and its precious double specimen out of the deep hole and lowered it onto a flat back truck. The whole operation was carried out with military precision. It was now simply a case of the truck taking our 'treasure', suitably covered, back to my department at the South Riding University.

Over the next few weeks my colleagues and I were able to give our precious find a thorough examination. We were able to establish that our treasure was indeed a Roman cavalryman, probably not surprising since Doncaster had been a garrison town with a cavalry unit. His dress told us that he was a soldier of high rank. All other indications were that he and his horse had had the misfortune to fall into a deep bog that had literally swallowed both of them up in a matter of seconds. The bodies of both man and horse were incredibly well preserved, as indeed were all items made of leather, such as boots, reins and straps. All the various items had been seen before, having been found during excavations at various sites both in England and Europe. Most could be seen in museums, such as the British Museum and of course the Museum in York.

But there were three items that, to our knowledge, had never been seen before, and ploughing through the numerous reference books on the Roman Empire that were in our possession, failed to reveal anything about them.

Around the neck of the soldier we found a thin thong of black leather, rather like a boot lace, tied with what we would now refer to as a reef knot. On the end of it, hanging down on the man's chest, trapped underneath his breast plate, was what looked like some sort of object made of glazed pot. It was exactly five centimetres across at its widest point, in the shape of a perfect hexagon and white in colour. The leather thong passed through a small hole close to the edge of one of the six sides.

But what puzzled me most of all were the Greek letters θ (theta)and π (pi) that were deeply engraved into one side of the piece...Why Greek letters? Why not Latin ones? And was the choice of letters of any significance? Today θ is used for a variety of reasons in science and maths. It is for example used to indicate the eighth brightest star in a constellation on star charts. And π, as all older children know, or should know, represents the figure you get when the circumference of a circle is divided by its diameter. $\pi = 3.14$...and goes on for ever...Yes, I found the letter choice most puzzling.

Then, as we were examining the horse's head we came across two very similar pieces of glazed pot, buried under clods of clay that had stubbornly adhered themselves to the leather bridle either side of the head. They too had black leather thongs threaded through tiny holes in them that had been used to attach them to the horse's bridle. I said very similar, for one of the pieces of the pot was a sort of pea green colour, the shape of an equilateral triangle, and had the Greek letter τ (tau) engraved into it, whereas the other was purple in colour, a strange shape that could be described as a rectangle sliced across its length at an angle and with the Greek letter ν (nu) engraved into it. Were all three pieces of pot somehow related? At that point it was impossible to say, but it seemed highly likely.

Our next task was to Carbon Date the carbon-containing parts of our find - the tissue of horse and man, and the leather objects, including the three thongs that we'd found, one round the man's neck and two attached to the horse's head and were threaded through the strange pieces of pot. This was done by our Chemistry Department, who came up with an age of almost two thousand years taking the objects back to between 20 and 50AD.

Once our studies of the soldier and his horse were complete I had to decide how they could be displayed so that the public could see and hopefully appreciate them. I initially considered trying to display them as they'd been found, but realised that it would be difficult to support them. They were now little more than skin and bone. Some sort of ugly metal framework would therefore be required.

Instead I took the decision to have the man and the horse displayed separately, the man lying on his back, the horse on its side, both in glass cases, to allow control of both temperature and humidity. I also had a very realistic cast of the man mounted on his horse made of resin by a local sculptor, who also made replicas of the shin guards, sword, breast plate and helmet. Clothes as realistic as she could get them were made by a dress maker friend of my wife. An old cobbler I knew, who still repaired shoes in his little workshop, made all the leatherwork, even down to the thin leather thongs that had been attached to the three pieces of pot. All this of course cost a lot of money, but a successful application for a Lottery grant enabled us to have all the work done.

Before final assembly I had to make two decisions. The first was to decide on the colour of the horse. Tufts of hair had indicated that it was either white of light grey. I decided to ask the students who had worked on the project what they thought. A quick vote chose light grey.

The second decision was to decide whether or not to include the three piece of pot on the display. But before doing this I asked my students for their opinions on what the pieces were and where they had possibly come from. There was overwhelming agreement that the pieces were probably lucky charms to protect the owner from 'evils', - a bit like the *Saint*

Christophers that people wore round their necks to supposedly protect them whilst travelling.

As to where the pieces had come from, my students were all of the opinion that the answer to that question was almost certainly a bazaar or market place in a Greek speaking part of the Roman Empire such as Athens, Crete or Cyprus.

Once assembled I placed the white hexagonal piece, on its leather loop, over the head of the soldier so that it hung freely on his chest. It stuck out like a sore thumb, totally out of place. Of course it had been hidden under the soldier's breast plate when we found him. For this reason I took the decision there and then not to bother with the piece. And for the same reason I decided not to display the other two pieces either.

It was my intention to work out how the three pieces could be in some way displayed separately. Meanwhile they would be locked away in my department's safe that already contained some very rare objects including gold Roman coins found when excavations at the old Doncaster railway plant were carried out.

After my team at the university had carefully placed on both man and horse all the replica items I had to decide, with others, where it would go. It was my intention that the striking figure, looking as closely now as he had two thousand years ago, would go on display in the entrance hall of Doncaster Museum. I knew that the curator of the York Museum wouldhave given his right arm for both displays, but I wanted to see them on show locally…And as it happened I got my way.

***

Chapter Twelve

Now to the second discovery of significance. This took place during a holiday to Israel by my good friend David Rogers and his family. Although David was Head of Science at the Donwick-le-Street Community College in South Yorkshire, he had a personal interest in the history of Doncaster, particularly the period when it was occupied by the Romans. In fact the Roman dominance during that period fascinated both of us. We also shared an interest in that period when the Holy Land was part of the vast Roman Empire and was well documented in the books of the New Testament.

This part of the story came directly from David as he described how the discovery was made after 'grilling' his two children - grilling because he'd had to know the exact facts since he and his family could well have been faced with an immediate problem on their return to their home just outside Doncaster. There had been the distinct possibility of the family being embroiled in some sort of legal action with the Israeli Authorities. Although the issue sounded serious, the fact that we discussed it over a pint in the *Fox and Hounds* appeared to slightly ease the problem and enabled us to draw up a plan of action. At this point David takes up the story.

Narrator – David Rogers, with help from his wife Marie and his two children Jemma and Jamie

My wife Marie and I, and our ten year old twins, Jemma and Jamie, were looking forward to Easter when we would be able to get away for a couple of weeks to somewhere hot. Although Head of Science at the local comprehensive I had strong religious beliefs that had stuck with me since the days when I'd been a choirboy at Wakefield Cathedral. In fact when I decided to become a teacher I had to give considerable thought as to which subject I would specialise in - science or religious studies - almost at the two extremes of what life is all about.

Recently I had read an article in *Science & Religion* on the Dead Sea Scrolls, and the likelihood that they would soon be digitally copied using the latest techniques and made available to everyone on the Internet. The whole article had caught both my scientific and religious imaginations and I made a decision there and then to visit the site of their discovery at the earliest opportunity, which of course had to be during the two week Easter holiday.

That opportunity came when Marie popped into *Sunshine Travel,* in Donwick-le-Street's main shopping centre, on the Saturday morning at the commencement of the February half term holiday. She was looking for a seven night family holiday during Easter, knowing full well that it would cost the earth at that particular time, our children and I not being able to go in term time.

Marie sat down at the desk and proceeded to set out her requirements to the assistant attending her, pointing out that the holiday to Israel had to be during the Easter holidays. The assistant rapidly tapped the information into the computer then waited for its response. After a few seconds the screen filled with data and a large grin spread across her face. And when she went through the information with Marie, Marie almost fell off her chair.

The assistant explained: "We've had a last minute cancellation...Very last minute...In fact earlier this morning...Can you fly out tomorrow at 12.00 noon from Manchester?...There's a seven night holiday for two adults and two children at the *Pater Noster Hotel*, a small family hotel in Tel Aviv, Israel." She then printed out the details and handed the sheet across to Marie, who studied it closely. It looked ideal. The holiday was on a half board basis, so no looking for meals in the evening. The full price included a sea view room, and their appeared to be plenty to do for the children. Both loved swimming and she was pleased to see that the hotel had a large pool. Above all, the total price was ridiculous - just short of £800 for the four. She had fully expected to pay at least twice that amount for a holiday taken at Easter.

Marie had to decide quickly, knowing full well that the holiday would be soon snapped up by someone else. Ideally she would have wanted to contact me, maybe even our two children, but I was somewhere on Donwick-le-Street Municipal Golf Course, playing in the monthly handicap, and our two children were roaming around Donwick's South Riding Mall with their friends.

It was decision time: "I'll take it."

The assistant tapped the confirmation details into her computer and printed out the relevant forms for Marie to sign, including the Visa payment slip. The deed was now complete. She hoped that I would approve of her actions. If our children didn't, then tough luck. The family were going to Israel tomorrow for a week's holiday. There was no turning back.

As Marie made for the door, feeling on the one hand quite pleased with herself, and on the other a little apprehensive, for it had all taken place so quickly, the assistant shouted across: "What about currency, Mrs Rogers?…And are you all right for holiday insurance?"

On the latter point she knew she was, for I had holiday insurance for the family through my bank that was renewed annually. On the former she knew she wasn't. She didn't even know what the currency for Israel was.

The assistant at the bureau-de-change desk soon put her wise: "The currency in Israel is the shekel, and the exchange rate this morning is 5.25 shekels to the pound."

On previous holidays we had usually budgeted for the equivalent of £80 per day, with a little extra for trips. £700 for the week's holiday seemed to be about the right figure. Our family didn't spend huge amounts on presents for ourselves or others, and although she like one or two glasses of the house red on an evening and I two or three pints of the local lager, our drinks bill for the week was more than reasonable. Marie wasn't happy using her credit card abroad, having on a previous occasion been in some way fiddled by a restaurant on the Costa del Sol, paying the bill twice. She therefore ordered £400 worth of shekels and £300 worth of Sterling travellers cheques, knowing that she could always cash in any unused cheques on her return.

As she walked out of *Sunshine Travel* she felt more apprehensive than feeling pleased with herself. She had just taken £1500 out of our family assets. What would she do if for some reason she hadn't thought of we couldn't leave for Israel tomorrow? There'd be absolutely no chance of getting our money back on the holiday itself, although the currency would be still available as and when we eventually took our holiday in Israel, as both of us intended to do.

Although not a strongly religious person, unlike me who knelt to pray every time I went into a church, she couldn't help looking up at the heavens and whispering to herself: "God…I hope I've got this right." As it happened she had.

That evening our household became a bit of a madhouse. My first task with the help of my son was to search the loft for the suitcases. Jamie loved going up into what had become known as 'Aladdin's cave', I using the loft space to accommodate everything that could not be found a home on the two floors below or in the garage. While I was moving boxes in order to locate the two cases we usually took on holiday, Jamie was rummaging through a box that was full of what could only be described as 'junk'. The box had come from his granddad's home just after he'd died. Jamie first pulled out a stamp album containing stamps from the whole world, but with a huge section of British stamps. He immediately recognised the present queen's head on many of them, but there were also stamps with another woman's head on them, and several with three different men's heads. Wanting to know who they were, he asked me as I struggled to free the suit cases from beneath a heavy coffee table that I'd refused to discard, getting myself covered in cobwebs in the process.

"Dad...Who's this woman on these stamps?"

"Queen Victoria...She ruled this country just over a hundred years ago."

"And these men?"

I pointed at the stamps. "Er...That's Edward the Seventh...That's George the Fifth...And that's George the Sixth."

"Are they valuable?" That question was uppermost in Jamie's mind.

"Well...Yes...Especially those." I pointed to a page that had mounted on it three penny blacks, four tupenny blues and eight penny reds.

I knew that Jamie's mind was already working overtime. Surely he was the rightful heir to the album, and since I didn't seem to be interested he decided to assume ownership of it. What was essential - his sister had to be kept in the dark otherwise she'd want her 'cut'.

I climbed down the loft ladder then asked Jamie to pass the two cases down to me through the hatch. After doing so he carefully descended the ladder, holding on to the rail with one hand and holding tightly onto the stamp album with the other. Finally I threw up the ladder, then closed and locked the hatch. As I struggled across the landing before descending the stairs with the cases I saw Jamie enter his own bedroom, lift up the mattress of his bed and place the album under it. I knew what his intention was - he would browse the Internet at the first opportunity in order to get some idea of what some of the stamps could be worth. I also knew that if he did manage to do some sort of deal on Ebay I would have to be involved in any money transaction. At that point his sister, mother and I would indeed take our 'cut'.

One of our holiday excursions was to the Dead Sea, more specifically to the area of Qumranwhere the Dead Sea Scrolls had been originally found in cliff side caves by Bedouin goat herders in the 1940s. There was little to see, but to me it was important to have been to the area where the discoveries had originally been made.

As those on the excursion were provided with lunch at a purpose built restaurant close by, Jemma and Jamie decided to do a little exploring on their own. Soon they were scrambling up and down the gently rocky slopes.

At one point there had been some sort of land slip, revealing the tiniest of cracks. Both children peered inside, but could see nothing apart from a narrow strip of sandy soil, that part of the floor that was being illuminated by the beam of sunlight passing through the narrow opening.

Not content with this, Jamie tried to squeeze through the gap, but his protruding ears prevented his head from doing so. He hastily gave up, remembering the time when he'd got his head stuck in the school railings because of his ears, and a fireman had to cut him free. It took ages before his mates stopped ribbing him about it.

It was now Jemma's turn to try, but she had a similar problem. In her case it was a tight squeeze because her thick curly hair almost preventing her head passing through the narrow gap. But she just managed to make it.

"Look around, sis...See anything?" enquired her brother.

"No...It's dark."

"Well feel around."

Jemma soon found that her eyes became accustomed to the dark and, using the bit of light there was, was able to see a collection of pots at the back of what looked like a shallow cave. Most were broken, but one or two were whole.

"Lots of pots, Jamie...All sorts of shapes...Mostly smashed...Some the size of an egg cup, others as big as a bucket."

Jamie's brain went into overdrive. The tour guide had given his group a detailed account of how the Dead Sea Scrolls had been discovered inside pots within cliff side caves. Jamie had taken it all in: "Feel inside the pots you can get your hand in, sis...Is there anything there?"

Jemma wasn't keen on the idea. The tour guide had also mentioned that the odd scorpion was known to live in the area. What if one was sleeping in one of the pots? It wouldn't take kindly to being woken up.

However, she had also heard the guide's words about the discovery of the scrolls and was just as keen as her brother to find something interesting. There were four large pots, all intact, set apart from the others. She decided to try those first.

The first revealed what appeared to be the mummified remains of a mouse or similar animal, it was hard to tell. Jemma wondered if it had fallen into the pot and not been able to get out. In the next she felt small particles of something filling half the pot. On extracting a handful and holding them in the light she came to the conclusion that they were seeds of some sort, or maybe even rice. The third pot was empty. Cautiously she felt in the fourth, fully expecting the sleeping scorpion to be there. To her relief it wasn't, or at least nothing appeared to bite or sting her. But there was something there. The shape and size immediately reminded her of a familiar object - a half used toilet roll, but not as soft. For a second a couple of questions flashed through her mind - did the goat herders of the past used toilet roll, and if so, what was it made of?

Jemma carefully extracted the roll from the pot, cursing to herself as she felt bits flaking off it as she did so. On holding it in the beam of light she realised that it was indeed some sort of rolled up thick paper, brownish in colour. She tried to think of something similar she had seen before. All she could think of was a roll of brown paper in one of the kitchen drawers at home, used for parcelling up objects before posting them off somewhere, except that this roll was much narrower and the paper much thicker..

Although Jamie couldn't see anything, his line of vision through the crack in the rock being severely restricted, he nevertheless detected excitement in his sister's voice: "Hey, Jamie…I think I've found one of those Dead Sea Scroll things…Look." She then held it in the beam of light so that her brother could see it.

"Bloody hell, sis…I think you're right…Pass it through."

Jemma carefully eased it through the narrow gap, trying to avoid any more flaking of the object. Jamie slowly lowered it onto the ground with equal care, then shouted to his sister: "Better get out of there, sis…It's half past one and dad told us to be back by two o'clock, at the latest."

Jemma, much to her surprise, managed to squeeze back through the crack in the rock quite easily and came to the conclusion that the reason for this was the fact that her hair was wringing wet with perspiration, or was it fear?

Both children stared down at their 'find', wondering what to do next. Jamie made a suggestion: "I'll roll it up in the towel I've got in my haversack...That will at least protect it." Both children had brought towels with them because the highlight of the excursion was supposed to be bathing in the Dead Sea itself. Once the rolling up process had been accomplished both children set off for the restaurant a ten minute walk away.

"Find anything interesting?" I asked, jokingly.

"A mummified mouse, dad," replied Jemma.

"An empty coke can and a crisp packet," added Jamie; "A bit disappointing, really...We thought we'd at least find one of those Dead Sea Scroll things."

"Oh...They've all been found years ago," I said, a big grin across my face: "This whole area has been thoroughly searched over the last sixty years...It's doubtful that any more will be found."

On hearing his father's words Jamie winked at his sister.

On the journey back to our hotel, Jamie and Jemma sat together on the coach. This gave them chance to discuss in whispered voices what to do with their 'find'. Their Guide on the excursion had stressed in no uncertain terms how any sort of important discover, especially of a historical nature must be handed in to the Authorities, and that it was a crime, possibly punishable by imprisonment in the most serious cases, to smuggle such items out of the country. Both children knew the action they should take, but the temptation was so strong to hang onto their treasure that they decided to do just that. It would go in Jamie's small suitcase that went in the hold of the plane. This wouldn't be x-rayed so all being well the scroll would not be discovered. There was the slight possibility that Customs at Manchester Airport would search all their luggage, but it was unlikely. They rarely checked the luggage of a family passing through. The thought of taking the scroll to school and showing it to their friends and teachers really excited them. It never occurred to them that once the initial interest had worn off they would be left with an object of worldwide interest and importance, but in their eyes nothing more than a rolled up piece of paper - a bit like a toilet roll.

On the last day of our holiday Jamie started to pack his small suit case. It was of the soft type with padded sides. Knowing the other cases would probably be piled on top of it in the plane's hold and that even if wrapped in a towel the scroll could easily get squashed, he looked for a solution to his problem.

Earlier, as the family had sat round the pool for the last time Jamie observed his sister tucking into some *Pringles*. These she extracted from a tube-like container made of strong cardboard, with a strong plastic top and bottom. The tube would be ideal for protecting the scroll. In no time at all the tube was emptied by the two 'vultures'.

As we were gathering our belongings from the side of the pool Jamie's mother spotted him placing the empty *Pringles* tube in his rucksack: "Can't see much point in taking an empty food container with us, Jamie...Throw it in the litter bin across there." She pointed to one on the other side of the pool."

Jamie, who always took a selection of felt tip pens and coloured pencils with him on holiday, replied: "I thought it would be ideal to store my pensand pencils in, mum...The zip on the case I've brought is broken and they fall out all over the place."

His mother simply nodded her head from side to side and whispered to herself: "Now why didn't I think of that?"

Back in the apartment the family packing was soon in full swing. Jamie and Jemma had a room of their own with bunk beds in it. This allowed them to pack there own things, unobserved. Jamie carefully extracted the scroll from a small cabinet just below the window where it had been hidden away behind his underpants. Since the apartment was on the ground floor people passing could easily glance in, he therefore closed the curtains, at the same time turning on the light.

"Hey, sis...Can you get me some toilet paper?...About five metres of it."

Jemma, wanting to get on with her own packing, frowned at him, but knew why he'd requested it. Reluctantly, she went to the bathroom andpulled off the required amount. It was just her luck to be spotted by her mother: "Er...What's with all the toilet paper?...Are you expecting the 'runs' on the plane?"

"Don't be daft mum...You know those small pot ornaments I bought...You know, the ones of the Three Wise Men on camels...I bought them during our excursion to Bethlehem...Well, I want to protect them in my case."

It seemed a good enough reason for extracting several metres of toilet paper from the bathroom, so her mum said no more.

Jamie first pushed a wad of toilet paper into the bottom of the empty *Pringle* tube. He then carefully spread out the paper across the floor and rolled the scroll over it, giving it a protective covering several layers thick. Carefully he slid the scroll into the tube, finding it a tight fit. Finally, he pushed a wad of paper on top of the scroll and carefully eased the lid onto the tube. All he had to do now was to roll the tube in his towel and place it in the centre of his case, surrounded by clothes. The job was now done, and to his satisfaction too.

Jamie knew that the time spent at Tel Aviv Airport would be a difficult time for him. He also knew that he hadn't to look in anyway nervous, suspicious, or guilty. He had to act like a lively youngster who was excited about flying home.

The only time he showed signs of panic was when the woman on the check-in desk asked me how many pieces of luggage I was putting in the hold. "One," I confidently replied. But Jamie wanted his small case to also go in the hold: "Er, dad…Can mine go in as well?…It will save you having to find a place for it above our seats in the cabin."

This did make sense to me because I usually ended up trying to find space for three pieces of hand luggage whilst at the same time being jostled by people trying to get past me.

Jemma decided to support her brother: "Mine as well, dad…And for the same reason."

As a result of all this, three pieces of Rogers' luggage went in the hold, all duly labelled by the woman issuing the boarding passes.

After an uneventful flight we arrived at Manchester Airport. It was now simply a case of going through passport control, collecting our luggage off the carousel and passing through Customs…Easy, thought Jamie, but how wrong he was.

Both children loved the carousel. It was all a bit of a game to them, guessing when their luggage would come along. If they were very lucky, all three cases would come at the same time. Less lucky, and two would come, with the third arriving a few minutes later. Extreme bad luck was when two arrived almost immediately, with the third being the last on the carousel. Fortunately the odds against that happening were very high indeed.

The large suit case did in fact arrive in a matter of seconds, Jemma's a minute later. But where was Jamie's? He couldn't understand where it was since all three had gone through the system at the same time.

As time passed, Jamie started to panic. His case wasn't there. The possibilities flashed through his mind - It had been left at Tel Aviv Airport. It was still on the plane. It had arrived at Manchester Airport, but had dropped off the baggage truck on its way to the carousel. But the biggest worry of all to Jamie was that someone else had accidentally picked it up thinking it belonged to them. His mother had bought his case in ASDA so there were literally thousands of them.

Jamie was about to ask me to make enquiries about lost luggage, when he spotted his case on the carousel. Since no more followed it he assumed it to be the last one - just his luck, he thought.

He ran round the carousel, his enthusiasm revived: "Better late than never, sis," he shouted loudly. Had the hall been full of people all would have heard, but our family were the only ones there.

Jamie grabbed the moving case and pulled it off the carousel. Just to make sure he checked that the name Rogers was on the label. But it wasn't. The name was McKenna. Someone called McKenna had accidentally taken Jamie's case. Surely it hadn't been taken purposely.

His heart sank. Not only had he lost his case with his clothes in it, including his new Nike trainers and a Sheffield Wednesday replica shirt. He had also lost the scroll, and that could have serious implications if it fell into the wrong hands, although he wasn't certain who the 'wrong hands' could be.

Hearing the bad news and seeing Jamie's obvious concern I strode across to the desk that appeared to deal with luggage problems in order to report the loss and to hand in the case that had been left on the carousel, but wasn't ours. Details were taken and the man behind the counter stated that he would get in touch with us when he had anything to report.

The following morning, just as I was tucking into my full English breakfast - a 'must' after a holiday abroad, I received a phone call: "Mr Rogers...This is Manchester Airport, I have some good news...Your case has turned up...Evidently someone's young son had picked up the wrong case, the mistake only being discovered when he tried to open it at home... Fortunately, the family only lives a stone's throw away from the airport, and the father's just this minute dropped it off, at the same time picking up the correct one."

The news was obviously well received, but picking up the case was now the problem. It would mean a trail across the Pennines. I had no alternative but to say: "I'll pop across tomorrow morning and pick it up...Do I come straight to your desk?"

"No need, Mr Rogers…We've a flight across to Robin Hood Airport this morning…The case will go on that…Do you live far away from the airport?"

My eyes lit up. Robin Hood Airport was just down the road from where I lived. The solution was ideal: "No…We live just a five minute drive away…What time will I be able to pick it up?"

"Well, the flight is due in at noon…I would suggest you call about one o'clock…All right?"

I enthusiastically thanked the man for his efficient handling of the problem and replaced the handset. Jamie breathed a sigh of relief at the news, but realised that if he didn't 'come clean' with his parents about the scroll it would only a matter of time before his deceit came to light. And when that happened the balloon would explode like a nuclear bomb.

As I was about to set off for Robin Hood Airport Jamie asked if he could come along. I, welcoming the company of my son, agreed. The case was duly picked up, Jamie checking that the three number combination lock attached to the zip was still intact. All indications were that whoever had mistakenly picked up the case at Manchester hadn't somehow worked out the combination and had taken a peek inside.

On the journey home Jamie decided to tell me the full story: "Er, dad…I think I've done something a bit stupid…" He then proceeded to give a full account of what he had done. He could have blamed half on his sister, but decided not to. But, knowing my daughter as I did, I knew that she would have been involved in some way. Besides, she had actually made the initial discovery of the scroll inside the cave.

I felt like exploding with rage at my son's stupidity, but decided that being in a car travelling at sixty miles an hour was not the best place to go off the deep end. Besides, the damage had been done. The theft, if indeed it was a theft, had taken place and had gone undetected. The clock couldn't be turned back. It was now a case of deciding what to do next with such a valuable item of treasure.

***

Chapter Thirteen

Narrator – Professor Peter Robertshaw

It commenced with a phone call from David Rogers. He revealed that he was in a bit of a fix over some sort of artefact that had been smuggled out of Israel. Naturally, as Professor in Archaeology at the university, and also a close friend, I was the obvious person to turn to. He didn't elaborate other than state that he could be in trouble with the Israeli Authorities. Since I knew about the rules and regulations governing the movement of objects of great historical importance, I was the one to come up with a solution, if indeed there was one. Obviously the issue had to be discussed, and what better place to do it than over a pint in the *Fox and Hounds*.

David first asked me what I knew about the Dead Sea Scrolls, admitting that when the Guide had been telling his group about them on the coach down to the Dead Sea he had fallen asleep. As it happened it was a subject that I had studied at great length, not only out of personal interest, but because they had probably been written and hidden during the period when the Romans were ruling the Holy Land, a period that I was supposed to be an expert on.

I therefore gave David a crash course: "Well now…Opinions differ on who actually wrote them and when they were hidden…What is not in doubt is where and when they were discovered and what they say…So here goes…972 documents found in eleven caves in and around Qumran on the north west shore of the Dead Sea…First ones found by Bedouin goat herders in 1946, the remainder found in the following ten years…Written on parchment and papyrus in Hebrew, Aramaic and Greek, covering a period from about 150BC to 70AD…Almost all of the Old Testament was covered…A people called the Essenes could have written them round about 60AD and hidden then in the caves during the Jewish Revolt against the Romans…Another school of thought is that they were written by scholars in and around Jerusalem and hidden in the caves as they fled from the Romans during the Destruction of Jerusalem in 70AD…Right, you now know as much as I do."

David gasped: "So they're pretty important, then?"

"You could say that, especially if you're Jewish…Why?"

"We think we've got one?"

"How do you mean, got one?…Got what?"

"A Dead Sea Scroll."

He then described to me the happenings of that day when his two children made their startling discovery. He also described how his son had kept it a secret until the time his suit case became lost then found at Manchester Airport after their flight home. Cagily, he reached under the table and lifted up an ASDA carrier bag from which he extracted a tubular carton labelled *Pringles*. He eased off the plastic lid, turned the tube slowly over and allowed whatever was inside to slide out onto the palm of his hand: "It's wrapped up inside the toilet paper."

I hesitantly took hold of what looked like a badly rolled up cylinder of toilet paper with the ends folded in. I cannot describe the temptation I felt to have a peek underneath the layers of paper, but I was acutely aware just how fragile both parchment and papyrus could be, having handled both on many occasions. Besides, the pub was quite full and it wasn't long before eyes glanced across at two middle aged men, one holding a *Pringles* carton, the other studying an unusually long tube of what looked like an oversized toilet roll.

The problem now was what to do next, but first I issued some advice to David, telling him that it was very important, indeed essential, that none of his family should breathe a word to anyone about the find. If word got out the tabloids would get hold of the story and the Government may feel it had an obligation to get involved, if only to appease the Israelis who may insist that the perpetrator be extradited in order to stand trial.

As far as the scroll itself was concerned I needed to consult my colleagues to see if we had between us the expertise to create the right atmospheric conditions in which to carefully unroll it. Some nine hundred and seventy had already been 'processed', if that was indeed the right word, so there was plenty of expertise around. It was up to us to dig it out. If indeed there was anything written on the scroll, for example in Hebrew, Aramaic, Greek, even Latin, we had experts on the university campus who would be able to carry out a translation.

And so we left it at that. David understood the part that he and his family had to play. I would work out how any writing found on the scroll could be translated. If my department didn't feel confident to do the work I would reluctantly have to consider passing it onto the British Museum, but I was loathed to do that.

Over the next few weeks my department worked tirelessly on the Dead Sea Scroll that had been acquired, albeit by highly irregular means. Its appearance immediately told us that it was a parchment scroll. After painstakingly opening up the first few centimetres we could see that there was indeed writing on it, and the writing was in Greek.

Having photographed the opening lines of script our next task was to gently spray the first few centimetres of the parchment with water in order to see if we could prevent it from fragmenting, and also to see if the black ink was water soluble, resulting in the print disappearing altogether.

We were lucky. The wetting process enabled us to fully open up the scroll, giving us a length of approximately three metres. The wetting process also had little effect on the ink, which may well have been made of a lampblack and animal glue mixture.

Once the whole scroll had been photographed, using high definition cameras, the photographs were passed to the university's Department of Ancient History where Professor Andreas Leptos, our expert in ancient Greek took over. He worked almost round the clock meticulously carrying out the translation. Of course everyone involved had willingly been sworn to secrecy, the privilege of being able to work on such an unusual, yet incredibly fascinating project being too good to miss. But one thing I didn't tell any of them was how the scroll came to be in my possession in the first place. I simply informed them that I had received it anonymously through the post. I would of course tell them the full story later when I was certain that the Rogers family were free from any sort of legal action.

Once the translation had been made to the satisfaction of Professor Leptos, who on several occasions had to guess at what was being stated because that part of the scroll was missing or illegible, several copies were printed, each copy running to seven sides of A4 paper. At this point the decision was made to make the details of the scroll available to the outside world. A full description of the scroll itself and how it had been processed would be placed on the university's website, along with photographs and of course the full translation, but not how the scroll had been obtained, other than that it had arrived anonymously through the post. An article would also be sent to *Archaeology Today* for publication in the next monthly issue. As a matter of courtesy a full report would be sent to the Israeli Antiquities Authority, with a request that the university would like to keep the scroll if the Authority had no objections.

Having received my copy of the translation from Professor Leptos I took it home that evening to study it. He had already informed me that unlike almost all the other Dead Sea Scrolls this one was devoted to a period covering the life of Jesus from his birth to his crucifixion, resurrection and ascension into Heaven. It was not unlike the Gospels of Matthew, Mark, Luke and John, but there appeared to be accounts of happenings that for some unknown reason none of the four had included.

As I read along, one such account towards the end, hit me between the eyes as I read through it. I read through it again and again, just to make sure that I fully understood what the text was actually stating. In fact I read it out aloud:

It was now the first day of the feast of the Passover and Jesus met his disciples at the home of a friend, Zachariah the potter. When all were assembled for what Jesus knew would be their Last Supper together he spoke to them saying - Today I will eat and drink with you for the last time. Later I will be betrayed by one of you, tried, found guilty and sentenced to die. I will rise from the dead and ascend into Heaven to sit at the right hand of my Father. This will be to fulfil what has been written in the scriptures.

But before we eat I wish to give you something to remember me by. Wear it with pride at all times, even when your enemies surround you. Always have faith in my Father, and it will protect you against all evils. When the time comes to pass it on, do so with care. My Father will guide you as to a suitable person to receive it.

Jesus then showed them thirteen small pieces of pot that had been made by Zachariah only days before. Some were the same colour, some the same shape. All fitted perfectly into a square wood frame a hand span in size making a Star with six points. Jesus, being a carpenter, had made the frame himself. Twelve of the pieces had a letter cut into them taken from the Greek. Some of the pieces had the same letter. The thirteenth had two letters. All had a small hole drilled into them near the edge.

As all the disciples looked on, Jesus said - I have called the star the Star of David, after the great king of the Israelites. The twelve surrounding pieces represent the twelve tribes of Israel.

Jesus then took out the centre piece, white in colour and with the letters θ and π cut into it. He threaded a thin leather thong through the

137

small hole, tied it in a loop and placed it over his head. He said to his disciples - Now you do likewise. Simon Peter you take one of the pieces of pot with ν on it. You Andrew take the other one with the ν and you James Zebedee take the α. You John also take the α and you Philip the ε. You Bartholomew also take the ε. You Thomas take the ο. You Judas also take the ο. Matthew you take the τ and you James Alphaeus the υ. You Lebbaeus take the ρ and you Simon also take the ρ. Jesus watched as they threaded the leather thongs he had given them, through the holes in the pieces of pot, tied them, then placed them over their heads as he had done.

Then Jesus said to the twelve - As man becomes more greedy, more perverted, more uncaring about his world, a time will surely come when my Father in Heaven will destroy it by a force beyond the understanding of man. Far worse than the destruction of Sodom and Gomorrah. Only when the thirteen pieces of pot are again assembled together by the leaders of the world, sworn to work in harmony for a better world, will my Father prevent this destruction. When this will be only he knows. But it will surely come to pass. Always be prepared.

Simon Peter then asked Jesus a question that was puzzling all the disciples - Master, what do the letters mean. Jesus replied - You do not need to know but those who follow you will. It will be up to them to work it out.

The account then described the Last Supper itself, in words very similar to those set out in St Matthew's Gospel.

The link was uncanny, if indeed it was a link. My Roman cavalryman had a white piece of pot engraved with the Greek letters θ and π, hanging round his neck on a leather thong when we'd found him. His horse had two pieces, a green piece engraved with the Greek letter τ, and a purple piece engraved with the Greek letter ν, attached to its bridle either side of its head. And here it stated on a newly discovered Dead Sea Scroll that at the beginning of the Last Supper Jesus placed a leather thong round his neck from which hung a white piece of pot, also with the letters θ and π engraved into it. He then proceeded to give out other pieces of engraved pot to his disciples. My three pieces of pot and those referred to on the Dead Sea Scroll couldn't be the same objects, surely. It just wasn't possible.

There was of course a very simple explanation. There were in fact many hundreds, possibly thousands of these pot shapes with Greek letters engraved into them. They had probably formed some sort of children's game, used to help with the recognition of the letters of the Greek alphabet and the building of words...Yes, that explanation made a lot more sense.

One thing however puzzled me - why, throughout the Middle East, where the Greeks and Romans had been so dominant, were there no records of identical pieces of pot having been found elsewhere? Maybe they had, but were considered of little or no significance.

My next task was to write down and study the individual Greek letters that Jesus had chosen for the thirteen pieces of pot:

θ-π-ν-ν-α-α-ε-ε-ο-ο-τ-υ-ρ-ρ

The choice puzzled me. The letters appeared not to have been chosen at random. And why were some duplicated, but others not? Why had Jesus chosen two letters for himself, but only one for the others? There appeared to be some sort of pattern, but it wasn't at all obvious to me what it was.

But something else kept niggling me - something I'd heard many years ago. During my early teens I'd been a choirboy at Wakefield Cathedral. In fact that's how I came to know David Rogers, he being a choir boy at the same time. The Eucharist was something I'd seen celebrated every Sunday for the best part of four years, in fact until my voice broke. At Easter the service was something most impressive, with the bishop present and lots of the clergy in colourful vestments. The service started with a procession round the cathedral, with the choir in good voice, singing the well known hymn *Jesus Christ is risen today*. Incense was sprayed abundantly until a point was reached when one couldn't see from one end of the cathedral to the other. It was truly a show of great 'pomp and circumstance'.

The readings also stuck in my mind and it was one of those that was causing that niggle, so much so that I had to pull a bible out of the book case in my study.

I knew that what I wanted to look up was towards the end of Saint Matthew's Gospel, but before doing so I decided to refresh my memory of the Sodom and Gomorrah story. I quickly found the account in Genesis,making a mental note of two passages in particular:

Genesis 18 vv 20 - 21: *And the LORD said, Because the cry of Sodom and Gomorrah is great, and because their sin is very grievous; I will go down now, and see whether they have done altogether according to the cry of it, which is come onto me; and if not, I will know.*

Well, it would appear that the citizens of the two towns didn't heed the good Lord's warning.

Genesis 19 vv 23 - 28: *The sun was risen upon the earth, when Lot entered into Zoar. Then the LORD rained upon Sodom and upon Gomorrah brimstone and fire from the LORD out of heaven. And he overthrew those cities, and all the plain, and all the inhabitants of the cities, and that which grew upon the ground. But Lot's wife looked back from behind him and she became a pillar of salt. And Abraham got up early in the morning to the place where he stood before the LORD. And he looked towards Sodom and Gomorrah, and towards all the land on the plain, and beheld, and, lo, the smoke of the country went up as smoke of a furnace.*

So, that was the end of Sodom and Gomorrah, if we were to believe the account in Genesis - a sort of local disaster...very local indeed. I wondered if those who were at the same time building pyramids in Egypt, well over a thousand miles to the south west, heard the news.

Now, this was only a tiny form of God's retribution on man for his sins. What Jesus had prophesied would happen was on a monumental scale by comparison.

But surely man was also committing similar sins in North and South America, Central Europe, China and Japan, even Australasia. Why didn't God destroy places in these areas? Or did he? But there were no records of him having done so. We do know that Pompeii was destroyed in 79AD when Mount Vesuvius erupted. All indications were that the town was a pretty sinful place - a bit like Sodom and Gomorrah. So was that God's retribution?

We do know, according to Genesis, that some sort of Great Flood took place, with Noah being instructed by God to build a huge boat, an ark, to save several species of the animal kingdom. Was this also an example of his retribution? And far, far more recently was man's discovery of atomic energy, leading to the building and dropping of the atomic bomb, bringing an end the WW II. Was this God's way of inflicting 'brimstone and fire' on Japan? Then followed the 'Cold War', that kept the peace because both sides had identical nuclear weapons and feared mutual annihilation.

The more questions answered, however unconvincingly, simply lead to more questions. Why were millions of innocent Jews murdered in the Holocaust? And surely the 2752 people who lost their lives when the Twin Towers came down on the 11th September 2001 were all innocent people. Couldn't God have somehow engineered some sort of mechanical malfunction that prevented the planes taking off? Or didn't he work in that way? In sheer desperation I abandoned trying to make sense of any of it.

But what I did know, not because I was a believer, but as a scientist, was that the most likely way the World as we knew it could be totally destroyed was by the impact of a large asteroid at some future date, as had already happened in the past, possibly, even probably, bringing an end to the reign of the dinosaurs. The Earth would suffer a climatic disaster, brought about by the billions of tonnes of dust in the atmosphere reducing temperatures to those experienced in the Ice Age. Both plant and animal life would find it difficult to survive. Man certainly would not.

Was this the message to mankind in our Dead Sea Scroll, a message that came from God, via his Son? This was the only natural disaster that I could think of that could wipe out all life. Maybe also a huge volcanic eruption, blanking out the sun and also producing ice age conditions across the world, but even then some species would survive. And what about some form of deadly virus? It may kill off the human race, but what about other species and vegetation? No...the asteroid idea seemed the only possibility, but when it would arrive was anybody's guess.

God's message had also given man a 'get-out', something to do with the pieces of pot being arranged in a particular way by the most powerful men in the world. Fat chance of that happening even if all thirteen pieces were available to them. I tried to imagine the President of the United States placing his piece in the square, then inviting the Chinese President to do likewise. But my imagination wouldn't stretch that far.

So far I, representing mankind, had only three piece of pot in my possession. Assuming that all three had genuinely been handed out by Jesus to his disciples, as our Dead Sea Scroll stated that they had, where were the other ten? I had to track them down...But what an impossible task to take on.

I first concentrated on the three pieces of pot I had. If one had belonged to Jesus at the time of his crucifixion and the other two had belonged to the disciples Matthew and Simon Peter, how had the three ended up in a bog at the side of an English river 2000 years later and 3700 kilometres away? It was time to study the bible again and seek out the passage that had originally niggled at my brain. This time I was into the New Testament, more specifically Matthew's Gospel, chapter 27 v 35. During Jesus's crucifixion the verse stated that:

They (the soldiers) then crucified him, and parted his garments, casting lots: that it might be fulfilled, which was spoken by the prophet, They parted my garments among them, and upon my vesture they cast lots.

Did the soldiers at the same time cast lots for the piece of pot on its leather loop that would have almost certainly been ripped from around Jesus's neck by one of the soldiers, before he was nailed to the cross? Were Matthew's and Simon Peter's pieces of pot also ripped from around their necks by the same soldier, for all the disciples, except Judas Iscariot, were there to witness Jesus's crucifixion? It would at least explain how the three pieces came to be in the possession of a Roman soldier. Did that soldier return to Rome, to be posted out to Gaul and onto Britain? If he did we had a plausible explanation, but the chances of all this happening were too remote to even contemplate. He could of course have passed one, two or all three pieces on to another soldier, a friend or relative who had somehow ended up thousands of kilometres away at the Britannia garrison town known at that time as Danum, but we know today as Doncaster?

Maybe each piece of pot was looked upon as some sort of lucky charm, although the one belonging to Jesus certainly hadn't worked that way for him. Could he have actually given his piece to a sympathetic Roman soldier, with such words as: "Keep this safe and it will keep you safe." We know from the scriptures that soldiers who had witnessed the crucifixion had been moved by the event. Matthew's Gospel chapter 27 v 54 states:

Now when the centurion, and they that were with him, watching Jesus, saw the earthquake, and those things that were done, they feared greatly, saying, Truly this was the Son of God.

All this was of course pure speculation, with no evidence at all to support it…But I had to literally clutch at straws. What at least was beyond doubt was that three pieces of pot, identical to those given out by Jesus to his disciples at the Last Supper had somehow found their way to Doncaster attached to a Roman soldier and his horse…How, was anybody's guess.

I then had a thought. There was a test that I could do, or rather have done for me on my three pieces of pot. I knew that our Chemistry Department had a mass spectrometer, a devise for analysing substances in great detail, giving the proportions of the elements in a particular sample. I caught up with Mike Leigh, Head of Chemistry, in his lab-cum-workshop.

"Mike, would it be possible to take a few bits of clay, analyse them in your mass spectrometer and work out where the clay came from?"

Mike pondered for a few seconds then replied: "Well, the analysis of the sample would be straight forward…The problem is what do we compare the results with…We would need a data bank of all the analyses of clays found throughout the UK…Do you have some idea where the sample may have come from?"

Understandably he'd assumed the area to be somewhere in the UK: "Er…No…Possibly somewhere in Israel…Around Jerusalem."

To this news Mike's reply was most encouraging: "It's more than likely that the Israeli Environmental Authority has analyses of the minerals found in that area, including clays…We can give it a go and see what we come up with."

When I showed him the three pieces of pot, at the same time telling him how I came by them and their possible significance, he saw an immediate problem: "Ah…They're glazed…The clay's underneath…It will be difficult to get a sample of it."

My heart sank. Breaking the pieces in half would reveal the clay, but that was the last thing I wanted to do to such valuable items.

After closely studying the pieces he came up with a suggestion: "If the glaze hasn't penetrated the holes we may be able to get a sample there by high speed drilling them with a slightly oversized diamond tipped drill…Le's give it a go, shall we?"

Mike passed the first piece of pot to his lab technician who I simply knew as Ted, who like most lab technicians could do almost anything, even probably turn base metals into gold. He in turn carefully clamped the piece below the drill, replaced the bit with a special one with a diamond tip. He then pulled down his goggles, switched on the drill and with the utmost care ran the bit through the hole. As he did so a neat reddish brown pile of powdered clay collected on top of the piece of pot. After switching the drill off and lifting his goggles he unclamped the pot and carefully tipped the powder onto a clean filter paper, at the same time writing the pot's Greek letter on the paper for identification. He then repeated the process on the two other pieces: "Here's your three samples Mike…Shall I now put them through the mass spec?"

"Go ahead, Ted…It's all yours."

The pieces of pot, now safely back in my hands enabled me to examine them closely for any damage. There was none. In fact it was impossible to see that the holes had been enlarged at all.

A few days later Mike called me into his office, which happened to be only a few doors down the corridor from mine. After sitting down and arranging two cups of coffee with his secretary, Mike presented me with three print-offs: "You were right about the origin of your samples, Pete…They did come from Israel…A tiny, ancient village called Artar, about four kilometres west of Jerusalem…I emailed the Israeli Environmental Authority and they sent me a list of clay analyses they had in their data base…As you can see, the analyses of all three of your pot samples shows two isotopes of aluminium and their percentages… $^{27}_{13}Al$ at 98.448%, and $^{26}_{13}Al$, a radioactive isotope, at 1.552%…Now look down the list from the Israelis…The clay sample taken at Artar, known to be a place where there was a thriving pottery industry in Roman times, has almost identical percentages, well within acceptable limits…There's no doubt that your three pot samples came from that area…A note on the list states that the deposits there were more or less worked out by the end of the 15th century."

I enthusiastically replied: "So…We can be pretty sure that my pieces of pot, found on my Roman soldier and his horse in a bog at the side of the River Don, came from clay extracted from a deposit close to Jerusalem?"

"Yes…I'd say a hundred percent certain," was Mike's equally enthusiastic reply.

I had started to make some headway, albeit very small. But one thing I would never be able to ascertain was how a hexagonal white piece of pot that may well have been round the neck of Jesus Christ just before his crucifixion, a triangular green piece of pot that could have belonged toMatthew, and a rectangular shaped piece of pot cut across at an angle, purple in colour, that could have belonged to Simon Peter or Andrew, all three being Apostles of Jesus, were now in the palm of my hand. If only all three pieces could tell their story.

***

Chapter Fourteen

My next quest was an impossible one - to locate the remaining ten pieces of pot that the disciples had taken with them after the Last Supper. These, along with the three pieces already in my possession, would fit perfectly together inside a square frame about a hand's span in size, forming a Star of David...a bit like a jigsaw puzzle but without the parts actually interlocking. This was *Christ's Holy Square*, as I'd decided to call it.

As I sat there at my desk, doodling on a piece of paper with a pen, I decided to try and work out the shapes of the other ten pieces. Why I'd never tried this before puzzled me. It was the obvious thing to do.

First I pressed my hand flat on the paper, spreading out my fingers and thumb. I then made two pencil marks, one at the end of my little finger, one at the end of my thumb. After removing my hand I joined the two marks together with a ruler and measured the length of the line. My ruler reading was 21.5 centimetres (8.5 inches in old money, as they say). I then drew a square of side 21.5cm. This gave me some idea of the size of Christ's Holy Square.

I knew from my maths studies at school that you could draw a six pointed star by first drawing an equilateral triangle, then drawing another of the same size on top of it, but upside down. By getting the position of the second triangle just right, a perfect six point star is produced. I also knew that this would be a Star of David. I therefore carried out this simple exercise.

On looking closely at the drawing I'd produced by this method, I could immediately see that there was a hexagon in the centre, but it wasn't a 'regular' one. (ie) with sides all the same length and angles the same size. For the time being I didn't let that worry me.

I then surrounded the star with straight lines, in effect putting it inside a rectangular box. This gave me the construction I wanted. Studying it closely I immediately saw that there were twelve shapes surrounding the central hexagon - thirteen shapes in all - one for Jesus and one for each of his twelve disciples.

I quickly acquired a piece of thick white card and constructed the Star of David again, but this time I commenced with the central hexagon first. By using a protractor to make its six 120 degree angles and hence its six sides all the same size, I ended up with a hexagon that was regular. I then

146

drew equilateral triangles, six in all, using the hexagon's six sides as base lines. This immediately gave me my Star of David. It was now simply a case of drawing a square round it, although it didn't turn out to be a square, but a rectangle. So…Christ's Holy Square wasn't a square at all. Not that it really mattered. It was near enough to one.

I now knew the shapes of all twelve pieces of pot that Jesus Christ had given out at the Last Supper and of course the one he'd kept for himself. I also knew the colours of three of them and the Greek letters inscribed on them. I left the hexagon white and using a black felt pen wrote the θ and π on it.

Since there were six equilateral triangles in the square, the piece of pot in my possession with that particular shape could in theory go in any of six places, but in three of these the triangle would be upside down. Of the three remaining places I decided, for no good reason other than it looked right, to choose the triangle sitting on top of the hexagon. I took a green coloured pencil, coloured the triangle green and wrote on it the Greek letter τ.

Finally I looked at the rectangular shaped piece of pot, cut across at an angle, purple in colour. It was obviously a corner piece, but of the square's four corners where did it go? There were in fact only two places - top left or bottom right. But in the bottom right position it would be upside down. Its position therefore had to be top left. I coloured the shape in the top left corner purple with my coloured pencil and wrote on it the Greek letter ν.

I was now pretty certain that I knew the positions of three out of the thirteen pieces of pot in Christ's Holy Square, but I would only be able to work out the other positions if some, and ideally all, of the other pieces turned up. What was the chance of that happening, I wondered? But if Jesus's prediction that the world would be destroyed if his Holy Square could not be fully reassembled by the most powerful people in the World, they had to turn up, somehow. Was it just possible that God above had specially chosen me to carry out the monumental task of locating all the pieces? It was just a thought.

My last task was to take a pair of scissors and cut up the square of card into its thirteen pieces. I then mixed all of them together before reassembling them, giving me what I'd originally started off with. I was like a child with a simple jigsaw puzzle. It was oh so simple. It was the weirdest of feelings to think that Jesus had had this very construction on the table at the side of him at the Last Supper, the only difference being that his pieces were of coloured pot with Greek letters engraved into them and tiny holes drilled through them. Mine were of card without the holes, but three did now have their Greek letters and also their correct colours .

I cellotaped together the three pieces that I knew the positions of. After carefully placing the pieces in a large envelope and sealing it I placed it in the top drawer of my desk. I then put the three valuable pieces of pot, possibly the most valuable objects in the whole World, back in the safe in my room, listening for the tumblers to drop as I locked it.

I'd succeeded in drawing a square, or near enough to one, and a six pointed star that fitted inside it. This revealed exactly how the thirteen pieces of pot that Jesus Christ had distributed to his disciples at the Last Supper fitted into it. I also knew how the three pieces of pot already in my possession fitted in. This was indeed Christ's Holy Square.

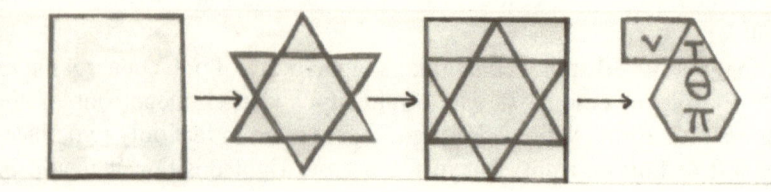

It was now time to give my first year students a little task in investigatory techniques. It would keep them busy during their Easter vacation. By using the Internet I instructed them to find out as much as possible about what had happened to the twelve disciples after Jesus's crucifixion, his resurrection and ascension into Heaven. I asked each one to present me with a report of their findings.

What I didn't tell them at that precise moment was why I wanted the information, which was quite simple, really. I had to assume that the small pieces of coloured pot had gone with the disciples as they went on their travels preaching Jesus's word. Of course some could have been lost in the following few weeks. More likely, the pieces would have been forcibly taken by over-zealous Roman soldiers. There was also the strong possibility that one or more of the disciples, knowing that the pieces could identify them as followers of Jesus, simply threw them away, hid them or destroyed them. What were the chances of the remaining ten being eventually found? A million to one against - possibly greater. But I had to try. My students' investigations would at least indicate the route the pieces could have followed. I had absolutely nothing to lose by pursuing this line of enquiry.

After their Easter break my group of students handed in their reports. Following the usual pattern, a few were excellent, showing real commitment to the task. Most were average, and one or two downright poor, showing no commitment whatever. These had probably been hurriedly completed the night before over a pint of crap lager and a takeaway. I prided myself in being able to predict, even at such an early stage, who would get a 1st class honours, and who would struggle to even get a pass…And I was usually right.

Since most of the students had used the same websites, for example Wikipedia, their findings were more or less the same. Some however pursued their investigation with more enthusiasm and came up with additional information. These reports I studied in depth.

If any of the ten pieces of pot had actually been found (too remote to even contemplate), there was a distinct possibility that they could be on display in some small local museum, maybe amongst the Greek or Roman pottery and jewellery exhibits. It was therefore obvious to me that such museums should if possible be identified and contacted. Using modern methods of communication such as email, this should have been a relatively easy procedure. But was it likely that a small museum in a remote town in Iraq or Iran had an email address? Quite honestly I didn't know.

As I looked through the reports I couldn't decide whether I was surprised or not at the distance some of the disciples had travelled. They were mainly uneducated men, with little or no wealth. Andrew and James were in fact fishermen, so how did they survive on their journeys? Who fed them? Did they do menial tasks in order to pay their way? Was their message well received, or did they have to cope with life threatening situations? Almost certainly, yes.

Thomas and Bartholomew, for example, had travelled as far as India. Simon Peter as far as Rome. Did this surprise me? I didn't know. Could one or more of them have made it to China, or Britain, or Central Africa, all reachable by land, apart from the twenty mile Channel crossing that the Romans had been making for years to Britannia? I didn't know that either.

I started to scribble down brief notes based on my students' findings. I simply wanted to know at a glance where the disciples had finally died.

If there was such a thing as a 'likely spot' to find their unique pieces of pottery, surely it had to be there. Finding the proverbial needle in a haystack would be child's play by comparison.

My brief notes, also showing the Greek letter that Jesus had allotted to them, revealed the following:

Simon called Peter (nu - ν) was supposed to have been crucified by Nero in Rome in 180 AD (surely this date can't be correct, being about 150 years after Jesus's death, unless Simon lived to a very, very ripe old age.) Since Rome had been extensively excavated and had some excellent museums, the odds of finding Simon's piece of pot were surely good.

Andrew (nu - ν) was known to have preached in Scythia (now modern Georgia), Thracia (modern Bulgaria), and died by crucifixion on an olive tree (how could they have possibly known the species of tree?) in Patria (modern Greece) where he was buried. Had Andrew's piece been discovered in any of these areas? That was the question.

James, son of Zebedee (alpha - α) didn't get very far. He was beheaded by Herod in Judaea and presumably was buried there. The chances of discovering James's piece of pot in that area were also surely good.

John, brother of James (alpha - α) apparently did well in terms of life span, dying of old age in Ephesus (modern Turkey). He had earlier been banished to the isle of Patmos by Dalmatian the king. What if his piece had at some point dropped into a crevice on that island and was still there, undiscovered, today? I hastily dismissed that thought from my mind.

Philip (epsilon - ε) was also crucified, in Hierpolis (Eastern Turkey), having preached widely in Phrygia (also now Turkey). What were the chances of finding his piece? Not good.

Bartholomew (epsilon - ε) preached in India, but was crucified and buried in Allanum, a town in Armenia (now South Georgia). Had his piece been discovered there some time between then and now?

Thomas (omicron - o) preached widely, ending up in Calamena, India, where he was killed by a pine spear (how would they possibly have known the species of wood the spear was made of?) and buried there. The chances of his piece turning up in some remote part of India were surely nil.

Matthew (tau - τ) had died in his sleep, presumably at a good age, in Hierees, a town in Parthia, near Tehran the capital of Iran. Fortunately I didn't have to worry about his piece of pottery. It was already safely locked away in my department safe. But to me one thing was pretty obvious - the piece had never found its way to Iran before eventually ending up attached to a horse buried in a South Yorkshire bog. More likely it had found its way directly from the Holy Land to the shores of Britannia via Italy.

James, son of Alphaeus (upsilon - υ) also didn't get very far. He was stoned to death by Jews in Jerusalem. The odds for finding the υ piece of pot were surely good, the stoning to death and burial being 'local' events and no doubt witnessed by many.

Lebbaeus (rho - ρ) died in his sleep, probably at a decent age, at Berylas in Mesopotamia. It was anybody's guess where his piece was hiding.

Simon the Zealot (rho - ρ) seemed to have done quite well, becoming the second bishop of Jerusalem. He also died in his sleep in that city and was buried there. This sounded as good a place as any to locate his piece, Jerusalem having one of the best museums in the world.

Judas Iscariot (omicron - o) hanged himself after betraying Jesus for thirty pieces of silver. Who found him? Who buried him? What happened to his piece? Maybe it too was in the museum at Jerusalem, amongst the Greek artefacts.

Most had died horrific deaths, four being crucified, suffering the same fate as their master. Their faith must have been so strong after witnessing his crucifixion, resurrection and ascension into Heaven, that they were not, presumably, prepared to denounce it. One thing was clear – the pieces of pot around their necks had not protected them against such barbaric acts, as Jesus had told them they would. But had they earlier lost their pieces? We of course would never know

To say that these events took place almost 2000 years ago the detailed information seemed to me surprising. Who made the observations? Who recorded them, and in what form? And where were the records kept? Are they in some form available today? Questions. Questions. Questions.

But this also gave me hope. If all that I'd read was to all intents and purposes accurate, the chances of actually locating the ten missing pieces of pot improved immensely. When all said and done the three pieces in my possession were 2000 years old, had travelled over 3000 kilometres and had still been found, almost as good as new, so why not the other ten pieces?

As I lay in bed that night, being a real pain to my wife Angela by my restlessness, I planned my next move. I took the decision to publish on the university's Archaeological Department website details of my three pieces of pot - their colour, shape and exact dimensions, and the fact that one had the two Greek letters θ and π engraved deeply into one side, and the other two the Greek letters ν and τ. And although only a minor point, the fact that all three had a tiny hole drilled near the edge to take a thin leather thong. I also added details of where and how they had been discovered. This gave the reader some idea of their age and therefore their possible origin. The entry also referred to our Dead Sea Scroll that had revealed Jesus's message predicting possible world destruction if man didn't mend his ways. Details of this had already been placed by me in the public domain.

On the following day, and much to my complete and utter surprise, my Department received an email from the Israel Antiquities Authority. It stated that three similar pieces of pottery were in their possession, two at the Rockefeller Museum in Jerusalem and one in the Eretz Museum at Tel Aviv. All three were on display in the Greek section and were labelled as probably having been part of a children's puzzle, possibly to help with their reading. The details from the email were as follows:

The first piece, in the Rockefeller, where the curator's name was a Dr Jacob Sheresh, was red in colour, shaped like a rectangle, cut across at an angle and had the Greek letter α engraved on one side. The email had a photograph of the piece attached to it that also included its exact dimensions.

The second piece, also at the Rockefeller, was blue in colour, the shape of narrow isosceles triangle. The Greek letter engraved into it was ε. Again a photograph was attached that included the exact dimensions.

The third piece, in the Eretz, where the curator's name was Moshe Schelach, was grey in colour, the shape of an equilateral triangle and with the Greek letter υ engraved into one side. But as the attached photograph showed, this piece was peculiar because for some reason, not immediately obvious, the υ was upside down, and judging from the position of the tiny hole, was intended to be worn that way.

The email finally added that since receiving the detailed report on our Dead Sea Scroll, including the scroll's translation, the IAA had searched for the pieces of pot in their own museums and had discovered the three. They also added that they would use their contacts throughout the Middle East in order to see if any of the other pieces could be located.

I immediately replied, thanking the IAA for acting so promptly, for their valuable information and of course for their offer of help in locating the other pieces that may be in nearby countries. It appeared that when it came to archaeology, political differences were set aside. I finally informed them that I would keep them abreast of any progress I was making.

With my Dead Sea Scroll notes in front of me I was quickly able to establish that the rectangular shaped piece cut across at an angle and red in colour with the Greek letter α, had belonged to James, son of Zebedee, who had been murdered somewhere in Judaea, probably not many kilometres from Jerusalem itself.

The narrow triangular piece, blue in colour, with the Greek letter ε had belonged to Bartholomew. Although he'd travelled as far as India, he'd been crucified in Armenia. So why had his piece been found in Israel? There were several possibilities - He'd lost it. He'd given it away. He'd hidden it. Any one of these could have taken place before he'd crossed the northern border out of the Holy Land.

The inverted triangular piece, grey in colour, with the Greek letter υ had belonged to James Alphaeus. He'd been stoned to death in Jerusalem. His piece had therefore probably been found on the doorstep, so to speak. When and where exactly, didn't really matter.

I'd already predicted that if any of these unique pieces of pottery, apart from the three found on my Roman soldier and his horse, were to be found at all, it was likely that they would be the ones belonging to the disciples who hadn't managed to travel very far. To date the score was two right, one wrong, Bartholomew letting my theory down. But it was early days, yet.

I enthusiastically pulled out from my desk's top drawer the large envelope containing the thirteen pieces of card that I had earlier cut out. Three of these I'd already cellotaped together in what I considered to be their correct positions in Christ's Holy Square. From the ten remaining pieces of blank card I chose three pieces that had the same shapes as the three pieces of pot known to be in two museums in Israel.

The first I chose was one of the two rectangular shaped pieces, cut across at an angle, and coloured it red. I then wrote on it the Greek letter α. Since there was only one position it could go in Christ's Holy Square - the bottom right hand corner, I placed it in that position and cellotaped it onto the other pieces.

The second piece, also one of two, had the unusual shape of a thin isosceles triangle that stood on one of its two sharp points. I first coloured it blue and wrote on the Greek letter ε. There were two possible places for it in the Square - on the left side and on the right. Placed on the right would mean that the ε was the wrong way round, so it had to go on the left. I therefore positioned it there and also cellotaped it in.

Finally I took the third piece - the shape of an equilateral triangle and one of five. First I coloured it grey, then wrote on it the Greek letter υ but upside down, as the photo had shown.

There was one glaringly obvious place for it to go in the Square - upside down at the bottom of the white hexagon. I therefore cellotaped it to the others in that position hoping that I was right.

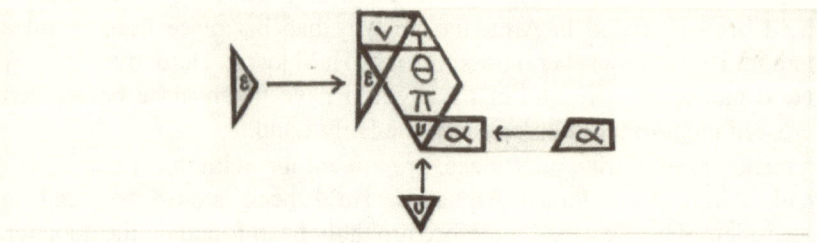

Playing a hunch, I dug out the piece of paper on which I'd earlier written all fourteen Greek letters after reading that part of the Dead Sea Scroll translation that had described the distribution of the pieces of pot by Jesus at the Last Supper. I studied the row of letters:

θ-π-ν-ν-α-α-ε-ε-ο-ο-τ-υ-ρ-ρ

I noticed that the four single letters – τ, θ, π and υ☐ all occupiedpositions down the centre of the Square. My hunch was that maybe the right hand side of the Square was identical to the left. If so it was possible to guess the positions of three of the other pieces - the ν, α and ε. I decided to cellotape all three shapes in and, using a pencil, faintly wrote in those letters, prepared to change them if I'd got them wrong.

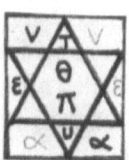

I stared at the nine pieces of card cellotaped together, feeling pleased with the progress I had made. I now had a good idea of the positions of all but four pieces in Christ's Holy Square.

A full week went by, with nothing on my department's daily email listings that was of any help to our project. My request for information had come to nothing after the first day's email from Israel. I'd been far too optimistic, requesting information about some pieces of pot that were 2000 years old and probably buried somewhere within a 2000 kilometre diameter circle centred on Jerusalem.

*** *

Chapter Fifteen

But I was wrong, for although the next communication didn't arrive by email, it did so by a more conventional route - landline telephone. It was the equivalent of steam radio as compared with the latest satellite digital receiver.

Expecting the call to be an internal one from another department I spoke into the hand set: "Peter Robertshaw here…Can I help you?"

I immediately heard crackling on the line, something unheard of on the internal system. Then a shaky voice spoke, fading in and out as it did so: "Doctor Robertshaw…My name is Doctor Javad Ashoubi and I am speaking from the Museum of Glassware and Ceramics in Tehran…You know, in Iran…Sorry the line is so bad, but an electric storm is raging overhead at the moment…It has also affected our internet access."

Realising that the call was of the utmost importance - it had to be coming all that way, and the fact that the line could be lost at any second, I quickly replied: "Hello Dr Ashoubi…Now, how can I help?"

"We have a similar piece of pot to the one you described on your website…Let me describe it to you…It is light brown in colour, the shape of an equilateral triangle and has the Greek letter omicron, o, on one side…A tiny hole has been drilled into the apex…It was discovered five years ago during the excavation of an ancient settlement a few kilometres north of Tehran."

He then gave me the length of the base and the vertical height of the triangle. Finally he added: "I will send you a picture of it by email if we can get up and running…Failing that I will use the airmail post…But I cannot guarantee that you will get it in less than two weeks…OK?"

I was just about to thank him and replace the handset, when he shouted: "My number at the museum is…"

He then rattled off a number that seemed to go on for ever. Fortunately I'd pen and paper at the ready and managed to scribble it down at high speed, hoping and praying that I hadn't missed a digit or got one wrong, otherwise a future call could well end up in the wilds of Outer Mongolia. After thanking him profusely, during which time the line went dead, I replaced the handset.

Excitedly I opened the top drawer of my desk and extracted the large envelope containing my pieces of card, some cellotaped together, some not. I extracted a piece of card the shape of an equilateral triangle, coloured it light brown and wrote on it the Greek letter o. I now had a problem. Since an equilateral triangle with the letter o on it looked the same upside down as the right way up it would fit in the Square in any of the four remaining positions. Having a one-in-four chance of getting it wrong I decided not to guess, and placed the piece on one side for the time being.

Of course, knowing the shapes and colours of all thirteen pieces of pot,and the Greek letters inscribed on them, was all very nice, but it did not solve the problem...the problem being that in order to fulfil the conditions as set out by Jesus at the Last Supper, and described on our Dead Sea Scroll, all thirteen pieces would have to be first located, then brought together at a central point so that the 'Square' of pieces could be reassembled, otherwise the World would be in great danger of total destruction.

On this front nothing appeared at the moment to be sitting menacingly on the horizon intent on wreaking World disaster, so it was my task to solely concentrate on locating the remaining six pieces.

But this relied totally on other people making contact. All I could do was wait in front of the computer...or within easy reach of my mobile and the office telephone, landline of course.

But what if some peasant in Outer Mongolia, who'd seen a programme about the newly discovered Dead Sea Scroll, on his local television, knew that Joe-the-Yakman across the valley, wore a similar piece of pot round his neck having found it amongst the ruins of an ancient settlement, wanted to contact me?

That night, as Angela and I watched yet another CSI repeat, I joking said: "Looks as if I'll need to look for some semaphore flags on Ebay and a correspondence course on reading smoke signals...Can't afford to leave anything to chance."

Here reponse was to give me a friendly nudge, propelling me off the end of the settee.

After four weeks, during which time I received nothing by email or by telephone that would help with locating the six remaining pieces of pot, disillusionment was beginning to set in. I became convinced that all the museums in those parts of the world where the pieces were most likely to be found, had by now checked their displays and come up with nothing. We were in effect at the end of the line. The missing pieces could in fact be anywhere - buried under some multi-storey car park in Damascus or Baghdad, or under a motorway in Turkey. Or they could have been accidentally or purposely destroyed and the fragments thrown anywhere. The task had been hopeless from the start.

We knew, if we were to believe the words stated by Jesus at the Last Supper, that God his Father would at some time in the future inflict on the Earth a destructive force beyond the comprehension of man if he did not mend his ways. We also knew that God had given him a 'get out clause', involving the thirteen pieces of pot that his Son had given out to his disciples at the Last Supper.

The answer seemed incredibly simple, and yet would be incredibly difficult to carry out. It appeared that the easy part should be the assembly of the thirteen most powerful leaders in the World in order for them to insert a piece of pottery into 'Christ's Holy Square'. There had for instance probably been occasions in the past when such people had been present together at the United Nations in New York. Only when the Square was complete with its thirteen pieces in place would God exercise his supreme power and prevent the destruction. By comparison it appeared that the hard part would be to locate all thirteen pieces of pot. That part appeared to be an impossible task.

But was the task in fact impossible? I already had three pieces in my possession. I also knew the location of four more, making a total of seven. I was in fact over halfway towards locating all thirteen. Was it just possible that I could complete the set? There was no doubt in my mind that I had to keep looking. I was also coming to the conclusion that God himself had given me the task of doing just that and was prepared to give me a helping hand.

At midday my office phone rang. I'd been expecting a call all morning from one of my First Year students who'd been ill for several days with meningitis. This was very likely to be it. The student, a girl called Susan Miller, had requested some work to do at home during her convalescence. Needless to say, she was one of my best students, and I was already predicting her to get a First in just over two years' time.

Assuming it to be her I picked up the handset: "Hi, Susan…Expected your call earlier…but better late that never…Eh?"

"Er…It's Dave Rogers…I've something very important for you…Can we meet tonight in the *Fox and Hounds*…Seven-thirty okay?"

"Not another bloody Dead Sea Scroll…Surely?" was my joking reply.

"No…But could be equally as important."

"What, then?…Don't keep me in suspenders."

"Wait until tonight." David then replaced his handset, not giving me chance to make a further plea.

At seven-thirty I entered the *Fox and Hounds*, having driven straight from work. The pub was only a ten minute ride away from the university, traffic permitting. David was standing at the bar waiting to be served having arrived just before me.

We settled in a quiet corner, pints on the table and well away from the crowd of young men, the yuppies, as I still called them, although the title had gone out of fashion. They were in the habit of calling for a drink before going home - something to do with 'unwinding after a hard day', whatever that was. Most were estate agents, and clerks in banks and insurance offices.

I asked David what his call was all about. Rather than tell me, he showed me. Without speaking a word he carefully pulled a screwed up handkerchief out of his pocket and slowly unravelled it. At first I saw what looked like the end of a thin black shoe lace drop downwards, then another, presumably the other end. At this point I had no idea what he was about to reveal.

He then took hold of the two black ends with his other hand and gently pulled. To my utter amazement a piece of pot, the shape of an equilateral triangle, yellow in colour, dropped downwards and would have hit the hammered copper topped table had he not stopped it from doing so by holding onto the two lace ends.

After examining it closely I knew immediately what it was, either a genuine piece from the Last Supper of Jesus Christ, some two thousand years old, or a good replica of it. At that precise moment I suspected the latter. I asked the obvious question: "Where the devil did you get it?…It could be the real thing you know."

Dave was familiar with my search for the thirteen pieces of pottery that had been mentioned in the translation of the Dead Sea Scroll he'd presented me with some weeks earlier. His reply was as astounding as it had been when he'd explained to me how he'd happened to have the Scroll in his possession.

"Well, Pete…The story of the kids finding the Scroll in some cave by the Dead Sea was hard to believe, but this is even more so."

After that story nothing would have surprised me about Dave's two venturesome children: "Go on...I'm all ears...It can't be more far fetched than the last one."

"As you know, we went on several excursions during our holiday in Israel...One of those was to Nazareth to see the very spot where Jesus was supposed to have been born...Well, all the tourist areas are plagued by young Arab boys trying to sell souvenirs, especially post cards of the various holy places."

"Yes, I know what you mean...When I visited the Pyramids and the Sphinx just south of Cairo I experienced something similar...They were a real pain." I nodded, indicating that I wanted him to continue.

"I only found out about the next part of the story after we quizzed Jemma about the piece last night...Not knowing that it was something very special, she'd put it in her top drawer beside her bed and forgot all about it...Evidently she'd tried to wear it at school, but had got a good telling off by the head teacher when she saw it, referring to it as a bit of cheap trash...Well, a couple of nights ago she'd had a coughing spell and got herself a glass of water, placing it on the chest of drawers by her bed."

By this time I was getting a little frustrated. All that David was saying was no doubt a true account of what had actually happened, but I wanted to hear where the piece of pottery had actually come from. Obviously I couldn't speed him up. I simply had to be patient.

After a good drink of his pint he continued: "The following morning, in her haste to get ready for school she knocked the half full glass over, spilling the water everywhere...As she shot through the door with her brother she shouted to her mother, asking her to sort the spillage out...As Marie soaked up the water she looked in the top drawer to see if any had got in...This was when she saw the yellow piece of pot."

We were at last getting somewhere, but what came next was hard to believe. After another drink the explanation finally came out, and what an explanation it was, too. In fact it was so good even an intelligent and imaginative girl such a Jemma just couldn't have made it up. And this was what added credibility to the story.

"Marie's initial reaction was one of annoyance...She'd told Jemma off on numerous occasions before about wasting her pocket money on cheap tatty jewellery sold from those stalls in the market...And she'd done just that again...Marie guessed that there wouldn't have been much change out of a five pound note."

I had to smile. Marie's estimate was probably out by a factor of a million, if indeed any price could be put on the piece at all.

Dave at last rounded off his story: "We tackled Jemma that evening and this is what she told us...The eyes of one of those scruffy urchins selling postcards evidently came to rest of a Walt Disney wrist watch that she was wearing at the time...She'd had it a couple of years, but now thought it a bit childish for her, so she thought she'd try a little bartering, just as her mother and I had been doing at a market stall close by a few minutes earlier...At first the young boy was only interested in handing over a pack of post cards, but Jemma's eyes had already focussed in on some sort object around his neck - a yellow piece of pottery, triangular in shape and with a strange sort of sign on it that reminded her of a tadpole with a big body and a long tail...The object had been threaded on what looked like a thin black shoelace and tied round the lad's neck...Evidently at first he wasn't prepared to let the object go, but the attraction of the watch was far too great and the two did a swop....And that's how we come to have it here in front of us this evening."

I felt like clapping, and probably would have done so had not the pub been full of the yuppy brigade. What a story...and it all made sense. too. There were however several questions I'd loved to have known the answers to, but obviously would never be able to ask. Where had the boy got the valuable object from? Had he simply found it whilst playing with his mates on the land surrounding his home? All the disciples would have probably passed through that area at some time after Jesus's crucifixion, resurrection and ascension. Had one of them dropped it accidentally or maybe buried it purposely so that he couldn't be identified as a follower of Jesus? But that would have been two thousand years ago. That couldn't be the explanation, surely.

Could the piece have been somehow passed down through the boy's family, having been found by some ancestor? I suppose that was a possibility, but again the huge time span involved between the loss of the piece and its discovery would have made that explanation unlikely. In the end I took a philosophical view. It didn't really matter how it had come to be round the young boy's neck. All that mattered now was that it was lying safely in the palm of my hand.

I closely studied the piece - the yellow colour probably as intense as the day it was made. There were no cracks or chips, and for a second I thought that it may have been some sort of replica after all, made out of plastic or even glass. The Greek letter ρ□'rho', did indeed look like a tadpole with a long tail and big head, as Jemma had observed. The tiny hole was there, exactly in the correct place to take the black lace. Originally a thin leather thong would have been used, but it was too much to expect that that too had survived for two thousand years. As I held it in the palm of my hand I knew instinctively that this was indeed the genuine article.

David then posed a question, not expecting me to have the slightest idea of the answer: "Don't suppose you can tell which disciple it originally belonged to...Can you?"

He had obviously forgotten the Dead Sea Scroll translation that had revealed which piece of pottery had been given to which disciple by Jesus, but I hadn't. I had made a point of memorising the details:"Jesus gave out two pieces with a ρ on them, one to Labbaeus and one to Simon the Zealot, both lesser known disciples...It is thought that Labbaeus died somewhere in Mesopotamia, quite some distance away...Simon became second bishop of Jerusalem and died there...So, doing some hefty speculating on my behalf, the piece is more likely to have belonged to Simon than to Labbaeus."

Just at that point one of the yuppies swayed past on his way to the toilet. As he did so, he glanced down at the piece: "Give you fifty pence for it, mate," he shouted jokingly.

Equally jokingly I replied: "Bollocks...But you can have it for a million...Genuine Russian Faberge...Just imported last week...Special order."

"And b..b..bollocks to you, too," was his drunken reply.

Both Dave and I smiled, but resisted getting into conversation with him,not wanting to attract any more attention. If only the yuppy brigade had known just how near they all were to one of the most valuable objects in the world...far more valuable than Leonardo Da Vinci's *Mona Lisa*, even his painting of the *Last Supper* itself. Now, there was an interesting point. Leonardo didn't know, couldn't know, that his masterpiece was incomplete. It should also have had Christ's Holy Square prominently positioned on the table along with the food and drink, and of course the cup that had held the wine that Jesus had described to his disciples as: "My blood of the new testament which is shed for many."

I know it sounds crazy, but that night I slept with the piece of pottery under my pillow, such was my fear of accidentally losing it. My wife Angela also thought I was crazy - such a fuss over such a small object. Her comments were however spoken tongue-in-cheek because she too was fully aware of the significance of the piece. She was a historian herself and had closely followed my quest to find the thirteen pieces of pottery that would, when assembled correctly, make 'Christ's Holy Square', as I now always referred to it. Her enthusiasm had so far been equal to my own, even though she on more than one occasion had called me a 'silly old bat'.

As I laid there, thinking about the piece, I realised that Jemma may have been lucky getting it past Israeli security at the airport. Had she packed it in the hold luggage, or was it in her hand luggage that would have been X-rayed? Or had she worn it round her neck, possibly covered by a round neck T-shirt? Fortunately, being made of pot instead of metal, the security scanner would not have picked it up, Thank God...But maybe that's what he'd intended.

I couldn't get to work fast enough the following morning. With the piece of pot safely wrapped up in a clean handkerchief and positioned deep in the zipped up inside pocket of my leather bomber jacket, I set off.

Unusual for me I drove like an idiot. Angela always said that I drove too cautiously, if indeed it was possible to do so, but I knew what she meant. I normally drove at twenty in a thirty mile an hour limit, and thirty when the limit was forty, much to the annoyance of drivers behind me who couldn't get past. On the motorway I rarely exceeded sixty, usually unaware of the forty ton juggernaut that was almost up my exhaust pipe. But on this occasion my mind wasn't on the job in hand. Uppermost was where my newly acquired piece would fit in the Square.

This led to some erratic driving. At one set of traffic lights I missed them changing to green, and had to be reminded by the driver behind me blasting his horn. At the next set I squeezed across the junction at amber, just missing a cyclist who'd anticipated the change and set off prematurely. How could such a small piece of pot have the effect that it was having, putting my and other lives at risk? But that was its effect. Fortunately for all, I survived the journey without any mishap.

Once seated at my desk I carefully extracted the piece of pot from my pocket and placed it in front of me. I then lifted out of the desk's top drawer the envelope containing the coloured shapes of card that I had already cellotaped together, nine in number. I sorted out one of the remaining four white equilateral triangles, coloured it yellow and wrote on it the Greek letter ρ. Looking at the Square I could see that there were two places where it could go, either side of the central hexagon in the bottom half of the Square. If my hunch was right, and I felt it was, these two places would be occupied by the two ρ pieces, so it didn't matter which I chose. I decided on the left hand one and cellotaped it onto the other pieces. I then remembered that I hadn't earlier cellotaped in the light brown o piece of card. There were only two places where it could go, upside down in the top half of the Square. I therefore inverted it and cellotaped it into the vacant position on the left hand side. The whole of that side of the Square was now complete with the three central pieces immediately to the right of it.

I then extracted from the same drawer the notes I'd made about the eight pieces I already knew about, having added the details of the eighth piece that had come my way via Jemma Rogers, the undisputed queen of 'barterers'. Four were already in my possession and four I knew the whereabouts of…three in Israel and one in Tehran.

Although I'd only actually held four of the pieces in the palm of my hand - Jesus's θ-π piece, Matthew's τ piece, Simon Peter's v piece and either Labbaeus's or Simon the Zealot's ρ piece, I'd seen coloured photographs of four more, including the piece found in Iran, whose photograph had arrived in the university post only that very morning. In my enthusiasm to cellotape into position my newly acquired piece from David Rogers I had neglected to even go through the post, let alone open a few envelopes. It was only the PAR AVION sticker that had drawn my attention to the envelope from Iran.

As I stared at the pieces I'd cellotaped together I was more and more convinced that the left hand side of Christ's Holy Square was the same as the right. As it happened, I'd cellotaped the pieces together on the back, this allowed me to draw a vertical line from top to bottom on the front, dividing the Square into two equal parts. I knew already that the individual shapes were identical either side of the line, the Star of David structure telling me that. I was also convinced that the colours and letters were identical. In effect one side was indeed a mirror image of the other, or almost, the letters themselves not being reversed. I therefore completed the right hand side of the Square, colouring the pieces, writing the correct Greek letters on them and cellotaping them into their correct positions.

164

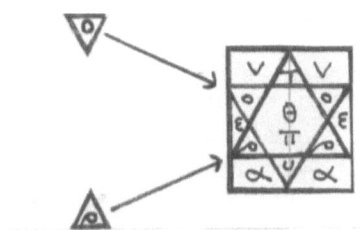

What was fascinating was the way Jesus had chosen letters down the centre of the Square, τ-θ-π-υ, that could be vertically divided in half. I couldn't help smiling to myself - how simple and yet on the face of it how complicated Christ's Holy Square was. If only I knew how he'd chosen his fourteen Greek letters I'd feel a happier man. But there was no possible chance of me ever knowing that.

Then, suddenly out of the blue, an expression flashed through my mind. Whilst reading various accounts of the Last Supper written throughout the ages, including descriptions in fiction, the expression 'Holy Grail' had been mentioned many times. During the Crusades it was thought that the Holy Grail was the chalice, probably made of silver that Jesus Christ had used to hold the wine, representing his blood, during the Last Supper. So-called clues were revealed indicating where the chalice could be found, leading to vast searches being made across the length and breadth of Christendom. Later it was thought that the Holy Grail was a collection of books or manuscripts describing a bloodline of Jesus. The writers, having studied Leonardo Da Vinci's painting of the Last Supper that appeared to show that a woman was seated at the table beside Jesus, thought that he may have had a wife. Possibly there were also children, and if that were so there could be relatives even living today.

But those who believed one or other of the two versions, or others for that matter were in my humble opinion all wrong. The Holy Grail was in fact Christ's Holy Square, complete with its thirteen coloured pieces of pot. It had last been assembled during the Last Supper two thousand years ago by Jesus himself. I suddenly had the strangest of feelings. I was convinced that God up above had given me the task of locating all thirteen pieces of pot, ready for the Holy Square's re-assembly sometime in the future. Would I be alive at the time to see it? I had no way of knowing.

My next task was to ask the Chemistry Department's lab technician, Ted, to drill out the tiny hole of my newly acquired piece from David Rogers, in order to get a sample of the clay so that he could analyse it in the department's mass spectrometer. Later that day he presented me with the results, alongside the results obtained for the original θ-π piece. Within acceptable limits they were identical.

My final task was to open the large office safe, used to keep secure some of the more precious archaeological items that we held at the university. Such items included the recently discovered cache of gold coins and jewellery that a farmer ploughing his fields just the other side of the A1 a couple of miles away, had unearthed. The valuable items had been dated to the time Henry VIII had destroyed the local monasteries. I placed the piece of pot that had originally belonged to either Labbaeus or Simon the Zealot, alongside my Jesus, Matthew and Simon Peter pieces. Carefully I closed the safe door knowing that inside were four of the most precious artefacts ever found on Earth.

As an archaeologist of many year's standing nothing surprised me when it came to the discovery of artefacts, the finding of the Roman soldier, still on his horse, probably lost without trace in a bog almost two thousand years ago, being a case in point. Had Doncaster Council not given permission for the new industrial estate to be built on the site, preferring to leave it as parkland for its citizens to jog around, walk their dogs, even fly their model aeroplanes, the soldier would never have been found. Even gold Roman coins had been found in the stomachs of fish being prepared for someone's dinner. And only recently the body of an ancient traveller, who'd had the misfortune to fall into the deep crevasse of a glacier whilst crossing some alpine pass, had emerged where the glacier had eventually melted. Carbon dating had revealed that the tragic loss had taken place over a thousand years earlier. As I said, nothing surprised me.

***

Chapter Sixteen

One of the young women who worked in my department as my second-in-command was called Rhoda Smithson, an unusual Christian name that she hated. (I prefer the word 'Christian' to the now politically correct 'first' name. I also prefer Angela referred to as my 'wife'. I don't particularly like the word 'spouse', and positively hate her being referred to as my 'partner', as if we were some sort of team in some sort of shady financial scam). But how could one hate a name given to one by ones parents in all sincerity? But Rhoda evidently did.

I can remember the first day Rhoda started with us. Her opening words were: "Hi...My name's Rhoda, but please call me Rho." And from that day on we did. But what was interesting about her name was the way she initialled the documents she'd either produced or checked through. At the bottom of each page was a single letter, and a Greek one at that. It was the letter rho - ρ, which, when you think about it did make sense.

I thought about initialling my documents with the Greek letter pi - π. I even considered asking all eight people who worked full time in my department to use a Greek letter when initialling documents, just to make the department that little bit different to the others. I did however dismiss the idea from my mind when I asked myself how Colin Gregory and Jane Hirst would initial their documents.

Rhoda and Ben her husband loved to holiday in Israel, where her grandma, aged ninety-five, lived in the city of Tel Aviv. Rhoda had earlier told me how her grandmother had been born of Jewish parents in 1916 in Gdansk, Poland, where her father was a welder in the huge shipyard there.In 1937 he became concerned about what was happening across the border in Germany, where Hitler was already flexing his muscles. Before the year was out he'd managed to move his family to England, taking up residence in the northern city of Leeds.

Grandma, at the age of twenty-one and unable to speak a word of English, entered the tailoring trade as a seamstress, a skill she'd acquired in Poland. Working at Montague Burtons in Leeds with strong, vocal and worldly women she soon learned to look after herself, holding her own with the rest of them - as Rhoda described her, a fiesty woman then and a feisty woman now. (Can a woman of ninety-five be feisty, I wondered?)

One thing was certain - Rhoda had inherited her feisty qualities from her grandma, as I knew to my cost. When I jokingly tried to 'pull rank' on her she usually responded with: "Don't you dare use that tone of voice with me…And balls to you, too."

Rhoda had told me that her grandma had married a train driver who was based at the Holbeck sheds, in 1939 and her mother, Ruth, had been born in 1945. She'd married in 1970 and Rhoda had come along in 1972. On retiring in 1976, her grandparents had visited Israel on holiday, fallen in love with the country and its people and emigrated there a couple of years later.

When Rhoda's annual holiday came up she and her husband naturally headed for Israel. They loved the country's chequered history and of course its people. Above all it enabled Rhoda to see her beloved grandma.

They flew out from Manchester on the Saturday. At seven o'clock on Monday morning the phone rang at my home. Angela and I were still in bed, but at least I was awake.

"Guess what?" I immediately recognised the voice .It was Rhoda on her mobile.

I hated calls that started in that way. The two words were either the forerunner of bad tidings, such as when the wife had pranged the car, or that some crazy revelation was about to follow, such as a female colleague at work, already pushing forty-five, was pregnant.

Fearing the latter, I first replied: "Have you any idea what time it is?" Following this with: "Go on…Amaze me."

"It's nine o'clock here…Oh, sorry…Forgot…We're two hours ahead of you."

This brought an unimpressed grunt from me: "Continue."

"I've got another piece from your puzzle…You know, Christ's Holy Square…Or I think I have."

This just couldn't be true. Surely the length and breadth of Israel had been gone over with the proverbial fine tooth comb looking for head lice, in an attempt to locate the pieces of pot that had been distributed at the Last Supper by Jesus Christ to each of his twelve disciples. Four pieces had already been located in that country. Surely not another.

"Describe it to me," I yelled down the phone, unnecessarily because her crystal clear voice sounded as if it was coming from the adjoining room with the door wide open.

"Let me first tell you how I acquired it…In Tel Aviv market there's a stall that sells absolutely everything…Ancient and modern, you know, just like the hymn book."

"Leave the jokes to me, Rho," I again yelled, but this time in sheer frustration.

"Well…One section's full of jewellery, some items quite modern, others donkey's years old…I was perusing the old section, looking for something a bit out of the ordinary, as a present for my grandma…It was there that I spotted it."

"Hope your phone's fully charged." I suddenly realised that I could lose the call at any second.

"No problems there…Anyway, It was hanging from what looked like a very thin gold chain round the neck of one of those dummies you see in shops, cut off just above the waist, and used to display necklaces and fancy pendants."

All this was very well, but what the devil was it? "Get to the point, Rho."

"Well…It's triangular in shape…Probably an equilateral…Yellow in colour, with a tiny hole at the apex where the chain passes through…But what caught my eye the most was the Greek letter engraved into the face of it…My name Rho, ρ…How about that for coincidence?"

At last…I knew what it was. But was it genuine? That was the question.

Before I could ask, Rho came back at me: "I know what you're thinking…Is it the Real McCoy?…Quite honestly, I don't know…All I can say is that out of the hundreds of items on display, there was nothing anything like it…If it had been a new line of jewellery some little sweat shop in the Far East would have been churning out pieces by the million, all different shapes and colours, and all with different Greek letters on them…And when I asked the stallholder, who looked older than Methuselah, if he'd seen anything like it before, he said no."

My next question was the cost. Had the stallholder known the true value of the piece the sky wouldn't even have been the limit…But he obviously didn't. Even then, if Rho had shown too much interest in it he'd have had second thoughts and upped the price: "So…What was the damage?"

"His starting price was three hundred shekels."

"What's that in real money?"

"Oh…About fifty pounds….When I started walking away he changed his tune: "Two hundred shekels," he shouted. I kept on walking.

169

"One hundred shekels…My final price…And you can keep the gold chain."

"I quickly reversed my steps, shook hands with him and sealed the deal."

Why were women always better at bartering than men? Angela was brilliant at it. I was rubbish: "So, you got it for about seventeen pounds, then?…Not bad for a little triangular piece of pot probably worth millions."

Rho grunted down the phone: "But even then I was bloody robbed…The chain was only gold plated…You could see the base metal underneath where the gold had been scratched off the catch."

"Do you know…Some people are never satisfied," was my unsympathetic reply.

I now had to wait patiently for Rho to return home. All I could do was to ask her to keep it in a safe place. I also suggested that she should remove the chain from the piece of pot, replacing it with a narrow shoe lace, or something similar, tie it round her neck and wear a high neck blouse or jumper to hide it from the checkers at airport security. Being made of pot, the scanner wouldn't pick it up. Since the 'Dead Sea Scroll' incident the security staff were evidently checking everything that looked a possible artefact.

Seven days later, on the Monday morning, well before nine, Rho burst into my office and placed the yellow triangular piece of pot on my desk.As I stared down at it I knew instinctively that it was indeed the Real McCoy. I also knew that it had belonged to one of two disciples - Simon the Zealot or Labbaeus. Since Simon had remained in Jerusalem, eventually being ordained its second bishop, and dying there, it seemed reasonable to assume that it had been his piece. Had it then passed into the hands of another holy person, maybe the third bishop himself? If it had, it was anybody's guess what had happened to it after that. I then remembered…I had assumed, using the same reasoning, that Jemma Rogers' ρ piece had belonged to Simon, so could Rho's piece have belonged to Labbaeus? Again, it was anybody's guess.

During the afternoon, by courtesy of the Chemistry Department, the tiny hole in the piece was slightly enlarged in order to get a sample of the clay. This was soon in the mass spectrometer and, as I'd hoped, or was it expected, such was my confidence, the analysis was almost identical to that produced by the clay from the θ-π piece, that had now become the standard marker to compare all other clay samples with.

I now had in my possession five genuine pieces of pot out of the total of thirteen that had originally occupied positions in Christ's Holy Square at the Last Supper 2000 years ago. I also knew the exact whereabouts of four more. Three were in museums in Israel and one in a museum in Iran. This made a total of nine. Where the devil were the other four? Was he, the Devil, in fact hiding them from me? Now, there was a thought. If he wanted to see the World destroyed, all he had to do was to make sure that just one of the four pieces wasn't found. He could then sit back and have a grandstand seat watching God destroy his own handiwork. How ironic that would be...But not of course for we who lived on planet Earth.

Over the next six months I heard absolutely nothing that would help my project along. The trail or trails because there were four of them, had gone cold, in fact ice cold. There were no requests for information from universities across the world, which surprised me since it was now common knowledge what God's message, through his Son at the Last Supper, had been.

But did it really surprise me? The answer quite honestly was no, and for a very good reason. With a high percentage of the World's population non-believers the message was treated with scepticism by those who bothered to give it any thought at all.

The atheists, who didn't believe in God anyway, simply adopted the attitude - no God, therefore no message, therefore no threat. The agnostics couldn't make up their minds one way or the other, and therefore adopted very much the same attitude. Even some of those who called themselves believers didn't take much notice, their attitude being - well nothing's happened in two thousand years, so why worry now? A more selfish attitude expressed by many was - well I won't be around when it does happen (note the assumption that it would happen), so why should I care?

Finally it didn't help when NASA expressed a view on the possibility of a rogue asteroid striking the Earth. They decided to go down the statistics line, quoting astronomical figures for the odds against such a strike. They even referred to 'advanced plans' that would swing into action in the event of an asteroid approaching Earth. Steps would be taken to prevent it impacting by either landing a team of astronauts on it to place nuclear explosives that would blow it to smithereens...or mounting a huge sail on it so that the solar wind would change its course, rather like a yacht. It all sounded a bit *Bruce Willis* to me. Unfortunately NASA's approach gave people the impression that this potential problem had already been solved, when this couldn't have been further from the truth.

Of course, those whose religions were based on Christianity and those of the Jewish faith, took the warning seriously and watched first with interest, then with increasing concern, at the limited progress I appeared to be making in locating all thirteen pieces of Christ's Holy Square. I'd already heard on the grapevine,(that being the University of South Riding's chaplain who had friends in high places, but evidently not as high as God himself), that the Archbishop of Canterbury had already discussed the issue with the Pope. Evidently their efforts had concentrated on trying to work out how the thirteen most powerful men in the World could be assembled together, possibly at the Vatican, but more likely at UN Headquarters in New York. Here they would hopefully be persuaded to place a coloured piece of pot into a wooden square specially constructed for that purpose. I was given to understand that the expression: "And pigs might fly," was used by the Archbishop at some point in the discussion.

I felt it my duty to keep the World informed of our progress and did this by publishing a monthly report on the University's website. But rarely did I get any feedback, such was the World's apathy.

As time passed even I started to lose interest. If the rest of the World didn't care about its future why should I? Besides, there were other projects that I wanted to get my teeth into. One such project was the excavation of an old graveyard at the side of a Norman church and therefore possibly dating back some nine hundred years, in the tiny village of Ribbleswell, up in the Yorkshire Dales National Park. The Company Yorkshire Water, digging a long deep trench by the side of the road that ran along the edge of St Stephens church graveyard in order to put in a new water main to the village, had broken into what appeared to be ancient graves, revealing several bones.

The Council, concerned about Health and Safety issues, had contacted the vicar, suggesting that the graves could be excavated and the remains placed in some sort of communal grave closer to the church. The vicar had sought advice from the Archbishop of York, who could not see a problem since there were only two gravestones in the churchyard. They were no more than half a metre tall and apparently engraved with barely visible identical crosses within circles, making it impossible to know who had originally been buried there. There were no objections from the villagers since, as far as they were aware, none of their ancestors had been buried there. They were only interested in getting their new water main as soon as possible, the old cast iron one, laid down in Victorian times, having failed on too many previous occasions.

At this point South Riding University's Department of Archaeologywas contacted by the vicar whose son had recently studied in my Department, and the letter he'd sent inevitably ended up on my desk. He first explained the present situation in some detail. This included copies of letters from both the Water Company and the County Council asking that the project wasn't unduly delayed. It then suggested a possible way ahead that included a thorough excavation of the site, followed by re-interment of the remains in a communal grave. This would have a simple headstone with some sort of inscription on it, the wording yet to be decided.

After a visit to the site with some of my colleagues in the Department of Archaeology a plan of attack was drawn up. Work would commence as soon as was practically possible and would hopefully be completed in a couple of weeks. It was planned that a start would be made at the edge of the road. We would then work inwards towards the church itself. This procedure would cause the minimum delay to the Water Company who obviously wanted to get on and complete their project before winter set in. Needless to say, my team and I were also eager to get started.

***

Chapter Seventeen

Then, completely out of the blue, came an email from the Curator of the National Archaeological Museum in Athens. Two identical pieces of pot to those that appeared on our website had been recently found by some children in a town on the island of Andros, just over a hundred kilometres east of Athens. They were now in safe keeping at the capital's museum until it was decided how to display them in a way that would show their true significance. Was I interested?

I felt like replying: "What a bloody silly question," but obviously couldn't. Instead I immediately sent an email asking for as much detail as possible - how and where they were found, by whom, and a description of each piece, including it exact shape, size, colour and any inscription on it.

Much to my frustration I heard nothing for over a week, when I expected a reply within twenty-four hours. When the reply did eventually arrive the reason for the delay was abundantly clear, and this now made me feel annoyed with myself for being so impatient.

The email was lengthy and read like a mini story. Although written by the Curator who, judging by his name was almost certainly Greek, the English was excellent :

Good morning Professor Robertshaw. I hope I find you well.
Sorry for the delay in getting back to you, but there were several facts that I wanted to first check out. Let me commence by describing how the two pieces of pot were found. Two young children from the town of Andros, on the Aegean island of the same name, were digging in the soft ground just outside the town where several small pieces of broken pottery had earlier been found. The two pieces, nothing like the others, attracted the children and they took them to school to show their teacher. Since both pieces were identical in shape but not in colour, nor with the same Greek letter inscribed on them, their teacher thought that they may have been pieces from some sort of children's game, where different pieces with different letters were placed in line to form words - a bit like the game of dominoes or scrabble. Such a game could have been used to teach children not only the letters of the Greek alphabet, but also how the letters could be arranged to form words. In fact the teacher proceeded to

make several identical shapes out of thin plywood, and with the help of his class painted them different colours and wrote different letters on them. The class then proceeded to place pieces in line to form words. Two weeks ago theschool happened to be visited by a team of inspectors. One of them, who has an interest in archaeology, had apparently recently read an article in 'Archaeology Today', written by your good self. It described the discovery of another Dead Sea Scroll, that appeared to give a more detailed version of the Last Supper, including Christ's distribution of the small pieces of pot to his disciples. Immediately recognising the pieces' significance he asked the two children if he could take the pieces with him when he left the school, in return giving each of them a Manchester United shirt, which they willingly accepted. I understand that the English team has quite a following by the children of the village. The Inspector contacted the Greek Antiquities Authority who in turn contacted me, suggesting that the rightful place for the two important pieces was the Museum at Athens. They also suggested that I immediately contacted you with the good news. Rather than give you a detailed description of the two pieces I have attached to this email a coloured photograph of them together, including their exact dimensions. If the pieces are indeed genuine you may well be able to tell me which disciples they originally belonged to. If you let me have this information I will endeavour to find out as much as I can about how those disciples happened to be in this part of the world.

I hope to hear from you soon.
Yours sincerely
Dr Stavros Democratos

After reading the email twice and thoroughly studying the attachment, just to make sure that all the information had sunk in, I referred to my list describing the thirteen pieces of pot making up Christ's Holy Square. I immediately identified the two pieces. Both had the peculiar shape of a rectangle, cut across at an angle. There were in fact four pieces shaped like this, forming the four corners of the Square. One of the newly found pieces was purple in colour, with the Greek letter ν inscribed into it. This one had been given to Andrew by Jesus at the Last Supper. The other was red in colour, with the Greek letter α inscribed into it and had been given to John at the same time. Although it didn't really matter if I couldn't find out how both pieces had somehow come together, to be found 2000 years later in the ground on the island of Andros, it would increase our knowledge of the apostles' movements before they eventually died. Clearly John or Andrew, maybe even both, had been on the island at some time, unless of course the two pieces of pot had been passed on, either forcibly or willingly, to a third party, as had happened to some of the others, including Jesus's own personal piece that had ended up in a Doncaster bog.

Maybe Dr Stavros Democratos could investigate on my behalf. I therefore sent an email in reply, informing him that the two pieces of pot had originally belonged to the apostles Andrew and John. Could he find out something about their movements?

After sending my reply I once more extracted from the top drawer of my desk the envelope containing the thirteen pieces of coloured card that I'd earlier cellotaped together. As I'd predicted, the two newly discovered pieces occupied positions in the Square where I'd already cellotaped them in.

There were now only two pieces of pot that I did not know the whereabouts of - a thin triangular piece, blue in colour with the Greek letter ε inscribed on it that went down the right hand side of the Square. This piece had been given to Philip by Jesus during the Last Supper. Philip had then preached widely throughout what was Asia Minor before eventually losing his life in Hierapolis, a hundred and sixty kilometres east of Ephesus. One account suggested that he may have been crucified upside down for his beliefs. So his piece of pot could be anywhere within that huge area.

The second piece was the shape of an inverted equilateral triangle, brown in colour with the Greek letter o inscribed on it. This piece had been given to Judas Iscariot by Jesus. It was this latter piece that particularly interested me. It appeared to be an accepted fact that Judas had committed suicide by hanging himself after betraying Jesus to the priests and magistrates. He must therefore have been buried in the vicinity of the house where the Last Supper had taken place. An area of land known locally as the Potter's Field has been suggested as his final resting place. Presumably the Israeli Authority had combed the area, but had found nothing. Could they be persuaded to look again, I wondered?

Much to my frustration a week elapsed before I heard from Dr Stavros Democratos again. As his first email had been, his second was again in the form of a mini story and grammatically near perfect.

Good morning Doctor Robertshaw. I hope I find you well.

Please accept my apologies for not getting back to you sooner, but I had several facts to check out. As far as I can ascertain the apostle Andrew preached widely in the lands that surrounded the Black Sea, ending up in Patria (modern Greece) and was crucified there, some say from an olive tree. Presumably he was buried somewhere in that area. The apostle John appears to have died of old age in Ephesus, having been earlier exiled on Patmos, an island in the Aegean Sea by Dalmatian the King. Although there is no evidence whatever to suggest that it happened, Andrew and John could have visited the island of Andros at the same time, possibly for a meeting that had been pre-arranged. For reasons we can only guess at, one being that the pieces of pot in their possession could identify their owners as being followers of Christ, both apostles decided to bury them in a safe place with the intention of retrieving them at a later date, something that they obviously failed to do. It was sheer good luck that the two children started digging at the exact location, but as you are no doubt aware many of our archaeological discoveries have been as a result of sheer good luck. Perhaps you'll find the following approximate distances interesting:

Ephesus to Patmos = 107km

Patmos to Andros = 161km

Athens to Andros = 107km

So as you can see, the distances involved were small, even though they would be covered by ships using sail. A meeting of the two apostles could easily have taken place on the island of Andros.

I have now to decide how the two pieces should be displayed in the museum. Should they be displayed as pieces of a children's game, along with the plywood pieces that the children's teacher has made? Or should they be displayed as two of twelve pieces that had been given out by Jesus to his disciples at the Last Supper? I strongly suspect that it will now be the latter. In order to display the pieces as accurately as we can I would appreciate it if you could send me by email photographs of the model that you have no doubt already made of Christ's Holy Square, showing the authentic pieces already in your possession in their correct positions, and where those not in your possession but you know the whereabouts of, probably go. This will enable me to do justice to the two pieces that I have in my possession.

I look forward to hearing from you in due course.

Yours sincerely

Dr Stavros Democratos

I was more than happy to help Dr Democratos in his determination to display his two pieces of pot as best he could, knowing full well how important it was to show such artefacts in the best possible way. I had yet to decide how I wanted the five pieces in my possession to be exhibited, and where. Although I would have liked them to be put on display somewhere in the north of England, York Museum being the obvious place at least in my eyes, the British Museum was probably the correct place in this country.

But was it in fact the right one? Surely the correct place for all eleven pieces already found, and the remaining two that hopefully would soon show their faces, was the Museum in Jerusalem. I was fully aware however how jealously the World's museums guarded their artefacts, even though by right they did not belong there. The Elgin Marbles in the British Museum were a good example. There was strong feeling in Greece that they should be returned to their home country, but the British Museum was determined not to let them go.

Above all, what was absolutely necessary was the total security of the eleven pieces already discovered. It was essential not to forget the threat of God, as portrayed by Jesus at the Last Supper. If the future of the World did come under threat by some yet undiscovered force, a force so great that every living thing on Earth, both plant and animal, would be destroyed, and God had given we humans a 'get out' route, then we had to be ready to take it.

After reading the Dr Democratos email I smiled to myself...we were almost there. The whereabouts of eleven of the thirteen pieces of pot were now known. We had to be optimistic that the remaining two would also eventually turn up.

Having gone to such trouble to locate the pieces it would be the height of stupidity to allow any of them to fall into the wrong hands, those being the hands of terrorists who would no doubt use them as bargaining tools, or the hands of collectors of rare artefacts, or indeed the hands of speculators who would pass them on for huge amounts of money. It was in fact debatable whether the pieces should be on display at all, and if they were, security would have to be equal to, or better than that of the *Mona Lisa* in the Louvre in Paris.

After thinking deeply about it I decided to contact the Curators of the museums in Jerusalem, Tel Aviv, Tehran and now Athens. I did this not by email or phone, but by personal letter to the effect that the pieces of pot in their possession should at least for the time being be locked securely away. If a threat to the World suddenly became imminent, and that threat could be removed by following the route laid down by God through his Son Jesus, then we had to be ready. For my part, I would be. Hopefully so would the custodians of the other pieces.

When I sent the information that Dr Democratos had requested I also included my personal letter. A week later I received his reply and was pleased to read that he agreed with me on every point I'd raised regarding security. He would lock the two pieces away, at least until a fool proof system could be designed to ensure their security, whilst at the same time being on display to the public. As he said - a bit like the *Mona Lisa*. I wasn't a hundred percent happy, but had to respect his desire to display what would be the two most valuable artefacts in his museum. And, according to the literature I'd recently read, he had some very valuable pieces there - the Mask of Agamemnon and the Theseus Ring immediately sprang to mind.

***

Chapter Eighteen

One thing that had always surprised me, even puzzled me, was the apparent lack of interest in God's threat of World destruction and my quest to locate the thirteen pieces so that they could then be used to avoid that threat, in the United States of America. There were many religious sects there that would surely have had an opinion on the whole issue. I could immediately think of The Episcopal Church, The Church of Jesus Christ of Latter-Day Saints (I remembered some years ago how their 'apostles' pestered us on our doorsteps in the UK), Jehovah's Witnesses, and then of course the so called 'Bible Belt' in the south of that huge country.

But all I'd heard from across the 'pond', as the North Atlantic was sometimes referred to more by the Americans than us, was the comment made by NASA to the effect that in the event of a rogue asteroid heading for the Earth they had plans to prevent a 'strike' taking place. It seemed that for a reason best known to themselves the country's religious sects, who always had plenty to say about women bishops, gay marriage and abortion, had been conspicuously silent about God's threat to the World.

A couple of days later my phone rang in the early hours of the morning. I reluctantly picked up the handset knowing that calls at that time often indicated that someone in the family or a close friend had suddenly become ill, been involved in some sort of accident, even passed away. I also felt annoyance at having my and Angela's beauty sleep interrupted. I was therefore surprised by the voice on the other end of the line. I immediately recognised the drawl of an American accent, female.

As I answered the phone I glanced at the radio alarm clock at the side of the bed. The time showed half past two. Fortunately Angela, lying at the side of me, continued breathing heavily in an obvious deep sleep.

Peter Robertshaw here…Can I help you…You do realise that it's the early hours of the morning here."

"Sorry, Professor…It's daylight where I live…I forgot all about the time difference."

I accepted her apology and asked her as politely as I could, to state why she wanted to speak to me at this unearthly hour.

"My name is Ella Makepeace and I am calling from Wakefield, a town just ten miles north of Boston, in the state of Massachusetts."

She paused, allowing me time to take in her opening statement. I immediately thought - what a coincidence - her home town sharing the same name as a city only a few miles north of where I lived. I wondered if she was aware of that, but didn't mention it, wanting her to get on, which thankfully she did.

"I think that I may have one of those pieces of pot you are looking for…You know, that make up the Holy Square of Jesus Christ…The work you are doing was recently discussed at our Bible Class after one of our members had stumbled onto your university website…At our meeting we expressed concern about the good Lord's threat to destroy everything on Earth…We were equally concerned that few people were taking the threat seriously."

After feeling initially hurt…stumbling onto our website indeed, I realised that this was no crank at the end of the line, but a very serious person. I asked her to describe the piece to me.

"I will of course do that…But first allow me to explain how I come to have it in my possession…I'm sure you'll find the story interesting…I also think that you will agree with me that I was incredibly lucky to find it…It was almost as if God himself wanted it to happen."

My heart sank. All I wanted were details of the piece - its shape and dimensions, its colour and anything inscribed on it. Since I knew that just two pieces were still missing, and of those two I knew their shapes, colours and the Greek letters inscribed on them, if this woman on the end of the line described anything different I would immediately know that the piece wasn't genuine. I could tell her so, thank her for calling me and put down the handset. Alas, life wasn't as simple as that: "Please continue", I replied, gritting my teeth at the same time.

"It all started with a journey of a lifetime…My husband and I had never been to Europe before…We wished to do so before we left this Earth because both our fathers had been on Omaha Beach on D-Day and had lost their lives there…Both are buried in the American Cemetery at Coleville…So we decided to take a holiday in Europe that would include a journey on the Orient Express from Paris to Rome, calling at Venice…We first spent a week in the French capital and this gave us the opportunity to visit the D-Day sites and to see both our fathers' names on the Roll-of-Honour displayed on a long circular wall at the cemetery…We of course went up the Eiffel Tower, visited Notre Dame and the Palace at Versailles…But to me the highlight of our days in Paris was our visit to the Louvre, especially the picture of the Mona Lisa."

I felt like pointing out to her that if the small piece of pot in her possession was genuine it was worth several times the value of the Leonardo de Vinci painting, but resisted.

I was beginning to become frustrated and wanted to shout down the phone: "Get to the bloody point, will you?" Instead I behaved like a polite English gentleman, hoping that when she met her Bible group next time she would point this fact out to them: "So…A trip on the Orient Express, eh?…I've always wanted to go on it, but never been able to afford it…Please go on."

"We boarded the luxury train at the Gare de l'Est, travelled through the Alps and onto Innsbruck, in Austria, before entering the Santa Lucia station at Venice…Such a romantic name for a railway station, I'm sure you'll agree…We stayed in Venice for two days and did the sights - St Mark's Square, the Bridge of Sighs and the Rialto Bridge…And of course the canals."

I was now tearing my hair out. I'd heard enough of her grand bloody tour of Europe. I therefore tried to move her on: "How did you come to acquire the piece?"

"Well, I've just mentioned the canals…We of course had a ride on a gondola - those men in tight trousers that row them…What a sight for a woman getting past her prime."

Unnoticed by me, Angela had not only woken up, but had moved her head close to the earpiece so that she could hear the woman's voice. At the woman's last comment Angela whispered: "Ah…Those men in tight trousers…Such pert bottoms."

I gave her a friendly dig in the ribs with my elbow.

I was on the verge of drifting off completely, when the woman finally got to the point: "As we walked along the side of one of the smaller canals we came across a crowd of people watching with fascination a mechanical digger lifting sediment out of the canal and depositing it in a large open tank on the canal side…"

"A skip," I whispered to myself.

"As the water drained away a small piece of what looked like pot caught my eye…Thinking it may be of interest I picked it out of the mud…After asking a workman with a hose pipe, there to keep the canal side clean, to wash in down for me, I studied it closely."

At long last we were getting there.

"The first thing I noticed was its shape - triangular...Then its colour, blue...In one corner was the tiniest of holes, and the piece had a funny shaped letter ε engraved on one side of it...I particularly noticed *that* because it was the first letter of my name - Ella...Coincidence...Eh?"

I was now getting excited: "Can you describe the triangle to me?...Where exactly is the tiny hole...And the colour, light or dark blue?"

"Er...You'd call it an isosceles triangle, but the two equal angles are very small...The hole is in one of the small angles...The colour is lightblue... I managed to buy a thin black lace in a shoe shop, threaded it through the hole and wore the piece round my neck...I thought it looked pretty cool, and so did my husband...It even brought complimentary comments from others in our group...By the way, if the piece is genuine can you tell me which disciple Jesus gave it to?...My Bible group will be dying to know."

I was pleased that the woman had some sort of mathematical background. The missing ε piece was indeed an isosceles triangle with very small equal angles and with the hole in one of those angles. I was now convinced that the piece of pot was the genuine article, even to the point of her wearing it as it was originally intended. To answer her question: "The piece was given to Philip by Jesus, but what is a mystery is how it happened to end up in a canal in Venice...None of the references about the disciple's travels before his death mentioned that he was anywhere near that city...Of course he could have been, or he could have passed the piece on to a third party...And it is possible, even probable, that it was forcibly removed from him by a Roman soldier...Who knows?"

The woman then went onto an entirely different tack: "By the way, we visited your country before returning to the States...London, Stratford-on –Avon, York."

I had to ask: "How did you travel up to York?"

"By train... One of your high speed ones, but not of course as fast as those in France...TGVs I think they call them."

Although I didn't say anything I fully agreed with her. I did however add: "Do you know that the line up to York passes through Doncaster, within a stone's throw of the university where I work?...Had you known that, and had you known that I was seeking information about these very special pieces of pot, we could have arranged a meeting and you could have left it in my safe keeping."

"True…True…But I can assure that it's in perfectly safe hands on our side of the Atlantic."

I was so tempted to ask her if she would be prepared to send it by post to me, but realised that I would never forgive myself if it somehow got lost in transit. Instead I made a simple request: " Do you have a computer?…If so, will you take a photograph of the piece and email it to me at the address on our website?…I'd also appreciate the dimensions of the piece."

Her reply was encouraging: "Yes, we have a computer at home…I'm not very good on it, but my husband, Harvey, considers himself a bit of a whiz kid…He'll send you a photograph of the piece, including its dimensions."

I looked at the bedside clock. We had been on the phone for well over an hour. I thanked her for the information she'd given me and finally added, knowing that the most likely place for a 'get together' of world leaders to re-assemble Christ's Holy Square would be the United Nations in New York: "And who knows?…We may meet up at UN Headquarters in the 'Big Apple' itself, in the not too distant future."

She hastily replied: "You do realise that if we did meet up at the UN it would be because all life on Earth was in imminent danger of being destroyed by some force beyond the comprehension of man?"

She was of course right. On second thoughts I hoped that I would never meet up with Ella Makepeace under such circumstances. But if I ever did manage to visit the United States in the future I would like to think that I would look her and her husband up in Wakefield, Massachusetts. I would imagine it would be a most interesting experience.

After writing down her telephone number I wished her a 'good day' then ended the call. I turned to Angela: "How about that for luck…Talk about divine intervention…What are the odds of thirteen pieces of pot, made and distributed by Jesus Christ two thousand years ago, not only surviving to the present day, but also being found - must be millions to one against?…It's almost as if God above, if indeed there is one, and many people believe there is, including ourselves, has used his powers to ensure that all the pieces are eventually found…What I want to know now is - where the devil is the final piece, the one belonging to Judas Iscariot?…Trust his piece to be the last one…Could it be that the devil himself had already acquired it?"

184

Angela smiled and replied: "Don't let's involve the Devil, or he'll put the kibosh on everything." She then pecked me on the cheek and added: "The Big Apple indeed…Who do you think you are, some trendy politician?" She then turned over, at the same time flicking the light switch.

As I laid there in bed staring at a patterned ceiling I couldn't see, I had a thought. If I'd been asked by someone, which of the twelve disciples' pieces of pot would be the last to be discovered, I'd have put my money on the one originally belonging to Judas Iscariot. If I'd then been asked to give a reason for my choice, in all honesty I would not have been able to give one. In fact, as I'd thought on many previous occasions, the piece belonging to Judas should surely have been one of the first to be discovered. His suicide had taken place in close proximity to the sites of the Last Supper and Jesus's crucifixion, so the piece couldn't have travelled far from that area. And yet the Israelis had been unable to locate it.

Surely my quest to know the whereabouts of all thirteen pieces was not going to fail at the final hurdle. But, with five pieces in my possession having travelled over three thousand kilometres, three having arrived in this country two thousand years ago in the possession of a Roman cavalryman and his horse, and two having made the journey within the last few months in modern airliners, not to mention one that had crossed the Atlantic, nothing surprised me anymore. I had to be optimistic.

***

Chapter Nineteen

We were on the move early, we being myself, Rho Smithson, Colin Gregory, Jane Hirst and Wendy Sutherland, all members of my department, and twelve of my first year Archaeology students. It was a fine sunny morning in June, almost the longest day of the year. We boarded our two minibuses that belonged to the university and were mainly used for taking sports teams to their away fixtures. One minibus contained the students, the other me and my staff and all our equipment. We were heading for the village of Ribbleswell, just north of Skipton in the Yorkshire Dales. Here we intended to carry out our survey of the local church's graveyard before its excavation and re-interment of any human remains found so that Yorkshire Water could lay down a new pipe to the village.

It was decided that we should take up residence in a close-by barn that the farmer had earlier converted into living accommodation for walkers who wished to pursue their activity in the Dales. We would stay Monday to Friday, returning to South Yorkshire at the weekend. My wife, Angela, wasn't thrilled with the idea, but she had an active social life with her many friends so I wasn't unduly worried about leaving her on her own.

As a matter of courtesy I had over the weekend contacted by phone the local vicar. During our brief conversation I asked him a question that had been puzzling me since our earlier visit to Ribbleswell - surely the parish records would tell us who were buried in the church's graveyard. Alas, no. Evidently five years earlier, after a Sunday evensong, an electric heater had been accidentally left on overnight in the vestry. Some vestments hanging on coat hangers a bit too near caught fire and in no time at all anything in the vestry that would burn, did so, and this included the parish records, which happened to be the only records in existence. So now we knew…We had no idea whose remains we were about to disturb.

On arriving at Ribbleswell our first task was to do a very general survey of the church's graveyard, including its approximate dimensions. The graveyard was now little more than a grassed area, like an unkempt lawn, with just two gravestones, barely half a metre tall, still standing upright

186

close to the north wall of the church. All that was visible on them, and only just, because the extremes of the hostile Dales weather - hot sun in the summer followed by hale, snow and icy blasts in the winter had taken their toll, was a circle the size of a large dinner plate with a cross inside it.

St Stephen's Church was small in size, no doubt catering for only a handful of people when built and, according to the vicar, who had six village churches in his care, only for a handful now. The graveyard ran along the northern side of it. We quickly ran out the tape and measured its length and breath, the length being twenty metres, and the breadth a mere five metres.

The two solitary gravestones were in line, two and a half metres apart. This gave us an approximate guide as to the length of a grave, if indeed there were any. Eight graves in line would cover the full length of the graveyard, and if we assumed that a particular grave was approximately a metre wide, there would be five going across. Equally, assuming that all the graves were occupied, that made a total of forty bodies, now as skeletons, under the ground. But it was all assumption. It could be that there was just a row of graves along the edge by a retaining wall that was slowly collapsing because of Yorkshire Water's trench, and one or two dotted around elsewhere.

Fully aware that any human remains would be anything up to a metre and a half under ground and therefore difficult and time-consuming for us to get to by manual digging, Yorkshire Water, keen to get on, brought in a mechanical digger. This would first be used to remove the bulk of the soil along a run the full length of the grave yard and two and a half metres wide. The digging process would then be repeated, thus eventually covering the entire site. Fortunately it hadn't rained for several days and the ground was quite hard. This should allow the digger to make good progress.

Since, having been informed by the digger's driver that the first run would take the whole of Monday to complete, I suggested that we as a group should travel up to Horton-in-Ribbledale and climb Pen-y-Ghent, one of the Three Peaks. It was a glorious day and this is what we did.

On Tuesday morning, after rising at seven and consuming a hearty typically English breakfast prepared by the farmer's wife, we arrived at the site to find that half the site had already been excavated by the digger. The operator had also removed the crumbling wall that would have had to be rebuilt anyway. A huge pile of soil and a separate pile of stone blocks stood at one end of the site and the digger operator was already adding to the pile of soil as he continued to excavate the remainder of the site. Both he and I had anticipated a problem when it came to the two gravestones. We therefore agreed that he should work round them, leaving both gravestones and possible graves beneath them, in place. When we eventually reached the point where we wanted to excavate the two graves he would lift the gravestones away and remove the metre and a half of earth below them.

It appeared to me that the area already excavated was not deep enough, but as the operator informed me, he had stopped digging when he'd started lifting bones to the surface. So, at that point any human remains present were not as deep as I'd originally thought they would be. Not to worry. It made our task that bit easier.

It was time to make a start. First we divided the area that the digger had already excavated, in half length-wise, then into eight plots breadth-wise, giving a total of sixteen numbered plots, as it happened the same number of 'bodies' we had in our party. This dividing of the site was done using white plastic tape pinned to the ground with tent pegs. Armed with spades, forks, trowels, large paint brushes and an ample supply of bin liners and smaller plastic bags, we made a start...well almost. One of my female students suggested that maybe we should be wearing face masks, wondering if there was any danger of being infected if the buried individual had died of some terrible disease such as the plague. She had a point, although I had never heard of anybody being infected in that way. I therefore handed out masks to everybody from the store I kept, mainly as a guard against inhaling fine soil particles.

My instructions to the group were simple: "First choose a plot then carefully dig down with the spade to a depth of no more that thirty centimetres...There obviously has to be a limit as to how far down we should go...If nothing is found, replace the earth and dig elsewhere within the plot...If something of obvious interest is unearthed, almost certainly a skeleton, use the fork to carefully release the earth surrounding it, then the trowel and finally the paint brush to remove any remaining earth...Do not disturb it at that point...Photograph it and draw a map of the plot showing where exactly the object is found...Only then carefully remove it and place it in a plastic bag, labelled with the number of the plot...If a skeleton is unearthed the same procedure is to be followed, with all bones found placed in a bin liner and labelled...Any objects found, and hopefully lots of bones, ideally making up complete skeletons, will be studied in detail back at the university, where as you are aware, we have some very sophisticatedscientific/forensic equipment."

I decided to concentrate my efforts on the skeleton that the digger had disturbed whilst excavating the trench by the crumbling retaining wall. Once the operator had spotted the bones in the earth lifted by his bucket he'd carefully replaced the earth and moved on. All I could therefore see were one or two bones breaking the surface. What I did immediately notice was the lack of any fragments of rotten wood from some sort of coffin. Presumably if one had been used it had rotted completely away. I knelt by the bones and armed with my trusty trowel commenced gently scraping the earth away, revealing more bones. Since the full skeleton had now been disturbed the bones were no longer in any arrangement I would recognise. Although knowing that a photograph would be of little value, nevertheless I took one.

All I could do now was to release the bones and pile them up at the side. I did this, carefully digging deep with my trowel to ensure that I did not miss any. The skeleton appeared to be complete and the eyeless sockets in the skull seemed to stare out at me. I now had to make sure that I located the small foot and hand bones as well as all those in the backbone. When I was satisfied that I'd got most of them, hopefully all of them, I carefully placed the bones in a bin liner, tied it up and labelled it. Finally I drew a sketch of the plot, with the skeleton along its length.

One of my students was working alongside me, and it wasn't long before he too unearthed some bones with his trowel. Again there was no sign of fragments of wood. As he carefully scraped away the earth more bones were revealed. At that point I joined him and together we eventually exposed the full skeleton. As I photographed it the others in the group gathered round, most of them never having seen anything like it before.

I addressed them: "You can now see what you're looking for…If you locate something work carefully so that you end up with a specimen as good as this." They nodded and moved back to their plots.

It was a shame to disturb the skeleton, but it had to be done, so my student carefully gathered up the bones and placed them in a bin liner. After tying it up he labelled it. Two plots had now been excavated.

As our excavation continued, working away from where the wall had been, it became clear that there were in fact two rows of graves along the edge of the grave yard that ran by the road. It was as if those in charge of burials in the past had decided to commence at a point furthest away from the church, and work towards it, thus avoiding having to walk over existing graves in order to create new ones, which did make sense. By the end of the day we therefore had the remains of sixteen people who at some time in the past had been buried there.

We collected up our tools and carefully, almost reverently, placed the bags of bones in one of the minibuses. It had been a good day, but I felt just a tinge of disappointment. To my shame I found bones uninteresting. I was hoping that some interesting artefact would be unearthed - a ring, bracelet or pendant, preferably made of gold, even a coin to give us some indication of the age of at least one of the graves…but nothing. We had so far found nothing but bones…lots of them.

When we arrived at the site on Wednesday morning I looked at what we'd managed to excavate so far, and how much more we'd still to do. We had in fact cleared two fifths of the site that had already been excavated down to a depth of about a metre and a half by the digger. This we had accomplished in two days. Weather permitting we should be able to complete our work by Friday evening, when we would be returning home for the weekend. Assuming that we'd completed our excavation on time, work on what we'd found would commence first thing Monday morning in one of my department's laboratories.

Thursday was a most disappointing day. As we systematically moved across the site towards the church we found nothing, not one solitary bone. It appeared, for a reason not at all clear to me or the vicar, that the area had stopped being used as a graveyard after the first two rows had been laid down just inside the crumbling wall. So why were there two gravestones, set in line, close to the northern wall of the church? Were there any human remains underground there? Friday, hopefully our final day, would settle the issue one way or the other.

When we arrived at the site at nine o'clock the digger operator was already sitting in his cab, eating his breakfast. The engine was running, providing sufficient heat to keep him warm, for it was a cool morning. After downing the remains of his tea or coffee, or whatever he had in his thermos flask, he jumped down, pulled out a long, wide nylon binder from a box at the rear of the digger and proceeded to wind it round the first of the gravestones, before looping it onto the digger's bucket. He then slowly and carefully lifted the stone out of the ground, not knowing if it would disintegrate as he did so.

As it hung there in the air, the lower two thirds of its length covered in thick clay, I quickly but rather foolishly, for the stone could have come loose and landed on top of me, pulled out my tape and measured its length. All of us were surprised to see that it was about a metre and a half long, with a full metre having been underground for God knows how long, and therefore hadn't been exposed to the elements.

The operator, after first rebuking me for my stupidity and setting a bad example to my students, lowered the stone to the ground a couple of metres away. With equal care he repeated the whole process with the second gravestone, which looked to be roughly the same size as the first. In fact the two gravestones appeared to be identical in every detail, including the engraved crosses within circles on the upper part of both of them that were just barely visible.

The operator's final task was to remove the remaining metre and a half layer of earth above the two graves, if indeed they were graves, thus bringing the remaining area down to the level of the rest of the site. As he did this there was no sign of fragments of rotten wood. If indeed there had been any coffins for these two graves there was certainly no sign of them now.

It was one of my students who spotted it first, pointing excitedly at writing on one of the gravestones. As it had been lowered to the ground some of the clay had been dislodged. A quick examination of the second gravestone also revealed similar writing.

As Rho and I carefully scraped the remaining clay off one of the gravestones, and a couple of students did the same with the other, the vicar arrived, immediately turned round without saying a word and headed back to the church. He returned minutes later with a bucket of water and two hand brushes. In no time at all, all the clay had been removed by the application of copious amounts of water, apart from that embedded in the letters and numbers themselves. I was now able to easily read both inscriptions. The fact that the lower third of the two gravestones had been below the surface for very many years had in some way protected them and the engraved letters on them from the hostile elements of gale force winds, intense rain and freezing temperatures that had raged above ground for God knows how long.

I read out loudly what had been written so that the others, some who were too far away to read for themselves, knew what had been engraved on the two gravestones:

John Brown   *Robert Brown*

Crusader

Born 1ˢᵗ April 1170

Died 10ᵗʰ December 1195
Aged 25

RIP

Crusader

Born 1ˢᵗ April 1170

Died 12ᵗʰ December 1195
Aged 25

RIP

"So...They were twins, then." commented one of the students.

"And both died within two days of each other," added another.

"And crusaders, too...What ever that is," added a third.

This prompted me to fall back into my lecturer role and ask my students a simple question: "So...Who can tell me anything about the crusades?"

There were twelve blank faces. Then I realised that it was unlikely that 'The Crusades' had appeared on any of the History syllabuses they had studied in their fifteen or so years of full time education. It was time to give them a crash course in the graveyard. But first we sat down on the church steps and ate our packed lunches, accompanied by both the operator of the digger and the vicar who, like a magician, miraculously produced a rucksack full of bottles of *Old Peculier*, a well known and highly respected local brew.

"Right...The Crusades...A crash course," I shouted so that all could hear.

"The crusades were military expeditions that took place in mediaeval times...They were blessed by the Pope of the time and were against the enemies of Roman Catholic Christianity...Military action was justified because a Just War was being fought...They were numbered, up to about seven, and took place over a four hundred year period between 1189 and 1588...As far as England was concerned, the Third Crusade was the most important...When Jerusalem fell to a Muslim called Saladin in 1187 Richard, son of the king Henry-the-Second, decided to gather together an army from all over the country to go to the Holy Land and re-take Jerusalem...On the death of his father in 1189 Richard-the-First became King and was known later as Richard the Lionheart, or Coeur de Lion, as the French knew him...You may have heard of him in Robin Hood films...In order to finance the campaign to the Holy Land he ordered the collection of funds from both rich and poor...This made him and the campaign very unpopular...He left this country in 1190, but didn't manage to re-take Jerusalem, but did agree with Saladin that Christian pilgrims would be allowed to visit and pray at the Holy Places in the city...Concerned that his brother, John, had his sights on his throne Richard left Palestine in late 1192, was shipwrecked just off Italy and imprisoned in Austria, then Germany, as he tried to make his way north across land to England...After a huge ransom was paid he was released in 1194. ...He then spent the next five years building and defending a castle in France where he died in April 1199...Those soldiers who had not lost their lives in the Holy Land returned home...They had been away from their families for almost three years...So there you have it...The Crusades in five minutes."

I asked if there were any questions. There was just one: "So...We could have buried here the remains of twins who had travelled to the Holy Land with Richard and returned home, only to survive a couple of years...Any chance that they could have been murdered?...You did say that the Crusades were very unpopular, and as far as I can see, their expensive mission failed....And another thing, Richard appeared to prefer France to England."

My student had a point, or several. The ill-feeling could well have been there long after the Crusaders' return. The only answer I could give her was: "Well. Let's first see if we find any human remains...And if we do, something may tell us how they met their deaths."

After my little open air lecture I asked the students for their ideas on something that was puzzling me - why had the two gravestones been erected in such a way that two thirds were below ground level, thus covering up the inscriptions that some stone mason had caringly and certainly skilfully carved into them? It just didn't make sense to me.

"Could they have gradually sunk over the years in the soft earth...They are very heavy?" asked one student.

Before I could reply one of the others offered his opinion: "But surely they wouldn't have sunk at exactly the same rate...And wouldn't they have leaned over a bit?"

It was a good reply. Give or take a couple of centimetres both had been just half a metre above the ground, and perfectly upright.

Another student then offered her explanation: "Maybe Crusaders were unpopular at that time...You've said already that huge amounts of money were collected from local people in order to finance the Crusades and there was much hostility to the idea of fighting a war thousands of miles away…Maybe the relatives of the two crusaders had asked for the stones to be set deeply so that others would not be able to identify them and violate their graves."

She certainly had a point. The collection of money had indeed been highly unpopular. In fact there had been wholesale riots throughout the country just before Richard had left these shores.

There was a pause as the students searched for other explanations. For myself I had no idea at all, and therefore didn't, couldn't, offer an opinion. Even the vicar sat there, silent, staring at the distant horizon, apparently searching for an answer, but not coming up with one.

It took an offering from the digger operator to bring a twenty-first century explanation to my question: "Health and Safety."

We all looked blankly at him. What the devil was he on about? Had the *Old Peculier* gone to his brain?

"Please go on," I encouraged.

"Well…A few years ago the Yorkshire Electricity Board dug a narrow trench along the edge of the graveyard to put down a new electric supply to the church…I remember them doing it…At that time you had to go down some steps to the graveyard …Maybe they discovered bones not all that far down, and the Council's Health and Safety people insisted that more soil be added to give more depth…That's why it's now level with the church…It also explains why the wall was in danger of collapsing, the additional soil pushing against it."

I glanced across at the vicar inviting a comment, and what he said added some credence to the operator's explanation: "I've only been here a couple of years, but I do know about the new electrical supply…We now use electric heaters and the old power supply wasn't as we say - fit for purpose…When I arrived the graveyard was already grassed over…But if you look across there (he pointed to a long narrow stone slab that was just visible above the surface), that could be the top of the steps our digger operator referred to."

I felt like pointing out that if the writing on the gravestones had only been covered with clay for a couple of years, having been previously exposed to the elements for eight hundred years, the words would have been eroded to the same extent as the circle and cross. But they obviously hadn't. Not wanting to dismiss the operator's explanation out of hand, bearing in mind that he'd been prepared to give the problem some thought, when I and nine of my students had remained silent, I replied: "Do you know I'd have never thought of that." He beamed, maybe thinking that he'd out-thought the professor...me, and my supposedly brainy gang of students.

The most likely explanation had been the one by the girl student. It's doubtful that the crusaders came home as heroes, especially since they'd returned without their king. Violating a crusader's grave would have been one way that people, who had earlier been fleeced of their hard earned money, could have shown their dissent, and probably did so.

***

Chapter Twenty

It was now time to excavate the ground below where the two gravestones had been. Since I wanted this meticulously doing, so that no stone was left unturned, to coin a phrase, I allotted three students to each plot - one digging where the head would be, another where the feet would be, and one digging between the two.My instruction was short and to the point: "If you reveal the smallest bone call me across…If we wish to know how their owners died their skeletons may give us the answer."

As the six students, already using their trowels, worked slowly and with great care, the rest of us thoroughly cleaned the two gravestones, carefully digging out the soil trapped in the engraved letters and numbers.

Suddenly a shout went up: "Found something."

We all rushed across, just as the student, who was working on the grave of the twin who had died first, brushed away some more earth to reveal the end bones of five toes. Carefully working back she revealed the ankle bones, then the tibia and fibula - the bones of the lower leg. Seconds later the front of the skull appeared, followed by the ribs. Brushing with the paint brushes now became a little frantic and I had to curb the enthusiasm of their operators.

Understandably, work stopped on the other grave as the three students working on it looked at what was slowly being revealed at the side of them. Soon the whole skeleton was unearthed, but told us nothing about the owner apart from the fact that he'd been, according to my tape, over six feet tall, and all the bones were whole, showing no signs of fractures.

After one of the students had taken several photographs and another had completed a sketch showing the skeleton inside the plot, it was time to disturb the bones in order to remove them. I decided to concentrate on the skull, carefully releasing the earth that had been holding it in position.

Finally I was able to lift it clear. As I did so, carefully tipping it slightly forwards, one thing was immediately visible. There was a jagged hole in the top and I could see bone fragments inside it. All indications were that the crusader had been hit on the head with a sharp heavy object. I guessed that a hammer blow would have resulted in such damage. Or had he fallen, smashing his head against a hard sharp corner or edge, like that of a stone step? Was he in fact murdered or had he had some sort of fatal accident? At this point we could only hazard a guess.

Almost reluctantly, and certainly as reverently as we could, we transferred the bones, all but the skull, to a bin liner that was then duly labelled. I placed the skull in a separate bin liner. When we eventually got down to examining the skeleton in the laboratory back at the university, especially the skull, I would contact Doctor Braithwaite, a pathologist at Doncaster General, and a friend of mine of many years standing. I would be interested to hear what he'd make of our crusader's head injury. In the doctor's long career he would have no doubt seen many similar injuries.

Because of the excitement all work had stopped on the other grave. This was resumed with great urgency and enthusiasm. The three students working on it now knew that almost certainly they too would unearth a skeleton. And they did. As in the previous unearthing, the feet appeared first, quickly followed by the ribs and finally the front of the skull. This time I stood back and let them get on with it.

Suddenly there was a deafening shout that reverberated round the graveyard, bouncing off the church wall: "There's something amongst his ribs...Look." She pointed, at the same time pushing her index finger between two ribs about three inches below the left collar bone.

I moved in closer and stared into the gap. I could see what looked like a brown leaf. Maybe one of the decaying ones had blown across from the rose bushes that were just in front of the church's west door.

As the student trapped the object between her two fingers and carefully lifted it out she realised that it was in fact a triangular piece of pot. When she placed it in the palm of her hand and proceeded to brush it vigorously with her paintbrush, revealing that it was a light brown in colour, I shouted: "Careful," for I'd suddenly realised what it was...or could be.

"Turn it over, please."

The poor girl almost panicked, having her tutor shout at her. As she hurriedly turned the object over, it almost dropped from her dithering fingers. At that point I knew exactly what the object was, the Greek letter omicron - o, engraved in its upper surface confirming it. If it was indeed genuine, and my gut feeling told me that it was, my student had in the palm of her hand the brown piece of pot that Jesus had given to Judas Iscariot at the Last Supper. We had in fact found the thirteenth and final piece of Christ's Holy Square.

I shouted excitedly: "It's the final piece of the Square." My colleagues and students knew exactly what I meant, having put up with my highs and lows for months, including the occasional tantrum, as I'd hunted for all the missing pieces. The student held out her hand and passed the object to me, probably glad to release it. As she did so I wondered if she realised just how valuable it was. To me it was, after the piece that Jesus had kept for himself, and that had turned up two thousand years later on a Doncaster building site, the most important piece in the Square. Why? I didn't really know, other than that Judas had betrayed Jesus, leading to his eventual crucifixion. That made it very special.

The vicar looked on, a blank expression on his face. He obviously had no idea what Christ's Holy Square was. Surely Ribbleswell wasn't so isolated that its vicar hadn't heard of it. I attempted to put him in the picture, keeping it as short and simple as possible: "Are you aware that at the Last Supper Jesus gave each of his twelve disciples a coloured piece of pot with a single Greek letter engraved into it, keeping a thirteenth piece for himself?"

His expression remained blank as he nodded his head from side to side. I therefore continued: "I'm almost one hundred percent certain that this piece is the one that Jesus handed to Judas Iscariot…I now have in my possession six of the pieces…I also know where the remaining seven are…Six in foreign museums and one with a private owner in America."

The vicar finally spoke: "So, Professor…Apart from being of archaeological interest why are the pieces so important to you?"

"Ah…You're obviously not aware that the destruction of the Earth could be imminent…Unless all thirteen pieces are reassembled to form Christ's Holy Square by the most powerful political figures in the World… God has, for his own good reasons, decided at some future date to destroy it."

"I vaguely remember reading something about it in *The Times*, but didn't think that it was being taken seriously…Over hundreds of years predictions had been made about the end of the World," replied the vicar, possibly revealing his own scepticism towards the threat.

"Well…We'll just have to see…If in the future the World does come under such a threat by some force that man cannot comprehend we at least have a 'get-out', albeit a most unusual one."

The vicar smiled, not at all convinced.

It was now time to carefully transfer the bones of the second grave into the bin liner. As one of the students carefully lifted the skull, briefly examining it as she did so, she spotted a hole in the top, and immediately shouted enthusiastically: "A hole…It's got a hole just like the other one."

"Looks as if they were both attacked at the same time…From behind…Maybe at night," speculated one of the students. And he could well have been right. Had the twins been bragging about their crusade exploits - the exotic foreign food, the good quality wine and the beautiful eastern women, whilst drinking in the local alehouse? Did some poor begrudging farm labourers waylay them in some dark alley, hitting them on the head with a blunt instrument? One could have died instantly, the other surviving the attack for just a couple of days. The burial would then have taken place, with the two gravestones being later sunk well into the ground in order to cover the inscriptions. The intention of the family could have been to lift them when the ill feeling towards the returning crusaders had subsided, but never did. It was all pure speculation, but wasn't it nice to speculate? Nobody could prove you wrong.

As we made our way to the minibuses, parked on the road that ran alongside the church, ready to make the long journey home to Doncaster, I glanced across at the site we'd been working on all week. The digger operator, after placing the two head stones close to the church wall, was already digging his bucket into the pile of earth and distributing it across the whole area. Since he could now do no damage he worked quickly, using the back of the bucket to smooth out the earth as he dropped it. I suspected that when he'd finished, the site would be as flat as a Wimbledon tennis court, but without the grass.

As we pulled away we waved to both him and the vicar, who probably couldn't wait to get his grassed area back as it had originally been. A new wall could be built, hopefully at Yorkshire Water's expense, and the new water main laid down to the village. In a few months' time a passer-by would not be aware that a major excavation had recently taken place. After we'd carried out our examination of the skeletons we would return them to the church so that they could be buried in a communal grave with a new headstone. I had however suggested to the vicar that the two Crusader gravestones should be sited somewhere, if only inside the church itself, maybe as some sort of 'feature' that would attract historians.

On our journey southwards I sat with Rho Smithson. It wasn't long before we started to discuss the unbelievable discovery of the piece of pot originally belonging to Judas Iscariot. How the devil had it ended up in a graveyard in North Yorkshire? I offered her a possible scenario: "Well...As far as we are aware the twins brothers travelled with Richard-the-Lionheart to the Holy Land...We also know that Richard's army failed to take Jerusalem, but he managed to negotiate with Saladin an agreement to allow Christian pilgrims to visit and pray at the Holy Places within the city walls...Maybe our twins took advantage of this concession, dressing as pilgrims and entering the Holy City...In some way, one of them managed to acquire Judas's piece of pot...He could have visited the Potter's Field where Judas was supposedly buried after his suicide, and stumbled on the piece...Or he could have seen it on a local market stall and bartered for it...At the end of their duty the twins simply returned home, one having the piece in his possession, but not having a clue what it was. Who knows?...In fact we'll never know, but as it happens, it doesn't matter... I've now got in my possession six of the thirteen pieces and I know where the other seven are...This now completes Christ's Holy Square."

Rho suggested another scenario: "Maybe one of the other disciples had acquired the piece immediately after Judas's suicide...He could then have gone on his extensive travels...We know that the disciples called at places such as Cyprus, Crete, the ports of Greece and Italy, all places where the Crusade fleets would have called on their way to and from the Holy Land. Maybe the piece had in some way been acquired by our crusader in one of those places...Admittedly it would have been a thousand years later, but the two pieces found by you on a Doncaster building site had been deposited there almost two thousand years ago."

I nodded in agreement. Her scenario was equally as strong as mine.

After an examination of the bones we'd found in the church graveyard at Ribbleswell, work that my students had excitedly carried out, but to my shame had not caught my imagination, the bones were returned to their bin liners ready to be taken back to the church so that they could be buried in a communal grave. Radio carbon dating of the bones using the university's Accelerator Mass Spectrometer gave the earliest age of 1200, and the latest 1400, give or take twenty-five years. Examination of long bone length, teeth and wear on the joints revealed that age at death ranged from young children to people well into old age. Some bones showed obvious signs of healed fractures, but the skeletons of two young children, buried side by side, had several unhealed fractures. Had there deaths been the result of some accident such as falling out of a tall tree or worse still being trampled underfoot by a herd of stampeding cows or horses? Maybe even the result of a vicious assault by an adult, possibly a parent. We would never know. Apart from our two crusaders there was nothing to indicate that the others had met their deaths at the hands of their fellowmen.

I wrote out a brief report of our findings and sent it to the vicar, hoping that he would find it interesting. I also asked him to inform the headteacher at Ribbleswell Primary School that I would be happy to give a talk on our findings to the children. Hopefully it would spark off an interest in archaeology in some of them, and who knows - in ten to fifteen years' time one of them may apply to the South Riding University for a place on a course run by my department.

But before I returned the bones to the church I asked my pathologist friend, Doctor Braithwaite, to pay us a visit in order to look at our two damaged skulls. This he duly did.

Surrounded by my students, all seated and eager to hear what our guest had to stay, I placed the two skulls on the bench in front of him, at the same time inviting him to examine them, speaking as he did so. Initially he didn't take up my offer. Instead he reached down to a haversack that he'd brought with him, extracted a skull and placed it on the bench at the side of the other two. He then produced a small hammer similar to one you'd find in any DIY toolbox. The students leaned slightly forward, wondering what was coming next. They weren't disappointed.

Doctor Braithwaite then invited Jane, one of my female students, to join him. She hesitantly did so, not quite knowing what to expect. To her and the others' surprise, including me, he asked her to commit an act of violence: "Take the hammer, Jane, and strike the top of the skull with the blunt end." He then put on a pair of protective spectacles, at the same time handing a pair to Jane who put them on. He then took the skull in his hands and held it in front of her.

Not having the slightest idea of how much force to apply she tapped the skull with the hammer. To her surprise it rebounded away, leaving no apparent damage.

"Again, Jane...This time a little harder," suggested Doctor

Braithwaite: "Let's see if we can do some real damage."

Jane, again hesitantly, struck the skull with considerably more force, causing the other students to gasp. But still the blow made little impact on the skull.

As the doctor took the hammer from Jane and placed the skull on the bench, at the same thanking her, he addressed the students: "This is the skull of an adult male, age at death forty-five, give or take a year or two...It is in the region of sixty years old...Who he was, I don't know...The skull was an exhibit in the Pathology Department when I arrived at Doncaster General some ten years ago...It's evidently borrowed on occasions by a local drama group when performing Hamlet...My little exercise was intended to show you just how strong the human skull is...It takes considerable force to fracture it...Obviously the sharper the object used the easier it is...A chisel being far more effective than a baseball bat...Of course, the hammer I'm holding in my hand would do the trick if sufficient force were used, as it would no doubt be by a determined attacker."

One or two of my male students smiled at the doctor's comment, thinking that had the hammer been in their hands they'd have certainly acted like determined attackers.

To move things on I asked Doctor Braithwaite what he thought of our two skulls from the Ribbleswell Church graveyard. I'd earlier labelled them **A** and **B**. He picked up the one labelled **A**, the one belonging to the Crusader who had died first. As he did so he continued his lecture, if indeed it was one. To me it was more of a friendly chat, but that was the nature of the man: "As you have already seen, the brain is well protected by a very robust cover of bone...But if sufficient force is applied it will eventually fracture...This force can be applied in different ways and these produce different types of fractures, of which there are four main types...But I will concentrate on the two most common."

I glanced at the faces of my student group, looking for signs of 'Do we have to be here, listening to all this? We're archaeology not forensic students'. I also knew that being Friday afternoon, and the evening binge drinking session in the Union Bar was the week's highlight, the girls would want to be off to their rooms in order to get tarted up, and the lads to look as way-out as they possibly could in order to attract the girls' attention. But I detected no such signs. In fact all eyes were riveted on the doctor.

He continued: "I'll try to keep it simple...When all said and done

202

you're not forensic scientists...First the linear fracture...The most common type accounting for about seventy percent of all skull fractures...Usually caused by a large blunt object such as a baseball bat or a plank of wood, even falling on a flat surface such as a concrete floor...Energy is applied over a fairly large area of the skull resulting in a fracture that is more-or-less a straight line...Hence linear, but there is no bone displacement...In most cases there is no physiological or neurological damage, although the person my suffer concussion or even become unconscious...As with all head injuries, medical advice should always be sought."

I nodded in agreement, at the same time thinking back to my rugby league days, playing in the Sunday League. A mate of mine took a kick to the head after going down in a massive free-for-all punch up involving all twenty-six players plus one or two subs. He was stretchered off, but seemed to recover and rejoined the game. That night he was rushed into Doncaster General, where a fractured skull was diagnosed. And for the next couple of days it had been touch-and-go whether or not he'd make it. Fortunately he did.

Doctor Braithwaite continued: "The second type of fracture is called a depressed fracture and accounts for about ten per cent of all fractures...Here the force tends to be concentrated on a much smaller area and can therefore do immense damage...This type of fracture can result from being struck with a hammer, a brick, even the pointed toe of a shoe or boot...For obvious reasons it is called a depressed fracture, the skull fragmenting at the point of impact and the fragments being depressed into the tissues below...Not only can the tissue be damaged it can also be infected by the environment - hair, dirt from the object used to inflict the injury, and dirt if the victim is on the ground - dog muck, rotting food, oil contaminated puddles...It doesn't bear thinking about, does it?"

The students nodded their heads. It certainly didn't.

Aware that time was passing I asked the doctor to compare the two skull fractures and comment accordingly. He did so: "Right...Skull A...Damage caused by an object probably circular in shape and about three centimetre across...A modern day hammer would inflict such damage, so a similar twelfth century object would have been used...Fortunately for us the fragments of bone are still inside the skull, and if I extract them and try to fit them together, like a jigsaw, on a wide piece of cellotape that I just happen to have handy, you'll see we have almost a perfect fit...The jagged edges would have been driven into the tissues below with tremendous force, enough to cause sufficient trauma to kill the person almost immediately."

"Any ideas how?" I asked, already suspecting that I knew the answer.

"Almost certainly from behind, with the victim not expecting it...Probably in a dark alley somewhere."

"And what about skull **B**?" I asked.

"Ah...This fracture is more interesting, for there appears to be just one main fragment and this is roughly triangular in shape...It's as if the fragment fractured inwards along the triangle's baseline...I suspect that it may have been caused by the sharp corner of a brick or something similar, striking the head at an angle, probably as the victim turned as his brother was hit...It's pure speculation, but I feel that it could have happened that way."

"And why did he live a couple of days longer than his brother?" asked one of the students, who had been totally absorbed by the whole proceedings.

"Ah...Not an easy question to answer...I suspect that the initial damage to the brain was not as severe, but death could have taken place later due to contamination...A brick picked up off the ground would certainly have been filthy, a few dogs having previously pissed on it."

On that comical note I decided to end the proceedings, thanking Doctor Braithwaite for giving up his valuable time to talk to us. At that point the students started to clap, slightly embarrassing our guest speaker. Also at that point I had a thought - would the Doctor like the two skulls to use in any future lectures he may give? Did it really matter if the skulls weren't buried with the skeletons of the two Crusaders? I thought not, but really it wasn't my decision. The final say should rest with the vicar of Ribbleswell Church. When I contacted him a couple of days later he thought it a worthwhile suggestion, especially if the skulls were in the hands of a practising pathologist who gave lectures about his work. And as the vicar pointed out, there would be sixteen skulls in the communal grave anyway as a result of the skeletons found in the graves just inside the boundary wall, so two skulls wouldn't be missed. Needless to say, when I told Doctor Braithwaite the news he willingly accepted the two skulls into his safe keeping.

It was now essential that the bones were returned to Ribblewell Church so that they could be interred in a communal grave. As luck would have it, one of my students lived on a farm just outside Skipton and went home every weekend. Her vehicle was a 4 X 4 truck and she offered to drop them off at the church on her next visit home. Hopefully she would not be stopped by the police and asked to explain why the back of her truck was full of human bones. To be on the safe side I advised her to keep to the speed limit on the A1.

Some months later Angela and I travelled up to the Yorkshire Dales for a long weekend at the *Bluebell Inn* at Kettlewell, the inn where we'd originally spent our honeymoon. On the Sunday morning, after a gigantic breakfast, typical of those served in these parts and verging on obscenity in their generous proportions, we decided to drive across to the village of Ribbleswell and visit the church. I wanted to show Angela where my students and I had earlier spent a week excavating the churchyard, and where the final piece of Christ's Holy Square, Judas Iscariot's piece, had turned up. I also wanted to see how it looked after the communal grave had been completed and the landscaping carried out.

After parking up at the side of the road we headed for the churchyard. Immediately we heard organ music and a quick glance at the church noticeboard told me that the eleven o'clock Holy Communion service had that very minute commenced. I whispered to Angela, not wanting to wake the dead: "Do you fancy taking communion?...We haven't done so for years."

Angela, possibly less religious than myself, nevertheless whispered back: "Why not?...We rarely get the opportunity to do so nowadays."

This of course wasn't true, for one obviously created the opportunity if one was keen enough.

We entered the church via the south door, the heavy wooden structure squeaking on its hinges as we did so. So much for not waking the dead. As we sat down on the back row of pews, with a congregation of ten villagers sitting in front of us, the vicar lifted his eyes from his prayer book, looked over his glasses and nodded. I assumed that he recognised me, but I'd no way of knowing.

At the appropriate point in the service the vicar, after taking communion himself, invited his flock to do so. Angela and I rose from our seats, joined the small queue of communicants who proceeded to kneel in a row at the communion rail. Following a practice that had been carried out in churches worldwide for the best part of two thousand years, the vicar first presented each communicant with a small disc of unleaven bread which they consumed He then followed this with a sip of wine from what looked like a silver chalice that had seen better days. The base was uneven and the top lip misshaped, indicating that the chalice had almost certainly been dropped on the floor, probably on several occasions during its life. The main body was also badly scratched.

I couldn't help comparing it with the one at Wakefield Cathedral that had been used every Sunday morning at the Solemn Eucharist during the period I'd been a choirboy there. It had also been made of silver, but there the similarity ended. This one had been twice as big both in height and width, encrusted with jewels of different colours and intricately engraved. Sadly, about five years ago a report in the *Wakefield Express* revealed that thieves had hidden in Saint Mark's Chapel after the Sunday Eucharist and stolen it before it could be safely locked away. When the Provost was asked to put a value on it he simply said: "Priceless." And it could well have been so.

After giving the Blessing the vicar walked to the back of the church and bade farewell to the members of the congregation, at the same time shaking hands with them as they passed through the now open south door. This of course included Angela and I. His words did in fact indicate that he had earlier recognised me: "Hello, Professor Robertshaw…Good to see you at our humble service…Don't forget to visit the churchyard…I think you'll be impressed."

After introducing Angela to him I informed him that we were indeed heading in that direction before returning to Kettlewell.

I was amazed at what I saw. All the work had been completed. There was little evidence that a long trench had been excavated along the roadside in order to lay a water pipe, the turves having been caringly placed back in position. A new wall had been built using the original stones, the new mortar being the only sign that it had been recently constructed. This looked more than adequate to hold back the depth of earth behind it. To my surprise the graveyard had been turfed across its whole area. The joints could still be seen, but it wouldn't be long before the turves had all knitted together, making the area as good as the putting green on a golf course.

But what surprised me the most was the newly constructed communal grave. It was set in the centre of the turfed area and roughly three metres square. It consisted of a low black marble wall no more than six inches in height and the whole area was covered in small chippings of white marble. Five rose bushes, now in full bloom, had been carefully positioned within the square, giving the appearance of the five dots on a domino.

I was also thoroughly pleased to see that the new headstone was in place at the west end of the grave, facing east. It was of black polished marble, standing about a metre high, and the inscription in gold lettering was clear for all to see:

This a communal grave for sixteen
people whose names are not known
and who were interred in this graveyard
between 1200 and 1400AD
Also interred here are two Crusaders
who had served King and Country in
the Holy Land

But what pleased me by far the most was to see that the gravestones of the two crusaders had been positioned either side of the main headstone, standing their full height, thus revealing their inscriptions, the letters having been thoroughly cleaned out making them easily readable. I had earlier suggested to the vicar that maybe they could be found a place inside the church, but there was no doubt that their rightful place was in the graveyard itself. The vicar had got it spot-on.

As Angela and I stood at the end of the grave, facing it with heads slightly bowed, we heard the church's south door close, the solid iron catch dropping into place. (why is it impossible to close a church door quietly, I wondered?). It was the vicar leaving the church. He spotted us by the communal grave and came across: "Come to see our handiwork, have we professor?...I think the stonemason's done a first class job, don't you?"

"Excellent," I replied, and continued: "I like the way you've included the two crusaders' gravestones...I suggested that you found a place for them inside the church, but I'm glad you didn't take any notice of me."

"Me too," declared Angela, adding that it had not been one of her husband's better suggestions.

I was about to bid the vicar farewell, when a question suddenly flashed through my mind. Aware that money was always tight at village churches, I asked him, a smile on my face, not in any way wanting to offend him: "Who paid for the turf?...Must have cost a bob or two...And who laid it?...Certainly did a good job."

He tapped the side of his nose before explaining: "To cut a long story short, I was in the *Fox and Grapes* one evening and happened to mention that the graveyard would need to be seeded in the Autumn…One of the regulars, a local farmer said that his brother ran a turfing company down in Lincolnshire that supplied most of the Premier League football grounds…There and then he rang him on his mobile, and within a week the turf was laid, and by them too…Evidently they'd had a few square yards spare from a big job…Didn't cost us a cent, either."

"A bit of divine intervention, then?"I replied, jokingly.

The vicar smiled: "Just a little."

As Angela and I moved across to the newly constructed wall so that I could take a photograph of the communal grave, one that I intended to send to the *Yorkshire Post*, along with a small article, I whispered to her: "With a bit of luck news will get around and visitors to the Dales will call at the church to see the grave…Maybe at the same time dropping the odd coin in the collection box."

Angela nodded in agreement.

***

Chapter Twenty One

It was in the 2nd of January 2012 edition of the *Yorkshire Post* that I saw it - a five line report on the right hand edge of page six, under the main column heading - *BRIEFLY* -

New asteroid discovered. Amateur astronomer Jamie
Telford, age twelve, and of Ambleside in Cumbria, using
a telescope he'd purchased from the internet supplier
eBay has discovered a new asteroid. The professionals
are now investigating his sighting.

That was all the report stated.

Although the report was obviously of interest to me, there was so little information given that I quickly moved on. Besides, I was thinking, probably unfairly, that the boy's no doubt affluent parents had splashed out on some sophisticated and therefore expensive equipment in order for their son to pursue his hobby which had led to this observation. Those poor youngsters who lived on the council estate close to where I lived would never get the opportunity to make such observations even if 'star gazing' had caught their imaginations. I made a mental note of the report and quickly found the sports page.

My team, Doncaster, had played at the weekend in Rugby League'sChampionship Division. They were floundering near the bottom of the table, but I tried to maintain an interest in how they were doing, although to my eternal shame I rarely actually watched them play. As Angela had pointed out on more than one occasion: "You either support them or you don't…There's no in between." And of course she was right. I had to make a greater effort.

That evening, as I picked up the paper again, this time to re-read an article about the discoveries made in Egypt using satellite photographs that revealed evidence of buried ancient cities, the brief astronomy article again caught my eye.

Later, out of sheer curiosity, I went on eBay to see how much a decent astronomical telescope would cost. Perhaps I could re-kindle the interest I had as a child. It started when my father made me a three inch refracting telescope out of a yard of drain pipe, the main lens and eyepiece having been bought out of a magazine called *Exchange & Mart*.

I guiltily thought back to earlier in the day when I'd considered the young boy Jamie Telford to be privileged. Had I also been privileged? For none of my mates on the council estate where I'd spent the first twenty years of my life, had a telescope.

To my amazement I could, if I wanted, purchase a telescope that would do the job, for not much more than the laptops and mobile phones that most of the kids nowadays had. Jamie Telford hadn't been privileged after all. He may even have saved up his pocket money for his telescope.

What I did know was that any old telescope would not do the job. It would have to take a camera and be mounted on its tripod in a very special way.

In order to make the observations that would reveal an asteroid the telescope has to follow the stars as they travel across the sky, movement caused by the Earth rotating on its axis completing one full rotation in slightly under twenty-four hours.

Shortly after the telescope had been invented astronomers worked out that if it was mounted in a particular way it would follow the stars as they moved across the sky. Such a mount, still widely used today, is called an *equatorial mount* and consists of two axes set at rightangles to each other. One of the axes is lined up at a point very close to the North Star, or α Ursa Minor as astronomers know it. The telescope is mounted on the other axis. It's all very simple, but it works perfectly when set up correctly.

But it wasn't until a camera was mounted on the telescope that the equatorial mount came into its own. Photographing the stars by simply pointing the camera at the sky and activating the shutter is not possible if pin point images are required. First there isn't enough light falling on the exposed film in the short time the shutter is open. And if the shutter is kept open longer in order to collect more light, 'camera shake' spoils the image. Of course the camera can be mounted on a tripod and the shutter left open for several hours. In this case each star will leave a curved trail of light on the exposed film. By doing this, beautiful pictures can be produced, particularly if the camera is pointed directly at the Pole Star, when a series of concentric rings of light is produced.

If the camera is connected to a telescope that is on an equatorial mount, driven by a very accurate electric motor that slowly turns the mount so that the telescope can follow the movement of the particular star being observed, all the light collected is concentrated at one point over the period the shutter is open, usually several hours. When this was done for the first time there were some surprises - stars that were thought to be single were found to be doubles, even triples and faint patches of light in the heavens were found to be wonderfully shaped spiral galaxies.

But how does this type of telescope help in the discovery of asteroids and also comets? Once the telescope is accurately set up it is found that if a particular area of sky is photographed on consecutive nights the photographs show all the 'fixed' stars in identical positions. But sometimes a point of light is seen to have changed its position. It could of course be one of the major planets, but their positions and movements are already known. It must therefore be an unknown object moving rapidly through space - an asteroid, meteor, or a comet that eventually develops a 'tail' as it approaches the Sun on its orbit. Comets have been known about for thousands of years, the ancient Chinese, Egyptian and Greek astronomers being aware of them. The most well known one is Halley's Comet, named after the English astronomer Edmund Halley. It pays Earth a visit every seventy-five/six years, making an appearance in 1066 when the Battle of Hastings was fought. It even appears on the Bayeux Tapestry, that shows the battle in a series of embroidered pictures. Its latest visit was in 1986, but far too many cloudy nights in the UK hindered good viewing. The next visit will be in 2061/2.

Asteroids and Comets must not be confused with 'shooting stars'. These are particles of debris that enter the Earth's atmosphere at high speed and burn up. We see this as a bright trail of light rarely lasting more than a second. Sometimes this debris comes from a larger object that has disintegrated forming very many much smaller objects. When these hit the atmosphere we get a 'meteor shower' where several trails are seen apparently coming from the same general area of sky. Famous meteor showers are the Leonids on 15-19th November, appearing to come from the constellation Leo - the lion, and the Geminids on the 7-15th December, appearing to come from the constellation Gemini - the twins.

To observe meteor showers one doesn't require any sophisticated equipment. A camera is placed on a flat surface such as a paving stone or a wall, if possible well away from street lights, and pointed at the sky, better still at the constellation where the meteors are expected to come from. The shutter is then left open for several hours. The exposed film picks up the trail of light made by each of the meteors.

Young Jamie Telford must have had a telescope with a camera

mounted on it that would follow the stars. He must have examined photographs on consecutive nights and spotted a point of light that had moved its position. He must have also had star charts that enabled him to see that the object shouldn't have been there, and was therefore a 'new' object. He must have revealed his findings to a professional body, probably the British Astronomical Association, who realised that he had found something special. Quite a bright boy.

A couple of weeks later in the *Yorkshire Post* the discovery was again reported, but this time as a fore-runner to a longer and more detailed article written by the paper's science reporter. The article heading was:

New asteroid now being officially tracked

Jamie Telford was only given a brief mention. It then went on to inform us that an organisation in America with the acronym LINEAR, standing for the Lincoln Near Earth Asteroid Research facility, had plotted the course of Jamie's object, almost certainly an asteroid, and were tracking it on a daily basis. It had been given the code – 2011JT82, JT signifying that Jamie had discovered it. Being 60km long, 44km in cross-sectional diameter and shaped roughly like a rugby ball, it was definitely of interest. It was at its last measurement **88 000 000 Km** from the Earth, being just outside the orbit of Mars, but its highly eccentric orbit meant that it would pass the Earth at a distance of about 320 000 Km, bringing it just inside the orbit of the Moon. It had been designated a **4** on the *Torino Scale*, but this had now been changed to a **7**. The course of the asteroid was not causing any concern and was at the moment being simply monitored. The reporter then went on at length to inform the reader that a similar sized object had struck the earth 65 000 000 years ago with a force of 26 000 000 Hiroshima atomic bombs (the reporter loved his numbers with lots of noughts). It was in fact known as a 'Global Killer'. The resulting climatic change, especially the massive amount of dust forced into the atmosphere, blotted out the sun. This had caused a huge drop in temperature creating a Nuclear Winter, where life was extremely difficult, if not impossible for most species, including the dinosaurs that eventually became extinct. Being the sort of reporter who appeared to believe implicitly what the 'experts' told him he assured his readers that there was nothing to worry about. The Earth had been threatened with such a catastrophe many times in its history, and here it was still happily getting on with its very existence.

As I put the paper down I whispered to myself: "Such blind faith...Hasn't he read all the information now in the public domain about the Almighty's threat, as relayed by his Son to his disciples and hence to the World, at the Last Supper?...Obviously not." For some reason unknown to myself I was already assuming that if God did decide to destroy all life on Earth it would be by asteroid collision. But what about increased solar activity, a killer virus, a huge volcano blowing its top or a rapid increase in climate change, even nuclear war? All these could have a devastating effect on life on Earth, although their effect would be by their very nature much slower?

After our evening meal Angela settled down to watching *Emmerdale*, her favourite soap, followed by *Coronation Street*, while I settled down to do the washing-up. She loved the way the fictional Yorkshire Dales village and the Lancashire Street had become the modern equivalents of Sodom and Gomorrah - funny really, since those two ancient cities had also got a mention when Jesus had addressed his disciples. She couldn't resist making one of her merry quips: "I wonder if the good Lord is thinking of raining fire and brimstone on a certain street in Lancashire and a certain village in Yorkshire...They certainly deserve it."

I had to remind her that if the good Lord decided to go down that particular route, most of the places portrayed on television in soaps, sitcoms and films would meet the same fate...Mind you, that maybe no bad thing.

But one elementary point, yet so important as far as we the readers were concerned was the fact that the reporter had told us nothing about the Torino Scale. I certainly hadn't heard of it before, neither had Angela, and she knew all sorts of obscure facts that the rest of us had never heard of. Had he assumed that the scale was already familiar to us and therefore needed no explanation? Or didn't he know anything about it himself?

Had it been the Richter Scale he may just have been able to get away with it. Most readers of the *Yorkshire Post* knew that it was to do with earthquakes, and that **2** on the scale probably means the odd tile dropping off a roof, whereas an **8** would indicate massive damage of property and if in a populated area huge loss of life - Haiti in January 2010 being a good example. What most people didn't know about the Richter Scale was that the degree of damage doesn't go up in equal steps, but rises rapidly as one moves towards **10**. But that didn't matter. Most people knew that high numbers meant massive damage to buildings and high loss of life, and that's all they needed to know.

It was time to increase my knowledge of asteroid threats, at the same time checking out what the Torino Scale was all about. I got on line and typed in - asteroids. As I expected there was a mass of information, some useless to my search. I was not interested in nightclubs called *The Asteroid* as apparently several were.

The first website I decided to look at was an obvious one - The North American Space Administration, more commonly known a NASA. The site's title was 'Asteroid and Comet Impact Hazards. It immediately referred to NEOs, or Near-Earth-Objects. These are small objects within our Solar System with orbits that being close to the Earth's orbit sometimes cut across it, making a collision in the future a possibility.

But how small or large would such an object have to be to cause real damage? Evidently one the size of an office block (seemed huge to me) up to forty metres in diameter, although the objects are rarely spherical in shape, would most likely burn up in our protective atmosphere before impact. At one kilometre diameter (frighteningly large to me) massive local damage would be done, especially if impact was in a populated area. At two kilometres diameter the energy released on impact would be in the region of a million megatons of TNT. Here massive amounts of atmospheric dust or water vapour, because impact would be highly likely out at sea, would cut out the Sun's light and heat, producing a global winter that living things, both plant and animal, would find hard to survive.

The website understandably mentioned that sixty-five million years ago an asteroid fifteen kilometres across struck the earth with an energy release of about a hundred million megatons of TNT, and that this led to the demise of the dinosaurs. (although I had read elsewhere that this was by no means a hundred percent certain). Asteroid 2011JT82 was estimated to be four times larger.

The next section of the website should have at least brought some comfort to me - details of who were looking for these highly dangerous objects, travelling round the Solar System at high speed, rather like cars on a Formula One Grand Prix circuit. Well, several bodies, but apparently only a few people, digital cameras pointing at all areas in the sky doing the bulk of the work. Of course NASA was involved in conjunction with the US Airforce (were they looking for aliens at the same time, I wondered?) There was LINEAR in New Mexico, NEAT in

Hawaii and Spacewatch, The Catalina Sky Survey and LOEOS in Arizona. It appeared that Arizona was a good place to carry out such work. But most people involved were in fact amateur astronomers. Where was the British contribution? Jamie Telford?

In spite of all this observational activity the next section of the website was far from comforting:

Question - When will the next substantial impact take place?

Answer - We don't know. Statistically one would take place once or twice every million years...or tomorrow. All the observational work being carried out is looking for possible impacts well into the future, not in a few days' time, when it would be far too late to do anything about it anyway.

Question - How much warning would we get?

Answer – Could be None. An undiscovered asteroid could arrive without any warning. All we would see was a flash of light and feel the ground shake beneath us, unless it landed right on top of us, then we would know nothing about it at all. Not a bad way to go, I thought. From that point on things would take place at frightening speed. A shockwave, possibly accompanied by a tsunami, would rush round the world not allowing us to make any sort of preparation for what was to come.

The only comforting news was that if some distant object was found by one of the search teams to be on a collision course with the Earth we could have a few years to think about what we could do to prevent the collision. Unfortunately the website gave no indication of what steps could be taken on the Earth itself other than that the area of impact, that would presumably be accurately known, could be evacuated. I'd read elsewhere that spacecraft could be landed on the object and explosive charges set to blow it apart. Even 'sails' could be attached that would catch the solar wind and change the object's course, a bit like a yacht. Presumably Bruce Willis, if he were still alive, would be recruited to undertake the highly dangerous one-way mission.

It was now time to find something out about the Torino Scale. I typed in the words and waited. Seconds later tons (as we used to say as kids) of websites were displayed. Where to start? I decided to look at the LINEAR site first, and this immediately revealed what I wanted - a simple explanation of the Torino Scale. I quickly read the relevant information, speaking aloud as I did so for the benefit of Angela who was getting bored with Deidre's hysterical sobbings in *Coronation Street*.

"Right...First an opening statement...A scale that assesses asteroid and comet impact hazard predictions in the 21st century…It's a scale with both colours and numbers …Right, here goes:

WHITE - 0 - likelihood of collision zero
GREEN - 1 - collision extremely unlikely, no public concern
YELLOW - 2 to 4 - a close encounter, meriting attention by astronomers
ORANGE - 5 to 7 - a very close encounter but still uncertain threat of global catastrophe
RED - 8 to 10 - a collision is certain, capable of causing climatic catastrophe, threatening the future of civilisation as we know it

So there it is…The Torino Scale in less than a minute."

Angela said nothing for several seconds, no doubt piecing together in her own mind what she intended to say. She then started: "So…This LINEAR organisation initially gave the asteroid a score of ONE on this Torino Scale - meaning a zero likelihood of collision…But changed its assessment to SEVEN, meaning there would be a close encounter, but still an uncertain threat of global catastrophe…It seems a bloody big jump to me - from ONE to SEVEN, and yet they say the asteroid is causing no concern and that it is being carefully monitored…It all seems a bit hit-and miss to say the future of all life on Earth is at stake."

Of course Angela was right. But some organisations, and I wondered if LINEAR would be one of them, would be reluctant to release information that could lead to human panic. Announcing impending doom for the human race would immediately lead to self preservation acts such as a run on the banks and the mass buying and hoarding of food and water, thus decimating the supermarkets. All work would stop as individuals chose to be close to their loved ones. Some, although I suspected not many, would literally 'head for the hills', thinking that maybe that would be the safest place to be. In other words whole countries would be brought to a standstill. Of all human acts, only one - being with one's loved ones - would make any sense. Hence the reason for keeping people in the dark until as late as possible, for if the asteroid struck the Earth all human action, even descending into subways and mines would be of no avail because the passing shockwave would suck the very air out of them. And if they managed to survive that, the tsunami would drown them.

216

But as had been pointed out two thousand years earlier the human race would be given a 'get out'. Unfortunately this depended on many factors. The most uncertain one was the assembly of the most powerful men and women in the world in one place, presumably the UN Headquarters in New York, but not necessarily so, in order to place one piece of pot in Christ's Holy Square. But even if all were prepared to participate, one huge obstacle loomed up - travel, or more correctly the lack of it. If airlines couldn't operate because their pilots had decided to be with their families, air travel would not be possible.

I scribbled down a theoretical plan on a scrap piece of paper what would be required:

1. I, with my six pieces of pot, would have to get to wherever the meeting was being held.
2. Three pieces from Israel, two from Athens and one from Tehran would have to make possibly longer journeys.
3. The piece in the possession of the American Mrs Makepeace would only have to make a short journey, assuming New York was the chosen place.
4. The thirteen most powerful world leaders would also have to make the journey, assuming of course that the will was there to do so. And that was by no means certain.
5. Finally, a wooden square divided into the thirteen compartments making up Christ's Holy Square would have to be constructed. I decided that I would do that, being a dab hand at DIY. Besides, I was probably the only one who knew the exact dimensions of each piece and hence the dimensions of the compartments within the Square itself. We didn't want a situation where one or more pieces would not fit into the Square when the leaders tried them, as the asteroid sped out of control towards the Earth.

It all looked so simple, and in 'normal' times it would be, but I suspected that if indeed air travel was on the go at all, the airports of the world would be pretty chaotic places if the end of the World was nigh.

Fortunately we were nowhere near that point yet, and hopefully would never be if LINEAR's predictions of a near 'miss' turned out to be correct. But just in case the prediction was wrong and a 'strike' was on the cards we had to have a plan 'B', and that had to be one that would fulfil the requirements as set out in God's message to the World. The atheists and agnostics, and maybe people whose religion was not Christianity would not like the idea, even pooh-pooh it, but it would still have to be done.

Meanwhile the asteroid would continue on its predestined course regardless of any action taken by mankind. As I pointed out to Angela as we climbed the stairs to bed: "The ideal scenario is for the asteroid to spiral into the Sun never to be a cause for concern again…Or it could narrowly miss Earth and continue its journey to the outer reaches of the Solar System to return many years into the future…Either way we wouldn't have to worry about it again."

She nodded her head in agreement, but just to avoid me being too complacent, she added: "But what if it's heading straight for us?…What then?"

I shrugged my shoulders and said the only words I could think of: "Head for the hills with a good bottle of wine."

***

Chapter Twenty Two

As I laid in bed, mind as active as it could be and my restlessness being a real pain to Angela, who was trying to get some beauty sleep (of course I never suggested that she needed it), my mind returned to the prediction of total annihilation of the World by God the Almighty through his son Jesus Christ, if man did not mend his ways. I had always assumed, without any grounds for doing so, that the method of destruction would probably be similar to that inflicted on Sodom and Gomorrah. Or maybe by a Great Flood similar to that when Noah built his Ark (assuming that both actually took place, of which there is some doubt), but on a world wide scale. It appeared to me that this could only be accomplished by some form of asteroid strike. I had already ruled out earthquakes, volcanoes or some sort of killer virus. They would all tend to be too localised to be effective in the short term. And climate change would take ages to have any sort of impact. But maybe God would want it that way, just to see how man would cope.

The following evening, during yet another night of appalling television. (Who wanted to watch two participants on *Big Brother* apparently having simulated sex?), Angela made a suggestion. A sudden change in the Sun's activity could result in the release of high energy radiation that could have a devastating effect on the human race - she'd recently read about it in one of the tabloids whilst waiting for her perm to take at the hairdressers. It was already well known that the Sun went through an eleven year cycle of activity, and that we were approaching a 'maximum' in the cycle. It was also known that bursts of radiation could disrupt world communication and electronic circuitry. But nowhere had I read that loss of life had taken place. It was however just possible that the odd aeroplane could drop out of the sky as its electronics had a nervous breakdown. I therefore came to the conclusion that the Sun could play no part in what was predicted to take place.

So…God's method of World destruction was going to be by asteroid impact. Nothing else in the short term would work…Or was I missing something?

That night, as I stared yet again at the invisible bedroom ceiling, something that I was making a habit of doing, my mind was as active as ever. In fact all my thinking on the issue appeared now to be taking place as I laid in bed unable to sleep. Had God, through his Son, left a clue somewhere along the line that would point us in the right direction? I thought not, but just to check I crept out of the bedroom, descended the stairs and entered the kitchen. After making myself a cup of steaming coffee to keep my brain alert I settled down in the lounge.

Although all the information I had gathered was stored on disk I'd also made hard copies of everything - just in case. I therefore had a box file crammed full of sheets of relevant information. To my eternal shame organisation wasn't one of my strong points, consequently the sheets were in no particular order. In fact the very top sheet gave details of the discovery of the Roman soldier in a Doncaster bog, the very first account in a long, long story. Second sheet down was the print-out of Dr Democratos's email describing how two children on the Greek island of Andros discovered two of the thirteen pieces of pot whilst playing near their home. As I said, the sheets were in no particular order. My mistake had been not giving Angela the job of keeping the file in order. Had I done so each sheet would have been placed in chronological order, numbered, with a contents sheet placed at the top.

Realising that I had to get a grip of the situation I decided to get the information in some sort of order as I looked through it, searching for God's vital clue - if indeed there was one, which I doubted. Why should he help us anyway?

I made my way through the sheets and pieces of card that I'd cello-taped together as the various pieces of pot, or their location, had revealed their shape, colour, exact dimensions and Greek identifying letter. I sorted the information according to the sequence of events, commencing with the finding of the white hexagonal θ - π piece of pot found on the Roman soldier in the bog, and ending with the finding of the brown triangular o piece in Ribbleswell churchyard, that had originally been given to Judas Iscariot by Jesus himself.

One of the last things I'd done was to make a master card, giving all details of the thirteen pieces of pot - order of discovery, colour, shape, Greek letter, the disciple who'd received it from Jesus, where it had been found, and most important of all, where it was now.

Below all this information was my drawing of Christ's Holy Square, showing all thirteen pieces - shape, colour, letter, all in their positions.

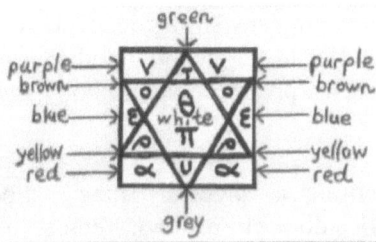

I was convinced that I had this correct because for a while now I had believed that the left side of the square was the same as the right. The halves weren't exact mirror images because the letters themselves weren't reversed, but what was interesting was the way the four letters down the centre τ-θ-π-υ could also be divided vertically in half and these were almost, but not quite, mirror images.

The letter arrangement obviously showed a pattern, but were there also other patterns? I started to arrange the letters in various ways:-

Going across the square:ν-τ-ν-ο-θ-ο-ε-ε-ρ-π-ρ-α-υ-α
Going down the square:ν-ο-ε-ρ-α-τ-θ-π-υ-ν-ο-ε-ρ-α
Placing double letters together: νν-οο-εε-ρρ-αα-τ-θ-π-υ

But after three apparently unsuccessful attempts to reveal some sort of pattern that could be interpreted as a clue, I gave up.

Then a flash of inspiration...Why hadn't I seen it weeks, if not months, before? Was it just possible that the fourteen letters could be rearranged in the same way crossworders solve anagrams, to give one or more Greek words that, when translated into English, would give me my clue, or even a message?

Since my knowledge of Ancient Greek, because that's what it would be, could be written on the back of a postage stamp, apart from the alphabet itself, I badly needed an Ancient Greek-to-English dictionary, but didn't possess one at home, nor indeed in my vast library at work. I did however have a colleague in the Classical Languages Department who knew Ancient Greek like the back of his hand. Professor Leptos had in fact earlier translated the Dead Sea Scroll that Jemma Rogers had found and smuggled out of Israel...and a good job he had done, too.

There and then I decided to pass the list of letters on to him first thing in the morning on my arrival at work, then wait and see what he came up with, if indeed anything at all.

At that point, not having any strong desire to pursue the issue further, I placed all the material in the box file and returned to bed, intensely annoying Angela when I pressed my cold body against hers in order to steal her wamth.

The following morning at precisely nine o'clock I found myself knocking on the office door of Professor Leptos.

"Enter," boomed a voice. It was his characteristic way of greeting his students. They in turn found it amusing to mimic him, behind his back of course.

I was immediately invited to sit down and asked if I would like a coffee. The water had evidently just that minute boiled in the tiny kitchenette that adjoined his office. Having rushed out of my home thirty minutes earlier without as much as a drink I gratefully accepted his offer.

"Now Peter…What can I do for you?…Not another Dead Sea Scroll, is it?"

"If only it was," I replied. The professor invited me to continue, which I enthusiastically did: "You of course know already that I have in my possession six of the thirteen pieces of pot given out at the Last Supper by Jesus to his disciples, and know the location of the other seven." He nodded and smiled, knowing that it was doubtful that anyone on the university campus didn't know. "Well, I wondered if the Greek letters on the pieces could be rearranged to give one of more Greek words that, when translated into English, may give us a clue as to how God intends to annihilate the World…Will you look at the list of letters and see if you can come up with something?" I then passed to him a slip of paper with all fourteen letters written on it. Since I felt it unlikely that any sort of Greek word would contain several double letters I kept them apart.

ν-ο-ε-ρ-α-τ-θ-π-υ-α-ρ-ε-ο-ν

Dr Leptos stared long and hard at the letters hoping, but not expecting, the answer to jump out at him. He was right…it didn't. He then started to talk to me as the thought processes passed through his mind: "As you are aware, Peter, in English certain letters frequently go together…Q is almost always followed by **u**, and **c** often followed by **k**…K is often followed by **n**…Think of the word 'knock', where both combinations occur…Well, in Greek, both ancient and modern, the same happens, with the following combinations being common…ευ, κα and πρ, but there are many others…In your list of letters there are several so that approach is not going to help."

This gave me the opportunity to make a suggestion: "As you are aware, there's a 'box of tricks' available where you type in the letters of a word, press a key and an anagram of the word is displayed…People who do crosswords sometimes use one, but it seems like cheating to me…Is there a similar box to use with Greek words?"

"As a matter of fact I have one, but only use it as a last resort…Having said that, if I'm well and truly stumped I do use it, as will probably be the case with your letters…But I'll try the hard way first, just to exercise the brain."

"Right," I replied, a little too abruptly: "I'll leave you to it…All I want is an answer and I don't really care how you get it."

Angela always said that the working of my brain was a total mystery to her. She'd tried to work it all out over the fifteen years of our marriage, but had failed miserably, much to her annoyance.

My next attempt at trying to understand the arrangement of the letters in Christ's Holy Square perfectly displayed this 'working'. I decided to replace the Greek letters with English ones. This required some careful thought along a certain channel and involved a lot of doodling with pen and paper, since crosswords had never been my strong point.

I required one or more words giving a total of fourteen letters and including five double sets of letters in order to fill the right and left vertical columns of the Square with identical letters.

Thinking that scientific words or expressions may offer me the best choice, by sheer good luck I stumbled on a nine letter word that contained two Ds two Is and two Ls, the last two letters being side by side. It also contained the letters S, T and E. I was almost there. Immediately a five letter word flashed through my mind that not only provided me with the second T and E, but also added W, A and R. My second word went perfectly with my nine letter word.

Feeling extremely pleased with myself I sketched out my Square and inserted all fourteen letters, ensuring that the five down the left side were identical to those down the right. The remaining four letters went down the middle, with two in the hexagon. It was too much to expect that a central vertical line would cut all four letters into equal halves, but the **W** and **A** did so very nicely. Finally I sketched out Christ's Holy Square at the side of my Square so that I could compare the two.

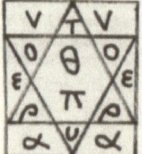 

I then wrote out the letters, working my way across, then down the Square. This gave me a random row.

I-S-I-L-W-L-D-D-T-A-T-E-R-E

It didn't give me a recognisable word or expression that the anagram would come from, but I felt that that didn't matter. It was now simply a case of rearranging the letters into my two chosen words…simple.

I now had to try my puzzle out on someone. Angela, who could do the *The Times* crossword in ten minutes, was the obvious choice. So, over morning coffee, I gave her a slip of paper with the fourteen letters in random order across it.

"What's this?" was her terse request.

"It's an anagram that I want you to solve."

"But it's not a word or expression…Anagrams are different words or group of words containing the same letters."

"Does that matter?…All I want you to do is come up with one or more words from those letters."

"How many words?"

"Two…Nine and five."

"Clues?"

I hadn't expected her to ask that, so I had to think quickly: "Er…Top up for a reliable start."

She glared at me no doubt thinking what a stupid clue it was.

Angela didn't need pen and paper. Her eyes ran across the letters and quickly picked out a five letter word that could be linked with 'top up': "Water…Topping up baths and swimming pools, even steam irons spring to mind."

After crossing out the five letters she rewrote the remaining nine. Within a matter of seconds she had the second word as well, one that

224

went nicely with the first.

She yelled out the answer: "Distilled…So the answer's 'distilled water'."

I should have felt a little peeved at her triumphalism, but I didn't, for she had shown me how Christ's Holy Square could give an answer as to how God intended to destroy the World. I hoped that when Dr Leptos came to solving the puzzle his thought processes would be along the same lines as Angela's.

Angela then felt that she had to give me a crash course on 'the cryptic crossword clue': "The clue should give the letters in the form of meaningful words that when re-arranged give the new word or words…The expression should also contain a clue…Let me just have a little think round your letters…"

This time she picked up a pen and started to scribble on the edge of the newspaper: "Well, it's not brilliant, but it will give you some idea…My cryptic clue is:

Diller wasted it to produce a liquid of high purity…Two words 9 and 5…

The anagram comes from the fourteen letters in - Diller wasted it…It's now just a case of trying to tie the clue to the words…Liquid of high purity should lead you to 'water', and water can be made pure by distilling it…This gives you the word 'distilled'…So the answer is 'distilled water'…Get it?"

I did indeed get it. But was I now ready to tackle *The Times* crossword? I didn't think so. Maybe I'd be better off getting one of those crossword books you see in newsagents that have EASY - MEDIUM - HARD crosswords and slowly make my way through it…if I had the patience…which I doubted.

My clue did however puzzle Angela: "Can't see how your clue and 'distilled water' are linked together…Please explain."

"Ah…In the good old days you had to top up your car battery with distilled water…If you didn't you'd find that the car wouldn't start…It was one of the weekly checks you made, along with oil and radiator levels and tyre pressures."

"You mean all those checks you don't make now?"

"To my eternal shame…Yes." My excuse was that I just didn't have the time. But to be quite honest, it was just sheer laziness.

That night, just after dinner, as Angela and I settled down in front of the television to yet another CSI repeat (they must make so many, that when they do eventually run a repeat a year later they hope you've forgotten the plot). Unfortunately Angela has the memory of an elephant and I got fed up of constantly hearing the words: "Seen it."

As I flicked channels the phone rang. This was not an unusual event, especially when you had a group of sometimes naïve students under your wing. We always assume that today's eighteen year olds are 'worldly'. Believe me they are not, and when they did have a problem, a phone call to my home number was often the answer - like the other week when one of my students, Rachel Frost, ended up at the local police station, accused of stealing another girl's handbag in the toilets of the *Carousel* night club.

I got the call just after midnight and, accompanied by Angela who drove to calm my nerves and stop me exploding, we set off for the station. Fortunately it had all been a big misunderstanding. A group of girls had apparently decided to move on to another night club, assuming that their friend, who had been in such a rush to go to the toilet that she'd left her *MOSCHINO* handbag behind, would follow them. Naturally the other girls had picked it up and taken it with them. Rachel, accompanied by her own identical handbag (evidently, according to Angela, they were two-a-penny), had also entered the toilet. When leaving, with her own bag, the other girl had seen it, assumed it to be hers and accused Rachel of stealing it. A heated argument had then followed, and before Rachel had had chance to open her bag and show the girl the contents, including her diving licence, the girl had punched her in the face, bursting her nose (very lady-like remarked Angela, sarcastically). A full scale scrap had then taken place with no holds barred. The management had called the police and both women had been arrested.

Anyway...it had all turned out right in the end and we took Rachel to A&E for a check-up before taking her back to her student accommodation. What had surprised me about the whole incident had been her presence at the night club on her own. Angela pointed out that that was not uncommon and sometimes, unfortunately, led to the lone girl being molested, even raped, as she made her way home in the early hours of the morning. As tutor-in-charge of my students I gave all of them a lecture on personal safety the following morning. I suppose it fell on deaf ears, but I hoped not.

Now, back to my phone call. It was in fact from Dr Leptos : "I've got a possible answer to our puzzle…I decided to give my students studying Ancient Greek the list of letters and sent them away for the day, armed with their laptops and dictionaries, trusting them to take the task seriously, but knowing that most of them would end up in the local pub…Anyway, we've got a possible answer, and one on the lines I know you've been thinking along for the last few weeks."

"Come on…Let's have it," I shouted, bringing a scowl from Angela, at my bad-mannered impatience.

"Well…We've come up with two Greek words that fill the bill…I'll spell the first one out to you…Got a pen and paper handy?"

Angela quickly passed me the necessary requirements.

"Right, here goes: First word **pi - epsilon - tau - rho - alpha**…Spelling **petra**."

I wrote down the letters in Greek and then their English equivalent:
πετρα-**petra**

"Now, second word…**omicron - upsilon - rho - alpha - nu -omicron - theta - epsilon - nu**…Spelling **ouranothen**…Got them?"
I quickly wrote down the Greek letters and their English equivalent:
ουρανοθεν **ouranothen**

I had indeed got them both, but when I counted up the English letters in both words the number came to five plus ten (ie) fifteen in total, one too many. Disappointed, I pointed this out to Dr Leptos. It was back to the drawing board.

"Ah," he replied: "You've probably written **theta** as **th**, that is two letters…But as a Greek letter theta is written as θ, that is one letter."

Exhaling in relief at not having to go back to the drawing board, I stared at the two words. The first word definitely rang a bell, as indeed it should have done. My brain started to trawl through its database and soon came up with an answer. I quickly conveyed this to Dr Leptos: "Petra…Greek for Peter, my Christian name…Peter the Rock…Is Petra in fact Greek for 'rock'?"

"You've got it in one," was his enthusiastic reply.

But I had to admit, nothing registered at all with the second word, my good doctor friend had therefore to help me: "Now…the second word was more of a problem, but one of my students came up with an answer…The Greek word I gave you, when translated into English, gives 'from heaven'."

My mind immediately put the two words together giving 'rock from heaven'...Or expressing it in modern language an asteroid, comet or meteor coming from the sky. I'd been right after all about the method to be used by God to destroy the World if man did not mend his ways. Jesus had excelled himself.

First, he had chosen two words that gave a total of fourteen letters, then displayed them in the thirteen sections of a Star of David surrounded by a square border, placing two letters in the central hexagon that he kept for himself.

Second, he had arranged them in a sort of pattern even though there wasn't one, just to tease us. It proved beyond any doubt that he'd been more than a simple carpenter. He'd had in fact a very sophisticated mind and obviously had a knowledge of Greek that must have been gained at a young age. How, I wondered? Of course the Good Lord himself could have been behind it all, but I doubted it.

After thanking Dr Leptos for his time and effort, at the same time informing him that I would further discuss the issue with him in the morning, I wished him goodnight and replaced the handset.

Typically, Angela's comment was: "So...That's the end of the story, is it?...Problem solved...Issue closed...Thank God for that...You've been a right pain in the backside over these last few months."

My reply didn't give her any comfort: "Alas, Angela, no...In fact the story could only just be beginning...Let's just assume that an asteroid is heading roughly in our direction, but all calculations show that it will miss us by a safe margin...Suddenly, and for no reason that the World's most brilliant astronomers can explain, it changes course, heading directly at us, giving us barely a week to prepare...What would we do?"

"Head for the hills with a good bottle of wine," was her unhelpful, yet understandable reply. She was probably right, too. It seemed in the apparently hopeless circumstances the most obvious and sensible course of action.

I closed my eyes and tried to visualise Angela and I sitting on the summit of Pen-y-Ghent, not the highest, but in my opinion the most striking of the Three Peaks of the Yorkshire Dales, with our picnic basket and that good bottle of wine. As the asteroid struck our atmosphere there was a blinding flash of light. (I must remember to keep two pairs of sunglasses permanently in the glove compartment of the car). The impact shook the Earth, presumably regardless of where it had taken place, the greatest distance from us being somewhere in the region of New Zealand. Then, hours later, or was it just minutes, the huge shockwave, maybe evena tsunami that had already crossed over Ireland and Lancashire, hit us. As it happened we saw it coming and just had sufficient time to link arms, raise our glasses and drink a toast to the good life we'd both undoubtedly had. We were then swept off the peak and into oblivion. What a way to go…surely much, much better than passing away after suffering terminal cancer, motor neurone or Alzheimer's Disease.

***

Chapter Twenty Three

'And it came to pass'. I wondered how many times this expression appeared in the Bible. But on this occasion it seemed the appropriate way to commence this chapter.

And it came to pass that the asteroid that the young English astronomer Jamie Telford had discovered months earlier with his amateur equipment had proved to be a bit of a headache for the 'experts'. LINEAR hadn't been able to understand how all their sophisticated equipment...state-of-the-art digital cameras, computer enhanced imagery and telescopes with pin point accurate motor drives, had failed to pick the asteroid up. Jamie had been able to do so with 'stone age' equipment by comparison.

Once LINEAR had it on their 'radar' they had measured its size and hence its mass and velocity, and had plotted its highly eccentric orbit. This revealed that its journey took it just beyond the orbit of Neptune when furthest away from the Sun, and within the orbit of Venus at its nearest point. It took a full twenty-five years to complete its orbit. Since it hadn't been seen previously, astronomers assumed that it had somehow strayed from its orbit within the asteroid belt, possibly as a result of a collision with another asteroid, and was now following its highly eccentric orbit around the Sun. Further investigations revealed that it had crossed the Earth's orbit on the 26th December on its inward journey, but the Earth had already passed that point and was some 180 million Km away. After going round the Sun it would again cross the Earth's orbit on the 23rd March as it commenced its journey to the outer reaches of the Solar System. But on that date the Earth would not have yet reached that point, being still 15 million Km away. It would in fact reach the point on the 25th April. So, the asteroid was not a hazard to the Earth, but had to be watched closely, just in case.

Then, on the 17th February the asteroid started to change course. LINEAR, feeling unease at their worrying observations, contacted all the other agencies involved in the search for such celestial bodies, to confirm that their findings were correct. They were. The asteroid, given the code name 2012JT82, was in fact changing course ever so slightly as each twenty-four hourly observation revealed. Rapid reassessments of its exact position when it next crossed the Earth's path gave a date of the 6th

April, the exact date when the Earth would reach the same point, and that a collision was inevitable. LINEAR immediately gave it a code RED - 10 on the Torino Scale. Impact would take place on that date, which happened to be in just forty-eight days' time, barely seven weeks.

The question now was - what could be done, if indeed anything at all? LINEAR, knowing with great accuracy the asteroid's exact orbit, position on that orbit and velocity, were able to predict the exact time of impactand where it would take place, assuming of course that there were no more subtle changes in its orbit. Impact would in fact take place on the 6th April at 02.30 GMT. in the North Atlantic, five hundred kilometres south - west of the Azores.

Initially the reaction round the World was one of total disbelief. People had constantly been told that there had been many 'near misses' in the Earth's past and there would no doubt be many in the future. But an actual impact due to take place in just forty-eight days' time was simply unthinkable. It just wouldn't, indeed couldn't take place.

Unfortunately, as the latest data coming from observation stations throughout the World was analysed it became clear beyond any shadow of a doubt that an asteroid, some 60Km by 44Km, shaped not unlike a rugby ball, was heading for the Earth and would strike it with unimaginable force.

There then followed a feeling of helplessness as the news spread round the World using all forms of communication, from simple word-of-mouth to the most advanced electronic methods. NASA reluctantly stated that there was insufficient time to mount any sort of mission to land on the asteroid and either blow it up or in some way change its course. (As I jokingly pointed out to Angela, evidently Bruce Willis wasn't available). But it wasn't funny at all. It was deadly serious. The President of the United States informed NASA to 'get its finger out' and get the problem sorted, at the same time pointing out that it had been a drain on the US economy for years and it was now 'pay back' time.

The other nations of the World, including mighty Russia and China, looked on helplessly, expecting the rival super power to come up with something. The rest of the World sadly fell into a state of abject resignation.

At this point I can only describe what happened in the United Kingdom, but there was little doubt that a similar pattern of events was being acted out worldwide. As had always happened in times of grave uncertainty, for example impending war, mankind acted in a predictable and perfectly understandable way. Realising that the Government was impotent to do anything about the situation, people had to protect themselves in what ever way possible.

A run on the banks took place, in the circumstances a totally pointless exercise since sleeping on a mattress under which had been hidden hundreds, maybe even thousands of bank notes, would not be of much help when the asteroid struck. And yet people with money in the bank felt the strong need to withdraw it. Of course some of the money was used to 'stock up' on provisions, but only while the supermarket shelves had anything on them. Which wasn't very long. Obviously people bought useful things like food and water while supplies lasted, but also, given the circumstances, useless things such as metal polish, paint and kebab sticks. It was simply a case of - if I've got it, you haven't.

All common sense seemed to have been abandoned, with frozen peas, burgers and chips being preferred to tins of corn beef, baked beans and fruit, people not realising that a loss of power would quickly make defrosted food inedible. Since at no time did the Government give its people any advice on what to expect, the people simply chose to disbelieve the predictions of the scientists, assuming that they would only have to survive hardship for a few weeks at the most.

Petrol stations were quickly emptied, even though those with a full tank had nowhere to go. This quickly led to diesel being in short supply resulting in the supermarkets' supply lines breaking down. The stealing of cars shot up, not to joyride in or sell on, but to siphon the fuel from.

But one thing did happen and it brought the country to a virtual standstill. Many workers - deliverymen, train and bus drivers, even pilots, decided to stay at home to be with their loved ones, at the same time preparing their homes for the impending disaster, refusing to accept that there was actually nothing they could do. It of course didn't help when Government advice, when it was eventually given, included running masking tape across all windows and glass panelled doors to prevent dangerous splintering, something I'd recently seen on *Dad's Army* that had showed the practice to be commonplace during WW II. But it soon became clear that such advice was only tinkering at the edges of a potentially deadly situation.

For a reason not easy to explain those in the utility services, particularly electricity, gas and water supplies, and the essential sewage system, kept working, as did the police, fire fighters, teachers and those in all levels of the medical services. Head teachers kept their schools open, but it wasn't long before the children started to opt out, preferring to stay close to home. But for how long would the workers keep working? Nobody knew.

One unusual, yet perfectly understandable effect, given the circumstances, was the way families slowly came together. A couple living with a couple of children suddenly found that their house population had increased by a couple of grandparents, who had used their precious petrol to travel halfway across the country. Some homes were invaded by four grandparents. Large family groups were seen out together, combing the shops for anything they could make use of. When quizzed about their closeness they responded by pointing out that if an asteroid struck they would at least all 'go' altogether.

Angela and I continued to work. We saw little point in staying at home. My students, who came from far and wide, initially continued with their studies, but some disappeared, and not because the university's kitchens had run out of food, because they hadn't. Our cook had a reputation for always preparing for the proverbial 'rainy day', consequently the larder was stocked to the ceiling with everything imaginable, as indeed were the freezers. We at the university hoped and prayed that we would not lose our power supply. Every day we gazed northwards to check that the power stations in the Aire Valley - Ferrybridge, Eggborough and Drax were still 'on load'. Fortunately all three had huge stocks of coal.

Those students who prolonged their departure asked me what Angela and I would do on impact day. I could have pussyfooted around the question, giving advice about making sure they had enough food and water, warm clothes, even toilet paper, and that how personal hygiene would become increasingly important.

Instead I was bluntly honest, treating them as intelligent people, as of course they were. They were entitled to know the facts, and that's what they got from me. I gave them the sequence of events as far as I knew them - the flash of light on impact, the shaking of the earth below them, a shockwave probably accompanied by a tsunami that would sweep their homes away with them inside. Death would be as near as damn it instant and therefore painless. And to the question - what do you and Angela intend to do? I gave our agreed answer - Head for the hills with a good bottle of wine. The students nodded. In the circumstances it didn't seem a bad idea and several made the comment: "Can we join you?"

My reply? "Why not...The more the merrier."

One piece of news that I was as pleased as punch to read was an email from a student called Mark Miller. An Australian, who had wanted to study Archaeology at South Riding University, Mark suddenly found himself over ten thousand miles from home. Fortunately for him he had managed to get aboard the last flight out of Heathrow to Sidney. His email had confirmed his safe arrival. Fortunately the email system was still in operation, but for how long?

The Government did eventually come up with one piece of advice that made complete sense - Stay put in your homes with your family - There's little point in going elsewhere. One thing it also did, to its merit, was to bring home every soldier, sailor and airman serving abroad. It was supposedly done on humanitarian grounds. They too deserved to be with their families. But many suspected that it had been done to support the police in the event of mass civil unrest.

Strangely, given the circumstances, this never materialised on any large scale. Could it be that the typical stiff upper lip of the British had come into force, with their 'we'll fight them on the beaches' attitude? Of course the incidence of petty crime went up, with looting and burglary more in evidence, but common sense quickly prevailed - what was the point of possessing twenty brand new flat screen televisions or state-of-the-art mobile phones, having previously broken into the local branch of *Currys*, if an asteroid was going to annihilate you in a few days' time?

Some decided that the only way out was to drink themselves into oblivion or to drug themselves silly. Unfortunately for them the medics decided that they were low priority, and as a result the death rate amongst such groups increased considerably. On the otherhand, the incidence of suicide fell. Did those at risk suddenly decide that they didn't want to go to a 'better world' after all, preferring to witness the end of the world on which they actually lived?

Understandably some people who lived in London decided to camp down in the Underground, a bit like they did during the blitz in WW II, not realising that when the shockwave did strike, it would probably suck theair out of the underground tunnels, and if it was accompanied by a tsunami, as it probably would be, the tunnels would fill with seawater in a matter of seconds. Coal mines and caves wouldn't offer any protection either, and for the same reasons.

There was however a positive 'spin-off' to all that was taking place, depending of course on your point of view. The nation's churches - Anglican, Methodist, Catholic, Jewish, Mormon, plus all the other minor religions, were soon bulging at the seams, as indeed were the Mosques. Praying became the most important aspect of many people's daily lives. In a country were the majority had probably turned their backs on religious belief, praying to some superior God suddenly became the answer to their problem. Maybe this was the first indication he was looking for to show that mankind was prepared to 'mend its ways'.

As the days passed one thing puzzled me beyond my comprehension. It was something that I had noticed in the weeks after I'd released details of Jemma Rogers' Dead Sea Scroll discovery and what it had revealed, on my university's website. At the time I had not only asked the museums of the world to search their collections for the unusual pieces of pot that Jesus had given out to his disciples during The Last Supper, I had also invited a response from the world's religious communities on what the Scroll had revealed.

The response had, to say the least, been pathetic. There had either been an apparent lack of belief in the story, or alternatively a resignation that 'what will be, will be', by the religious leaders of the world, especially in those countries with strong beliefs - Italy, Spain, the South American countries and on the continent of Africa.

That silence prevailed now, and the question was - Why? Did they believe that there wasn't a problem? Did they believe that if there was, it would simply go away? Or was it simply a state of utter hopelessness, where God had let them down, or would do so on the day of judgement?

Why, when a possible solution to the problem was well documented, and had been for two thousand years, weren't the religious leaders of the world asking there political masters to 'pull their fingers out, and get the problem sorted,' as the US President had bluntly put it to NASA'? But silence prevailed. Nothing but silence.

Even Geat Britain appeared to have abandoned the idea of taking the lead, which was in itself unusual, given that it still believed that it was the 'world's saviour'…But I was wrong.

***

235

Chapter Twenty Four

On the morning of *Domesday minus Thirty* (it all sounded like the title of a Bruce Willis SiFi movie), I'd journeyed to work on almost deserted roads. Most people were now staying at home, apart from those who occasionally, but usually fruitlessly trawled the supermarkets. There I discovered the strangest of emails on my works laptop. I studied the strangely styled address. I'd not seen it before, but that was not unusual. I received emails from all over the world and most had weird and wonderful addresses.

I opened it and read its contents, being immediately certain that the sender was not a regular user of the email system. It was in fact set out like a formal letter.

The email stated:

Dear Professor Robertshaw
I would like to invite you to a meeting with the Archbishop of York, Joel Logongo, and myself in order to discuss the impending collision between the Earth and an asteroid, and to look into a way of preventing the catastrophe. The meeting is to be held at Bishopthorpe Palace, York at 10.30am on Thursday 7th March.
If you are able to attend please let me know as soon as possible. In the event that you can, please bring with you all the information in your possession about Christ's Holy Square.
If the date proves to be a problem for you please suggest an alternative one and we will make the necessary arrangements.
Yours sincerely
William Colton - Archbishop of Canterbury

It was a letter from the top man in the Anglican faith. At last, I thought…Action.

After a quick phone call to Angela, informing her of the email and asking her if she would also like to accompany me, I emailed my reply to the Archbishop accepting the invitation.

It was now simply a case of gathering all the information together and waiting for the day to arrive. I had already decided to take the risk of transporting the six pieces of pot that I had in my possession, knowing full well that neither Archbishop had set eyes on a single piece, let alone handled one. What a thrill they would get, knowing that not only had the disciples handled the pieces, Jesus Christ himself had done so.

But the idea was fraught with danger. What if a piece became lost? Worse still, what if we were ambushed and robbed on our journey to York, and the robbers took the pieces? They wouldn't of course know what they were, and it would be sheer folly to try to explain to them their sacred significance and hence their value. But in the eyes of a robber everything would have a 'value' and for that reason the pieces would be taken from us, by force if necessary. Would Angela and I be prepared to risk our lives for them? I honestly didn't know. I didn't even know if the pieces had any sort of protective power. According to Jesus at his Last Supper they had, but according to the way several of their original owners had met their fate, they hadn't. So, would that protection be there for us? When all said and done, we were in possession of six pieces. Surely that meant something.

The day before we were due to make our visit to York I'd removed the six pieces of pot from the safe in my office at the university and managed to get them home without incident. It was now a case of finding a safe place for them on our journey north to York. I thought initially about the car glove compartment, but quickly realised that that was the first place any robber would look whilst ransacking the car. I thought about carefully wrapping them up and placing them in the inside pocket of my jacket. But wouldn't that be the first place a robber would look for my wallet? I'd already decided to carry the minimum amount of cash, certainly no more than fifty pounds. And since no one now accepted credit cards I decided to leave mine at home. So, the problem was - where to place the pieces of pot for maximum security?

Typical of her, Angela came up with a possible solution: "Tell you what…I'll place them inside my bra…And woe betide anyone who tries to molest me."

I'd forgotten to earlier inform you that my dear wife was a Black Belt at judo and could wrestle most men to the ground if need be, as I'd found to my cost on more than one occasion as we often sparred with each other on the garden lawn.

This sounded a brilliant idea to me. I knew, having bought her underwear on many occasions at birthdays and Christmases, that she had, dare I say, an ample bust, to be exact a 38DD, so I knew that there would be ample space to conceal the pieces, three each side. I offered to do the concealing, but withdrew the offer when she threatened to deck me.

The following morning we were both on the move early. As Angela was dressing she tried out her method for concealing the six very precious pieces of pot. First she carefully wrapped each piece in a couple of paper handkerchiefs to provide padding for the sharp corners, then she positioned then inside her bra, underneath her breasts to avoid unsightly bulges being seen from the front. After a little adjustment in front of the mirror in order to ensure as much comfort as possible we both agreed that maximum security had indeed been accomplished.

Since I always travelled better on a full stomach I decided to have some breakfast, as indeed did Angela. We hadn't much in stock, but we did have ample bread for toast and ample marmalade to spread on it. The bread had been made by Angela in her newly acquired bread machine. We'd seen it on offer in *Argos* a few days earlier. Evidently bread machines had been considered low priority by the hoarding masses, hence the good price. I wondered if it could have been a case of modern families being so brainwashed into eating white, tasteless sliced bread, that the actual use of a bread maker in the home would have been completely foreign to them. Angela had earlier stacked up on the basic ingredients, intent on having a go at making a loaf or two. The machine meant that she didn't need to do all that 'kneading'.

Alas we did not have any butter or spread to scrape on and off our newly made bread, but our supply of marmalade was considerable, Angela having passed through a 'jam making' phase that had of course also included marmalade, long before the asteroid crisis had raised its ugly head.

The car's tank was about half full, the fuel I'd managed to accumulate on my visits to my small local garage, where I had for years had all my servicing done. The old proprietor, a one man band with a couple of young apprentices was now looking after his 'regulars' as far as fuel was concerned. His ration was five litres to non-regulars, ten to regulars, twenty to special people…and I was a special person. Evidently this sort of thing had been common during the last war and had more recently been seen in television's *Dad's Army* where Jonesy the butcher gave an extra sausage to special customers, usually blonde blousy women.

And so, briefcase in my hand and priceless pieces of pot in Angela's bra, we left home at just after eight o'clock, heading for York. Within minutes we were passing through the tiny village of Burghwallis (what a regal sounding name, I thought. Did King Edward-the-Eighth ever pay a visit there with Mrs Simpson?).

At this point we had a choice of route. The quicker one would take us north on the A1 to link up with the A64, the Leeds to Scarborough trunk road, just north of the picturesque village of Aberford. This would be all dual carriageway and hence a steady speed of seventy plus miles an hour if one wasn't too worried about petrol consumption, which I definitely was. Or, we could join the A19, head north across the M62 to Selby then onto York. Both routes ended up on the York bypass where, presumably we would pick up the signposts directing us to the village of Bishopthorpe and hence the Palace.

Since the last thing I wanted was a breakdown on the faster, but more isolated motorway route, for there would probably be little traffic on it apart from the odd delivery lorry, I decided to stick to the A19 that passed through several well spaced villages where help could possibly be mustered if required.

As it happened, the road was surprisingly busy. Where everybody was going I'd no idea. Then, as we approached Selby, the reason became clear. Just on the outskirts of the town was a Farmers' Market. Evidently there were still crops in the ground that had to be raised, and the local farmers were doing just that. I was tempted to stop and try to purchase something, if only a bag of carrots or a couple of cauliflowers, but knew that parking would be impossible. Besides, I had an urgent appointment to keep.

As I drove steadily along I spotted some sort of ambulance behind me, the driver keeping his distance, with no intentions of overtaking, which was unusual for an ambulance driver. They usually drove like 'bats out of hell'. I guessed he was heading for one of the York Hospitals with a non-urgent patient. At least it indicated that the health of one individual was being catered for in these apparently hopeless times. Of course the ambulance could have been empty.

We were within a couple of hundred yards of the York Bypass when a black BMW, the driver on his own, pulled sharply in front of us and braked. Unable to pull out and overtake I had no alternative but to hurriedly stop. Instinctively I glanced in my rear view mirror to check that no vehicle was up my exhaust pipe intent on running into me. In the distance I saw that the ambulance had pulled in at the side of the road and also stopped. Why, I had no idea, nor did the driver's action concern me. There could have been a hundred-and-one reasons why he had decided to do so.

Hastily a young scruffy individual jumped out of the BMW and, brandishing a hand gun, ran back towards us. As I wound down my window in order to ask him what the hell he was doing, he shouted: "Out of the car and get your fucking hands up."

In a state of near panic I hurriedly got out and raised my hands, at the same time managing to stammer: "OK…K-keep cool…We'll do w-what you say." There was little point in arguing with a man waving a gun in your face.

Angela, however, was determined not to be intimidated. As slowly as she could she opened her door and alighted from the car, handbag in hand.

"And no trouble from you, bitch," shouted the gunman, obviously irritated by her defiant action. Little did he realise that he had made the biggest mistake of his life referring to Angela as a 'bitch'.

I looked across to her and mouthed: "Take it easy…Nothing stupid."

But my dear wife wasn't the sort to be intimidated by anyone, even one pointing a gun at her. She casually moved in front of the man, eyeballing him: "We've nothing of interest to you…Now piss off."

I cringed. What the hell was she playing at?

Not having any idea how to deal with a defiant woman, and feeling uncomfortable at the thought of having to do so, the gunman nervously shouted: "Oh, I love a bitch with attitude…Now pass your fucking handbag across…And no funny stuff."

As Angela slowly raised her hand, fingers gripping the bag, the man momentarily took his eyes off her, focussing instead on the bag. Mistake number *one* on his behalf.

What happened next took place faster than the eye could see and therefore the brain could register. Angela kicked out with her left leg, catching the barrel of the gun with the pointed toe of her shoe. The accuracy was uncanny.

More by accident than intent the gunman squeezed the trigger as the gun left his hand and shot up into the air. The bullet whistled past Angela's left ear, hit the car's windscreen making the neatest circular hole in it before embedding itself in my headrest. As the gun fell the man tried desparately to catch it. Mistake number *two* on his behalf. Angela like lightning moved forward and grabbed the man by the shoulders, pulling him towards her. Up came the knee straight into his balls. In obvious agony he bent over and grabbed himself in an effort to relieve the pain.

Mistake number *three* on his behalf. Angela again lifted her knee but this time into the man's face, and I was sure I heard the crack of breaking bone...nose, cheek or jaw. The man dropped to his knees then keeled over, hands holding his face, blood seeping through his fingers.

Angela picked up the gun and as if throwing a hand grenade tossed it yards into a field of oil seed rape bordering the road: "Come on...Let's continue our journey," she shouted as if nothing unusual had happened.

Without hesitation I climbed into the car. She did likewise, making herself comfortable and fastening her seat belt. As I started the engine she said: "Don't say a word...Not a bloody word."

I looked at her in exasperation. What had she expect me to say?...Poor bastard, you nearly killed him?...I was just about to crack him, when you beat me to it?...a bit stupid tackling a man with a gun? I immediately realised that there was nothing I could say that seemed appropriate. I therefore took her advice and kept my mouth shut, thankful that I had a wife who when it came to the martial arts had few equals.

But one thing still preyed on my mind - how lucky Angela had been. Had she leaned a fraction to the left during her flykick the bullet would have hit her in the face with fatal results. It was as if a guardian angel had been looking after her, and maybe it had. Or, had the fact that she had six pieces of Christ's Holy Square inside her bra something to do with it? I was convinced that it had.

As I accelerated away from the scene of our hold up I saw two separate sights in my rear view mirror. One was the gunman, still in obvious pain, staggering to his feet, the other the ambulance speeding past him, the driver apparently unconcerned. I couldn't help thinking - very strange. Had the Health Service broken down after all? The ambulance soon caught us up and I could see its two occupants waving to me, through my rear view mirror. Were they congratulating us, I wondered? At that point the driver dropped back and I lost him at the road junction.

As I'd predicted we did eventually pick up the signs to Bishopthorpe and it wasn't long before we found the drive leading up to the Palace itself.

Like many stately buildings the Palace had a most impressive gateway, with a clock above the archway showing exactly ten-thirty. The gap, appearing to be just wide enough to allow the car through, led us into a courtyard where we parked up to the right of a large set of stone steps that led up to the main entrance that had Gothic columns either side.

As if having been waiting for our arrival a middle aged woman dressed in a smart black trouser suit descended the steps and came across to welcome us: "Good morning...Mr and Mrs Robertshaw?...I'm Jane, one of the Archbishop's secretaries."

"Er...Yes...We have an appointment with the Archbishop at ten-thirty," I replied hesitantly, not quite knowing who I should say our appointment was with, there being in fact two Archbishops.

"Just follow me please...Both William and Joel are waiting for you in the drawing room."

I was a little taken aback at the familiar use of Christian names, but may be that's how they addressed each other here. We were about to find out.

Once through the main door we walked along an impressive entrance hall, also in the Gothic style. At the end of the hall was a closed door. The woman knocked and entered. As we passed through, she announced us, speaking directly to one of the two people present in the large well windowed drawing room: "Archbishop...Peter Robertshaw and his wife Angela."

The Archbishop, with a large grin on his face spoke quietly to us: "Welcome to Bishopthorpe Palace...I'm Joel Logongo, Archbishop of York and this is William Colton, Archbishop of Canterbury...I trust you had a good journey...Now...Tea. Coffee?...You'll no doubt have been on the road for some time."

I was about to describe the incident with the gunman, in answer to the Archbishop's assumption that we'd had a good journey, when Angela replied: "Uneventful...In fact we only saw an ambulance on the road...Good to see that the Health Service is still functioning."

"Good indeed...Such dedication in these difficult times," was the Archbishop's reply.

Such bloody dedication, indeed, I whispered to myself.

Reagrding the drinks enquiry, Angela replied on both our behalves: "Coffee, please."

The Archbishop nodded to Jane, who promptly disappeared, to reappear five minutes later with a large tray containing four mugs with something steaming inside them, plus a plate of chocolate digestive biscuits, accompanied by a stack of four side plates.

We were invited to sit down on two of the several easy chairs in the large room. As we did so I looked round the walls of the room where there were paintings of previous Archbishops of York. Angela's eyes focussed immediately on the picture of Joel Logongo's predecessor, David Hope. Her obvious interest brought a question from the present one: "Any special reason why the picture of Archbishop Hope has caught your eye?"

Angela knew full well that I had been a choirboy at Wakefield Cathedral and had attended Queen Elizabeth Gammar School in the city, but she had never revealed to me what she was prepared to reveal today about her father. In fact over the years she had revealed very little about him, other than that her relationship with him had at times been 'explosive' because of her totally independent attitude. Now, apparently prepared to show some recognition of him, she smiled: "My father went to Queen Elizabeth Grammar School with David Hope and both were in Wakefield Cathedral choir in the early nineteen fifties."

This came as a big surprise to me, but this was neither the time nor the place to have it out with her as to why she'd kept it a secret all these years.

The Archbishop smiled: "Wakefield's Grammar School and Cathedral seem to have been a breeding ground for bishops...Are you aware that Robert Hardy, a former Bishop of Lincoln also attended both also in the nineteen-fifties?...By the way, David is now a vicar up in North Yorkshire."

Angela nodded. The name Robert Hardy definitely rang a bell with her, and she did know of David Hope's move to the country because it had been well reported at the time in the *Yorkshire Post*.

As we sipped our drinks I heartily tucked into the chocolate digestives. I hadn't had one for ages, the hoarders having hoarded all of them long ago. As I did so Angela glared at me, knowing that if I wasn't curbed the whole plateful would soon disappear. She'd seen it so many times before.

At that point the Archbishop of Canterbury took over: "Could we first get rid of all the formalities. It will make our discussion far easier...Please address me as William and my colleague as Joel...We'd like to address you as Peter and Angela...All right?"

243

Both Angela and I nodded in agreement. There was no doubt that any discussion would flow more freely if we didn't have to keep repeating the word 'Archbishop', not to mention whether we were addressing York or Canterbury.

William continued: "Thank you for agreeing to see us, Peter, and at such short notice too…Joel and I have for some time been concerned at the apathy being shown throughout the country, indeed throughout the world, at the situation mankind finds itself in…Our government appears to be at a total loss as to what to do, or say…And we in the Church are reluctant to say or do anything for fear of being accused of meddling in matters that don't concern us…When we have expressed concern about the plight of the homeless, for example, we have been told in no uncertain terms to leave the problem to the relevant Department, and not 'rock the boat' by criticising the role of Government…Far too often we have been told to keep our nose out of Politics…In the past we have stated our views openly and been criticised for it…Issues such as the institute of marriage, teenage pregnancies, abortion and more recently so-called mercy killing, spring to mind…Far too often, and may I say to our shame, we have tended to sit on the fence when controversial issues were being discussed…Anyway, enough of me trying to justify our guilt…Please tell me all you know about Christ's Holy Square, the threat made by God and how you see the way forward to prevent the annihilation of the World as we know it."

I initially gasped at the enormity of what William had said, and the task in front of me. I could tell by the way he'd spoken, in many ways with a tone expressing a feeling of total helplessness, that he expected me to have some answers. For a second I felt deep-down annoyance - why wasn't the Astronomer Royal here, the Head of the Military, even the bloody Prime Minister himself? Why was it all being left to a humble Professor of Archaeology at what could only be described as one of the country's minor universities?

But the Head of the Church of England and his Deputy (if indeed the Archbishop of York could be described as a 'Deputy'), had asked to see me personally, and here I was seated in front of both of them. It had to be a privilege. And indeed it was.

I was about to start when William intervened, stressing the importance of the media - press, radio, TV and of course the Internet, not getting wind of our meeting. It would indicate that we were acting unilaterally, and the Government would again feel that we were interfering in a problem that was basically theirs, although of course it wasn't.

I commenced by telling my story, starting at the very beginning, when I received a call from John Pemberton, Head of Cultural Affairs at Doncaster Council, informing me of the discovery of a well preserved Roman soldier on his horse, in boggy ground on the banks of the River Don. This immediately led me to the discovery of three of the pieces of pot that Jesus had given out to his disciples at the Last Supper.

"Where exactly were the pieces positioned," asked Joel, leaning forward in his chair, obviously curious to know.

"Maybe as one would expect, one of the pieces, in fact the one that Jesus had originally kept for himself, was attached to a thin black leather thong and positioned round the soldier's neck, just underneath his metal breastplate...But strangely the other two pieces were found on either side of the horse's neck, attached to the bridle...Maybe the soldier looked upon them as lucky charms that would protect his horse in battle...But this is pure speculation."

Joel then asked the question that I knew was coming: "Have you brought the three pieces with you?"

I hesitated, not quite knowing how to reply. Angela spotted this and did so on my behalf: "Er...they're here, Joel, inside my bra..." She pointed with the index fingers of both hands at her chest: "In the circumstances we felt that it was the most secure place to hide them...We didn't want to lose them in some sort of hijack on the way here."

Joel couldn't help letting out a little titter. As he admitted, he'd heard that prostitutes often stuffed bank notes down their bras for safe keeping. Here was another example of their versatile use.

Angela then added: "May I suggest that when Peter has finished telling you his story I nip to the toilet, extract the pieces we have in our possession and show them to you."

Both William and Joel nodded enthusiastically, agreeing with her suggestion.

Before saying another word I opened my briefcase and extracted a large buff unsealed envelope. I turned it upside down allowing a square of card, made up of thirteen individual pieces of card cellotaped together, to fall onto the coffee table in front of me. Each piece, except one, was coloured. All had a special shape and all but one had a Greek letter written onto it. The central piece had two letters.

I then pointed to the three pieces that represented the three found in the Doncaster bog, at the same time stressing that the pieces of card were correct in size, shape, colour and the Greek identifying letter. This I placed on the coffee table in front of the two archbishops, pointing out that I was almost a hundred percent certain that the arrangement of all thirteen pieces wihin the Square was correct. Finally I expressed how I had originally thought that the three pieces may have been part of some sort of Greek children's spelling game, where pieces could have been laid in a row spelling out a word...a bit like a word in 'scrabble'.

This led me nicely onto our second discovery, or more correctly Jemma and Jamie Rogers' discovery inside a cave close by the Dead Sea in Israel. After briefly describing how the discovery had been made I pulled out the transcript of the relevant section of the Scroll and read it out to William and Joel, finally adding: "And this was the point when I realised that the three pieces of pot found in a Doncaster bog had in fact been given out by Jesus to his disciples at the Last Supper, and that one of the pieces had actually belonged to Jesus himself."

"Was there any way of dating the three pieces of pot in your possession?" asked William, no doubt looking for evidence that they and the pieces mentioned in the Dead Sea Scroll could in fact be the same pieces.

I had to be honest: "No, but we were able to carbon date the soldier, his clothes and his horse...These were two thousand years old, give of take fifty years, in fact round about the time Jesus was living and dying in the Holy Land...We also managed to prove, using a complex high tech method that I won't go into, that the clay used to make the pieces of pot had been extracted from deposits very close to Jerusalem, deposits that haven't been worked for five hundred years...It's not conclusive evidence, but it does at least indicate that the pieces are very old and came from the Holy Land, not elsewhere in the Roman Empire."

William nodded, accepting my answer.

Wanting to move my story on I then mentioned how placing the transcript of the Dead Sea Scroll and details of the three pieces of pot that I had in my possession, on my university's website had led almost immediately to responses from two museums in Israel, to the effect that they had three similar pieces of pot on display there. They too had described them as possibly part of some children's game. And this had been followed by a phone call from Tehran, informing me that its museum also had a similar piece. As I spoke I pointed to the four new pieces.

"So, Peter, you now had three of the pieces in your possession and knew the possible location of four more?" This came from Joel, wanting to confirm that at that point in my story seven of the thirteen pieces had in fact been discovered.

I nodded, but had to add: "Of course we were unable to carry out tests on the clays used to make these pieces, but their shape, dimensions,colour and Greek identifying letter led me to believe that they were in fact part of the thirteen-piece set."

"Ah...I can see now how the Holy Square is building up...Very clever." Joel obviously appreciated the amount of thought that Jesus had put into the puzzle, for that's what it was...a puzzle.

"Please continue, Peter...I'm finding the story most fascinating and cannot wait for the next instalment." William was now perched eagerly on the edge of his chair.

I did so: "Right, now...The next two pieces found their way into my possession in very similar ways...One of my colleagues at the university, in fact my second-in-command, named Rhoda, went on holiday to Israel in order to visit her grandma who, as a young child, had managed to escape with her parents to England just before the Nazis invaded her homeland of Poland in nineteen thirty-nine...Anyway, Rhoda was browsing in a Tel Aviv market one day when she spotted on a stand of old jewellery a yellow coloured triangular piece of pot hanging from what looked like a thin gold chain...It particularly caught her eye because of the Greek letter engraved into it, rho, ρ,...She didn't particularly like her Christian name, preferring to be simply known as Rho...In fact she signed all her letters and documents with the single Greek letter...After a little bartering she managed to buy it for a few shekels, having a sneaking suspicion what it could be...Tests later showed that the clay used was identical in composition to the three pieces already in my possession."

"What a lucky find," commented Joel, further adding: "And after two thousand years as well."

"Lucky indeed," I replied, at the same time pointing out the eighth piece on the constructed, cellotaped Square.

Both William and Joel gazed at the pieces and I could sense that they were itching to get their hands on the real thing...But they had to wait a little longer.

I was about to continue my story, when Joel unexpectedly chipped in:

"Time for a coffee break, I think...I'm sure, Peter, you are thirsty with all this talking."

He was right, too. I was gagging for a drink and the sustenance of a chocolate digestive. Jane was at hand, and in no time at all we were all sitting there, sipping our steaming coffee, and in my case tucking into my fifth chocolate digestive. I could tell by Angela's glare of disapproval that she was annoyed at my greed in the austere conditions. The word 'pig' would have undoubtedly been shouted in my direction had we been at home.

I was about to resume my story when Angela asked where the toilets were. Jane, who was at the time collecting the empty coffee mugs, offered to show her the way, and both disappeared.

I took a deep breath and recommenced my story: "As I said earlier, two of the pieces were found in almost identical ways...Jemma Rogers, the young girl who, with her brother, had found the Dead Sea Scroll, had been visiting one of Jerusalem's holy sites when a young Arab boy, selling post cards spotted her Walt Disney wristwatch, and had set his heart on it...At first he only wanted to do a straight swop for some post cards, but Jemma spotted a strangely shaped piece of pot on a thin loop of black leather around his neck and indicated that she wanted it in return for the watch...Eventually the attraction of the watch was too strong for the boy, and they did a deal..."

Joel couldn't help repeating himself: "Talk about luck."

"Luck indeed," I replied. I then finished off this episode in my story: "Jemma stuck it in a bedroom drawer when she got home and forgot all about it...Some months later, while her mother was cleaning her bedroom, she stumbled on the piece...Of course she knew immediately what it was...Or could be, for she was obviously familiar with the Dead Sea Scroll story." I pointed to the relevant piece of card, cellotaped to the others, the ninth we knew the whereabouts of.

I was about to press on when Angela returned to the room. A quick wink told me that she had managed to extract, painlessly I hoped, the six pieces of pot from her bra. A discrete tap on the side of her handbag also told me that they were safely in there.

Before I could commence my last 'lap' Joel pointed first to the right hand side of my card Square then to the left: "So, one side of the Square is a mirror image of the other?...Jesus Christ must have given considerable thought to his choice of letters to achieve this."

I replied, correcting him on his first observation and totally agreeing with him on his second: "Well, not quite a mirror image because the letters aren't reversed...We always think of Jesus as a simple carpenter, but he was a well educated young man."

As Joel nodded in agreement Angela glared at me and whispered: "Don't be so petty."

After a shrug of the shoulders I glanced at my watch. The time was already twelve-thirty. I had been talking for all of two hours, but there was still much to tell, so I needed to press on: "My next stroke of luck came in the form of a phone call in the early hours of the morning from, would you believe it, America...To cut a long story short a certain Mrs Makepeace, holidaying in Italy, visited Venice...As she watched one of the canals being dredged by a mechanical digger she spotted in the sediment a strange shape, possibly part of a shattered piece of pottery...Closer examination revealed a blue triangular piece of pot that she wiped clean and placed in her pocket...And would you believe it, it was one of the thirteen...Its colour, shape, exact dimensions and an identifying Greek letter all indicated its authenticity...But just to check I asked her to take the piece to her local university chemistry department, which she did...The clay analysis was forwarded to me and I compared it with those from the five pieces already in my possession...They were identical." I then pointed to the tenth piece of card, already cellotaped into its position.

I was almost there: "We next got two pieces for the price of one, so to speak...The two were found together by children on the small Greek island of Andros...They too were thought to have been parts of a children's spelling game...In fact the children's teacher made similar pieces out in wood at the same time painting them so that they could be placed together in a line to form words, a bit like a line of dominoes...An Inspector with an interest in archaeology paid the school a visit, recognised the pieces for what they were and contacted the museum in Athens...The curator passed on the information to me...Tests on the clay revealed it to be identical to the other pieces." I pointed out to Joel and William the two pieces of card in the Square that represented these two pieces of pot.

There was now only one piece of card cellotaped in position that I had not so far referred to. It was triangular in shape, brown in colour and had the Greek letter o engraved into it. I paused to see if either Joel or William would remember and comment accordingly.

I wasn't disappointed. Joel studied the Square, pointed at the piece and smiled: "So, Peter…Where was the last piece found?…And let me guess…Did it belong to Judas Iscariot?"

"Got it in one, Joel…And it did belong to you-know-who…And would you believe it, we found it here, in England…In fact not many miles from where we are sitting." I then proceeded to describe our find in Ribbleswell Church graveyard. Joel immediately chipped in: " I remember it…I was in fact consulted on the possible implications if the remains of individual graves were re-interred in a communal grave…As far as I could see there weren't any, and I understand the re-interment went ahead."

I nodded to him: "If you've a spare day in your busy schedule perhaps you could pay the church a visit and see the tasteful way it has been done." I then wished I'd said nothing, Such a visit would surely be of low priority when the fate of the World was at stake.

As a final act I pointed to the piece of card within the Square which represented Judas Iscariot's piece of pot. I breathed a sigh of relief and followed it with a final statement: "So there you have it…I and now you know where all thirteen pieces of pot making up Christ's Holy Square are located…The serious bit comes next…What do we do with the knowledge?"

To my utter surprise both William and Joel started to applaud to show their obvious appreciation. I wasn't one to be embarrassed easily having worked for several years with students who were in the habit of speaking their own minds and questioning my opinions. But on this occasion I held my hands up appealingly. It was all too much. Later, Angela informed me that my cheeks had taken on the colour of beetroot. Although probably an exaggeration it proved to me that embarrassment was definitely part of my makeup.

At that point I had a thought. What did the two archbishops think to the 'Holy Grail' stories? I decided to sound them out: "You've both no doubt heard of the Holy Grail…Do you believe there is or was such a thing?"

William answered first, but only briefly: "I personally doubt it…But it makes a good story."

Joel added a little more: "The weakness in the story is that no one can agree what exactly it is, or was…Some say a chalice, possibly of silver, used by Christ at the Last Supper to hold the wine that he said represented his blood…Others say some sort of manuscript, maybe similar to one of the Dead Sea Scrolls…Some even suggest it refers to the womb of the Virgin Mary…Like William I have my doubts about all the versions."

In I plunged: "What about it referring to Christ's Holy Square?…Most people now accept that such an object was present at the Last Supper, and that Jesus took pieces of pot from it and gave them to his disciples…Was the Square in fact the Holy Grail?…To me its claim is stronger than all the others."

Both shrugged their shoulders, preferrng not to agree or disagree with my very personal theory.

This was the time to show William and Joel the six pieces of pot that were in our possession. Responding to my nod Angela opened here bag and eased out six folded paper hankies with the pieces inside. As she did so she carefully placed each one on the coffee table in front of her. I in turn unfolded the hankies to reveal each piece in turn. As I gently placed the piece on the table I gave additional information regarding the piece's original owner. Quite intentionally, Angela kept Jesus's white hexagonal piece, the largest, until the last. This allowed me to describe its owner as someone very special indeed.

Both William and Joel handled the pieces with the utmost care and reverence, no doubt thinking that they were fragile items that would break in half if the slightest pressure was applied. It was easy to forget that all thirteen pieces had survived intact for two thousand years. It was unlikely that they were now going to crack when being ever-so-carefully handled.

Their reaction to having the hexagonal piece that had belonged to Jesus himself, in the palm of their hands, was particularly interesting. Both in turn closed their fingers around the piece, at the same time closing their eyes and, I assumed, silently saying a prayer. They then opened their fingers and kissed the piece. For the first time in their lives, and possibly the last, they would handle something tangible that had belonged to the very person who had been the founder member (apart from God himself) of a belief that had dominated their day-to-day existence for most of their lives. They were very privileged…and I think they realised it.

After this brief ceremony, if indeed that was an appropriate description of what had just taken place, I carefully collected up the six pieces. As I passed then one at a time to Angela she carefully wrapped them up before placing them back in her hand bag. Later she would return them to the security of her bra before we commenced our journey home.

At that point I thought I'd finished my long account of how I'd managed to locate all thirteen pieces of Christ's Holy Square, but William's final question showed me that I had missed out a vital section, maybe the most vital one of all: "What I can't work out is why Jesus engraved each piece with a Greek letter…If he'd given an alpha piece to his favourite disciple, possibly Peter, and an omega piece to Judas who later betrayed him, I could have understood it…Or used alpha and omega, meaning the beginning and the end, on his own piece, I could have understood that too…But the letters seem to have been chosen and given out at random…Have you any ideas about this?"

I realised that after two hours of talking I hadn't referred to the choice of letters at all. It was essential that I did so now: "I realised too that surely Jesus hadn't chosen the letters at random so, once I had all fourteen I asked a colleague, an expert in Ancient Greek, to look at the list…He managed to re-arrange the letters and came up with two words that when translated into English spelled out - rock from heaven - that I interpreted as meaning an asteroid impact…And it looks as if that is about to take place, unless we can do something to prevent it…The reason why we are here today discussing the issue is to hopefully do precisely that."

William smiled: "So, the answer to my question came down to the method a crossworder would use to solve an anagram?…It's hard to imagine that Jesus was familiar with anagrams, but he obviously was."

I glanced at Angela before replying, remembering how she had pointed out that anagrams are different words or expressions with the same letters: "Not strictly an anagram, in the true meaning of the word, but you're on the right lines."

William again smiled: "It's all a bit too complicated for me."

Angela shook her head in disgust at my pettiness.

Just as I was about to begin my second phase, one that both Angela and I had given considerable thought to, knowing that William and Joel would ask us how we saw the way ahead, Joel suggested that we broke for lunch. It was then that I realised that our get-together with the two most powerful men in the Anglical Church would take up a full day.

During an excellent, though traditional, lunch of cucumber sandwiches, followed by homemade, or was it palace-made apple pie, washed down with a strong cup of Yorkshire tea, Joel explained how his staff regularly combed all the food outlets they knew of, sometimes travelling several miles down to Selby Farmers' market, in order to keep the household going, in just the same way all households were having to do.

It was now our turn to applaud him, or rather his staff, for doing such a good job, and treating us as special people, which we didn't think we were.

***

Chapter Twenty Five

It was now time to get down to the nitty-gritty of the whole problem. William immediately got the ball rolling with a simple question that had the most complicated of answers: "So, Peter, where do we go from here?"

I replied as honestly as I could: "Well...The answer to your question is simple, but implementing it will be nigh impossible...Let me put it this way...In just thirty days' time the Earth will be struck by an asteroid roughly the shape of a rugby ball, 60 kilometres in length and 44 kilometres in diameter, travelling at about twenty-five thousand miles an hour...That's about seven miles a second...The resulting explosion will be beyond the comprehension of man...I can give you the size in megatons of TNT if you like, but the figure is meaningless."

He nodded in agreement. What would a number with tens of noughts mean to a man-of-the-cloth? Nothing.

I pressed on: "Initially there will be a blinding flash of light as the outer layers of the asteroid burn up in our atmosphere...The flash will be seen round the world turning night into day...Then will follow a shockwave,accompanied by a tsunami, because the impact is predicted to take place in the North Atlantic,south-west of the Azores...These will kill most living things in their path...Any living thing that manages to survive will then be faced with the onset of what scientists have called a 'nuclear winter', produced by the sun's heat and light being blocked out by dust that had been blasted into the atmosphere...The Earth will in effect become a giant snowball in space."

"Ah...The extinction of the dinosaurs...You paint a ghastly picture, Peter...Now tell me how we prevent this happening." Of course William knew the answer to his question already, as did I, but how could the answer be implemented?

I kept my own version as simple as I could: "ONE - A place acceptable to all the leaders of the World has to be chosen where the re-assembly of Christ's Holy Square can take place...Jerusalem is probably the obvious place since the original prediction that God would destroy the World if man didn't mend his ways, was made there...But sadly, in the present political climate in the Middle East, I don't think the Holy city would be acceptable...The Vatican could be a possibility, even here in Westminster Abbey...But for me the place should be the United Nations Headquarters in New York."

William first smiled and I wondered if my mention of Westminster Abbey had a certain appeal to him. He then spoke: "I agree, but this can only be done through diplomatic channels...The church couldn't have any influence in that decision...It would be up to the UN Secretary General to get the consensus that would be required."

I nodded in agreement: "And this is where our Prime Minister will need to get involved...Now...TWO - Assuming that UN Headquarters is chosen, a date has to be agreed when the re-assembly of the Square will take place...This date must allow for any last minute hiccups that could jeopardise the whole plan...I would suggest a minimum of ten days before the asteroid is due to hit the Earth, that we know will be on the 6th of April, unless it again changes course...That would make the date the 27th March, in twenty days' time...THREE - I would then see my role as twofold...To get myself to New York with my six pieces of the Square, and to contact my friends at the museums in Jerusalem, Tel Aviv, Tehran and Athens, asking them to also get the pieces in their possession, six in total, to New York by the agreed date."

Joel, taking it all in, spotted that my answer was incomplete: "But that only gives twelve pieces...There are thirteen."

"Ah...Sorry, Joel...As I said earlier the thirteenth piece is already in America, only a stone's throw away in comparison to my six pieces...I would of course contact Mrs Makepeace and assume that she would get her piece to New York by the agreed time...If I get all-round cooperation from my contacts all thirteen pieces of the Square will be in New York ready to be placed in the wooden frame that I have already constructed to take them...I know the exact dimensions of all thirteen pieces and have made the Square to accept them."

"Do you see travel as a problem?...The airlines must be in a chaotic state at the moment." Joel had pointed out an obvious problem, to which I didn't fully know the answer...But I did have a sort of one.

"I would hope, given the seriousness of the situation, that each country's airforce, assuming it has one, would provide the necessary transport if civil aviation wasn't available...I would certainly expect the RAF to get me to New York in the event of BA or Virgin not being able to do so...In fact I rather fancy a trip across the Atlantic in a Tornado."

Angela glared at me for being so flippant.

William had sat quietly, presumably taking in all that I'd said. He then asked a question that, quite honestly, I hadn't thought of, assuming my role to simply get all thirteen piece of pot to the 'assembly' point: "You've obviously given this a lot of thought...How do you see our role?"

I had to think fast, wanting to give the impression that I had at least considered his question. Angela, knowing how to interpret my facial expressions after years of practice, was aware that I was struggling for an answer.

Quick as a flash she came to my aid: "Funny you should ask that question, William...Peter and I discussed it on our way here...Perhaps you, Joel, could contact the Prime Minister as a matter of urgency and put him in the picture about this meeting...Hopefully he will agree that the UN Headquarters is indeed the place where the re-assembly of Christ's Holy Square should take place...He will obviously know how representations to the UN Secretary General are made, possibly through our Ambassador...It would also make sense for him to contact the US President, not only as a matter of courtesy, but also to put pressure on Israel if it refuses to release the three pieces in its possession...Hopefully Turkey would be able to negotiate with Iran if it proved to be a stumbling block...It goes without saying that the PM is made to appreciate that time is of the essence...That could be your task, Joel."

Angela's intervention had given me time to think about William's role. I came up with one, but wasn't sure how important it was: "Do you think, William, that it would be a good idea, maybe indeed essential, to contact the Pope about our meeting?...As I see it, this is principally a Christian problem, and appears to have a Christian solution, even though it is obviously going to involve all the non-Christians of the World, of which as you know there are very many...Above all I feel it is essential that you as representative of the Anglican Church and the Pope as representative of the Catholic Church put forward a united front and are in fact present when the Square is re-assembled."

William nodded in apparent agreement, then, fully aware that the problem would not require any sort of solution from us, nevertheless asked an interesting question - one that would have to be answered by someone, and soon: "How would you go about choosing the thirteen World leaders who would be asked to place a piece of pot in the Square?...I'm just curious."

Now this was a question that Angela and I had given a lot of thought to back at home, even though we knew full well that we would not be in any way involved in the process, thank God: "Well now...First and foremost it cannot be a religious decision, but a political one...I looked it up - the United Nations has a hundred and ninety-three member countries at the moment, all recognised sovereign states...There are five permanent members of the Security Council - America, Russia, China, France and of course the United Kingdom...One would assume that those five would be part of the thirteen...The question is - how do you choose the remaining eight?...Not easy."

William smiled: "Not easy indeed...So how would *you* make the selection, Peter?...You must have thought about it."

I had: "Well...Drawing names out of a hat is one possibility, but what if Japan missed out but Angola didn't, no disrespect to Angola...Would we be happy with that?...Surely God would be looking for leaders whose countries have real influence in the World...I would now look at the six continental areas and choose a country from each, except Europe which would already be represented by Russia, France and the UK...From North America, along with the USA, I would also choose Canada; South America, I would chose Brazil; Asia, along with China, I would also choose Japan; Africa, South Africa; Australasia, Australia...This would give ten countries in total...We now need three more to make up the thirteen...I suppose that these could be drawn out of a hat, but I'd personally choose another South American country -Argentina; another African country - Kenya; and another Asian country - India...That's how I would choose my thirteen countries, knowing full well that there would be opposition from many quarters...But it's one of those situations where you just can't win."

"Well...Your method seems as good as any to me...But it will be interesting to see how the thirteen are eventually chosen, assuming of course that we get that far." William looked at his watch: "Goodness me it's almost four o'clock...I'm sure that you and Angela would like to be on your way while it's still daylight...Joel, can you organise a cup of tea for our guests before they commence their journey?... And perhaps you'd like to show them your splendid chapel...I believe it's the highlight when people are shown round the Palace."

After we'd drunk our tea and I had consumed yet another two chocolate digestives, Joel moved towards the door, indicating that Angela and I should follow him. But she intentionally excused herself: "Must pop to the toilet before we set off." At the same time she winked at me. It was her way of telling me that she was about to return the pieces of pot to the safety of her bra.

Joel first showed me the Great Hall, used for conferences. Its long central table seemed to go on forever. Evidently it had been made out of one long length of tree trunk. Its walls were also used to display paintings of past Archbishops of York. The Chapel was most impressive, with its stain glass windows and large wood wall panels, evidently carved by a Bavarian carpenter. Finally he took me outside and onto the river bank. Here he pointed to a mark quite high up on the wall: "As you are no doubt aware, Peter...The River Ouse regularly floods...This mark shows the highest it's been...No doubt it did considerable damage at the time."

I was tempted to point out that if the asteroid struck, the tsunami produced would rush across the Plain of York and Bishopthorpe palace would end up being hundreds of feet under water, but resisted.

As we returned to the entrance hall there was Angela, waiting with my brief case in hand. Both Joe and William thanked us for putting them well and truly in the picture about the situation as we saw it, including how we saw the way ahead, a way that had to be followed if the total annihilation of the World had to be prevented. I knew that I would now have a frustrating wait, for I couldn't take unilateral action. I was one small cog in a huge machine that had just started turning, albeit very slowly. Time was indeed of the essence.

That evening, as Angela and I were watching the BBC News at Ten, a bulletin caught our immediate attention, and what we saw and heard both surprised and worried us. It was dark and the reporter, fully illuminated and standing in front of the Gateway at Bishopthorpe Palace with a large furry microphone nearly stuck up his nose, was giving his report:

It has been revealed within the last hour that throughout today a meeting has been taking place between Professor Peter Robertshaw, a leading expert on the asteroid that is predicted to hit the Earth in thirty days' time, supposedly guided by God, and the Archbishops of Canterbury and York in the building just behind me, which is Bishopthorpe Palace, the residence of the Archbishop of York. What was discussed is not yet known, but already members of the country's Security Service have on the instructions of Downing Street, been in touch with both Archbishops and Professor Robertshaw in order to ascertain what the meeting was about. We have heard that in view of the uncertain situation the Prime Minister has asked to be kept informed. Meanwhile the asteroid is still heading for the Earth.

At that point the picture was changed to a spectacular shot of Halley's comet. The fact that the threat was from an asteroid and not a comet didn't matter to the News producers. They wanted maximum impact. Besides, who, apart from those with an interest in the subject, would know the difference anyway...And did it really matter?

The report was of course inaccurate as far as we were concerned because no one had been in contact with us. That was about to change.

As I started to flick channels and Angela moved to the kitchen in order to make us both a warm drink, the doorbell rang. Half expecting one of my students to be stood on my doorstep with some 'despairing' tale, I opened the door. To my surprise two middle aged men stood there. One immediately spoke in a quiet, friendly voice: "Good evening, Professor Robertshaw...Sorry to bother you at this late hour...My name's John Seymour and this in Robert Shields...We're both members of the Security Service...Do you mind if we come in, rather than hold a conversation on the door step?"

At that point he waved some sort of Identity Card in front of me, but the print was too small to read, although the photograph did appear to match his face. As he placed the card back in his pocket, an almost undetectable smile spread across my face. Had someone asked me how I would have expected members of the Security Service to look, jokingly I'd have said - wearing long dirty raincoats and trilby hats - and yet here were two in front of me dressed just like that. It was just like a shot from John le Carre''s *Tinker Taylor Soldier Spy.*

Having a good idea what they wanted, and with absolutely nothing to hide, I invited them in. As I showed them into the lounge he continued: "Again, sorry to bother you at this late hour, but may my colleague and I have a word with you and your wife?...It's about your meeting with the Archbishops of Canterbury and York earlier today."

At least we'd been forewarned that such an intrusion was imminent.

As they sat down Angela entered the lounge with our drinks, placing them on a couple of coasters on the coffee table. She looked suspiciously at the two men then glared at me 'why did you let them in?' written all over her face. I simply shrugged my shoulders. After asking the two men if they too would like a drink she disappeared into the kitchen.

As I said - with absolutely nothing to hide and wanting to get rid of them as quickly as possible I decided to give them a full, unabridged account of our earlier meeting with the Archbishops. The only thing I didn't do was show them the six pieces of pot that I had in my possession. They were already in my safe and I had no intentions of getting them out, certainly not without a search warrant. As it happened they didn't appear to be sufficiently interested in them to demand a viewing.

As the two were about to leave, apparently satisfied at what they'd heard, I felt the desire to know how the Security Services had 'got onto us'…So I asked.

The one who appeared to be the senior of the two, smiled: "You've been under surveillance ever since the day the asteroid changed its course and started heading for the Earth…You must appreciate that being in such an important, even powerful position, as you obviously are, we felt that it was important to keep an eye on your movements…We also felt that with your knowledge, and the fact that you were in possession of six of the thirteen pieces of pot, you were at risk from terrorist organisations, with your kidnapping being a real possibility…You were followed up to York…I won't say how…And when it was discovered who you were visiting, the reason immediately became of interest to us…By the way, as you are probably already aware, since there's been a report on it on the national news, both Archbishops have been spoken to by our colleagues…The Prime Minister has asked to be kept informed, and he will be briefed first thing in the morning."

Both men rose, again apologised for disturbing us at the late hour and thanked us for our cooperation. They then made their way to the entrance hall and I let them through the front door. As I closed it I breathed a sigh of relief. Thank God such a visit didn't take place on a regular basis.

Minds still active and with no desire to go to bed Angela and I got to thinking about our journey up to York. How were we followed up there? Then I remembered. As I'd picked up the A19 just outside the village of Burghwallis I had spotted one of those large, square and colourful paramedic ambulances, in my rear view mirror. I thought nothing of it at the time. Why should I? Why shouldn't an emergency vehicle be on the road, maybe taking a patient up to a hospital at York? In fact our journey was interesting, even comical. When we came to a rise in the road the ambulance dropped well behind us, at times disappearing completely. Later, on a downward section of the road, it would speed past us, the driver and his colleague giving us a wave as it did so. It was almost like a game of cat-and-mouse.

Then we came to the incident with the gunman. At exactly the same time as he'd stopped us, the ambulance driver, having obviously seen what was happening, had pulled in at the side of the road not wanting to get in any way involved.

Later, as we'd left the A64 and taken the winding road to Bishopthorpe I'd lost sight of the ambulance altogether and assumed it had gone on to York. In fact throughout the journey I'd been glad that it had been there. Hopefully, had we had a breakdown, or worse still an accident due, say, to a blow-out, the driver and his colleague would have been there to offer assistance.

Now I realised that *they* had been the ones keeping us under surveillance. Had they somehow become involved during our gunman incident their cover could have been blown. And had they stopped to assist him they'd have lost all contact with us. No doubt they'd followed us to Bishopthorpe Palace itself, observed that we'd stayed there all day, and reported back to Headquarters, probably by the ambulance's radio or some sophisticated communication equipment. It all seemed a bit James Bondish to me, but nevertheless very clever. And had they also accompanied us on the return journey home? I'd no idea. Maybe they'd thought it unnecessary, but in the event of them having done so, I had not spotted them.

But maybe not clever enough, or rather not secure enough, for when the *Sun*, the nation's leading tabloid newspaper made its appearance the following morning on the news stands and on people's hall carpets having been pushed through their letterboxes, the headline stated:

Archbishops' Asteroid Quest

It appeared that either the contents of the radio message had somehow been intercepted and sent to the newspaper by someone wanting to make a quick buck, or there had been a leak within the Security Service itself. One thing was certain...the leaked information had not come from Angela and I, and I doubted that the two archbishops had been responsible. What about the crew of the ambulance? I suppose there was a possibility.

The headline, accompanied by a full page photograph of Bishopthorpe Palace, was followed by a detailed report of my meeting with the two archbishops. It then went on to give a detailed account of how I'd pursued my quest to locate the thirteen pieces of pot that Jesus had given out to his disciples during the Last Supper, and that would now need to be assembled together in the form of a Star of David by the most powerful leaders in the World in order to persuade God not to destroy the planet.

The reporter had certainly done his research, for he'd included in his article the fact that a woman who lived in an American town that shared the same name as a well-known Yorkshire city, had one of the thirteen pieces, and that another had been found in a Dales churchyard, the chance result of Yorkshire Water digging a trench to lay a new supply pipe.

As I read through the article I felt both annoyance and elation - annoyance at the intrusion into my and my wife's personal lives, elation at the publicity that I and hence my university were getting. Mind you, if God did indeed destroy the World, then it would all count for nothing. My task was to make sure that didn't happen.

This one article had the desired effect in that it prompted the Government into action. To date it had seemed impotent, although no doubt 'things' were going on behind the scenes. That evening the Prime Minister addressed the nation on the five main TV channels, all at the same time, intended on persuading those watching not to flick channels as always happened when a party political broadcast came on. I wondered at the time if *Sky* had been consulted about its cooperation. The fact that it continued to follow its schedule indicated that either it had not, or had but decided not to cooperate.

He commenced his address with a 'no punches pulled' account of what was predicted to happen to the Earth on the 6th of April when an asteroid would collide with it. He bluntly stated that all life on Earth would come to an end, although the timescale was unpredictable. (He could have perhaps mentioned that maybe some primitive insects and bacteria would probably survive, but what would have been the point?)

But - there was a way out for mankind, and the meeting between the Archbishops of Canterbury and York, and an archaeologist named Peter Robertshaw had taken place, as stated in the press, in order to plan the way ahead. The PM then assured the nation that he had already been in touch with both Archbishops, and as a result he would be crossing the Atlantic to first see the President of the United States, then the Secretary General of the United Nations to 'get the ball rolling', as he put it.

Meanwhile we had to be optimistic that the predicted catastrophe could and would be avoided. It was therefore in all our interests to get back to normal life as quickly as possible. There was nothing to be gained by simply idling our time away at home, feeling sorry for ourselves. It was now a time for optimism - things were on the move. Let's get some order in our lives again - transport back on line, children back at school, our supermarket shelves again bulging at the seams with products we desire. He finally ended his address with - Trust us...We have the problem in hand.

Maybe it had all been a bit optimistic, but it had the desired effect. The following morning the TV News had reporters and cameras out on the ground reporting that bus and train drivers had already reported for their early morning shift, tankers were streaming out of the oil refineries and delivery wagons were already cluttering up the high streets of our towns and cities. Even the schools were reporting near full attendance, pupils wanting to get the latest gossip from their mates - texts and emails were all very well, but there was nothing to beat the hustle and bustle of the playground. Suddenly there was a feeling of optimism in the air. Even the sun shone to greet the new day.

As I watched it all unfolding on the TV in my office at the university I looked upwards, at the same time whispering to myself: "Please God, we are trying our best to meet your conditions...Help us."

***

Chapter Twenty Six

Suddenly, as if it had all been predetermined, the world sprang into life to preserve itself. It was like a huge machine, full of cog wheels that would rotate at different speeds when the machine was switched on. The simplest example I could think of was a wind-up clock, where the cog controlled by the balance wheel moved quickly and the cog attached to the spring moved so slowly that the eye couldn't detect it. And all this appeared to kick off as a result of my meeting with two archbishops.

The first cog sprang into motion when the Prime Minister left for America the following day, arrangements having already been made for him to see both the US President at the White House and the UN Secretary General in New York. With him was the Foreign Secretary whose PPS had a transcript of my meeting with the two archbishops that I'd been asked to hastily produce. This had required Angela and I to work through the night in order to produce the document. Her contribution had been essential to ensure that nothing was missed. With little to lose by doing so, I included details of how I would choose the thirteen leaders who would place a small piece of coloured pot into a wooden frame to build up Christ's Holy Square. I wasn't optimistic that even part of my method would be used, apart from possibly the inclusion of the five permanent members of the Security Council. I included it to show the possible thinking of a layman with no political axe to grind. The full transcript had then been emailed to an address that I had already been given for that specific purpose.

Within a matter of days of all this activity, in New York the second cog started to rotate. The Secretary General of the United Nations, having first taken advice from his closest confidants, had not only deciding that the General Assembly Hall would be the venue for the re-assembly of Christ's Holy Square, but that it would take place at 12.00 hours on the 27th of March. This would be ten days before the 6th of April, the predicted date when the collision between the Earth and the asteroid would take place.

The venue and date were immediately transmitted round the World by the media and were widely reported on the internet. It was essential that the world's population were in no doubt as to the seriousness of the situation, and that there was a 'way out' that would require maximum cooperation from all the national Governments of the world.

I knew that the third cog had started to rotate when a week later it was widely reported in the UK media that the two archbishops had left for Italy on a prearranged meeting with the Pope at the Vatican. I wondered when I heard the news what contribution the three of them could make, since the majority of the World's population did not follow the Christian faith. But there again it was a Christian problem - it had to be if God and his Son Jesus Christ were involved in the solution. And although it would have been the height of arrogance to think that it was possible to read the mind of the Almighty, surely he would expect the Heads of the Anglican and Catholic Churches to be present at the re-assembly of the Square. This would ensure that the Leaders of the World were sincere in their commitment to the cause.

For my part I was in a bit of a quandary as to how to get my cog, probably the slowest in the machine, rotating. I knew exactly what I wanted, indeed needed, to do, but didn't quite know how to do it. My role was to ensure that on the day Christ's Holy Square was due to be re-assembled by the world's leaders, all thirteen pieces of pot were there. If one piece, for what ever reason, was missing, the Square could not be completed. We had to assume that God would see it as mankind's lack of commitment, and allow the asteroid to continue on its way until it impacted with the Earth.

But how to fulfil my role - that was my problem. The easiest part was undoubtedly getting my six pieces to the re-assembly point. Now knowing that it would take place in the General Assembly Hall at UN Headquarters in New York, I could simply jump on a BA or Virgin plane at Heathrow now that transatlantic flights had resumed. I would of course ask Angela to accompany me to provide security for the six pieces of pot, using her well-tried method.

The next easiest part of my role should, and hopefully would, be to ask Mrs Makepeace to ensure that her piece arrived at the re-assembly point on the appointed date. I knew that she lived in Wakefield, in the state of Massachusetts. I pulled out from my bookcase a copy of Philips New World Atlas, found Wakefield and, using the map's scale, measured the distance between it and New York. It was a mere two hundred miles, funnily enough the same distance between Yorkshire's Wakefield and the English Capital. No doubt 'the motor car country of the world' had an excellent motorway between Wakefield and New

York. At a steady fifty-six miles per hour the journey time would be less than four hours. Or maybe there was an airport at or near Wakefield. Didn't the Americans take an internal flight whenever they could?

The following day, at a time when I knew she would be up and on the move, unlike when she rang me in the middle of the night, forgetting about the time difference, I phoned Mrs Makepeace in America. I had an email address somewhere in my files so I could have contacted her electronically, but it was an impersonal way of communication, hence the call: "Good day, Mrs Makepeace...Peter Robertshaw calling from England."

"Goodness me...A call from England...How exciting...We never get calls from England."

I could have immediately killed her enthusiasm by pointing out the serious nature of my call, but decided not to: "I hope that you and your husband are keeping well...How's the weather in Wakefield this morning?...In our Wakefield, just up the road from here we have a dry and sunny day." I was assuming of course that the good weather in Doncaster, where I was calling from, did in fact extend the twenty miles north to Wakefield.

"Oh...The weather is brilliant here today...We would normally have some snow at this time of year, but we have been clear for several weeks now...Must be all that global warming we hear so much about nowadays...Now, you haven't called me all the way from England just to ask me about the weather..."

"Er. No...I want you to do me a big favour." I put it this way in order to win her cooperation. I could have demanded action from her, but realised that I had to be a bit diplomatic. The last thing I wanted to do was to give the impression that I was pressurising her.

"It all sounds very intriguing...Please elaborate."

"You of course know the importance of the piece of pot that you found in Venice...You also know what was said by Jesus during the Last Supper regarding his Father's threat to destroy the World if man did not mended his ways...Well, as you are no doubt fully aware an asteroid is predicted to strike the Earth on the 6th of April...You are also aware, because we discussed it at length during our last conversation, that this can be prevented by all thirteen pieces of Christ's Holy Square being re-assembled by the most powerful leaders in the World."

There were a few seconds of silence on the line before Mrs

Makepeace replied: "Ah...I know what you're going to ask me...You want me to take my piece somewhere so that along with the other twelve the Square can be re-assembled...I hope I haven't to fly to Europe...At my age I can't cope with the hassle."

"Quite the contrary, Mrs Makepeace...It is I who will be flying across the Atlantic, along with many others, because the point of re-assembly is in fact the UN Headquarters in good old New York...It will take place, all being well, at twelve noon on the 27th of March...It is essential that you are there with your piece."

Almost before I'd got out my last word, her reply came flowing back down the line: "Oh, good...Just up the road, then?...We always have a day up in New York to do our Christmas shopping ...You know, presents for all the grandchildren...Everything's so much cheaper up there...We can make it in just over three hours...We could get there by train, but my husband enjoys the drive...We'll have no difficulty in getting there in good time."

I breathed a sigh of relief, appreciating that there was one thirteenth of the Square that I didn't have to worry about, or seven thirteenths if I counted the six pieces in my possession: "Thanks, Mrs Makepeace...Your cooperation is much appreciated...I look forward to meeting you on the 27th...And hopefully it will all turn out right in the end." I felt like adding that if it didn't we would all end up in Heaven or Hell, but realised that it wasn't the time to be flippant about the possible destruction of the human race.

My main problem was how to get the six pieces of pot on display in three of the World's museums - three in Israel (two in Jerusalem, one in Tel Aviv), two in Greece (Athens) and one in Iran (Tehran), to the re-assembly point. What worried me was whether the countries' Governments would place obstacles in the way. I didn't anticipate problems from Greece, an EC country, but what if Israel insisted on placing one, two, even all three of its pieces in the Square, before releasing them? And if they did would that lead to a boycott by some other countries? I honestly didn't know. And what about the piece at present in the museum in Tehran? Would Iran want something in return, such as being allowed to continue developing its nuclear programme unhindered? Again I honestly didn't know?

I had of course no power to apply any sort of pressure, other than to point out the urgency of the situation. All I could do was contact the curators of the museums and ask them to make every effort to get their pieces to the re-assembly point on the appointed day, and leave it to them to sort out how they intended to do it. It made sense for the two Israeli curators to work together, and they probably would.

And this is what I did, but using the personal touch of phoning rather than the impersonal way of email. I already knew that all three curators had a good command of English having spoken to them previously, so phoning would not be a problem due to language difficulties.

My first call was to the curator of the Rockefeller Museum in Jerusalem, a certain Doctor Itzik Goresh. I decided to keep the call very formal: "Good day, Doctor Goresh...This is Professor Peter Robertshaw, calling from England...You may remember contacting me some months ago about the two pieces of pot that you have in your possession...The ones that Jesus gave out to his disciples during the Last Supper..."

"I do indeed remember, Professor Robertshaw...I am also aware that you have managed to locate all thirteen pieces, a task that I know must have demanded a great deal of dedication on your behalf."

Feeling quite embarrassed at his comments, I replied: "Thanks for your kind words, but I have been incredibly lucky...It's almost as if God himself was in control of the situation, not making it easy, yet making it possible."

"God does indeed work in mysterious ways, Professor," was the Doctor's reply. He then continued: "I've been expecting your call, or email, because I've kept myself abreast of what's been going on regarding the asteroid's changed course...I am also aware of your Prime Minster's visit to see the US President and the Secretary General of the UN...And also your two archbishops' visit to the Vatican."

"You are well informed, Doctor... You therefore have a good idea why I have called you..."

"Well...Yes...I assume that an attempt is going to be made to re-assemble Christ's Holy Square in order to prevent the destruction of the World, as predicted by Jesus during the Last Supper...I already know the venue and the date, both having been widely broadcast by the media...In fact since the announcement a day hasn't gone by without it being the main news item."

I smiled to myself. The good Doctor appeared to know almost as much as I did: "You are indeed remarkably well informed, Doctor...As you've said, there has been a great deal of activity behind the scenes, so to speak, in order to ensure that the re-assembly goes ahead, as indeed it has to, otherwise the end to all life on Earth is well and truly nigh…As you will be aware the 27th of March is ten days before the predicted impact of the asteroid with the Earth…What we all must do is ensure that all thirteen pieces of pot that made up the original Christ's Holy Square are there for the re-assembly…This is in part the reason for my call to you."

There was a pause of several seconds before the Doctor replied: "Right…Let me tell you about the plans we in Israel have already made…First, the urgency of the situation is such that the Government has taken over the transfer of all three pieces we have in our possession, including of course the piece in the museum in Tel Aviv, to New York…They will travel by military aircraft in order to ensure their absolute security…I and my colleague, Doctor Schelach up at Tel Aviv, will of course travel with them…The pieces will no doubt be secure within the aircraft, but it is essential that they are not damaged in any way…That will be our role."

On hearing the news I didn't know whether to breathe a sigh of relief, or not. Was I happy with the military involvement? Or would I have preferred the pieces to be travelling on a commercial plane, as indeed mine would be? I didn't rightly know. But…three more pieces were hopefully going to get to UN Headquarters in time for the re-assembly, so I should have felt elation. And after a second's thought I did.

But what about the piece in a museum in Iran? I wondered if Doctor Goresh had any thoughts on my question. I therefore decided to ask him: "As you are aware, Doctor, there is one piece in the Museum of Ceramics and Glassware in Tehran…Knowing that relations between your country and Iran are, to say the least, tense, do you anticipate any problems here?"

Again there was a pause of several seconds. It appeared to be his 'style', and I could imagine any lecture given by him being full of such pauses. I even suspected that he wore spectacles that he looked over the top of, or took off altogether during each pause, waving them in the air to emphasise a point. I had over the years seen many lecturers have such a style.

His reply didn't surprise me: "Well…As you are no doubt aware we in Israel are very concerned about Iran's nuclear programme…In fact way back in 1981 we bombed the Osirak nuclear reactor…If they can develop some sort of atomic bomb we are concerned that our country will come under threat...We would of course take steps to protect ourselves from such an attack...It may come as a surprise to you, but we would like to see the leader of Iran being one of the leaders to place a piece of pot in the Holy Square...We would hope that that would show the country's commitment to peace rather than being a potential threat in our part of the World...I know that our Prime Minister has already made his views known to the UN Secretary General who will ultimately have to choose the thirteen leaders."

As I listened to the Doctor I found myself nodding at the phone, something I often did when communicating by this method. What he'd said made a lot of sense, but he hadn't really answered my question. Maybe he felt that Iran would be a problem, but did not want to openly say so. I did however find his reply interesting, and pointed out why: "As a small exercise I decided to make my own choice of the thirteen leaders...Some were obvious, like the five permanent members of the Security Council, others not so...But in my final list Iran did not figure...After listening to you I can see why that country's leader should be on the list...I suppose the question is - how committed to World peace would the leader be?...But doesn't that also apply to other leaders who would be asked to place a piece in the Square, including your own?...Would, for instance, those countries with nuclear arsenals, including of course yours and mine, be prepared to get rid of them?"

Again the long pause: "An interesting point, Professor...But please remember that during the so-called 'Cold War', which your country was more involved in than mine, it was the threat of nuclear retaliation, leading to mutual annihilation, that in fact kept the peace...No, I don't think that is what God's threat is all about, otherwise he would have struck immediately after the first atomic bomb exploded over Japan during World War Two, an act that heralded the nuclear age...No, I think it's far more basic than that...More along the lines set out in his Son's preachings and teachings...The extremes of poverty, even in so called civilised countries, such as your own...Millionaire footballers with little talent living alongside pensioners who die of hypothermia in the winter...A lottery supported by people who can ill afford to do so, but see a win as the only way out of their meagre existence...The wealthy do not buy lottery tickets...The world banking crisis brought about by man's greed, but still the obscene bonuses continue...The breakdown of family life in many countries, leaving young people with no one to guide them by example into adulthood...Lack of respect for each other...For life itself...Even in your country, once thought to be the best country in the world to live, prompting I believe Cecil Rhodes to state that in the lottery of life being born British was to win first prize, the incidence of gun and knife crime are now a worrying feature...Older people want to live in Spain, younger people want to seek a new life in Australia...Now, in answer to your problem - I do believe that there will be a problem with Iran."

I had to be honest - I was surprised at his verbal attack on Britain. He obviously had a low opinion of us...Could this attitude be related in any way to the smuggling of a Dead Sea Scroll out of his country by a Briton, albeit a child? It was just a thought...And this coming from the citizen of a country that had its fair share of internal problems. I strongly felt like taking him to task, including his misquote of Cecil Rhodes, but realised that there was little to be gained by doing so. Instead I rather too abruptly thanked him, told him that I looked forward to meeting him in New York, and replaced the handset.

Angela, aware that I was uptight as a result of my call, to the point where I was about to throw the phone across the lounge, poured me a whisky in order to calm me down. After two more I had to admit I felt a good deal better.

The following day I booked two return flights for Angela and myself to New York's Kennedy Airport on 25th March. This would allow us a couple of days to get our bearings before the main event at the UN. If all went according to plan we intended staying a few days, possibly going inland to see the Great Lakes and Niagara Falls, something both of us had always wanted to see.

And if things didn't go according to plan we would return home, buy our bottle of wine and head for Horton-in-Ribblesdale. Here we would pitch our tent and calmly prepare for our final journey into the unknown.

Some hours before the predicted time of the asteroid's impact we would climb to the summit of Pen-y-Ghent and admire the view before the tsunami swept us into oblivion. It sounded strange to think that if all this came to pass we would be going to meet our Maker, he having just, and intentionally, destroyed us. To both Angela and I, who were members of the Christian faith and who had strong beliefs, it would take some getting our heads round.

I now had to contact the curator of the Museum of Glassware and Ceramics in Tehran, a Doctor Javad Ashoubi. Was I going to have a problem here? I hoped not.

I dialled the long number he had earlier given me, taking great care to get it right. After what seemed to be an eternity my call was answered, but by a woman and in a language I didn't recognise. I had no alternative but to reply in English: "This is Professor Robertshaw, calling from England…Is it possible to speak to Doctor Ashoubi, please?"

There was a pause and I suspected that the woman was seeking advice from someone close by her. She then replied in near perfect English: "Er…Doctor Ashoubi does not work at the museum anymore…He's on extended leave…Can I ask you what your call is about?"

The warning bells immediately rang within my brain, the words of Dr Goresh coming to the fore - I do believe that you will have problems with Iran. I now had a problem. What should I say to the woman? How much should I reveal, assuming that she wasn't au fait with the situation? Was she a genuine replacement for Dr Ashoubi, or was she a member of some sort of Secret Service? I had no idea. Should my reply be guarded, or should it be completely open? And if guarded, would the woman be more suspicious than she probably was already? Questions. Questions. Questions, and so little time to come up with some answers.

I made a decision - speak to the woman as I would to Dr Ashoubi. But I decided to commence with two probing questions: "Are you aware that your museum has a small piece of coloured pot, one of thirteen which is believed to have been given out by Jesus Christ to his disciples during the Last Supper?"

Again a long pause before a reply, indicating to me beyond any doubt that the question was being relayed to the third party in the room: "Er…Yes. I am aware." Nothing more was said.

I had no alternative but to press on by asking my second question: "And are you aware that during the Last Supper Jesus stated that at some time in the future the Earth would be destroyed unless the thirteen pieces were re-assembled together in the form of a Star of David by the Leaders of the World?"

This time the woman's reply was almost immediate and I suspected that she may have been presented with some brief notes, hastily scribbled down by the third party, setting out the significance of the piece of pot in the museum's possession: "Yes…I know all about the importance of the piece…I also know of the threat to the World…But we in Iran are of the Muslim faith and we follow the words of the Koran…We do not attach any credibility to the story you have quoted, as indeed we do not to much of what it states in the bible, which is now widely believed by the world's religious scholars to be little more than a collection of fairy stories...Our astronomers have assured our Government that the asteroid's course presents no danger to the Earth, and will pass by at a safe distance...The so-called re-assembly of this Holy Square is therefore unnecessary...It therefore goes without saying that our piece of pot will not be leaving our country...Nor will our President be attending any sort of re-assembly ceremony in New York if invited, which, given our country's strained relationship with the United States, will probably not be the case."

Her words left me speechless. How could her country be thinking along such lines when the rest of the World were hoping and in fact praying that a solution to the problem could be sorted out before 'impact' day? The cogs in the giant clock were already turning, some quickly, some slowly. And now one big spanner was about to be thrown in the works bringing the whole mechanism to a grinding halt. Without the piece in the Tehran museum Christ's Holy Square could not be completed, and the consequences of such incompletion were well predicted.

I had to reply...but what to say? Should I clinically lay out the facts and leave it at that? Should I plead with her, all the time being aware that it was highly unlikely that she would have any sort of power to change her country's mind on the issue?

But I had to make some sort of constructive response: "I'm sorry that your country has adopted the attitude it has...I assume that you are aware that observers throughout the world agree that the asteroid's change of course will result in a collision with Earth on the 6th of April...There is no doubt about that...The result will be the total annihilation of most of life, both plant and animal, on the planet, including of course all the people of Iran...Do your advisors realise that?...If your leader does not cooperate there is absolutely nothing that you can do to save your people."

Again the long pause. It even passed through my mind that she had put down the receiver. Then she spoke: "We in Iran do not accept that there is a threat to life on Earth and therefore will not be taking any sort of action."

As a last resort I decided to try a different approach: "You do realise of course that the other main Muslim countries in the World - Pakistan, Egypt, Iraq and Saudi Arabia, to name just four, all accept that if the Holy Square is not re-assembled in time the asteroid will strike the Earth with unimaginable force, and are actively supporting the policy being pursued by the United Nations Secretary General..." I didn't in fact know if what I'd just said was correct, but the ploy was at least worth trying.

This time her reply was immediate: "Our country has made its decision and will not change it."

Realising that I was not going to get anywhere I decided to end the call: "Well...I can only hope that your country has a re-think, otherwise it is the accepted view that the World as we know it including of course your country and all its people, will come to an end on the 6th of April...Good bye." I reached out in order to replace the handset, when I realised that I had just one more question. I rapidly fired it at her: "By the way, what has happened to Dr Ashoubi?" I then heard the receiver click into position, breaking the line. I leaned back in my chair, wondering - what constituted 'extended leave' in Iran?

Knowing that I had done all I could to persuade the Authorities in Iran to allow the piece of pot that presumably was still on display in Tehran's Museum of Glassware and Ceramics, to cross part of Asia, most of Europe and then the Atlantic Ocean to New York, I was at a loss as to what to do next.

After only a few seconds' thought I made my decision. The problem and therefore its possible solution had now to be pursued at Government level. I quickly logged on, typed in the email address that I had earlier been given to allow me direct access to someone close to the Prime Minister, then composed my message. I briefly described my failed attempt to get the piece of pot that was on display in a Tehran museum, on its way to UN Headquarters. I suggested, as a matter of urgency, that the Foreign Office should get involved directly with the Government in Iran. There was nothing more I could do.

Fortunately I had more luck with the curator of the museum in Athens, Stavros Democratos. When I contacted him he informed me that he had already sought advice from his Government. The Prime Minister had been made aware of the situation and had taken the decision on advice from his Foreign Office to leave all arrangements to Stavros himself.

At my suggestion he, accompanied by Mrs Democratos, arranged to fly from Athens to Heathrow, stay the night in London, then join Angela and I on our flight across the Atlantic. Although the company would be welcome I had an ulterior motive - by Stavros and I travelling together it ensured that eight of the thirteen pieces of pot would at least arrive at UN Headquarters together, and on time. It was all a case of cutting down the odds of something going wrong.

With the three Israeli pieces travelling by military aircraft in the capable hands of Doctors Goresh and Schelach, and Mrs Makepeace making the two hundred mile journey by car, this hopefully meant that twelve of the thirteen pieces would arrive at their destination, and on time. But all this would be in vain if the piece held in Iran wasn't allowed to cross the country's borders.

***

Chapter Twenty Seven

Time was passing and the World was waiting. But feet were being dragged and for an unacceptable, yet understandable reason - the choosing of the thirteen World leaders who would be required to place a piece of pot in Christ's Holy Square. Despite several meetings in camera between the Secretary General of the UN and his closest advisors the list had not yet been finalised, thus giving some indication of how difficult the task was. And yet it had to be done, and quickly.

Once the list had been drawn up the leaders chosen had to be notified and at the same time asked to be participants in the re-assembly of the Holy Square. Travel arrangements had then to be made, possibly easy from countries with functioning airports. But what about those where the airports were still in total chaos? People were still wanting to get out, refusing to accept that even if they managed to get to the most idyllic country in the World it would be of no avail if the asteroid struck the Earth?

Of course there was method in their madness, for if the Square was successfully re-assembled in New York and the Good Lord above did change the asteroid's course, preventing its collision with Earth, they would already be, in their eyes, in their country of choice, ready to start their new life there. News reports from many African countries were revealing airport chaos, and for this very reason.

The travellers had to be able to scrape together the air fare, and many were doing so, some committing crimes in their quest to raise the money. European countries were popular destinations, especially the UK. The reason given for entering the chosen country was to take a holiday or to visit relatives, but once in that country they would then simply disappear, hoping to take advantage of any chaos that the country was experiencing as a result of the asteroid threat. But once the threat was over they'd be there, ready to commence their new lives.

On the 15th of March the Secretary General at long last revealed his list to the World of the countries whose leaders would be requested to place a piece of pot in Christ's Holy Square, knowing full well that it would be controversial. Countries expecting to be on the list were left off, and less obvious ones included. Immediately the list was broadcast worldwide using every method available. Radio was still extensively used to reach isolated areas, such as in the wilds of eastern Europe, northern Asia and central Africa, this still being the only means of communication. Of course television was the main communicator of information, now closely followed by the internet, although the elderly in many countries were still suspicious of it, even in so-called 'advanced' countries.

I had first hand experience of this. My and Angela's parents, all four in their seventies, would not accept a computer into their homes, even though I had offered to pay for them, set them up and give the parents a crash course on how to get the best out of them. But no - the reason being: "Far too old to take it all in."

I received the news, not by any of the 'modern' forms of communication, but by the most basic - the landline telephone. As I sat at my desk at work, studying the latest information the university's Astrophysics Department had furnished me regarding the course of the asteroid as it continued its final journey towards the Earth, my phone rang. A little annoyed at being disturbed I lifted the handset and barked abruptly into the mouthpiece: "Yes?"

"Er...Got out of the wrong side of the bed this morning, did we?" It was Angela. She'd been asleep when I'd left for work early in order to beat the traffic, now back to normal - bumper to bumper through the centre of Doncaster between eight and nine o'clock.

"Sorry, love...I was engrossed in a report produced by the Astro department on the asteroid's latest course."

Playing 'hard to get', and no doubt with a big grin across her face, she replied: "I've got some important information for you, just this second given out as a bulletin on the BBC News channel...The Secretary General of the UN has just published his list of the thirteen countries...But if you don't want to hear it I won't bother telling you...Only joking...Got a pen?...I'll read it out to you."

I quickly grabbed pen and paper: "Sorry...Go on...I'm ready." As she read out the list I scribbled down the names of the countries:

America - Russia - China - France - UK - Germany - Japan
Brazil - Australia - South Africa - North Korea - Iran - Israel

I thanked Angela for furnishing me with the information and told her I would discuss the list with over dinner, I then replaced the handset.

I closely studied the list in front of me. God, some shocks there. As I expected, the five Permanent Members of the Security Council - America, Russia, China, France and the UK were there. Then came the more obvious ones - Germany, Japan, Brazil, Australia and South Africa, the last three countries obviously representing the southern hemisphere. But no Canada - that was a surprise. Then the shocks, two presumably included by the Secretary General because he and his advisors considered them to be a future threat to World peace - North Korea and Iran. But the biggest surprise of all was Israel. Had it been included because of its sometimes strained relationships with the countries that surrounded it, and of course with Iran? Or had it been included as a matter of 'right', because the original distribution of the thirteen pieces of pot had taken place in that country at the Last supper of Jesus Christ? I wanted to believe that the latter reason was the case. One thing was certain, the Secretary General had not, and probably would not reveal the reasoning behind his final choice.

Now that the list had been produced it was simply a case of waiting for the World's response, or more specifically the responses of the chosen nations. In most cases this was immediate, with the names making the air waves (and presumably cyber waves, whatever they are) buzz with commitment.

Within twenty-four hours we knew that the five members of the Security Council would be there. I had wondered if China would prove to be awkward, but no. A statement from Beijing expressed enthusiasm for the proposed, and indeed essential, 'get-together' in New York. With a population approaching one and a half billion about to be wiped out if action wasn't taken, minds tended to be concentrated.

This was immediately followed by the more obvious nations - Germany, Japan, Brazil, Australia and South Africa - the last three the southern hemisphere contingent.

After three days of silence Israel responded, the reason for the delay not being at all obvious to me. Had there been some sort of unease at being included in the list when much larger countries with huge populations and different religions, India and Pakistan springing to mind, having been excluded?

But there was an uncomfortable silence from Iran and North Korea.

The date had now moved on a couple of days, to the 17th of March. The

278

re-assembly of the Square was due to take place in just ten days' time, on the 27th. God would no doubt be 'up there', looking down and waiting…waiting.

But still no response from Iran and North Korea.

Then, news started trickling out of both Tehran and Pyongyang, the two countries' capitals, that students were on the streets, peacefully protesting. This had happened before in Tehran, but with security as tight as an iron glove in Pyongyang, it had previously been unknown on any sort of scale.

As the various social websites of the World started buzzing with reports of the protests the situation started to become clear in the two capitals. In Tehran the protests had started in a low key way on the campuses of the University of Iran and the Sharif University of Technology. But it had soon spread to the spacious Azadi Square, with it massive Tower, sometimes referred to as the Freedom Tower, that had been constructed to a height of some fifty metres in white marble to commemorate the Persian Empire.

In support of the students more people joined the protest, particularly the young, and started to congregate in the Square determined to have their voices heard. At first the powers of law and order looked on as the protesters with their banners and posters kept a silent vigil.

But it wasn't long before the students became restless and decided to take action that took the form of taunting the police. This immediately became confrontational and the police responded. At first they attempted to quell the protests, using the well tried methods of tear gas, water cannon, rubber bullets, but it wasn't long before live ammunition was used, resulting in several protesters' deaths. But this only made the situation worse, as more young people entered the city from the outskirts of the capital. There attitude was simple and indeed made a lot of sense. If the asteroid did wipe out all life on Earth the elderly had already lived their lives, but the young had their lives ahead of them, an attitude that was also supported by the elderly. They were not prepared to have their leaders 'dragging their feet' on such an important issue.

Not only was Tehran brought to a standstill, but much of Iran was as well, as people of all ages assembled in their own towns and cities to voice their protest at their leader's refusal to travel to New York and carry out what they considered to be his 'duty'. This had nothing to do with religion. It had all to do with survival.

The North Korean Authorities looked on uneasily at what was happening six thousand kilometres to the west of their country, realising that the actions of the Iranian people could quite easily be copied by the people in their own country because the reason for the protests was identical. They tried to place a blanket ban on all forms of communication with the outside world. They hoped that by doing so they would be able to contain the small and so far peaceful protests that were already taking place within the country's borders.

But the Authorities did not appreciate just how quickly technology had moved on. Despite their attempts to block all incoming information about what was taking place in Iran, the details still came streaming in on the various social networks. This could only have one effect - encouragement to the country's young people. If it could happen in Iran why not in North Korea?

Although most of the universities in the capital Pyongyang had been closed, the students being found physical work in factories, on building sites and farms. This done was in order to increase production and help to get the country's failing economy back on its feet. But two of the city's universities - the University of Science and Technology, and the Medical University were kept open. It was essential that the training of future engineers and doctors continued. As a result there was a ready supply of students waiting to take to the streets and mount a peaceful protest. Soon they were joined by those who lived in the surrounding areas, taking full advantage of the excellent public transport system. As word of the protest spread like wild fire, the Metro, trams and trolley buses were soon bulging at the seams as young people decided to head for the city centre in order to make their voices heard.

As in Iran their reason for protest was simple, and their banners stated it- they had the whole of their lives before them and were not prepared to see it snuffed out in an instant, just because of some idealistic, yet misguided, intransigence of their political leaders.

Typical of the Korean people the protest was peaceful, as they gathered at three of the city's main rallying points - the Arch of Reunification, blocking the highway that ran south to the Demilitarised Zone separating the country from its neighbour South Korea; the Arch of Triumph, so large that it even dwarfed the Arc de Triomphe in Paris; and the Workers Party Monument, with its hammer, sickle and paint brush representing the roles of the factory worker, those who worked on the

280

land, and the artistic and intellectual.

But it wasn't long before they all headed for the Kim II Sung Square, the official rallying point for any event that celebrated the country's successes. Banners were raised, simply asking their country's Leader to make the journey to UN Headquarters in New York and do his 'duty', as the Secretary General had asked him to do.

The Authorities, quickly realising that the protest was escalating out of all proportion and could soon get out of control, brought in the army to support the riot police. They initially charged at the protesters, but found it difficult because tens of thousands had all sat on the ground and linked arms. Water cannon had little effect because many of the protesters had had the good sense to bring rainware with them, and many of the protesters appeared to have also come prepared for a tear gas attack, wearing a variety of face masks. Warning shots were fired into the air, but to no avail. The protesters now packed so tightly that had they wanted to move they wouldn't have been able to, stayed put. They'd even brought supplies of food and water. On previous demonstrations they had submitted to the mighty force of the state...but not this time.

Of course the whole of the World was now watching, almost with bated breath, wondering what the Government would do next. Previously the whole might of the country's huge military machine had been rolled out as a show of strength, intent on sweeping the protesters aside, but not on this occasion.

The following day was warm and sunny, and the protesters were in good voice, chanting out their protest slogans and waving their banners. Since they were still sat peacefully, arms still linked, the riot police, totally out of character, decided to take up positions along the edges of the huge Kim II Sung Square and wait. What exactly they were waiting for wasn't at all clear, but a message had percolated through their ranks that something dramatic was about to take place.

Like many of the world's great Squares the Kim II Sung had a large government building with a substantial balcony overlooking the Square. This was used by the representatives of Government to take the salute at rallies that showed the country's military strength, with a march past by the army, followed by tanks, missiles on carriers and armed vehicles. And it was on that balcony that those in the Square observed activity, particularly the positioning of microphones in the centre of the balcony. Some sort of statement was about to be made...but what, and by whom?

At precisely midday the balcony filled with men, dressed in simply styled grey suits, who left a space in the centre as they lined up. Many protesters had no idea who the men were, but when the central space was filled by a man who had moved forward from the back, the more knowledgeable ones immediately recognised him and passed the word round. Like 'wild fire' the information spread throughout the seated protesters. It was their country's Leader.

The vast crowd, realising that some sort of statement was about to be made, hopefully to the benefit of all of them, stood up and cheered. Even the riot police, totally out of character for such a well disciplined force, hammered their shields with their batons. Everybody appeared to be celebrating...but celebrating what? So far not a word had been uttered by their Leader.

The Leader then raised both his arms, hands pointing upwards and palms facing outwards. The effect was almost immediate, the Square becoming as silent as a grave yard. Everybody was waiting in anticipation.

Leaning slightly forward, he spoke into the microphone:

"Comrades...As your Leader, I greet you...Today I have good news...I, as the Leader of the Democratic People's Republic of North Korea, will be travelling to United Nations Headquarters at the request of the Secretary General in order to place North Korea's piece in the Holy Square of Christ...This shows how important our great country is in today's World...I know that you will now want to celebrate my momentous decision to play my part in saving our planet...Please do so peacefully...Show the rest of the World, whose eyes are on us today, how we in the Democratic People's Republic of North Korea respond to such good news."

The country's National Anthem was then blasted out over the public address system. As the last note faded the thousands of people present again cheered, this time with added enthusiasm. Their voice had been listened to.

Then, on obvious instructions from 'high up' in order to avoid any sort of confrontation through sheer puzzlement, the riot police moved slowlyback, removed their helmets and body armour, and stored them away in waiting vans. They then commenced gently herding those protesters on the edges of the huge crowd towards the many exits of the Kim II Sung Square. Slowly, ever so slowly, the Square emptied. It was difficult to imagine that a Square full of thousands of people in any other city in the World would have emptied in such an orderly and disciplined manner.

When I saw the pictures on my television screen of what had taken place in the North Korean capital I mentally placed a tick at the side of that country's name. This added to the ticks against the names of the eleven countries whose leaders had already committed themselves to placing a small piece of coloured pot in Christ's Holy Square. Only one more tick was required.

Meanwhile, just over six thousand kilometres to the west, in Iran, the protest had hit a brick wall. Despite the now massive demonstrations of the people throughout the country, the Government stubbornly 'dug its heels in' and refused to move on its already stated policy. It would not be sending its leader to UN Headquarters in New York to partake in some sort of mumbo-jumbo ceremony designed to save the World. Nor would it allow the triangular piece of brown coloured pot, part of an exhibit in the Museum of Glassware and Ceramics in Tehran, to leave the country.

The full force of the military had been brought in to support the police and all indications were that the protest was going to end abruptly and if necessary, bloodily. The Government, determined not to have its policy determined by mindless protesters, decided to take decisive action, and in Iran this normally meant swift and ruthless action.

But not on this occasion. With the rest of the world looking on, waiting in anticipation and ready to criticise, the Government decided to give the protesters twenty-four hours to disperse, with a hint that it was prepared to discuss the whole issue the following day. Would this be enough to appease the protesters? And was it just possible that something would happen that would change the Government's position?

Unfortunately, as the rest of the World look helplessly on at the so-far intransigence of the Iranian Government, time was passing. The day that the asteroid would collide with the Planet, bringing such devastation that most, if not all, life would be extinguished, was fast approaching. It would take some sort of momentous event, maybe even a miracle, to prevent this happening. It would of course be too much to expect the Lord above, who was about to destroy the World, to come up with a miracle to save it.

***

Chapter Twenty Eight

During the next few days those leaders who had agreed to re-assemble Christ's Holy Square, including the leader of North Korea, started to arrive at Washington DC's International Airport. There they took up residence in their countries' embassies and consulates. They would have to make the two hundred mile journey to New York for the re-assembly ceremony. The UN Secretary General still hoped that the government of Iran would have a change of heart and that its leader would also arrive in New York before the day of re-assembly.

I and Stavros Democrates duly arrived on the 25th of March, accompanied by our wives. Between us we had eight of the thirteen pieces of pot in our possession, Angela having six pieces of pot inside her bra, just to be on the safe side. This had been a little uncomfortable for her during the long flight, but as she put it: "It's for Harry, England, and Saint George, …Or rather the World," misquoting Laurence Olivier's famous line in the film *Henry the Fifth*.

In my suitcase, carefully packed, was the varnished wooden square that I had made to take the thirteen pieces of pot. British Embassy officials had already made arrangements for us to stay in a small but excellent hotel overlooking the East River, just a short taxi ride from UN Headquarters. The Greek authorities had made similar arrangements for Stavros and his wife.

The following day, early on, I received a call on the apartment's internal phone. It was from a man who called himself Ed Irving, who evidently held the position of chief aide to the Secretary General. He asked me to attend UN Headquarters with Christ's empty Holy Square in an hour's time. Where he'd got my number from I'd no idea, unless the British Embassy had given him the name of our hotel. Maybe the Embassy used the hotel on a regular basis. He must have assumed that I had the Square with me. When all said and done it was what this whole business was all about.

I stared at the Square and whispered a little prayer as I carefully placed it in my shoulder bag. Although I had accurately measured the dimensions of the six pieces in my possession I had to construct the Square based on the dimensions given to me by email and over the phone. I could only hope that these had been taken with the utmost accuracy. Heaven forbid that a particular piece would be too big to drop into the Square in its allotted position. The embarrassment would be too great to bear.

I then reached under my pillow for the six pieces of pot in my possession. I had placed them there for safe keeping no doubt naïvely assuming that in the event of a break-in during the night the intruder would not have looked under the pillow. The pieces were still wrapped in paper handkerchiefs, All I had to do was push them deep into my trouser pockets three either side, with a large man's handerchief pressed down on top of them.

As I prepared to leave the apartment I suggested to Angela that she should take a taxi into the city centre and simply explore. I then asked the hotel receptionist to call me a taxi, which she duly did. I was heading for UN Headquarters. I was also feeling intense excitement.

After signing in at the main reception desk, at the same time being given and accepting my security tag that I proudly hung around my neck (where the devil did they get my photograph from?), I was escorted to the main Assembly Hall where I was introduced to a young, well groomed and extremely good looking guy. This was, according to his security tag, Edwin Irving, senior aide to the Secretary General himself.

I immediately looked around me. What an impressive hall it was. To the front, on the wall facing the area where the assembly assembled, so to speak, was a huge rectangular gold coloured panel with the circular UN emblem on it. Either side of this were smaller rectangular shapes displaying the UN flag. Could these also be television screens, I wondered? Set out at the front of the hall, facing forwards was a greenish coloured marble dais behind which were three cream leather seats where presumably the Secretary General sat with two of his assistants. Immediately in front of this was a tall black marble dais where those addressing the Assembly made their speeches. In front of this was a small carpeted area, then came the seated area divided into four sections separated by aisles. Here the delegates from the various member nations, along with their advisors and interpreters, sat at long green topped tables with microphones set out at intervals. At the ends of these tables were the plates with the nations' names on each side so that all could clearly see them.

It was then that I noticed in the area in front of the tiered rows of seating a polished wooden table, approximately the size of a pool table, that had been placed in the centre. Its top had been inlaid with red leather, looking a bit like the tables used as writing desks and seen in antique shops.

The aide asked me to place my constructed wooden Square in the centre of the table. I did so and stared at it, realising just how lost it looked on the large table, covering a mere fraction of the total area. Although measuring a mere eight inches by seven inches and therefore very slightly rectangular in shape, it was referred to as a Square. Its irregular dimensions were dictated by the shapes and sizes of the thirteen pieces of pot that had to fit inside it. I wondered why Jesus hadn't made the pieces of pot substantially larger, then realised that he had intended them to be worn round the neck on a thin leather thong. Larger pieces would have been both cumbersome and uncomfortable, and would have drawn eyes immediately to them…not always what one would want.

Of course all this preparation would be of no avail if the thirteen pieces of pot were not there at the ceremony. I had my six with me. In fact they were wrapped up in paper handkerchiefs and positioned deep in my two trouser pockets for safe keeping. But had the others arrived? At that point in time I didn't know if they had. It was therefore time to find out, and the only person who could tell me was the aide standing beside me: "Er…Have all the other pieces arrived yet?"

He looked at me, apparently puzzled by my silly question. Of course they've all arrived. We wouldn't be going through this ceremony otherwise: "The three pieces found in Israel arrived a couple of days ago with the Israeli delegation. They are safely locked away…The two pieces found in Greece were deposited with me earlier this morning by the curator of the museum in Athens who I believe you travelled to New York with. They too are locked away…The piece already on American soil in the possession of a certain Mrs Ella Makepeace arrived at nine o'clock this morning…Having telephoned ahead giving details of her impending arrival from Wakefield, just a four hour drive away, I met her outside the UN building…She handed the piece over, said she was going shopping in New York with her husband, and promptly sped away in order to park up somewhere…Unfortunately we do not have the piece from Iran…What we can do about that I have no idea."

Neither had I.

Feeling a touch upset at Mrs Makepeace's decision not to make herself known to me as I thought we'd earlier agreed, I asked the aide to take me through what was now going to happen. This he did. We were going to carry out some sort of rehearsal of the re-assembling ceremony. He produced a black velvet bag approximately a foot square with a golden cord draw string at the top. Anticipating that he would ask me to produce the six pieces of pot in my possession I carefully extracted them from the depths of my trouser pockets.

The aide now went through the procedure that would be followed the next day. He first sat down on one of the seats that would be occupied by the Russian contingent, including its leader. He then asked me to carefully place the six pieces of pot in the black velvet bag, continuing: "Ask me, as President of Russia, to approach the table, remove one of the pieces from the bag and place it in the Square in a position indicated by yourself."

I was initially embarrassed at the request, but nevertheless played my part in the rehearsal. I shouted out my requests: "Would the President of Russia please approach the table, take a piece of pot from the bag and place it in the Square in the position indicated by myself?"

The aide slowly rose from his seat, descended the stairs and approached the table. I held out the bag, holding it tightly at the top, and the aide placed his hand inside. Slowly he extracted a green triangular piece with the Greek letter τ engraved into it. I pointed to a triangular section in the Square and the aide carefully placed the piece into the space. It fitted perfectly, as I knew it would.

The aide smiled: "This will be the procedure tomorrow...The Secretary General will invite each Leader in turn to approach the table...I will hold out the bag...And I want you at the side of me to show where each piece goes...Can you see any problems?...If so, let's iron them out here and now."

I thought for a few seconds. I could immediately think of one, but surely it had been sorted out already: "In what order will the Leaders approach the table?"

Initially the aide looked blank, surely the order didn't matter. I therefore pointed out the simple practicalities: "Well, no it doesn't matter...But surely the Secretary General will be reading the country names from a list, otherwise he has to memorise thirteen names...It would be easy to get one wrong...Think of the reaction if he called the Leader of South Korea instead of North, or Iraq when he meant Iran...Remember, this ceremony is going to be televised throughout the world...We don't want any cock-ups, do we?"

The aide immediately saw my point: "Er, no...What do you

suggest?"

I was already thinking ahead: "Well, you could first invite the five permanent members of the Security Council, then follow them with the remaining eight...But the trouble with that method is that it would place countries in an order of importance...Who would be first?...Who would be last, and would that country be offended by being last?...No, I would place the countries in alphabetical order...It's the simplest and least complicated way."

The aide searched around in his jacket inside pocket and extracted a small notepad. The top sheet had a list of names on it - the names of the thirteen countries whose Leaders had been invited to take part in the re-assembly ceremony. He tore off the sheet and handed it to me: "Please read them out in alphabetical order...I'll write the names down again, and we'll see how the list looks."

I looked through the list, worked out the order and read it out: "America - Australia - Brazil - China - France - Germany - Iran - Israel - Japan - North Korea - Russia - South Africa - United Kingdom."

He smiled at the order. America, although not the host country since UN Headquarters was looked upon as neutral soil, was first on the list. Was that fitting, he wondered? And the United Kingdom, the country that had led the way in organising the ceremony, last. Was that also fitting? I felt that it was, my country rounding the proceedings off. And what about Israel immediately following Iran? Then I remembered that unless something 'out of the blue' happened Iran would not be represented anyway.

At that point the aide's face took on a serious look, and he asked a question that as it happened had been foremost in my mind for several days, although I had tried to push it into the background: "Do you think that there is any point in going through with the ceremony when one country is missing and one piece of pot will not be positioned tomorrow?...At the end of the ceremony the Square will be incomplete...Surely it is too much to hope that God above will accept an incomplete Square and an absent Leader, especially one whose commitment to world peace is absolutely essential?"

I honestly didn't have an answer: "Quite frankly I have no idea...All I can suggest is that the ceremony goes ahead and we see what happens...Maybe God will see that we have made a determined effort to fulfil his conditions, and give us credit for doing so...This could take the form of a slight change in the asteroid's course, making it just miss the

288

Earth, but giving us all a scare that may encourage us to permanently change the way we as nations get on with each other."

The aide nodded: "I suppose that's the best we can hope for."

I then had a quick thought: "Of course the whole world will witness the event and there will be wholesale condemnation of the government of Iran for not being represented…And of course the nation's people will be far from happy with the way their country will undoubtedly be despised by the rest of the world…As far as I'm aware, there is no time limit to the re-assembly process, other than it obviously has to take place before the asteroid hits us…After tomorrow there will be some nine days before the day of impact…Hopefully world pressure can be brought to bear on Iran that will change its intransigence and become involved…Both Leader and piece of pot could be in New York in a matter of hours if the will is there."

Again the aide nodded: "I suppose all we can do is hope…And pray."

It was now my turn to nod.

On the same day as I and the senior aide to the Secretary General of the United Nations were rehearsing the re-assembly ceremony in New York, almost eleven thousand kilometres to the east, a middle-aged man with a middle eastern look about him, but dressed as a businessman, possibly from a western company, entered the Museum of Glassware and Ceramics, in Iran's capital city, Tehran. The Museum was set well away from where the protests were taking place and a decision had been made to keep it open, hoping to attract some of the extra people who had entered the city, many out of sheer curiosity. That middle-aged man now takes up the story.

***

Chapter Twenty Nine

Narrator – Jesus Nazarene, the Son of God

My name is Jesus, Jesus Nazarene, although most people of the world know me by my biblical name, Jesus Christ. They also know that a person of that name appeared on this Earth just over two thousand years ago. Well, I am that person and again here on Earth, making my second coming. When and how I arrived is not important...sufficient to say that I have been here long enough to know of man's complex ways. I am here for a specific reason which will become apparent as my story unfolds.

Having entered the building by the open large double door I moved quickly across the ground floor of Tehran's Museum of Glassware and Ceramics, viewing the exhibits as I did so, obviously knowing exactly what I was looking for. I suddenly stopped at a marble plinth about half a metre high with a square glass display cabinet on top of it. Its height was such that all but the shortest of children could see the exhibit inside, and for a good reason too.

The exhibit, entitled:

A Greek child's word game - dating back to about 50AD

consisted of eight pieces of coloured pot, all the shape of an equilateral triangle and with a Greek letter engraved into each one. The eight pieces were set out in a long row, every alternate triangle being upside down. The eight pieces spelled out a Greek word.

One piece, however, was slightly larger than the others and positioned with a small space either side of it in order to make it stand out from the other pieces. This was 'my' piece, the one I had given to my disciple Thomas at the Last Supper.

The description of the exhibit stated that the larger piece, with the Greek letter omicron - O engraved into it, had been found just outside Tehran five years ago during the excavations of an ancient town. It was thought to be about 2000 years old and could have been a piece from a Greek children's word game, where pieces with different letters engraved into them were placed in line to form a word. The other pieces, made recently, showed how they and the original piece could be placed together to form such a word.

I closely studied the row of letters.

Being a scholar, with the ability to speak in many tongues, I translated the word into different languages, speaking to myself as I did so, - Latin, Arabic, Hebrew, finishing with English, a language I had recently mastered. The Greek word 'daktulos' translated into *finger*, and gave for example to the English language the word 'dactylography', which is the science of fingerprints.

As I stared at the exhibit I smiled. Only the α, τ, υ and ο pieces appeared in my Holy Square, but the α piece was entirely the wrong shape, and all but the ο piece, were of the wrong colour. In fact the vibrant colours used had obviously been chosen to catch the eye.

After I'd been gazing at the exhibit for several minutes a member of the museum's staff, presumably a guide, an attractive young woman, dressed in accordance with her role, came up and started to talk to me: "You are obviously interested in the exhibit…Do you understand what it is about?"

I immediately replied, at the same time smiling: "Oh, yes…A Greek children's game, where words are built up from different lettered pieces of coloured pot…The word 'daktulos' means one of these…" I hesitantly stuck up my index finger knowing that in some parts of the world such a jesture was offensive. Fortunately she did not see it that way. Maybe young Iranian women had not been exposed to such a crude jesture.

"Ah…You are a linguist, then?"

"Well…You could say that…But my native tongue is Hebrew."

"Ah…Israeli?"

"I prefer Jewish…My birthplace was a small town called Nazereth…I don't suppose you've heard of it."

"Oh, indeed I have…It was the place where Jesus Christ was born some two thousand years ago…We have several exhibits relating to the Christian religion in the museum, even though we are a Muslim country…Any good museum should not be selective in what it exhibits…We have for example a very good section that covers The Crusades."

As I and the guide were having our conversation three women, two in black jihabs, one in light grey that covered all but their eyes, making it impossible to guess at their ages, came up to study the exhibit, although they appeared to be waiting for a chance to speak to the guide. As they did so they spoke quietly to each other, presumably about the exhibit itself.

I already knew that the Curator of the museum, a Dr Ashoubi, had been in contact with the English Professor Peter Robertshaw. I also knew that the professor had in his possession six similar pieces of pot, three having been found in an English bog, two in Israel and taken back to England by tourists and one found in a English churchyard. I therefore assumed that the Curator was now likely to know the true significance of the piece of pot in his museum's exhibit. It was therefore time for me to meet the doctor if at all possible.

Just as the guide was about to leave me in order to speak to the three women, I asked her what to me was a perfectly reasonable question: "Is it possible to have a word with Dr Ashoubi, please?"

The guide was visibly taken aback at my request, and the three women promptly noticed this. They also observed her abrupt response: "How do you know of Dr Ashoubi?"

"Oh, I'd reason to contact him some weeks ago when I read on some English university's website that this museum had an unusually shape piece of coloured pot on display, not unlike three pieces found in that country on the body of a Roman soldier extracted from a bog...I was just seeking more information about it."

"Dr Ashoubi does not work here anymore...He's on extended leave." At that point she hurriedly moved away, obviously not wanting the conversation to continue.

Since I had seen all I wanted to see in the museum I exited by the large open double doors and headed down the street in order to work out what I should do next. I'd barely gone a hundred metres when I heard the sound of shoes hitting the pavement behind me. Someone was chasing me, about to mount an attack...a robber maybe. Or someone was simply trying to catch up with me.

I turned, prepared to fend off any attack, only to find the three women I'd earlier seen in the museum, trying their hardest to catch me up. The one dressed in the light grey jihab arrived first and gasped out a question: "May we have a word, please?"

I, a gentleman through and through, immediately stopped and waited several seconds before I answered allowing all three women to get their breath back. I then replied: "Of course you can…Haven't you just been in the museum back there, looking at the same exhibit as myself?"

"We have," replied the woman in grey: "Since you asked the museum's guide, to us a very important question, perhaps I should introduce myself and the others…We are the daughters of Dr Ashoubi, and we called at the museum to confront the management over the sacking of our father, but failed to do so."

I initially smiled, knowing that my suspicions about Dr Ashoubi's 'extended leave' were correct. I quickly removed my smile when I realised that the issue wasn't funny at all: "Please go on."

The woman, who had decided to make herself spokesperson, was obviously extremely well informed, and explained: "When the UN Secretary General released the names of the thirteen leaders he'd chosen to re-assemble Christ's Holy Square, the leader of our country being on the list, my father was invited by the *Tehran Tribune* to write an article on the whole issue…He did so, including the history behind the Holy Square and God's threat to destroy the World, and that how re-assembly of the Square would persuade him not to go through with it…Obviously my father stressed in his article how essential it was that not only did the piece of pot in his museum make its journey across the Atlantic so that it could be placed in the Square, but also that our leader should make the same journey in order to carry out his duty…He pointed out in his article that our nation should be proud of being chosen as one of the great nations of the world…But my father's article did not go down well with the Government …He was accused of meddling in matters that did not concern him, removed from his job as museum curator and placed under house arrest at his home…the Authority's version of extended leave."

I didn't express any surprise, for what the woman had said had simply confirmed my suspicions. I did however need to speak to her father, and therefore sought his whereabouts. Unfortunately what she told me wasn't helpful: "We live in a small town called Now Shahr, about a hundred and sixty kilometres to the north of Tehran, on the coast by the Caspian Sea…But the house has a police presence to prevent our father escaping or receiving visitors…We and our mother are allowed to move freely, but you would have no chance of getting to see him."

Realising that a journey north would be a waste of time I asked the woman to give her father a message: "Would you please inform him that you met a Jew who called himself the Nazarene, in the museum, and he said that he would make sure that the triangular piece of pot, light brown in colour and with the Greek letter O engraved into it, would be taken by him to New York...And that once this has happened, as it surely will, it may persuade the leader of Iran to also make the journey."

The woman asked the question that she knew her father would ask me if he were here: "How do you propose to get the piece out of the museum?...All the exhibits are alarmed in order to prevent such an act of theft."

I simply smiled as I answered her: "Oh, it will need a bit of a miracle...But I'm pretty good at that sort of thing, having had a lot of practice...And is it theft to take what is rightfully mine?"

All three women looked at me, puzzled. Was I some sort of con artist, or plainly mad? Only a fool would try to steal something from a museum in Iran, where theft was simply not tolerated.

I detected this puzzlement, and my final comment simply added to it: "Please pass on my message to your father...He will be able to work out who you've been speaking with, and will also know how I intend to take the piece of pot out of your country."

The three women, certain that I was indeed quite mad, nevertheless assured me that they would pass my message on to their father.

Earlier in the day I had noted from a board on one of the large double doors that Tehran's Museum of Glassware and Ceramics closed at five o'clock. At precisely half past four I returned. This time I circled round the exhibit that had occupied all my interest a few hours earlier, preferring to look at the other exhibits. The young guide, who had previously conversed with me, now appeared to avoid me. I got to thinking - was it because I'd expressed an interest in Dr Ashoubi, who I now knew was under house arrest on the shores of the Caspian Sea?

As it happened, this lack of attention didn't worry me. In fact it was just what I wanted. Without attracting the slightest attention to myself from the handful of viewers in the large room I slowly moved back to the Greek children's word game exhibit. Closing my eyes and pressing the tips of the fingers of both hands together, I whispered a prayer: "Please, Father, may it be thy will that the piece of pot that I gave to my disciple Thomas, is now returned to my care."

Slowly the **o** piece of brown coloured pot rose from its position within the Greek word δ-α-κ-τ-υ-λ-ο-ζ, passed silently through the wall of the glass exhibit case and came to rest between the palms of my hands. As I carefully placed the piece in my trouser pocket, pulling my handkerchief over it I whispered three words: "Thank you, Father."

My mission now complete, I made my way through the open door, just as an announcement was being made over a public address system that the museum would close in ten minutes' time. At that point the young guide, along with her colleagues, moved to the door in order to thank those leaving, for their interest and support. When the last one had exited the museum the large double door was closed and firmly locked. Inside the room the senior guide's last duty was probably to press the code into the alarm system and set it. Since the numbers of visitors had been less than anticipated during the previous two days, a decision had evidently been made to close the museum until further notice. This information was displayed on a notice that one of he guides pinned to the main door after she and her colleagues had exited the building by a side door.

As I moved away from the museum I observed the guides, no doubt keen to support the protest, cross the road. They then headed for Azadi Square several streets away, arriving just in time to find many protesters, who were prepared to give the Government time to have a rethink, slowly dispersing. As they did so they had to pass the rows of riot police, with the army in the background. All had been instructed to hold their ground, but take no action. Disappointed at the lack of 'action' the young guides joined the protesters as they left the huge Square.

I looked at my watch. Time was passing and I had to get to Tehran's Imam Khomeini International Airport as soon as possible. I had no idea where it was, but knew of several men who would...if only I could catch the attention of one of them.

I needed bit of luck, and as it happened I got it, for round the corner of the museum came a taxi, the illuminated sign on its roof indicating that it was open for business. I managed to flag it down, quickly jumped in and told the driver where I wanted to be. I then eased back into the rear seat and relaxed.

Fortunately for both the driver and myself the route to the airport took us well away from the streets where the protesters were dispersing. After a hair raising drive lasting about thirty minutes the taxi pulled up outside the double glass doors that led into the departure area of the Airport.

My entry into Iran had been unconventional, to say the least, sufficient to say I had simply 'dropped in'. I now wanted to fly to

America by a more conventional way, that is by air. But that had implications.

At that point I panicked, unnecessarily as it happened. I thought I had no money to pay the taxi driver, nor to pay for my flight out of Iran. As the driver looked expectantly, I felt in my jacket inside pocket. I had to at least give the impression that I was looking for some money. To my immense surprise and relief I felt some sort of package. I pulled it out to find it was an unsealed envelope containing a large number of American dollar bills of various denominations. The driver's eyes lit up at the sight. He mentally converted the fare from Iranian rials to dollars, no doubt doubling it in the process and willingly accepted the dollar bills as I peeled them off and passed them to him. As the taxi moved away I closed my eyes and for the second time whispered to myself: "Thank you, Father."

I now had to book a flight, if possible direct to New York. Was it possible to do so? I had no idea. For no other reason than that I came to it first, I stopped at the Lufthansa desk. Unable to competently speak Persian, the language most people spoke in Iran, nor indeed German, I decided to try English: "Is it possible to book a flight to New York please, direct if possible?"

The young woman, dressed in western attire replied in English, at the same time tapping keys on the keyboard in front of her: "Er yes, sir...But you will have to change at Frankfurt International...Shall I see when the next flight is...And if there's a seat on it?"

"Please," I replied, at the same time looking at my watch. It was exactly six-fifteen.

Within a matter of seconds the computer screen filled with information. The woman turned it round so that I could see it: "You're in luck, sir...There's a flight LF128 departing at 19.20 hours, arriving at Frankfurt at 21.55...There is then a flight out from Frankfurt at 02.25, arriving atNew York JFK at 04.45...There is just one seat left...Would you like me to book it?...I can give you the cost in Iranian rials, or would you prefer it in American dollars?"

Knowing that I had several dollars, although not the slightest idea how many, I hastily replied: "Please book it...And in dollars, please."

"That will be three thousand five hundred and ninety-eight dollars, exactly, sir...Cash or credit card?"

I had never thought of a credit card. Was there one in the envelope containing the money? I checked, and to my surprise and relief there was. As I extracted it from the envelope I noticed the name on it…Jesus Nazarene.

Since I had a large amount of money and a valid credit card in my possession, presumably I also had a passport. As it happened I had, not in the inside pocket of my jacket, but one of the outside ones. I looked at the outside cover, discovering that although I had been born in Israel I was now, possibly for convenience, an American citizen. On opening it at the information page I first glanced at the photograph. Was I as handsome as that, I wondered? I then checked the name, discovering that I was indeed Jesus Nazarene, but obviously my date-of-birth was wrong, in fact some two thousand years out.

After entering the details in the boxes on her screen the woman asked me to tap my PIN number into the machine on the counter. For the second time I panicked. How could I possibly know what it was? I glanced at the large digital clock on the wall behind the woman. It showed **18:29**.

I tapped in the four numbers, and shouldn't have been surprised when they turned out to be the correct ones. The transaction now complete the woman handed me my passport, credit card and the all-important ticket, complete with boarding card for my flight: "Have an enjoyable flight…And by the way, sir…In all the years working on this desk I have never seen the name Jesus Nazarene before…There can't be many of you around. "

I smiled at her: "No…There certainly aren't."

As I walked away I whispered to myself: "In fact only one." I then paused, closed my eyes and whispered, for the third time: "Thank you, Father."

After booking in and with boarding card safely in my hands I headed for security and passport control. As I walked along the long spacious corridor, mingling with the other travellers, I suddenly had a worrying thought. Would the security sensors pick up the small triangular piece of pot that at that moment was deep in my trouser pocket? I had no idea, but realised that if it was detected not only would the piece be confiscated, I would also have some explaining to do. Certainly I'd be arrested.

Having no real idea what to do I decided to place the piece between the dollar bills inside the envelope. Naively I thought that maybe the sensory 'rays' would not penetrate the paper layers and detect it, not appreciating that they were designed to pick up metallic objects, not ones made of pot.

Once through security and passport control I headed for one of the cafés in the departure lounge. I'd ample time to grab a bite to eat. After settling down with a bowl of some sort of soup, a bread roll and a glass of water, paid for with eight willingly accepted one dollar bills, I got to thinking. My time and date of departure from Tehran was 19:20 on the 26th of March. Studying the print-out that the booking clerk had given me I noted the arrival time in New York was 04:45 on the morning of the 27th. Surely it wasn't possible to fly across part of Asia, the whole of Europe, calling at Frankfurt, and then the northern Atlantic in just over ten hours. Then it occurred to me – something to do with time zones. I'd be crossing several of them, but going backwards in time.

The Secretary General of the United Nations had chosen the 27th for the ceremony to re-assemble Christ's Holy Square. That would give me time to book in at a hotel, have a quick nap, followed by a bite to eat. I then had to make my way to UN Headquarters, arriving in good time for the re-assembly ceremony that was due to take place at midday. I definitely had to be there.

After an uneventful flight I arrived on time at New York's JFK International Airport. After first setting my watch to local time I quickly passed through Security, thankful that I had an American passport, and headed for the taxi ranks. Not having the slightest idea about a hotel I decided to ask the taxi driver, stressing that I wanted a hotel that was small, clean and reasonably priced, and that I would be only there for a couple of nights. It would help if it wasn't too far away from the UN building.

The driver no doubt having been asked the same question many times before had come to an arrangement with the owner of a hotel only a few minutes away from the airport. He therefore dropped me off there.

I booked in, was shown to my room, that although basic was totally acceptable to me being a simple man, and collapsed on the bed. Having found it almost impossible to sleep on the plane I was now dead on my feet. I needed a few hours' sleep, but was acutely aware that I had to get to United Nations Headquarters in good time for the ceremony. It was essential that I didn't fall into a deep sleep. But just before putting my head on the pillow I extracted the precious piece of pot that my visit to first Tehran then to New York was all about, from deep in my trouser pocket. I first unfolded the handkerchief that was wrapped round it then unnecessarily checked it to see that it hadn't been damaged in any way

298

on its eleven thousand kilometres journey. Finally I placed it in one of my shoes, pushing a sock in after it. This was the only form of security I could offer it.

I awoke with a start and grabbed my watch from the bedside table. The time was already ten o'clock. The ceremony at UN Headquarters was due to take place at midday. I ordered toast and coffee in my room, washed and shaved using the razor that the hotel provided, and generally smartened myself up. My final task before leaving my room was to place the piece of pot back in my trouser pocket, as deep down as I could get it. After paying for my room from my envelope of dollars I asked the clerk behind the desk to get me a taxi. When I asked the driver to take me to UN Headquarters I got a surprised look. The driver didn't expect to get a fare to that destination from such a basic hotel.

I thought I knew a bit about New York, but had never been there before. I'd seen all the pictures of it, but those couldn't prepare me for what I was now witnessing. Why didn't some of those tall buildings topple over, I wondered? Why didn't all the cars crash, forming several big heaps of mangled metal? After being in the taxi for only a few minutes I knew the answer to my second question, marvelling at the skill of my driver as he weaved his way through the traffic.

In what seemed only a few minutes my taxi pulled into the area specifically for the dropping off of passengers at UN Headquarters. A quick glance at my watch revealed a time of eleven o'clock...one hour to re-assembly. I now had to not only get into the building, I had to actually get into the Assembly Hall itself and let someone in authority know who I was and why I was there...not going to be easy.

Security around the building was frightening, with a high concentration of police with very visible firearms. This of course was not surprising since assembled there today would be some of the most powerful people in the world including their delegations. The crowds of people, mainly there out of sheer curiosity, were kept behind barriers, the only ones allowed in close being the numerous press photographers and television camera operators. Those actually being allowed in appeared to have security passes which were thoroughly scrutinised. My task of actually getting into the building appeared to be hopeless.

As I puzzled what to do a cavalcade of cars pulled up close by the taxi rank. It was obviously a delegation of people from one of the UN member countries and numbered about twenty. All had highly visible identification tags the size of a CD case hanging from a yellow ribbon looped around their necks.

As the delegation passed me on the other side of a barrier that happened to have the slightest gap in it, I squeezed through, unnoticed, and joined the

back of the group. As the tight body of people approached the large open doorway I immediately became aware that I too had an identification tag round my neck, just like all the others. I should have been surprised, but I wasn't, knowing that the tag had come to me from the same source as the envelope of dollars, the passport and the credit card.

As the group passed into the building their movement was slowed to a crawl as each individual passed through a rectangular security frame similar to that seen at airports. At the same time any bags in their possession were X-rayed. The security people were not taking any chances at such a prestigious event, with the world's media transmitting every detail. Not having my overnight bag with me I passed through the security frame without any bleeps sounding off. I noted that as I did so a burly security man the size of a gorilla glanced at my ID tag, making sure that the photograph was that of the person round whose neck it was hanging. In my case it obviously was, the one who'd placed it there having made sure of that. Yet again I closed my eyes and whispered to myself: "Thank you, Father."

Once in the Assembly Hall the delegation was shown by one of the many guides to its place, indicated by a large label showing the country. I was evidently a member of the ISRAELI delegation, which when you think about it, was entirely appropriate.

At this point I broke away from the group at the same time spotting an unattended clipboard on a table. I quickly grabbed it then, looking like a man with a purpose, I became one of the many people milling around in the area where a large table, standing on its own, had been positioned. I guessed, as it happened quite rightly, that the table would eventually be used for the Re-assembly Ceremony.

I moved unnoticed towards the table studying its red leather top as I did so. There, already in position at the centre, was what looked like a square frame of varnished wood, similar to the one that I'd made to hold the thirteen pieces of pot that Zachariah the Potter had made for me in time for the Last Supper with my disciples two thousand years ago. It did however differ in one respect – this square had a transparent cover that could be closed and fastened. At that moment it was open so that the internal structure was clearly visible. Also on the table was a black fabric bag with a gold coloured draw string pulled tightly at the top.

As I moved in closer to study the Square, just to make sure that the thirteen sections were of the correct shape and together made a Star of David, one of two men on the other side of the table, looked suspiciously at me and called across: "Er…Can I help you?"

Rather than trying to explain my obvious interest in the Square at the centre of the table, I decided to plunge straight in: "My name is Yesus Nazarene (I intentionally pronounced the 'J' as a 'Y', thinking that it sounded more like a genuine forename)…I have just flown in from Iran…I have in my possession the thirteenth piece of pot, the one that makes up the complete set…The Holy Square can now be fully assembled." As I spoke I eased out of my jacket pocket my passport that had tucked inside it the boarding pass that clearly showed that I had indeed flown from Tehran's Imam Khomeini International Airport to JFK within the last twenty-four hours.

As the man opposite me studied my passport and boarding pass I in turn studied him, or rather the ID tag hanging from his neck. The name on it was Professor Peter Robertshaw, a name I immediately recognised and a person I admired for his sheer tenacity. Here in front of me was the man who had devoted in recent months all his time and effort to locating the thirteen pieces of pot that I myself had distributed to my disciples two thousand years earlier.

***

Chapter Thirty

Narrator – Peter Robertshaw

I studied the name on both the passport and boarding pass. The man's name was given as Jesus Nazarene, an American, who had indeed arrived from Tehran within the last twenty-four hours. I wondered how he had then got through the security system, one designed to prevent a person not having a legitimate right to be at the ceremony, getting anywhere near the Assembly Hall. I realised however that I didn't have the time to quiz him about it, nor did it now matter. He was here, beside me. The time of the re-assembly of Christ's Holy Square was rapidly approaching.

Again I studied the name - Jesus Nazarene. It was so close to Jesus the Nazarene, so close to Jesus of Nazareth. Was I in fact looking directly into the eyes of the Son of God? His age worked out to be thirty-six, which seemed about right, give or take a couple of years. Jesus Christ's age at death wasn't known accurately, anyway. Was I in fact witnessing what many of the Christian faith had been waiting for, for two thousand years - the Second Coming of Jesus Christ? Had he in fact arrived and was standing next to me at this very minute?

My mind flashed back to my time as a choirboy at Wakefield Cathedral. Every Sunday morning for the best part of four years, until my voice broke, I had sung the words of the Creed as part of the Solemn Eucharist. I slightly moved away from the man in order to recount them, eventually singing them to myself to my favourite Mass - the Darke in F. I remembered that other favourites of mine had been the Vaughan Williams Masses in D and G minor. But I'd hated all those by Palestrina:

…And the third day he rose again according to the scriptures. And ascended into heaven and sitteth on the right hand of the father. And he shall come again with glory to judge both the quick and the dead. Whose kingdom shall have no end.

So here was a prediction of Christ's Second Coming. I had no idea how far back the words of the Creed went, but I suspected a long time.

Of all the people who were present in the Assembly Hall this day the man standing beside me had the greatest claim of anyone to be there.

It was now most important that I checked that he did in fact have the thirteenth piece of pot on his person. Knowing how difficult it would have been to get the piece out of Tehran's Museum of Glassware and Ceramics, then out of Iran itself, I wanted to know how he'd done it. But again time was pressing so those questions would have to wait until later: "You say you have the thirteenth piece...May I see it?"

The man placed his hand deep into his trouser pocket and carefully extracted a folded handkerchief. This he placed on the table, gradually unfolding it as he did so. Sure enough a small triangular piece of pot, brown in colour and with a tiny hole in one of the angles, was revealed. There was however no inscription on it, not surprising because it was upside down. I gently turned it over, and there was the Greek letter **O** engraved into it. Although I was a hundred percent certain that the piece was genuine I nevertheless extracted a plastic six inch ruler, with both metric and imperial units on it, from my jacket inside pocket. I always carried it with me when I knew that I would be handling these precious items. I had got into the almost obsessive habit of regularly checking the dimensions of them...just to make sure.

The piece looked to be a perfect equilateral triangle, but if it had been slightly out by as little as a couple of millimetres the eye wouldn't have detect it. I measured the lengths of all three sides. All were identical, as they should have been. The size was also correct. But just to make sure I carefully removed all twelve pieces from the black bag having first slackened off the gold string round its neck. As I did so I placed them face up on the red leather top. These had earlier been placed in the bag in readiness for the re-assembly ceremony. This enabled me to immediately locate the other **O** piece, because of course there were two. I first placed the two pieces side by side in order to check that the shades of brown were identical. They were. I then placed one piece on top of the other. They were identical in both size and shape, as I was confident they would be. Only then did I breathe a sigh of relief. There in front of me were all thirteen pieces of pot in a row across the table.

As I carried out this small exercise I was acutely aware that the man's eyes were focussed on the pieces, especially the white hexagonal one. If he was indeed Jesus Christ, and I was now convinced that he was, he'd last seen and handled all the pieces two thousand years ago. The temptation to pick them up again, feel them, even place them back in the wooden frame that I had made specifically to take them, must have been very strong. But he resisted the temptation to do so.

I was sorely tempted to do the same, but that would have defeated the whole object of the ceremony that was about to take place. God definitely did not want to see me re-assemble the Holy Square, nor indeed to see his own Son do likewise. He wanted to see the Leaders of the world do so, at the same time committing their particular nation to a new era in the way they lived their lives, cared for others, cared for all the other living things, both animals and plants that share the planet with them. He wanted them to care for the only place where they and those who were to follow them could survive - the Earth…Their Earth. This was what God wanted to witness. It was my role to see that he did.

Curious to see what was happening, the aide to the Secretary General came across to where Jesus and I were standing. He had been consulting with the Secretary General who, along with his two Deputies, had already taken up their positions behind the huge marble dais on the stage at the front of the Assembly Hall.

I took the aide on one side and explained the situation to him, stressing that the man at the side of me had just flown in from Iran with the thirteenth and final piece of pot, and that I was convinced that he was indeed Jesus Christ. We were in fact all witnessing his Second Coming. The aide's eyes focussed on the pieces of pot that I had set out in a row across the table, and proceeded to count them. He then carefully placed them back in the bag.

At this point Jesus Nazarene asked the aide a most unexpected question, in fact one showing extreme impertinence: "Is there any possibility of me addressing the Assembly after the re-assembly of the Square has been completed?…I have something important to say to all who will be present in the Hall…I have a message from my Father in Heaven."

The aide initially stared at him, speechless. He was of course aware that since the United Nations' inception many important debates and speeches by some of the most prominent people in the world, John F Kennedy, Golda Meir and Yasser Arafat immediately springing to mind. But never before had a request been made, let alone allowed, for someone to make a speech from the floor of the Hall not having been earlier invited to do so. Obviously unable to make a decision himself the aide returned to the stage in order to consult with the Secretary General.

Understandably the Secretary General initially looked puzzled. He stared down at Jesus Nazarene from his elevated position, trying to form an opinion about him. He whispered to himself: "Who the devil (a strange choice of word in the circumstances) are you?"

His aide, a man of vast experience and a good judge of people, appeared to believe that the man was in fact Jesus Christ, the Son of God, his opinion having been influenced by me, a British archaeologist with impeccable credentials. I was the man who had managed to locate all the pieces of pot that this immensely important meeting was all about, and I was totally convinced of the man's true identity.

This placed the Secretary General in a difficult position. He did have the power to change the very tightly planned format of the Re-assembly Ceremony to include a speech from this man, but if he did allow it, was he setting some sort of precedent that may be taken advantage of at some future date?

After a lengthy discussion with his two Assistants he made his decision. He would allow the speech to take place, with the proviso that he would immediately intervene if it became in any way politically offensive to any nation, or indeed confrontational. This decision was taken back to the man by the aide.

I was pleased about the decision for I had a good idea what the man was going to say. His Father would not be happy that one of the world's leaders had failed to turn up. This was not acceptable. The question he would want answering was...what is the General Assembly going to do about it?

At this point I spotted the Archbishops of Canterbury and York taking their seats alongside the United Kingdom delegation that now included the Prime Minister, his foreign Secretary and the UN Ambassador. I nodded across acknowledging them. I then cast my eyes around the huge hall to see if I could see the Pope anywhere. Was there a separate desk for Vatican City, or would he be there as part of the Italian delegation? I had no idea, nor could I see him.

Acutely conscious of the passing time I moved quickly across to where the two archbishops were sitting. Fortunately formal introductions were not necessary, I having met them earlier, so in I plunged, putting them in the picture about the man who at that moment was talking to the aide.

Both were already aware that one of the pieces of pot, required to complete the Holy Square, would not be present in the hall, nor was one of the Leaders who had been specifically chosen by the Secretary General. But they sat up rigidly in their seats when I mentioned that the man standing only a few metres away from them was called, according to his passport, Jesus Nazarene, and that he had just flown in from Iran with the missing piece. How he had managed to acquire it I had no idea.

Although I was clear in my own mind what the answer was, I floated the question to them: "Could this man be Jesus Christ himself?…Could this in fact be his Second Coming?"

Both men, knowing that their faith accepted that there would indeed be a Second Coming at some time in the future, nodded to each other. If the world was in danger of being destroyed in a few days' time the Second Coming had to take place before that event in order to fulfil the scriptures, where several references were made to such an event.

I then informed them that the man had asked to address the whole Assembly, and that the Secretary General had agreed to his request. Both holy men again nodded to each other. It was obvious to them that the incomplete re-assembly of the Holy Square, his Holy Square if he was in fact Jesus Christ, could not be simply left at that, incomplete. The Leaders present could not be allowed to simply leave, with the problem of the impending destruction of the world still unresolved. Maybe a speech by this man would shake them into some sort of action, although it wasn't at all clear what that action could be, or should be.

It was now midday and the Secretary General brought the Assembly to order. On the aide's instruction to one of the guides in the hall, three chairs were fetched and positioned along the side of the table allowing those who would be sitting on them to face the assembled delegations. The aide indicated that I and the man should sit down. He then took up his seat beside us.

After an opening speech, where the Secretary General stressed in no uncertain terms why we were all assembled there, he described how the re-assembly of Christ's Holy Square would be carried out. The Leaders who had been asked to take part would approach the table in alphabetical order according to their country, remove one piece of pot from the black fabric bag being held by the aide and place it in the Square in the position indicated by Professor Robertshaw, in other words, me. Not surprising, I felt honoured at being directly involved in the Ceremony. I knew that Angela would be proud of me, as she watched the whole procedure on the television in her room back at the hotel, along with the billions of people throughout the world.

The Secretary General, after again bringing the Assembly to order,

306

for his words had understandably caused much noisy discussion amongst the delegates, produced a list of the countries, in alphabetical order, as I had earlier suggested. This was definitely not the time for any cock-ups.

He then got the process he'd described, on its way, commencing with the President of the United States, America being first on the Secretary General's list. The President slowly rose from his seat, moved across to the nearest aisle and approached the table. The aide held the bag out and the President reached down into it, pulling out the first piece of pot. It was triangular in shape, green in colour with the Greek letter τ engraved into it. On my indication he carefully placed it in its correct position in the Square. He then nodded to me reverently (why I didn't rightly know), and moved slowly away from the table, returning to his place. He had carried out his duty.

Jesus Nazarene looked at me and whispered: "I gave that piece to Matthew."

I nodded, at the same time mouthing: "I know."

The Secretary General named the second country - Australia. The procedure continued without a hitch, the Leaders of Brazil, China, France, and Germany all choosing their pieces, with me indicating where in the Square they went. With six pieces now in position the Square was almost half full. At this point I glanced at one of the two huge television screens that had been installed on the Hall's front wall, either side of the United Nations' circular emblem. On both screens was a picture of the Square. I glanced upwards and spotted the camera that was taking it. As the Leaders approached the table other cameras zoomed out in order to show the whole process of them randomly choosing a piece of pot then placing it in the Square. At this point both the aide and I were in the picture. After each piece had been positioned the camera zoomed in so that the Square filled the whole screen. I remembered seeing something similar when watching an international chess match on television some months earlier.

The Secretary General had now to make a difficult decision. - whether to invite the Leader of Iran to approach the table, knowing full well that he was not there, or to move on and invite the Leader of Israel. He decided to choose the latter option, not in any way wanting to embarrass Iran by calling out its name. Had he done so every eye in the Hall would no doubt have focussed on the empty section where the Iran contingent should have been seated...but wasn't. There may have even been a vocal outburst from some of the younger members in the

Assembly who were going to have their short lives abruptly ended if God went ahead with his threat.

In my opinion the Secretary General had made the correct decision.

On being called, the Israeli Leader approached the table and chose his piece. Without waiting for me to show him he placed it in its correct position in the Square. As he did so I recognised the piece as one of the three that had been found in Israel and until recently had been on display in a museum in Jerusalem. The Israeli Leader would no doubt have been earlier shown by one of the curators where in the Square all three pieces went. Nevertheless I nodded to him indicating that he was in fact correct.

Then followed the Leaders of the remaining five countries - Japan, North Korea, Russia, South Africa and finally the United Kingdom. As the UK Prime Minister approached the table he gave me a friendly wink. Was he possibly showing his appreciation for the role I, a fellow citizen of the UK, was playing in the re-assembly process? I hoped so. Maybe if all went well and the asteroid could in some way be spirited onto a non-destructive course, I would be offered a knighthood...It was just a wild thought.

Although the re-assembly process was now at an end it was not complete, for one piece remained in the bag and there was one place for it in the Square. As luck would have it, or was it some form of divine intervention, the piece in the bag had belonged to Jesus Christ himself...in fact to the man who was at that moment sitting at the side of me. I looked at the Square and the empty space in its centre where the largest piece, the white hexagon with the Greek letters θ and π engraved on it, should now be in position, but sadly wasn't.

Just to be sure that the piece was still in the bag I felt inside and pulled it slowly out, placing it on the table in front of me. Of course the overhead camera picked up my action and those still watching the television screens saw me do this. I suspected that most, if not all, were willing me, and if not me, someone else, to drop the piece into the waiting space in the middle of the Square. The Square would be complete. God above, if there was one, and I was convinced in my own mind that there was, would witness this and use his powers to change the course of the asteroid. We could then all go home...job done.

But of course it wasn't as simple as that. I knew it and so did the man sitting beside me. For the second time within the space of an hour he had looked at the piece...his piece. How strong the temptation must have been to also fulfil the viewers' wishes. But he was acutely aware that he wasn't there for that reason, neither would his Father have approved of such action.

Having witnessed our inaction and therefore thinking that the ceremony was now over, several delegates became restless, wanting to be off, for there was little point in prolonging their stay. They also thought that their restlessness would hurry the Secretary General into making a declaration that the meeting was now at an end, even though the 'end' had been far from satisfactory.

The meeting was not however at an end for there was still a speech to be made, and to be listened to. The Secretary General once again brought the Assembly to order. He then uneasily introduced his guest speaker, not quite knowing what to say about him. He decided that the best way was to invite the guest to introduce himself: "Before I declare the meeting closed I have invited a very important person to address you…All I will tell you is that he arrived in New York only a few hours ago having travelled here from Iran…In his possession was the thirteenth piece of pot that had been in a museum in that country's capital, Tehran…But as you see there is still one piece on the table and therefore the Square is incomplete…I will leave it to him to explain why."

The Secretary General's words caused further confusion, with the Leaders of the various nations asking their aides what the devil was going on. Surely this man from Iran, who had brought the final piece of pot to the meeting, was that country's representative. Maybe the country's Leader was ill and had been unable to make the arduous journey. Surely it was now simply a case of this person placing the final piece in the Square, thus completing it. What was the problem?

The man rose to his feet and the aide escorted him to the smaller marble dais just below the larger one behind which the Secretary General and his two Assistants were sitting. Immediately the assembly settled down, to a point where one could have almost heard a pin drop. After the Secretary General's brief, almost mysterious introduction, they were eager to hear what this man had to say.

Of course the man in front of them was used to addressing large numbers of people. He had done so on a regular basis, albeit two thousand years earlier. On one occasion he'd even fed them all, even changed their water into wine, but on this occasion he'd no intention of doing anything like that. Had he done so he would have been considered some sort of magician, like the ones on television who could change elephants into cars and houses into airliners…and he definitely was not a magician.

He took a deep breath and commenced his speech:

"Perhaps you will allow me to introduce myself…My name is JesusNazarene…I was born two thousand years ago in a small town called Bethlehem, although I spent my early life in Nazareth, now a large city in the country of Israel, and lived in the area known as Judaea for my thirty-six years of life on this Earth."

At this point he paused, knowing that a ripple of whispering would spread across the assembly, which of course it did. Almost every person in the Assembly Hall had heard of Jesus of Nazareth, regardless of the religion they personally followed, and he did indeed live some two thousand years ago. So, how could he be here now addressing them? Quite simply he couldn't. Was this man some sort of crank, or a drunk who had somehow bypassed all the security checks and found his way by accident in the Assembly Hall? Alternatively, had the Secretary General somehow been hoodwinked into letting a man who was obviously a fraud address the United Nations?

When the assembly had again settled down he continued:

"That was my First Coming on this Earth…Just before I left it I asked a local potter to make me thirteen pieces of pot of different colour and shape that would fit into a wooden square surrounding a six point Star of David that I had constructed to take them…These I gave out to my twelve disciples, with the message - preach my words abroad, which I'm glad to say most did…I kept a thirteenth piece for myself which I gave to a Roman soldier just before my crucifixion…I then gave them my Father's ultimatum – that he would destroy the Earth and all life upon it if man did not mend his ways…This could be avoided by man showing his commitment to making the World a better place for all living things, by the most powerful Leaders in the World sometime in the future reassembling my Holy Square to show this commitment…At that point my work on Earth was at an end and after my crucifixion I ascended into Heaven to join my Father."

On hearing him mention the Roman soldier I smiled to myself. Could it have been *my* Roman soldier, the one found in a bog at the side of the River Don, in Yorkshire? There was of course no way of knowing for certain, but it could have been the same soldier, who had become custodian of the piece throughout its journey from the Holy Land to the wilds of Britannia. I wondered if Jesus knew this, and the fact that two other pieces were also found, on the horse on which the soldier had been mounted.

The man continued:

"It gives me great pleasure to see that after two thousand years all thirteen pieces have been located and are now on this table, twelve within the Square, one piece, my piece, outside it...This final piece should be placed in its position in the Square by the leader of Iran, who had been invited by the Secretary General to do so...Sadly that has not taken place...You may be thinking that I could solve the problem by placing the final piece in the Square myself...But let me tell you now that my Father in Heaven would not accept a Square that had been completed by his Son, nor would he accept one that is incomplete...It is up to you, as representatives of the world's people, to make sure that the Square is completed...How you do this is entirely up to you...I have played my part by bringing the piece from Iran to this Assembly...I can do no more...It is now up to you... But I can tell you this...If the Square is not completed, in ten day's time my Father will destroy the world, your world...This is no idle threat...It will take place."

Having said all he wanted to say he turned, slightly bowed to the Secretary General then moved away from the dais and returned to his seat at the side of me.

Initially the Assembly was stunned into silence, most of the delegates still focussing their eyes on one of the large television screens, even though all it showed was the dais from where the man had delivered his speech. The cameras then moved slowly round at the same time zooming out to show the full Assembly Hall.

At first the delegates talked amongst themselves, trying to make sense of what they'd just heard, but soon those from one country were moving across the Hall to have discussions with those of other countries. I studied the names of the countries where this was taking place and noted a pattern - the mainly Christian nations appeared to be forming some sort of alliance, as indeed were the Muslim nations. There also appeared to be an alliance of countries that were not officially 'religious', although many in those countries did practise their chosen religion. It appeared that the United Nations were no longer united, dividing instead into three distinct camps. And it wasn't long before shouting and finger pointing between the camps started to take place.

The Secretary General, a man of great experience, quickly assessed the situation. All that was now taking place in the Hall was being transmitted worldwide to millions, if not billions, of people. To them the Hall must have appeared to be in total chaos. The Secretary General was definitely not having that. His, and the whole reputation of the United Nations were at stake.

With difficulty he brought the Assembly to order, asking the delegates to return to their places, which they reluctantly did. He then invited each of the three camps to choose a spokesman who would make a brief statement to the Assembly. The Muslim speaker put forward the point of view that the leader of Iran had the right not to be involved in a ceremony that he did not believe in. The non-religious speaker expressed that in the circumstances, where the whole future of the world was at stake, the completion of the Square must take place, but offered no opinion as to how this should be done. It was up to the speaker representing the Christian nations to make a concrete proposal. This was seconded, and the proposal was put to the whole Assembly.

The proposal was worded in the following way:

This Assembly proposes that the Secretary General, representing the wishes of the United Nations General Assembly shall ask the Government of Iran to send its leader to UN Headquarters in order to complete the Holy Square

A vote of all one hundred and ninety-three nations present then took place, with the result being announced by the Secretary General after the votes had been counted: "The result of the ballot is as follows :-

For- 160
Against- 22
Abstentions - 11

I declare the motion carried and will now carry out my duty, immediately contacting the Government of the Islamic Republic of Iran."

I studied the results as they appeared on the television screens. The majority for the motion was overwhelming, being over eighty percent. It was obvious to me that even some of those nations who'd supported Iran's right not to attend the Assembly, had voted for the proposal, as had several of the so called 'non-religious' nations. Would the Government of Iran be persuaded by this massive support for the motion? I'd no idea, and neither had anyone else in the Assembly Hall, for that matter. What I did know was that if the Square was not completed in the next ten days the World as we knew it would be destroyed. Plans for Angela and I to fly home, gather our camping gear and of course a good bottle of wine, and head for the summit of Pen-y-Ghent, where we intended to spend our last hours, were already formulating in my head. Was this an indication of my lack of faith in the Secretary General's ability to influence the Government of Iran, I wondered? I hoped not.

Slowly the Assembly Hall emptied, but some leaders and delegates lingered behind, no doubt discussing what they had witnessed that afternoon. I saw my own Prime Minister move across the Hall to where the US President was sitting. I could tell by the mannerisms of both men that an intense discussion was taking place, no doubt along the lines...Where do we go from here? Even the leaders of Russia and China were in deep discussion, something rarely seen, the interpreters certainly earning their pay.

As the UK delegation made its way towards the exit, including the two archbishops, both clergymen suddenly left the group and headed up into the centre of the hall, obviously looking for something...or someone. I watched them closely, curious to know what or who they were looking for.

I didn't have to wait long. They soon spotted their objective, who I immediately recognised as the Pope, seated with the Italian delegation. Its members had also remained seated and were in deep discussion. I would have loved to have moved in close and tuned in to the holy men's conversation, but obviously I couldn't. I did however wonder what the three had made of the whole procedure, and whether they too were asking the question...where do we go from here?

Since my task as I saw it was now at an end I closed the glass lid of the Square and pushed the catch across, thus trapping the twelve pieces in their positions. I then placed the thirteenth piece back in the black bag and pulled the gold cord tightly. Finally I handed both Square and bag to the aide, at the same time asking him to place both in a safe and secure place: "I've a feeling that you will need both in the next few days for I am optimistic that the Iranian leader will agree to the Secretary General's request and come 'on side' in the interests and indeed survival of the World's people."

He replied, a doubtful look on his face: " I wish I shared your optimism, Professor…But if an Iranian delegation does wish to pay the UN a visit I will of course be ready to welcome it with open arms."

As I was about to say goodbye to him I noticed a man break away from the delegation that had occupied the Pakistani desk. He hesitantly edged his way towards us, obviously wanting to make a comment or possibly ask a question: "Could you please remind me of the name of the man who has just addressed the Assembly with such thought-provoking words?"

Wanting to be as helpful as possible the aide replied: "He calls himself Jesus Nazarene…Flew in from Tehran only yesterday with the thirteenth piece of pot."

The man smiled, bowed his head slightly and said: "Thank you."

I watched the man move away to rejoin his delegation as they passed through the large open door. As they did so I got to thinking. There was no doubt in my mind that the man had simply been confirming what he already knew.

It was now time for me to depart. I therefore said my goodbye to the aide. As promised, I had arranged to take Angela inland from New York in order for both of us to see the Niagara Falls. The ninety minute flight from JFK to Buffalo Airport was already booked, starting a two day stay at a hotel called the Holiday Inn, one highly recommended by a colleague back home. We would be flying out at eight in the morning so I wanted to get back to my room in order to pack, then get a good night's sleep, for we had to be on the move by five in the morning, at the latest.

It was also time to say goodbye to the man who had been at the side of me throughout the ceremony. He had been talking to some of the delegates as they were leaving, but had now rejoined us.

But how did one address the Son of God? I had no idea, neither did I intend running the risk of offending him by guessing and coming up with the wrong title: "So, where do you go from here…Surely there's nothing more that you can do?"

He smiled: "I'm afraid I'm going to have to return to Iran…There's obviously still work to be done…I see my role as being on the side of mankind, having been a member on two occasions, albeit two thousand years apart…This is what my Father expects of me."

There was no comment I could make, not being able to understand or appreciate the relationship between a man on Earth and his Father in

Heaven: "Well, I wish you well in your mission back in Iran...But be careful...Remember that you stole and smuggled out of the country the thirteenth piece of your Square...Admittedly it did belong to you in the first place, but I doubt that the Iranians will see it that way."

"I know of the dangers, but they cannot be greater than preaching in the temple in Jerusalem in front of hostile Pharisees and Sadducees, and surrounded by Roman soldiers, as I did."

"But remember what happened to you there."

He just smiled, resisting making a comment.

After saying goodbye to the Son of God (how many in the world could say that?), I made my way along a route that would take me out of the grand UN building to where I would be able to pick up my taxi. As I walked along I rapidly went through the sequence of events that I had earlier witnessed.

All those present in the Hall had seen the almost, but not quite, re-assembly of Christ's Holy Square. All had then heard a speech by a man who professed to be the Son of God. Finally all had taken part in a vote whose overwhelming result had revealed that most wanted the Secretary General to ask the Government of Iran to 'play its part' in the saving of the world. All they could do now was return to their home countries and wait - wait for one of two things to happen.

Either the Secretary General's appeal to the Government of Iran would be successful, or it would not, and God would wreak his vengeance on the World. All the Leaders of the various countries could now do was to ask their people to somehow prepare for the worst possible scenario. But how does one prepare for one's inevitable death in just ten days' time? Tidy up your financial accounts? Why? Forgive those who had harmed you in the past? Not much point now. Renew relationships that you had allowed to lapse, especially within families? A bit late in the day for that. The list seemed endless once you started.

I suspected that we would hear reports of people taking their own lives, and in large groups and whole families too, rather than wait for death coming as a result of an asteroid hitting the Earth. Were this to happen it would be most unfortunate, for I was personally optimistic that the Leader of Iran would make the journey to New York, if only at the very last minute - a bit of brinkmanship.

I was even of the opinion that if he did not make the journey God, who I felt was a compassionate God, would accept that Man on Earth had made a determined effort in the brief time available. He had tried to fulfil the conditions that God had laid down two thousand years earlier, and had been revealed only a few months ago in a recently discovered Dead Sea Scroll. I had to feel that way because it had been me who had led the quest to locate all the thirteen pieces of pot so that Christ's Holy Square could be re-assembled at UN Headquarters. We had got so near, and yet so far from accomplishing this. Surely God would take all our efforts into account.

At the Lincoln Near Earth Asteroid Research Establishment, commonly known as LINEAR, at Socorro in the US State of New Mexico, the televisions on the wall of the main observation centre were showing the same pictures as those being transmitted worldwide from UN Headquarters in New York. The observer team had been waiting impatiently for the thirteenth and final piece of pot to be placed in Christ's Holy Square. They knew that that simple act would result in the asteroid they'd been tracking for some weeks, changing course, moving into an orbit round the sun that would take it close to the Earth, but harmlessly by-passing it.

But alas that very act had not taken place, the all-important thirteenth piece being positioned on the table in the UN Assembly Hall no more than twenty centimetres from the Square itself, but sadly outside it. The Square was therefore incomplete. The question now was - would God up above carry out his threat and allow the asteroid, its original harmless course having earlier been changed by him, to strike the Earth in just ten days' time with such force that all life on the planet would be destroyed?

No one of course knew the answer to that question. But observations still had to be made to check one way or the other, and it was up to LINEAR, along with other stations throughout the world to come up with the evidence.

As the sun was setting in Socorro preparations were already in progress for the night's observation programme. The main telescope was already lined up on the asteroid, even though there was still too much natural light to see it. In an hour's time it would be 'all systems go', with the sophisticated digital cameras taking a series of rapid snapshots that would be overlaid, all of course computer controlled, in order to 'see' where the asteroid was in relation to the fixed background stars. The stars would then be erased, leaving the asteroid. Its present position, speed and future course could then be calculated.

As the first results were analysed the looks of disappointment on the observers' faced said it all. The asteroid's collision course hadn't changed in the slightest. A check of the results confirmed that it would indeed strike the Earth with immeasurable force at 14:30 on the 6th of April, just southwest of the Azores. The impact would be on such a devastating scale that the extinction of almost all living things would take place. Only the most tolerant plants and animals, such as simple grasses and primitive insects would survive...certainly not man.

What was evident was that God had not shown any compassion. Man had tried his best to assemble the world's most important Leaders together, as decided by the UN Secretary General in order to re-assemble his Son's Holy Square...but on this occasion man's best had not been good enough.

This unfortunate news was relayed back to UN Headquarters. The Secretary General had hoped that he would not have to send his communique to the Leader of Iran. He now realised that it should be already on its way, to be delivered by the US Ambassador in Tehran as soon as possible.

***

Chapter Thirty One

They say that 'God moves in mysterious ways, his wonders to perform', so wrote the English poet and hymn writer, William Cowper, some two hundred and fifty years ago. During my choirboy days I remembered singing the hymn, although the words did not make much sense to me at the time. I was now about to witness what exactly they meant.

What had taken place at UN Headquarters had of course not only been seen by those representing the Government of Iran, including its Leader, but also by its millions of people. All this had taken place before the official communique from the Secretary General had dropped on the Iranian Leader's desk.

As far as the Iranian people were concerned what they'd seen on their television sets and heard on their social network sites had one of two effects. On the one hand some, mainly the old and uneducated, objected vehemently to their country's Leader being given some sort of ultimatum, not by the other nations, but by a Christian God. On the other some, mainly the young and educated, were still disappointed that their Leader had not been present in the UN Assembly Hall when the ceremony, one that had been witnessed by the whole world, had taken place. Everybody knew that Iran, their country, had not been represented, and that annoyed them intensely. How could their country be considered a 'world player' when it was absent from such an important event?

This situation again quickly developed into a wholesale protest, this time more violent because Iranian was fighting Iranian instead of being united against the Government. Taking advantage of the situation the Government was content to simply keep control of the violence, ruthlessly stepping in to prevent the damaging and looting of property. And it didn't help when on the morning of April 1st it openly declared that it was not prepared to be dictated to by the United Nations. The country's Leader would not be travelling to New York to take part in some sort of mumbo-jumbo ceremony.

It was now time for Jesus to take up the story again since he was, for the second time, directly involved.

Narrator – Jesus Nazarene

That evening, following Iran's declaration, two events took place in that country that were apparently unconnected, indeed couldn't be connected, but yet they were. I, who had flown out of the country's Imam Khomeini Airport only a couple of days earlier, flew back in and was promptly arrested by the authorities who, as a result of a phone call from an official in the Pakistani Embassy in Washington, had been warned to keep a lookout for a man called Jesus Nazarene, travelling on an American passport, who may try to get back into the country.

I was first questioned on why I had returned to Iran in such a short time, making a round journey of some twenty-two thousand kilometres in the space of only two days. I honestly replied, getting straight to the point: "I have returned to warn you of impending catastrophe in your country…But it can be avoided if your Leader is prepared to fly to New York and place his piece in the Holy Square."

The immigration official, a man insecure in his position and realising that he was well out of his depth, made a call to some higher authority, who too realised that someone at Government level needed to be consulted. This duly took place and within the hour such a high ranking person arrived from Tehran, some thirty kilometres away from the airport. His first question to me was on an entirely different theme: "Could you tell me how you managed to get the piece of pot out of the Museum of Glassware and Ceramics?...Security at all public buildings had been stepped up during this period of unrest." He had obviously checked first to ensure that the piece had in fact gone missing. The one that had turned up at UN Headquarters could have been a fake.

Determined not to be intimidated by the high ranking official, I simply smiled before answering him: "Oh…I just spirited it out of the case and into my hands…it was as simple as that."

It was now the official's turn to smile: "As easy as that, eh?…I suppose you can walk on water, heal the sick and pass through walls?"

"Well…I can certainly do the first two…But have not tried the third."

The official, now getting annoyed, realised that he wasn't going to get anywhere questioning me about what had already passed. He therefore asked about the impending catastrophe: "So…What is this catastrophe going to be?"

"All I can tell you is that your country will be attacked from the skies…But not by another nation…I must stress that." I did not want Iran to think that another nation was preparing to attack it, and make a pre-emptive strike. Were that to take place it would indeed be a disaster and could throw the whole world into conflict…something that on the face of it would not matter if my Father in Heaven destroyed the World in five days' time. But I was optimistic that 'something would happen' that would lead to my Father not taking such devastating action.

The official looked puzzled. If not an attack by another nation then by whom, or what? Realising that he too was out of his depth he left the room in order to make a phone call to those higher up the chain of command than himself. He needed to seek advice on what to do with the information he'd just received…and what to do with me.

The advice was simple…the military machine would be put on full alert to counter any threat from the sky…and don't release me. I may be needed for further questioning.

The sky over Iran's nuclear installation at Arak, a town two hundred kilometres south west of Tehran had already darkened as night set in. It was a crystal clear night, with the Milky Way, that wide band of diffused light that crosses the sky, showing that the galaxy of which our sun is a member, is a thin spiralling nebula slowly rotating in space. A group of young boys, living on the outskirts of the town, who were returning to their homes having attended prayers at the local mosque, looked up at the clear sky as children of all countries did. They were curious about what exactly was going on up there. Could there be life like there was on their own planet, they wondered?

Suddenly the group became aware of a bright light in the sky, far brighter than the brightest star, moving very quickly towards them from the west. The light appeared to have a fiery tail streaming out behind it. The boys had seen brief trails of light in the night sky on many previous occasions, but those had lasted barely a second. Their teacher at school had told them that they were meteorites - small pieces of rock that had entered the earth's stmosphere at high speed and had simply burned up. But this was different. It was brighter, obviously larger, and continued burning as it sped across the sky.

The brilliant object then changed direction and appeared to be heading straight for them. What could they do? Running was pointless, for the fiery object may chase them. There was only one thing to do - lie flat on the ground, bury their faces in the sand and pray as they had done earlier in the mosque.

Protecting their faces with their hands they sneaked a look through their open fingers and saw the object hit the ground some distance away from them, to the west of the town. On impact there was a flash of light, followed a few seconds later by a noticeable 'thud', and then silence. Being too far away for the children to investigate, they ran home to tell their parents what they had just seen.

Typical of parents, they tried to explain. It must have been a military aircraft. You occasionally saw flames coming out of the rear of their engines. Something to do with afterburners, explained one knowledgeable father to his son. Maybe the plane had caught fire and crashed. Another parent had a different explanation. He reminded his son that the builders of the new Arak motorway down to the Persian Gulf occasionally used explosives when the route was blocked by a rocky outcrop. Since they wanted to get the work done as quickly as possible they were now working through the night.

The children listened, but were far from convinced, and for two very good reasons - Aircraft made a lot of noise. The object they'd seen in the sky had been silent. And the motorway being constructed was to the south of the city. The flash and thud that they'd seen and heard were definitely to the west.

Of course those who lived in the area west of the town saw the light in the sky and its descent to the ground if they happened to be outside, as some were as they made their way home from work. Whether inside or out all heard and felt the thud because the ground shook in the same way it did when an earthquake struck, as it had over the years in that area.

The men rushed to where they thought some sort of explosion had taken place, and it wasn't long before they came across a large crater in the soft sandy ground, surrounded by the flattened remains of several buildings that only minutes earlier had been part of a huge industrial estate. Their estimates put the crater at about fifteen to twenty metres across, with a depth of about ten metres. As they cautiously peered into it they detected a dull red glow, and smoke and steam were rising from it, being clearly visible in the headlights of cars that had been driven to the scene. There was little doubt what it was. A meteorite had fallen from the sky and impacted on the outskirts of their town. The men looked across to the glowing lights of Arak's Heavy Water plant, no more than a kilometre away. It had been a near miss. Fortunately the nearest houses had been at least a couple of hundred metres away, and although the shockwave produced by the impact had caused some structural damage, no one had been injured.

Even at that late hour news travelled fast, and it wasn't long before the Head of Internal Security in Iran's national government was informed of what had taken place. He was at the time attending a formal dinner at the Turkish Embassy in Tehran, where closer cross-border cooperation was being discussed. Understandably he wasn't best pleased at being asked by one of his aides to take a phone call.

The Head had already been informed of the 'threat from the skies' made by a man who had just flown into Imam Khomeini International Airport from New York, having earlier made a provocative speech to the UN Assembly. And just to be on the safe side he had put the military, especially the airforce, on a code red alert. He was therefore pleased to hear from his advisors that although a meteorite had in fact struck the Earth, just to the west of Arak there had been no loss of life, nor had the city's Heavy Water Plant been in any way affected. One thing was certain - no other country had been involved. As the Head of Internal Security put it to his Turkish counterpart, having returned to the dinner hall: "It had simply been a meteorite…Some sort of Act of God."…And indeed it had been.

He and his Turkish counterpart were good friends of many years' standing, and the Turkish politician felt that he could say exactly what he thought to his friend: "Has it occurred to you that this is the warning that the man who'd given his speech at the UN referred to on his return to your country?…Had the meteorite struck a bit further to the east it would have devastated your heavy water plant, putting back production for years."

The Iranian politician laughed off the suggestion: "You don't honestly believe that, do you?…Are you honestly suggesting that some God above has intentionally directed a meteorite to hit my country, but to just miss a vital nuclear istallation?"

"Yes…I am suggesting exactly that," replied his Turkish friend.

Knowing that there was little they could do until daylight the men who had discovered the meteorite crater started to make their way home. As they did so they suddenly became aware that another bright light had appeared in the sky, apparently heading towards them. It too was travelling at high speed and had a fiery tail.

Suddenly the light became two. In a matter of seconds the men realised what was taking place. Another meteorite was on its way towards them, but had now broken into two pieces. As one knowledgeable man pointed out: "Meteorites often come from the same source, usually some larger object that has disintegrated in outer space...This is obviously the case here...But on hitting the earth's atmosphere the one meteorite has split, becoming two."

All the men were now no doubt thinking the same thing. If the pieces of glowing rock were on the same trajectory as the previous one then both could strike the ground exactly where they were standing. Realising that there was little they could do, they, like the children had done a few minutes earlier on the other side of town, fell to the ground and prayed. They too sneaked a look through open fingers and were pleased to see that both fiery objects had passed overhead and were heading east on identical courses, one being slightly behind the other.

Just before the two meteorites disappeared over the horizon, now well clear of Arak, both appeared to change course, one heading north, the other heading south.

As the men, now safe, stood up and watched both objects fall below the horizon they witnessed two distinct flashes of light, albeit very faint, almost a minute apart. Each flash was accompanied a few minutes later by a distant rumbling sound. It was not unlike a distant flash of lightning, accompanied by the rumble of thunder.

There was no doubt in the men's minds what had taken place. Both meteorites had struck the earth, one roughly north east of where they were standing, and one a bit further away and to the south east. The question was - where exactly?

As the Head of Internal Security was about to make his closing speech he was again interrupted by one of his aides: "There's another phone call for you. Sir...Sounds urgent."

"Can't it wait?...I'm about to make my closing speech...Tell who ever it is to ring back in an hour."

"I think that you should take the call now, Sir...It's to do with what happened at Arak about half an hour ago...There have been two more meteorite impacts."

Unhappy with the situation the Head left the room in order to take the call in private.

"Yes?" he yelled down the phone.

Sensing that the Head of Internal Security was annoyed at the intrusion, the caller first apologised before passing on the vital information: "Sorry to disturb you, Sir, but there have been two more meteorite impacts...At Qom, some hundred and twenty kilometres north east of Arak and at Natanz, two hundred kilometres to the south east."

The Head immediately recognised the names of the towns and knew of their importance; "Any damage to the uranium enrichment plant at Qom?"

"No, Sir...The meteorite impacted in the ground some distance away from the plant itself, unfortunately hitting the Qom to Aliabad highway...The crater has cut all means of transport between the two towns."

"And what about the uranium enrichment plant at Natanz...Any damage there?"

"No, Sir...In fact the meteorite impacted in the middle of the town's only fooball pitch." Chuckling down the phone he added: "Looks as if the local team will have to play all its coming matches away from home." He then realised that the Head would probably not be in the mood for jokes.

The Head, determined to bring the conversation to a quick end, gave his instructions: "Get the necessary plant in and immediately sort out the highway problem...I want it open within forty-eight hours...With regard to the football pitch at Natanz, organise some diggers and bulldozers to fill in the crater and level it off...It will be a bit uneven, but I'm sure the team will manage...Their hardly English Premier Division, are they?"

"Right, Sir...I'll get on with that straight away."

The Head returned to the Assembly Room and made his closing speech, suggesting that both countries should jointly patrol the four hundred kilometre border in order to stop the flow of drugs across it. Finally he gave brief details of the three meteorite impacts that had fortunately done little damage, neither had there been any loss of life or even injury to the three towns' citizens. He then sat down next to his Turkish friend.

"Three meteorite impacts, then?...All near some form of nuclear installation...Sheer coincidence?...Or some sort of warning?" asked his friend.

The Head, on hearing of the first impact, was convinced that it had indeed been sheer coincidence. But two more impacts, uncomfortably close to Iran's nuclear installations...that was hardly coincidence. Iran was a huge country, most of it uninhabited. The meteorites could have impacted hundreds of miles from where people lived, but they appear to have sought out those towns near to nuclear installations. And was it significant that there'd been no loss of life? Were the three meteor impacts indeed some form of warning? The attack, as predicted by the man who had spoken at the United Nations and was now beng held in a secure room at Tehran Airport, had certainly come from the skies and had not involved any other nation. So...what next? It was essential to interview the man again.

Of course the news of the three meteorite impacts spread like wildfire throughout the Iranian nation. Details were not only shown on national television, but all the social network sites were buzzing with the news.

Some people of course were prepared to accept one version that was being put around by government loyalists that the three meteorites, presumably all from the same source in space had by sheer coincidence hit the ground close to three of the country's nuclear installations. It was as simple as that.

Others, possibly the young and more clear thinking, with access to the latest forms of communication, tied together the three events that had taken place during the last forty-eight hours. They were my speech to the United Nations Assembly, my arrest at Tehran Airport where I had predicted an 'attack from the sky', and the three meteorite impacts close to the three most politically sensitive places in the whole of the country. This was definitely not sheer coincidence. It was a case of someone, whoever that someone was, 'making a point'.

The official who had earlier interviewed me at Tehran Airport was instructed to interview me again, possibly with a bit more respect this time. He had been instructed to find out the answer to one question - What happens next?

This time I spoke with more confidence, knowing that the three meteorite impacts had caused consternation at the highest level of government: "Well...these were just a warning of what could happen...If your country's Leader still refuses to go to New York and complete my Holy Square as he has been asked to do in the Secretary General's communique to him, then more impacts will take place, but this time with more devastating effect...My Father is giving your country one last chance to carry out this simple duty to mankind."

Again my message was relayed to the highest levels of government, and again there was obstinacy, the attitude still being that The Islamic Republic of Iran was not going to be dictated to by anyone, certainly not a man sitting in a detention room at Tehran Airport, nor from his so-called Father in Heaven.

Still in detention I looked at my watch, which also showed the date - it was the 2nd of April. All life on Earth would be extinguished, in just four days' time unless my Holy Square was completed by the Iranian Leader. Time was indeed running out for mankind. A further warning was required, and soon.

That evening the men working at the secret nuclear facility at Khvareh, in the centre of the Dasht-e-Kavir Desert were celebrating. They had built in record time a uranium conversion plant to convert 'yellowcake', a powder obtained from a uranium bearing ore, into high grade uranium oxide, by a series of chemical processes. This was used to produce the fuel for nuclear reactors of the pressurised heavy water type. Since the plant was largely self controlled, using the latest computer technology, the men had retired to the town, some five kilometres away in order to carry out their celebrations.

At precisely midnight a young boy, lying in bed but still wide awake, was staring through his uncurtained window. He hated the curtains being drawn, plunging his bedroom into total darkness. He found it frightening. As soon as his mother had tucked him in and left his room he'd got out of bed and pushed the curtains back.

He stared out towards where he knew the plant was, some two kilometres away, although he couldn't see anything because at night the lights were turned off to avoid the plant being seen from the sky by a passing spy satellite. He was about to go back to his bed when he saw an intensely bright light with a glowing tail behind it rise above the horizon in the west. It then proceeded to cross the sky, but when almost overhead it changed direction and plunged to the ground. It had to be a crashing aeroplane, thought the boy, it couldn't be anything else.

The impact with the ground produced a flash of light followed by a thud that shook the whole area. This was immediately followed by a shock wave of air that struck the boy's house and others in the street, with massive force. Fortunately for him the huge flash of light had frightened him into jumping back into bed and pulling the thick bed clothes over his head. This simple act protected him from the shower of glass that resulted when the window shattered into the room as the blast of air hit it.

As dawn broke over the town of Khvareh the extent of the damage became clear. The houses closest to the devastated plant, including of course the young boy's house, had stood up to the blast remarkably well, but their windows had been blown inwards by the blast. Otherwise there had been only superficial damage such as some of the terracotta pantiles being ripped off the roofs and chimneys blown over. People had of course been shaken, but otherwise fortunately unscathed. It appeared that the only person to have seen what had actually happened was the small boy.

Later, in the town's main square he was asked to describe what he'd seen, which he did as vividly as he could. Many of those listening to him immediately assumed that the plant had indeed been hit by a crashing military aircraft. They were always flying overhead. But the town's elders weren't so certain. Although they'd been inside their homes at the time of impact they hadn't heard the slightest sound, certainly not the wail of a dying aircraft about to hit the ground.

The men who had worked on the plant had of course already been informed of what had happened at Arak, Qom and Natanz. Had the same now happened at Khvareh? The general opinion was that it had.

The plant, that had earlier shined, as the bright stainless steel reflected the sun's rays, was now a twisted mass of piping and corrugated metal, surrounding an obvious steaming crater in the ground. There was no chance that the five men who had been on security duty could have survived.

But by far the most worrying effect resulting from the devastation was the presence of the highly radioactive yellowcake as a fine layer of dust covering all exposed surfaces. It could even be detected in the air by its unpleasant metallic taste.

The scientists who had worked on the plant immediately recognised the danger. Within the confines of the plant many had had to wear protective clothing when moving around. Now they and the town's population had no protection at all. There was only one answer - evacuation, and quickly.

The chief chemist at the plant suggested that the residents should as quickly as possible place some form of tightly woven cloth over their mouths and noses. It was essential that they inhaled as little of the powder as possible. They were then advised to pack into a bag some clothes, food and water, as well as items that they considered valuable or essential to them, such as mobile phones, laptops and of course any medication they required. They should then leave the town as quickly as possible by what ever means were available. Many did have cars and they were asked to offer lifts to those who didn't. There were also plant lorries available that had not been in the vicinity of the blast and hence were undamaged.

Over the next few hours the small town of Khvareh, with its population of just under six thousand, was evacuated as its citizens made their way along the desert road to the nearest town, that of Qarmsarteh, some ninety kilometres to the west.

Of course it wasn't long before the news of the devastation at the Khvareh's nuclear installation reached the highest level of government. Advisors were quickly called in and listened to by ministers. It was clear that what had taken place at Arak, Qom, Natanz and now at Khvareh - all plants part of Iran's nuclear programme, could be repeated elsewhere. Three were fortunately still intact, but one was now a devastated mass of twisted metal, with the close-by town uninhabitable because of radioactive contamination. What next? Could the plants at Bushehr, Gachin and Isfahan be next in line for devastation by a falling meteorite? It was anybody's guess.

One thing was obvious to the government of the Islamic Republic of Iran. If meteorites, although relatively small in size, could be directed with such accuracy by what appeared to be some 'controlling' force, maybe some form of God up above, the threat of world annihilation by a huge asteroid in just four days' time suddenly became a distinct possibility. Action had to be taken…and fast. Very fast.

The name-of-the-game was now 'saving face'. Iran was a proud nation and had never showed weakness when faced with adversity. Any action had therefore to be carried out in as covert a way as possible.

***

Chapter Thirty Two

As the scheduled Lufthansa daily flight from Tehran's Imam Khomeini Airport to New York's JFK, via Frankfurt, commenced its take off at twenty past seven that evening, there were only a handful of people on board. With the imminent destruction of the world, who would want to travel half way across it? Better to stay put with family and friends. This showed a lack of confidence in the Government's - 'It's all mumbo-jumbo…Nothing will happen…Trust us', attitude. Well, they didn't, and when news flashed across the country that one of its nuclear installations had been devastated by a meteorite crashing to the ground, and that three others had had near misses, this confirmed that their lack of trust was justified.

Those who had decided to make the journey to the United States were American business representatives who were determined to get home to their families before the asteroid struck the Earth.

But there were two people on board with entirely different missions. One was me, the man who had just spent almost twenty-four hours incarcerated in a room in the immigration suite at Tehran Airport. I had been questioned intensely, but had not in any way been mistreated. In fact my interrogators had treated me with the utmost respect, almost awe, not quite knowing who they were dealing with. I was then suddenly released without any sort of explanation and placed on the plane back to the United States.

As the plane took off on its long journey the immigration officials breathed a sigh of relief. They too had been informed of the devastation that had taken place in their country, devastation which had been predicted by me, the very man who'd they'd earlier interrogated. No doubt they thought…thank God he was no longer on Iranian soil making further predictions.

I, sitting at the rear of the plane and not having slept for the best part of twenty-four hours, immediately dropped off. I had no interest in who was travelling on the same plane, nor was I worried about the plane arriving safely at its destination. Although I suspected that the air traffic controls of the various countries to be overflown may not be at their safest, it was important that I arrived safely back in New York, and my

Father in Heaven would make sure I did.

Also on the plane, but sitting at the front, were three men who had boarded it by the 'back door', not having been seen by the other passengers who had had to book in, pass through the various security checks, then hang around for the best part of two hours before boarding. The men, as I later discovered, were in fact the Leader of Iran, accompanied by two of his aides. The Leader's mission was simple - to as covertly as possible cross the Atlantic Ocean to New York's UN Headquarters, place the thirteenth and final piece of pot in Christ's Holy Square and return. He would insist that this was done in total secrecy, certainly not within full view of the world's media.

Since there were so few passengers on the flight all were allowed into the VIP lounge at Frankfurt Airport for their mid-journey break. The atmosphere was strange, to say the least. The Leader of Iran did not appear to be recognised by the other passengers even though his face was a familiar one on Iranian television. So was it a case of the others being in such awe of him that they preferred not to be in anyway involved with him? It was difficult to say. Certainly they did not acknowledge him, preferring to keep themselves to themselves.

My position was entirely different and particularly interesting because I had never seen the Leader and hence had no idea what he looked like. But I suspected that the Leader knew who I was, having seen me at the 'Holy Square' ceremony at UN Headquarters, as shown on worldwide television. The Leader had probably viewed the ceremony many times over and wondered. Surely with such important people as the US President, the Prime Minister of Russia and the Chinese Leader being prepared to place a tiny piece of coloured pot in some sort of wooden square, not unlike a child's first jigsaw, it couldn't be one big confidence trick, could it?

And yet the Iranian Leader had chosen not to attend. With hindsight he must have wondered why he'd allowed himself to be pressured by his ministers into not doing so. Anyway, he was now making amends, but didn't want to show any kind of weakness to the rest of the world. He would insist that the event he was going to take part in was not in any way recorded for all the world to see and comment on. 'Face' had to be saved.

The second lap of the long flight to New York's JFK Airport was only an hour old when I, again trying, but failing to get to sleep, was nudged by one of the hostesses. As I opened my eyes, startled, she whispered to me: "There's a man up at the front who would like you to join him."

I, led by the hostess, shuffled unsteadily up the central aisle, my stiff legs not quite working properly. As we reached the front seats where three men were sitting the hostess spoke quietly to the man who had approached her about the person sitting near the back of the plane: "Here is the man you wanted to have a word with," she then pointed to me before backing away, turning and heading down the aisle to join her colleagues at the rear of the plane.

One of the men vacated his seat to allow me to sit down. This I did, not having any idea at that point who the three men were. The man now standing explained: "Thank you for joining us…Let me introduce ourselves…This is Karim Aziz, the Leader of Iran…We two are his aides, travelling with him to New York."

I should have been surprised, but I wasn't. I always knew that at some point before the 6th of April, the day chosen by my Father to destroy the world, the Iranian Leader would make the journey to UN Headquarters in order to place the thirteenth and final piece of pot in the Holy Square. I had always thought that journey would be made under secrecy in one of Iran's military aircraft, but apparently not.

But now thinking about it, surely the Americans would not allow an Iranian military aircraft within a thousand kilometres of its airspace. Travelling by commercial aircraft therefore made complete sense. A representative at the Pakistani Embassy in Washington DC had probably been made aware of the Leader of Iran's impending visit and made the necessary arrangements at the American 'end'. This would include making the President himself aware of the visit. And the Secretary General of the United Nations would also need to know. It would be his responsibility to ensure that the Leader had access to the Holy Square in order to carry out his final task, unseen by the media. This would be simple to organise because the Square, still missing one piece to complete it, was at that very moment in exactly the same position it had been left in after the re-assembly ceremony just three days earlier. At the side of the Square was the black felt bag still containing the missing piece…Iran's piece…My piece.

On more than one occasion the uniformed security guards who had been given the job of protecting the Square all round the clock had been tempted to remove the final piece from the bag and place it in its correct position just for the sheer hell of it. Surely no harm could come by doing so.

They did however resist the temptation when one of their reliefs informed them of what he'd just seen on the world TV news. Three nuclear plants in Iran had suffered near misses and a fourth been totally destroyed by meteorites, killing some of the plants' personnel. The relief said that it was all to do with the wooden Square in front of them. Maybe if they interfered with it in some way a meteorite would come down from the sky, seek them out and strike them dead.

The Secretary General, having taken advice in the form of a discrete word with first the Pope and then the Archbishops of Canterbury and York, had decided that Christ's Holy Square, incomplete as it was, should remain on the table until one of two things happened. Either the Square would be completed and the annihilation of the world avoided, or it would not. In which case it would suffer the same fate as everything and everyone would suffer when the asteroid struck the Earth with devastating force. All thirteen pieces would return to me, their original owner, who as all life was being extinguished on Earth, would swiftly collect them up. I would then again join my Father in Heaven, as the Nicene Creed, sung or read every Sunday in many churches throughout the Christian world, stated:

And the third day he rose again according to the
scriptures and ascended into heaven and sitteth on
the right hand of the father.

Maybe the 'third day' part would be a little out, for when the asteroid struck few would survive very long, including myself, at least in my human form. For the second time I would ascend into Heaven. For the second time I would sit on the right hand of my Father, and for the second time it would all be according to the scriptures.

The leader of Iran then spoke to me: "You now know who we are, and you no doubt have a good idea why we are on a plane to New York."

I nodded: "I suspect, indeed hope, that you are going to the United Nations Headquarters in order to place the final piece in my Holy Square...Am I right?"

"Yes...You are correct...My government and I decided that in the interests of the world's survival and also world peace I would make this memorable journey...My country does not have an embassy in the United States, but we do have a representative in the Pakistani Embassy in Washington. He has already made the necessary arrangements with the Secretary General...By the way, would you like to join us?"

"Yes...I would appreciate that...Would you believe that the last time I saw my Holy Square with all its thirteen places in place, was two thousand years ago during the Last Supper with my twelve disciples?...You may be aware that shortly afterwards I was betrayed by one of them, tried, found guilty and crucified...On the third day I rose again and later ascended into Heaven to join my Father...The same Father who has vowed to destroy the world in three days' time if you do not place the final piece in its central position in the Square."

The Leader smiled, almost mockingly, then immediately regretted it, realising that I, sitting at the side of him had detected it. But I let it pass for I knew that I had the upper hand. The Leader, now feeling a bit uncomfortable and maybe even thinking that a mere nod of my head to my Father in Heaven could result in a meteorite being directed at the very plane they were all flying in, made a simple request: "We of the Muslim faith know little of you and your faith...Would you please tell me about yourself and how your Father's threat to the world came about?"

Over the next hour of the flight I narrated my story, commencing with the prediction of my birth in the scriptures. I then gave a detailed account of what I'd been told about my birth to parents called Mary and Joseph, of the three wise men with their gifts of gold, frankincense and myrrh, and the journey into Egypt to avoid Herod's cruel action of killing newly born boys because he'd been informed by his prophets that a 'king' had been born.

After Herod's death my parents returned to Israel and settled in a village called Nazareth. This was the reason why I was called Jesus of Nazareth, or as stated on my passport - Jesus Nazarene. I then described my mission to spread the word of my Father, setting out a code on how man should lead his life for the good of all others. This code has throughout history been followed by many people, but a few did not do so and this led not only to local wars, but wars on a world scale such as the two Great Wars, both within the last hundred years. More recently the so-called Cold War had prevailed - a sort of stalemate situation. But it was ultimately realised that had war actually broken out, life on Earth as we knew it would have come to an end in a nuclear holocaust.

I then rounded my story off with the situation as I saw it today. I purposely did not mention nations by name, but made it obvious who they were: "The super powers have realised that some sort of nuclear conflict between them would be futile, and are now prepared to lead the way in developing better relations between nations...The formation of the European Community has ensured that European wars, that have plagued so much of world history, are now a thing of the past...But the Middle East is still a headache for my Father, and for me, because that is where I was born and spent all my life...There was conflict there then...There is conflict there now...Even countries hundreds of kilometres away present a threat to the region, as you are no doubt aware." This comment was aimed directly at the Leader's own country, but I purposely did not mention it by name.

"As much as anything it is this problem that my Father is trying to address, by getting nations to come together to declare their peaceful intentions...This declaration would be shown by their Leaders placing small, insignificant, yet so important pieces of pot in an equally small, almost pathetic wooden frame...My Father hopes that this simple act will get nations thinking how peace throughout the world can be achieved...Otherwise his mission to make a world for his creations, both animals and plants to live in, in complete harmony, will have failed...If he feels that this point has been reached he will bring it all to an end and try again elsewhere...Within his Universe there are many places ready to take on this role...One has only to look into the night sky."

The Leader was obviously taken aback and deeply moved by my strongly expressed words. Never before had he felt quite that way. How could a man be prepared to sacrifice his life for the love of others? He knew of course of examples where men and women had sacrificed their lives in order to save others. Only the other week two children had got into difficulties whilst swimming in the fast flowing River Safid some hundred and fifty kilometres to the west of Tehran. A woman, a total stranger, unknown to the children had managed to get both of them to the bank where waiting parents pulled them to safety. But unfortunately the woman lost he grip and was washed away in the fast current. Her lifeless body had later been found some distance down the river. The Leader remembered how the selfless act had been widely reported in the Iranian press and on national television.

Being a keen mountaineer himself, spending any free time he had climbing in the Reshteh-ye-Kuhha Mountain Range, north of Tehran, and an ardent reader of anything to do with his beloved sport, he had read of fallen climbers sacrificing their own lives by cutting themselves free in order to save the other members on the rope. But were such selfless acts carried out, out of love for their fellow men? It was a difficult question. It all came down to your interpretation of the word 'love'.

The Leader thanked me for being so open with him. He then explained why he was so interested: "As I stated earlier we of the Islam faith know very little of your religion, and I suspect that the vast majority of Christians know very little of my faith...Let me be as open with you as you have with me...I too have a God, as you do...his name is Allah and is one God...I understand that your God is three persons - a Trinity of Father, Son and Holy Spirit."

I nodded. I also realised that the Leader knew more about Christianity than he was prepared to admit.

He continued: "Your religion says that you, the Son of God, were sent down to Earth to carry out God's work...We have Muhammed, not the son of Allah, but a great prophet who set out how Allah expects us to lead our lives...This is set out in his Qur'an...You of course have your Bible, which agrees with the Qur'an in many ways."

I again nodded, fully aware that most people of my faith had not even heard of the Qur'an, or Koran as it was often spelt, let alone knew anything about it.

The Leader rounded his words off: "Finally, your faith has a place called Heaven, where believers enjoy eternal life...We too have such a place...We call it Paradise where all our desires are met...We do agree on a place called Hell...Both of our religions think of Hell as a place of eternal punishment and torment."

After my religious lesson from the Leader I asked what to me was an obvious question: "You have shown by your words how similar our two religions are...So why, over the centuries, have Muslims and Christians been at war with each other? The Crusade Wars were a good example of this, where both Muslim and Christian claimed the Holy Land, more specifically the City of Jerusalem, as its own."

The Leader smiled: "But you earlier mentioned the two Great Wars, fought mainly in Europe...Funnily enough in those wars Muslim and Christian often fought side by side...And during the so called Cold War Muslim countries were not involved at all...It is therefore difficult to work out what has gone wrong in the last thirty or so years to put the two religions in conflict with each other."

Again I nodded. I too had difficulty in working it all out. What I did know was that the very country where I'd been born, spent all my life and had died a horrible death, appeared to be playing some part in putting Muslim against Christian, or in this case, Jew. I'd always hoped that my sacrifice would lead to 'peace on earth', but all indications were that I had failed. I hadn't anticipated man's greed, intolerance, lack of respect for others and the environment that they shared with all other living creatures and plant life. The Earth was in a bit of a mess, a situation that was getting steadily worse. I'd failed. It was now up to my Father to stop the rot. The threat of world annihilation was the first step, the assembly of the world's Leaders, pushing to one side their supposed grandeur in order to perform the simplest of acts, being the second. This second step was almost complete, but not quite. Hopefully it would be within the next twenty-four hours.

The Leader's arrival, at his request, went unannounced, at JFK International, where he, his two aides and myself passed through unnoticed, (except by a small trusted group of immigration officials who were expecting the Iranian Leader). Who would be interested in the passengers on the 4.45 flight from Tehran via Frankfurt? No one. Had the Leader been met by some high level government entourage his presence on American soil would have been given top priority, leading to considerable and probably hostile media coverage.

The three Iranians were immediately picked up, again unnoticed, by a representative of the Pakistani Consulate in New York and taken to a hotel a short taxi ride from the UN building. I already knew where the taxi ranks were and in no time at all I was again booking in at the hotel I'd stayed at on my earlier visit to New York.

The following day, at noon, I received a phone call from the aide to the UN Secretary General, asking me to meet him in the Assembly Hall in an hour's time. He did not elaborate, but I guessed the reason why.

When I arrived I was met and greeted in the foyer by the aide, who vigorously shook me by the hand. As he quickly ushered me to the Assembley Hall he whispered: "Thanks for making this possible."

I whispered back: "My Father's been pulling a few strings too."

The aide's reply: "I understand so."

Once in the Hall he less enthusiastically shook hands with the Iranian

Leader, who was already there with his two aides, and thanked him on behalf of the Secretary General for travelling thousands of kilometres in order to place his country's piece in the Holy Square.

The three of us made our way to the large table that still had my Holy Square positioned at its centre. The black satin bag with the gold draw cordwas beside it. Instinctively I looked through the Square's transparent lid just to check that the central piece was absent…It was. I then felt in the bag to check that the missing piece was there…It also was.

The two UN security guards who were evidently part of a team who had been given the responsibility for looking after the Square since its reassembly, moved to one side. This allowed the Leader to get closer to the table where he was able to study the Square. He had of course seen it before, but only on television, when the camera had zoomed in, thus allowing the Square to fill the huge television screen. He was now looking at the real thing.

His immediate thought probably was - what a pathetic object it looked, sat there on the table, covering only a fraction of its area. The frame hadn't even been made by a craftsman. The joints were rough and the staining and varnishing had been poorly done. How much more impressive it would have been, crafted in silver or better still, gold. How on Earth could its completion with small, different shaped pieces of coloured pot wield such power?He no doubt found it hard to get his head round his question.

Narrator – Chuck Oldfield, Security Guard at United Nations Headquarters, New York

At this point the aide to the Secretary General, who knew we'd been on duty since early morning, told me and my mate Phil to go home, which we gratefully did. We had no idea what was going on, nor did we care. Our duty was done. We could now go home, have a bite to eat then get our heads down for a couple of hours. We both lived on the outskirts of the city and had been on the move early in order to get to the UN building by six o'clock, the time our shift had commenced.

As we made our way home, sharing a car to ease the problems of parking, I asked Phil, who was skilfully weaving his way through the heavy traffic, a question: "I wonder, Phil, what's going on there?…Any ideas?"

"No, Chuck…But that man with the two body guards looked familiar to me...I'm sure I've seen him before, maybe on TV."

"Give us a ring if anything comes to mind."

"I will."

Tired and hungry, we left it at that.

Narrator – Jesus Nazarene

The General Secretary's aide, knowing that there was no point in pussy-footing around, released the catch on the Square and lifted the transparent lid. He then spoke to the Iranian Leader, rather too abruptly, showing a lack of due reverence: "We all, Sir, know why you are here...Would you like to extract the final piece of the Square from the black bag and insert it in the remaining empty place...This will then complete the Square, thus fulfilling the conditions laid down by the Father of the man standing beside you." He then turned to me: "Do you have anything to add, Mr Nazarene?"

I had: "Just one thing...I would like to have seen this simple yet so important act given worldwide coverage so that all could witness the Islamic Republic of Iran's commitment to world peace...But my Father did not stipulate that that should take place as a condition of his plan to bring the world to its senses before it is too late...All he wanted to witness was the completion of the Square, my Square, as a positive sign of the world's commitment, not only to peace, but also to a completely new approach to the ownership and welfare of the planet on which you all live...I say 'you' because I of course have another abode, up in Heaven with my Father...My role is, and has always been, to represent him on Earth....That is why I was present at the previous ceremony, and am here now."

The aide nodded vigorously, his way of not only agreeing with my words, but also to express his thanks to me. He then spoke to the Leader: "When you're ready, Sir."

The Leader stepped forward, cagily placed his hand in the bag as if half expecting some creature inside to snap at it, and carefully extracted the thirteenth and last piece of pot - the white hexagonal piece that had been round my neck during that brief period in my life between the Last Supper and my crucifixion.

He first placed the piece in the palm of his hand, staring at it as he did so. I could tell by his facial expression that the feeling was strange. The piece probably felt warm, a warmth that would intensify almost to the

338

point where the piece became too painful to hold. But instead of putting it down he gripped it tightly. At the same time his breathing seemed to shorten and I suspected that his heart was beating twenty to the dozen (to quote an old English expression that I'd heard somewhere on my travels). For a few seconds a thought flashed through my mind…If he died there and then? would he rise into a Christian heaven?…And how would his death be explained to the people back home? Would it get out that he had in fact been taking part in what could only be described as a 'Christian' ceremony? And if it did, would his country's status in the word be enhanced or diminished?

As it happened I did not have to worry about such thoughts, for as fast as the Leader's worrying symptoms had appeared, his breathing and no doubt his heart rate had returned to normal. I visibly breathed a sigh of relief.

The leader then carefully held the piece above its allotted place, slowly rotated it to ensure that the Greek letters θ and π where the same way up as all but one of the other twelve letters were. Finally he gently released the piece, allowing it to drop the couple of millimetres into the space. It fitted perfectly. The Leader stepped back and bowed slightly, probably not knowing quite why. Christ's Holy Square was now complete. He had fulfilled his duty, albeit reluctantly.

I now stepped forward, reached out and slowly closed the clear lid, activating the catch as I did so. It was essential that none of the pieces fell out. I then picked up the Square in both hands and raised it, pointing it at the ceiling. I then lifted my eyes, staring at an invisible point way above where I knew Heaven was. I whispered to my Father, quoting words from his very own prayer: "Thy will be done on Earth as it is in Heaven." My final act was to carefully place the Square back on the table.

At this point the Leader indicated to the UN aide that he would like to leave the Assembly Hall. Using his cell phone the aide summoned someone to escort the Leader and his small entourage out of the Hall and eventually out of the UN building. There presumably he was met by a private car, probably provided by the Pakistani Consulate to take the party back to its hotel. The Leader obviously did not want to stay on American soil longer than he had to, and no doubt he and his aides would soon be making their way to JFK International for their long flight back to Tehran.

I suspected that the Leader was confident that he'd pulled it off. His departure from Tehran's Imam Khomeini International Airport had only been witnessed by a handful of trusted workers, all members of the country's security 'machine'. At JFK he and his aides had been discretely escorted from the plane by the 'back door', members of the security service being used in preference to immigration officials who could have friends in the media. He had also been assured by the Pakistani Consulate that his secret was safe with them. And the UN aide and myself, who had both witnessed his act of completing the Square, had nothing to gain by revealing what we'd seen.

At this point the UN aide suggested to me that the Square should be left on the table so that now the Iranian Leader had left the Assembly Hall the cameras could be switched on, focussed on the completed Square and the pictures transmitted throughout the world. When all said and done this was what the peoples of all nations were waiting for. Many had already accepted that life as they knew it would come to an abrupt end in a few days' time. Others had maintained an optimism that at the very last minute 'something' would happen, but they had no idea what. They certainly didn't expect an Iranian Leader to make the journey to New York in order to carry out the one act that they thought could, indeed would, change the course of the approaching asteroid.

But it was my opinion that we should wait, at least until the Iranian Leader had touched down again on Iranian soil. He would then be able to defend his action rather than having possibly to do so whilst still in the air. I knew that coup d'etats often took place in countries when their leaders were abroad. The cameras could then be switched on so that the world could be made aware of the momentous event that had earlier taken place. The viewing public would not be too concerned about how the Square had been completed, only that it had been. Maybe the Son of God, me, had carried out the act...Who cared?

My Father would have witnessed the event and would already be changing the course of the asteroid ever so slightly, just to take it off a collision course with Earth.

Just to make sure, I decided to remind him with a short prayer. For the second time the aide observed me lift my eyes to Heaven: "Now is the time for you to fulfil your promise to mankind, Father."

***

340

Chapter Thirty Three

Narrator – Chuck Oldfield

But the Iranian leader had been seen by me and my mate Phil, and later recognised by me after seeing a news bulletin on television. We were also prepared to take financial advantage of our good fortune…Let me explain.

When Phil and I, who had earlier been trusted with the job of keeping Christ's Holy Square safe in the UN Assembly Hall, arrived home after completing our shift, our wives already had breakfast on the go. For my part, as I walked through the door the aroma of frying bacon hit me. When I moved into the kitchen I found my wife Janice already cracking the eggs. While she was doing this I switched on the television and commenced flicking the channels until I found the one I wanted – the CNN channel transmitting the hourly news.

I enjoyed the news because it enabled me to converse confidently with those attending the UN building. It never ceased to amaze me how they wanted to seek my views on the affairs of the moment, almost as if they wanted those of the 'layman', not the supposed 'expert'.

The first report described what had recently happened in Iran. Spy satellites had picked up evidence of what looked like four explosions at Arak, Qom, Natanz and Khvareh, all nuclear installations. There had been speculation that some sort of attack by another nation could have taken place, and to allay fears within his country its Leader had come on television to reassure the nation. This he did by first explaining that some days earlier the nation's astronomers at the Imam Khomeini Observatory in the Zagros Mountains had reported that a small meteor out in space had broken up and the remnants were heading for the Earth. Purely by chance they had landed on Iranian soil and purely by chance had landed close to the four scientific sites. No mention was made that they were nuclear installations. Fortunately only one of the plants had actually been hit and there'd been minimum loss of life.

I immediately realised that the man talking on the television screen was the same man as the one I'd been standing next to in the UN Assembly Hall only an hour earlier. It had been the Leader of Iran. The television pictures showing him must have been pre-recorded before he'd left the country.

I immediately phoned my colleague: "Guess what, Phil…That man we saw in the Assembly Hall was the frigging Leader of Iran, would you believe?…I've just seen his face on the telly."

"God, Chuck…Bet your friend at the *Herald* would give his right arm for such info…It would be a real exclusive for him…Any chance we could cash in?"

"Don't know, Phil…Let me have a bite to eat…I'll then make a phone call before we meet up and decide what to do."

"Good idea…I'm half way through a steak…I'll pick you up in an hour."

Five minutes later I made my call: "Hi, Cec..Can we meet?"

An hour later Phil and I were having a beer in *Joe's Bar,* just round the corner from where we both lived. Perched on a stool at the side of us was Cecil Gee, one of the *Herald's* most experienced reporters. Over the last five years a steady stream of low level information had passed between Cecil Gee, Phil and myself, mainly about who had arrived at UN Headquarters by the 'back door' rather than by the main entrance. Cecil had even provided me with a camera that had been embedded in the centre of the badge on the peak cap I always wore, indeed expected to wear as part of my uniform. Unfortunately a few days ago the camera had been damaged beyond repair when my wife, thinking that the cap was smelly and greasy, decided to sponge it down in the sink. It hadn't done the precision-made, yet plastic lens any good when she'd vigorously scrubbed the badge with an abrasive pad to remove a film of grime.

"So, Chuck…What yer got for me?…Must be pretty big, you not prepared to give me any hint over the phone."

I smiled: "This is big, Cec…Real big…Certainly worth a buck or two."

Give us a hint, Chuck…Can't go throwing the paper's cash around on rubbish."

I obviously wanted to prick Cec's curiosity, but didn't want to give anything away: "Er…Iran."

"Iran?…What about Iran?" Cecil obviously knew all about the country's Leader's refusal to take part in the Holy Square ceremony at the UN since it had been extensively covered by all the world's media. He had also seen the news a few minutes earlier showing the damage to

342

the nuclear installations in Iran, and the leader's explanation of what had taken place. So, what else could be new about a country that the average American knew nothing about, and cared even less about?

"It's about the Iranian Leader." I released a little more information.

This puzzled Cecil. How could a security guard at the UN be privy to some information about the Iranian Leader that he, one of the most respected and knowledgeable reporters on America's Eastern Seaboard, hadn't heard the slightest whisper of? He had to know: "Ok...Let's talk money...That's what you want isn't it?"

I enthusiastically nodded.

"Right...How about five hundred?"

"Yer jokin', Cec...It's worth a thousand at least." I realised that whatever the figure was, I would have to share it with my mate Phil.

"Go on, then...A thousand...But it better be good, or I'll go frigging spare."

"Cash up front, Cec...Yer know the deal."

"Reluctantly, Cecil reached inside his jacket, pulled open the zip that his wife had specially sewn in to foil any slick pickpocket, and pulled out a battered, sealed buff envelope. He had many contacts within the city and always carried a considerable quantity of cash on the off-chance that something out of the ordinary would come up from one of them who would then need some recompense. He passed the unopened envelope across to me, at the same time not releasing his grip: "So, Chuck...Let's have it."

As my finger and thumb squeezed on the corner of the envelope I said: "He was in the Assembly Hall this morning, wasn't he, Phil?"

Phil enthusiastically nodded, even though he had no idea what the Iranian Leader looked like. He therefore had to take my word.

"Yer sure, Chuck...How do you know it was him?" Cec wasn't convinced.

"Saw his face of the telly this lunchtime...Talking about some meteorites hitting Iran...It was the same man in the Assembly Hall...I swear."

Cecil informed us that he knew all about the 'strikes' in Iran, the spy satellites having relayed their information back to receiving stations in America, and the information had been broadcast on all the various news channels. All indications were that the damage had in fact been caused by some sort of shower of meteorites that had been too big to burn up in the atmosphere. I bet he'd secretly hoped that some sort of missile attack had been carried out by some other nation because that would have been 'real' news. But alas that apparently had not been the case.

Cecil had to take my word that I had in fact seen the same man at UN Headquarters only a couple of hours earlier.

Narrator – Cecil Gee, reporter, New York Herald

As it happened this did not come as a surprise to me, for I had always been of the opinion that 'something' would happen before the asteroid struck the Earth, as had been predicted by the world's most prominent astronomers. It all made sense to me. The Leader of Iran had made the journey to New York under a veil of secrecy in order to complete the Holy Square. I told Chuck and Phil that I was prepared to bet my next month's salary that just after they'd been dismissed by the UN aide, the Leader would have placed the thirteenth and final piece in its allotted place.

After assuring Chuck that I would provide him with a new camera for his cap badge I quickly left *Joe's Bar*. I had a very important journey to make and precious little time to make it. Perhaps I could just succeed.

The journey to JFK airport took an eternity and I cursed every second of the way. It seemed as if every traffic light, every driver, every pedestrian was against me. As I approached the airport I could see the planes taking off. Was I too late, I wondered? Was one of the planes in fact carrying the Iranian Leader back to his home country?

After parking in the short stay car park I rushed across to the closed doors of 'Departures'. They sluggishly opened and I again cursed as they did so. Why had everything been stacked against me, I wondered? I looked up at the screen displaying the Departures. The top line said it all.Lufthansa LU129, bound for Tehran via Frankfurt, had left just five minutes earlier. Which plane had it been, rising into the sky as I'd approached the airport? Was the Iranian Leader on it? I would never know for certain.

As I again approached the doors, this time to make my exit, they again reluctantly opened. More curses. After finding my car I simply sat inside it, with no intentions of starting the engine. I'd fed the meter for an hour's stay so there was no hurry.

I now had to make a decision - to either go ahead and write an exclusive article on the presence of the Leader of Iran at UN Headquarters, or not to bother because I had no actual proof. I only had the word of my security guard contacts, and they could well have got the identification of the Iranian Leader simply wrong. Having said that, Chuck Oldfield had never let me down before.

It took me only a few seconds to decide…I would write the story.

The following morning my article appeared in the *New York Herald.* The headline was:

Iranian Leader in New York to complete Christ's Holy Square

My long and detailed story commenced with God's message, set out in a recently found Dead Sea Scroll, that unless man mended his ways he, God, would destroy the world. But this could be avoided by the leaders of the world coming together to complete the Square with the pieces of pottery that Christ himself had given out to his disciples at the Last Supper. All thirteen pieces, against huge odds, had been located by the diligent work of Professor Peter Robertshaw, a British archaeologist, and were at that very moment at the United Nations Headquarters in New York.

My article continued by describing how an asteroid had been discovered to be on a collision course with Earth that would annihilate all life on the planet. The completion of the Square would avoid this taking place.

In considerable detail my article then described the almost complete, but not quite, re-assembly of the Square at the UN, even though the ceremony had been widely covered on television only a couple of days earlier. At this point I stressed the absence of the Iranian Leader, followed by the consequences of his absence.

Finally my article described, with my imagination working overtime, how the Iranian Leader, on humanitarian grounds, had secretly flown across the Atlantic to New York and had placed the final piece in the Square, before returning home. I rounded my article off with the following three sentences, the last allowing the reader to boast: "I knew that already."

The world's astronomers are at this very moment looking for a change in the asteroid's course to take it away from a collision with the Earth. If such a collision were to take place it would result in conditions that would eventually lead to the extinction of most of the life on the planet. It is thought that such conditions led to the extinction of the dinosaurs some sixty-five million years ago, conditions that were also produced by the impact of an asteroid.

Although the first part of my final statement was not a figment of my imagination, for what took place next was entirely predictable. Obviously the world's astronomers were hard at work. But my last sentence was almost, but possibly not quite, true, the jury still being out on what exactly had led to the demise of the dinosaurs.

Earlier, when it had become common knowledge that twelve of the thirteen pieces of pot had been added to the Square, observations had commenced to see if there was any change in the asteroid's course, the hope being that twelve pieces would be enough to persuade God to show compassion on the planet and its inhabitants. Much to their disappointment, the astronomers hadn't detected such a change. The asteroid was still on its collision course.

But now the situation had completely changed. As soon as the *Herald*, with my article prominently displayed in it, hit the news stands and appeared on the worldwide web, making it instantly available to all interested parties, the astronomers commenced their observations with a renewed enthusiasm, for the Square was now complete. God's demands had been fulfilled to the letter.

Of course it was daylight in America when the *Herald*, that included my article, appeared on the news stands so no observations of the asteroid, designated the code 2012JT82, could be made. But in those parts of the world where it was already night time the sophisticated equipment required to observe any changes in the asteroid's course was already in action.

The first positive results came from the Siding Spring Observatory, some four hundred kilometres north-west of Sidney, Australia. The observers, using a similar technique to those at LINEAR in New Mexico, reported that a change in the asteroid's course had been detected at precisely 00.01 hours the previous night. The change had been slight and the observatory, not wanting to give false hopes to the world, had decided to re-check their readings the following night. When they did so their earlier observations were confirmed. The asteroid had indeed changed course and the most recent calculations indicated that if its present course continued unchanged it would definitely miss the Earth. It would be a near thing, the asteroid passing within the moon's orbit at a distance of 320 000 kilometres at its closest point.

Just two hours later, as the rotating Earth moved nightfall round its surface, the Zijinshan Observatory, located at Purple Mountain in Jiangsu Province, China, an observatory with an enviable reputation for discovering new comets and asteroids, was also observing the asteroid's slight change in course. But had also withheld revealing the news to the world without first checking their equipment and making further observations. On such an important issue it was essential that the hopes of the world were not raised by false information. As soon as the Australian astronomers revealed their results to the world the Chinese astronomers followed suit, confident that their original observations had indeed been correct.

It was some fifteen hours later that LINEAR'S telescopes in Socorro, New Mexico, were able to focus on the asteroid, and then only to confirm that it had indeed changed course and would now miss the Earth by some 280 000 kilometres, not 320 000 kilometres as had been calculated by the Australians the night before. A possible explanation for the difference in distance was that the asteroid was increasing in velocity. LINEAR did however confirm that it no longer presented any risk to the Earth. God had kept his side of the bargain. It was now up to man to keep his.

When I revealed that the Leader of Iran had secretly flown to America, visited UN Headquarters and placed the thirteenth piece of pot in Christ's Holy Square before returning home, the news was vehemently denied by Tehran. The idea was unthinkable. How could he possibly have made the journey when his presence in his own country had been witnessed by many people? In fact he'd been seen on national television inspecting the installations at Qom and Arak, both slightly damaged by the meteorites, or at least someone very much like him had visited the sites.

Most Iranians were prepared to believe that it had been their Leader making the inspections, although others had their suspicions that he had in fact made that journey to UN Headquarters in New York. As far as the world at large was concerned it didn't really matter who had placed the final piece in the Square. Someone had and as a result the asteroid had changed its course and was now heading harmlessly towards the sun, where it would swing round it, then head out towards the outer reaches of the Solar System, predicted to return in twenty-five years' time. Would we be faced with all this palaver again, I wondered? Hopefully not.

Narrator – Peter Robertshaw

Those responsible for the day-to-day running of the United Nations Headquarters were now faced with a problem - what to do with Christ's Holy Square. It was still positioned in the centre of the table that itself was standing just in front of the dais used by members of the General Assembly to make their speeches. It had done so under security guard since I had placed it there, empty of course, several days earlier. Now it was complete, all thirteen sections being occupied by their coloured pieces of pot, each with a Greek letter engraved into it. Not only was the Square important, its completion having in some mysterious way changed the course of an asteroid heading for the Earth, it was highly valuable - in fact priceless.

If the twelve pieces of pot had in fact been given out by Jesus Christ to his disciples at his Last Supper with them, with the thirteenth piece being kept for himself, it was hard to think of a more valuable object than the completed Holy Square. The Koh-I-Noor diamond? No. The world's most valuable painting, maybe Leonardo da Vinci's *Mona Lisa*, or even his *Last Supper* which failed to show the Holy Square on the table in front of Jesus? No. And what about the gold death mask found in Tutenkamun's tomb? No, not even that.

Who in fact owned the Square? I had made it and had located the thirteen pieces that went into it, personally supplying seven and making arrangements for five to be delivered to UN Headquarters. Was it therefore mine? Surely I had a strong claim. Or did it belong to the man who had stood beside it during all the proceedings involving it - the man who called himself Jesus Nazarene? If his identity was indeed genuine, all thirteen pieces of pot belonged to him. He had commissioned the making of them two thousand years ago. Surely he had the greatest claim of all. I, for one, would not argue with that.

One thing was certain - the completed Square could not stay where it was. It would only be a matter of time before the odd piece of pot was taken as some sort of souvenir. Maybe the whole Square would be stolen. There were no doubt plenty of wealthy individuals within New York itself who would give their right arms to own it, not at all worried how it came to be offered to them. Worldwide the wealthy would queue up to bid for it. All would be aware that they would never be able to display it openly, but that would not be important to them...Possession would be the 'name of the game'.

As I now knew, for Jesus Nazarene told me when I later met him at UN Headquarters, he had been directly involved in deciding the fate of the Square. At the request of the Secretary General, his aide had contacted Jesus, inviting him to come to UN Headquarters. On his arrival he was quickly taken to the Assembly Hall where the aide was waiting for him.

The aide explained the problem: "I need your advice, Mr Nazarene...The completed Square on the table in front of us obviously cannot stay there indefinitely...It will not be long before pieces go missing...What do you suggest should happen to it?...When all said and done you are the rightful owner of it."

Before Jesus could give an answer, the aide continued: "The Secretary General has made some suggestions which I have jotted down on a piece of paper." He extracted the paper from his pocket and proceeded to read from it: "The Holy Square could:

1. be kept at UN Headquarters, on display, but heavily protected under armour plated glass and fully alarmed, as a reminder to all who attend the UN building that it represents - *Peace on Earth, Goodwill towards Men*...words that your Father's angels spoke to the shepherds close to the inn where you were born some two thousand years ago.

2. be returned to Israel - the place where the thirteen pieces of pot originally came from...Possibly to be displayed in the Museum in Jerusalem.

3. be kept in New York, where one of the many museums would pay handsomely for the Square...Maybe such a payment could then be used for charitable purposes somewhere in the World.

4. be returned to the Englishman Professor Robertshaw...He personally collected seven of the pieces of pot and located the other six, and had of course constructed the wooden frame to hold them...Surely he has some sort of claim as well.

As I now know, for Jesus had made me aware of the fact, he already knew what the fate of his Holy Square would be. He also knew that it would not be to the liking of the Secretary General or his aide. But that could not be helped. His intention was to take it with him when he made his 'Grand Exit', what ever form that would take.

There were of course many throughout the World who would want to see the Square and its contents destroyed beyond recognition. To them it represented a religion that was alien to them, in fact one that their ancestors had fought bloody wars over. Jesus was of course fully aware of this, but was determined that total destruction was not going to be the fate of the Square.

When the aide asked Jesus what his plans for the Square were, he was evasive, not wanting to give the slightest hint. What was essential was that the Square was not interfered with in any way until he was ready to make his move. But in order to have that impact he required a little information, and he knew that the aide would be able to furnish him with it: "Tell me, Sir...When does the full General Assembly meet again in this splendid hall?"

The aide, having the timetable at his fingertips, willingly supplied the information: "This month is the busiest in the UN calendar...There are many resolutions to be discussed and passed, but not to do with world security. That is done in the Security Council, not in the General Assembly...This month there will be discussions on the drought in East Africa; the world's stagnant economy; improving the Tsunami early warning system in the Pacific; and the moratorium on whaling in the Antarctic...The work never seems to end."

The aide knew the meeting schedule off by heart: "In just two days' time the whole issue of drought in East Africa will be discussed...We need to find ways of diverting the precipitation that falls in the Ethiopian Highlands eastwards in much larger quantities than at present...We also need desalination plants on Eritrea's coastline with the Red Sea...Regarding Somalia, we have problems with political instability...This is hindering us in that area...The present situation cannot be allowed to go on, year in, year out."

Jesus nodded in full agreement and wondered why so little had been done in the area over the years. The Ethiopian Heights got more than their fair share of rain, his Father in Heaven saw to that. It was man's job to move the water to where it was needed most. Oil and gas were moved huge distances. In fact on the other side of the continent the West African gas line was over six hundred kilometres long...So why not water?

Jesus's second question was even more strange and the aide was taken aback by it.

"I would like to address the full General Assembly again...Can that be arranged?"

Obviously the aide could not give him an answer. Only the Secretary General himself could allow such an address. And bearing in mind that Jesus's earlier address had been controversial to say the least, even damned insulting to some, the aide was not optimistic.

But this man Jesus Nazarene was someone very special who oozedcharisma, holding the assembly spelled bound during his earlier address. Maybe the Secretary General would again allow him to speak, especially since the Holy Square was now complete and the asteroid was no longer a threat to the Earth.

The aide moved away to make the phone call, but did not expect an early decision. Speakers at the United Nations were arranged months in advance, not in a couple of days. If Jesus Nazarene was to speak he would have to be somehow 'slotted' into the busy timetable of the discussion on East Africa, possibly right at the end after all the Resolutions had been passed.

The aide, making his phone call some distance away, gave Jesus the opportunity he'd been waiting for. As he told me later, he was able to place, unseen, a written message under the Square's top left corner piece. He quickly scribbled the message on a scrap of paper, lifted the piece out of the Square and placed the paper in position, dropping the piece back on top of it. No one would know it was there…except him.

The aide rejoined Jesus, having made his call to the Secretary General's office. He also, as a matter of courtesy, decided to text me. He felt it was essential that I was aware that Jesus Nazarene had not only made 'plans' for the Square, he had also made a request to address the full Assembly again.

As it happened I and my wife were on the *Maid of the Mist*, a boat that at that very moment was sailing worrying close to the foot of Niagara Falls. The two of us were clothed in waterproof apparel so although I heard the phone ring out its characteristic tone I was unable to get to it. Fortunately I was able to read the text once I had changed and dried out.

The message was short and to the point:

Request your presence at UNHQ tomorrow 2pm - Ed

I vaguely remembered the aide at some point previously introducing himself as *Ed*, so the text had obviously come from him. As it happened Angela and I had already planned to return to New York for a couple more days before returning to the UK. I therefore texted back:

Will be there - P

Jesus Nazarene had hung around hoping, but not expecting, a reply to the aide's call to the Secretary General. He therefore decided to take his leave, having the aide's assurance that as soon as a decision was made he would be informed of it.

After reading my text reply the aide's phone rang as he was placing it in his pocket. Jesus Nazarene, just about to exit the Assembly Hall, hesitated. Was it the call he was waiting for?

It was. The Secretary General had made his decision. Jesus would be allowed to address the General Assembly at the end of the afternoon session on the water crisis in East Africa. Maybe he would even be able to contribute in some way to the discussion that had already taken place. If his Father could alter the course of an asteroid heading for Earth, surely he could make it rain a bit more on the Ethiopian Heights.

Jesus, hoping that he would be allowed to speak, had already formulated in his own mind what he intended to say to the General Assembly if he got the opportunity. And this would be followed up by his plans for both himself and his Holy Square. It had to have the maximum impact...And it would.

His Holy Square had been re-assembled by the most powerful Leaders in the world, including the Leader of Iran, although his presence in New York had been vehemently denied within his own country. This act hopefully indicated man's commitment to world peace, to a better understanding between nations to the benefit of all, not just a few, and a serious re-think of what man was doing to the planet.

But Jesus, from bitter personal experience, knew only too well about human frailty. It would be all too easy for man to continue in his old ways. He therefore intended by his actions to make man realise that this whole business had not been some 'mystic game' where a rogue asteroid heading for Earth had somehow changed course.

There were already rumblings in the press that maybe the asteroid had not been on a collision course after all. The various astronomical institutions had simple got their sums wrong. Even the reputable Cecil Gee had written a short article headed:

Was it all a hoax?

If the world at large started to think along those lines nothing would change. Jesus was determined to carry out some sort of act that would remind the world that what had taken place in the Assembly Hall a few days earlier had been deadly serious. His act had to have impact, and he was determined that it would. It would also follow a pattern that was not only familiar to him, but to every Christian throughout the world.

Before Jesus left the Assembly Hall he asked the aide to place the Holy Square in a safe place. He also asked him to make the Square available to him on the day he addressed the General Assembly. The aide assured him that he would do so.

***

Chapter Thirty Four

Narrator – Milad Mansouri, New York cabbie

My colleague Jalal Haghighi and I had drawn up our plans on the day a man professing to be Jesus Christ, the Son of God, had addressed the United Nations General Assembly. He had humiliated a country that we still looked upon as our own even though we had left it at the age of five. This humiliation had taken place in front of the whole world, the man pointing the finger, a finger that said: 'By not completing my Holy Square your leader and hence your country are letting the rest of the world down'.

It had annoyed us even more when a *Herald* reporter stated in a long and detailed report that our country's leader had secretly entered the United States, completed the Square and then returned home. That had been a down right lie.

Jalal and I were cabbies in New York and had been for the last twelve years. As children, only five years old, both of us had entered the United States with our parents, from Iran in June 1980, a year after the fall of the Shah and just before the country was plunged into a war with Saddam Hussein's Iraq which started in September of that year. Unfortunately for our two families the United States gave its support to Iraq and this had repercussions for all of us.

Initially we were ostracised, being looked upon as some sort of enemy of the state. And it didn't help when we moved into a couple of corner shops in the area where we lived. We were soon accused of depriving Americans of homes and jobs. Graffiti was sprayed on our doors, dog dirt pushed into our letter boxes and the odd brick launched through our windows. Jalal and I were also bullied at school as we struggled with the language and the material demands of our American peers.

But by working hard in our shops, prepared to open our doors at all hours for the benefit of the local community, our two families slowly gained respect as hard working citizens. We were contributing more than our fair share to society, unlike the layabouts that lived in the same area, of which there were many. Nothing had been too much trouble for us. If some sophisticated young woman required a particular French

Sauvignon Blanc, we got it for her. If an old timer, well past his sell-buy date, wanted an unusual brand of pipe tobacco, we hunted it down for him. And when some spoiled little brat had developed a liking for Branston's Rich and Fruity Sauce whilst holidaying with his parents in England, our shop on the corner managed to find a supplier in the US.

Over time the attitude of the local community changed. Our two families were no longer looked upon as 'undesirables' who should be on the next plane back to where ever we came from. We were now an important, indeed essential part of the community in which we lived.

It was in the year 2001, to be precise the 11th of September, that all our hard work paid dividends. When the World Trade Center towers came down, the result of a well organised Al-Qaida aerial attack, Muslims throughout the country, but especially in New York itself, came under scrutiny. In some quarters there were hate campaigns against them. But somehow our two Iranian families came through unscathed. Even Jalal and I, young men of only twenty-five and could have been looked upon with the utmost suspicion, did not experience this, being well known hardworking and respected cab drivers. Our appointments to the job had raised a few eyebrows in certain quarters, the attitude being - New York cabbies should be New York born and bred. But those who had felt that way had been unaware of one very important fact - the official at City Hall responsible for the appointment of the city's cab drivers was also a regular customer at the stores run by our two families. To coin a phrase - strings had been pulled.

Jalal and I had developed an interest in football at quite an early age. We seemed to have a natural flair for the game and were soon playing in our school team. As we got older we joined our local club and both of us had trials for New York's elite club The Manhattan Kickers. It was therefore not surprising that when the opportunity arose, we both crossed the Atlantic to attend the 2006 World Cup in Germany. Although the trip wasn't cheap we'd saved hard for the event, working overtime whenever we could.

Although our birth country Iran and adopted country the United States were knocked out in the early group matches we did see both national teams play - Iran drawing with Angola in Leipzig, and the United States losing to Ghana in Nuremberg. We then stayed on to see the Final in Berlin where Italy beat France 5 - 3 on penalties.

After the Final both Jalal and I decided to delay our return journey by stopping over in England for a few days. Both our families had friends in that country, going back to their lives in Iran, and had kept in touch during the intervening thirty or so years.

We flew from Frankfurt International, landing at Birmingham Airport where a friend, also a cab driver, picked us up. It was during our three day stay that we were introduced to a cleric called Abouzar Ghazi. He held special prayer meetings at his own home, well away from the local mosque, for a select group of men. Jalal and I were invited to attend during our brief stay and it was here that we were recruited to *Mujahid*, a new group similar to, but completely independent of *Al Qaida*.

During the few meetings we attended, Ghazi, acting as tutor, gave lectures on post war Iraq where chaos still reigned, the never ending Afghan conflict, and the way Iran was being portrayed to the World as a nation intent on some sort of nuclear ambitions. And then there was the Palestinian - Israeli dispute that was if anything slowly getting worse, with no end in sight. Ghazi's aim was to convince his listeners that all these conflicts were an attack on Islam, and that action had to be taken to, as he put it - "Get our own back."

He finally informed his audience that when the time was right, targets would be identified and the details of the action to be taken, described. Meanwhile, go home, lead normal lives and don't draw attention to yourselves…Just wait.

And Jalal and I did just that, returning to our homes in New York and carrying out our duties as friendly, loyal and hardworking cabbies. No one suspected that we had in fact been converted to a belief that the rest of the World was against the religion we held so dear, and that revenge was the only way to combat it. But for the moment we were simply abiding by the instruction….*Just Wait.*

We continued our daily attendance at the local mosque for prayer, as good Muslims we were expected to do. Our non-Muslim friends and colleagues at work accepted this dedication, sometimes with a degree of envy at not having such a strong faith themselves. Neither of us had ever shown the slightest interest in politics.

But, although only five years old when we'd left the country of our birth we were still immensely proud of it, due mainly to the fact that our parents had always encouraged us to be so. We both spoke Persian fluently and had intentionally developed a good knowledge of the history of Iran, using the internet to do so. It was therefore not surprising that when Iran was widely criticised for not taking part in the re-assembly of

357

the Holy Square ceremony, and then this was followed up by lies that Iran's Leader had secretly entered the United States in order to complete the Square, we both felt annoyance. How dare this man who called himself Jesus Christ, the Son of God, say such things?

The feeling to take some sort of action was unbelievably strong, but we had to be careful. It would be so easy for both of us to destroy all the goodwill that had been built up over the years towards ourselves and our families.

On the evening of the day when Cecil Gee's article - *Was it all a hoax?* had appeared in the New York Herald both Jalal and I finished our shifts and arrived home just after midnight. After parking up at the end of the street on which we both lived we said our good nights and headed for our homes.

Since in the area where we lived the post often arrived late in the day we were both in the habit of checking our post boxes when we arrived home from work. I collected the pile of envelopes and entered my home. Jalal did the same.

He decided to sort through the pile there and then, and came across an envelope, small in size, with no address or stamp on it, but with his full name neatly printed on the front of it. Knowing that there was little point in opening it under the street's poor lighting he entered his home. Once through the door and with the hall light now on, he carefully opened the envelope, extracted a credit card size piece of paper and read what was neatly printed on it... There were just three words:

Kill the Christ

At the same time as Jalal was reading the message, I was sorting through my pile of envelopes and discovered an identical one to that which my friend had just opened. Thinking how unusual it was to receive such an envelope, unaddressed and unstamped, but with my full name printed on it, I opened it first, eased out the piece of paper and read its message:

Kill the Christ

The message was identical to the one received by my friend.

During the process of conversion in England all those present had been informed that any instruction sent to them would not be by phone because there were now ways of tracing such calls, especially by cell phone. Another way would be used, and had been on this occasion. Someone, Jalal and I hadn't the slightest idea who, had walked past the two post boxes, probably in the dark, and simply slipped the envelopes through the slots.

There had however been an element of risk. What would have happened had one or both of our wives collected the post, seen the envelopes and opened them? But the person who had delivered them was on safe ground for he knew that it was unthinkable for a Muslim wife to open a sealed envelope with her husband's name clearly written on it. It would have shown a total lack of respect for his privacy.

Remembering not to use his phone Jalal ran the couple of hundred yards to my home. He'd left his wife, fast asleep in bed, and my wife was also asleep. In the kitchen and over a cup of tea, both of us having been teatotal all our lives, we compared our pieces of paper. They were near enough identical and had obviously been written by the same hand:

Kill the Christ

Once compared, I took both pieces of paper, ignited one of the cooker's gas rings and burned the two pieces to ash, remembering when being told about the dangers of phone calls, that anything written must be memorised then incinerated.

Jalal spoke first: "So, we know what, or rather who, the target is…My question is…Why him?…I know he's been a bit outspoken about our country and our leader…But surely that doesn't warrant us killing him…Besides, how are we expected to carry it out…We're not assassins."

After a pause in order to work out my reply, I expressed my views: "Well, one reason could be that he insulted our country and its leader in his speech to the UN…But I don't think that's the main reason…Remember that many of *Mujahid* are not from our country and would therefore not feel as strongly about his words as we do…No, remember who this man is…Think back, Jalal, to our childhood when our Christian and Jewish classmates at school celebrated their Christmas - decorations, singing carols, giving presents on Christmas morning…All celebrating the birth of Jesus, the Son of God, two thousand years ago…Then remember how in our religious studies at high school where we were told that Jesus was crucified for saying that he was King of the Jews, something that didn't go down well with the scribes and elders, who were jealous of him...How he rose from the dead and a few days later ascended into Heaven...This is the same Jesus visiting the Earth again, even speaking at the UN...Some call it his *Second Coming,* and had been predicted in their Bible."

All the time I was talking Jalal was nodding his head, remembering all that I had described. He remembered, for example, how his parents had given him presents on Christmas morning even though his family did not recognise the Christian celebration. This Jesus Nazarene was indeed someone special. What a coup it would be if *Mujahid* could kill him in some spectacular fashion. That would at least balance out a few of the deaths being suffered by Muslims in Afghanistan, killed by the infidel armies there.

But how to carry out the act? We weren't assassins, familiar with the methods used to kill someone. Neither had we ever handled a firearm. And our only experience with a knife was in the kitchen. And as far as bombs were concerned even handling fireworks made us feel uneasy, especially when our children were around.

One thing was certain - what ever we decided, if indeed anything, it had to be soon, assuming of course that this Jesus Nazarene was still in New York. He appeared to be in the habit of crossing the Atlantic at a moment's notice. We had to assume that he was. Surely the writer of the two messages had in some way checked, otherwise leaving the messages would have been pointless.

Luck often plays a part in successful terrorist attacks - the suicide bomber, intent on detonating his bomb whilst standing at the side of the target, usually some important person, suddenly finds that the person is surrounded by several equally important people - a case of killing several birds with one stone. Or the bomber who leaves his bomb unnoticed on the top deck of a bus hoping to kill or maim the people on board, seeing from a distance two other buses pull up either side of the bus where he'd just left his bomb. On detonation, carnage takes place on all three buses. And could the planners of the attack on the World Trade Center have thought in their wildest dreams that both towers would have collapsed to piles of rubble in such a short time, if indeed collapsing at all? Yes...luck can have an important role in terrorist attacks.

An opportunity came completely out of the blue and was the result of uncanny timing. As Jesus Nazarene left United Nations Headquarters after his discussion with the Secretary General's aide about what should happen to the Holy Square, he headed for the cab rank feeling elated. The Secretary General had given him permission to address the General Assembly a second time.

As it happened only two cabs were waiting, one driven by me, the other by Jalal. We both immediately recognised Jesus Nazarene, having seen him on television when he'd earlier addressed the UN General Assembly.

He climbed into Jalal's cab and told him where he wanted to be taken. I decided to follow at a distance, not quite knowing why. Maybe I would be able to see where Jesus went after Jalal had dropped him off. This information would come in handy if we decided on some sort of action against him in the near future. But at that point I hadn't the slightest idea of what that action could possibly be.

On reaching his destination Jesus climbed out of the cab, paid Jalal and thanked him. Seeing a news stand on the opposite side of the street hedecided to cross in order to purchase a paper, probably the *Herald* since Cecil Gee was in the habit of writing about him. What would the article be about today? Maybe how the Leaders of the world intended to change it for the better. That *would* make interesting reading for the man who called himself Jesus Nazarene.

I suddenly saw my chance. An idea, admitted a crazy one, flashed through my mind in a split second, but the timing had to be spot on. Not thinking of the possible consequences I eased down the accelerator in order to pick up speed.

As Jesus, possibly not used to heavy traffic and therefore not fully aware of what was going on around him, emerged from behind a large confectionery van that was parked in order to make a delivery, the front of my cab hit him. Although I immediately jumped on the brake pedal the collision threw his body into the air. As it impacted with the sidewalk his head struck with considerable force.

I immediately climbed out and rushed back to where Jesus was lying in the road, lifeless with blood already coming from his ears, nose and mouth.A crowd soon gathered round and in a matter of seconds the traffic was brought to a halt, my cab blocking one lane, the crowd the other.

Fortunately there was a one way side street close by and this allowed access to the paramedics' ambulance and a police car that had been summoned by the driver of the delivery van. After a quick assessment of the man's condition the paramedics supported his head with a neck brace before placing him on a stretcher which was then quickly wheeled to the waiting ambulance. With siren screaming it sped off in the direction of the nearest A&E Department.

It was now the task of the two police officers to find out exactly what had happened. With note pads in hand they started to interview the witnesses, of which there appeared to be many since the street was filled with shoppers. Eventually the officers compared notes: "Looks like the guy stepped out from behind the van straight into the path of the cab, Jim…Driver didn't have a chance…Looked in bad shape when the paras took him away."

"Any idea who he is, Bob?"

"Yes Jim…While the paras were examining him I checked for ID…I first checked the man's outside jacket pocket but found nothing…I then checked the inside pocket and as luck would have it I found his passport… How many people carry their passports around on the streets of New York?...Not many, but for some reason this man did."

The police officer, having hung onto it, opened it: "Name of Jesus Nazarene, Jim…DOB gives an age of thirty-three…Maybe some sort of tourist."

"Not in that gear, Bob…He's too well dressed, wearing a collar and tie under a suit…Could be some sort of businessman."

Later Jalal told me that he'd seen the whole incident through his rear view mirror as he'd moved away. The man he'd dropped off at the side of a street lined with parked vehicles of varying height, had decided to cross it. He'd stepped out from behind a delivery van without apparently looking, and been hit by my cab following a few yards behind. As he pointed out - I'd had no chance of stopping, or so it had seemed.

Immediately, Jalal had stopped his cab, blocking his half of the street, got out and ran back. He had been an eyewitness to an accident that had involved his friend. It was important, indeed essential, that the police officers, who had already interviewed many of the crowd, took his statement too.

As Jalal and I stood together, waiting to be interviewed by the officers, we of course knew who the man was, unlike the officers who, although they knew his name, had apparently no idea who exactly he was. Hadn't they seen the same man make his speech at the UN? It had been on every news channel.

Suddenly one of the crowd shouted out: "Eh...Didn't the guy who's just been knocked down, make a speech at the UN a couple of days ago...You know, when all the world leaders completed what to me looked like some sort of kid's jigsaw puzzle...All different coloured pieces of pot...Remember?"

Several of the crowd shouted: "Yer...I remember."

"Didn't he say something about being the Son of God?" continued the member of the crowd who'd first recognised Jesus.

"Yer...But he looked like an ordinary guy to me," shouted someone else in the crowd.

I was initially shocked at what had happened, for I couldn't decide who was at fault. Had I in fact intentionally run Jesus Nazarene down? I saw him commence his crossing of the street by first moving behind the parked delivery van. As he emerged from the van's protective cover I seemed to squeeze the accelerator pedal just before I hit him. Could I have stopped in time, or did I purposely run him down? Assuming that he was dead (he certainly looked it), had I in fact carried out my duty to 'kill the Christ' without actually realising it? I wasn't at all sure.

Or, was it just an unfortunate accident, beyond my control - just one of those things that happened every day somewhere on the streets of New York? The man had stepped out from behind the delivery van and I'd had no chance of stopping, even if I'd wanted to. Of course I hit the brakes, but far too late. It was almost as if the man had committed the act deliberately, like those who took their own lives by stepping at the last second into the path of a train travelling at high speed. Again, assuming he was dead, did he in fact commit suicide?

As one of the officers measured the lengths of the skid marks using a tape that he'd brought from his squad car, his colleague, accepting that there was little more that could be done at the scene, started to get things back to normal, the number one priority being to get the traffic flowing again. After fetching a bag of sand from his car and spreading it over the already congealing blood, the other officer examined my cab. Noticing the damage to the offside headlamp he decided that the vehicle should be examined by an engineer. Maybe the brakes had been faulty. He therefore summoned a breakdown wagon, which arrived minutes later using the near-by one way street, and took the cab away. Meanwhile Jalal had pulledhis cab into a layby further up the street.

The police officer who appeared the senior of the two decided that both Jalal and I should be interviewed and our statements taken, back at the station. We were therefore whisked away in a squad car.

After being kept apart so that we couldn't concoct a common story, our statements were taken. I stated that the man had just appeared in front of me from behind the van. I'd had no chance of avoiding hitting him. Of course I immediately braked. The skid marks on the road showed that. When asked if I was speeding I said no, adding that I was in a stream of traffic, my colleague being in front of me having just dropped the man off. All this seemed to agree with the statements that had been taken from members of the public who had been closest to the incident.

Jalal's statement, setting out what he'd seen through his rear view mirror, was probably the most accurate of all the statements taken by the police because he'd probably had the best view, seeing the man as he moved out into the path of my cab from behind the delivery van.

The police officers conducting the interviews appeared to be satisfied that all indications were that the man had indeed stepped out into the path of the cab without looking. Had it been a deliberate act? Only the New York District Coroner allotted to the case would be able to decide that, based on all the evidence presented to him or her.

As Jalal and I were leaving the police station he was given a bit of not- too-friendly advice to the effect that he should spent more time with his eyes on the road ahead and less on his rear view mirror, I was instructed to return the following day for further questioning, after my vehicle had been thoroughly examined.

As we were passing through the door a call came through from the local hospital's A&E Department. Sadly, Jesus Nazarene had been pronounced dead on his arrival there.

The message on the piece of paper flashed through my mind:

Kill the Christ

Well, I had certainly done that.

Had it been an accident, or had I deliberately run down the man who called himself Jesus Nazarene? At that point I had no idea. My intention to eventually kill him had not been in doubt, but did Jesus do the job for me by deliberately stepping in front of my cab? Quite honestly I did not know the answer to that question either. I also did not know whether I should have been feeling sadness at what had happened, the death of any individual always being a sad event, or feel elation at a job well done?

My mind was now in turmoil because I had no idea how I should have been feeling.

Jalal, obviously not feeling the same way, phoned for one of our colleagues to pick us up and take us back to base. Here, on instructions from our supervisor, we both made statements for the Company's legal department, to be available in the event of some sort of claim being made on behalf of the dead man's family. Everybody had some relatives, how ever distant they may be. But not in the case of Jesus Nazarene. He had no next-of-kin, at least not on this Earth.

That afternoon, after having been sent home to get over our ordeal, Jalal and I checked our post boxes, as we were in the habit of doing daily. We both found small sealed envelopes, unaddressed and unstamped, with our names neatly printed on them. Before entered our homes, thus avoiding our wives seeing the envelopes and enquiring what they were about, we opened them and eased out a slip of paper. The message was short...Just two words:

Well Done

News about the death of Jesus Nazarene had obviously travelled fast. To where and to whom we had no idea.

***

Chapter Thirty Five

Narrator – Dr Henrietta Percival, Pathologist at Bethesda District Mortuary, New York City

That evening I was called back to the mortuary in order to carry out an autopsy on the body of a man called Jesus Nazarene to establish the cause of death. Once done, my report commenced with an account of my external examination of the body. This had produced some interesting observations. There was scarring above and below the centre of the hands and feet, and one on the left hand side of the front of the body just below the rib cage. The scarring to the hands and feet appeared to be as a result of recent injury, but it was difficult to say how they had been caused. I certainly had never seen anything like it before.

On examining the body's interior I found that there had been considerable damage. There was transection of the brainstem, fracture dislocation of the atlas vertebra with respect to occiput, multiple head injury, pulmonary oedema and a ruptured spleen - all injuries consistent with a body being hit by a vehicle at speed, propelling it into the air before it crashed to the ground. It was impossible to tell whether they were the result of an unfortunate accident, some deliberate act on behalf of the cab driver, or indeed an act of suicide by the deceased. It would be up to the coroner to determine that.

In the morning details of the accident would appear in the local press and hopefully next-of-kin would come forward. They would then be able to claim the body for burial in line with the Jewish tradition.

Having finished my gruesome yet essential task I placed the internal organs inside the body cavity before stitching up, there being no reason to keep them for further examination. I did however take a blood sample for toxicology tests, just in case the man had been under the influence of alcohol or drugs when he'd been struck by the cab. I then dictated the details of my findings into my computer, placed the body of Jesus Nazarene back into the stainless steel cold storage cabinet and closed the square polished door.

It was time to call it a day, a very long day, the reason being that I had also carried out autopsies on an old man and his wife who had been found dead in their bed by their daughter. All indications were that they had died of carbon monoxide poisoning and this view had been strengthened by a police report stating that a gas fire set on a low heat had been found in the bedroom.

But on my examination of both bodies I had found evidence consistent with the two elderly people having been suffocated, possibly with a pillow. Here too I'd only been able to record my findings. Others would have to decide what exactly had taken place in the bedroom where the unfortunate couple had been found.

I washed down, changed into my 'going home' clothes and after switching off the multitude of lights, quietly closed the door of the mortuary on my way out. It was important not to wake the dead...But that is exactly what I did do, or appeared to do, for a sequence of events later took place that had last been played out over two thousand years earlier, albeit a modern version. This sequence had been well documented by the four Apostles in the New Testament. Luke described it in the following way:

Very early in the morning they (Mary Magdalene and Mary, mother of James) came to the sepulchre...And they found the stone covering the entrance of the sepulchre rolled away...And they entered in and found not the body of Jesus. And it came to pass, as they were much perplexed thereabout, behold, two men stood by them in shining garments: And as they were afraid and bowed down their faces to the earth, they (the two men) said onto them, Why seek ye the living among the dead? He is not here, but is risen. Remember how he spake to you, saying, The Son of man must be delivered into the hands of sinful men and crucified. And the third day he did rise again.

As I approached the Bethesda District mortuary the following morning to commence another day of investigating how the dead met their demise, I met up with my assistant John Atkin as we both passed through the main door and made for the elevator. John had worked with me for far too many years to remember. The time was just eight o'clock. Both of us liked to make an early start.

"Wonder what today will have in store for us?" enquired John knowing that no two days were ever the same, and often full of surprises.

I smiled: "I don't know, but it could involve a man I did an autopsy on yesterday evening...By the name of Jesus Nazarene."

"How so?"

"There was something about him on the late news channel last night...Evidently he was the man who addressed the UN General Assembly a few days ago, professing that he was the Son of God...He was also involved in that business where small pieces of coloured pot were placed into a wooden frame by all the leaders of the world, including our own President...So he is, or was, some sort of special person...I should have recognised the face or the name, or both, but nothing registered at the time, neither did the scarring to the hands and feet, which should have pointed me in the right direction...The poor guy had been crucified, for God's sake... Probably I'd been up country with my father doing a bit of fishing when this Jesus guy made his speech at the UN."

As I walked with John along the long cold corridor that led to the mortuary, what had happened to Jesus Nazarene two thousand years ago, assuming of course that he was in fact the Son of God, was uppermost in my mind. I was a devout Christian, albeit a scientific one, and was therefore familiar with the Easter story that described a crucifixion, a resurrection and finally an ascension.

John pushed open the door, held it open and allowed me to pass through. Immediately we were both startled by how bright the large autopsy room was. Neither of us had switched on the multitude of fluorescent lights that hung from the ceiling as we'd entered and, looking up, we could see that none of them were actually on. So where was all the light coming from?

We both moved to the centre of the room then looked across towards the far wall where the rows of cold storage cabinets were. This was where the intense white light appeared to be coming from. And both of us immediately saw what the source, or sources, of light were.

At the side of an open cabinet door, which happened to be the one where the body of Jesus Nazarene had been stored, stood two men in shining white garments. Both stood either side of the platform that allowed the cabinet's stored body to be slid in and out as and when required. I immediately noticed that the body of Jesus Nazarene was not there, so where the devil (a wrong choice of word in the circumstances) was it?

Both John and I moved cautiously towards the men, at the same time staring into the empty cabinet. We had no idea how to react. Was the situation threatening? Were our lives in danger? We had no idea. Should one of us at least say something?

We didn't have to, for one of the garmented men spoke first: "Why seek ye the living among the dead?...Jesus Nazarene is not here...After being killed by an evil man for telling the truth about the Iranian leader's visit to New York, he is risen from the dead, as he was two thousand years ago after being crucified...And as he did then, he will first reveal himself to mankind, then ascend into Heaven and sit on the right hand of his Father."

The man's answer offered an explanation as to why Jesus Nazarene, assuming he was alive, wasn't there in the room, but offered no explanation as to where he actually was. I decided to pluck up the courage and asked: "So, where is Jesus now?"

The man's reply was only of partial help: "I cannot tell you...But what I can say is that he will keep his appointment with the United Nations General Assembly tomorrow afternoon, when he has requested to address all those who will be present."

At that point the two men in white garments slowly faded into nothingness, plunging the large room into semidarkness, for it had no windows to allow in natural light, and neither me nor John had previously switched on any of the lights. The only lights visible were the small indicator squares that showed that the cabinets' refrigerating systems were functioning correctly. This bright red glow was sufficient to allow me to walk across to the battery of light switches on the wall without bumping into the autopsy tables and trolleys that were dotted around the room. The room was then flooded with light as the fluorescents fired up.

At first neither of us knew what to say. It was as if we'd been struck dumb by what we'd just witnessed. Both of us had scientific backgrounds and knew that what could and what could not take place was governed by scientific laws such as Einstein's Theory of Relativity. But even $E = mc^2$ could not explain how a man born two thousand years ago could have been alive just twenty-four hours ago. Neither could it explain how a dead man who'd had an autopsy carried out on his body rise from the dead and leave the room, presumably assisted by two men in glowing white garments, who had themselves then faded away to nothing in front of our very eyes.

Funnily enough both of us were prepared to accept that two thousand years ago a man name Jesus had been crucified, had risen from the dead within a sepulchre assisted by two garmented men, and then entered the community before ascending into heaven, but surely it couldn't happen a second time round.

So, what *had* actually happened during the night in the autopsy room? Suddenly John nudged me: "CCTV."

The whole room was covered by six closed circuit television cameras as follows:
1.   main double swing door
2.   cloakroom
3.   refrigerated cabinets
4.   autopsy tables
5.   storage wall cupboards
6.   elevator doors

The cameras were not only able to pick up normal light images, but also infra red ones for when the room was in total darkness, as it was through the night. The system had been installed a month earlier after the body of a drug mule had been removed during a night break-in. It was thought that the mule, a sad, illiterate Jamaican woman, had several condoms of heroin or cocaine somewhere within her digestive system that the autopsy that had not yet been carried out, would have inevitably revealed.

The CCTV system had been wired up so that the autopsy room monitor was one of several in the hospital's security suite, all focussed on some part of the hospital building. Both of us would have to go there in order to view what the cameras in the autopsy room had picked up. Conveniently for both of us the autopsy room and the security suite were on the first floor, barely twenty metres apart.

Once we were seated in front of the monitor John asked the security guard, who had just come on duty, to run back the system's disk so that the previous two hours' recording of the inside of the autopsy room could be viewed. The huge monitor screen was divided into six sectors numbered 1 to 6 in the left top corner. Each showed what its individual camera had picked up. At the press of a button the whole screen could show the recording of an individual camera...all very high tech, and in infra red, too.

Eagerly, all three of us stared at the monitor as the replay commenced, all six pictures initially being displayed. The time in the top right hand corner showed 06:00hrs and the replay showed real time. It would take a straight two hours to view the whole recording.

The guard, realising this, pressed the fast forward button. This moved everything quickly on, but allowed an expert eye to detect if something was happening, albeit only as a blurred image. At that point the recording could be stopped, run back, then run forward at normal speed allowing the viewer to see what exactly was taking place.

As the time passed 07:25 nothing unusual had been observed, but when it reached 07:32 the keen eye of the guard, used to looking for such blurred images, even being able to spot one of a dog or cat as it walked past the hospital's main entrance, spotted something on the screen's sector 3, the one showing images from the camera pointing directly at the refrigerated cabinets storing the bodies of the dead: "There," he shouted enthusiastically, at the same time freezing the image.

Both John and I moved our heads closer to the screen. Yes, there was no doubt about it, something was taking place, but it was impossible to work out what from the still picture.

The guard slowly move the time back until the fuzzy image disappeared. He then ran it forward at normal speed, finger on the button ready to stop it again.

This time the image, or rather two images, were as clear as a bell. Both images were of men dressed in glowing bright garments, so bright that the cameras, designed to automatically switch onto infra red when the light intensity fell below a certain value, had difficulty in deciding what setting they should be on. The men appeared to be reading the names on the refrigerated cabinets, no doubt looking for a particular one.

The guard again froze the picture, amazed at what he was seeing. Why the hell hadn't his mates, the two guards on duty until eight o'clock, reported the incident to the police, and then gone to the autopsy room to investigate? That was the procedure, laid down by the hospital authorities. He looked in the logbook that would, or should, have shown details of any unusual sightings, entered by either of the two guards on duty. But there was nothing. All the log said was - *Nothing to report - Everything normal*, followed by the guard's signature.

It then dawned on the guard studying the log book what had probably happened. The security suite had a dartboard in one corner and the night shift were in the habit of playing a game of 501 during their final tea break, that usually took place round about seven o'clock in the morning. Both guards on duty had completely missed what had been going on in the autopsy room between the hours of seven and eight, and had been displayed on just one sixth of the monitor screen.

"Run the disk back," I yelled, immediately apologising for my ill mannered tone of voice.

The guard, fully understanding my impatience, smiled as he ran the disk back to 07:25. And as all three of us stared at the screen he allowed the picture to progress at normal speed. What it revealed was amazing, to say the least.

At 07:25 the camera revealed nothing other than a still infra red image of the body storage cabinets, But as the time approached 7:26 the camera picked up what appeared to be two small glowing volumes of luminous gas each no more than the size of a tennis ball, floating at a height of about a metre. Over the next minute the two volumes expanded and changed shape to that of a rugby ball standing on its end and now approximately two metres in height. During the next minute the shapes materialised into two men, with heads, thoraces and abdomens standing on two legs. The arms followed next. Once perfectly formed, their bodies became covered with glowing white garments. The men then moved in front of the storage cabinets and were seen to be pointing at the name plates on the cabinet doors.

The left arm belonging to the man on the right could then be seen reaching out and opening one of the square cabinet doors. It was the second one up from the floor and third one in from the left wall. I winked at John. We both knew whose body was in that particular cabinet...the body of Jesus Nazarene.

The other man standing on the left then took hold of the sliding table and slowly pulled it out to its full extension. On it, covered with a white sheet, was the body they were looking for - the body of Jesus. Slowly the man pulled the cover away, revealing the naked body. He then bent over and gently kissed the forehead. Slowly the top half of the body rose into a sitting position and appeared to stretch its arms outwards, as one would do to relieve any stiffness in the muscles and joints. It was clear that a conversation of some sort was taking place between the two men. I cursed under her breath. Why the hell hadn't the whole system also been wired to pick up sound?

Jesus, with the help of the man, slowly eased his legs over the side of the metal table and placed his feet tentatively on the floor. When he had established his balance he walked slowly around, stretching his legs outwards as he did so. No doubt those muscles and joints were also stiff.

While all this was going on, the other man had moved across the room and out of the field of view of camera 3. The guard quickly pressed a

372

button that now brought on screen what camera 2 had been picking up. The second man was seen heading for a closed door with a large sign saying 'CLOAKROOM' on it. He pulled it open and passed through, disappearing as he did so. Seconds later he re-appeared with a whole lot of clothing across both arms.

Both John and I immediately knew what was happening, or rather about to happen. In the cloakroom there were open shelves, closed lockers and hanging spaces where those who worked in the autopsy room kept spare clothing, just in case it was required, such as having to make a sudden court appearance or comfort grieving family members of some deceased relative. There were jackets and trousers, shirts, ties and jumpers, even shoes, socks, underpants and a variety of scarves, hats and caps. And these only belonged to the men. There were also items of female clothing - trouser suits, skirts, blouses, cardigans, bras and briefs, and of course stylish shoes.

The man with the clothing moved out of the camera's field of view, and the guard quickly switched back to camera 3, which picked him up as he moved to where Jesus was standing. The clothes were placed on the metal table and the three men commenced sorting through them, putting on one side what appeared to be items that would make up a full set of clothing.

Jesus then, with the help of the other two, put the clothes on. There was nothing he could do to hide the visible damage to his face, but the brim of a slightly oversized trilby cast a shadow over it, as well as covering the damage to his head. After obviously getting the approval of the other two men Jesus appeared to say farewell and head for the door leading out of the autopsy room. The press of a button brought in camera 1 and this showed Jesus exiting the room, the double doors closing behind him.

Noting the time of 07:50 in the corner of the monitor's sector 1, I asked the guard to move the picture back to camera 3. Here the two men appeared to be tidying up. While one was wiping the table down with paper towels from a dispenser, the other was seen to be neatly placing the unwanted clothing over his arms and, as camera 2 showed, carefully placing them back in the cloakroom. The man then joined the other, as sector 3 again showed.

As the time moved onto 08:02 two figures suddenly appeared on the screen from the right.

"Us," shouted John, enthusiastically, at the same time pointing at the monitor: "That's where we made our entry...We must have just missed Jesus Nazarene...We used the elevator...I bet he used the stairs."

As the three of us stared closely at the screen we could see that a conversation was taking place in the autopsy room. I recalled that conversation, or rather the question that one of the garmented men had asked John and I. I repeated the question to myself: "Why seek ye the living among the dead?...Jesus Nazarene is not here." Well, how could he be? The three of us had just seen him rise from the dead, get dressed into clothing that would enable him to merge into any crowd unnoticed, and then leave the hospital. Where he'd gone was anybody's guess. What we did know was that Jesus Nazarene would, according to the garmented men, make an appearance at UN Headquarters, where he would address the General Assembly. What he would say, and what he would do after his speech, was anybody's guess.

Narrator – The Author

On leaving the hospital's autopsy room Jesus Nazarene followed the WAY OUT signs that led him first to the descending flight of stairs then the main door where he exited the hospital unnoticed. It had been a hectic night in the reception area and there were still staff hurrying around. Who'd notice a well dressed man, even one wearing a trilby, walking confidently towards the already open door? No one.

Once on the hospital's concourse Jesus made for the cab rank. He wanted to get back to his hotel as quickly as possible. He was hungry, not having eaten for well over twenty-four hours. Smelling of antiseptic he needed a shower and being extremely tired he wanted to get his head down. Above all he wanted to give some thought to his speech to the UN General Assembly in a little over twenty-four hours' time. He had a good idea what he wanted to say, but needed to think about the exact wording.

As luck would have it, a cab arrived at the same time and dropped off its fare, an impressive looking man carrying an oversized brushed aluminium attache case - maybe some sort of medical consultant or a business rep. Jesus thought. The driver was about to move away when Jesus rushed up and jumped into the rear of the cab. When the driver, unhappy at the way someone had assumed that his cab was for hire and jumped in without as much as a word, turned round and glared at his passenger, he gasped because he immediately recognised him. It was the man his colleague Milad Mansouri had knocked down and killed the

374

previous day. Jalal Haghighi, not having been affected by the accident to the same extent as his colleague, had been allowed to resume his duties as a cabbie. But Jalal was certainly being affected now.

He knew that this Jesus guy had died, that information having been relayed to the police station from the hospital while Milad and himself were being interviewed. Was he therefore in effect looking at a ghost? He had no idea. His strong Islamic faith did not allow him to believe in such things, but how could the presence of a living man in the back of his cab who had been dead less than twenty-four hours earlier, be explained? Quite simply it couldn't. He would certainly have to give considerable thought about telling Milad of the sighting, and hoped that the *unknown one* who had issued the order to 'kill the Christ' would not instruct both of them to this time do the job properly…and permanently.

At his destination Jesus Nazarene felt in all the pockets of his borrowed clothes, hoping that the owner, or owners, for the items could well have belonged to more than one person, had left the odd coin or bill…But nothing. Failing that, he hoped that his Father would have already spirited some money into his Son's trouser pocket as he had a passport and a credit card during his trip from Iran to the United States…But no. He had no alternative but to appeal to the taxi driver's generosity.

Fortunately for Jesus, out of sheer guilt Jalal Haghighi had already decided to waive the fare, with the explanation that since he'd been instructed by his base to pick up a fare just round the corner from where they were, he had to make the journey to the area anyway. Jesus breathed a sigh of relief when Jalal shouted: "Had to come here anyway, mate…So have this one on me." He then sped away, not wanting to get into any sort of conversation with a 'dead man'. Jesus shouted his thanks wondering at the same time if New York cabbies in such circumstances were in the habit of showing such generosity. He somehow doubted it.

As Jesus passed through the hotel's reception he noticed a young bellboy behind the desk, one he hadn't seen before. Without hesitation he asked for his room key, and without hesitation the boy gave it to him. Although not recognising the man he assumed that he had a legitimate reason to ask for a key. He did however look suspiciously at the recipient's badly bruised face and the antiseptic aroma that surrounded him. Had he recently been released from some A&E department after being in some sort of fight, or been the recipient of a good mugging?

Seconds later Jesus entered his room, ordered a full breakfast then showered. Although extremely tired he decided to give some thought to his speech to the UN. With note pad and pen at the side of him he heartily tucked into the two sunny side up fried eggs, the two huge rashers of grilled bacon and a separate plate of hash browns. Inevitably he got fat all over the pad as he jotted the key words he would use in his speech..

***

Chapter Thirty Six

The gathering of people at the Headquarters of the United Nations the following day was like the 'gathering of the clans'. Everyone was there -well almost - the Secretary General, the representatives of most of the 193 member countries of the General Assembly, Jesus Nazarene and Professor Peter Robertshaw. And although his presence could not be detected, apart from maybe by Jesus, no doubt God himself was there looking down from above. Of course the World Leaders, who had been present and had played such an important, indeed essential, part in the ceremony to re-assemble Christ's Holy Square, were not there - nor did they need to be.

Professor Robertshaw and his wife Angela had just flown into JFK from Buffalo after their couple of days exploring the Niagara Falls area. The cab from the airport had dropped the professor off at UN Headquarters, before taking Angela back to her hotel. Their luggage went with her, his personal bag containing his laptop went with him, as it always did. Angela would watch the proceedings at the UN on her room's TV when the transmission commenced in the afternoon.

News had spread like wild fire that the man who called himself Jesus Nazarene, the Son of God who had earlier addressed the General Assembly after the re-assembly of his Holy Square, would be addressing the Assembly again in the afternoon. It was now widely accepted that the Iranian leader had in fact made the journey to New York in order to complete the Holy Square. It was also widely known that as a result of this action the asteroid that had been on a collision course with Earth was now on a harmless orbit that would take it round the Sun before heading for the outer reaches of the Solar System. What surprisingly hadn't hit the headlines as yet, was the fact that Jesus had been killed in an unfortunate automobile accident in a New York high street. Several individuals had witnessed the incident and Jesus had been identified at the scene. Surely ace *Herald* reporter Cecil Gee had got wind of it and had fast tracked an exclusive report into the morning's edition, but apparently not.

What wasn't known, except by a cabbie named Jalal Haghighi, who couldn't make up his mind whether to take his close friend Milad Mansouri into his confidence or not, was that Jesus Nazarene was alive and apparently well. How, he had no idea. Three other people were also aware of the fact - the pathologist who had carried out an autopsy on his body, her assistant and a security guard. They had seen Jesus Nazarene rise from the dead in the autopsy room, helped by two men in white glowing garments, get himself dressed and apparently leave the hospital. The pathologist, after considerable soul searching felt that she had no alternative but to pass the information on to the hospital authorities and the police. Both organisations, having great difficulty in getting their heads round what they'd heard, decided that for the time being they would sit on the information, not wanting to be the possible subjects of ridicule.

There would no doubt be some red faces in both organisations when news eventually perculated through to them that Jesus was already in the UN Assembly Hall, looking forward to making his speech.

Jalal Haghighi could not make up his mind what to do. There was no doubt that the man he'd given a lift to was the same man that his colleague had earlier knocked down and killed. Admittedly the man's face had been badly bruised, even slightly distorted, but there was no doubt that it was the same man. How he had somehow risen from the dead, Jalal had no idea. But what he did know, from his study of the religions of the world, was that the same man had risen from the dead once before, some two thousand years ago, so why not again?

Immediately after dropping the man off, Jalal had pulled his cab into a lay-by, switched off his FOR HIRE sign and, using his cell phone, called the only name he'd ever heard of at the *New York Herald*, that of the well known and highly respected reporter Cecil Gee.

After taking Jalal Haghighi's call and telling him that he would get back to him within the next ten minutes, Cecil Gee made a hasty call to one of his contacts in the UN building, security guard Chuck Oldfield: "Hi Chuck, it's Cecil...Heard anything about this guy, Jesus Nazarene, being killed insome sort of road accident yesterday afternoon?"

"No, Cec...But what I do know is that he is standing in front of me in the Assembly Hall at this very moment...He looks as if he's gone fifteen rounds with Mike Tyson judging from the bruising round his face...Preparations are already being made for him to address the whole Assembly this afternoon after the debate on the East African drought...He's talking to that Professor Robertshaw guy at this moment."

Thanks, Chuck…Will be in touch." Cecil Gee, having ended the brief call, got to thinking…If Jesus Nazarene was indeed capable of rising from the dead, and his past record indicated that he was, he would have to do so again in order to ensure his second appearance at the UN General Assembly, because that was this man's style. He was the supreme expert when it came to communicating with the public as he had been two thousand years ago. He had ruffled a few feathers then and no doubt he would be doing so again in a couple of hours' time.

Cecil Gee was now in a bit of a dilemma…what to do next? The day's edition of the *Herald* had of course been on the news stands for several hours, and the next one would not appear until the early hours of the following morning. By that time Jesus Nazarene's second appearance at the United Nations would have been transmitted round the world. There was little point in the reporter spending his precious time producing a report that would already be old news. Maybe a few lines about the road accident itself would suffice.

But weren't the public entitled to know what had actually happened? A New York cabbie had witnessed the accident, been told by the police that the victim had died, then had later picked up the same man outside the Bethesda hospital and drop him off at his hotel. How? It just didn't make any sense. Maybe some sort of inquiry was called for.

There was little point in Cecil Gee describing in any sort of detail the appearance of Jesus Nazarene at the UN when millions, maybe even billions throughout the world had already seen his speech live on their televisions.

For the first time in his highly successful career Cecil Gee had no alternative but to sit on possibly the most important story he'd had the opportunity to report on. From his point of view the timing of the story breaking had been the worst possible.

Narrator – Professor Robertshaw

At noon three people came together in the UN General Assembly Hall. They were myself, the principal aide to the Secretary General and Jesus Nazarene. Neither I nor the aide had any idea that Jesus had in fact been killed in a road accident, had received an autopsy on his body and had then risen from the dead, all within the last twenty-four hours. He was smartly dressed in clothes that he'd managed to acquire from somewhere…we later found out where. But not all the evidence could be hidden, Even though he insisted on keeping his trilby tightly down to his ears his face was severely bruised. How could he explain that away?

"Looks as if you've been in the wars Mr Nazarene…Feel all right?" asked the aide, politely.

"Yes…I was beaten up by a couple of men on the way back to my hotel after appearing here…Said they were Iranians, and told me to keep my nose out of their country's affairs…They then ran off."

"Did you contact the police? " I asked, assuming that such a racist act would surely not be tolerated on the streets of New York.

"Er, no…Couldn't see the point…It all happened so quickly, the police would have had no chance of catching them."

I could sense that he was uneasy about his explanation. Maybe itwasn't quite the right tale. Maybe he was deceiving the aide and myself, being economical with the truth. I found this strange for throughout his short life two thousand years ago he had always preached both truth and honesty. Was he now going against all that he'd stood for all those years ago?

The debate on the drought in East Africa was due to commence at two o'clock precisely…precisely being the optimum word, the Secretary General made sure of that. By one-fifty all who intended to be present were expected to be in their places…and they were.

Jesus Nazarene and I took our seats below the main dais, the one that would be used by the speakers taking part in the debate. As the Secretary General took his place he glared disapprovingly at the trilby Jesus was wearing. No one wore headwear of any sort in the Assembly Hall, apart from those wearing national dress, as was the case where delegates came from some Arab and African countries. Obviously there was no objection to the yarmulkes worn by many of the Israeli delegates. In fact it was a bit of a puzzle as to why Jesus Nazarene wasn't wearing one, being of the Jewish faith…but there again surely he was a Christian.

The aide, spotting the Secretary General's glare, climbed up the stairs to where he was seated and whispered in his ear: "He was attacked in the street after he'd appeared here…Some foreign thugs, I understand…Face a bit of a mess, hence the hat."

The Secretary General nodded, feeling a degree of sympathy for the man. On this occasion he would make an exception, but he would not allow it to set some sort of precedent otherwise some of the younger delegates would soon start turning up in baseball caps advertising Adidas or Nike. The Secretary General was definitely not having that.

As the second hand of the watch on the Secretary General's wrist climbed to the top of its circular path, indicating two o'clock, he nodded to the Georgia delegate who would be chairing the session.

She rose from her chair and in excellent English read out a statement. This immediately brought the many interpreters into action :

"We are here today to debate and vote on Resolution 81/345, that calls upon all Nations to accept that the drought crisis in East Africa is a human tragedy that is totally unacceptable, and to take the action urgently required to alleviate the human suffering that is taking place in that region."

After a brief introductory speech, where she *recalled* the excellent work that had already been done on the water crisis in East Africa, *expressed concern* about the continuing political instability in the area that hindered any sort of real progress, *welcomed* the help and expertise that was now coming forward from some of the wealthier nations, and *called upon* all those nations involved to treat the human tragedy that was taking place before 'our very eyes' with the same urgency as a major earthquake hitting a highly populated area of the world.

Following procedure she invited those who intended to speak in the debate to come up in turn to the dais and do so. First to speak were those who lived in or close to the area, who described the problem, the devastating effect that it was creating, and how they saw the problem being solved. They finished their speeches with an urgent plea for financial and practical assistance.

Then followed the delegates of those nations who were being asked to supply that assistance. They of course were conscious that a certain Jesus Nazarene was listening to them. This was the man who had somehowsmuggled the thirteenth piece of his own Holy Square out of Iran. This was the man who had persuaded the Iranian Leader to make the journey across the Atlantic to New York and place that thirteenth piece into the Square, thus completing it. This was the man whose Father had then changed the course of the asteroid, in effect saving the World. For all these reasons this man was someone very special...and he would definitely be listening.

The speech makers were of course fully aware that Jesus had established a religion that had already lasted two thousand years, and would no doubt go on a great deal longer. It preached as one of its main themes helping one's fellow man. Well, if there was ever a need for that it was the drought crisis in East Africa. Those who inhabited that area hoped that Jesus would be hanging onto every single word uttered by those delegates whose countries were at the moment 'dragging their feet' on the drought issue.

Eventually the debate came to an end. It was then time to vote on the Resolution. This was quickly done and the result declared by the Chairperson, the delegate from Georgia. She again spoke clearly in English: "The result of the vote is as follows:

Votes for the Resolution - 164
Votes against- 9
Abstentions - 10

This gives an overwhelming majority of 155...The resolution is therefore carried...Time is off the essence, it is therefore important that Working parties are immediately set up to plan the way ahead...There can be no 'pussy-footing' around...I now declare this session closed." She turned, nodded to the Secretary General and sat down.

I smiled to myself at the Chairperson's choice of expression. I could just imagine the fun the interpreters were having translating 'pussy-footing'. I was also prepared to bet that she had in the past spent some time in the UK, where there was plenty of pussy-footing going on, especially within government.

At this point some delegates, assuming that the proceedings were now at an end, stood indicating that they were preparing to leave. The Secretary General, realising what was taking place, quickly brought the Assembly to order. The session's agenda had been earlier circulated to all delegates, but it appeared that some had either not seen the last item on it, or had chosen to ignore it. Why was this Jesus individual treated with such reverence anyway? He seemed to click his fingers and a space was found for him on the agenda. This allowed him to address the General Assembly, a privilege given to only a few very important individuals, such as Presidents and the occasional Prime Minister.

The Secretary General made a brief statement: "Last item on the agenda...An address by Jesus Nazarene...You will remember that he addressed this Assembly only a few days ago with some thought provoking words."

Those present in the Hall came to order and again took their seats, some reluctantly. When all was quiet the Secretary General nodded to Jesus Nazarene, who had already stood up in readiness. He slowly left his seat, moved up the stairs and took up his position behind the dais. All eyes were on him, as indeed were the 'eyes' of every television camera in the hall, waiting in anticipation. What would the man who professed to be the Son of God say to them?

What took place next was clinical in its nature, mesmerising to the observer. Slowly, in fact very slowly Jesus did in effect a partial striptease.

First he took off his hat, dropping it to the floor. This immediately exposed the bruising on his face. But it also revealed something else, as those closest to him could see. Some sort of line was visible around his skull, just above the forehead, with what looked like a series of short lines along it. They were in fact seeing the stitching that had taken place to hold on the skull cap that had been removed by the pathologist during the autopsy.

Jesus then took off his clothes in order - his shoes and socks, followed by his trousers, revealing white boxer shorts. At this there were gasps in the Hall, especially from some of the female delegates, their traditions not allowing them to set eyes on a naked, or near naked man, except their husbands.

This placed the Secretary General in a dilemma…what should he do, or at least say? But for some reason he felt dumbfounded. It was as if the power of speech had been taken away from him. He opened his mouth, but nothing came out. His aide, unable to understand why the Secretary hadn't rebuked Jesus, opened his mouth to speak, but he too found himself unable to. In fact every single person in the Hall had been similarly afflicted. Fortunately our inability to speak lasted barely a minute.

Jesus continued his striptease. His jumper, tie and shirt followed. Finally he removed his vest. There he now stood before the entire United Nations General Assembly dressed only in a pair of white boxers. His appearance was in fact similar to how he had been portrayed in the many paintings and crucifixion sculptures throughout the world, the tightly pulled up boxers looking not unlike a loin cloth.

The whole assembly stared at him, or rather his body, their eyes

383

immediately focussing on a 'Y' scar running down it from shoulders to belly button, again the result of the autopsy. But there were also five other scars, looking as if they were the result of recent injury, but in fact were some two thousand years old. One was at the side just below the ribs. The other four were visible on the palms of the hands and the tops of the feet. If there had been any doubt in the minds of those in the Hall as to who exactly was standing in front of them there was no doubt now. He was indeed Jesus Christ the Son of God…the one who had been crucified during the Roman occupation of the Holy Land.

Jesus gripped the dais with both hands then spoke to the Assembly, again in English as he had before: "As you can see, I've been in the wars…Let me tell you what happened…Yesterday I was knocked down in the high street by a cab and killed…I know it was a deliberate act of revenge carried out by a man who objected to me interfering in his own country's affairs…I had also been accused of blasphemy against the country's leader…You may remember that two thousand years ago accusations of interference and blasphemy led to my crucifixion…At least on that occasion I did have a trial, with Pontius Pilate making some sort of effort on my behalf…On this occasion I didn't, one person acting as judge, jury and executioner…My body was taken to a local hospital where later an autopsy was carried out on it…As you can see, I bear the scars.

"But there is one more act that I and my Father in Heaven wish to carry out, and in order to do so I had to first die then rise from the dead, and this is what I have done, as I did two thousand years ago…And here I am…How I got here is unimportant, sufficient to say that I had a little help from a couple of my Father's heavenly friends.

"But before that final act can be carried out I need to remind you of the significance of what took place in this Hall a few days ago when the re-assembly of my Holy Square was carried out by the twelve most powerful leaders in the world, with the thirteenth piece added a day later…

This showed their commitment to making this world, your world, a better place for all…Your world is a bountiful place in all that man needs - huge mineral wealth, abundant food potential, ample fresh water…But these must be well managed, not greedily squandered…Man has the ingenuity to do this, my Father has made sure of that…But man's ingenuity can be his own worst enemy, the gun and bomb being unfortunate, regretful inventions…The largest Continent on your planet has everything and yet it is where the poorest of the world live in large numbers. You need to ask the question - why has so little been done about their plight?"

As Jesus took a sip of water from a glass placed at the side of the dais by the Secretary General's aide a ripple of whispers spread across the Assembly. One could sense that those present were not prepared to accept their share of the blame for the state the world was in, with discrete glances across at those delegations from the countries of Africa, the continent that Jesus was no doubt referring to. One could almost hear the accusations... Why don't you put your own house in order?...When such countries were incapable of doing so because of continuing conflict within or on their borders.

Replenished, Jesus continued, and on a different note: "Your world is changing, and one of those changes is beyond your control...Your Sun is going through one of its 'warming up' stages...Regardless of what you do your world will slightly increase in temperature...Your polar ice caps will melt releasing huge quantities of fresh water into the oceans causing a rise in sea level...The oceans will warm slightly producing instability in the atmosphere, and more extreme weather will result...One change that is already taking place, but appears not fully understood by your scientists is the effect this extra heat is having on the Earth's crust...This is slightly expanding, creating instability leading to an increase in both earthquake and volcanic activity...There will also be an increase in harmful solar radiation resulting in an increase in skin cancers."

As those in the Hall continued to listen in silence, the only sound being the whispers of the interpreters, they marvelled at the knowledge of someone who had always been portrayed as a simple carpenter all those years ago. And here he was giving the world's leading scientists a lesson on climate change.

"All this is already taking place and you'll have no control over it...Accept it and concentrate on what you can control...The Greenhouse Effect is very real and already taking place as your life styles make heavy demands on the environment...CO_2 emissions are a major problem, both from domestic and industrial sources...These in some way must be cut by changing to alternative forms of energy production...And don't rule out nuclear power just because of the odd hiccup...Use the ingenuity that my Father has given you to solve the problems...Failing that, use carbon capture, but appreciate that to be effective it will have to be done on a massive scale...Fresh water supplies will become increasingly a problem in many areas of the world and this will inevitably lead to conflict...In fact we are already witnessing this in the area at the centre of your debate today...The Earth already gets ample rainfall for its needs, both for plants and animals, including yourselves, and this could well increase in the years to come...But it has to be channeled to the areas where it is needed...Save every drop that falls...It is sheer madness that in times of heavy rainfall most of it flows back to the sea...If some picturesque valley has to be flooded, so be it, get your priorities right...Although the sort of plant required to move large quantities of water great distances has to be robust and therefore expensive, the technology is hardly rocket science, to quote one of your favourite expressions."

The last comment produced a smile on most of the delegates' faces, breaking the serious nature of Jesus Nazarene's speech. They were always being told by their advisors that something wasn't 'rocket science'. NASA had a lot to answer for.

After another sip of water Jesus continued: "And now to the main thrust of my speech – the role of man...My Father in Heaven did not create him in his own image with the desire to kill his own kind in order to solve his problems...He gave him a brain, the most advanced in the animal kingdom, to enable him to solve his problems by reasoning, negotiating and compromise...But far too often he behaves little better than those animals who have to kill in order to survive...Sadly, since man set foot on this Earth, killing of one's kind has been common and widespread...and still is...It's as if man glories in it...Well, I warn you now, my Father will not tolerate it any longer...Never before in the history of the World has it been more urgent for men to come together and work in harmony, putting conflict aside for the benefit of all...Never before in the Earth's long history has it been so essential for man to combine his efforts to combat the problems ahead...There is no place for complacency or selfish desires for power, wealth, land, whether at the individual level or nationally...At present extreme poverty and obscene wealth sit side by side in almost all countries of the world. How can that be?"

As the Assembly took on board the last two statements a ripple of whispered comments went round the Hall, some prepared to accept that both applied to their country, others quite adamant that they didn't apply to theirs, and yet it was common knowledge that they did.

It was now time for Jesus Nazarene to round his speech off, and he did this in the form of a 'no nonsense' warning: "My Father has given the world, your world, a second chance to reform, by deflecting the path of an asteroid away from the Earth thus preventing the total annihilation of most living things, certainly the human race…He believes that the simple and yet so important act of your leaders placing small pieces of pot in a wooden frame has shown their commitment to change for the benefit of all, and in this case 'all' includes the numerous plants and animals who share the planet with you."

As these comments were being taken on board by the various delegations there was much nodding of the head showing obvious agreement. There was indeed growing concern at the spiralling increase in world population, the depletion of the world's rain forests, so essential for the health of the atmosphere; that some species of fish were on the verge of extinction; and that creatures such as tigers in Asia and rhinos in Africa could disappear altogether in only a few years, apart from in zoos and safari parks.

"Now, here is the 'deal', using a word familiar to many of you…The world, or rather its human inhabitants, are being served 'notice', to use another familiar word, to put their house in order…From this day on my Father will be looking for change, commitment, and not just by a few dedicated individuals, but by whole nations, following their Government's lead, which is so often lacking…The large, rich and powerful nations will be expected to take the lead, not only in their own backyards, but by giving assistance to those countries too poor to make real change without making conditions for their people even worse…My Father has asked me to inform you that he will review the situation in just ten years' time, appreciating that changes cannot be made over night, so to speak…But, and this is no idle threat, if he is displeased at what he sees, he will annihilate all life on this planet…How, you may ask…Well, he and I know, but your astronomers, even with their most advanced computers do not, that in exactly ten years' time, to the day, the deflected asteroid makes its return and will again be on a collision course with the Earth…He will simply allow it to continue that course…This time there will be no 'third chance'." At that he sat down, sipping his glass of water as he did so.

I thought about his final sentence…no third chance. Surely he meant second chance. Then I got to thinking. Jesus had counted his first visit to the Earth, where he'd been crucified in order to save mankind, as his first chance. His second chance to mankind had just been given, but in just tenyears' time there would be no third chance if things had not substantially improved.

***

Chapter Thirty Seven

The reaction to this 'threat' was interesting. As one observed the delegates and their entourages one could detect two distinct reactions. Some were almost laid back as if to portray a 'no urgency, then' reaction at the news that they had ten years to put the World's house in order. Others reacted with deep and serious discussion, where people huddled together.

Ten years was an incredibly short period of time to make any real impression. Eyes were directed at the laid back nations, and the odd finger discretely pointed as if to say "you're the main offenders".

It was now time for Jesus Nazarene to round off his appearance at the Headquarters of the United Nations, and he did this in great style, as one would expect of him. But this would take place outside the UN building, not inside the Assembly Hall.

As he made his way back to his seat, leaving his untidy pile of clothes on the floor, he beckoned to the Secretary General's aide. He in turn came towards him, wondering what was wrong. Jesus whispered to him: "Could you please fetch me my Holy Square?...I believe it was locked away for safe keeping."

The aide had indeed done so, knowing full well that had the Square been left on the table in the Assembly Hall some, if not all, the small pieces of pot would have 'walked', maybe even the completed Square itself. When all said and done, in terms of value, it was the most valuable object in the whole world.

The Square had been locked away in a safe within the Headquarters' admin centre. The aide disappeared and five minutes later returned with it. He passed it to Jesus, not having any idea what he intended to do with it.

Thinking that proceedings were now at an end those in the Hall prepared to leave. The Hall was becoming noisy. Jesus, realising that soon he would not be heard, shouted out: "Would you all please follow me?...I have one more thing I want you all to witness." At that he moved quickly towards one of the Hall's exits, carefully carrying the Holy Square in both hands in front of him. Those close by who had heard him, out of sheer curiosity followed him out of the Hall. Those further back, not wanting to miss out on anything, eagerly followed them.

I had already worked out what Jesus was going to first say, then do. I quickly caught up with him as he made his way to the UN building's main exit. As we both passed through I whispered: "I think I know what your intentions are."

Jesus Nazarene's reply was also a whisper: "If you do, please don't say anything…You must appreciate that to have maximum impact it must be a complete surprise to the masses."

I nodded in agreement knowing I'd worked it out correctly. I also appreciated that it did indeed need to be a complete surprise to the masses.

As Jesus slowly walked along he lifted the transparent lid of the wooden frame that protected the thirteen pieces of pot and held them in their allotted positions. He then carefully extracted the central white hexagon with the Greek letters π and θ engraved into it, and gave it to me, with the words: "Please accept this as a token of my gratitude for all the hard work you put in, locating all the thirteen pieces…Look upon yourself as the custodian of the piece on my behalf…Who knows, I might need it again."

I at first hesitated even though the piece had been in my safe keeping for several months, apart from the last few days. In fact it had been in my possession from the day it had turned up in on a Roman soldier who had had the misfortune to fall into a Yorkshire bog almost two thousand years ago. But the fact that Jesus himself was offering it to me made it very special. Was I worthy of being custodian of it? Gratefully I accepted the piece, wrapped it up in a clean handkerchief and stuffed it deeply into my trouser pocket for safe keeping. He in turn closed the lid and activated the clasp.

News travels fast in New York. The Assembly Hall's internal television cameras had transmitted the debate and vote on the water crisis in East Africa and had kept on running to show the thought-provoking speech of Jesus Nazarene. Quick thinking television stations within the city sensed that something dramatic could well take place once Jesus was outside the building, especially since he was naked apart from a pair of white boxer shorts. They therefore rushed their reporters and camera teams to the UN building. When Jesus emerged, with the delegates following him as if he were a modern day Pied Piper, the media were ready, waiting.

As if knowing their place the delegates and their entourages gathered as a large group in front of Jesus and were quickly joined by people who'd been sightseeing in the area.

I pushed my way to the front, ending up within two metres of him. He spotted me and smiled in acknowledgement. I hoped he saw a friendly and reliable face in the circumstances, for I knew that the next few minutes would be difficult for him, taking him back over two thousand years.

Not knowing how long I would be standing there, and with my arm beginning to ache, I placed the bag containing my laptop on the ground, trapping it between my feet so that it wouldn't topple over.

The sightseers in the surrounding streets sensed that something was 'on the go' when they observed the numerous taxis and vans with satellite dishes mounted on their roofs rushing past them heading for the UN building. They too headed in the same direction. News does indeed travel fast in New York.

Jesus looked around him and was pleased at what he saw. It reminded him of the time two thousand years ago when he had addressed the 'five thousand'. On that occasion he had not only addressed them, he had also fed them, as the apostle Luke had later described in his Gospel:

For there were about five thousand men...Then he (Jesus) took the five loaves and two fishes, looked up to heaven and blessed them. He then broke them and gave them to his disciples saying, feed my flock

Well, I doubted that he intended feeding his 'flock' on this occasion...But you never knew with this man.

Jesus now felt that his time had come. Taking the Holy Square in his left hand he first checked with his right that the catch holding the transparent lid firmly closed, was in position. The last thing he wanted was for the small pieces of pot to fall out. He then lowered the Square to his left side. Finally he raised his right hand above his head, fingers pointing to the Heavens.

This simple act had the effect of calming down the assembled mass. Within seconds an eerie silence spread across the whole area. Everybody seemed to be waiting for something to happen...And they didn't have to wait very long.

Jesus spoke in a loud clear voice, intending that all would hear him: "It is now time for me to join my Father in Heaven...May the Lord bless you and keep you...May the Lord make his face shine upon you and give you his peace, from this day on and for ever more…Amen."

It was in fact the Christian 'Blessing' that all clergymen, (and now women), from village priest to archbishop would give their congregations at the end of a church service.

A mumbled 'Amen' rippled across the assembled mass, as people who recognised the word repeated it.

Jesus then took the Holy Square in both hands and raised it above his head, pointing it to the sky. This act seemed to be some sort of signal, to whom wasn't exactly clear. What *was* clear was that what happened next could not have been man-made. Although it looked like a magician's trick, it certainly wasn't one.

From the unusually low dense cloud base that was below the tops of some of the city's skyscrapers, a column of the same dense cloud, approximately five metres in diameter, slowly descended vertically to the ground, completely engulfing Jesus Nazarene and those closest to him, including me, making us invisible to the thousands present. At the same time the temperature plummeted, encouraging me to push my hands deep into my jacket pockets.

Suddenly I became aware of movement behind me and before I could react felt my bag slide away from between my feet. Taking advantage of the 'pea soup' fog conditions some opportunist had stolen the bag containing my laptop.

I spun round, but not being able to see a hand in front of him I'd no chance of seeing the culprit, let alone apprehending him, or maybe her.

Equally slowly, the column rose, taking Jesus with it, but leaving everybody else behind, including me, staring up in utter amazement. On the one hand we couldn't comprehend why we'd been left behind, but on the other were thankful that we had.

As our eyes followed the cloud skywards we saw it reach the cloud base where it simply merged into it, completely disappearing as it did so. For the second time in his life Jesus had ascended into Heaven, his role on Earth having been completed.

I looked down to where he had been standing to see if he had left anything behind, if only his white boxer shorts. He certainly wouldn't be needing them once in Heaven. To my utter surprise there was my bag, lying on the ground exactly where Jesus had stood. The thief had obviously removed the laptop, discarding the bag which had a faulty catch, looked a bit tatty and had obviously seen better days. He had then merged back into the crowd. It was of little concilation to me that I'd at least got my bag back.

But I was wrong. The bag felt heavy when I picked it up, and I could feel something square and flat inside it. My laptop hadn't been taken after all. There was no need to check. Had the potential thief, in the presence of Jesus, suddenly had a fit of conscience, dropped the bag and made a hasty retreat? Highly unlikely, but what other explanation was there? By the way, there were no boxer shorts.

For some reason, one that probably the multitude of people were individually unable to explain, they burst into unanimous applause, making the large area reverberate with joyous sound. Those of a more religious persuasion, presumably of a Christian belief, started to chant: "Christ has risen, Hallelujah…Christ has risen…Hallelujah." Soon the chanting was taken up by most of those who were present, making the whole area sound like a football crowd supporting their favourite team. Of course they should have been chanting: "Christ has ascended", because he had already risen, in the autopsy room. But who cared about the exact wording? No one.

A silent calm then descended on the whole area as all those present realised the enormity of what they had just witnessed. As they wondered what to do next, half hoping that Jesus would return to Earth the same way he'd just left it, the heavens suddenly opened. In a matter of seconds it was raining torrentially. This was immediately accompanied by a thunder and lightning display of firework proportions. The head and shoulders of members of the crowd, packed like sardines in a tin, were soaked to the skin in a matter of seconds. There was no way of making an early escape. And it didn't help matters when a flash of lightning forked down and struck the conductor of a close-by building, giving the impression that the whole lot was going to crash down on them. Had an airliner flown into one of the skyscrapers above the cloud base? Memories of 'nine - eleven' suddenly came flashing back.

Then, as fast as the storm had descended on the area, it abated. The electrical display abruptly stopped and the sky slowly cleared, revealing a glorious sun. Again the applauses rang out, or rather slapped out, because the sleeves of shirts, jumpers and jackets were soddened…But who cared? It was a time for celebration. Jesus Christ had risen from the dead and ascended into Heaven, just as he had two thousand years ago. And all those present had been privileged to witness the final act. How would it affect those delegations that had been present? What message would they take back with them to their governments? Only time would tell.

Knowing that getting a cab back to my hotel would be out of the question for maybe an hour or more, the demand being so great, I decided to walk. The further I could get away from the UN building the more chance I had of getting one. As luck would have it, I'd only been walking ten minutes when I managed to flag one down. The cabbie had evidently dropped off a fare no more than half a mile away and was already returning to the UN building, knowing that there was business there to keep him busy for the next couple of hours.

I knocked on my hotel room door. Angela having a good idea who it was, but still having a quick looking through the spy hole just to check, opened the door to let me in. After a kiss and a cuddle from her as a form of greeting I stripped down to my underpants and tossed the still wet clothes onto the bedroom floor. After putting on a white dressing gown, supplied by the hotel, I collapsed into an easy chair positioned directly in front of the television. On my lap was my bag, which I held tightly, even though there was now no need to do so.

Angela was the first to speak, describing what she had seen on her television set and what she knew I had actually witnessed. Her question was short and to the point: "Well...What did you make of that, then?"

"I'd a good idea that Jesus Nazarene would go out in style so to speak, and it probably wasn't difficult to work out how he would do it...When I saw him remove his clothes it just confirmed my suspicions...We were going to witness his ascension, presumably into Heaven."

Angela smiled: "So what did you make of this ten year threat...Seems a bit far-fetched to me."

"Is it no more far-fetched than the threat that was set out in the Dead Sea Scroll unearthed earlier by those two children?...That was certainly real...In fact we were just a couple of days away from world annihilation, if we believe what Jesus told us...And don't forget all the evidence produced by the world's leading astronomers. "

"And did you believe him?"

"Well, yes...I'd no reason not to...And don't forget, the asteroid did change its course and would have collided with the Earth, with devastating effect, had it not done so...Its course had been changed by something, or someone, presumably God."

Angela nodded in agreement. There was no doubt, according to the world's experts, that the collision would have taken place: "So, do we go through all this again in ten years' time?"

"I've no idea…A similar ceremony could take place at the UN, but this time without the Holy Square…Jesus took that with him when he ascended into Heaven…I suppose he could return it to us in some way just before the ten years are up…He seems capable of doing anything."

Wanting a record of what I'd just witnessed both inside and outside the UN building I unzipped the bag containing my lap top. It was time to type it all in while it was still fresh in my mind.

As I eased the lap top out I realised that there was something else in the bag, also square and flat, but slightly smaller. To my utter amazement I extracted the Holy Square and immediately came to the obvious conclusion - during the thick fog, when I had felt my bag being removed from between my feet, Jesus had been the person who had removed it in order to place his Holy Square inside it, presumably for safe keeping down on Earth. During his ascension he'd left the bag behind assuming that I would see it and immediately claim it, as I obviously did.

Angela immediately took the Square from out of my hands and stared at it, fascinated. She'd obviously seen it before, in the Robertshaw household back in Doncaster, where I had constructed it and placed in it the six pieces of pot that I'd had in my possession at the time – the three found in a Doncaster bog, the two brought back from Israel by Rhoda and Jemma, and the one found in a North Yorkshire graveyard.She'd also seen the seven pieces of coloured card that I'd cut out to take the place of the missing pieces. But now the Square contained all the original pieces of pot. Well almost, because the central white hexagonal piece, the one belonging to Jesus himself, without doubt the most valuable piece, was missing.

Angela spotted its absence immediately: "Where the devil's the centre piece?...It was there when Jesus took possession of the Square after his speech…The television camera zoomed in on it, and all thirteen pieces were there…I saw them."

I simply smiled, but said nothing. Instead I eased out of my chair, went into the bedroom and retrieved the piece, still wrapped in the handkerchief from the pocket of my soddened trousers. On returning to the lounge I unfolded the handkerchief and passed the piece to her, again without a word.

"So, how do you come to have it?"She asked, dying to know.

"Jesus gave it to me…Asked me to act as custodian of it…Said he may need it again in the future."

Angela shook her head, not in the least surprised at the revelation. In fact nothing surprised her anymore about the whole issue of Christ's Holy Square. She placed the piece on the rug in front of the fireplace then carefully opened the catch on the Square and, much to my disapproval, because it seemed to me such an irreverent act, slowly turned the Square upside down, allowing the pieces of pot to fall also onto the rug.

I screamed: "Careful, for God's sake…They're fragile," as I saw and heard the various pieces collide as they landed on the rug.

Angela initially felt both annoyance and guilt - annoyance because I'd shouted at her, guilt because she knew I was right to criticise her action.

Of course I knew what she wanted to do. Just as a simple exercise she wanted to see if she could place all thirteen pieces back in the Square in their correct positions. It would be like doing a children's jigsaw puzzle.

As the pieces fell from their positions in the Square to the rug beneath, a folded piece of paper suddenly appeared and proceeded to float down also landing on the rug. Angela, again shook her head, picked up the paper, unfolded it and discovered that there was a handwritten message on it. She read the words out:

"Look after my Square for me.
I'll see you again in 2022.
Jesus N."

I smiled, not showing the slightest surprise. Not only had Jesus placed his Holy Square, the most precious item in the world, in my hands for safe keeping, he had also stated that on the second day of 'Judgement', in the year 2022, he would again make his appearance.

Angela asked what to her was an obvious question: "How does he know that you will be alive in that year?…You'll be seventy years old…In ten years so much could happen – a fatal accident, a fatal disease…You're already got type 2 Diabetes and your blood pressure's sky high…You're overweight, eat the wrong food and drink too much…So you don't know what's just round the corner."

I again smiled: "Don't forget…If we believe that his Father in Heaven is all-powerful he will ensure that I survive to at least that year."

Angela smiled: "And what about me?"

"Oh…You'll just have to take your chances."

Her reaction was to push me with such force that I fell off my chair.

Out of sheer curiosity Angela then asked another question: "I wonder when he placed the piece of paper in the Square?...Once he'd shed all his clothes, apart from his pants, he'd nowhere to hide it."

I thought back to the proceedings in the Assembly Hall, but could not think of a time when Jesus had the opportunity to place the paper under one of the pieces of pot without being seen. He must have therefore done it earlier having first written the note, but when, I had no idea. Or could he in some way have 'spirited' the paper into the Square? Jesus had earlier described to me how he'd managed to extract the piece of pot from an alarmed display cabinet in Tehran's Museum of Glassware and Ceramics, so he was certainly capable of 'spiriting' a piece of paper inside the Holy Square. But at the end of the day how it had got there didn't matter. It was there and its message was clear. I would be seeing Jesus again in just ten years' time. And hopefully Angela would too.

***

Chapter Thirty Eight

Since arriving back in England I had been faced with a problem – what to do with Christ's Holy Square. Only two people on Earth and one in Heaven knew that I was in possession of it. The question now was what should I do with it?

The simple answer was to lock it away in a safe place for the next ten years, probably in my university department's safe, but I hated the idea of items of archaeological interest being locked away. Their rightful place was on display so that the public at large could not only see them but also appreciate them, especially if they were items of beauty such as pieces of jewellery found in an Egyptian tomb. But I knew that, to be fair to the majority of museums throughout the world, they had so many items of interest that it was impossible to display them all. In such circumstances museums did on occasions devote a whole section of their display areas to a particular theme (eg) *The Egyptians, The Romans, The Crusades*, thus allowing as many items as possible to be exhibited. Art galleries did the same, with *Turner, Monet* and *Picasso* exhibitions. Sometimes valuable exhibits crossed continents and oceans to be put on display.

It was for this reason that I was determined that Christ's Holy Square, although only a small item, would go on display, preferably in the British Museum. Unfortunately the real item had been seen by millions of people on their television sets ascending into Heaven in the hands of Jesus Christ, or so they had been led to believe, therefore an excellent copy was required for display.

Of course the wooden Square itself, the one the public had seen on their television screens, could not have been genuine. The original one was made by Jesus himself two thousand years ago and had either been destroyed by Roman soldiers, the Square having belonged to a person accused, tried, found guilty and executed by crucifixion, for subversion. Or it would have been discarded, thrown into a fire or onto a rubbish heap where it would have simply burned or rotted away over time. The descriptive notes attached to any exhibit would of course point this out to the viewer.

But first I had to come up with a plan to deceive everybody, except of course my wife Angela. I intended to have the genuine thirteen pieces of pot displayed for the benefit of the public. They would think that they were viewing an excellent copy, but they would be wrong.

I first contacted the Curator of the British Museum, Tom Colley, who was a personal friend of several years' standing. Tom's interest in the 'Christ's Holy Square' story had commenced when I'd informed him of the discovery of a Roman cavalryman, sat on his horse, in a bog at the side of Yorkshire's River Don. It had ended when a column of 'fog' had carried Jesus Nazarene and the Holy Square up to Heaven, only a few days ago.

Numerous emails and phone calls had kept us in contact during the intervening period between these two momentous events, indicating that the whole issue of Christ's Holy Square had really caught the Curator's imagination. I therefore decided to take him into my confidence, and for two very good reasons - his genuine interest in the subject, and the fact that the centre of the Christ's Holy Square exhibit in his museum would contain the thirteen genuine pieces of pot. They would in fact be the twelve pieces that Jesus had distributed to his disciples all of two thousand years ago, a thirteenth piece kept for himself. Only the wooden Square would not be genuine.

In this way the pieces could be displayed to the public instead of being locked away in some university's archaeology department in the depths of South Yorkshire. The deceit would also hopefully ensure that no attempt would ever be made to steal the valueless copies, made only weeks earlier. Had it been known they were the genuine article the exhibition would have required a security system on a par with that used to protect the Louvre's *Mona Lisa* in Paris. The 'copy' could be simply protected by its glass case, a sophisticated alarm system being unnecessary.

There was just one condition that I had to insist on – that in ten years' time, when Jesus was expected to make his 'Third Coming', I would again take possession of his Holy Square.

Unfortunately Tom Colley was knocking on it years, probably into his late fifties, and it was anybody's guess who would be in charge of the British Museum in 2022. Hopefully there would be no problems when the new person, who obviously would have to be made aware of the situation, took over.

But for a reason that I found difficult to explain, I wanted my own personal copy of Christ's Holy Square. Did I think that the original one on display in the British Museum could somehow go missing? The security protecting it was almost non-existent, but there again it didn't need to be anything sophisticated. The toughened glass was deemed more than sufficient, for in terms of actual value the wooden square and thirteen funny shaped pieces of coloured pot, since a copy, was probably less than five pounds. Or did I feel that in ten years' time there may be difficulty in getting my hands on the Square, and would have to settle for a good copy? I had no idea.

My next task was therefore to see my good friend Josh Moorcroft, Head of South Riding University's Ceramics Department. Josh was some distant relative of William Moorcroft, the founder of the well-known Stoke-on-Trent factory which had been producing fine pottery for years. Josh was an excellent potter himself and was reputed to be able to 'throw a pot' better than anyone else in the country. How this had been determined had never been explained to me. Had there been some sort of competition, I wondered? Or maybe his family connection had been sufficient for him to assume the title. What I did know, having seen him on many occasions at the 'potter's wheel', was that he was very good, especially when drawing up the clay to make a tall, thin vase.

Anyway, this was neither here nor there. Josh was more than capable of making thirteen coloured pieces of pot, complete with Greek letter inscriptions, of the shapes and dimensions required to fit in a wooden square. I would of course construct the square myself. Hopefully it would be better than my first attempt, which I admit had been a bit rough.

At the same time as I placed my order with Josh I took him into my confidence and told him of my plan to enable the genuine Holy Square to be displayed in the British Museum. The public at large would simply see it as an excellent copy. I also showed him the thirteen individual pieces of pot so that he could see their exact shapes, measure their dimensions accurately and match up their exact colours to the numerous colour charts he had. His final task was to make notes of the size, shape and exact position of the fourteen Greek letters Jesus had originally used.

And so, over the next few weeks three tasks were completed. First I constructed the Holy Square to the same dimensions as the previous one I'd constructed, and as near as damn it to the same dimensions that Jesus must have used to construct his Square two thousand years earlier. The

Square had taken me hours to construct, the pile of discarded pieces showing that only perfection had been acceptable. When all said and done the exhibit would be on display to the world. Needless to say, Angela's sarcastic comments about the pile were unprintable.

Josh Moorcroft duly produced the exact copies of the thirteen pieces of pot. When he showed them, understandably I wanted to compare them with the genuine article. Since the copies were virtually identical I had to be careful not to mix the two sets together. Fortunately, Josh had stamped a tiny 'M' on the underside of each piece so that it could be differentiated from the real thing.

Finally, once the completed Holy Square, the copy of course, was ready I placed it in the top drawer of one of my office's filing cabinets for safe keeping. I, accompanied by Angela, then took the genuine Square down to London, to the British Museum, and presented it to Tom Colley, with the simple request - display it in a prominent position, with the best description you can come up with. I couldn't resist making one or two suggestions, totally unnecessary of course, Tom being more than capable of producing a first class display.

How:

- Christ had constructed it, commissioning a local potter to make the thirteen individual pieces.
- all the pieces had been distributed to his disciples, lost, then re-discovered.
- the re-assembly of the genuine article by the most powerful leaders in the world had resulted in the prevention of the total annihilation of the world by some rogue asteroid.

It would of course be pointed out that the object viewers were looking at was an exact copy (the individual pieces of pot having been made by the great British potter Josh Moorcroft), the original having been in the possession of Christ himself when he'd ascended into Heaven. Of course reference needed to be made to the description of the Last Supper, as set out in a recently discovered Dead Sea Scroll. In fact a piece of the scroll would be included in the exhibit, with a translation in English. I left all the wording to Tom and his team, confident that they would do a good job.

Tom Colley duly obliged, and although one of the smaller exhibits, Christ's Holy Square quickly became the most 'must see' item in the British Museum, as the *Mona Lisa* was at The Louvre in Paris. The visitors accepted that it was actually an excellent copy of the Square, most having earlier seen the genuine article ascend into Heaven in the hands of its owner, on their television screens. Little did they know that they were indeed viewing the 'real' thing – the most precious and valuable article in the whole world. I personally felt that the deceit was fully justified.

That evening, as Angela and I were watching a BBC *Horizon* programme on Climate Change, I glanced at the date at the top of the *Yorkshire Post*, it was Monday 10th September 2012. Jesus had informed us that he would see us again in the year 2022. It was anybody's guess what would happen in that year, but we had to assume that something would.

Meanwhile, all Angela and I could do was to enjoy the next ten years of our lives through both work and play, and that is what we intended to do.

***

Chapter Thirty Nine

Narrator - God

The time has now moved on to 2022, and as the tenth anniversary of my Son's second ascension into Heaven approaches I look down on the Earth for one final time. This, following my assessment, will enable me to make my decision. Do I destroy the Earth and all that lives upon it…or do I give it yet another chance?

Unknown to the world's leading astronomers, but known to me because I have been in control of its route through space, is a very large asteroid approaching the Solar System having been 'caught' and pulled in by the Sun's gravitational attraction. It is this that I have decided to use to destroy the Earth and all that lives upon it if that is my verdict. It will all depend on whether or not human kind has really made a determined effort in the ten years I gave it to mend its ways.

I wondered if the English boy Jamie Telford, who had discovered my asteroid ten years ago, was still hunting the heavens looking for them now and would spot my new one before the experts?Or had he moved onto 'pastures new'? Maybe he had risen to some dizzy height in the scientific world, or had he decided to become a pop star or a professional footballer instead? Perhaps my son Jesus can check that out for me, but it will have to be done quickly because Jamie will also suffer the same fate as the rest of mankind if I decide to allow my asteroid to enter a 'collision-with-Earth' orbit round the Sun.

Of course the time had to eventually come when my asteroid was discovered by the experts using the latest equipment available to them. As my Son had discovered, young Jamie Telford had indeed moved onto 'pastures new', those being as an undergraduate studying Chemistry at the South Riding University…a bit of a coincidence. In fact I understand that my son's Earthly friend, Professor Peter Robertshaw had already met him and they'd reminisced about Jamie's original discovery all of ten years earlier.

It had been said by the Earth's leading astronomers that an asteroid could not 'sneak' into the Solar System without being detected, the equipment now being so sophisticated. They even boasted that such an asteroid's distance from Earth could be measured to within one kilometre, and if on a collision course, its time of impact could be calculated to within one hour, and its point of impact to within a hundred square kilometres of the Earth's surface. On this occasion I'd allowed their equipment to discover the asteroid out in deep in space.

The discovery, made by a Chinese astronomer named Liu Zheng at the Zijinshan Observatory, up in China's Purple mountains, immediately became common knowledge. Checks were quickly made as a matter of urgency to verify the discovery. Once carried out, the disturbing information about the asteroid became common knowledge. This was displayed twenty-four hours a day on dedicated channels in order to keep the world's population informed on what was going on. Some information remained constant, some was changing second by second.

For example this was being displayed at that very moment on one of those dedicated channels being transmitted throughout the British Isles where my son's friend Peter Robertshaw lived.

Asteroid 2022LZ31 Torino Scale 10. Code RED – collision with Earth certain, causing climatic catastrophe threatening the future of civilization as we know it. It is described as a 'Global Killer' of all living things both plant and animal
Date – 1st June 2022
Time – 10:09:30 BST
Length – 60 km
Diameter – 44km (roughly ovoid in shape)
Mass – 7.3 x 10^{15} tonnes (assumed to consist mainly of iron)
Velocity – 48 000km/hr
Distance from Earth – 27 072 000km
Impact date and time – 24th June 2022 11:24:30 BST
Impact Point - 35 degrees 10 minutes N, 33 degrees 05 minutes W, placing it approximately 800 kilometres south west of the Azores, in the North Atlantic
Countdown to impact – 23 days: I hour:13 minutes:00 seconds

Those who still bothered to study the table, which were now very few, either refusing to believe my threat outright, or accepting its implementation as being inevitable, immediately saw that three numbers were falling second by second...the time, falling; the distance of the asteroid from the Earth, falling; the countdown, falling; Only one number was increasing, the velocity of the asteroid, as the Earth's gravitational pull increasingly acted upon it.

Of course, man discovered asteroid 2022LZ31 far too late for him to do anything about it. It had entered the Solar System, almost colliding with Pluto, and was on a highly eccentric orbit that would take it round the Sun. It would then travel out to beyond Neptune, except that I would or would not guide it onto a collision course with planet Earth.

So, the question was – what could man have done, if indeed anything at all, had the asteroid been discovered earlier? Two suggestions had been made as far back as 2012, when it had been thought that asteroid 2012JT82 would pass the Earth at a worryingly close distance. Both had been made by scientists at NASA's Jet Propulsion Laboratory at Pasadena.

The first suggestion had been to launch a manned mission to rendez-vous with the asteroid. Nuclear explosives would be planted at strategic points and these would hopefully split the asteroid into two or more smaller pieces. Since their masses would now be considerably smaller than the original, the gravitational pull of the Earth, Venus, Mercury and of course the Sun, would change the courses of the 'bits', taking them away from the Earth. In theory it had been thought a workable plan with a high chance of success. Of course, the astronauts had to first get there, land, do what they had to do, and get off...not of the easiest of tasks.

The second suggestion had been a bit more 'airy-fairy', with no one having any real idea what would happen, if indeed anything at all. It had been known for many years that the Sun emitted a continuous stream of high energy particles in all directions. This stream had been given the name – the *solar wind*. The particles were responsible for the occasional breakdown in radio communication, particularly during periods of high solar activity, such as when the eleven year sun spot cycle was at its maximum. They were also responsible for the phenomenon that man knows as The Northern and Southern Lights. The particles can even reach the Earth's surface and be responsible for that most unpleasant of human ailments, malignant melanoma – more commonly known as skin cancer.

Scientists wondered if some sort of huge sail could be somehow constructed on the asteroid that would 'catch' the solar wind causing the asteroid itself to be ever so slightly deflected – a bit like the course of a yacht being changed by the wind. A small deflection millions of kilometres away would send the asteroid on a different course, so that it would pass the Earth at a safe distance.

"So, was either idea tried? The simple answer was, no. NASA had always been convinced that although asteroid 2012JT82 would pass worryingly close to Earth there would be no noticeable effect to cause any real concern. Of course, after I'd put it on a collision course with Earth it was too late. The World's leaders had no alternative but to complete my son's Holy Square, committing themselves and their countries to making the World a better place. It was far too late for NASA to do anything about it then…And it was far too late now.

***

Chapter Forty

Narrator – Peter Robertshaw

Angela and I had faired pretty well during the intervening ten years. We had both retired in 2020 at a reasonable age of sixty-eight, and had led full lives from that point on. We could have retired earlier having earned well and been sensible with our money, but job satisfaction had encouraged us to continue. We'd had no children, Angela being unable to do so, and therefore the patter of feet, tiny and larger, had never featured in our household. We'd purchased a converted barn north of the village of Selside, close to the Settle to Carlisle railway line, in our beloved Yorkshire Dales and this had allowed us to pursue our new pastimes in ideal surroundings.

I had taken up the three related hobbies of painting, sculpture and pottery. I had taken over a large room in the loft, one that had windows in the roof allowing lots of natural light to stream in, and converted it into my studio. During the conversion there had been a slight panic when the floor creaked as the heavy pottery kiln was installed, otherwise all had gone well. Now I disappeared for hours on end, only appearing to eat and sleep,covered in paint, clay or marble dust depending on what my project was at the time.

One thing I did do before retiring was to remove Christ's Holy Square from the filing cabinet in my office in the Archeological Department of South Riding University. This was the near perfect copy that I'd earlier made of the genuine article, the one that at that very moment was on display in the British Museum, having been so for the last ten years

Tom Colley, who had been curator at the time I'd presented the museum with the genuine Christ's Holy Square, had also retired. The assistant curator, Henry Jackson, had been appointed to the top job and was already fully aware that the museum was in fact in possession of the genuine article, not some excellent copy. For this reason I didn't expect any problems when, during this year I would request to take possession of the museum's genuine article, as had been arranged with Tom.

At home I had specially constructed a hidden cupboard behind the kiln in my studio. No opportunist burglar who happened to break into the barn while I and Angela were away from home would find it. This was where the copy of the Square was kept, and would eventually hold the genuine article when I took possession of it from the British Museum.

Angela had always wanted to write and illustrate children's stories and compose poems, but had never had the time to do so during her working life. She too had taken over a room, one facing roughly south-east, with Pen-y-Ghent in the distance forming a picturesque backdrop. She'd converted it to an office, housing her computers, printers and art material. She'd published some e-books, but had always preferred the conventional route of producing books that her readers could hold in their hands and turn the pages over. After the initial enthusiasm for e-books it had been found that more and more people, including children, were returning to 'paper' books.

One thing we did do was to eat together in the evening and discuss the progress we had made in our individual projects. This took place in the oak beam ceilinged lounge and in front of the huge wood burning fire, a welcome sight on dark cold nights. Television was unbelievably bad, with only a handful of channels worth watching out of the hundreds, possibly thousands, now available. 3D sets were now common place, but the technology had never caught our imaginations.

Angela continued her story writing. I too had decided to write my own book. Throughout my mission to first locate, then bring together the thirteen pieces of pot that made up Christ's Holy Square, I had kept a detailed diary. It was now time to convert it into an informative piece of non-fiction, and this is what I did. The story, with the title – *Christ's Holy Square – A Mission Impossible*, was much along the lines of Dan Brown's world number one novel, *The Da Vinci Code*, published over nineteen years earlier, in 2003. Hopefully my story would be as popular.

Angela and I had travelled widely together, concentrating mainly on the great cities of the world, with their famous art galleries, museums and architecture. But we certainly weren't opposed to a holiday in the sun, mixing with the other holiday makers. Surprising to our more academic friends, Tenerife's Playa de las Americas was our favourite resort. We enjoyed the hustle and bustle of the place and still enjoyed setting out our sunbeds on the beach, swimming in the sea, and generally watch the world go by.

Above all, we had kept in good health, mainly due to eating well and taking plenty of exercise. This took the form of long walks with our Belgian Shepherd dog, *Tala*, named after a Cypriot village that we had visited during a holiday on the island to see the mosaics at Curium.

Sadly, Tala had died in 2020 at the relatively young age of eight years, having eaten some poisoned chicken up in the Dales that had been laid down by some unscrupulous gamekeeper intent on killing red kites.

Unable to cope with the absence of a dog in the household I decided to get another one. By sheer good luck I'd been on the *Dog Trust* website and spotted that the Leeds branch had a two year old Belgian Shepherd bitch that had lost her elderly owner in a car accident. Within a matter of days I had picked her up. She was as black as coal, as Tala had been, and had soon settled into her new way of life. And just as Tala had been, she was as keen as mustard. Since she hadn't responded particularly well to her name of *Poppy* I decided to re-christen her *Tala 2*, which quickly became just *Tala*. Of course she needed regular exercise, and this kept both Angela and I on our toes, keeping us fit and healthy, apart from the odd ache and pain.

Although there'd been no doubt in my mind that God had had something to do with my and Angela's good health over the last ten year, I now had my doubts. Within the last month, after weeks of a persistent throbbing headache, I was diagnosed with an aggressive form of brain tumour. It was deep seated and surgery, even using the latest pinpoint computer-controlled robotic scalpels, was not an option nor were radio and chemotherapy. The prognosis was poor and I'd been given six months at the most to live.

But I had an appointment with Jesus in June 2022, and obviously I wouldn't be able to keep it if I were dead. I had visions of falling off my perch immediately after that appointment, even if God decided to give mankind another chance.

On the morning of the 10th of June, just two weeks before Asteroid 2022LZ31 was expected to strike the Earth with such devastating force that almost all life would be annihilated, I phoned Henry Jackson, the British Museum's curator. It was time for me to pick up the genuine Christ's Holy Square. This would be replaced with the excellent copy that I'd had in my possession since 2012.

If Jesus and I were going to meet up as he had promised, I had to have in my possession a Square that contained the thirteen pieces of pot that he'd had made for himself over two thousand years ago by Zachariah the potter. It was no good presenting him with copies, however good those copies were. I was convinced that that meeting would take place sometime on that final day. I also had a good idea where.

Unfortunately when I rang the British Museum Henry Jackson was not available, having been summoned to Scotland Yard to discuss the Museum's security. It was felt that the Museum could be subject to attacks of looting during the remaining few days before the asteroid struck the Earth. I therefore had to speak to the receptionist on the other end of the line.

Not being prepared to explain in detail my business with the curator, to her I simply asked her to inform him that Peter Robertshaw would be travelling down from Yorkshire to see him the following day. I did however mention that my visit would be to do with the Christ's Holy Square exhibit. I certainly didn't anticipate any problems. When all said and done the exchange of the two Squares had already been arranged, and indeed expected, even though not due to take place until the year 2022.

Early the following day, after a quick breakfast, Angela and I made preparations for our journey down to London. We in Yorkshire always insisted that we went 'down' to the capital, not up, a description that those living nearer the capital, often used. Having the previous evening removed my copy of Christ's Holy Square from its hiding place it was now time to place it in my shoulder bag, first ensuring that the brass clasp was tightly fastened. The last thing I wanted was for the pieces of pot to become dislodged and start rattling around in the bottom of the bag, or worse still fall out of the bag altogether. I'd dropped Tala off at Smiths Farm, just across the Settle - Carlisle railway line, the previous evening, so we did not have to worry about her for the rest of the day.

Angela and I travelled down to Horton-in-Ribbledale railway station in our ten year old Ford Fiesta in order to catch our train to Leeds, and hence down to London. The car had only 40 000 miles on the clock, was running like a sewing machine, and we didn't see the point of replacing it with some new-fangled electric one.

Having parked up at the station we both boarded the Carlisle to Leeds train, finding it full. It was now common knowledge that the Earth was in danger of being hit by a huge asteroid, so where were all the people going, or coming from? Or had they decided to travel the iconic Settle to Carlisle line for the last time? On talking to those around us, some who had travelled from as far afield as Kent and Cornwall, it was clear that some had.

The train down to the capital was equally full. Fortunately we had reserved our seats for the two and a half hour journey. We should have been travelling on the new HS2 train had the Government 'got their finger out' and got it built. It was intended to rival Japan's *Bullet* train, travelling at three hundred miles an hour and cutting the journey time to less than an hour. But alas we would be taking over twice that time.

What was surprising was the fact that the train was running at all, but like almost all the public services it was a case of 'business as usual', even though the world could be coming to an end in just over a week's time. Very few people throughout the whole world believed that it would - and that was the problem, or was it? Surely the best thing possible for the world's population to do was to carry on as normal, otherwise man's last few days on Earth would be intolerable. Of course the idle and the criminal, fueled with drugs and liquor, were already making life a living hell for those who wanted to lead near normal lives in the closing stages of their and their planet's existence. But civilised life had to continue, right to the very end...and in most countries it appeared to be doing just that.

After taking a taxi manned by a talkative driver who provided stimulating and informative conversation on our short journey from Kings Cross to the British Museum, both Angela and I entered and quickly found one of the guides. I, assuming that my previous day's message had been passed on by the receptionist, informed the guide that the curator, Mr Jackson, was expecting me, even though he actually wasn't. As it happened, the message had indeed got through. The guide contacted the curator on her mobile then took Angela and I to his office. There I introduced myself and Angela to Henry Jackson.

"Hello, Mr Jackson...My name's Peter Robertshaw...I was for many years Departmental Head of Archaeology at South Riding University before I retired...I was also a professional associate and personal friend of Tom Colley your predecessor...This is my wife, Angela."

Henry Jackson confidently replied: "Good morning Professor ...I do indeed know of you, and of your exploits...Tom spoke at length about you, especially your involvement in the whole Christ's Holy Square saga...Quite a story, the way you managed to locate all thirteen pieces of pot, that were then used to bring together the leaders of the world and, following words set out in a newly discovered Dead Sea Scroll, asked them to commit themselves and their countries to look after the Earth and all that live upon it, both plant and animal...And of course to witness Christ's second ascension...That must have been a very emotional experience for you…I was at university at the time and watched the whole saga unfold, on television."

"It was indeed an emotional experience, one I will remember to my dying day, which as it happens could be in just a few day's time." My replied was rather abrupt for I wanted to get onto the job in hand rather than get bogged down, describing and discussing past events to do with the Holy Square. I quickly followed my reply with my request: "You will no doubt remember that I had an understanding with Tom Colley that I could take possession of the Holy Square on display in your museum, replacing it with a copy that I have in my possession, sometime during the year 2022?…Since the end of the world could be imminent I would like to make that exchange as soon as possible…Could that take place today?…I have the copy with me."

"Er, sorry, Professor…Although I am aware that you are in possession of an excellent copy of the Square, I remember Tom telling me that, I cannot remember him saying that at some point in the future an exchange would take place…Besides, the exhibit has now taken on a new and significant importance…People in their droves are visiting it and praying…They stand in front of it, hands together and eyes closed, asking God to forgive them all their sins, and asking him to save the world from destruction…I've even seen parties of school children with their teachers, praying, in this day and age a most unusual sight…In such circumstances I don't feel that I can replace the genuine Holy Square with some copy, one made only a few years ago…And I'm sure that God, if there is one, would not want me to do so."

I was initially taken aback. I certainly hadn't expected this. Feeling first like a grenade with the pin halfway out, ready to explode, then totally helpless, wondering what I could do if the curator 'dug his heels in', I paused before replying. What *could* I in fact do? There was no one I could appeal to. Nothing had been put down in writing, a shaking of hands being considered sufficient. Tom Colley had died a few years ago, so that avenue was closed. The museum's governing body probably wasn't even aware that its museum had been in possession of the genuine Holy Square for the last ten years, so there was no point in making any sort of appeal there.

After taking some deep breaths in an effort to calm myself down and stop my heart exploding with the pressure, I decided that I had no alternative but to appeal to Henry Jackson's sense of decency. At the same time I was prepared to reveal exactly why I wanted the genuine article: "Don't you feel any obligation to abide by what your predecessor and myself had agreed?"

"Er, in the circumstances, No…I cannot see what difference it makes as far as you are concerned…genuine article or copy."

"Well…I know that you will find it hard to believe, but just before Jesus Christ ascended into heaven for the second time he gave me the genuine article for safe keeping, at the same time stating that he and I would meet again…I am certain that that meeting is going to take place just before the asteroid strikes the Earth…I therefore feel it only right that I should be able to present him with *his* Holy Square, not *my* copy…Surely you can see that."

"Would he know the difference?"

I could have exploded at the question. I felt like shouting at the man - *of course he would know the bloody difference, you stupid man…He's Jesus Christ, the Son of God.* Instead, I made my final appeal: "So, you won't budge on the issue, then?"

"As I said before…In the circumstances, no."

I reluctantly accepted defeat. If I did happen to meet up with Jesus on the final day I would simply have to explain and apologise. Hopefully he would understand…Maybe even ask his Father to strike Henry Jackson dead. Immediately I felt ashamed at thinking such a thought.

As a final request I then asked the curator if I could visit the Christ's Holy Square exhibit. I had last viewed it some six years ago when I and Angela had travelled down to the capital in order to attend Tom Colley's retirement party.

At that precise moment the exhibit was closed to the general public, the room having been temporarily roped off. The stand supporting it had become unsafe, the result of people pressing against it. Some minor strengthening was therefore being carried out even though it would only be required for a matter of a few days. Since the workmen were on their tea break the exhibition room was empty of people. Henry Jackson therefore instructed the guide to remove the rope barrier and allow Angela and I into the room. He then made his excuse to leave, claiming that he was a very busy person. After a quick meaningless handshake and an equally quick: "Goodbye…Must go…Work to do," he disappeared. I shook my head in disgust. Angela, a much more vocal person, said exactly what she thought of Henry Jackson: "Ignorant bastard."

The guide, observing that visitors were staring into the room, one even attempting to push the rope barrier aside in order to gain access, quickly moved to the door, pulled it slightly closed and took up a position just outside it. This meant that both Angela and I were able to view the Christ's Holy Square exhibit with not another person in sight.

The exhibit was as we both remembered it, except that the glass lid that I had made to prevent the pieces of pot falling out, had been closed on our previous visit. It was now open. This did at least make the pieces slightly more visible. I reached into my shoulder bag and carefully extracted my excellent copy, (although I say it myself), of the Square. I then undid the clasp and lifted the lid, thus allowing me to compare the two sets of pieces of pot more closely, all thirteen of them. What struck me most of all was how close the colours were - the yellow of the four ρ pieces, the red of the four α pieces and the green of the two τ pieces. Josh Moorcroft, who had made the copies for me, had certainly done a brilliant job. Would Jesus really be able to tell the difference?

Then, the strangest of things started to take place. As I, Angela standing at my side, held the copy in front of me, and at the same level with the Square inside the glass display case, the two α pieces in each Square rose out of their set positions and slowly, but definitely, passed through the glass barrier and exchanged places. The four ρ pieces then did exactly the same, and this exchange continued until the final two pieces, the white hexagonal ones, Jesus Christ's personal pieces, completed the exchange. Angela rubbed her eyes and shook her head, wondering if she'd just had some sort of dream. By all the laws of physics known to man, what she'd just witnessed just couldn't take place - and yet it had.

I initially could not believe my eyes, but then I got to thinking. Hadn't something remotely similar taken place in Tehran's Museum of Glassware and Ceramics ten years ago? Jesus Nazarene had 'spirited' the brown o piece out of the exhibit. I remembered him describing to me how the piece had simply passed through the glass wall and into the palm of his hand. I had to come to the obvious conclusion that at least for that brief moment I had been given the same powers that Jesus had possessed. Or had it all been nothing to do with him? Had some superior being, that surely being God himself, simply carried out the exchange? I knew that he was in the habit of moving in mysterious ways, but this was a bit special, to say the least. But that didn't matter. I now had in his possession the thirteen genuine pieces of pot. The wooden Squares themselves hadn't changed places, but that didn't matter because both had been made by me within a month of each other ten years ago, the original having been constructed by Jesus himself two thousand years earlier, That had presumably disappeared after the Last Supper.

I first carefully closed the glass lid of the Holy Square in my possession and activated the clasp. This ensured that the pieces of pot could not move from their fixed position, or worse still fall out. I then gently eased the Square back into my shoulder bag.

Both Angela and I hastily said our goodbyes to the guide, at the same time thanking him for his help and cooperation. Little did he know that that cooperation had enabled the 'forces at work' to exchange the thirteen pieces of pot outside the glass exhibition case with those inside. We then hailed a taxi that took us back to Kings Cross.

Our train was already waiting and within ten minutes we were on our way back to Leeds. We couldn't get away from the capital fast enough. As we sped northwards we looked at each other and smiled, no doubt thinking exactly the same thing. The uncompromising, pompous and ignorant bastard Henry Jackson – to quote Angela, had no idea that his precious Holy Square was now in fact my copy. I was almost tempted to call him on my mobile and inform him to that effect, but resisted. He wouldn't have believed me anyway, knowing full well that any attempt to tamper with the glass case would have inevitably resulted in permanent damage to it. Even now I couldn't work out why the glass hadn't shattered.

***

Chapter Forty One

As the 'day of judgement' approached, the day when God would, or would not, allow asteroid 2022LZ31 to collide with the Earth, annihilating all human life, most of the other creatures, and destroying almost all the vegetation, Angela and I drew up our plans for that fateful day.

Throughout the world people appeared to be adopting one of two attitudes towards their fate, whatever it would be. Millions moved into their churches, synagogues and mosques, and continually prayed asking for forgiveness, thinking that God could be persuaded to save mankind by deflecting the asteroid away from planet Earth.

But the overwhelming majority of the world's population either simply refused to believe that the collision would occur. The so-called 'experts' had simply got it wrong. Or, they accepted the inevitable, but refused to go down without an act of defiance. And that took the form of celebration. Vast street parties were planned and it was anticipated that, as far as the United Kingdom was concerned, these would be similar to those that had taken place in 2012 when Queen Elizabeth the Second's Diamond Jubilee had been celebrated. In other countries the celebrations would be similar to those held on New Year's Eve. Huge firework displays were planned, especially on some of the tallest buildings in the world, and of course on such iconic structures as the Sidney Bridge, San Francisco's Golden Gate and the London Eye, to name just three.

A considerable number of people throughout the world thought that some sort of manmade conspiracy was afoot, toe-the-line or face annihilation, as if the path of a huge piece of rock hurtling through space towards Earth could be controlled by one man...a bit like the villain in a James Bond film. Maybe it could all be done by deflecting laser beams with huge electromagnetic fields, or maybe just by simple mirrors.

It appeared that the overwhelming attitude was along the lines - if we're going out, let's go out in style. No point in being depressed or feeling sorry for ourselves. Surprising, or maybe not so surprising, little civil unrest was recorded, at least in Britain.

Angela and I were only able to comment on our observations of what was taking place in our own country. We found the behaviour of most of the people strange in such unusual circumstances. There was for instance little evidence of food hoarding or the looting of goods from stores, the attitude apparently being – what's the point of having ten state-of-art television sets or twenty loaves of bread, when you'll be dead in a few days' time? The whole atmosphere was most strange. Many people continued to go to work – Power and water workers, so the lights were on and toilets were flushing; teachers were at their workstations, trying to convince their children that school was the best and safest place for them, rather than aimlessly roaming the streets getting into mischief or being in danger…and school attendance, in the circumstances, was surprisingly high; nurses were still in their wards, and A&E departments still functioned, treating all the run-of-the-mill accidents, such as dog bites, cut heads and sprained ankles; the police were still sorting out binge drinkers and druggies, just like they had done on Friday nights for as far back as they could remember, and the firefighters were still standing by their engines. It was even not uncommon to see joggers continuing their 'keep fit' routines in their local parks. How they would have explained their strange action in these unique circumstances could only be guessed at, but it would have been interesting to hear. Maybe they thought that being fit in heaven or hell would be some sort of asset…and maybe it would.

The Government was at a loss as to what to do, or say. In fact only one message came out of the Prime Minister's office at 10 Downing Street. This was displayed on the screens of all forms of visual communication from the personal wrist TVs to screens the size of a lounge wall - stay calm, act responsibly, maintain law and order, and stay close to your loved ones. Perhaps understandably, it specifically failed to mention anything about impending doom and what the worse-case scenario could be. Panic had to be avoided at all costs.

But although there seemed to be a blanket ban on the transmission of information by a Government sponsored body there was nevertheless much speculation by those who presumably knew about such things. They were the astronomers who had observed asteroid impacts on other planets such as Jupiter, the geologists who knew all about earthquakes and tsunamis, and the biologists who had for years been setting out various scenarios for all living things on Earth if the planet was suddenly faced with a massive drop in temperature. This could be the result of the Sun's light and heat being blocked out by dust in the atmosphere as a result of an asteroid impact or massive volcanic activity. The picture all the experts painted was indeed a black one.

417

What *was* known was that if the asteroid continued on its present course it would strike the Earth roughly in the middle of the North Atlantic, some 800 miles south west of the Azores. On the grand scale of things the exact coordinates didn't really matter.

Those experts who were prepared to voice an opinion were in general agreement that the following sequence of events would probably then take place, although some of the numbers had by their very nature to be only approximate:

    1)   – the asteroid, known to be roughly the shape of a rugby ball 60km in length and 44km in diameter at its widest point and made largely of iron ore would approach the Earth from the SW and hit the Atlantic Ocean at an angle of about 60° and at a speed in the region of 64000km/h. The resulting impact with the ocean floor would cause the asteroid to explode, creating a fireball that would also include molten debris from both asteroid and ocean floor. This,along with many billions of tonnes of dust and water vapour, would rise upwards and outwards into the atmosphere. The pieces of rock, some probably still glowing, would eventually fall back to Earth some distance away from the point of impact, and if falling on land would start uncontrollable fires as vegetation ignited. The fireball the size of over a hundred suns would be seen by all those people where it rose above their horizon. A crater of a size impossible to calculate but of unimaginable dimensions would be created on the ocean floor and the initial displacement of sea water outwards would be massive.

    2)   – The impact would produce a seismic shockwave that would literally shake the planet as it travelled outwards at frightening speed. Earthquakes would be widespread with Richter scale readings sufficiently high to cause structures to collapse, depending on their distance from the asteroid impact.

    3)   – The resulting explosion would produce an airblast that would in turn produce a hurricane spreading outwards at a speed far greater than anything that the Earth had experienced since man had set foot on the planet. This hurricane would travel thousands of kilometres destroying everything in its path – all but the strongest buildings would be flattened, even trees would be uprooted, or at least stripped bare of their foliage. It was thought that some living creatures with lungs could be killed by

literally having the air sucked out of them as the airwave passed by.

4)   – Finally a tsunami, produced by the huge displacement of water, would spread outwards in an ever increasing circle, eventually developing into a wave that could peak at a height in the region of fifteen hundred metres as it approached land.

Three of the four phenomena - the seismic shockwave, the air blast and the tsunami would spread out in all directions at different, yet frightening speeds. It was thought that this combination of events, the result of an asteroid striking the Earth just off the Yucatan Peninsula in the Gulf of Mexico, some 65 million years ago, could have led to the extinction of the dinosaurs…although there were other schools of thought on this.

But it was the tsunami that would ultimately do the most damage as it spread out equally in all directions like the expanding circle seen when a stone is tossed into a pond. I dug out my Philips New World Atlas and quickly found a map of the World. Using the longitude figures along top and bottom and the latitude figures up both sides I worked out the point of impact at Latitude 38° N and Longitude 26° W, marking it with a black dot. It was approximately in the middle of the North Atlantic.

After measuring the length of a line joining the black dot to the centre of the British Isles I drew a circle centred on the dot with a radius of that measurement, with a pair of compasses. It was now easy to see which land masses would have been hit by the advancing tsunami by the time it reached the place where I lived. The circle also showed me how much of the Earth's surface would have already been affected by the time the tsunami reached the British Isles.

Using some simple maths that I had learned at school and had stuck in my mind I was able to work out the area in relation to the total area of the Earth's surface. Already approximately 8% would have been affected by the tsunami. Fortunately almost all this would have been sea, but it would then start to pass over land that was not high enough to be above it, and that inevitably included thousands of kilometres of coastline where many of the world's population lived.

I studied what fell within the circle. The first land to be hit would be the islands making up the Azores, a mere 800 kilometres to the north-east from the point of impact, They would be simply swallowed up by the advancing wave. The Canaries would be hit next. There, only Tenerife's Mount Teide at a height of over 3000 metres would be high enough to poke its head above the advancing waters.

Canada and the African continent would come next, with only the Atlas Mountains in Morocco offering any resistance. Spain would be the first European country to be hit, with only the Sierra Nevada and the Pyrenees hindering the tsunami's relentless advance into the Mediterranean Sea .

After passing over the islands of Bermuda as if they weren't there, America's eastern seaboard, some 3000 kilometres away from the point of the asteroid's impact would be the first major land mass to be hit as the wave moved west. How far a tsunami 1500 metres high would spread inland was anyone's guess. But one thing was certain, all in its path along the coast, buildings, whatever their strength and height, would be reduced to rubble by the advancing waters. It went without saying that all human and non-aquatic animal life would be exterminated in a matter of seconds.

At a distance of 3600 kilometres the British Isles, along with the Islands of the Caribbean, would be next on my imaginary list. And last of all within the circle the tsunami would hit the South American continent. But of course it would not stop there. It would continue to expand outwards at frightening speed, seeking out all land below about 1500 metres in height.

How long this expansion would go on nobody knew. Could the tsunami in fact travel all the way round the World, moving into the Pacific Ocean having passed over the narrow strip of land that joined North and South America, and cutting across southern Africa and into the Indian Ocean? Or would it simply move through the Mediterranean Sea, cut across Saudi Arabia and enter the Indian Ocean that way? Nobody of course knew.

What was known was that a high number of the World's population lived on or close to a coastline. It was therefore inevitable that most would be annihilated by the advancing waters unless they could in some way be evacuated to higher ground, but that higher ground was not easy to find. In fact in the British Isles there was no high ground at all, even Ben Nevis, at a height of 1343 metres, would succumb to a tsunami over 1500 metres high.

So, what *would* be the effect on the British Isles? How far would the tsunami travel inland?Since no one actually knew, one could only make a calculated guess.

A small tsunami maybe only a few metres high and approaching from the south-west, would be split by the Cornish Peninsula, half going north into the Irish Sea and the Bristol Channel and half going east into the English Channel. But the path of this tsunami that could be as much as a 1500 metres in height, would not in any way be controlled by coastlines. It would simply rush across land masses as it came to them. Just how far that penetration would be could only be guessed at. And since there was no ground above fifteen hundred metres in Ireland and Great Britain, would a wave of that height simply pass over both land masses as if they were not there, rush across the North Sea and hit the coastline of Europe? Would it eventually reach the Alps, even the Urals? Again, nobody knew. Any land above 1500 metres, would in theory poke its head above the swirling waters, but it was anybody's guess how a mass of water, moving at over 800 kilometres an hour, would act when meeting such high ground. Would it for instance simply wash over the top, as a wave in a rough sea would pass over a large pebble on the beach? Again, nobody knew.

Presumably an observer in orbit around the Earth would see the high ground, such as Tenerife's Mount Teide, the Pyrenees and the Alps as islands, until the waters eventually receded, being drawn back into the crater that the asteroid had created on the floor of the Atlantic Ocean. This was of course likely to be the eventual outcome unless the tsunami managed to travel round the World and pour back into the huge crater on its return.

But would people get any sort of warning of their impending doom? It had been predicted that the first physical effect those living in the UK would experience would be a seismic shock or earthquake of unpredictable magnitude – the worst case scenario being as high as 9 or 10 on the Richter Scale - a magnitude rarely experienced on the Earth. This in itself would cause considerable damage to most manmade structures. The nation's people had already been forewarned in good time to find a safe haven out in the open air, well away from buildings that would inevitably collapse.

Parks, school playing fields and large supermarket car parks, even football stadiums, soon became favourite places of occupation for those who lived in the larger towns and cities. Such areas initially looked like orderly holiday campsites, but soon resembled shanty towns and third world refugee camps. Many people had already headed for the nearest countryside using whatever forms of transport were available. Residents headed for the nearest open space, for example those of Manchester and Sheffield headed for Derbyshire's Peak District. Those of Leeds and Bradford headed for the Yorkshire Dales. Such people, often as whole family groups, took up residence in the many farmers' fields, making sure not to pitch camp too close to a dry stone wall that could collapse on them. In no time at all tranquil pastures also took up the appearance of third world shanty towns and refugee camps, as did the nation's National Parks.

Since the air blast produced by the asteroid's impact would move outwards at high speed, experts estimating that to be in the region of the speed of sound, around 1100 km/h, what effect would it have? Would the prediction by some that the air would be sucked out of the lungs of those living things that had them, killing them instantly, come to pass? Or would they survive only to be drowned shortly afterwards by a tsunami anything up to 1500 metres in height and travelling according to the same experts, at about 800 km/h?

What people of all nations would know was that the earthquake, air blast and tsunami would be on their way long before they actually arrived. The asteroid's course through the Earth's atmosphere and its eventual impact with the planet would be observed by the network of satellites that had already been put in place specially to observe such an event. These images would flash round the World, leaving everyone in no doubt that their planet and hence their lives were about to change forever, and most likely come to an end.

So, what would be the time scale as far as the British Isles were concerned? The signals from the satellites recording the event would take a fraction of a second to reach the receiving stations in the UK and the pictures would be transmitted to the nation at about 11:25 on the morning of the 24th of June. Some enthusiasts with appropriate communications technology would receive the information direct from the satellites, but the vast majority would be glued to their latest form of visual communication, watching the news coverage of the event as it unfolded. All would be spellbound at the apocalyptic sight.

The seismic shockwave, travelling at an estimated speed in the region of 15000 kilometres per hour, would arrive about fifteen minutes later, at 11:40. The Earth's crust would be shaken violently and the vibrations would travel round the world at this frightening speed.

The shock wave, in the form of an air blast, would take about three and a quarter hours, arriving at 14:40 in the afternoon. The tsunami would arrive an hour and a quarter later, at just before 15:55. All times, by their very nature, could only be approximate.

What individuals would do in the intervening periods would presumably be entirely up to them – have a party, get drunk or stoned, or both. Make mad passionate love with a loved one, or a total stranger. Would it really matter? And of course pray, as no doubt many would.

Could they protect themselves in any way, say by moving underground, a bit like they did during the Second World War when the air raids started on London and the underground railway stations provided a safe haven? That may give some protection against the air blast, assuming that the structures had somehow survived the earlier earthquake, but not a very good idea when the 'enemy' was a tsunami 1500 metres high.

What about a boat? You could then simply float on top of the wave, a bit like Noah did in his Ark, or you could surf it on a board.But how would you launch your boat or board on a 1500 metre high wave? Not easy.

No doubt some would head for the hills - Ben Nevis, Snowdon, Scafell. Surely they would be safe up there. Well no, they wouldn't be. The mountains simply wouldn't be high enough.

What would also happen although little mention was made of it, presumably because it was thought that most would fall back harmlessly into the Atlantic Ocean, was the mass of debris, glowing red hot, that would be blasted into the atmosphere by the asteroid's impact. But if some did shower back to Earth and impact on land, the distance between the point of impact and the nearest large land mass, Africa, being about 2000 kilometres, it would set alight anything that would burn. The debris would be sulphurous in nature filling the atmosphere with poisonous sulphurdioxide that would ultimately fall to Earth as acid rain. Only the most hardy plant life and those creatures that over time had developed the ability to survive in such conditions, those living close to active volcanoes, for example, would have any chance of continuing to do so.

And these were the reasons why the Governments of most countries offered no advice on what to do. They simply didn't know what was going to happen, other than that a combination of earthquake, air blast, tsunami and possibly red hot debris falling from the sky, would in the very short term kill billions of people. Over a longer period of time conditions would make it extremely difficult, if not impossible, for all those living things that had managed to survive the initial effects of the asteroid's impact, to continue to do so…and that definitely applied to the human species. Our Government therefore re-iterated what it had said earlier - stay calm, maintain law and order, and stay close to loved ones. And to their credit, this is what the vast majority of people did.

***

Chapter Forty two

Angela and I had already made our arrangements, knowing exactly what we intended to do. On the evening of the 23rd of June 2022, the day before the asteroid's impact was due to take place, the latest predicted time being 09:24 hours local time, local time being mid North Atlantic time, which meant about 11:24 UK time, we would gather together what we considered we would need. I had already done my own calculations on the sequence of events that would follow, not being prepared to rely entirely on the Government's 'official' figures.

According to my figures the satellite signal would arrive in my living room and hence on my television screen at about 11:25. The seismic shock, or earthquake, would hit the UK twenty-two minutes later, at 11:47. The air blast of hurricane proportions would arrive about three and a half hours after impact, at 14:58. Finally, the tsunami would hit the west coast of Ireland and then the UK at 16:06. All the times had to be approximate because no one, not even the best brains in the country, knew with any degree of accuracy what the time scale of the various events would be. My figures would therefore probably be as accurate as anyone else's.

Our plan was to travel the few miles to Horton-in-Ribblesdale in our trusty Ford Fiesta, park up and commence the walk to the top of Pen-y-Ghent, not the highest of the Yorkshire Three Peaks, but in my opinion the most attractive, accompanied by our dog Tala. There we intended to settle down, have a picnic and drink a good bottle of red wine, at the same time celebrating our life together.

Because we would be up there several hours before being swept into oblivion, we decided to take something to occupy our minds. I planned to take my mobile water colour paint set with me. Over the previous few days there had been many computerised images on television showing what we could expect when the asteroid struck, the huge rising fireball featuring prominently on most of them. I had decided to paint my own version of that catastrophic event.

Angela decided on a writing pad for composing a final children's poem, and a set of felt pens to illustrate it. As we painted and scribed we would eat our picnic and drink our wine. After tucking into her own food - chicken and rabbit, no expense spared on this final day, Tala would probably sleep.

Although our 'masterpieces' would be destroyed at the same time as our deaths, that somehow wouldn't matter to us. We could not think of a more ideal way of leaving this Earth. Just to be on the safe side I decided to include a lightweight tent, just in case the weather decided to turn unpleasant on our last day in this world.

We woke early the following morning to glorious sunshine. Being only three days after the year's longest day the sun had already risen above the horizon, the horizon being Pen-y-Ghent itself, at five o'clock and was already high in the sky. Angela and I decided that we should leave our home at about midday. The combined journey of car down to Horton-in-Ribblesdale and walk up to the summit of Pen-y-Ghent would take about two hours. Lunch would therefore be at about two o'clock. The air blast would arrive just before three o'clock, and the tsunami at just after four - assuming of course that everything went according to plan, that plan having been drawn up by God himself, and the times worked out by myself.

It was now seven o'clock. We therefore had some five hours to kill (a funny expression to use in the circumstances) before leaving our homestead for the last time and heading for the hills. There was little point in not commencing our day as we always did, with a hearty breakfast, and Angela soon had the frying pan on the Aga, with four rashers of bacon sizzling away. At our age the days were long gone when we felt that we had to be health conscious. It was all a bit late in the day to worry about our cholesterol levels, and gobble down a measured amount of Swiss muesli.

"So, Angie, how do you intend to spend your morning before we head for the hills?" I had plans of my own, but wanted to hear what my wife had in store.

"Oh, not much…I know it might sound pretentious, even arrogant, even a bit daft, but I don't care…Assuming that the asteroid does strike and annihilates all life on Earth I would like some future visitor maybe from a planet orbiting one of the stars we see in the night sky, to see a record of my work…I therefore intend to pack the best of it, including copies of all the books I've written, into some sort of substantial, waterproof container, packed with expanded polystyrene to make it float, and leave it on that patch of high ground at the end of the paddock…Hopefully the tsunami will pick it up as it passes by and drop it somewhere when the waters recede, as I assume they will…Who knows, the package may end up on the slopes of some mountain in the Alps, like the Matterhorn or Mont Blanc."

I at first couldn't see the point of it all, and was tempted to say so, but then realised how important it was to her. The task would also fully occupy her mind for the next couple of hours…No bad thing in the circumstances.

But I was curious to know how exactly she was going to do it: "So, Angie, how do you intend making everything waterproof?…And won't the package have to last hundreds, even thousands of years?" I wasn't at all convinced that it could be done, and was certain that it would be a complete waste of time. Who would eventually be around to open the package and admire my wife's work, anyway? No one. But I didn't want to dash her enthusiasm, so I said nothing.

Angela explained what she intended to do: "First I'm going to pack my chosen items in those plastic bags that you can seal at the top, you know, like food bags…I picked up a pack from the hypermarket in Skipton last week…I then intend to place the plastic bags inside a couple of those plastic bags that you can connect to the vacuum cleaner to suck out all the air, then seal…Finally I will place them inside a large fabric feed bag containing blocks of expanded polystyrene to make it float, then sew up the top…As I said, hopefully it will soon come to rest somewhere as the waters recede…I'm confident that my idea will work."

I wasn't so sure. Making packages a hundred percent waterproof was a notoriously difficult task. But I decided not to point this out to her. Besides, my idea for occupying *my* mind was just as daft, as my wife knew it would be.

"So, Pete, how do *you* intend to spend the next couple of hours?" She was itching to know."

"Er, I'm not going to tell you…It's a secret."

"Oh, come on…Don't be shy."

Embarrassed, I told her.

"Well, first I'm going to charge up the car's battery…It's been a bit dodgy of late and I don't want to find that the car won't start when we commence our final journey down to Horton…I then intend to wash the car…At the moment it's covered in mud after yesterday's journey up to High Rise Farm to see the Browns…I have no intentions of us going to meet our maker in a dirty car….I'm then going to wash the dog…She's plastered with mud after chasing the Brown's Alsatian round the yard yesterday…If Tala is going to meet her maker I want her to look her best." We had already made the decision to take Tala with us to the top of Pen-y-Ghent. The horses, poultry and cats sadly would have to be left behind. At least when the tsunami arrived their deaths would be quick and hopefully painless.

Angela knew that both my jobs would take me the full two hours. I would first wash the car down with the hosepipe, leave it to dry in the sun, then wipe it down before polishing it, maybe at the same time T-cutting out any stubborn mark or scratch. Finally, I would stand back and admire it. Tala would be next, first washed down, again with the hosepipe, which she loved provided I did not direct the jet of water at her face. She would then be shampooed, thoroughly rinsed and allowed to dry off in the sun, before I brushed her thick coat into place. Tala loved being groomed as long it was done gently, with no pulling. She soon issued a warning in the form of a spine-chilling growl, even to me, if she was being hurt in any way.

And so, during the morning of our final day on Earth Angela and I carried out our time-consuming tasks. It was essential that we did not allow any time to sit down and feel sorry for ourselves.

As Angela and I consumed our final breakfast on Earth I switched on the television. All the major channels were running programmes on the impending disaster, the transmissions appearing to flit between the studios in the UK and what the satellites were picking up over the North Atlantic.

But even though the end of the world was nigh some TV channels chose to broadcast films, and strangely enough British comedy films too. Channel 314 was showing *Carry on Camping* starring Sid James, and Channel 321 was showing *Trouble in Store*, a black and white film starring Norman Wisdom. I wondered if they'd been put on in order to keep the viewing children occupied. Some chance of that, I thought. Perhaps understandable in the circumstances none of the channels was showing Bruce Willis 'disaster' films.

Then, at precisely 11:00 BST, some twenty-four minutes before impact was predicted to take place, the strangest of things happened. All transmission ceased. I tried all the TV channels, both terrestrial and satellite - nothing. I switched on the digital radio - again nothing. I even tried my 'stone age' analogue radio with its FM, SW, MW and LW wavebands – again nothing. As a last resort I tried my state-of-the-art phone - also nothing. In fact all forms of communication were out. We, and I assume everyone else in the UK, and maybe the whole world, were isolated from what was, or was not, taking place somewhere in the North Atlantic. We were in fact completely in the dark.

So, what had happened? There was only one explanation I could think of. As the asteroid approached the Earth it had somehow disturbed, even destroyed, the electromagnetic waves, being transmitted by the satellites just as they were about to record what was, or was not taking place at sea level. We therefore had to assume that Asteroid 2022LZ31 had in fact struck. The sequence of events that had been predicted to take place would now start to do so. The plans that Angela and I had made for our last day on Earth would go ahead.

What I did know however, as did all those throughout the world who had taken a serious interest in the sequence of events that were predicted to take place, was that shortly after the asteroid had struck, a seismic shock would travel round the Earth within the crust producing earthquakes of unpredictable size, although quakes of 10+ on the Richter Scale had been suggested. I also knew that the seismic shock would reach the UK at approximately 11:40.

Fully aware that our converted barn, with its heavy Yorkshire stone roof, wasn't the strongest of structures I and Angela quickly moved out of the building and into the garden, sitting on the two sun loungers that we had positioned there for long summer evenings. Tala was also with us, and we could see our three cats basking in the hot sun in the middle of the paddock. The two horses, three goats and ten hens were already out in the field adjoining the paddock, so as far as we were aware none of our animals were in danger of being hit by any falling masonry dislodged by the quake.

Since both of us had lots to do, Angela saving her books and artwork for posterity, me cleaning the car then the dog, we decided to get on, fully expecting the ground beneath our feet to be violently shaken at any time.

As the two of us got on with our tasks I suddenly felt the ground beneath my feet shake. Since I had experienced the sensation on many occasions before it didn't surprise me in any way. Quarry blasting for limestone was a feature of the Yorkshire Dales and the quarry down at Ribblehead regularly blasted the hillside. The fact that such an activity should be taking place on the very day an asteroid was due to strike the Earth didn't at the time seem strange to me. Maybe it was business-as-normal down at the quarry, the workforce not believing the asteroid 'story'. Seconds later the old windows of the outhouse rattled and its equally old door swung open on its rusty hinges. But both had happened before when blasting down the valley was taking place.

Then I got to thinking – surely the idea of quarry blasting taking place was a non-starter, so had the vibration under my feet and the shaking of the outhouse, a rickety structure, actually been caused by the seismic shockwave passing under my feet? Had it been so weak, barely five on the Richter Scale, that only the old building had been affected by it?

I shouted across to Angela: "I think the seismic shockwave has just hit us, but so small that it only rattled the outhouse windows...Did you feel anything underfoot?"

"As a matter of fact I did, but didn't mention it for fear you'd laugh at me...But you could just be right...It could have been the seismic wave...No one has any real idea how it would dissipate as it spread through the Earth's crust...We are almost three thousand miles away from the point of impact...And isn't the crust very stable in this part of the world?"

Angela was of course right. In fact the stability of the rock strata in the north of England had led to the decision to bury nuclear waste in a huge vault deep underground, assuming that even an earthquake of huge proportions would not disturb it. I nodded to her and replied: "Maybe we have just witnessed the first indication that the asteroid has struck the Earth," I looked at my watch to check the time. It showed 11.45, just five minutes after my predicted time for the seismic shock to arrive.

Angela did the same and yelled out: "My watch has stopped...There's no digital display...I only had a new battery put in a couple of days ago,"

My reply understandably annoyed her: "Oh...Mine's going fine...Of course you can always rely on the old wind up type," which mine was, my father having left me his very expensive gold cased *Omega* in his Will.

This got me thinking, and just to check I ran into the house and looked at all the clock faces, of which there were six in the various rooms. All but one had stopped at precisely the same time, that being twenty to twelve. I was convinced that the breakdown in all forms of communication and the electronic time pieces ceasing to function, were in some way related. It was as if their circuits had in some way been 'blown'. Of course my clockwork watch had been unaffected, neither had the grandfather clock in the lounge, its pendulum happily swinging from side to side.

I shouted across to Angela: "Presumably the air-blast will now be on its way, with the tsunami not far behind…Better make sure we're at the top of Pen-y-Ghent when they strike."

"We'll be there," was her confident reply.

At precisely midday, I still being a 'stickler' for time although totally unnecessary in the present circumstances, Angela and I loaded up the Ford Fiesta. In went the packed lunch, including two bottles of our 'good' red wine, our writing and painting equipment to occupy our minds until the air blast or tsunami killed us, and with the most important item of all - Christ's Holy Square. I lifted the lid to do a quick check that all thirteen pieces of pot that Jesus Christ had had specially made for his Last Supper, were there, before placing it in the bottom of my rucksack. I was determined that when death struck me I would be holding the Square tightly in my hands so that hopefully I would be able to give it to its rightful owner. In fact the last message received by me from Jesus had been in the form of a written note. It had been hidden under a piece of pot in the Square that he had left in my safe and capable hands after his second ascension into Heaven:

Look after my Square for me.
I'll see you again in 2022
Jesus N

That note was still inside the Square, under one of the thirteen pieces, but I could not remember which one, not that it mattered.

When all was ready Tala jumped into the back of the car. She'd certainly no intentions of being left behind. Little did she know that it would be her final journey into the hills. I jumped into the passenger seat, with no intentions of driving. The brain tumour was now pressing on my optic nerve and I was slowly losing my sense of sight. Driving was difficult and even though I was confident that we would meet no traffic on our journey down, and certainly no pedestrians, I did not want to risk an accident. We had a timetable to stick to. There could be no delays. Angela, fully aware of the situation, jumped in the drivers' side and closed the door

The short journey to Horton took no more than ten minutes, the road being deserted. This was normally a rare sight, particularly in late June when the Dales attracted visitors like a magnet.

As Angela parked up in the village car park I looked across at the Pen-y-Ghent café, which was surprisingly open. My mind flashed back thirty years, when I'd set foot in the café for the first time. As leader-in-charge at the Adwick-le-Street youth club I had led a group of youngsters up Pen-y-Ghent, Whernside and Ingleborough, on their annual Three Peaks Charity Walk, which commenced at Horton-in-Ribblesdale.

Why was the café open, I wondered? Who would be walking in the area on their last day on Earth? Then I looked along the track that those who intended tackling Pen-y-Ghent would take. My failing sight just managed to pick out people in red, yellow and blue jackets striding purposefully along it. Angela informed me that there were six in total…quite a large group in the circumstances. No doubt they would have called at the café before starting. It was great to see that even on their last day on Earth some dedicated people were determined not to allow the unusual circumstances to alter their pastime of hill walking in the Yorkshire Dales.

Knowing that we had ample time to get to the summit of the lowest of the Three Peaks, but possibly the most attractive, Angela and I, accompanied by Tala, set off at a steady pace. Tala initially shot off in the direction of the group which were just disappearing over the brow of a hill half a mile up the track. A quick whistle from me brought her back to my side.

The usual approach to the summit of Pen-y-Ghent is from the south via Brackenbottom, but one has to scramble up the hill's southern rocky face – not an easy task for the very young and those in their twilight years, nor for a dog. Angela and I therefore decided to approach the summit via the easier northern route.

Our steady amble along the well-worn track, one that had been walked by hundreds of thousands of people, mainly youngsters, who had tackled the Three Peaks as a charity event, took us towards two sights that we had seen many times before, but never tired of seeing again. We first picked up the sound of a distant roar on the slight breeze. This became louder as we followed the track. Ahead lay two spectacular waterfalls, one plunging into Hull Pot, the other into Hunt Pot, both waterfalls plunging into the depths of the earth through huge chasms in the ground known as pot holes. There had been recent heavy rain in the area over the previous week and the becks feeding both waterfalls were in full spate.

I took photographs of both waterfalls, as I always did when visiting the two sights. It all seemed a bit pointless and for two good reasons. The photographs would never be displayed, and I would have difficulty in seeing and therefore appreciating them, anyway. Nevertheless I still felt that I had to go through the motions.

We then continued along the track in a roughly north east direction until we reached the long summit slope. After turning due south we ascended the gentle slope to the summit itself. I looked at my watch. It showed exactly two o'clock. The ascent had taken just under an hour and a half - not bad for a couple of seventy plus year olds. Strangely, the group of walkers had disappeared. Maybe they'd squattered behind a dry stone wall for a bite to eat.

Asteroid 2022LZ31 had been predicted to strike the Earth two and half hours earlier. Assuming it had, the air blast would already be on its way, predicted to arrive just before three o'clock. Would we be able to survive it? There was a considerable depression in the summit's eastern slope, deep enough for both of us, plus Tala, to crouch down in. Hopefully the blast, approaching from the west, would pass over us, partially taking our breath away, otherwise leaving us relatively unscathed.

The tsunami, due to arrive just after four o'clock, was in my opinion entirely unpredictable, Could it really travel 3600 kilometres across the Atlantic Ocean, then across the land mass of Ireland before hitting the west coast of England and moving inland? I found it hard to believe, but greater minds than mine had predicted that the wave would do just that. I stared westwards, across to Ingleborough Hill, higher than Pen-y-Ghent. Would the wave rush round it, leaving it looking like an island, or would it simply wash over the top, fully submerging it? If it did in fact have a height in the region of 1500 metres it would indeed do the latter, for Ingleborough was a mere 723 metres high by comparison.

The air blast would arrive without warning, but surely we would be able to see the tsunami as it approached us. From my visits to the Elvington Airshow I knew that a plane flying towards the viewing gallery even at the speed of sound, took several seconds to reach and pass overhead, so a huge wave, possibly a mile high, would surely be visible seconds before it struck Pen-y-Ghent. We would just have to see. As long as we'd time to link arms, clink our wine glasses and have a good swig before saying our goodbyes, I would be more than happy. Tala would of course be tightly wedged between us, totally oblivious to what was about to happen to her - no bad thing.

***

Chapter Forty Three

Narrator – God, having a conversation with his Son, Jesus.

'And it came to pass' - as I believe I've stated before, a favoured biblical expression if ever there was one - that at the commencement of the year 2022 I had looked down on planet Earth. How had it faired since the year 2012, when my Son, Jesus, on my instruction had given its inhabitants the ultimatum – mend your ways or face total annihilation? It was now time for me to do my assessment, in consultation of course with him, although the final decision would be mine and mine alone.

Before the discussion commenced I handed him a thin tablet of stone with a list written on it. It was not unlike the one I had given to Moses with the *Ten Commandments* on it, although much smaller: "Here, Son, before we start...I have jotted down the areas that are causing me the greatest concern...Study them before we start...The areas are not in any order of priority."

Jesus studied the list, reading the ten areas aloud as he did so:
- global warming
- devastation of the rain forests
- depletion of food stocks
- plight of wild animals
- nuclear proliferation
- hunger and drought
- pollution of land, sea and air
- man's inhumanity to man
- man's cruelty to animals
- man's attitude to sex.

I saw him raise his eyebrows and glance at me as he read out the tenth and last item on the list. It didn't surprise me.

As the discussion developed I made it clear that I was far from pleased at what I'd witnessed of man's actions, or rather inactions over the previous ten years. I of course knew all the figures and statistics that could be made to prove anything. I had no intentions of trying to baffle my son with 'science', showing him numerous weird and wonderful graphs that man had produced, indicating God knows what (no pun intended). All I was interested in was what *I* saw with my own eyes as *I* looked down on the Earth, and how it affected *me* emotionally. And in my opinion man had done little to improve the lot of himself and that of those animals and plants who shared the planet with him. I quoted several examples to my Son, roughly working down the list that I'd earlier given to him, but not emphasising any sort of order of importance. It was just as I saw it.

"As you can see, my Son, global warming has continued at a steady rate over the period, mainly due to the continued use of fossil fuels…Ocean temperatures have continued to rise and both ice caps have shrunk considerably causing all sorts of problems for my creatures who live on them…Below sea level the coral reefs are being destroyed at an alarming rate, thus destroying the habitat of those creatures who for millennia have lived upon them…The devastation of the equatorial rain forests has continued thus destroying the very lungs that the Earth has…Man has for years underestimated the importance of them as extractors of carbon dioxide and providers of oxygen, not forgetting the habitat they provided for my creatures." I kept emphasising *my* creatures, because in my eyes each one was important to me. When all said and done I had created them, whether they be ant, tiger or man.

I wanted, indeed expected, my Son to come to the defence of mankind, and he did so.

"But Father, as you are aware, man has made a determined effort in the areas you have mentioned…A vast replanting programme has been introduced in the Amazon Basin, man having seen the error of his ways…There has been a move away from the fossil fueled motorcar in favour of the electric car in many countries, and more electric power is now generated in nuclear plants, a way that I know you are in favour of, although not liked by many people on Earth…Regarding increasing sea temperatures, you are aware that the sun has contributed there, as its energy output has slowly increased…Unfortunately little can now be done about the coral reefs, but as you are also aware *Operation Polar Bear* has moved some animals from the Arctic to the Antarctic, and all indications are that they have settled in well and are already breeding…So in my humble opinion man has, and is, making a determined effort to improve the world…His world…Your world."

I decided to take issue with a couple of the points my Son had raised: "The rainfall in the Amazon Basin has dropped dramatically, and the trees will take years to mature, if indeed at all…And the use of fossil fuels in transport is almost on a par with what it was ten years ago."

I then pressed on: "Let me now turn to food stocks...I see the practice of growing crops to produce fuel still continues, when the land should be used to provide the needy and their animals with food...What has and still is taking place on the continent of Africa is nothing short of a world scandal...And what did happen to the promises that were made in 2012 to get water to the drought ridden areas in the Horn of Africa?...As far as I can see, nothing...Another scandal is the appalling waste of food that takes place every year by the wealthy nations...How this can be allowed when others are starving makes me lose all faith in the very man I have created...And do you know that in some parts of the world fish are actually thrown away, dead, because it is illegal to land them...In heaven's name what is the sense in that?...And another thing, I note that the practice of throwing food away because it is the wrong shape or the skin is slightly marked, continues unabated...This practice seems to be prevalent with fruit and vegetables - apples and pears with blemished skins, misshaped carrots, potatoes and tomatoes, all being destroyed...Has the world gone completely mad?" I was beginning to get really het up.

"Calm down Father...Calm down...The picture's not half as bad as you have painted...Man has already realised the folly of his ways and stopped using cereal crops for the production of ethanol...And you know as well as I do what the problems are in Africa...In some areas fighting continues almost unabated as the various tribes try to seize power...How can one have reliable water and food supplies when there is no law and order?...In fact I sometimes feel that you could do more to bring stability to some of those war- ridden countries."

I felt that my son's last comment was a blow below the belt, and said so: "Not a fair comment, Son...You know that it is not my role to determine how mankind should conduct itself...Oh, it would be so easy for me to do so, I have all the power I need, but man has to sort out his own problems and suffer the consequences when he gets it wrong...The Romans discovered that to their cost, you having first-hand experience of their regime...Napoleon discovered it, and more recently two World Wars had to be fought, and won, to bring the world back to some sort of order...But it annoys me intensely when man behaves little better than a wild animal...I didn't give him a sophisticated brain to slaughter his fellowman...I kick myself every day for allowing the firearm in all its various forms to have been invented and developed by him...Think how

437

much better the world would be had that invention not taken place."

Jesus reluctantly nodded in agreement. On many occasions I had suggested intervening, only to be told by him not to get involved. The last time was in the year 1999, when the World Trade Center twin towers were brought down...I was on the verge of creating a magnetic storm of such force that on that day not one plane would have got off the ground in the whole of the United States, when Jesus persuaded me that the plot should be allowed to go ahead, his reasoning being that the resulting world abhorrence of such a heinous act would ultimately lead to making the world a safer place. Sadly, this has not happened, and, looking back, I still feel that I made the wrong decision.

Jesus continued: "Regarding the wastage of food, whether it be due to people overbuying or the supermarkets demanding so-called perfect items from their producers, I have definitely noticed a change in the attitudes of consumers...Governments for the first time have played a part here, with powerful, hard hitting campaigns about food wastage...One advert I saw, made by the British Government, showed bin wagons spreading food of all types, including meat and fish, over a huge field...The next shot showed the field being invaded by the world's poor, who commenced eating the food as if there were no tomorrow...The sequence certainly pulled no punches...Hopefully it will have the desired effect...Another campaign showed two groups of children, one eating perfect fruit and vegetables with apparently no taste, and commenting to that effect, the other eating and obviously enjoying fruit and vegetables of the strangest shapes imaginable...Hopefully, this too will have the desired effect...Now, regarding fish stocks, you know as well as I do that the European Community's fish quota policy was changed some years ago...I have to agree, the 'throw away' policy was quite mad, and as the creator of those fish I can see why you were initially upset, then intensely annoyed...I know that you have always accepted that animals would, and indeed should, be used to provide food for man as long as they are given the best possible care when alive and slaughtered in the most humane way possible...As you are aware I do not agree with the Halal method of slaughter...It is cruel and gives no regard to the animal being killed...The word 'ritual' is used to describe the method...Well, it's no sort of ritual to me...And like you I too abhor the hunting and killing of animals merely for sport.. .It is only a small step between shooting a bear dead for sport and shooting a man dead in some sort of confrontation."

I nodded to him in total agreement on many of his comments, but the wastage of food, for whatever reason still appalled me. The needless cruelty to animals and the way they were slaughtered upset me most of all, and this in itself was enough to make me decide that mankind was not worth saving.

Jesus also needed another reminder: "Are you aware, Son, that there are now only a handful of elephants and rhinoceroses roaming wild on the continent of Africa, and only a few tigers roaming wild in the whole of Asia...Most have been hunted down and killed by poachers who sold their body parts to misguided people who thought they had magical properties...I tell you this - when the very last elephant and tiger in the wild are slaughtered I will breathe a sigh of relief for I know that such majestic creatures, my creatures, will never be hunted and ruthlessly slaughtered again...On many occasions I have been on the verge of striking the poachers dead...And looking back I wish I had...A bolt of lightning would have easily done the trick."

Again Jesus nodded in agreement, but still felt the need to put up some sort of defence for mankind, albeit a weak one: "Fortunately, as you are aware, Father, there are huge areas of land in many countries of the world where such animals are allowed to roam freely...There are also excellent zoos, so there's no danger of the animals ever becoming extinct...And hopefully the supply of the so-called magic potions will dry up, and those who misguidedly use them will realise that they didn't work anyway, such creatures should be perfectly safe...But I agree with you, it's sad that only a few are still roaming in their natural habitats."

My Son felt that I appeared to be more concerned about the planet's animal life than the plight of humans, and felt the need to point this out to me: "But Father, why are you concentrating so much on how the planet's animals are treated...Surely human life is more important."

I quickly put him right: "But, Son, all life on Earth is important and has been part of a long evolutionary process that I myself instigated, then controlled along its course...Man was just the end product, the final version, so to speak, of that process...In the grand scale of things there is in fact little difference in the make-up of man himself and the so-called 'higher' animals such as gorillas and chimpanzees...Man was the final version, but sadly over time he has lost some of the assets I'd originally given him...His memory is not as good as an elephant's - it is true they never forget...His eyesight nowhere near as good as that of an eagle...Hearing is nowhere near as acute as that of the humble rabbit, and his sense of smell very poor when compared with that of a dog…So he's not as perfect as he may think…That man Darwin was certainly on the right track when he proposed his Theory of Evolution…The so-called higher animals did evolve from the so-called lower ones…It had all taken place as he'd described…And his theory in no way clashed with any sort of religious belief either…What some people still can't accept is that I have been in control of the process from the start, and because evolution never actually stops I'm in control of it at this very moment, although where I go with the human being I haven't yet decided…Do I try to change him for the better, or destroy him and start again, maybe somewhere else?"

Before allowing my Son to respond I moved quickly on: "Pollution is still a concern to me, with the ground being the favourite place to get rid of waste, especially of the toxic type…Many countries are still burying their waste instead of recycling it…Some even transport it to poorer countries – a case of out of sight, out of mind…Regarding pollution of the atmosphere, while ever huge quantities of coal are being burned the pollution will continue…I accept that the electric car is becoming more acceptable, but the love relationship with the gas-guzzler is still as strong as ever…And what has happened to the wholesale move to public transport, as so many countries promised?...But the biggest worry is water pollution, or more correctly sea pollution…I am still seeing oil erupting up uncontrollably from wells on the ocean floor and having a devastating effect on wild life…When I see birds covered in oil and on the verge of death my heart bleeds for them…Fortunately there are still those humans who are prepared to go to their aid."

Again my son tried to show man in a good, or at least half good light: "I think you are a bit out of date on ground pollution, Father…The United Nations banned the transport of waste to third world countries some time ago…."

"But it's still going on illegally…Same countries involved and always to poor countries on the African continent."

"Ah… But you have to realise that although the transfer of waste to such countries is illegal it provides a living for very poor people, enabling those who sort through it to provide for their families."

I fully understood the point Jesus was making, but still the practice was wrong, and he knew it. I couldn't help sarcastically commenting: "Some living."

This brought me onto the issue that worried me the most - nuclear proliferation. I found it interesting, almost amusing, that man not only measured nuclear explosions in megatonnes of TNT, but also the impact of the asteroid that was about to strike the Earth, assuming that I allowed it to do so. Of course the nuclear explosions so far experienced on Earth were merely fireworks compared with the bang that my asteroid would make, again assuming that I allowed the impact to take place.

It was now time to detail my concern to my Son: "At the time I made my vow to give mankind just ten years to improve the lot of all living things on Earth there were several nuclear nations, with two flexing their muscles...Since then there have been several worrying situations involving the development and testing of ballistic missiles that could carry nuclear warheads across most of the world...Pakistan and India, both nuclear powers, are still at loggerheads and both appear to be on continuous alert...To its credit Israel has shown remarkable restraint even though it is surrounded by hostile nations...But one hostile move will bring an immediate retaliation, setting the whole Middle East alight...But Israel is not blameless...Its must really sort things out with the Palestinians...Both Russia and China disappoint me...They could exercise far more influence on the World for the good of mankind than they do."

I knew that these points also played heavily on the mind of my Son, and he forcefully expressed his feelings: "It worries me too, Father...If the balloon does go up other nations will get drawn in too...Don't forget Britain and France are also nuclear powers and would not stand idly by if friendly nations came under attack, and friendly nations include all those in the European Community, and would also include Turkey...This gives some indication how widespread a conflict in the Middle East could quickly become...And I haven't even mentioned the Far East."

My mind first went back to the Second World War, where the atomic explosions that had brought the war to an end had been restricted to just one country, and in terms of land area a small country too, although thousands lost their lives. Then followed the Cold War some fifteen years later. which had fortunately been restricted mainly to Europe and North America, and equally fortunately had not turned 'hot'. Had it done so, my decision to bring life on Earth to an abrupt end would have been carried out there and then. Today's uncertain situation was on a different scale and could well include the whole world, as the nations aligned themselves to those who they thought were in the right, whatever that right was...and I alone, would decide that.

Jesus then put a point of view that rather surprised me, and did not appear to fit in with his 'give mankind a chance' approach.

"Just think how many of the world's population would lose their lives in a nuclear war, even if it could be contained to the Middle East, which I doubt would be possible...In most cases death would be instant, in others over a short period of time, but then the radio activity would move round the world on the breeze insidiously killing the innocents abroad...I would personally rather see the asteroid strike the Earth, with the subsequent result, than witness some prolonged nuclear conflict...But of course you, Father, must decide, and you haven't much time to do so."

Although the original list had not been in any order of importance I had purposely not mentioned anything about the last item on the list – man's attitude to sex. It was now time to round off our discussion with this very important topic, one that probably grieved me the most. It had both worried and disappointed me for more years than I wished to remember.

It all seemed to revolve round the 'six Ps' - procreation, parenthood, promiscuity, prostitution, paedophilia and the pill. I decided to set out my views, knowing that they would bring much comment and criticism from my Son. So be it: "As you are aware, Son, I designed all life on Earth, both plant and animal, to be able to reproduce itself...To keep it simple, thus avoiding problems, I created two forms -male and female - that would come together in a variety of ways to reproduce exact copies of themselves, except that some would be male and some female in order that the process of reproduction could continue indefinitely...Of course over time some slight variations have crept in, for example in humans we have different coloured skin, hair and eyes, and huge differences in height and weight... And I know that on occasions males and females find themselves attracted to their own sex...I am also aware that some males find themselves in female bodies and vice-versa, and I am comfortable with such slight variations ...But generally speaking my method of procreation has worked well, and I am proud of my achievements in this whole area."

Jesus was quick to reply: "On the last two points you raised, Father, we have both known that they existed for very many years, certainly during my first coming on Earth when the Roman Empire was all-dominant...Such humans were in the past ostracised, but I am pleased to report that recently there has been greater understanding and tolerance, and this has been to man's credit."

442

I, of course, knew that this was true, and because of this increase in tolerance and understanding it wasn't an area that particularly worried me, but what did was the way the sex act, as I had intended it, had been degraded, at least in the human species. Sex between the male and female of the species was purely and simply for procreation and for most of the animal kingdom it still is. This was my intention. But since pregnancy in humans can now be prevented, especially by the use of the birth pill, sex has become little more than a meaningless pastime, a game, a profession, a means of exercising power and inflicting hurt.

I had to accept that promiscuity amongst members of the human species had always been present, and along with prostitution, had played their part in bringing down great empires, the Holy Roman Empire being but one, I had to admit the advent of the birth pill had dramatically increased the practice...not what I intended. I had hoped mankind would have progressed beyond this. I had allowed the invention of the birth pill to take place so that loving couples could plan both the timing and size of their families, and yet the birth of babies in areas of the world where there isn't enough food to support them or where there is military conflict, has continued almost unabated. Birth control is frowned on, and the use of a condom by the male of the species is still refused point blank. Why, I asked?

Jesus again came to the support of mankind: "But father, you gave both male and female of the human species a sexual desire, a most powerful one too...Of course they will want to experience this in order to show their love for each other, although it worries me that children as young as ten areexperiencing it...And since pregnancy can now be avoided by the birth pill sex has become a well practised act...On the whole this has kept mankind both physically and mentally healthy, although I have to agree that there has been a dramatic increase in those diseases transmitted by the sex act...On the second point you raised, you are partly to blame...You allowed a belief to develop that frowned upon, even banned, the use of any form of artificial contraceptive, this belief even forming an important part of some religions today...Hence an uncontrolled birth rate in some of the poorest areas of the world...And even where the use of the birth pill is allowed, it is often unavailable because of the cost...The reluctance to use a condom is interesting...There is an expression that I have heard on several occasions during my visits to at least one English speaking country, it is *riding bareback*...It's nothing to do with horseriding, by the way...It's a coarse expression used by bragging men, often drunk, to describe them having sex with some poor girl without using a condom...A sort of status symbol...I suspect that this is taking place in the poorer countries of the world where uneducated men take the same attitude...And don't forget that in such countries large families are looked upon as being essential because the death rate in the young is high and those who do survive are expected to look after the old."

Although I tried to keep 'with it' as far as the latest expressions used by the modern world were concerned, I had to admit that I hadn't heard of *riding bareback* before, except referring to riding a horse without a saddle.

My Son's comments nicely led me onto my next area of great disappointment – prostitution and the pimping (a seventh 'p') that went with it. Here the sex act, my very special act to create children, and also a means of expressing one's love for one's partner, was simply for sale. There was no love, no commitment, no creation, just a fee paid for an act. It degraded the woman, and the expression *just a bit of meat* was one I'd often heard used to describe her. Linked closely with this appalling attitude towards women is the practice of what has become known as *gang rape*, where several man, as many as ten, follow one another having sex with some unfortunate woman, usually very young, even a child, and obviously against her will.

Of course prostitution and pimping usually went hand in hand, except that the relationship was often little more than a 'slave and master' one. This led inevitably to further degrading of the woman, whether she accepted this or not, whereas the pimp, almost always a man, assumed an importance well above his station.

Promiscuity and prostitution inevitably hit the poorest countries the hardest and were largely to blame for the AIDS problem. I had created the HIV virus hoping that it would reduce the above two 'evils'. But to my disappointment it did not, and it grieved me even more when I discovered that babies were being born with the disease, passed on by their mothers. I definitely hadn't intended this.

I looked at Jesus, expecting him to be highly critical of my 'AIDS' policy, but he simply made a comment: "Well, since your policy hasn't worked perhaps you should point the world's virologists in the right direction to find a cure for the disease."

I nodded, indicating that if it wasn't already too late I would give his suggestion some serious thought.

I now wanted to bring up the institution of 'marriage', something I had encouraged almost from the outset for men and women to live together in a loving relationship that would provide the ideal environment for the children created by that relationship. Here yet another 'p' came into its own – parenthood.

My Son was already familiar with my strong belief in marriage, but I decided to remind him of it: "My ideal marriage is a ceremony which can take place anywhere - in one of the great buildings of the world, forexample a famous minster, cathedral, mosque, synagogue, but can also be the smallest village church or even a mud hut in the middle of Africa...It will be conducted by someone who represents me on Earth, for example an archbishop or a humble village priest...The format of the ceremony will not matter as long as at some point the two getting married commit themselves to each other in a loving relationship that will ultimately create children...For some reason that I personally failed to fully understand some religions decided that they would not marry divorced people in a holy place, and therefore other places, called 'registry offices', a poor choice of expression for such important places, became available...It has encouraged me to see that most of the people who have had to resort to the use of such places have committed themselves to each other in a loving and often child creating relationship...I feel that on the whole the institution of marriage has worked pretty well."

Jesus nodded in agreement, supporting, in particular, one area that I had mentioned: "I suppose the word 'office' came into use because the ceremony was often conducted in an office type room in some important building serving the town or city, such as the Town Hall...And I do agree with you that such places have served the community well, particularly for the more mature who wish to get married for a second time...Second marriages have a high success rate...And does the type of building matter, or who conducts the ceremony, so long as the loving commitment of the two participants is present?"

Of course my Son was correct, but of late I have seen a change in attitude. Everything in the garden was definitely not rosy. I have observed that marriage has in some people's eyes become little more than a 'showing off' event, where huge expense, often ill-affordable, is involved that always has to include a 'no expenses spared' wedding dress, a lavish reception and of course the obligatory honeymoon in some exotic and supposedly romantic location such as the Maldives,

445

(one of my creations although highly popular with non-believers). Lists of presents are even drawn up in collaboration with a well-known high street store. In many marriages children, some born outside wedlock, are proudly paraded almost like trophies won in a previous contest.

Sadly the attitude that so many getting married now adopt is – *let's give it a go and if it doesn't work out, no harm done.* Equally sadly I have also observed that many such marriages end up in divorce within the space of just five years. And harm *is* done, especially when children are casualties.

Jesus again nodded, apparently in general agreement with me, but did add: "Regarding marriage being a show-off event, a lot depends on the ages of the participants...To a young couple it is a 'dream' event and I think they genuinely feel that their marriage will last forever...It's the older participants, those well-heeled financially and with children from previous relationships, that we see the show-off event...Go to such events, as I have, and listen to the comments of onlookers...*I'll give it five years* being a common one."

What was in danger of becoming almost a 'fashion' was the worrying practice of literally *killing the kids*, just to get back at your partner. It mainly involved the father, but also occasonally the mother. This was quite a recent phenomenon and it worried me greatly. I was in the process of coming up with a solution, but the problem was not easy to solve. It was very much to do with a change in attitude to the 'sanctity of life', and this puzzled me. If those who carried out the act had a strong religious faith that made them feel that their murdered children were going to a 'better place' I could try to understand the practice...But I know that this is the furthest thought in their heads, hatred of their ex-partner being uppermost...A truly sad and unacceptable state of affairs.

This took me onto another word beginning with 'p' – paedophilia. Why do all the ills of mankind begin with 'p'.

Of course paedophiles, mainly men, have been around almost since time began. Sodom and Gomorrah were riddled with them, as was Pompeii. One could even argue that they played their part in the fall of the Roman Empire that you my Son are, or were familiar with.

Jesus smiled, then commented: "Do you know, Father, I saw very few paedophiles in the Holy Land...I came in contact with lots of young boys and the occasional young girl who acted as interpreters for the many Roman soldiers...One called Jacob, who interpreted for two soldiers who followed me around and who eventually were converted to my cause, particularly springs to mind, but there wasn't the slightest indication that their relationship with the boy was anything but proper."

I nodded, accepting all my Son had said, but time had changed...the Internet had been invented. To this day I wasn't certain that allowing its invention was a good idea. It would have been easy for me to have slightly changed the physical properties of the elements used in the microchips, thus making a computer inpossible to construct...but I allowed the invention to go ahead, seeing its potential to improve the lot of mankind at all levels.

I turned to Jesus and ranted off again: "As a result of the Internet we now hear of men with thousands of images of young children on their computers...Why?...Why?...I know they're only 'looking', but it's a fine line between looking and the desire to 'touch'...And what's all this 'grooming' about?...Funny how words suddenly change their meaning...Until recently animals such as horses, and women, sometimes also men were groomed to enhance their appearance...Now, 'grooming' appears to be some sort of process commencing with contact, leading onto flattery which is followed up with some form of enticement that ultimately ends up in a young girl, highly impressionable and often with low self- esteem meeting up with an older man. At this point the danger to the girl becomes very real, with her running the risk of sexual abuse which has on occasions led to her eventual death...And all this is done over the Internet and again brings us back to paedophilia.

I was determined to continue, not allowing my Son to reply: "And what is all this self exposure about on mobile phones and the various forms of personal communication...Why, in God's name, (I really had to stop blaspheming myself) should a young girl or boy want to show off their private parts to those they trust, only to find that thousands, possibly millions of people worldwide, including paedophiles, also have access tothe images?...What the Devil (why have I introduced him now?) are their parents (Oh God, another 'p'), playing at to allow it?...Don't they talk to their children about such dangers?

And whilst I was moaning about parents, or at least some of them, the majority doing a good job in often very difficult circumstances, I felt I had to further comment on parenthood: "Have you ever heard of the expression 'good practice'"?

My Son nodded, indicating that he had.

"It's used a lot in Britain, but I suspect other nations have a similar

447

expression…I believe the French refer to it as *la meilleure pratique*…It is used in both local and national government and is self-explanatory, quite simply the best way of doing something…But I've never heard it used when referring to the bringing up of children…Surely 'best practice' is where children are brought up by their two natural parents who have made their commitment to each other through marriage and who have created a loving and caring household…But no…It is thought equally good to bring children up with a lone parent, with gay and lesbian couples…But it isn't, is it?…Best practice means the 'ideal', and although many lone parents, some who may have lost their partners for example, and gay and lesbian couples, some who sadly adopt a child just to make a 'point', do an excellent job, in my opinion it is not the ideal…Not best practice." At that, I decided to shut up. I'd had my say and my Son knew exactly where I stood on the ways mankind had conducted itself over the last ten years (ie) the length of time I'd given it to mend its ways. He also knew that I'd been far from impressed.

After sitting silently for several seconds, no doubt working out what to say in defence of mankind for what could turned out to be the last time, my Son spoke: "You can't have it both ways Father…you've given men and women their strong sexual desire to ensure procreation…You can't be surprised when it throws up occasional unwelcome behaviour, hence your paedophile…As far as young people exposing themselves on the Internet is concerned, it's all to do with self-esteem, or lack of it…In two thousand years I cannot think of a time when young people, especially those who live in the wealthier nations, have so little self-esteem…They join gangs for security…They carry knives, even guns for security…They drink and drug themselves into oblivion to make themselves supposedly feel better and to gain approval from their peers…And they expose themselves on the Internet also seeking approval…Sadly they occasionally take their own lives thinking that they are going to a 'better place', but not believing that better place is with you

"Regarding 'best practice', you and I are on the same wavelength…It does worry me that as mankind moves into the future, if you decide to allow it to do so, children will be conceived not knowing who their parents are, maybe not having parents at all…Who would actually look after them throughout their formative years I have no idea…Fortunately all other forms of life, both plant and animal, will continue to procreate as they've always done…unless mankind interferes there as well."

My Son was beginning to look shell-shocked after having to come up time and again with some sort of defence for mankind against my onslaught, but I had to have my say. It was now time to round the discussion off. I commenced this by expressing what was uppermost in his mind, something that immensely saddened me...It was the increase in a lack of faith in me and all I stood for.

I was saddened to hear, more and more, three expressions that showed this to be the case:

You've got to live for today
You've only one life
This isn't a rehearsal

I've even heard such expressions quoted at marriage ceremonies, even at christenings. And the people most likely to use them are middle-aged and entering into a new relationship after leaving a failed one. It's as if the three quotes were being used to justify their action.

I could see by the expression on Jesus's face that he was searching for, but not coming up with some sort of defence on mankind's behalf. He did however make one final attempt: "Maybe it's due to all the uncertainty in the world...The effects of climate change, the threat of nuclear conflict, a world in depression...Maybe people see no future for themselves, hence the 'live for today' attitude."

My answer was abrupt and to the point: "Well, if that's the attitude of mankind I may as well end it all now...Perhaps the Earth needs a period of time to recover without mankind's interference...Then perhaps I can start all over again."

Jesus offered no further defence, knowing that it would probably be futile anyway. He simply replied: "Well the final decision is yours, Father, and yours alone...I will of course support you whatever you decide, as a good Son would."

The decision was mine indeed, and I thanked my Son for his input.

As Jesus was about to leave, evidently he had an appointment with someone on Earth called Peter Robertshaw, he asked me a question that I'd never thought of and hence did not have an answer to: "Will you tell the world of your decision, possibly through me using my United Nations connections?...I can always make a 'third coming' ...Or will your decision come as a complete surprise to the world, what ever it happens to be?"

I remained silent for a few seconds, not to make my decision, I'd already made that, but to formulate a plan to delay the world knowing that decision for as long as possible. I did not want mankind wasting time,making plans in pointless self-preservation. My reply to my son was brief, in fact just three words, ones he had used himself: "A complete surprise."

This could only be done by a breakdown in world communication, and I had the power to do this, having tried it out before, albeit only on a small scale. I would use the main body in the Solar System, another of my creations, to bring it about…the Sun.

It just so happened that the sun's latest eleven year sun spot cycle which was last at its maximum in 2012, would reach its maximum in 2023, before tailing off. It was therefore near its maximum at this very moment. This high concentration of sun spots was always accompanied by an increase in solar activity, and the sun was particularly active at the present time. This was the sort of activity that could interrupt the Earth's radio communication, and this is exactly what happened, with a little help from myself, of course.

Several hours before Asteroid 2022LZ31 was predicted to strike the Earth an explosion of monumental proportions took place on the surface of the sun, but it went unnoticed by all but the world's keenest solar observers. Most astronomers were fully occupied observing the asteroid, looking for the slightest indication that it would miss the Earth. As far as the world's population were concerned they saw nothing. Even the sun spots were invisible to them without special observing equipment. Besides, who was interested in the sun? Surely there was a more important celestial object to worry about.

The resulting flare shot outwards from the surface of the sun and in a matter of seconds a massive stream of charged particles was heading towards the Earth at almost the speed of light. Within twelve minutes it had covered the 150 million kilometres and was already causing maximum disruption to all forms of radio communication, as the complex circuitry in all electronic equipment had the equivalent of a nervous breakdown. Both terrestrial and satellite radio signals went down, as did mobile and landline phones. The result of this was that apart from the inhabitants of the Azores and possibly those living on the

Canaries, the nearest inhabited areas of land to the point of impact, the rest of the world's population would not know if the asteroid had struck the Earth, or not, which of course was what I intended...But within a short period of time they would know.

***

Chapter Forty Four

Narrator – Peter Robertshaw

As we sat on the summit of Pen-y-Ghent consuming our picnic and glasses of wine Angela became aware that something was taking place on the western horizon and described it to me, my deteriorating eyesight not being able to detect it. The crystal clear summit of Ingleborough had suddenly become dark and fuzzy, but it didn't look like the characteristic cloud that sometimes hung over it. Could this be anything to do with the asteroid impact? Could it be a bank of debris being forced ahead of the rapidly moving air blast? Was it in fact the first indication that something nasty was approaching us from the west at a frightening speed?

It was only when it cleared Ingleborough and slowly crept towards Pen-y-Ghent, also eventually enveloping its summit, that we were certain that it wasn't related to some devastating event that had already taken place some 3600 kilometres to the west. It was in fact a bank of mist, a regular sight in the area at this time of year

As the mist enveloped us the temperature immediately plummeted. We both extracted our waterproof jackets from our rucksacks and put them on. Tala, with her double coat of a soft under layer of fine fur and waterproof outer layer of long thick black hair, was oblivious to the cold and damp conditions. The sudden formation of the mist should not have surprised us. After days of continuous rain the ground was saturated. The days' intensely warm sun was simply evaporating the moisture, which was then rising into the atmosphere. On cooling, it formed the mist.

Suddenly, Tala became agitated. She'd either heard something or picked up some sort of scent. Maybe a rabbit was close by. Not happy, she started her blood curdling growl, enough to frighten the dead, and I reached down and took hold of her collar. The last thing I wanted was for her to charge off into the mist and confront what was disturbing her.

Both Angela and I suddenly became aware of someone approaching us from the north. At first we saw an ill-defined grey shape that quickly became the well defined form of a person. Man or woman, we had no idea. The only people in the area were the group we'd seen earlier heading north towards Plover Hill. They must have doubled back to cover the summit of Pen-y-Ghent itself, and we were seeing the first of them emerging out of the mist.

As the person, wearing hiking gear, including good quality boots and hooded waterproof jacket, approached us, Tala let out a warning bark and tried to free herself from my grip in order to defend us, to the death if necessary. She only calmed down when I greeted the person. "Welcome to our camp...Funny sort weather...Don't think it was forecast."

"Hello, Peter...Angela...God, you do take some finding." He then lifted his head to look skywards and whispered: "Sorry. Father...No blasphemy intended."

At that point I knew exactly who was facing us. It was Jesus Nazarene, or Jesus Christ, the Son of God. He'd earlier said in his written message to us that he would meet us again, and here he was. I could not think of a more fitting place nor fitting time for that meeting to take place - on the summit of Pen-y-Ghent, minutes before the world was due to come to an end.

Before I could reply he added: "I first tried the hill over there, (he pointed at Ingleborough)...You weren't there so I tried this one...And here you are."He then confidently held the back of his hand in front of Tala's nose so that she could smell it. This she did giving at the same time a faint whine before flopping onto the ground. Our visitor was friend, not foe.

At that point the mist slowly dispersed, allowing the hot sun to again shine upon us. I quickly came to the conclusion that it had enveloped us in order to allow Jesus to make his appearance - in fact his 'third coming'. His second ascension had taken place in mist, maybe also his first, so why not his 'coming'? Funny how the word 'descension' was never used. In fact was there such a word? I didn't think there was.

But how had he crossed the valley in such a short period of time? The bank of mist had left Ingleborough and arrived at Pen-y-Ghent in a matter of minutes. Had he made the same journey and in the same time? I decided to ask even though I was confident I knew the answer: "How did you get across the valley?...It's a good six mile slog."

A big grin spread across his face: "You know how I ascended into Heaven in New York...Well, I ascended from that hill (he pointed in the direction of Ingleborough), and descended to this one, all inside the bank of mist...A bit like a plane taking off at one airport and landing at another."

I smiled, wishing I hadn't asked.

His attire interested me, but what should I have expected? Jesus in a white gown? That would have been entirely appropriate at the top of some hillock in the Holy Land two thousand years ago, but not on top of Pen-y-Ghent's cold misty summit in 2022. Besides, hadn't he appeared at the United Nations in suit, shirt and tie way back in 2012? On the other hand his second ascension in the same year had been in just a pair of boxer shorts.

It was now time to establish why exactly Jesus was here, and more to the point, why he wanted to see me; "So, Jesus...Now you are here, what happens next "

"Well, first you can give me a glass of that wine...The wine I tasted two thousand years ago at my Last Supper was little more than vinegar...I trust yours will be of better quality."

As I poured him a glass I assured him that it would be. Costing an arm and a leg, as we say in Yorkshire, it wasn't cheap. As her sipped the wine he smiled: "Good...Good...A heavy, fruity bouquet with a hint of strawberries...Kept for a while in an oak barrel...Yes, very good."

I felt like telling him that he'd been watching too many food programmes on television, but realised that he probably wouldn't know what I was on about.

Before I could ask my first question again, Angela plunged in with the one and only question that she wanted an answer to: "So, Jesus...Has the asteroid struck, or hasn't it?...We have a hunch that it hasn't because there has been no seismic activity...I assume you do know."

"Indeed I do, Angela, and I'm sorry to have to tell you that my Father in Heaven has decided to allow the asteroid to crash into the Earth...He looks upon the World as a sort of modern day Sodom and Gomorrah ,where man thinks of no one but himself...He's very disappointed at how his ultimate creation has turned out...I tried to persuade him to give man another chance, but he has decided that he doesn't deserve one...Impact has already taken place, and the air blast and tsunami are already on their way... As you are probably aware, the air blast will arrive first, the tsunami a couple of hours later...By taking evasive action you will be able to survive the air blast, but not the tsunami."

Both Angela and I were staggered by the news, for we had beenconvinced that God would indeed give man another chance to mend his ways. I felt like asking Jesus if he was certain about what he'd told us, but knew that he was. The question now was - what do *we* do next?

I looked at my watch. It was happily ticking away unaffected by the damaging effect of the burst of energy that Earth had received from the sun. Angela's watch, usually so accurate, reliable and maintenance free, was now a useless objcct on her wrist, its printed circuits having been 'blown'. The time was 14:40. According to my predictions the air blast would hit us at 14:58. If we intended to take some sort of evasive action from it we had to take it now. The blast, if we were to believe the predictions, would hit us at about the speed of sound from the west, blowing us off the summit and down the eastern flank of the hill. Even if we survived we would be badly injured. It was therefore time to take that action.

Angela and I looked down the eastern flank and I located the deep depression in the slope some twenty yards below the summit that I had seen earlier. If we could lay face downwards in it we would get some protection from our padded jackets and we could use our rucksacks to protect our heads. Any debris that was being carried on the blast and happened to fall on us as the stream of fast moving air curved over the summit and dropped into the valley below hopefully would not injure us.

The three of us then had a brief chat on how we should breathe as the air passed rapidly over us. Should we hold our breath as long as we could? Should we breathe deeply and slowly, or in short gasps? I had sufficient scientific knowledge to know that when air moved over a curved surface, such as a plane wing, the air pressure dropped on the underside and this produced the 'lift'. So how would this fast moving air affect us? Would the air in our lungs be sucked out, a bit like being connected up to a vacuum cleaner? We had no idea. Hopefully, if our breathing was adversely affected it would only be temporary and not in any way damaging to us. For a second it flashed through my mind - was Jesus, the Son of God, immune to such a worry? Of course Tala wasn't party to our discussion and would breathe normally. As it happened we decided to do the same, not expecting any lasting adverse effect.

It was time to move. Angela and I collected our belongings and moved down the slope to our haven. Tala, not having any idea what was going on, nevertheless followed. We laid down on our stomachs, heads uppermost because the indentation was deepest there. I then persuaded Tala to lie between us, head also uppermost and bearded lower jaw resting on the soft ground. I had already decided to protect her head with the OS map in its large plastic cover that I had brought with me. It wasn't brilliant, but it would at least offer some protection, unless she received a direct hit from a large piece of rock that had been picked up by the fast moving air.

Jesus stayed at the summit, looking west towards Ingleborough. Presumably there would be some indication that the air blast was on its way. He then saw what he was looking for. Stretching across the horizon, from north to south, with Ingleborough in the centre, was a developing narrow bank of what looked like cloud. Jesus knew that he was witnessing the front edge of the air blast, charged with dust. The distance between the summits of Ingleborough and Pen-y-Ghent was just six miles. At a speed approaching that of sound the air blast would take no more than thirty seconds to reach him.

It was time for him to make his move to join Angela and I. On reaching us he too laid down, pulled his anorak hood over his head and hoped for the best. But of course he had the best protection possible…that of his Father who was no doubt looking down on the developing scene.

I only hoped that the group making their way south from Plover Hill had seen the atmospheric disturbance over Ingleborough, realised what it was and taken evasive action. They too had to descend the eastern flank and find some sort of natural depression to crouch down in, with whatever they had available to protect their heads. Over the last few days there had been numerous programmes on television predicting and describing what would happen when the asteroid struck the Earth, including protecting oneself from the air blast.

When the front of the air blast hit Pen-y-Ghent's western flank it had to rise over it, scouring the ground as it did so. Anything that wasn't securely fastened down was picked up - dead and weakly rooted trees, insecure fences and rocks up to the size of a football, and of course lots of dust, even though earlier rain had slaked much of it down.

The air blast seemed to hug the ground as it descended the eastern flank, showering us with debris. Fortunately anything of a size that would cause us injury, missed us and Tala, and all we suffered was a covering of small twigs, grass and dust. As we'd hoped, our breathing was unaffected, although personally I had held my breath when the blast was at its height.

After about two minutes the air blast rapidly abated and finally stopped, at least where we were. It was now blasting its way uncontrollably across Yorkshire towards the East Coast. Would York Minster, Whitby Abbey and Flamborough lighthouse withstand it? I had no idea. And much more important, how would the people in its path, fair? Not that it really mattered because a huge tsunami was already on its way determined to engulf them.

When we felt it was safe to do so we brushed ourselves off, returned to the summit and looked around us, surprised to see that there was very little debris there. Concerned about the group coming off Plover Hill Angela looked north to the point where she'd last seen them, a good mile away. She spotted the yellow jacket that one of them was wearing and expected to see the group walking south to eventually join us. How would Jesus introduce himself to them, I wondered? "Hello…I'm Jesus Christ, the Son of God," somehow didn't ring true.

To Angela's surprise she noticed that the group had commenced their descent down the western flank and were apparently heading back to Horton. I wondered if they were aware that in less than three hours' time a tsunami of monumental proportions would rush round Ingleborough, maybe even washing over the summit itself, depending on the height of the wave. This had been estimated at anything from five hundred to fifteen hundred metres, the higher figure being the more likely. One thing was surely obvious to the group - the higher you were, the more chance there was of survival. I was however certain in my own mind that even we on Pen-y-Ghent at a height of well over six hundred metres, would not be safe. Horton itself could be hundreds of metres under water. No one knew how far the wave would advance and no one knew when it would recede, and if it did where it would recede to. Would it return across Britain, the Irish Sea, across the Irish mainland and out into the Atlantic, eventually filling the crater that had been created by the asteroid? Again nobody knew. What was certain, nothing would be able to stand in its way whichever way it was moving.

As the time of judgement approached, that being approximately four o'clock, Jesus addressed Angela and myself, and in so doing shocked us: "It is now time to give both of you a choice…Either you can stay here and wait for the tsunami to sweep you into oblivion, as it surely will…Death would be by drowning and very quick…Or, you can ascend into Heaven with me…It is not my or my Father's desire that I stay here, only to be swept away and be drowned by the wave…In such circumstances my death would be meaningless, unlike my sacrifice two thousand years ago that even up to this day has influenced how many people lead their lives …The choice is yours."

I felt like pointing out to him that since mankind was about to be annihilated for its 'sins', a bit like Sodom and Gomorrah, but on a World scale, his mission on Earth had in the eyes of his Father in Heaven largely been a failure. But in the circumstances I refrained from doing so.

I did however point out one very important fact, one that I'm sure Jesus was already fully aware of, his Father having informed him: "As you are no doubt aware, for you seem to know about most things, I have a tumour on the brain and will be dead within six months, so what's the point of rising into Heaven with you?...May as well stay here and end it all quickly."

Jesus smiled: "Oh, ye of little faith." He then gently placed his hands on my head, looked up to heaven and whispered: "Please, Father, may it be thy will that this demon leaves this man."

I couldn't help smiling at his choice of word, one he'd used two thousand years ago, at a time when diseases were thought to be caused by demons that had to be banished from the body.

The sensation was strange. The throbbing in my head that had been there in the background for several weeks, slowly eased, then disappeared altogether, and when I looked across the valley at the summit of Ingleborough, the sight that had previously been fuzzy to me, slowly became crystal clear. The pressure on the optic nerve had obviously been lifted. Had I in fact been cured? I had to assume that I had.

My appreciation was expressed in one simple word. I could not think of anything else to say: "Thanks."

Both Angela and I were taken aback at the choice Jesus had put before us. Although we had no idea what death by drowning would be like, it couldn't be pleasant. But what would ascension into Heaven be like? Would we in fact die and if so, how? And if we didn't die what would happen to us? It passed through my mind that as we ascended we would eventually be unable to breathe, a bit like climbing Mount Everest without oxygen. Is this what would happen? Jesus had been through the process twice and had lived to tell the tale, so to speak, so why not us?

But two points were now uppermost in my mind – the first a question. Wouldn't we still end up in Heaven even if we were drowned by the tsunami? If we were believers in the Christian faith, as we undoubtedly were, that is what would happen to us. We would be killed by the tsunami and our spirits would leave our lifeless bodies and rise into Heaven. This is what we of the Faith had been led to believe. Whether we chose death by ascension or death by drowning we would still enter Heaven. Or wasn't it as simple as that?

The second point was this – Jesus gave the impression that he wanted us to rise into Heaven with him rather than drowned in the swirling waters directly below us. Why? Surely he didn't envisage us returning to the Earth sometime in the future to carry out some sort of role. What would be the point anyway? One thing was certain. The Earth would be uninhabitable. There would be precious little sunlight due to the amount of dust the impacting asteroid had forced up into the atmosphere. Temperatures would fall below freezing and there would be precious little, if indeed, any life, and that which had survived would be primitive in nature. The Earth would in fact be a giant snowball moving through space. And these conditions could persist for tens, hundreds, maybe even thousands of years. In such circumstances what role could we possibly play? None

Having given not too much thought to Jesus's question, principally because death by ascension was infinitely more attractive than death by drowning, Angela and I took barely thirty seconds to decide. Who would want to be swept off the top of Pen-y-Ghent by a tsunami, racing along at eight hundred kilometres an hour, heading for God knows where and carrying with it God knows what…trees, buildings, cars, dead animals, even dead people picked up by the wave as it swept across the country? There could even be dead friends of ours from close-by villages such as Ingleton and Horton, not that that would matter because we also would be dead.

Angela answered for both of us: "We're coming with you…We're going to ascend into Heaven…Care to give us some idea what to expect?"

Jesus smiled: "Oh, I can't do that…It has to come as a surprise…But I can assure you that it will be a pleasant experience…I'll say no more."

I suddenly had a thought. We had Tala with us. What would happen to her? I wasn't prepared to abandon her to her fate, even if her death would be rapid and hopefully painless. If she couldn't come with us I was prepared to stay with her, right to the death.

Jesus saw me looking down at my faithful friend and instinctively knew what was passing through my mind. He spoke to reassure me: "When I gave you the choice of accompanying me into Heaven or staying here I naturally included Tala as well…My Father would not have easily forgiven me had I not done so…It may surprise you, but he thinks as much about his animals as he does about we humans…And contrary to the belief of most humans who considered themselves to be believers, the spirits of all animals whatever their complexity or simplicity also enter the Kingdom of Heaven…Not only are your parents in Heaven, so is Tala number one…I wonder what Tala number two will make of her? "

I smiled, first at Jesus's choice of word. Was he in fact 'human'? He certainly looked it, almost a younger version of myself, then at the idea of Tala 1 meeting Tala 2. Tala 1 was hugely protective of both Angela and I, quite prepared to have a scrap with any dog who came too close to us. But Tala 2 was exactly the same. I'd visions of one almighty scrap taking place, and in Heaven too. Would God approve of me forcing my way between the two dogs, probably using my boots in the process, in order to separate them? Then it occurred to me…Tala 1 would be without her body. That was under a cherry tree in the garden of the smallholding where we'd lived. Whether Tala 2 would have hers, as yet we didn't know because Jesus had not informed us what would happen to us when we 'ascended' into Heaven.

Up to that point I had totally forgotten all about the Holy Square that was lying at the bottom of my rucksack. It had never occurred to me that had the rucksack taken a direct hit from some descending rock during the passing air blast, both wooden frame and thirteen pieces of pot would have been destroyed. I could have ended up with a pile of pot fragments only fit for making some sort of mosaic, albeit a very special one.

I had to at least tell Jesus that I had the Square in my possession, but before I handed it to him I decided to quiz him on a subject that had always puzzled me: "After first hearing about the Square and the important role it had played at the Last Supper, it became my humble opinion that *it* was the Holy Grail, not the chalice you used in your first communion service, and has been searched for throughout Europe for the last two thousand years…Am I right?"

His reply couldn't have thrilled me more: "Indeed you are, Peter…My Holy Square obviously played a far greater role in the proceedings than the chalice…When all said and done my distribution of the twelve pieces of pot to my disciples, then sending them on their way to spread my word, laid down the foundations of what is now known as Christianity…By the way, I did not coin the expression 'Holy Grail'…Others did."

I smiled at him, pleased that he agreed with me. I also felt like asking him a pertinent question - since his Father was in the process of destroying the World, hadn't Christianity failed? But being in a precarious position with the tsunami rapidly approaching I decided against it. I did however ask him another question, one that I was itching to know the answer to, purely out of sheer curiosity: "I don't suppose you know where the chalice is, do you?"

Jesus smiled: "As a matter of fact I do…My Father followed its route as it moved across the continent of Europe about eight hundred years ago…It's present location, only a few miles from where we are standing at this moment, will surprise you…It is used every Sunday morning in the Holy Communion service at the church where you found the piece of pot I originally gave to Judas Iscariot…I believe it's called Ribbleswell…One of the two Crusaders who were re-interred in the churchyard had acquired the chalice in a bazaar just outside Jerusalem and had brought it back to England with him…Of course he had no idea what it was."

A tingle of excitement shot through me like an electric shock, the result of knowing that some ten years ago I had received Holy Communion in a ceremony where that self-same chalice had been used to hold the wine representing the blood of the man who was standing in front of me. It was the strangest of feelings to know that my lips had sipped from the same chalice as his.

It then occurred to me - in the search for what many people considered to be the Holy Grail, hadn't anyone visited Ribbleswell Church, seen the chalice and just wondered, asking themselves the question: "Could this just be the one?"

Of course had they known about the two Crusaders buried in the churchyard they may well have put two-and-two together and come up with the right answer, but they hadn't had that knowledge. It took the excavation of the graveyard by my team of students to reveal the presence of the two Crusaders, as shown by their gravestones.

And another thing - most searchers had probably been looking for a stunning piece of silverware, probably encrusted with a range of precious stones, a bit like the one stolen from Wakefield Cathedral. By comparison the Communion chalice at Ribbleswell Church was misshapen, scratched, looked like something that had been rescued from a skip and had ended up at a car boot sale. It couldn't possibly be the one used by Jesus Christ at his Last Supper…but evidently it was.

I had been custodian of the Holy Square on Jesus's behalf for the last ten years. It was time to return it to its rightful owner: "Please take it…You can then decide what you want to do with it, although I can't imagine in the circumstances what."

Jesus had of course last seen the Square on the day he'd ascended into Heaven for the second time, the time when he'd given it to me for safe keeping. Well, I had kept my side of the bargain and had now handed it back to him.

As he received it, he spoke: "Thanks, Peter…When I left it with you I knew that it was in the safest of hands and would make its appearance on this day…I hope my action later on this evening doesn't make you feel that your conscientious efforts have all been a waste of time."

As he forced the Square down into the front pouch pocket of his anorak I smiled at him and nodded, not having the slightest idea what he intended to do with it. I did however expect something a bit out of the ordinary and I knew I wouldn't be disappointed.

It was at that point that we became aware that the tsunami was well and truly on its way. The first thing we noticed was a darkening of the sky in the west just above Ingleborough. It was as if the sky's lower edge had been painted across with a dark grey strip that had the thinnest of white lines painted along the top of its entire length. We quickly realised what it was. We were seeing the top of the wave as it rushed towards Ingleborough itself. The white strip was where the wave was breaking over. Imagine surfing on that, I thought.

Angela and I had earlier planned for this very moment, and it was now time to implement that plan. She had always assumed that there would be just the two of us. I'd always had a hunch that Jesus would make an appearance before my death, his written message - *I'll see you again in 2022* told me that…And here he was standing at the side of me.

Angela acted quickly. Out came our two glasses and the bottle of 'good' red wine. I quickly filled them then passed the bottle to Jesus. There was just time for our toast, but what should it be? As Angela and I clinked our glasses, then clinked the bottle Jesus was holding, he took the decision out of my hands: "To a new beginning…" he shouted. And not having the slightest idea what that new beginning would be, and whether it would include us, Angela and I shouted: "To a new beginning…" The wine was quickly consumed, Jesus unceremoniously emptying the bottle in one go.

At that point we saw the full height of the wave as it hit Ingleborough, although the hill made little impression on its advance, for the wave simply crashed over the summit, almost as if it wasn't there. I knew that Ingleborough was over six hundred metres in height. The wave looked considerably higher. A guestimate of almost fifteen hundred metres had been earlier predicted by those who supposedly knew about such things. The studiers of tsunamis produced by undersea earthquakes hadn't been far off the mark.

What Angela and I were witnessing was something we'd seen during our childhoods on numerous occasions on the beaches of Bridlington and Scarborough, albeit on a micro-scale by comparison – a big wave washing over a large pebble. The pebble had stood its ground, as indeed Ingleborough was doing right now.

I already knew that the distance between Ingleborough and Pen-y-Ghent was about six miles. The wave had been predicted to have a speed of about five hundred miles an hour. A quick and rough calculation told me that it would hit us in just under a minute. If Jesus intended to take some sort of evasive action for himself, Angela, I and a dog, it had to be now.

As the wave engulfed Horton, leaving the village under hundred of metres of water, it headed towards us at lightning speed, Jesus quickly came between us and linked his arms with ours. Tala looked up at me appealingly, trembling as she did so, poor dog. For the first time in her life she was frightened and didn't know the reason why. I crouched down and placed my arms under her body. Although she weighed a ton I was determined to lift her off the ground, something I had not been able to do for the last twelve months, but somehow I now found the strength to do so. Jesus made sure that one of his arms was still threaded through one of mine.

With the towering wave now filling a good proportion of the western sky as it raced towards us, Jesus looked urgently heavenwards and shouted: "It is time, Father…It is time…Take us into your care."

I suddenly found myself being lifted off my feet, at the same time Tala became weightless. I then started to rise rapidly skywards, or was it Heavenwards? I had no idea. What I did know was that Jesus and Angela were rising too, our arms still linked together. To any observer we would have looked like three ascending rockets, but without their fiery tails. Within seconds we were accelerating upwards at frightening speed. Presumably God had realised the seriousness of the situation and 'got his finger out', so to speak. At one point I was convinced that the wave would sweep us from our precarious position or at least wash over our boots as it rushed past, heading uncontrollably in an easterly direction. Fortunately I was wrong.

When the wave passed over Pen-y-Ghent's summit, looking not unlike the large wave passing unhindered over the pebble on Bridlington beach, we were already well above it and could look down and gasp at the sheer size and destructive power of it. As far as the eye could see to the west there was water…Nothing but water. To the east I could still land, but in seconds the wave would be heading towards the eastern horizon.

As I looked downwards I saw first a yellow dot in the swirling waters, then a red one, then a blue one. They were almost certainly the lifeless bodies of three of the walkers we'd seen earlier heading back to Horton. They'd never had a chance.

Seconds later Angela, looking down and pointing, shouted enthusiastically: "Look, Pete, there's the package containing my work…I told you my idea would be successful."

All I could see was a small white square shaped object heading eastwards in the swirling waters. It could have been anything white that the wave had picked up, a white out-building door for instance or a white fertilizer sack. But there was no point in dampening her enthusiasm. I shouted in return: "You certainly did, Angie…Looks as if your work's heading for Denmark…Of course it could get stuck on a wind turbine in the North Sea."

"Ha…Ha," was her 'not amused' response.

I then whispered to her, not wanting Jesus to think that I was in any way concerned: "How high do you reckon we are?"

She thought for a second before answering: "Well…I'm not experiencing any problem breathing so I suspect we are well below ten thousand feet…Being well wrapped up we're not feeling the cold."

Angela's answer immediately got me thinking. We'd both been up to that altitude whilst on holiday, to the summit of Mount Teide in Tenerife, and the Jungfraujoch in the Swiss Alps, and on both occasions we'd felt out of breath. At our present height we were breathing quite normally.

Jesus then asked us a strange question: "Would you like to see the extent of the damage done to the Earth by the tsunami so far?…But in order to do so there is one condition that you may or may not like, or be happy to go along with."

Jesus's question puzzled me. I could already see below me the damage done, but only to a fraction of the Earth's surface. How could we possibly see any more…unless we ascended higher, much, much higher. In fact Jesus gave me the details: "At present we are at an altitude of just under three thousand metres, but all we can see is water almost from horizon to horizon…Too get the best view I want to take you to an altitude of about 2000 kilometres."

Both Angela and I gasped at the figure, knowing that at a mere eight kilometres, roughly the height of Mount Everest, we would be unable to survive on the rarified air, not being in any way acclimatised to such a height.

Jesus smiled: "Of course, since your bodies are unable to survive above about eight kilometres you will have to die in order to reach that altitude…In fact your bodies will not be there at all, only your spirits…But you did express earlier that you wanted to join me in Heaven…Well this is the first stage in the process, so to speak…Are you happy to go along with that?"

He spoke in a matter-of-fact way as if what he was suggesting was an everyday occurrence.

But then I suddenly became aware of feelings of possible guilt. Was I in fact a worthy person to enter the Kingdom of Heaven? I thought that on the whole I was, but perhaps some sort of inventory on my life was in order. Besides, my precarious position tended to concentrate the mind. Both God and his Son would know of my 'sins' so perhaps it was a good idea to re-familiarise myself with them…But how?

I soon had the answer…use as a guide the code of conduct that God himself had set out for the Children of Israel in tablets of stone given to Moses on Mount Sinai, namely *The Ten Commandments*. Although now looked upon as 'dated', if one was honest most were still very relevant today. I could not remember them all or their order, but that didn't matter. I whispered to myself the ones I could remember and asked myself how well I'd done, trying to be as honest as I could.

Thou shalt not kill - This was easy. I had definitely not killed anyone. But thinking back I nearly had. I remembered the incident well, even though it had taken place many years ago, in fact when I'd been at university. I was mugged at an ATM, the mugger crashing my face into the screen as he snatched my cash. I'd just called at the Off-Licence and had a four-pack of lager in a carrier bag. In sheer rage I extracted a can and launched it at my assailant as he casually walked away, not wanting to draw attention to himself. My aim was good, in fact very good, and the edge of the can struck the mugger on the back of the head. He fell like a stone. The paramedics quickly got him to A&E where he was diagnosed as having a fractured skull. For the best part of a week it was 'touch and go' for him. Fortunately for him, and for me, he made a full recovery. Although charged with GBH, having supposedly used disproportionate force, a sympathetic judge convinced an equally sympathetic jury that they should come up with a not-guilty verdict…which they did.

Thou shalt not worship any other God but me, nor bow down and worship other idols – Since I had been of the Christian faith all my life I had no interest in worshipping another God, nor any form of idol. But I did come pretty close to idolising the whole Leeds United team during the 1970s when they won everything before them. And as far as an individual was concerned I did idolise the team's centre-half Jackie Charlton.

Thou shalt not take God's name in vain - I think all of us were guilty of this, with expressions such as:

Oh my God!!!

For God's sake!!!

Good God!!!

being common in every day talk. Hopefully God wasn't too offended by such expressions.

Thou shalt keep the Sabbath holy – Keeping the Sabbath holy was an interesting one because the day had changed from Saturday to Sunday centuries ago. Many people did essential work on that day, such as the police, nurses, fire fighters and those manning other essential services. But was it really necessary for almost every shop in the country to be open most of the day? But there again, whole families looked upon a visit to some huge shopping mall with a meal in a fast food outlet thrown in, as a family bonding exercise. Looking back, Angela and I had rarely spent a Sunday in, preferring to visit a mall or garden centre before calling for a pub lunch. All premises were staffed by young kids who wanted to make a bob or two to help pay their way through some form of higher education or vocational training. Surely God could see the merit in that.

Thou shalt honour thy father and mother – As a child and throughout my adulthood I'd had an excellent relationship with my parents. My father had been an excellent role model and both friends and relatives had remarked how like him I was. He had been a professional rugby league player as a young man, and a real hardcase too, so I'd been told. But off the field he'd been a gentle giant and had the knack of disciplining me without actually knocking seven bells out of me. One thing I sadly regretted...I never hugged him, nor he me. Why, I don't really know. Maybe it wasn't the done thing at that time. Even on his deathbed at Wakefield's Pinderfields Hospital I struggled to kiss him on the forehead. But I did and felt a good deal better for it. It was a way of not only saying farewell, but thank you. I can remember a short period in my teenage years when I was a real swine to my mother. I was feeling my feet and couldn't help showing it. This took the form of wholesale defiance and obnoxiousness. Fortunately my 'horrible' period didn't last long and from that point on I treated my mother with the greatest respect. Sadly she died suddenly and on her own, not giving me time to say how much I loved her.

Thou shalt not steal – This was an interesting commandment. As children we all 'nicked' the odd apple off a neighbour's tree, or a sweet out of one of those *pick 'n' mix* displays in Woolworths. I even took home items of stationery, books, CDs and laptops from the university so that I could carry on my work there. This seemed perfectly acceptable to me, although some would have said that it was a form of 'stealing'. But I was basically an honest person and this was shown beyond any doubt when I found a small plastic wallet containing 500 euros on the floor of a local bus. To cries of: "You must be mad" from some of my colleagues I returned it to the travel agent who had issued it, their slip and a credit receipt also being in the plastic bag. A week later I'd popped into the travel agent and the woman in the bureau-de-change informed me that the owner had been traced and had been in to pick up the currency. Since I'd left my name and telephone number I'd half expected at least a 'thankyou' from the individual who had lost the wallet, maybe even a little reward, but nothing. For the briefest moment I thought - you *were* mad - but I knew deep down that I'd done the right thing.

Thou shalt not commit adultery – To my eternal shame I had committed adultery on just one occasion. Rhoda Smithson had just joined my department staff and after our Christmas 'do' I walked her home, just down the road from the *Quarry Inn* where it had been held. Her husband was away on a weekend course down in London and Angela was visiting her parents in Harrogate.

Since I was well over the drink/drive limit Rhoda offered me her spare room for the night, which I gratefully accepted. Anyway, one thing led to another and we both woke up the following morning in the same bed and and completely naked. Need I say more?

Should I have confessed my sin to Angela? I don't know, but I didn't. Would God hold this against me when he comes to do his assessment of me? Hopefully not.

Thou shalt not give false evidence against your neighbour – I suppose I'd been guilty of this as well, but for a very good reason in my opinion. We had a young next door neighbour, a bit of a tearaway, who incessantly held wild noisy parties. The Council refused to take action until I had built up a dossier of dates and times, sound levels (they even provided me with a sound meter) and an account of the behaviour, which I duly did. Perhaps understandably I exaggerated everything, painting the worst possible picture. In court and under oath I was asked if my dossier was a true record, to which I replied: "Yes". Since the neighbour lived in a council owned property he was fined for his unreasonable behaviour and threatened with eviction. Needless to say he moderated it, and needless to say he didn't speak to me again. I always felt guilty about my high handed attitude.

Thou shalt not be envious of thy neighbour's possessions, including his wife – Finally to the question of envy, expressed in the bible as 'coveting'. I had never been an envious person. Possessions such as cars, watches, phones, ipads, the latest electronic gadgetries, had never interested me. And since my one night stand with Rhoda I had never looked at another woman, let alone envied the husband or boyfriend walking down the street with a stunning woman on his arm. Angela couldn't understand my apparent lack of interest and frequently commented that senility had come early to me.

So how had I done over the years? According to my reckoning I'd broken to a greater or lesser extent five of the ten commandments…hardly a brilliant record, but I suppose it could have been worse. It hardly made me a suitable candidate for Heaven. But who was perfect? If God only took in 'perfect' people, then Heaven must be a pretty empty place. And if we assumed that the alternative to Heaven was Hell, although Jesus had never mentioned such a place in all our conversations, then by comparison with Heaven it must be a pretty overcrowded place. All Sodom and Gomorrah would be there, for a start.

As I was still doing my personal assessment, trying to improve certain aspects of it Jesus moved away from us in order to talk with his Father, what about I'd no idea nor could I guess. Below us the World was slowly being consumed by the tsunami as it moved relentlessly outwards from the asteroid's point of impact in mid Atlantic. By now the eastern horizon was a line of water. In fact as I turned a full circle all I could see was water. It was like being in a small boat in the middle of an ocean.

I looked at my watch, still ticking away quite happily, totally unaffected by what was going on around it. The time was six o'clock in the evening. The tsunami had passed under us about two hours ago. Accepting that it would probably have slowed down as it passed over land with varying contours it could already be hundreds of kilometres to the east, now crossing central Europe having skirted round the Alps. But of course the tsunami was spreading outwards as an ever expanding circle with the point of impact at its centre. It was relatively easy to picture its expanse across Europe, but what was happening in other parts of the World? I was about to find out,

Jesus returned to us and spoke: "It is now time for you to enter the Kingdom of Heaven so let me explain what is going to take place...We are going to rise further, way past the point where you will be able to breathe...At this point you will pass into unconsciousness and quickly die."

I looked at Angela, a look that told her that I was far from happy with what Jesus had just said. Being the more philosophical one, she simply smiled, at the same time saying: "Well, we can't stay here forever."

She was of course right.

Jesus continued: "Your material bodies, now lifeless and therefore useless, will fall away leaving your spirits here, ready to rise into Heaven...But first I intend to take you on a journey to see the extent of the tsunami...I will also take you to the point of the asteroid's impact."

At that point Jesus again linked arms with us. On seeing this, Tala, jumped into my arms. She'd certainly no intentions of being left behind. The four of us then started to slowly ascend, passing through a layer of thick cloud as we did so. To what height was anybody's guess.

Dying was painless. I vaguely remembered experiencing difficulty breathing, but it only lasted a few seconds. Unconsciousness came quickly, presumably followed by death. It was at that point that I became aware that my body was leaving me. I had heard and read of occasions where people in hospitals had had an 'out of body' experience where they ended up just below the ceiling looking down on their lifeless bodies lying on the bed. It appeared that at that precise moment they had 'died', only to come back to life again seconds later.

My body seemed to slip away, downwards, then accelerate in the direction of the ground thousands of metres below me. Presumably there would be some sort of splash as it hit the water at God knows what speed. I could vaguely remember reading somewhere that a falling body reached a terminal velocity of about 200km/hr depending in how 'streamlined' it was, so presumably that would be the speed. Of course I would not feel anything on impact because my body was already dead.

As all this was happening I became aware that Angela's and Tala's bodies were also accelerating away, downwards. All three of us had died, but our spirits were still there, together.

So what did our spirits look like? Well, that was the surprising thing…all three of us looked the same as we had done before, like 'ghosts' of ourselves. Throughout history ghosts had reportedly been seen, usually in castles and stately homes, even old inns, and almost always in human form…prisoners, soldiers, kings and queens, even pub landlords. I had never believed such reports, yet here in front of me were the ghosts of Angela smiling away, and Tala happily wagging her tail. The scene was uncanny. I moved across and gave Angela a hug, but she wasn't there…and yet she was speaking to me. I then stroked Tala, but she too wasn't there, although she gave me an appreciative bark.

I looked across to were Jesus was standing, if indeed one could 'stand' in space, but standing seemed more appropriate than 'floating'. He looked the same as he had before, so had he died as he had on two previous occasions, and was I therefore looking at his spirit, or ghost? Were the two words in fact interchangeable? Quite honestly I had no idea, nor did it matter. But what I did know was that both words were used in the New Testament. I felt the urge to touch Jesus, just to check…solid body or spirit, but quickly realised that as a spirit myself I would not be able to 'feel' a solid body, anyway.

At that point Jesus came across and spoke: "It may surprise you to know, but we are now at a height of sixteen kilometres, about twice the height of Mount Everest, the highest point on Earth, but as I said before, we must go much, much higher in order to see the full extent of the tsunami's progress…About two thousand kilometres above the Earth's surface should do."

The distance staggered me. Even travelling at the speed of sound it would take in the region of two hours...But I was wrong. As if by magic we again started to ascend, but this time at a frightening speed. It suddenly occurred to me...how fast could spirits, or ghosts, travel? The speed of light? Even faster, making journeys to the outer reaches of the Universe, distances measured in thousands of light years, a distinct possibility? Now there was a thought. What if the spirits of dead people could then be 're-materialised' (if there is such a word), thus enabling them to time travel and explore the Universe. And finally...what if this was already taking place, and had been since man had set foot on his Earth?

In what appeared to be the blink of an eye we'd evidently risen to the required height. According to Jesus we were now at an altitude of exactly 2500 kilometres. How he knew the exact figure I'd no idea for he had no equipment to measure it, but he apparently did. Unfortunately because of the thick cloud that was at that moment covering the entire Earth we could see nothing.

This however did not appear to be a problem. Jesus simply asked his Father to do the necessary. As if by magic the cloud below us started to disperse, revealing the surface of the Earth in what should have been all its glory, just as the astronauts returning from the Moon had seen it... the Blue Planet with its land masses clearly standing out, the most beautiful sight a human being could witness, stated one astronaut...except that that wasn'tnow case. What we saw instead was devastation...utter devastation. One couldn't help but feel sorry for what was taking place... and anger, downright anger. It had taken God billions of years to create the beautiful world that we knew had been below us just before the asteroid had struck. He must have had a damned good reason for destroying it all in what was the blink of an eye in the grand scale of things. But Angela and I could not see in our wildest dreams what that reason was. All we could do was to accept that he had got it right, for he was the God Almighty.

It was now time for Jesus to take us on a 'grand tour' to see the extent of the tsunami's devastating effect, assuming that we would like to see it. I wasn't so sure I wanted to, and I suspected that Angela would feel the same. Tala, no doubt bored to tears, had fallen asleep so I decided to leave her where she, trusting that I would be able to find her again.

One thing did worry me...the intensity of the Sun. I was already aware that astronauts had to wear protective glasses when out in space and here we were without such protection. But I need not have worried because as Jesus explained, the eyes of spirits were not affected by the sun's damaging radiation.

He then informed us where we were going: "As you are aware, when the tsunami was formed it spread out in the form of an expanding circle, as the rings do when a stone is thrown into a pond...This continues until the tsunami hits land... At this point it slows down, passing over low lying land, skirting round land that will be above it, such as mountains...As it does so the circle becomes slightly distorted, but we will still be able to see the effect of the tsunami...We are going to join that circle roughly over Poland, where it has already reached, and travel quickly along the advancing front in an anticlockwise direction...Let's go."

With the advancing front breaking directly below us we started to move quickly in what was a northerly direction. At that height we could see the Swiss Alps to the south-west poking their heads above the water, and the mountains of Scandinavia to the north-west that we proceeded to pass over. The unhindered tsunami had already passed through the Greenland – Europe gap and was heading for the Arctic Ocean. The dot of land that we could just make out was probably Iceland. A good half of Greenland was already under water and the tsunami was speeding across Canada, with the tsunami rushing across Hudson Bay. Far in the west the Rockies could be seen, a formidable barrier for the advancing waters. At this point the sun moved behind the Earth. This should have plunged our view into darkness, but a full moon behind us illuminated the Earth enabling us to still see what was going on below us.

We were now over the central Unites States. Half the country was already under water, including of course the whole length of the Eastern Seaboard. It was hard to imagine that the great cities of New York and Washington were hundreds of metres under water. I could see some high ground poking its head above the waters, but my lack of geographical knowledge of North America did not enable me to identify it.

Angela reminded me: "The Appalachians,"

I nodded to her, having heard of them before.

At this point Jesus pointed out that we had now completed half our journey, having travelled a distance of just over 16000 kilometres in barely twenty minutes. God knows what speed we were travelling at.

The unhindered wave front had already passed over the Caribbean Islands and was heading for the isthmus joining the two Americas where it would spill over into the South Pacific making the Panama Canal surplus to requirements, not that it would ever be used again. As the tsunami continued its south westerly journey it would swamp the many south sea islands before hitting New Zealand quickly followed by Australia.

Also unhindered by land the tsunami had already reached the continent of South America where a good third of Brazil was under water. How strange it was to see the advancing front moving rapidly up the Amazon Basin. The Andes too, also to the west, would form a formidable barrier to the advancing waters. To the south the tsunami, again unhindered by any form of land mass, was heading for Antarctica. What would happen when it met the vast ice shelf, I wondered? Presumably the ice would break up and ride over the wave…or would it?

As we continued our high speed journey, moving quickly across the gap between South America and Africa the Sun rose above the horizon, lighting up what should have been a glorious Earth. But what we witnessed was further devastation as the tsunami continued its advance. It had already passed over West Africa covering the whole area that was the Sahara Desert. How strange it was to see thousands of square miles of sand that only a few thousand years ago were thought to have been covered in lush vegetation, now under water.

The Mediterranean Sea being narrow, with numerous large islands and an irregular coastline, hindered the tsunami's advance to some extent. As we looked down it was about to engulf Sicily, although Mount Etna had no intentions of succumbing to it. As we looked westwards we could make out Morocco's Atlas Mountains to the left and Spain's Sierra Nevada and the Pyrenees to the right. The Italian Apennines were now directly below us.

Our journey was now almost complete. Looking to the east we could see the Ural Mountains. Would that be the natural barrier that stopped the tsunami's eastward advance, I wondered? Or would it cross the lower land between the Urals and the Himalayas? In a southeasterly direction it would no doubt cut across the Middle East engulfing Saudi Arabia and entering the Indian Ocean, to continue its journey. Would this advancing front eventually meet up with the one that would hit Australia having crossed the Pacific Ocean? If it did, then what?

Of course the tsunami could 'run out of steam', so to speak, and start to be drawn back to the impact crater that the asteroid had originally made. I visualised it being like the plug being pulled out a sink's plug hole, thus allowing the water in the sink to escape down the hole. This of course would compound the damage done by the advancing tsunami as it withdrew at a similar speed to the crater were it had been originally born. What an awesome sight that would be, for the damage done would be laid bare for us to see.

Almost uncannily we ended up at our exact starting point. I of course knew this because Tala, now awake, was there waiting for us, tail wagging, and no doubt pleased to see us.

Angela and I assumed that our journey through space was now at an end,but we were wrong. Jesus wanted to show us one more sight. He explained: "I now want to take you to a point directly above the point of asteroid impact...This means travelling to the centre of the circle we've just been round, a distance of about 4000 kilometres, but we'll be there in about five minutes."

The speed of travel no longer surprised me. I was getting used to it.

On reaching the point I looked down from my elevated position, but all I could see in the failing sunlight was a dark coloured cloud covering a large area of the Earth's surface. This had undoubtedly formed as a combination of the upper layers of the Earth's crust, pulverised to dust, and the vast quantities of seawater, converted into steam by the huge release of energy, were blasted into the atmosphere. Occasionally gaps in the cloud appeared. When this happened I could see a red glow, the sight one witnessed when looking into the crater of an active volcano as the red hot larva looked for an escape route. I got the impression that a long time would have to elapse before the crater would cool enough to allow the water which had been displaced by the impact and had produced the huge advancing tsunami, to return.

As we stood, or was it 'hung', in our elevated position Jesus put both Angela and I on the spot, so to speak: "So...What do you think of what you have just seen...And please be honest...Feed back is useless if it isn't honest?"

I decided to answer first, knowing that Angela would want to give some thought to the question, certainly more than I was prepared to give.

"Well now...I am staggered by the devastation caused by the impacting asteroid...In my wildest dreams I could not have imagined what I am now witnessing...What worries me is that although the majority of the World's population will have been consumed by the tsunami, dying instantly, those who did reach high ground or already live there will have survived...What will happen to them?...Surely the atmosphere will already be coming too poisonous to breathe...Will they die a slow and painful death?"

Jesus declined to respond to my concerns. Instead he looked at Angela, waiting for her response to his original question...what did she think of what *she'd* witnessed?

Angela, that angered look in her eyes that I knew so well, was indeed ready: "I am appalled at what I've seen...Words fail me...The total devastation; the totally unnecessary loss of life, both plant and animal, including of course the majority of the human race...How in heaven's name can a God be loving and at the same time allow this to happen?...What faith there was, and I must admit that that wasn't much judging from the results of surveys throughout the World in the weeks before the asteroid struck, will have disappeared altogether now...Not that it now matters."

Angela had for a brief moment forgotten that most of those who had voted in those surveys were probably all dead by this time. I expected her to say more, but she was so annoyed and upset, she did not continue expressing her feelings. Both disgust and helplessness were written across her face.

After a few seconds' thought Jesus responded: "Well that is the point...That *faith* that was their until relatively recently had all but disappeared as man pursued his selfish needs...My Father gave humanity ten years to put its house in order...In fact you, Peter, played a prominent role in setting up the meeting that gave those with both national and international influence to make those changes...But did they? There's very little evidence that they did...Of course they tinkered on the edges of the numerous problems, but showed little enthusiasm or commitment...My Father and I had a long discussion during which I tried to put forward some sort of a defence for mankind, knowing deep down that I was on shaky ground."

Angela, aware of whatever she said, could now make no difference, still felt she had to have a final say: "But all that takes no account of the billions of innocent, helpless people who could have had no influence at all on the changes your Father wanted to see... But they too suffered the same fate as the so-called guilty."

Jesus smiled and came back confidently: "Ah…But you don't know of my Father's future plans as I do…I think you will be pleasantly surprised Angela, for he will prove to all, believers and non-believers, just what a loving God he is …At this point I will say no more…But first I will ask him to draw a veil over what is taking place below us so that you can concentrate on what I'm about to tell and indeed show you."

I could understand the point he was making, but the scene below fascinated me and I could not take my eyes off it. It was like what I imagined Dante's Inferno to look like, and yet it had a beauty about it; the swirling clouds opening up then closing allowing views of the scene below; the varying colours of the glowing larva from the brightest yellow to the dullest red; the waters that had the temerity to try to fall back into the crater being immediately blasted out in the form of clouds of white steam that mingled with the dark coloured dust clouds. Much to my disappointment a veil of high cloud moved across concealing the view below. I now had no good reason not concentrate on what Jesus was about to say to Angela and I.

The scene over two thousand kilometres above the Earth was strange, to say the least. As I stood there, or was it floated, still in my hiking gear, but now in 'spirit' form, I could see in front of me Jesus. He too was still in the clothes he'd been wearing when he'd met us on the summit of Pen-y-Ghent. I could also see Angela, wearing similar gear to me. And there was Tala, faithful Tala, looking the same as she always did, black as coal.

But were we now in Heaven, or weren't we? I had to know, and only one person could tell me. It was time for him to level with us: "So, Jesus…Is this Heaven or isn't it?"

Jesus smiled: "Heaven is where you make it, Peter…So yes, this is indeed Heaven…Now let me explain how you can take advantage of being here…First, you can see what and more importantly who you want to see by simply thinking about it or them…So think of the possibilities…People and Places…Remember the two 'Ps'…By the way 'People' also includes animals…I thought you may wish to see how Tala 1 is getting on."

I thought that he was pulling my leg, until I tried out what he said was possible. My mind drifted back to the time I took Tala 1 on her morning walk up the track leading to what we called the Top Field. She walked so far then bounded back to me. The images were as clear as if the walk was taking place at that very moment.

Then it occurred to me. Could Tala 2 see Tala 1 being fussed by me? If she could her protective nature would kick in and she would probably attack Tala 1, assuming that I was about to be attacked by her. It would be the first dog fight in Heaven. But she showed no indication that she could see what was going on, nor picked up Tala 1's scent.

Jesus smiled, knowing exactly what I was thinking: "Tala can only see the other dog if she thinks about her, but at this moment there's no reason why she should do...And of course spirits have no smell."

This made sense to me even though seeing Tala 1 in the first place, didn't.

Now it was Angela's turn to try out her new powers, and I'd a good idea who she would think about first...her mother. They were very close right up to her death in 2012, a year we always remember because it was the same year the asteroid almost struck the Earth, being deflected at the last minute by God himself.

At that point presumably her mother appeared to her, but she seemed lost for words. Eventually she spoke, as if talking to a long lost friend. "Hello, mother...How are you?...Haven't seen you for such a long time."

Her mother no doubt replied, probably pointing out that she'd seen her daughter only the other day, but I didn't hear that reply, nor could I see her.

Thinking about her myself immediately rectified that.

Jesus looked on fascinated at our choices of using the new 'technology', if that was indeed what it was. He explained further: "Now Angela, introduce your mother to Peter."

Angela, no doubt feeling strange, almost silly, about introducing an invisible person to me, nevertheless did so, not realising that I had already 'tuned in' to her mother.

"You of course remember Peter, my husband?" On the face of it, it was a silly question, but no doubt she had difficulty wording it differently.

Immediately her mother, having tuned into me, moved forward and proceeded to hug me: "Of course I remember him...Best thing that happened to you marrying him...You were going off the rails at the time...All that binge drinking and tarting around...You needed calming down, and he did it...Jim and I thought it would never last, but it did."

Jim was of course Angela's father. Someone I got on brilliantly with. It came as a shock to us all when he suddenly died whilst playing golf in the year 2000.

A common expression in the English language is 'spoilt for choice', and this was the case here…who to see next? Over the next hour we covered our relatives and friends, the list far too long to go through. Both of us realised that and knew that we would have to draw a line at some point. We could always think of others as and when we wanted to.

At this point Jesus informed us that he had to go: "Sorry, but I to leave you…There is something I urgently need to attend to…I will be in touch later." With that he simply faded away.

***

Chapter Forty Five

We were now left on our own and the question was…what to do next? After a moment's thought Angela came up with a brilliant suggestion: "Let's go back to our smallholding…See what it's like…See if our animals are all right."

"Great idea," I shouted, at the same time hugging her, but not feeling. At the same time she took hold of Tala 2's collar. I grabbed the collar of Tala 1, apparently holding it, but not feeling it. I then nodded to Angela, my indication that we should both be thinking about the same thing…our former home. The problem now was…at what period in time? We could have chosen those few hours just before we set off for Horton-in-Ribblesdale earlier in the day, but what would have been the point? It wasn't exactly a happy time, with the World about to be destroyed.

Angela made the decision "Let's go back a couple of years, to the time before you became ill and were diagnosed with the brain tumour…In fact to the day we had our new kitchen fitted…Or rather the day after, the fitting day being total chaos."

We of course had to both think about that day, and we did.

As if by magic our converted barn came into focus, and I assumed that Angela was seeing an identical image. There was Tala 2 treating the fitters who were still on site, with the utmost suspicion as she had on that day two years sgo. But where was Tala 1? Then I remembered…She was buried under a tree in the garden, having died a few years earlier. Had we wanted to see her we would have had to go back to when she was alive, but at that time Tala 2 would not have been born. It was a case of not being able to have both at the same time. At that precise point Tala 1 simply faded away.

It came as a bit of a surprise, although it shouldn't have done, to find that everything was as we remembered it. Our animals were out in the field, munching away. Our cats were fast asleep on the sunbeds we'd left in the garden throughout the summer. Inside the house the power was on and a cold blast hit us when we opened the freezer door. When we switched on the television the usual late evening programmes were available.

"Let's make a drink and have a bite to eat," suggested Angela. It was a brilliant idea. We hadn't eaten since our packed lunch on the summit of Pen-y-Ghent just before the tsunami struck, resulting in our eventual deaths and presumably our resurrections.

As we sat there in our dining room tucking into chicken masala, one of Angela's specialties, we gave each other brief accounts of our 'meetings' with friends and relatives. We probably did this to show each other that we were both capable of doing so. We then started to speculate where we went from there. If we were in fact in Heaven and could therefore 'see' places and people, could we continue living our lives as before? Was that what Heaven was all about? You died, separated from your material body and assumed a 'spirit' form that then allowed you to continue living at a time of your choosing. In other words you just continued your life, but in a different form, continuously repeating periods where 'good times' prevailed. Life would be bliss and go on forever. Amen.

As we were speculating what we should do next, with retiring to bed being the best suggestion there was a knock on the door. This was strange. If we assumed that all those who knew where we lived, were dead, having succumbed to the tsunami's advance, such as neighbours, who knew we were here? Tala had also heard the knock and took up guard by the closed door, ready to attack any intruder.

I decided to shout through the door: "Who's there, please?"

"Jesus...I've called to see how you're gpoing on...And to give you an invitation."

As I grabbed Tala by the collar Angela confidently opened the door knowing that it could only be one person, and one she knew.

The reactions of Tala was interesting. She obviously recognised the voice having first met Jesus at the top of Pen-y-Ghent earlier in the day. She was able to think about who owned it and hence visualise the owner, showing this by giving her characteristic friendly bark. When I shook Jesus's hand, and he hugged Angela kissing her on the cheek, Tala whimpered, indicating her approval of the visitor. She moved onto the hearth rug where she flopped down in front of the glowing embers.

"We've eaten up, I'm afraid, but would you like a drink of something...Tea?Coffee?A beer?Even a glass of wine?"

"Will the wine be the same as we had on the top of Pen-y-Ghent?...I really enjoyed that...Shame I had no glass and had to rush it."

He had too, drinking it hurriedly from the bottle like a 'wino', as the tsunami approached.

Angela produced the bottle and showed him the label: "Same wine, although I cannot guarantee that it was bottled at the same time." She then poured him a glass.

"Good...Good...Just like this morning's, but better in a glass."

After Jesus encouraged us to talk about our 'day' he got on to the reason why he had paid us a visit: "I'm having a bit of a get-together tomorrow evening and I'd like you both to come along."

Angela immediately answered for the two of us: "We'd love to come, but at what time, and where will it be...More to the point, how will we get there?"

Jesus smiled: "I'd like you to be there at eight o'clock...Regarding the venue, at ten minutes to eight I want you both to move into the garden and think about me...Holding hands as you do so will speed things up...A sort of doubling-up effect...I will then appear and escort you to where our get-together is being held."

"Any clues?"asked Angela jokingly.

"No...I want it to be a complete surprise to you both," was Jesus's evasive reply.

After consuming two bottles of the excellent wine, during which time all three of us went through the happenings of the day, Jesus took his leave. As I opened the door he expressed how he was looking forward to seeing us the following evening.

The day was pleasantly warm. The sun was still well above the western horizon, sunset being at a guess about nine-thirty. I decided for our surprise meeting with Jesus to wear a pair of light linen trousers and a casual generously fitting short sleeved shirt. The emphasis was on comfort. I decided to tie a jumper around my waist just in case it came cool later in the evening, for we had no idea what time our get-together would end.

Angela decided on a pair of check shorts that came just below the knee...quite trendy, I commented. Her top was a flimsy blouse with large sleeves, her bra being clearly visible through the very thin material. As she pointed out: "Comfort's the name of the game." She too tied a jumper round her waist just in case.

At ten to eight, as Jesus had suggested, we took up a position in the garden and held hands, at the same time thinking of the man himself.

Sure enough, as if by magic, his image came into my mind, and I assumed into Angela's as well. I expected him to also be casually dressed much the same as myself, his anorak and walking boots that he had been wearing the previous day not now necessary. He was in fact wearing grey cords, a black jacket with a white shirt underneath and stout black shoes. Understandably his attire puzzled Angela and I. Where had he acquired them? Where had he changed?

Behind Jesus, in the distance, I could see a track with a prominent white building with less prominent buildings either side of it. Behind the buildings were tall thin trees, possibly poplars or cedars, types not seen in the Yorkshire Dales. I tried to place the scene, and could only come up with an Italian or Greek village...or could the village be in Israel?

Jesus was the first to speak: "I'd like you to accompany me to the village just up the track...Our little get-together is in the large house you can see...It belongs to a very good friend of mine...There we will have supper with some very important people...Come, they are waiting for us."

At this point it should have come to me where we were and what was about to take place, but at the time it never occurred to me.

Angela, with a mind far quicker than mine, had already worked it out, or at least part of it. As Jesus strode out in front of us she whispered to me: "It's going to be a re-enactment of the Last Supper...His friends are going to be his twelve disciples."

It suddenly made sense to me...the old Israeli village, a large building owned by a friend, that would be Zachariah, and his friends the twelve disciples. But what would be the point of such a meeting? What role could they possibly play in the modern world?

The assembly room was on the first floor of what was a large villa. We therefore climbed an outside staircase to it. As we entered the open door we could see the whole scene set out in front of us. The first thing that struck me was the way Leonardo da Vinci had almost got it right. In his painting of *The Last Supper* he had obviously never witnessed the scene, only read various accounts of it that had been written fifteen hundred years before; the long refectory table running the whole length of the room, covered with a patterned table cloth on which were plates, glasses, bread rolls and fruit; the three windows allowing a view of the distant countryside, the low sun still making it clearly visible; thirteen people sitting at the table.

But there the similarity ended. Unlike the da Vinci painting where the twelve disciples had been told that one of them would betray Jesus and had reacted accordingly, today there were thirteen individuals sitting still, silent and with a confused look on their faces. They appeared to be anticipating some sort of message, but not having any idea what that message would be. There was also another difference and a major one, too. There on the table, prominently positioned, was Christ's Holy Square. Leonardo couldn't have included it in his painting because he'd known nothing of its existence.

Jesus smiled at me: "I assume you've already worked it out, Peter ...Although the Supper we had two thousand years ago was supposed to be the last one, the present circumstances on Earth have dictated that we should have another, but a very special one as you can see...You, Peter, and maybe you Angela, should recognise most of those sitting at the table."

I did, immediately. There were thirteen people sitting there (not twelve had they been the disciples). Most were wearing modern attire – suits over a collar and tie, but three were wearing clothes that one would go sailing in and included high visibility life jackets. One was even wearing a brightly coloured shirt and white shorts.

Looking round I immediately recognised some of the faces, having seen them, together, just ten year earlier. These were some of the thirteen World leaders who had placed (the Iran leader a couple of days later), a small piece of coloured pot in the Square that I had constructed for the event at the United Nations...the event that led to God the Almighty deflecting asteroid 2012JT88 from its collision course with planet Earth...also the event where God, through his Son Jesus, gave the World leaders the ten-year ultimatum. But why didn't I recognise them all? Was it just a lapse of memory, or something else? Angela, detecting my puzzled look, came up with the likely explanation: "The UK Prime Minister who held that post in 2012, went on to win the next two elections, so that's why he's here...Whereas the American president is only allowed two sessions in charge...We therefore have a new face at the table...On the other hand some leaders seem to go on forever, especially in non-democratic countries...This is why some faces are the same as those we saw ten years ago."

As it happened, it didn't matter who the leader actually was, only that he was present representing his country.

So, how had the leaders got here? More to the point, why were they here? Jesus explained to Angela and I. "All thirteen were engulfed by the

483

advancing tsunami…It just so happened that they were on or near the coast where it would have its maximum effect."

I couldn't help making a comment: "I suppose your Father in Heaven had something to do with that." He smiled then continued.

"Although my Father had already decided to give the World yet another chance, one it didn't deserve, he also decided to give mankind a scare, and a very real one, too."

Angela and I moved forwards, dying to know how the asteroid's impact and its consequences for mankind could possibly be reversed. The complete annihilation of the World was already well under way. Billions of humans had already died, most of the land members of the animal kingdom had and it was only a matter of time before the vegetation in all its forms would succumb to the toxic conditions – a salty environment on land and an acidic, dust-ladened atmosphere. How all this had affected the sea population was anybody's guess, but if life was ever to start again on the Earth maybe this would, for the second time, be the starting point.

Jesus had managed to re-assemble all thirteen leaders. How had he done it? More to the point, why? What was the point? It was all too late.

Jesus decided to put Angela and I out of our misery: "When the two asteroids struck…"

"Two asteroids?...But there was only one…Wasn't there?" Angela pointed out the obvious mistake to Jesus.

"Er, No…Didn't I tell you?...Several hours before impact my Father decided that in order to ensure that all thirteen leaders lost their lives in the resulting tsunami, this could only be achieved by the asteroid splitting into two, one impacting in the North Atlantic near the Azores and the other in the South Pacific near the Islands of Samoa."

This got me thinking: "But when you took Angela and I on our grand circular tour to witness the devastation caused by the tsunami, wouldn't we have seen evidence of the Pacific tsunami as we passed over the isthmus joining North and South America…But we didn't…Why?"

"Ah…If you remember, the whole of the Pacific was concealed by black toxic cloud, thus obscuring the effects of the Pacific impact…You remarked at the time, Peter."

Casting my mind back I did and I remembered Jesus's reply…perhaps it's better if you don't know why…and left it at that. He was now prepared to explain: "I was worried that you would think that my Father hated the human race to such an extent that he was determined that no one would survive…He therefore decided to go for the 'overkill', hence the two asteroids…But there was method in his madness, as you will see."

I suppose it made sense. If you wanted to kill a room full of people, one hand grenade would probably do, but two would be better. Similarly some people have survived a bullet to the head, but not two.

Jesus then gave us the main reason for the two-asteroid impact: "My Father obviously knew where all thirteen leaders would be at the time of the two impacts…In fact his 'guiding' powers ensured this…Let me explain…All the thirteen leaders had to be near the coast for certain death to take place…It was no good if one or more of them were well inland or sitting on top of a high mountain…For example the Iranian leader could have been in Tehran, over six hundred kilometres from the nearest coastline, and the Brazilian leader residing in Brazilia even further at well over eight hundred kilometres."

The point he'd raised was interesting and of course true, so where exactly were all these leaders when the two asteroids struck? I was long passed the point where Jesus surprised me, and his explanation followed this pattern.

"The Chinese, North Korean and Iranian leaders were in conference in Shanghai to discuss Iran's and North Korea's nuclear aspirations that were causing world instability…This was already hitting China's booming economy…There had already been some civil unrest and the two nations were being blamed for it…The British, French and German leaders were attending an EU meeting in Paris, but had taken time off to go fishing at La Rochelle where the French President has a yacht, hence the sailing gear …The US President found himself holidaying with his family at Disneyworld in Florida…The Japanese and Australian leaders were attending a trade conference in Tokyo…Russia's leader was at some sort of environmental crisis meeting in the Iceland capital, Reykjavik along with other Scandinavian leaders…A large tanker had run aground in the Baltic spilling thousands of tonnes of oil into the sea. …The South African and Brazilian leaders were attending a conference in Recife to discuss South Atlantic security…Evidently there had been an increase in the level of piracy on the Africa-South America trade routes…The Israeli leader was in Haifa opening a new university…Within the space of twelve hours all thirteen leaders had succumbed to the two tsunamis …Like you their spirits left their useless bodies behind and entered the Kingdom of Heaven…And here they are."

One thing immediately puzzled me. I remembered Jesus telling me that only 'believers' could enter the Kingdom of Heaven. It had been a well- publicised fact that the leaders of Russia, China, Iran and North Korea did not believe in a God who could change the orbits of asteroids, so how could their spirits enter the Kingdom of Heaven? I put the question to Jesus and he in turn explained: "Seconds before the tsunamis struck the cities of Shanghai and Reykjavik the four non-believing leaders, knowing that they were about to lose their lives, decided to pray to my Father asking him to forgive all their sins…It was a bit like Paul's conversion on the road to Damascus, except that it took place in the blink of an eye…My Father, being a forgiving God, accepted them into his Kingdom…And as I said - here they are."

The leaders' action didn't surprise me, and I suspected that millions of non-believers suddenly decided to believe as the tsunamis approached. Who wouldn't?

Jesus now explained to Angela and I what would happen next: "Zachariah…You remember him, don't you?"

Both of us nodded indicating that we did. Jesus continued: "…will provide us with supper…You will sit together at one end of the table, I at the other…At the end of supper I will celebrate my communion as I did two thousand years ago, except that the leaders will now be my disciples…After that I will explain to them their mission."

I had to ask the obvious question: "But how will they communicate with each other and you with them?...I can't see any interpreters, electronic or otherwise."

"Ah…Can you cast your mind back to that passage in the New Testament when my disciples spoke with many tongues to a large crowd of people who spoke many different languages…I had given them this power so that whoever they met up with on their travels they would be able to communicate with them…Our thirteen leaders will also have that power."

And he was right, too, for as Zachariah served the food – some sort of lamb stew with ample newly baked bread, followed by all the common fruits, washed down with red wine, they did indeed communicate. It was fascinating to see the Russian leader speaking French to the French leader to his left, and vice-versa, and the Chinese leader speaking to the US President in English, with the US President reciprocating in Chinese. Even the French leader, who on principle rarely spoke English although he spoke it fluently, was happily chatting with the Australian leader in English.

When all present appeared to have had their fill Jesus addressed them making English his language of choice, not that it mattered, the thirteen leaders having become instantly multilingual: "Before I explain to you why you are here I would like you to join me in my communion." He then took a plate of bread provided by Zachariah, broke it up into small portions and moved along the front of the table inviting all us to take a portion, which we all did. As he did so he recited to each of us the following words: "Take, eat…This is my body." After eating a portion himself he indicated that he wanted the rest of us to do the same, which of course we did.

At this point Zachariah re-entered the room with a chalice full of wine, but not any old chalice. I immediately recognised it as the one he'd used at the Last Supper two thousand years ago; the one that had been later purchased by a Crusader in a bazaar and brought back to England. There it had ended up as the communion chalice, used every Sunday morning in Ribbleswell Parish Church. Jesus saw me staring at it and winked: "…Decided to retrieve what was rightfully mine, before I met you on the top of Pen-y-Ghent…It was in my haversack at the time, but decided not to tell you…I didn't want you jumping to any conclusions."

I whispered to Angel: "I stopped jumping to conclusions as far as Jesus was concerned, some time ago."

He took the chalice from Zachariah, held it above his head with both hands, said a prayer, then drank. Again he walked in front of the table, but this time he invited us to drink from the chalice. As we did so he recited to each of us: "This is my blood that I shed for many."

It was to say the least a strange sight, seeing the leaders of the former non-believer brigade taking Holy Communion. I wondered what their countries' citizens would have made of it had they witnessed the sight.

The serious part of the meeting now over Jesus explained to the thirteen leaders why they were there, and it was certainly a 'no punches pulled' performance: "My Father, a caring, loving and compassionate Father, has decided in his wisdom to give mankind on Earth one final chance to amend its selfish, greedy and couldn't-t-care-less ways…This is the 'deal' - He is prepared to roll back time to the point just before the asteroid, given the code 2022LZ31, split into two pieces and impacted on the Earth…This means that all of you will be resurrected and returned to the point where you were before the tsunami struck." He looked across at the US President and smiled: "I believe, Mr President, that you were exploring Disneyland's 'World of Harry Potter' with your family at the time." The President nodded.

"And you, Prime Minister..." His eyes focused on the United Kingdom PM: "...were in the process of landing a good sized tuna, just off the French coast." The PM also nodded.

"On your return, around your necks will be one of the pieces of pot that make up my Holy Square...Some of you may remember re-assembling it at the United Nations way back in 2012."

I expected him to make some comment about the Iranian leader arriving two days late to that event, but he didn't, presumably not wanting to embarrass him. He did however say more: "Professor Robertshaw, who you have all seen before, will distribute the pieces to you in a few minutes' time...Those who took part in the 2012 ceremony will be given the same piece...Those who weren't there will be given the piece your predecessor placed in the Square."

At this point I panicked. How the hell was I expected to remember who placed which piece in the Square? Jesus detected my look and nodded as if to say – you'll be ok – and he was right, too, for I immediately remembered the order...quite an achievement after a lapse of ten years.

I moved into a position so that the Square was in front of me on the table. I slowly opened the catch and lifted the glass lid. To my surprise this revealed a bundle of thin black leather laces tied in a loose knot lying on top of the pieces of pot. I easily untied it. Next I picked up the Square making sure it was level so that no piece fell out, and moved to the front of the table. Then, in turn, I extracted each piece and gave it to the relevant leader along with a black leather lace. The order was as follows:-

τ – America
υ - Australia
α – Brazil
o – China
ρ – France
ρ – Germany
$\Theta\pi$ – Iran

ν - Israel
o - Japan
ε - North Korea
α - Russia
ε - South Africa
ν - United Kingdom

Without being told, each leader threaded the lace through the tiny hole in the piece of pot, tied the two ends to make a loop and placed it over their heads, allowing the piece to rest on their chests.

Jesus still had more to say, this being the principle part of his Father's ultimatum: "Wherever you are when you return to Earth, and some of you will be hundreds, even thousands of kilometres away, you will return home immediately, meet up with your Governments, then in ten days' time make yourselves available at United Nations Headquarters in New York in order to re-assemble my Holy Square…You will then make a speech to the Assembly where you will state in no uncertain terms what your country intends to do in the next twelve months …yes, twelve months…to improve the World…your World for the benefit of mankind…My Father is looking for massive, ground-breaking schemes to improve the environment, the lot of poor people, World poverty and financial equality…To make the World a safer place by clamping down on militant groups and terrorists and the increasing phenomenon of piracy…My Father wants to see the institution of marriage between a man and a woman strengthened, and a much greater emphasis on the way our children are being brought up in what appears to be a sexually driven World, and this means a radical shake-up of the Internet and its social networks…I could go on, but these are some ideas to be going on with…Please don't treat this ultimatum as some idle threat, with the attitude…he'll give us another chance, and another, and another…Believe me, to coin a typical American phrase – you are drinking in the last chance saloon."

Strange as it may seem, there were nods of agreement at all that Jesus had said. The World had become a horrible place to live, and things had to change for the better. But Jesus wanted more than a mere nod. He wanted a verbal commitment: "Do you agree with my Father's terms, if so, say 'Aye' as I ask each of you." He then moved down the line asking each one in turn. There were thirteen 'Ayes'.

After the holy communion ceremony and his 'ultimatum' speech Jesus invited all of us to move from our seated positions at the table to one where we could look over the room's large balcony. We should have been looking down onto a large courtyard, except that the courtyard wasn't there. It had been replaced by a direct view of the Earth below us.

As in a SciFi film we could see it as a giant ball moving through space, but whereas most distant shots of the planet showed its beauty –

the distinctly shaped continents surrounded by water and the polar ice caps. Named the 'Blue Planet', it had been a good description. But what we were now looking down on looked nothing like this. The continents looked nothing like their former familiar selves, their coastlines having disappeared under the expanding circles of water as the two tsunamis advanced. The familiar mountain ranges of the Himalayas, the Andes and the Rockies enabled me to get my bearings, but I had to guess where the Pyrenees, the Alps and the Atlas mountains were.

As sixteen pairs of eyes stared down at a scene that showed a mortally wounded planet Jesus asked us to watch carefully. The two irregular shaped circles that indicated the tsunamis' wave fronts appeared to have stopped, although at that distance one couldn't be certain. Then, before our very eyes, the circles started to contract. The movement was barely visible at first, but quickly speeded up. As this took place land that had previously been under water was now being revealed. There could be only one explanation – the two tsunamis had 'run out of steam' and were now receding, a process that would ultimately end when all the waters had returned to the craters created by the two impacting asteroids.

Suddenly, and without warning, the leader of Israel simply disappeared, soon followed by the Russian leader. The leaders of China, North Korea and Iran were next. Both Angela and I, puzzled looks on our faces, asked Jesus what was going on.

He explained: "What you are witnessing is not due to the tsunamis receding…Their wave fronts would have continued expanding outwards until the two eventually met."

More puzzled looks from Angela and I.

Jesus continued and his explanation not only surprised us, it worried us: "Within the last few hours my Father has discovered some very disturbing happenings out in deep space…I cannot say anymore at the moment…All will be revealed at a later date…As a result of this he has decided to give mankind another chance because it needs to be at full strength for what is to come."

'Be at full strength for what is to come', what the devil is he on about?

Jesus put us half in the picture: "My Father has decided to move time back to just before the asteroid split into two…He will then direct it away from the Earth."

"So all that we have witnessed taking place – the two asteroid impacts, the resulting seismic shocks, air blasts and tsunamis, didn't…So what happens to all those people who lost their lives?" I was determined to put Jesus on the spot.

Although his reply surprised us we were able to see his, or rather his Father's reasoning: "The experience of dying and the reasons for it will be permanently imprinted in their memories, and will be there even though the time has moved back and they are again alive…The elements of both thankfulness on their behalves and forgiveness on My Father's must be present."

"A bit of a frightener, then?" I ventured.

"Yes…You could say that…Now, why have the leaders of Israel, Russia, China, Iran and North Korea disappeared?…Let me explain…Asthe tsunamis retreat, the result of my Father's 'going back in time', their wave fronts eventually pass the points where the leaders were originally engulfed…They will find themselves alive at that point, but the happenings that they have experienced will also be imprinted in their memories, and for the reasons I have already given…Soon it will be our turn to depart."

And he was right, too, for we were indeed the next to 'go'. I could only assume that the leaders who hadn't disappeared would eventually do so as the two retreating tsunamis passed their original 'death' points.

I suddenly felt lightheaded, physically sick, almost drunk, followed by what must have been a state of unconsciousness. Inevitably I asked myself the question – am I being 'resurrected', or is a different process taking place?

What seemed only seconds later, although to be honest I had no concept of time, I suddenly found myself on the summit of Pen-y-Ghent wearing my outdoor gear. Angela was already there in similar attire, and in the blink of an eye Jesus materialised also in his outdoor clothing.

But where was Tala? In the process of our going back in time she had somehow got lost, or so it seemed. I shouted in desperation: "Tala…Tala."

Jesus, concerned at my despair, quickly responded: "She's still on your smallholding in Heaven sunning herself in the paddock…You will be unable to bring her back, but I can." He lifted his eyes to Heaven and whispered: "Please Father may it be thy will that Tala is returned to us."

Almost immediately Tala 'landed' some twenty metres away and came bounding towards me. But was this her spirit, or her real body? I soon found out when she launched herself at me and almost knocked me over. She was real, as were Angela, Jesus and of course myself.

As I looked around me everything was blurred and I immediately realised that my brain tumour was still with me. Time had in fact gone back to a point before Jesus had cured me.

As I screwed my eyes up trying to focus, Jesus twigged what was wrong. He moved across to where I was standing, gently placed his hands on my head and spoke: "Please, Father, remove this demon from my friend."

Again I smiled, demon indeed, why not tumour? But I'd certainly no intentions of arguing the point. Instead I whispered the words: "Thank you."

I looked outwards at the now crystal clear scene and soon spotted the group of walkers on Plover Hill in their red, yellow and blue anoraks. It was anybody's guess at what was going through their minds at the moment. I had to assume that they too had the earlier experiences imprinted in their memories.

As I looked to the east and south the rolling landscape looked dry and undisturbed as it did before the tsunami had struck, the result of the roll back in time. To the west was Ingleborough in all its glory, and just behind it on the horizon I thought I could just make out the shimmering sea. Was that the front of the now receding tsunami, I wondered? Or had it never been there in the first place? Confusion. Confusion. Confusion.

As Angela and I were preparing to descend to Horton-in-Ribblesdale by the same route we'd used earlier to ascend, earlier being almost two days ago, several questions for Jesus flashed through my mind, all being of the utmost importance: "Where is the Holy Square?...The last time I saw it was...er... up there..." I pointed skywards, or was it heavenwards? "...minus its thirteen pieces of pot...But don't you need it in New York in ten days' time?"

Jesus smiled: "Er...I don't, but you do, or will...I want you to be there to organise the re-assembly of my Holy Square as you did ten years ago...And regarding where it is, it's in the pouch of my anorak." He pulled across the zip, carefully extracted it and handed it to me.

On receiving it I couldn't help but notice the roughness of its construction. The angular cuts at the ends of all the sections (I stopped counting after ten), were way out. Most of the angles were 60°, but some were 30° and the pieces making up the four corners 45°. I remembered drawing lines on the thin wood strips using a protractor and cutting them with a saw with a blade that was far too thick. I then sandpapered the ends, making matters worse. Having glued the pieces in place I also remembered trying to disguise the inaccuracies by filling the gaps with plastic wood. Still the joints stood out like a sore thumb. Surely I could do better.

But would it be all right to have another go? I decided to ask Jesus: "May I construct another Square?...I'm not happy with this one."

"By all means...The one I made two thousand years ago was very similar to yours, but the wood was darker...God knows (sorry Father) what happened to it, but I suspect that Zachariah hid it to avoid any sort of recrimination, and just forgot where he'd put it."

I thought to myself - what a find that would be if it turned up in some bricked up cavity in the cellar of a house being demolished in or near Jerusalem. Like the thirteen pieces of pot it would be priceless, and together they would be the most valuable item in the whole world. I felt like asking Jesus why his Father hadn't 'tracked' it, like Tala could be tracked using her microchip? But thought better of it. I'm sure his answer would have been beyond my comprehension, involving some sort of 'box of tricks' to detect carbon-14.

My next question was about communication, or rather the lack of it. Just before the two asteroids had struck the Earth a giant explosion had taken place on the surface of the Sun. This had sent a stream of high energy particles towards the Earth that had put out of action all forms of communication. This had included all equipment containing electronic circuitry, even the humble digital wristwatch. The result of this had been to make the World's population completely unaware of what was happening...until the seismic shock, air blast and tsunami hit them. I asked Jesus when he thought normal communication would be resumed. His answer surprised me.

"Ah, let me explain...Before my Father allows this to happen it is essential that all mankind, and animals too although it is not important to them, should have their recent experiences imprinted in their memories...I believe I earlier explained the reason for this to you ...The two tsunamis are still receding and there are areas in the world that are still under water, for example the Azores in the Atlantic Ocean and the Islands of Samoa in the Pacific Ocean...Only when their peoples are back with the living will my Father allow all forms of communication to resume."

I looked at him, puzzled. It all sounded so complicated...And more was to come.

"It is of course very likely, indeed certain, that some people who were already living on high ground or managed to make their way to it were not reached by the two tsunamis and were therefore not engulfed by it.. They therefore did not die and may not even be aware that the Earth was hit by an asteroid...Some may have been able to look down into the valleys below and see the swirling waters, but how many, I wonder? "

My puzzled look had now changed to an eye-glazed-over expression as my mind had lost all sense of reasoning. And what he said next only made matter worse.

"Of course they too will experience time moving backwards, and when my Father restores all the various forms of communications they will all be displaying information that those watching will have already seen and heard...Any electronic device displaying the date and time will show them having gone backwards...What these people will make of this, God only knows...Sorry Father for the blasphemy."

And Jesus hadn't finished: "We therefore have four groups of people:

- Those who were engulfed by the tsunami and lost their lives. When time moved back they discovered that they were alive and well. But imprinted in their memories was all they'd experienced.
- Those who lived on high ground, made it to high ground or were beyond the tsunamis' wave fronts when they started to recede. None of these people died, but the restoration of communication made them acutely aware of what had happened...something that they will remember for the rest of their lives.
- Those who are the Leaders, just thirteen in number. They all lost their lives when the tsunami engulfed them, only to re-appear at the points where they were engulfed. They are fully aware of what has happened, including their appearance at my Last Supper. There they were given the thirteen pieces of pot with the instruction that they must appear with it at the UN in order to re-assemble the Holy Square. There they will also be expected to make a speech setting out their country's intentions for making the World a better place for all that inhabits it.
- We ourselves, just three in number. We did not lose our lives to the tsunami, but rose directly into Heaven where we witnessed the devastating effect of it. You two later joined me at my Last Supper and took part in the distribution of the pieces of pot to the thirteen Leaders. Finally the three of us were returned to the

summit of Pen-y-Ghent when my Father rolled the time back.

"By the way, all members of the animal and plant kingdoms that died when the tsunami struck, also re-appeared alive and in good health as the time rolled back. My Father would not have accepted anything less."

It all sounded so confusing, although Jesus appeared to know what he was talking about. It then occurred to me...If there was no communication, with all electronic equipment having had the equivalent of a nervous breakdown, there could be no flight. The thirteen Leaders who would rely on such a mode of transport would not be able to get home in order to muster support for the imaginative, groundbreaking and far reaching programmes to improve the World, that were hopefully going through their minds at this very moment.

I pointed this out to Jesus and he responded: "Ah...never thought of that...I'll get my Father to solve the problem straight away."

Seconds later the small digital radio that at that moment was lying at the bottom of my rucksack burst into sound with Queen's *'We are the Champions'*, and Angela's wristwatch started to bleep, indicating that the battery needed charging. As soon as she exposed it to the sun the bleeping stopped. It appeared that 'communication' was back in business.

It was inevitable that news flashed round the World at the proverbial speed of light and it wasn't long before the vast majority of the World's population realised that something very strange had happened to them, something involving a devastating tsunami that had killed them...and yet there they were unscathed...How? Not surprising, the word 'miracle' was bandied around.

But some people apparently had not suffered in any way at all...Why? Questions! Questions!

So, the next question was...had the asteroid actually struck the Earth, or not? The World's leading astronomers had predicted that without doubt it would. There was no possibility of it missing the Earth at the last minute, so to speak. Collision was inevitable. And there was concrete evidence to that effect from those who had been on high ground and had not only felt the seismic shock and the air blast, but many had also seen the swirling waters of the tsunamis as they had advanced, then receded, through the valleys below.

The evidence was less convincing for the vast majority who only had their memories to rely on. But how reliable were those images? Could they be memories of events that they had previously seen on their televisions, images of which there'd been many leading up to the predicted asteroid collision? There had certainly been disaster films where people had lost their lives to huge tsunamis.

By now the World's thirteen Leaders had arrived home. Their first task was to put their respective governments in the picture, before addressing their nations. When they did the latter some were surprisingly open on what had happened to them, leaving their peoples in no doubt.

***

Chapter Forty Six

Back at our smallholding Angela and I, with Tala fast asleep at our feet, sat glued to the television screen as the UK Prime Minister made his speech to the nation. We assumed that similar speeches were being made across the World, not only by the privileged 'thirteen', but also by the leaders of all the other nations once they knew what had happened, and what was required of them, for all nations were expected to make some contribution to world improvement.

What was interesting, and something I had never ever seen before, was the way the PM's speech was broadcast on every single TV channel. There was no way of flicking channels to avoid it. One could of course play a game or watch a film. Alternatively one could simply switch off. And in consultation with all the Providers the Government was able to get the Internet switched off for the length of the speech. It was all a bit 'Big Brotherish', but maybe necessary.

Angela, assuming that she knew what words the PM would probably be using, had a thought: "I wonder what the peoples of Russia, China and all the other non-believing peoples of the World will make of an ultimatum made by a God they do not recognise?"

She certainly had a point.

Just before the PM commenced his speech I set the recorder. I wanted to listen to his words at least a couple of times in order to check the accuracy of what he had to say.

"As all of you are aware it was predicted some time ago that an asteroid of considerable size would strike the Earth, the predicted date being the 24th June 2022."
He failed to mention God's ten-year ultimatum.
"This asteroid, classed as a code RED on the Torino Scale…"
He failed to mention what this meant. Maybe he didn't know.
"…would in effect annihilate all human life, most animal life and much of the vegetation…It would be the end of the World, Our World…So, did this asteroid impact actually take place? …Well, yes it did…In fact the asteroid split into two pieces just before impact, one part crashing into the North Atlantic, the other into the South Pacific…How do I know this when all other citizens of the United Kingdom do not?"

Had he forgotten that Angela and I, living in the UK, also knew?

"Good question....As most of you are aware, because it was well publicised at the time, I was attending a conference in the French coastal resort of La Rochelle along with the leaders of other members of the European Union."

I don't suppose he could have mentioned that he'd been fishing.

"Earlier all communication on Earth had broken down, the result of a massive explosion on the surface of the Sun which sent a stream of high energy particles towards the Earth...This damaged everything that contained electronic circuitry, from the complicated navigation systems in aircraft to the humble household washing machine...Because of this breakdown in communication no one in the British Isles was aware that the asteroids had struck the Earth...It was only when the great tidal wave, known as a tsunami, struck, that most of you became aware of what had happened...Unfortunately at that precise moment you lost your lives...What happened next you are going to find hard to believe, but take my word for it, it actually happened."

This was going to be good.

"God above decided to give mankind another chance, for a reason that he has not yet given us ...He did this by moving time back to just before the asteroid struck the Earth...In fact he changed its orbit to ensure it wouldn't...This of course meant that you regained your lives...I know it sounds strange, even impossible, but the fact that you are sitting at this moment in your living rooms watching and listening to me, proves that what I say is true."

He could have asked them to check that being engulfed by a giant tsunami was firmly imprinted in their memories, but chose not to.

"Again I pose the question that I'm sure all of you are asking yourselves – how does he know all this, but we don't?...It is sufficient at this point to say that I do, along with the twelve most powerful Leaders in the World."

I suppose that he could have mentioned that he had attended, along with the other Leaders, a 'last supper' organised by Jesus Christ, this time in Heaven.

"We too lost our lives when the tsunami struck, but in our case we entered Heaven and were given an ultimatum by God that unless we committed our nations to making far-reaching improvements to the World, to the benefit of mankind, but also to include all animal and plant life, the end of the World would not be some science fiction fairy tale...It

would definitely take place...We were told that we had to show our commitment in two distinct ways:

1) *By placing a small piece of coloured pot into a specially shaped wooden square, known as Christ's Holy Square, at the UN Headquarters in New York as we did ten years ago...Remember God's ultimatum then which we failed to meet, hence the new ultimatum now...This has to take place in just ten days' time and I will be leaving for New York tomorrow to meet up, hopefully, with the other twelve Leaders.*

2) *To give a speech setting out what contribution the United Kingdom intends to make to improve the World...I will be working on that speech between now and making my journey across the Atlantic.*

"So now you know as much as I do about the strange happenings over the last couple of days...There is no doubt in my mind that God's ultimatum is real and that if no improvements are made, and quickly, he will wreak his vengeance on us all...This no idle threat."

I suppose he could have gone on to describe how this would happen and when, but chose not to. Maybe he felt that he had said enough. I did however know because Jesus had told me. The asteroid that had just missed the Earth would continue its journey, rounding the Sun before heading back into the depths of the Solar System. In so doing it would again cross the Earth's orbit when the planet was at that exact spot. The resulting collision would take place in exactly one hundred days' time. God had chosen this for his 'final showdown' with mankind.

The PM finally rounded off his speech: *"The policies that the United Kingdom will be introducing will be unpopular to many people, making huge changes to their daily lives...The emphasis will be on major environmental improvements; equality at home and an attack on poverty overseas...But it has to be done and I expect all of you to support me...Good night and God bless you all."*

At this point the transmission ended, to be replaced by pictures of 10 Downing Street, Buckingham Palace and several other well-known places throughout the United Kingdom including Liverpool's Liver Building, York Minster and the River Forth rail bridge. All this was accompanied by a choir singing *I vow to thee my country* from Gustav

Holst's Planet Suite – "Jupiter - The Bringer of Jollity". It could have been worse. "Mars - The Bringer of War", being chosen instead.

As the music commenced, Angela and I sang the words that had been written by Sir Cecil Spring Rice sometime during the nineteenth century. It was one of several hymns that we had learned off by heart at our primary schools many, many moons ago.

The following morning I was on the move early. After taking Tala for a quick walk I snatched a slice of toast and a cup of strong coffee, before retiring to my study. It was time to commence my re-construction of Christ's Holy Square.

My first task was to locate my original scale drawing of the Square. All the diagrams, notes, maps, photos etc that I had in my possession were in a large box file. All had been prepared or collected by me over the period that had commenced with the discovery of a Roman soldier on a horse in a Yorkshire bog, and ended just after the ascension of Jesus into Heaven ten years ago just after his speech to the UN. Knowing that my filing system was non-existent I proceeded to plough through hundreds of loose sheets.

Luck was obviously on my side for in less than a minute I had located the sheets that I wanted. Although I say it myself the drawing I'd earlier made of Christ's Holy Square was a bit of a masterpiece. All the joints were shown as thin lines and the angles had been measured accurately with a protractor. All the dimensions had been written in and I'd even coloured in the thirteen sections where the pieces of pot went, at the same time writing on each section the appropriate Greek letter in black felt tip pen. Since the glass cover had been an afterthought it wasn't shown on the original diagram.

It was now a case of measuring out the various lengths of the individual pieces of wood from a long length exactly 15 mm square in crossection and cutting them off. For this I had purchased a special saw from the local DIY that would enable me to accurately cut the 90°, 60°, 45° and 30° angles that were required.

It took me the best part of the morning to make all the cuts, taking my time and above all not forcing the saw blade through the wood. As I did this I got to thinking – how did Jesus go about doing this two thousand years ago? What sort of equipment would he have used?

Eventually I ended up with the eighteen pieces that went inside the Square and four pieces that would form the Square itself...quite an achievement I thought to myself. One thing I'd learned from past experience was not to sandpaper the rough edges. How ever carefully you did this you spoiled the angular cut ever so slightly. But the ultimate test was still to come.

My next task was to accurately glue the four outer pieces onto a plywood backing board to make what looked like a picture frame. I already knew that the Square wasn't in fact a square at all, but a slight rectangle. If I didn't get this exactly right the eighteen individual inner pieces would not fit perfectly inside it.

Fortunately I had got it just right, and as I stuck the individual pieces into their correct positions the Square slowly took shape. Had it been sheer skill? Or had there been an element of luck? Had there indeed been some sort of divine intervention, since there seemed to have been plenty of it floating around recently?

My final task was to varnish it to give it that professional look, but before I did so I proudly showed Angela my handiwork. Before passing judgement she disappeared, to appear seconds later with the Square, empty of course, that Jesus had given me earlier. Now for the 'ultimate test'. Was my new Square considerably better that the old one?

Angela compared the two: "Um...Not bad...Not bad at all...Your third attempt is a hundred percent better than your first two...But you haven't done the ultimate test, have you?"

"What's that?" I shouted abruptly.

"To see if all thirteen pieces of pot will fit in perfectly...If they don't it's back to the drawing board...Can't have a situation where the President of the United States can't get his piece into its allotted position...Think of the embarrassment for him and the humiliation for you, with billions watching, the World over."

I knew that she was teasing me, and replied: "Oh ye of little faith."

But she was right. The ultimate test would be when the thirteen Leaders of the World attempt to place their pieces of pot in the positions indicated by me. If one didn't fit I would hope that the earth would open up and engulf me.

All I had to do now was varnish the empty Square, giving the inner sections the thinnest of coatings so that the pieces of pot would not in any way stick once in position. This I did, afterwards placing it on the top of the kiln that was still slightly warm after I'd switched it on in order to heat up the studio. It had been a coolish sort of start to the day for the time of year.

I'd never been happy with the covers that I'd made for the two Squares – the one in my possession and the one still in the British Museum. On both I'd used a picture frame with the backing board removed, glued the glass in then hinged it to the Square so that it opened and closed like a book cover. A crudely made catch kept it in place. It looked a real amateurish job and I was very conscious of the fact.

The following morning whilst in my local DIY store in Skipton I spotted exactly what I wanted - a metre length of wood with an 'L' shaped crossection. Glued upside down along three edges of the Square, a precisely cut piece of glass would neatly slide into the gap…Perfect. Within minutes of arriving home I had finished the construction, including the glass cover. Christ's Holy Square was now ready for its momentous journey across the Atlantic.

Late that afternoon, as Angela and I were inspecting what had to be done in the garden, my mobile that I had placed on the patio table, started to play Dire Straits' *Sultans of Swing* (I was prepared to bet my next month's pension that only I in the whole world had it as their ring tone). I fully expected the call to be from a friend or a past colleague checking up on Angela and I after all this asteroid kerfuffle.

A refined male voice, Oxbridge almost certainly, came on the line: "I wish to speak to Professor Robertshaw…Is he available?"

I felt like shouting into the mobile - of course I'm bloody available, but resisted doing so. Instead I answered courteously: "Peter Robertshaw speaking…Can I help you?"

Oh, hello Professor…I'm speaking from 10 Downing Street on behalf of the Prime Minister…It is his desire that you and your wife join his party on its flight to JFK Airport late tomorrow afternoon…Accommodation has already been arranged for you at a hotel just round the corner from the British Consulate in New York."

This welcome invitation came completely out of the blue. I had envisaged combing the Internet for the cheapest flight and accommodation, no doubt paying well over the odds.

The voice on the other end of the line assuming, as it happened quite rightly, that I would accept, continued: "I have taken the liberty of sorting out some train times for you…If you catch the 08.53 Carlisle to Leeds train, which calls at Horton-in-Ribblesdale at 10.24, this will give you ample time to catch the Leeds to London train at 11.05…You will then be picked on your arrival at Kings Cross at 13.38, assuming the train is on time, and taken to Heathrow where the PM will meet you in the Executive Suite...Your flight to JFK is at 15.50 hours...How does all that sound?"

"Brilliant," I shouted into the mobile. I then had a thought...how much would I have to pay, if indeed anything at all? I obviously couldn't ask the PM's spokesperson straight out. I had to be chose my words carefully: "Er...Should I keep any receipts?"

"No need, Professor...I will send all the relevant tickets electronically to you...Just print them out and show them when you board the trains...Obviously you won't need tickets for the flight to JFK." There was then the slightest titter down the line: "By the way...The PM has asked me to remind you not to forget Christ's Holy Square. " At that, the line went dead, the call being at an end.

As I studied the notes that I had hurriedly made during the call I felt a slight degree of satisfaction. The PM rated my presence at the UN meeting as important...maybe even essential.

It was now all hell-let-loose at the Robertshaw household, as Angela and I made our preparations for our short stay in New York. While she stayed at home, packing, I took Tala up to Smiths Farm and arranged for their teenage son, Jamie, to pop down to our smallholding in order to feed the animals while we were away.

Whilst at Smiths Farm the conversation inevitably got onto the PM's speech to the nation and the memories that both Jim, his wife Mary and their children had of being engulfed by the tsunami. They of course assumed that Angela and I had been afflicted in the same way. This placed me in a difficult position. Should I agree that it had been a weird experience and leave it at that? I could hardly say that we'd been 'to Heaven and back' (as opposed to Hell) and as a result had not been hit by the giant wave. I therefore quickly changed the subject, describing my call from the PM's office, and our forthcoming trip to New York. This also enabled me to describe how I saw my role at the UN meeting.

Jim couldn't resist making a comment: "So...You will be carrying out a similar role to that ten years ago, supervising the completion of this Holy Square thing." He had obviously remembered the images he'd seen on his television all those years ago.

The following day our journey down to London and onto Heathrow went without a hitch. The trains were on time. We didn't even find someone occupying our reserved seats, which surprised us because Horton – in-Ribblesdale was the tenth station on the line and the train appeared pretty full. Since the London train started from Leeds we were amongst the first passengers to take up our seats.

As we alighted the train at Kings Cross an exceedingly smart young woman in a fashionable black trouser suit came up to us and introduced herself as Hazel. She would be our escort to Heathrow. But how did she instantly recognise us? There could only have been one answer – the PM's security department must have done its homework. No doubt the department had a dossier on us including photographs that probably went back to the time ten years ago when Angela and I met the archbishops of Canterbury and York at the latter's residence at Bishopthorpe Palace. This had been the starting point that had led up to the re-assembly of Christ's Holy Square at UN Headquarters…and here we were again doing exactly the same thing…Talk about events going round in circles!!!

Hazel took us out of the station where a shiny black Jaguar was obviously waiting for us driven by a man in a flat peaked hat – the chauffeur. As I climbed in I couldn't help but notice the darkened windows. It passed through my mind that the vehicle could also be bullet proof.

In what seemed only a few minutes we pulled into what appeared to be a prohibited area at Heathrow Airport. On entering the building we were asked for our passports, which were first scrutinised then scanned. We were also asked to put our hand luggage through the X-ray machine. For some unexplained reason the young security man asked me to open my attaché case, which I did, not having anything to hide. This revealed of course Christ's Holy Square, wrapped up in a tea-towel, which I unwrapped for him. Hating to see an empty Square I had earlier placed coloured pieces of card, complete with Greek lettering into the thirteen sections. The man studied it closely, puzzled, before asking: "Some sort of kid's game?"

Not wanting to go through a detailed explanation as to what the item was and what part it would be playing at the United Nations in the very near future, I simply nodded, adding: "Yer…For teaching backward kids to read."

He accepted my explanation, apparently not noticing that all the letters were from the Greek alphabet.

After a short walk along a linking corridor we entered a door with 'Executive Suite' displayed on it in gold lettering. Here Hazel introduced Angela and I to the Prime Minister, not aware that the three of us had been together in Heaven just a few days earlier.

The PM's entourage numbered ten and included two familiar faces – those of the Home and Foreign Secretaries. Bearing in mind the nature of his trip to the UN, I suspected that the others covered such areas as Overseas Development, the Environment, Health, maybe even Defence.

We had only been in the air an hour when it was announced that a meal would be served. This news was very welcome to Angela and I since we had last eaten at the unearthly hour of five o'clock that morning. Menus were distributed by the cabin crew and we were invited to make our choices. Both of us chose the *beef wellington* followed by *apple pie and cream*. Angela, being the wine buff, chose a quality French chardonnay, and we rounded our meal off with a liqueur coffee. One thing was obvious – when one travelled with the PM one travelled in style.

After our meal I expected, but did not particularly relish, some sort of conversation, maybe even interrogation, with one of the PM's aides, maybe even the man himself. But no, we were thankfully left alone. This allowed us to doze. Angela quickly fell into a deep sleep, happily snoring away, much to my embarrassment. As I kept tapping her my mind started to speculate how the session at the UN would pan out. My mind inevitably tried to work out how Jesus Nazarene would 'play it'. Presumably he would insist on making a speech at some point, the content of which I could only guess at…but what then? Would we for instance witness another ascension into Heaven, making three in all? I doubted that he would 'go out' that way, so to speak. He'd know that that was already being predicted, and he would hate to be considered predictable. It just wasn't his style.

The rest of the flight was thankfully uneventful, and just after eight in the evening, local time, we touched down at JFK. After being whisked through some sort of special passport control set up for the PM's entourage including of course us, cars were waiting to take us to our hotel. I was worried about our two small suit cases, but was assured that we would find them in our rooms when we arrived at our destination…and they were, too.

Since I had managed little sleep on the plane, and Angela could sleep anytime, anywhere, we both fell onto the huge king sized bed and simply zonked out. Even then my mind was working overtime, trying to envisage how the meeting at the UN would go. For instance, would it be a re-run of the one ten years ago, plus the thirteen Leaders' speeches? I'd no idea.

Finally I did drop off, but of course not off the bed. Being half the size of a badminton court it was impossible to do so.

***

Chapter Forty Seven

Narrator- Peter Robertshaw

The meeting of the United Nations General Assembly was scheduled to commence at twelve noon. This was unusually early, but the Secretary General had no doubt been aware for several days that thirteen speeches, given by thirteen World Leaders would be taking place. These would inevitably take up a considerable amount of time. Even at thirty minutes a speech one was talking about a finishing time well into the early evening. He no doubt hoped that they would not ramble on about the World's present unsatisfactory state being nothing whatever to do with their own country, but at great sacrifice to themselves, his people were prepared to play their part for the greater good. Instead he hoped that the leaders would give a brief outline of what they and their countries intended to do. Twenty minutes' max should be sufficient. Then it would no doubt have occurred to him. Jesus Nazarene would also be present and he would want to address the Assembly. What he would say and how long it would take him to say it was anybody's guess. And would he make another spectacular 'exit'?

By eleven-thirty the following morning all the various parties were assembled in their allotted places. Ensuring maximum security around the vast UN complex had been a nightmare for the police, but fortunately, apart from some minor violations of the city's parking laws, everything had gone smoothly. There were no banners expressing 'SAVE THE WORLD', for that was exactly what the meeting was all about.

I'd arrived at eleven, having left Angela at the hotel. I had earlier convinced her that the day's proceedings would probably be uninteresting, even boring, and suggested that maybe she would like to hunt for bargains in New York's numerous stores. The idea apparently appealed to her.

I of course had Christ's Holy Square with me, minus the pieces of coloured card, and had immediately placed it on a table that I recognised as the one we had used ten years ago. I remembered its strangely carved legs, looking a bit like Red Indian totem poles.

In order to avoid any cock-ups in procedure the Secretary General's aide asked me to check that all thirteen Leaders were there. This presented me with a test of memory for I had to identify thirteen faces I'd last seen a few days ago in Heaven. Finding where they were, or should be, was easy. All I'd to do was look for their country's label, and to my delight all thirteen were there. But what pleased me most of all, for I didn't expect it, was the way all were displaying their individual pieces of coloured pot, on their black leather loops around their necks. It was as if they were displaying them as some sort of badge of honour or achievement, the way Olympic champions displayed their medals when attending functions.

At precisely midday the Secretary General got the proceedings started. He kept his opening address brief, presumably hoping that the thirteen Leaders would take their cue from him and do likewise. He first thanked those in attendance for doing so. He then outlined the procedure he wanted the Leaders to follow. When called by his aide they, in alphabetical order, would approach the table at the front of the Hall, remove the pieces of pot from around their necks and wait for me to snip the leather loop with a pair of scissors so that the loop could be removed. I would then indicate where in the Square the pieces were to go. The Leaders would place them in their alloted positions. Finally they would make their speeches to the Assembly.

It was now a case of getting the procedure started. It seemed fitting that it should be started by the host country, although the UN complex was not considered to be American soil, and the Secretary General called the President of the United States. He, with an air of authority, strode up to my table with a swagger the likes of which I'd seen in so many old cowboy films, removed his piece of pot and waited for me to do my snipping, before placing it in the Square in a section indicated by me. It was the triangular τ piece that went at the top between the two ν pieces. It was the piece that Jesus had given to Matthew two thousand years earlier and had turned up on a Roman soldier, on a horse, in boggy ground beside a Yorkshire river.

The President then took up his place behind the dais, pulled out a single sheet of paper from his jacket inside pocket and placed it on the slightly sloping surface. He was now ready to address not only the General Assembly of the UN, but also the whole world, for the television cameras had already zoomed in.

I had earlier decided that during the speeches I would make a note of proposals which appeared to me to be the most important, and I hoped that God above would agree with my choices.

These were my notes for each speaker:

America – *The setting up of an international humanitarian task force, well resourced, to respond within twenty-four hours to a natural disaster anywhere in the world. (He commented how ashamed he felt that his country had been slow to react to the 2010 earthquake that had devastated Haiti, a small island in America's backyard).*

Australia – *The easing of immigration restrictions. Australia, a huge country in terms of area with a population of just over 40 million, could take in many more people, especially from the overcrowded Indian subcontinent. This would produce a better quality of life for such people.*

Brazil – *An acceptance that allowing the devastation of the Amazonian rain forest had been a huge mistake. Replanting of trees on a massive scale was already in progress and would continue as rapidly as possible. Growth would be inevitably slow, but the action being taken was better than no action at all.*

China – *An appreciation that his country was now the economic dynamo of the world and that this had inevitably led to huge strains on the environment. Initiatives were already in place to improve the situation, especially in the areas of air and water pollution. Being a major nation his country had a role to play in relieving world poverty, especially in Africa. One trade that he was determined to stop was that in ivory, rhino horn and other animal parts. Involvement in Africa would enable him to do this. On the domestic security front his country was concerned about North Korea's military ambitions. These were producing fear and therefore instability in the general region and these were affecting trade with other nations. Meetings between the two countries had already taken place to improve the situation, and many were anticipated.*

France – *Disappointment was expressed at how Africa, a continent that had been heavily colonised by his country in the past and where it should have left a positive legacy, was the most backward continent in the world, with conflict, malnutrition and general poverty all unacceptably high. His country intended to set up as quickly as possible a working party of interested groups to improve the lot of the African people. The road would be bumpy, but the determination was there.*

Germany – First of all a candid acceptance that his country had been responsible for two world wars during the twentieth century, hence his country's reluctance to get involved in any sort of universal army. He did however accept that his country, one of the wealthiest in the world should contribute to reducing poverty, particularly in Africa. His country would therefore be wholeheartedly supporting France's African initiative.

Iran – Following an assurance to the surrounding countries that his country's nuclear aspirations were entirely peaceful, he stated that the programme would continue, but with Russian help. Hopefully this would allay the world's fears. He had already been in talks initiated by China that had also included North Korea. These had taken place, again to allay the world's fears of both nations.

Israel – An acceptance that the present hostile relationship with the Palestinians was responsible for much of the unrest in the Middle East and that positive meetings had already taken place to improve the situation. Regarding his country's attitude towards Iran he felt it necessary to stress that his country had a right to defend itself by any methods it considered appropriate. He did welcome both Russia's and China's involvement with Iran.

Japan – As in the case of Germany there was an acceptance of the role played by his country in the Second World War and this had led to his country's reluctance to get involved militarily in any world conflict, preferring to support environmental and humanitarian initiatives. His country was already the leader in electric car technology, and had stopped whaling in the Antarctic. It would be supporting France in its African initiative. His country did feel threatened by North Korea and expected China to curb that country's nuclear ambitions.

North Korea – An aggressive defence of his country's nuclear and missile programmes, stressing that it had the right to defend itself. Such programmes were inevitably costly and therefore made his citizens poor, but it was a price worth paying. His country was not a threat to other countries and would welcome any initiative on China's behalf to guarantee his country's security. Regarding its relation with South Korea his country was already in meaningful discussions, with reunification high on the agenda.

Russia – A disappointment that his country, a major world player had been unable to exercise more influence in making the World a better place. This would change with immediate effect. His country would *match America, rouble for dollar, in its humanitarian aid initiative, and would also be supporting France in Africa. His country's aid to Iran's nuclear programme would hopefully remove suspicion from that country. On the environmental front his country would soon be the world leader in electric car technology and had already made a breakthrough in the design of a new revolutionary battery.*

South Africa *– First an expression of disappointment that his country, the major one on the African continent, had been unable to exercise any real influence to improve the lives of so many people. It was an embarrassment to his country that Africa, a continent rich in fossil fuels and minerals, with a plentiful supply of sun and rain, can grow anything, and with ample manpower, was so behind the rest of the world. It was indeed a disgrace. His country would willingly work alongside other countries, such as France, Germany and China to rapidly improve the situation. Like the Chinese leader he too was determined to stop the trade in animal parts, especially ivory.*

Finally it was the turn of the Prime Minister of the United Kingdom to place the final piece of pot in Christ's Holy Square. As he approached me he winked, a simple way of showing recognition. A quick snip with the scissors and his piece, one of the two **v** pieces, was released from its black leather loop. Since there was only one vacant space in the Square I did not need to indicate to him where it went. Christ's Holy Square was now complete. I never thought I's see the day again, but here it was.

The PM then moved to his position behind the dais, extracted his notes from his jacket inside pocket and placed them in front of him. It was only then that I realised that all thirteen Leaders had used notes, some clearly hand written. Why, I wondered? Had the notes been hurriedly drafted together on the Leaders' planes to New York? The Assembly Hall had a sophisticated autocue type system that enabled the speaker to wirelessly link any type of recording equipment to it. The text could then be displayed in most of the world's languages on a screen in front of the speaker that was invisible to the Assembly. An instant translation in the required language was wirelessly sent to the various delegations…But not one Leader had used the technology. In a world dominated by electronic gadgets that could do almost anything, pen and paper had still been used…Quite unbelievable!

Of all thirteen speeches the one that I was without doubt most interested in was the one to be given now…the one by my Prime Minister…the one that would declare to the world what my country was prepared to do. I would be listening to it very closely and no doubt making copious notes about it.

The United Kingdom *– In the past Britain, with its huge Empire covering a good proportion of the inhabited world, had assumed a sort of world policeman role – send a gunboat – being an expression occasionally heard even now, albeit jokingly. That position changed many years ago as members of that Empire gained their independence. But the United Kingdom found it difficult to sit back on its laurels and let the rest of the world get on with it. It had fought in two world wars and Korea, kept out of Vietnam, but did get involved in Iraq and Afghanistan. It then gave support to those who wanted to change the regimes in Ethiopia, Egypt, Libya and Syria. Even today it still continues to exercise influence throughout the world and is at present one of the five permanent members of the UN Security Council, alongside the USA, China, Russia and France.*

But now it has a new challenge, one laid down by God himself – to improve conditions on Earth for the benefit of all life upon it – not only human, but also all animal and plant life.

It is clear to all that the continent of Africa is the world's biggest headache. In fact one world leader who preferred to remain anonymous recently referred to the continent as a 'basket' case.

This should have provoked a hostile vocal response from the leaders of the African nations, but it didn't, the comment having received worldwide coverage only a few days earlier. Besides, they knew it was true.

As stated earlier, this continent has everything – ample sun and water, a huge range of vegetation, oil and gas, unimaginable mineral wealth and a massive willing workforce. But many areas are riddled with corruption, poverty, malnutrition, disease and with low life expectancy. One has to address the question – Why? Why have the African nations been unable to 'get their act together' to make their continent a success? Why did the continent of South America, similar to Africa, although smaller, develop along different lines and is now looked upon as a successful continent, with one country, Brazil, one of the world's leading nations?

It is for this reason that Britain has decided to make the continent of Africa its number one priority. Along with its European neighbour Germany it will be supporting France in its African initiative – the aim being a United Nations of Africa, where health, wealth, education and general prosperity will top the agenda. Of course South Africa, as stated earlier by its leader, will also play a major role in this initiative. The journey will be bumpy, and at times seem impossible to complete, but if the will is there success will ultimately be achieved.

Understandably, there were gasps from the various African contingents, both Britain and France always having been looked upon with suspicion, going back to colonial days. But all of them knew that Africa as a continent could not continue failing its people as it had done for so long. The PM continued:

On the environment front within Europe the UK has at last been able to exercise influence on the EU's fishing policy which had dictated that the quite mad practice of throwing back millions of tonnes of dead fish a year in order to supposedly preserve stocks, was to be stopped.

Finally on our domestic front we are pushing ahead with our 'buy an electric car' policy, our nuclear energy programme is on track and this will see the elimination of all our coal fired power stations. Our domestic recycling programme is one of the best in Europe. Poverty both in young and old has all but been eliminated.

Ten years ago the United Kingdom took God's words, as expressed through his son, Jesus Christ, to heart and we will continue to do so.

The PM looked across to where Jesus was sitting and gently nodded his head. Jesus in turn nodded back. No other Leader had mentioned him in their speech.

Policies both at domestic and international levels were introduced to enhance the wellbeing of people both at home and abroad. Our animal welfare policies are already without doubt the best in the world, but we feel that there is still much to do on that front. We welcome Japan's whaling ban and support wholeheartedly those countries that are determined to stop the trade in animal parts especially ivory. I know, having spoken personally to Jesus, that his Father has been appalled at the way so many of the world's animals, all his creations, are treated. Jesus said that his Father had always accepted that animals would provide food for man. All he wanted was for man to give them the best life they could whilst alive, and to slaughter them as humanely as possible. We have consistently failed him here and are still doing so. I do not need to go into details. You should be aware of the practices used in your own countries, and if you aren't I suggest that you familiarise yourselves with them.

At these words an element of fury rushed through my veins, and had not the PM been addressing such an esteemed Assembly I would have certainly take him to task. For years in the UK the slaughter of animals according to Halal Law had been practised, much to the disapproval and protestations of the non-muslim population, who are still well in the majority. Successive governments have turned a blind eye and a deaf ear in, as they've consistently put it, the interests of racial harmony. One thing that was certain…I would be taking this up with him when we got back to the UK…maybe even during the return journey on the plane. I have never been able to stand hypocrisy. One thing was certain – both Jesus and his Father would have made a note of the PM's dual standards. *God has decided to give mankind another chance. Do we deserve it? I doubt it. It is now up to us not to let him down. We have set out what we intend to do to make the World, our World, a safer place where we can all live in harmony and lead fulfilled lives. As a top priority we must attack world poverty, and in doing this we will get on top of malnutrition, disease and poor education. Let us now return home, inform our people what is expected of them, and get on with our declared intentions.*

The PM stood perfectly still for several seconds as if drained of energy and waiting for it to return. He then slowly turned round and nodded to the Secretary General indicating that he had finished. He in turn returned the nod. I glanced at my watch. The time was exactly six-thirty. The PM, my PM, had spoken for forty minutes, longer than any other speaker. To be fair, they had kept their speeches brief with lots of vague statements of intent, but little actually set in concrete. Maybe they hadn't had time to add the 'meat to the bone', so to speak. Of course it could have all been a bit of bluff – giving the impression that they were full of ideas, committed to making a difference, but when it came to delivering, it would all be lacking. It was always the risk one took when giving the benefit of the doubt to others. God obviously knew that, but still went ahead. Hopefully man would not let him down, even though man did not have a good record on that score.

As all those present, feeling that the proceedings were now at an end, started to prepare for their exit from the Assembly Hall, Jesus Nazarene, who had been sitting by my side throughout the session moved across to where the Secretary General was sitting. He whispered something into his ear and there was no doubt in my mind what was said. It was a request to address the Assembly.

The Secretary General rose and indicated with the palms of his hands pointing upwards that he wanted the Assembly to come to order. This it reluctantly did…not surprising because those assembled had been bombarded with good intentions for the best part of seven hours, with only a short recess after the Iranian leader had spoken. If those present felt anything like me they were drained of mental energy and were also famished.

The Secretary General spoke: "To round off the session I have asked Mr Jesus Nazarene, a person who is well known to many of you, to say a few words…I understand that he has some very disturbing news for us…Jesus Nazarene."

This immediately puzzled me. I had spent time with him on Pen-y-Ghent Hill, at a re-enactment of the Last Supper in Heaven and during the long session in the Assembly Hall. We had discussed a great deal, covering many areas, but on no occasion had he said anything that could be remotely described as 'disturbing'. I was in for a big surprise.

Jesus moved to the dais. He'd no notes, not that he needed any. He was indeed the artist when it came to public speaking having years of practice, albeit two thousand years ago. He first thanked all those present who had contributed to the session, knowing full well that some would not fulfilltheir promises to make the world a better place. He then initially paused in order for his audience to focus on him, wondering what was coming next.

"Over the last few hours I have listened to the Leaders of the most powerful nations on Earth declare how they intend to cooperate together on joint projects in a variety of areas – peace and stability, the environment, health and welfare – to name but a few…But when you have heard what I have to say you will realise just how essential this cooperation will be, especially cooperation between the major military powers, although all nations will need to make a contribution."

One could hear the gasps at Jesus's last sentence. There was puzzlement written across the faces of many in the Hall. Was this man actually suggesting that the likes of America, Russia, China, even France and the UK, should pool their military expertise in some sort of joint military project? If so, for what purpose? The Americans and Russians already had joint space projects such as the space station and there was already talk of a joint mission to Mars. Both nations were also confident that by pooling their expertise a mission could be mounted to combat any future asteroid threat provided its discovery was early enough to take action. The World's leading virologists were confident that they had the know-how to get on top of, and eliminate any rogue virus that either evolved on Earth or came in from outer space. The world's leading environmentalists felt that they were already getting on top of the problems caused by climate change. And the commitment made by the Leaders today would hopefully make conflict between nations permanently a thing of the past. So…what else was there to fear? Jesus proceeded to put us right.

"What I'm going to say now, please do not treat as some sort of joke or make-believe threat…The information has come directly from my Father in Heaven…If you are inclined to snigger at information coming from that source I would suggest that you speak to any one of the Leaders who have appeared at this dais today…They know the true picture."

Any thought of having a behind-the-hand snigger at this Jesus guy's communication with his Father (did he use electronic mail?), quickly disappeared. He appeared to be deadly serious.

After a slight pause, just to let his words sink in, Jesus continued: "My Father has informed me that the Earth…your Earth, my Earth, has been under observation by an alien power ever since your scientists discovered radio communication, and radio signals started being transmitted out into deep space….Some of you I'm sure are aware that the nearest star system to our solar system is that of Alpha Centauri a mere four light years away…Perhaps I could remind you that light travels at 300 000 kilometres a second, as do radio waves, so the Alpha Centauri system is so far away that light leaving it at this phenomenal speed will reach us in four years…It follows that radio signals transmitted from Earth in the direction of our nearest star system also will take four years…For example members of such an alien power could have watched the 2016 Olympics in Rio de Janeiro just two years ago had they wanted to do so, the TV signals arriving sometime during 2020…The signals from the 2018 Football World Cup in Russia will already be well on their way and may be eagerly awaited if they haven't already arrived."

At these last words smiles went round the Assembly, The thought of some alien power watching our Olympics and the World Cup somehow appealing to those present. Maybe in years to come some sort of event could take place between us and them.

Jesus's next words quickly put an end to such thoughts: "This alien power, a very advanced people have developed the means of travelling across deep space at speeds only dreamt of on Earth…Their space crafts are able to travel at a quarter the speed of light meaning that a journey from their system to ours takes about sixteen years... My father has informed me that a massive invasion force has already taken off heading for Earth...Its arrival could be in as little as twelve years' time...some time during the year 2034...The question is, when the time comes what will we on Earth be able to do to combat such an invasion?"

He paused to allow his message and question to sink in. The rumble of noise produced by numerous conversations came from all areas of the Hall, and this also included a few words that passed between the Secretary General's aide and myself.

"How can his Father possibly know that?...NASA hasn't identified any threat from deep space."

My reply was short and to the point: "Well, he is the God Almighty."

In a lull in the noise level Jesus continued: "The ensuing battle that will take place will be on a scale beyond our present comprehension...What took place in World War II will pale into insignificance by comparison...One thing is certain, it will have to take place out in space, otherwise planet Earth as we know it will be destroyed forever...What is equally certain, a whole new range of weaponry will need to be developed, and it is in this area where cooperation between nations will have to take place...New space craft will have to be developed, armed with weaponry that will be able to overcome the enemy and win the war...May I suggest that your scientists look at the armoury seen in the many films that have been made on the subject of war in space, such as Star Wars and even Star Trek, in order to get some idea of what may well be required, science fiction may indeed need to become science fact."

Initially there were more behind-the-hand sniggers at Jesus's words...Star Wars and Star Trek indeed...But soon the words sank in as those assembled realised the seriousness of the situation, assuming of course that God's words, predicting this future conflict, were true. Was there some sort of sign that his Son could give mankind that the impending threat was very real?

Jesus read the minds of those present. He knew exactly what they were thinking. They wanted evidence, and he was prepared to give them some:

"Six months ago radio telescopes in both the northern and southern hemispheres picked up an object in space somewhere between the orbits of Mars and the Earth...It was already known to be an asteroid about the size of a large house and its orbit had been accuratedly plotted…It would pass within the orbit of the moon at a distance of about 300 000 kilometres from Earth…It presented no threat…Then the observers saw that the asteroid split into two…Although a rare event it had been seen before and caused no alarm, even when the smaller piece changed course and headed directly for the Earth. Being only the size of a double decker bus it would simply burn up in the atmosphere…But this object, being made of a material with too high a melting point, didn't and for a very good reason…It wasn't an asteroid at all but an alien space craft, in fact one from the Alpha Centauri star system…It had used its close proximity to the asteroid to avoid detection before breaking away…It should have landed intact somewhere, but hurricane force winds in the area caused it to crash…What its mission was we will never know."

There was now complete puzzlement on the faces of the Assembly. Why didn't the world at large know about this intrusion?…Well, as Jesus now revealed, a very select group of people did, but the incident was considered so sensitive that a clamp-down on the release of information was immediately enforced.

"The alien craft crashed in the desert some twenty kilometres due north of the Barringer Crater in the Arizona desert, more commonly known as Meteor Crater…It was discovered by a hiker who thought it was some sort of advanced military craft that had crashed…He, using his mobile phone, contacted a news reporter friend who lived in and worked from Flagstaff, only sixty-five kilometres away…Within an hour the reporter was viewing the crash site."

Jesus paused, knowing the effect his words would have. How could he, a mere member of the public with apparently no connections with any scientific, military or political groups, be privy to such Earth-shattering knowledge? Of course, most in the Hall could not get their heads round the fact that he had a personal connection with his Father, God himself.

As the volume of conversation throughout the Hall rose to a deafening level, the topic being obvious, I glanced across to where the American contingent, including the President, were sitting, or rather now standing, he furiously gesticulating to his advisors. I got the impression that he may well not have known anything about the incident, the military having kept it all under wraps. Of course all those in the Hall assumed that he did know, but had kept the information to himself – so much for cooperation between nations, they were no doubt thinking.

The Secretary General struggled to bring the Assembly to order, but eventually did so. It was essential that Jesus Nazarene should continue and reveal what else he knew. When silence had been established he nodded across to the speaker, an indication that he wanted him to continue.

"The reporter, a retired airman, who had flown missions in Vietnam, and more recently in Iraq and Afghanistan, had a vast knowledge of the world's military aircraft, but had seen nothing like the crashed plane, if indeed it was plane, for its unusual design made it virtually impossible for it to stay in the air...He climbed up onto the mangled mass and peered through the transparent canopy using a torch provided by the hiker...To his horror he saw the remains of what could only be described as some sort of creature crumpled up in the cockpit...Its appearance resembling nothing like a human being, but more like the aliens he had seen in some of our science fiction films, the creations of film makers' imaginations."

Jesus's account got more unbelievable by the second, and there was still more to come.

"The reporter immediately contacted a friend who held a senior position in the US Military and put him in the picture...Within the hour helicopters flew in with military personnel and a eight kilometre exclusion zone was created round the crash site...Later the wreckage was transported under wraps to Edwards Air Force Base some six hundred kilometres away...Obviously all the activity was witnessd by local people, but the official version released to the media was that an advanced version of the F-22 had crashed, killing its pilot, and the plane had been taken away for detailed examination to ascertain why it had crashed...The pilot's name would be released when next of kin had been informed...The story did however have an unfortunate twist to it...The hiker had continued his walk, but had later been knocked down and killed in a hit-and-run incident as he crossed one of the highways in the area...Needless to say the driver was never apprehended."

I personally shook my head in disgust. The hiker had obviously been eliminated in the interests of security...a security so tight that it had been decided at some level not to even inform the President. Presumably fear of a leak within the White House was too greater risk. He was now being accused of sitting on the knowledge when the world at large should have been made aware of the worrying situation. He didn't, quite simply because he couldn't.

Typical of Jesus, he came to the President's aid: "For reasons best known to itself the US Military decided not to release any information...Even the President was not informed, It was my Father who put me in the picture about the incident, and I can now reveal the following to you – the craft did indeed come from the advancing Alpha Centauri fleet...A sort of forerunner... Being made of a material unknown to man, that had an extremely high melting point it did not burn up in the Earth's atmosphere...It evidently crashed because during its design it had not been expected to meet up with the hostile weather prevailing over the state of Arizona at the time...Presumably the atmospheric conditions on the mother planet orbiting Alpha Centauri are always relatively calm...The alien has been carefully extracted from the wreckage under strict quarantine conditions in case it was host to a virus that could wipe out the human race, and at this very moment is undergoing forensic examination...Now that this story is in the public domain I am confident that the findings will be released to the world...In fact I am certain that the President will insist on it." He then looked across to where the man was sitting and received an agreeing nod of the head. The President had obviously had enough of all this secrecy.

Jesus now issued his final warning: "This alien was no doubt on some sort of mission...It could have been a peaceful one, suggesting some sort of alliance...Or it could have been a hostile one – accept our terms or face the consequences...In our own interests we have to assume the latter and prepare accordingly...Let me remind you what I stated earlier in my speech...You need to develop a completely new range of weaponry, and this can only be done through cooperation between those nations who are capable of doing so...I am reliably informed that the craft did have weaponry on board, and this will point you in the right direction as to what will be required...Now go and get on with it." Jesus took a deep breath indicating that his speech had had a draining effect on him. He slowly moved back to his place and sat down. Even then he managed a wink in my direction, as if to say – that's given them something to think about...and it had, too.

One thing was certain, Jesus had no intentions of making some sort of grand exit as he had previously done. He'd proved his point and his power on a previous occasion and did not feel the need or the desire to do it again. Besides...he would be needed on Earth.

Before the hubbub from the Assembly had time to start up again the Secretary General quickly brought it to order. It had been a long day and it was time to round things off. He then thanked all those who had attended and participated, for doing so. His final statement was: "We now have a great deal to think about…If the threat to our planet is as serious as Mr Nazarene has described, and I have no reason to think that it isn't, there is work to be done…As an organisation the United Nations can only do so much…It can for instance act as a meeting place for those nations who because of their expertise and wealth will be expected to come up with and implement those ideas that will not only stop this advancing alien force, but also to defeat it…But there is no reason why those countries should not host such meeting themselves, and that is what I would like to see…Now, to quote Mr Nazarene…Go and get on with it."

As the various delegations slowly made their way out of the great Hall, noisily conversing as they did so, I got to thinking. What had this meeting been all about? Surely it was supposed to be about improving the conditions on Earth to the benefit of all that inhabited it, both animals including ourselves, and the huge variety of vegetation. But once Christ's Holy Square had been filled in, so to speak, and the thirteen Leaders had made their 'this is what we intend to do' speeches, Jesus did not refer to the original aims of the meeting, nor did the Secretary General. It was as if all that had been promised would now have to be put on the back burner so that the efforts required could be diverted to this new and greater threat.

I wondered what God would be making of it all, and suspected that he would not be very impressed, but rather extremely annoyed. He'd stopped the annihilation of the Earth by asteroid impact in order to give the world another chance at getting its 'house in order'. If this didn't take place the asteroid may as well have devastated the Earth rather than some alien force from another star system doing so. And another thing puzzled me…where did this 'turn the other cheek' philosophy that his Son had always advocated, fit in? Here he was recommending that mankind arms itself 'up to the hilt' in order to fight the war to end all wars in outer space. Was the threat so serious that one simply could not afford to turn the other cheek? I personally found difficulty in getting my head round it all.

***

521

Chapter Forty Eight

Eventually the great Hall emptied, well almost, leaving just the Secretary General who was sitting deep on his cushioned seat, looking both physically and mentally exhausted, for it had indeed been a long session…his aide, Jesus Nazarene and myself.

All that needed to be said had been said, and not one of the four of us wanted to continue any sort of discussion. Having said that there were two questions, nothing to do with the day's proceedings that I wanted to ask, so I did so: "What now happens to the Holy Square?…It obviously cannot stay here on the table." (I felt like adding that all or part of it would probably be stolen if it did so, but resisted).

The three of us looked at Jesus, since it was his Square, hopefully expecting him to have a suggestion of some sort…and he had, too. First he picked up the Square, at the same time checking that the glass cover had been slid back into position, then walked across and climbed the stairs to where the Secretary General was sitting. Here he held the Square in front of him, offering it to the man: "I would like to see it prominently displayed somewhere in this great Hall…Although it is only small I'm sure that it could be made the centre point of a larger display telling its story…Maybe even showing how my good friend Peter managed to seek out all the thirteen pieces of pot, worked out how they all came together and built a Square to take them…There could also be a small length of a Dead Sea Scroll to show the part it played in the story…I want all who enter this great Hall for what ever reason, on official duty or as sightseers, to make a point of studying such a display, at the same time appreciating its immense significance."

To me this was the ideal solution. There was little point in Jesus returning to Heaven with it. Equally, there was little point in me taking it home with me. What would I do with it, other than again lock it away? I had earlier supported the suggestion that had been made by the curator of the Museum in Jerusalem that it should be on display there. But there was no doubt that it would be seen by more people if it was on display at the UN. The Secretary General agreed and said that he would make the appropriate arrangements.

My second question was directed at Jesus himself: "So…What do you intend to do now?"

His answer surprised me: "Well...If it's all right by you I'd like to take you up on your offer of spending some time with you and your good wife Angela...I rather fancy living on a smallholding in England's Yorkshire Dales, waking up to a view of Pen-y-Ghent each morning...I may be able, in complete obscurity, to observe how mankind tackles the planetary problems that face it and has committed itself to sort out...And at the same time cooperate to prepare for the alien invasion that we know will come in the not too distant future...If you are agreeable and it can be arranged perhaps I could fly back to the UK with you and your good wife."

I was highly delighted with his request and knew that Angela would have no objections. In the short time she had known the man she had certainly been impressed by his levelheadedness, vast knowledge and modern approach to life, something she found strange in a man originally born two thousand year ago.

Regarding Jesus's suggestion that maybe he could fly home wih us, I would have to check with the British Consulate to see if it could be arranged. I doubted very much that the Prime Minister would object. On our earlier journey to New York he had whispered to me how he was still scared of flying. One thing was certain, with Jesus on board there'd be no danger of the plane falling out of the sky. His Father would certainly make sure of that.

Jesus and I left the UN building together and once outside exchanged phone numbers. After saying that I would be in touch we went our separate ways. He took a cab to the hotel that he always used when in New York. Since it was a warm evening with lots of people milling around I decided to walk back to my hotel. I had earlier been seated for the best part of seven hours and my whole system felt as if it had seized up.

As I walked along in the warm evening air I at last felt relaxed. The UN session was now over and appeared to have been a success, with the Leaders having made their commitments to improve their planet. Of course the news that Jesus had revealed was worrying, but we did at least have time to come up with a solution to the problem. From a personal point of view I couldn't decide whether the news worried me or not. Would Angela and I in fact be around when the battle in space commenced, if indeed it did commence? We had no children and hence no grandchildren to worry about.

There was also another reason why I was in a relaxed mood. For some time now I had worried about Christ's Holy Square being in my possession. It had either been in the safe at home, where I worried about a break-in, or it had been on my person, where I worried about being mugged. It was now in the hands of UN security and would probably next show its face when it formed the centre piece of the display that would shortly be put together in the Assembly Hall.

On my arrival back at the hotel Angela was waiting to be taken out to dinner. She'd only had snacks all day having been glued to her television watching the proceedings at the UN. I too was famished, having only had a coffee and a sandwich during one of the breaks. I quickly showered and changed. I was now ready for a visit, accompanied by my dear wife, to a small, but excellent Italian restaurant just round the corner.

But first I had an important phone call to make that simply couldn't wait. I had to get Jesus on the plane that would take us back to the UK in the morning. My call was answered by Jeremy, one of the PM's aides who I had met for the first time on the outward flight, then during our coffee-and-sandwiches break earlier in the day, when the PM's fear of flying had again come up in the conversation.

As I made my request on Jesus's behalf I jokingly pointed out to Jeremy that the best security that his boss could have, with a hundred percent guarantee that the plane would land safely at Heathrow, was to have Jesus on board. Jeremy saw the point and said that he would first clear it with the PM then make the necessary arrangements. All Jesus had to do was present himself at JFK no later than 11.30 hours in the morning. I assured him that Jesus would be there. To ensure that, I immediately phoned Jesus to inform him that all had been arranged and that our taxi would pick him up at eleven o'clock, and to be ready. He assured me that he would be.

I was now ready for my large helping of spaghetti carbonara. Angela, having been extremely patient waiting for me, was no doubt ready for her Calzoni, neither of us being adventurous in our choice. We knew what we liked and usually stuck to it. I did however lash out on a bottle of Montepulciano D'abruzzo at fifty dollars…such extravagance.

It was anybody's guess what happened when the US President arrived back at the White House. Oh to have been a fly on the wall. I bet the air was blue with some very choice language being used by the President in order to make his point. All we could assume was that something did take place, for when we were at forty thousand feet over the Atlantic on our journey home to the UK the plane's young communications officer approached us. He presented the Prime Minister with some type written sheets, at the same time enthusiastically shouting out so that we all could hear: "Just picked this up on the air waves, sir...The US President has made a statement on NBC...Something about levelling with the world on what had happened in the Arizona desert...Didn't reveal much more, but directed listeners to a report on the NASA website...I did that and printed it out for you...There are some photos as well."

The PM thanked the officer then quickly scanned through the sheets, four in number. As he did so one could see the expression on his face change. He'd previously been in an up-beat mood, pleased at his personal performance at the UN, which I had to agree was good. He was still a relatively young and inexperienced politician. I couldn't help smiling as I whispered to myself those words so often used by not very well educated football managers when describing the performance of one of their young players: "The lad done good."

When he'd finished his silent reading he shouted across the aisle to where Jesus, Angela and I were sitting, inviting us to join him, which we of course did, finding space wherever we could. Once we were settled the PM spoke: "I'm sure you heard the officer when he handed me this document, so you at least know what it's about...but of course not its contents...Rather than try to give you my interpretation of it I will read it out verbatim." And this he proceeded to do.

The report was quite detailed, filled with scientific and medical jargon some of which the PM had difficulty in reading. Without going into too much detail I have decided to précis it down, not an easy task with a scientific, medical or technical account. It is so easy to miss an important fact...But here goes:

First the report described the alien craft that had crashed in the Arizona desert several weeks ago. It gave its dimensions as being twelve metres long, shaped like a dart that one would throw at a dart board, and with four, two metre wide tail fins set at 90° to one other, indicating that the craft probably took off and landed vertically. Unlike a dart the extending point was hollow and appeared to be the barrel of some sort of gun, but it was unclear what sort of gun it was. Further investigation would be required. The body contained a raised transparent canopy.

At the centre of the four tail fins was an exit pipe a metre in diameter.

This provided the forward propulsion, although it wasn't clear how this was done. It was thought that some sort of ion drive was used, but how the ion stream was generated in the first place was, as yet, unknown. Further investigation would also be required. The body was constructed of a complex material that had been made by bonding Carbon, Tungsten and Tantalium together, giving it a melting point of exactly 3170°c. This was the reason why it came through the atmosphere unscathed. The transparent dome-shaped canopy was of pure diamond just one centimetre thick, again with a high melting point. How it had been so precisely shaped could only be guessed at.

The whole craft was coloured a dark blue, the colour having probably been chosen to make it almost, but not quite, merge into the deep space background. There was no indication that the craft had been painted. The colour appeared to have been electrochemically deposited using a process similar to anodising. It was thought that the craft was on some sort of reconnaissance mission, not on an offensive task, although it appeared to be capable of defending itself if the need arose.

Second was the question - why did the craft crash? The weather prevailing at the time over the Arizona desert was to say the least, hostile, with high velocity swirling winds of tornado proportions, torrential rain and lightning. It was thought that as sophisticated as the craft obviously was it had been unable to cope with the extreme conditions. Maybe such conditions were never experienced on the planet where the craft had been designed, built and tested. Maybe they were always calm compared with those that can be experienced on Earth. The craft simply could not handle them.

The third dealt with the pilot, if indeed that was what he, or it, was. For ease of explanation I will refer to him as a 'he', although of course he could be a 'she', even an 'it'. An autopsy revealed some very interesting points. His body was covered with skin not unlike our own, but distinctly green in colour, and beneath that was a muscular structure, also green, again not unlike our own. There was no hair anywhere on the body.

All this covered a skeleton, but there the similarities with an Earthling were slight. Starting from the feet and working up, there were no individual toes, just two thick flat triangular bones, rather like paddles. (Had he lived part of his life in a liquid environment?). From foot to knee there was just one thick bone, not two as all mammals on Earth possess. Knee to hip was also one bone. The joint was a ball-and-socket, but had a cylindrical knee cap to prevent over-bending in any particular direction.

The pelvic girdle was an inverted triangle of solid bone, simple in structure, with three simple joints, two for the legs, both ball-and-socket,and one for the base of the spine which was in four sections of equal length joined together also with ball-and-socket joints, allowing considerable movement.

The rib cage was hardly a cage. Both front and rear were thick, curved and triangular in shape, inverted, with space in between for vital organs. The upper arms were connected to the top of these triangles, both with ball-and-socket joints. Below the elbows, also ball-and-socket, were single boned forearms, unlike mammals on Earth. Like the feet the hands were in the form of paddles, but much smaller and with two fingers and a thumb extending beyond.

A single hollow bone sat on top of the main triangular structure and formed the neck which supported the skull. The skull resembled an inverted cone, domed across the top and connected to the neck by yet another ball-and-socket joint. The skull apertures – the eye sockets, the nasal and the ear apertures were also triangular in shape. The mouth was not unlike that of a human on Earth, with upper and lower jaws, and a tongue, but there the similarity ended, for our alien had just ten teeth, five in the upper jaw and five in the lower. These appeared to be made of a quartz-like substance - extremely hard. The two eyes were also not unlike our own in basic structure, namely a lens structure at the front and a light sensitive layer at the back. But there were two distinct differences – the alien's eyes could 'see' in both infra red and ultra violet parts of the spectrum, and an evolutionary development that we humans would love to possess - the ability to zoom in and out. This meant a complex double lens structure. The sense of hearing was difficult to assess, the autopsy unable to reveal anything that would tell us. But one could confidently assume that it would be superior to ours, almost certainly having a higher and lower frequency range than we humans. The sense of smell would no doubt be the same, with the ability to detect chemicals in the atmosphere that we were unable to, more like the acute sense of smell that an animal such as a dog possesses.

There were two orifices in the lower body, probably to allow it to get rid of waste products, but there were no obvious signs of reproductive organs. Having said that...what exactly were we looking for? An additional orifice or some sort of appendage?

The evolutionary pattern had definitely favoured the triangle for its structures, and also the ball-and-socket joint. Was nature able to construct a triangle more easily? And were these aliens very agile creatures?

Now to the internal organs commencing with the brain, it was much larger than ours, but similar in appearance and structure. At the moment it was impossible to assess its capabilities. One had to assume however that any race capable of developing crafts that could travel across space at a quarter the speed of light, with at least one craft having already reached the Earth, they must be a race of highly intelligent beings. It had to also be assumed that they had developed offensive weapons that we on Earth could only dream of.

Our alien had just one lung, positioned low within the chest cavity. A liquefied oxygen supply within the body of the space craft indicated that he breathed the gas, just like us. (Why couldn't he have breathed some complex gas unknown to man on Earth instead of boring oxygen, I wondered?)

The heart was more complicated in structure than ours, having no less than six chambers. The two central chambers, one above the other, circulated blood in a loop from the lung to the brain only. The four other chambers appeared to circulate the blood in much the same way as in mammals on Earth, through a network of arteries and veins. The 'blood' was interesting. It was green in colour, and analysis revealed that it was copper based. In fact it had an almost identical structure to that of haemoglobin, except that the active metal was copper and not iron.

The digestive system was interesting…and worrying. From mouth to anus, if that's what it was, there was one continuous tube, approximately ten metres in length. There was no stomach, or other digestive organs such as the liver, pancreas and duodenum, just the long tube where all the digestion appeared to take place. Within fifteen centimetres of the tube's end it split into two, both tubes connecting to the two external orifices.

The worrying aspect was the system's contents that appeared to consist of partly digested flesh from another alien. So, were we dealing with a race of cannibals? And if they succeeded in defeating us in some sort of battle was our fate to be kept as animals in captivity and eventually eaten? I preferred not to think about it.

Finally there was what appeared to be a complex nervous system linking all parts of the body to the brain via a cord passing through the bones of the spine, not unlike our own. The impulses were electrical in nature and showed this form of energy to be a necessity wherever in the Universe one went.

How did the alien communicate? He had a mouth with a tongue, so could he speak, and if so, in what sort of language? Or was communication by telepathy, using thought waves?

So, how had our alien died? What did the autopsy reveal? All indications were that on forward impact with the ground he, not in anyway being strapped in, had shot forward, striking his head on the diamond canopy with considerable force. This had broken his neck, and this had been the cause of death. Unbelted car accident victims often suffered the same fate on Earth.

And what had his mission been? There was nothing inside the craft that gave a clue – no messages in any shape or form. All the investigators had in their possession was an alien craft that had been piloted by an alien pilot. But there *were* two possible scenarios for such a mission:

Either – the alien could have had a fit of conscience and decided that he could no longer go along with the invasion. He had acquired the craft and headed at high speed for Earth to warn us, even help us to prepare, using his vast superior knowledge. Unfortunately he would not be able to carry out his mission. We'd now be well and truly on our own.

Or – he had been sent to spy on us, to see if we had any idea of the impending invasion, and if so, how well were we prepared for it? Maybe he had already acquired the necessary information that showed that we were incapable of detecting relatively small objects in deep space, such as an invasion force, and therefore did not know of its presence. The question was – had he been able to relay that information back to the invading force, before his demise?

Because of our awareness of the advancing force, thanks to Jesus Nazarene and his Father, it should not be able to surprise us. We now had the time to make our preparations, hopefully unknown to the aliens. It would be *us* who would have the element of surprise, not *them*.

It was essential that we now developed the technology to make our fighting space craft invisible, not only to the naked eye, but also to any type of advanced detecting equipment. American scientists were close to their goal, but not close enough. We knew that the Russians and the Chinese were working on the same problem, and all our three countries were almost there. Cooperation between the three of us was essential to achieve our goal. Once achieved, the technology would be refined and applied to the crafts that would form our defensive shield. The plan would be to position in deep space many such craft, all invisible and armed with the necessary weaponry to destroy the advancing force. This would be the war to end all wars...and we would be victorious. This last sentence appeared to be from the lips of the President himself

The Prime Minister breathed a sigh of relief at having finished, folded the sheets and placed them on his lap. His comment was brief: "So, there you have it...There's really little else to say."

But I was now thinking on slightly different lines and once I'd got my thoughts together I decided to speak: "I personally found the report that you, Prime Minister, read out, absolutely fascinating...I should be feeling apprehension, but no, I'm brimming with confidence for the future of mankind on Earth...If there's one single threat that will bring the nations together it is the one from outer space, not from a rogue asteroid, but from a alien people set on destroying us and taking over our planet...We're definitely not having that."

Of course it was easy for me to show such enthusiasm, I did not need to worry. At our ages it was highly unlikely that I and my wife Angela would be around to witness the grand event...unless we were able to observe it from our position up in Heaven. After pausing to allow my words of optimism to sink in I continued, but on a different theme: "This whole episode has also verified several important ideas that we suspected were correct, but were never certain about...They are:
  - that life does exist in at least one other part of the universe
  - that such life is similar in many respects to our own
  - that such life can be more advanced than anything found on Earth
  - that such life can travel huge distances at fantastic speeds across space in purpose-built crafts
  - that as far as we are aware this form of life has made no attempt to communicate with us on Earth

On hearing my words Jesus smiled and couldn't resist making a comment, which quickly developed into a statement: "Of course my Father, and hence me, have always been aware of these facts, but he had decided that man himself should make the discoveries...This did not take place however, man's scientific and technological development not progressing rapidly enough...Since an invasion is now on the horizon, so to speak, my Father felt that you had a right to know...Hence my revelation at the United Nations…Man now has time to prepare, and it's up to him to do so…The crashed alien and his craft should point man in several relevant directions."

The assembly, sitting, standing, perching across the aircraft's cabin had listened in silence to Jesus's words. Even when he'd finished the silence continued, nobody wishing to comment. The Prime Minister, aware that the discussion, if that's what it had been, although only three people had actually spoken, had run its course, suggested that we should all try and get some sleep. Once back in the UK work had to commence on two distinct fronts. As far as the UK was concerned the promises on world improvement, particularly those involving the continent of Africa, had to be fulfilled. But the UK, with its vast wealth of talented scientists, engineers and technologists would be working with those of the other advanced nations on what eventually became known as *Operation Sahara*.

***

Chapter Forty Nine

Jesus quickly made himself at home in the Yorkshire Dales. Our converted barn had been reconstructed internally to give an area that had been intended by the previous owner to provide self-catering accommodation for those who wished to explore the Yorkshire Dales. Jesus simply took up residence in that area. He kept himself very much to himself, doing all his own cooking only joining us when invited to do so, usually in the evening to watch television. On the occasions that he joined us on our visits to Skipton to pick up provisions and the items we used in the pursuance of our hobbies, he always called at Barclays bank. Using his card he drew out sufficient cash to fulfill his needs, which included a regular payment to us for his accommodation. This annoyed us intensely because he was there as our guest, but he insisted on making the payment, threatening to leave if we refused to accept it. As a compromise, and at Angela's suggestion, we decided to send the money to four animal charities – the RSPCA, PDSA, IFAW and the Dog Trust, the last one dear to our hearts, being where we got Tala from.

Jesus walked a lot on his own exploring his surroundings which included climbs up the Three Peaks – Pen-y-Ghent, a hill he already knew quite well, having previously 'flown in' rather than having climbed it, Ingleborough and Whernside. When I'd asked him about his climbs he'd always said that they had brought him nearer to his Father.

But his greatest pleasure was undoubtedly taking Tala for a walk, usually once a day. In fact Tala so looked forward to it that when Jesus appeared on the scene she made a bee-line for him. I couldn't help feeling a tinge of jealousy at the thought that *my* dog was maybe changing her allegiance.

Angela and I had always been church-goers and when we arrived in the Dales we immediately became regular Sunday morning worshippers at the church in Horton-in-Ribblesdale. When Jesus joined us he expressed a desire to also become a regular communicant there. This required careful thought, and for a very good reason. What would happen if he was recognised? His face had appeared on worldwide television on no less than two occasions; the first when Christ's Holy Square had been assembled by the world's great Leaders at the UN after I had managed to locate all thirteen pieces. Here he'd made a speech critical of mankind and followed it up with his spectacular 'ascension' into Heaven. This was followed ten years later by a similar ceremony following the distribution of the thirteen pieces of pot in Heaven, the world's Leaders having all died in the tsunami and having later been returned to Earth. At this ceremony Jesus also spoke, but this time at length about the threat of invasion by an alien power from outer space. By this time he was a very familiar figure.The question now was, how could his identification be made impossible to the other members of the Horton-in-Ribblesdale congregation?

First I suggested that he should change his name, Jesus Nazarene being too much of a give-away. As we watched an old *Horizon* programme on a History channel the work of Isaac Newton featured prominently. This gave us our name. Jesus would be known as Isaac Newton. If asked about it, the explanation would be that his father, John Newton, was himself a keen astronomer (which of course Jesus's Father was…and is) and decided to name his son after the eminent scientist.

But a change in name would not be enough. When Jesus had appeared at the United Nations some weeks ago he sported a huge beard that covered most of his face. He had it now. We decided that it had to go. After some clever handiwork by Angela with a pair of scissors, followed by a shave by Jesus himself with an overburdened razor, he emerged clean shaven. More to the point he was now hopefully unrecognisable, which had been the aim of the exercise.

When we asked him, for the first time, to join us at church he enthusiastically did so. On that occasion we did feel a little uneasy. Would someone recognise him inspite of the steps we had taken to hide his identity? Fortunately no one did. On that occasion Jesus, or was it Isaac, took holy communion for only the second time on Earth. How strange it must have been for him to hear the vicar, the Reverend Davies, say the words that he himself had spoken all of two thousand years ago at his Last Supper: "Take…Eat…This my body," as he received the unleavened wafer, and "Take…Drink…This is my blood," as he sipped the wine from the chalice.

It wasn't long before his enthusiasm to be involved led to an invitation from the vicar to start reading the lessons from the lectern, often reading his own words as quoted in the four gospels. Later he was invited once a month to give the sermon from the pulpit. As the vicar had put it to his congregation: "You must be fed-up of hearing me drone on week after week…I have therefore invited Mr Newton to take over once a month."

There were nods of enthusiastic approval by members of the congregation, the general opinion being that listening to their incumbent was like watching paint dry. It gave Jesus great satisfaction often choosing one of his own parables as his theme. He used no notes – he didn't need any, unlike the Reverend Davies who used several sheets, sometimes getting them in the wrong order, sometimes dropping them on the floor of the pulpit, much to the amusement of his congregation.

Jesus's only disappointment was that his audience numbered barely thirty people instead of the five thousand, and more, that he'd been used to, but that couldn't be helped. He soon became a familiar figure in the Dale, mainly as a result of joining us on on our shopping sprees, but also by stopping to talk to the local farmers as they made their way along the country lanes on their tractors, or tended their sheep on their quad bikes.

The community was small and closely knit, so when somone became ill or had a bad accident the news became common knowledge in a matter of hours, with concern being shown by all, and that included Jesus himself.

About a month ago young Johnny Smith, whose parents owned the farm just up the track from our home, had a nasty accident falling off a quad bike. He had jumped on the bike being ridden by his elder brother, Mark, who tried to shake him off by swinging the bike from side to side.

Eventually he succeeded and his younger brother crashed to the ground hitting his head on the yard's concrete surface. Knowing that it would take ages for an ambulance to get up to the remote farm Johnny's parents lifted their son as gently as they could into the 4x4 and headed for Skipton A&E. After an assessment of the boy's condition it was decided to fly him by air ambulance down to Leeds General Infirmary.

It soon became clear that the boy had had a massive bleed into the brain and tests showed that there was no brain activity. Only a life support machine was keeping him alive. That evening Angela and I decided to drive down to Leeds to give the parents, who had not left the boy's bedside, some moral support. Jesus asked if he could come along. As we were sitting in a separate sideroom, simply staring helplessly at the boy, the specialist asked the parents to step outside. The time had come to talk about turning off the life support machine.

As the discussion was taking place outside Jesus stood, walked across to the boy and placed his finger tips on the boy's forehead. As he did so I heard him mumble something. He then returned to his seat. The specialist, at the request of the parents, agreed to monitor the boy's condition for the next twelve hours, just to make sure.

At this point Angela, Jesus and I, accepting that there was nothing we could do, decided to make our way home. It was a long journey and I would be driving at night, not something I enjoyed. We arrived home at two o'clock in the morning and I decided to make a relaxing cup of cocoa while Angela did some toast. As we sat there trying to get our heads round how a bit of brotherly horseplay had come to this my mobile rang. As Angela put it: "Who the devil's calling us at this unearthly hour?"

Rather abruptly I shouted down the phone: "Hello."

"Hi Peter...It's Bill Smith...Some sort of miracle seems to be taking place...The monitors have started showing some minor brain activity and our Johnny, although in a coma, appears to be trying to breathe on his own...The specialist has stressed that we must not build our hopes up, but we can't help it...I'll ring you again, about ten in the morning."

"Good news, Bill...Thanks for ringing...Look forward to hearing from you in the morning." I kept my reply brief, not knowing what else to say. As the three of us sat there staring at the glowing embers in the fireplace Angela spoke: "I hope they don't build up their hopes only to have them dashed."

Jesus simply said: "Let's at least be optimistic."

As Angela and I lay in bed, unable to get to sleep I got to thinking...surely Jesus had nothing to do with the boy's turn for the better...We had both seen him place his hand on the boy's forehead. We had both heard him mumble something. It was too much of a coincidence. And of course he had a previous record of doing this sort of thing. He'd cured me of my brain tumour, and of course he'd carried out many such healings two thousand years ago.

I nudged Angela and told her my thoughts. She, always the cautious one, admitted that it was possible that Jesus had played some part in the boy's slight improvement. It was however essential that none of us built up our hopes.

As promised, Bill rang at ten the following morning and the news was good...in fact brilliant. Johnny had been taken off the life support machine and was breathing normally. He had opened his eyes and smiled, apparently recognising his parents and brother. The specialist had stated that he had not seen anything like it in his twenty years of practice, and had actually used the word 'miracle' even though all his medical training didn't allow him to accept that such an event could take place. It was so tempting for me to tell Bill that maybe Jesus, who Bill of course simply knew as Isaac Newton, may have had something to do with his son's improvement. But had I done so I would have had to reveal who exactly Isaac was, and it wouldn't have been long before the news had become common knowledge throughout the Dale, quickly followed by the nation at large.

That morning Jesus took Tala for her daily walk, and I decided to join them. As we strolled along, both of us taking it in turns to throw a tennis ball for Tala to retrieve, I decide to broach the subject, trying to choose my words carefully: "Good to see that young Johnny Smith has taken a turn for the better…Shows just how resilient the young human body can be."

Jesus simply nodded in agreement, but chose not to say anything. I therefore continued: "I noticed that you placed your fingers on his forehead…"

"Yes…Just to check his temperature…You know, how you do when you think a child's burning up."

His answer was not at all convincing, so in I plunged: "Or did you lay your fingers on him to heal him, just like you did when you healed me, and the deaf, blind and crippled two thousand years ago."

Jesus just smiled, at the same time saying: "At my birth my Father gave me special powers, to be used sparingly…This is the second time I have used them in all those years, although I have been tempted to do so on many, many occasions…Johnny's accident took place in my 'back yard', so to speak, and I felt I had to act…The fact that the young boy is now on the mend indicates my Father's approval…By the way, there will be no relapse…Perhaps you would like to inform the parents."

I would indeed, but I would need to choose my words carefully. I could hardly say…By the way, Isaac is actually Jesus Christ the Son of God and he has just performed a miracle on your son. My words could only be in the form of reassurance and optimism, but one day I would tell them what exactly had happened to their son, maybe tell the son himself.

Meanwhile there was one person who deserved to know immediately and that was Angela. When Jesus and I returned home with a very weary dog we found Angela in the field adjoining the paddock looking for eggs laid by our free range hens. Since she'd been feeding the goats when Bill

536

Smith's call came through she hadn't heard the good news. I therefore quickly put her in the picture: "Bill called earlier…Young Johnny is off the live support machine, breathing on his own and showing signs of coming out of his coma…Good news, eh?"

Angela, always the cautious one, replied: "Don't let's build up our hopes too soon…There's a long way to go and he could have a relapse."

Before I could reply, Jesus couldn't resist making a comment choosing words that I had definitely heard before: "Oh ye of little faith…Trust in the Lord my God."

Angela simply smiled, preferring not to reply. She knew exactly what Jesus meant, for she too had witnessed his action at the hospital the previous night.

The following morning we woke up early to a glorious day. The sun was already above the horizon, that being the summit of Pen-y-Ghent. It was wall-to-wall blue sky and there appeared to be little wind. As Angela and I tucked into our bacon and egg we heard a tap on the kitchen door. Jesus entered with his walking gear on, not an unusual sight because there was still a chill in the air and he presumably had come to take Tala for her walk. As Tala dashed towards him in anticipation he spoke: "I fancy tackling Pen-y-Ghent today, so I prefer to leave Tala here…All right?"

It was a strange request for all three of us knew that Tala was more than capable of making the walk. I glanced at Angela: "Fancy joining Jesus?...We haven't done Pen-y-Ghent for ages…It's such a glorious morning, and I'm sure Tala will be ok."

Angela nodded enthusiastically, a mouthful of fried bread preventing her from replying, but I detected a look of slight disappointment in the eyes of Jesus. Did he want, for is own good reason, to be on his own during his walk? He then smiled and said: "Of course I'd like you to join me, but can we be on our way within the next half hour?"

"Oh, I'm sure we can make that…We've only to get our walking gear on."

As Angela cleared the dining room table, placing everything she could in the large kitchen sink, already full of bubbling hot water, I dived into the cupboard where the clothing and boots were kept. Within ten minutes we were both ready.

The walk started off uneventfully, but soon took on a very serious side to it as I will describe shortly. As we walked along at a leisurely pace we met several groups of walkers along the track, all no doubt having been attracted by the glorious weather. One group in particular caught my eye. It was a large group, I counted ten in total, with an age range I guessed between about twelve and fifty plus.

Seeing the group immediately brought back happy memories for me, for I had been part of such a group on many previous occasions. I had, during my years as a youth worker, led my members on our annual Three Peaks Walk on no less than six occasions. It was always a sponsored event with local charities benefitting.

I couldn't resist getting into conversation with the leader who informed me that they were from an Academy in Wakefield that had a youth club attached to it. This was their first Three Peaks Walk. It surprised him when I told him that I knew the Merrie City well, having sung in its Cathedral choir many moons ago and still shopped there at least once a month with my wife.

The young group quickly moved ahead of us and soon disappeared up the track. Tala initially followed them as the youngsters called her, but returned to us when she realised that the gap between them and us was rapidly widening.

As the three of us plus Tala rounded a bend in the track that crossed a laddered stile over a dry stone wall, we saw the group in some disarray. One youngster was laid on the ground, the others in a loose group gathered round.

As we approached, Angela grabbed Tala and put her on the lead. Jesus and I quickly moved into the group wondering if we could be of assistance, even though we had no idea what had happened. The leader explained: "A couple of the lads decided to race to the stile wanting to be first across it…Just before they reached it Jimmy here collapsed on the ground holding his chest…When the rest of us reached him he had already stopped breathing and I couldn't find a pulse."

My immediate response was: "Have you contacted the emergency services?" I assumed that there was at least one mobile phone within the group. But I was wrong, as the leader explained: "I told all the group to leave their phones in our minibus down at Horton so that they could concentrate on the walk without any distractions…I decided to bring mine in case of emergencies…but guess what, the bloody battery's flat…Have you got one?"

As it happened I had. When out in the hills one could never assume one's complete safety. Not only could you fall ill, you could have an accident. You could also become lost or disorientated in the heavy mists that had the habit of enveloping you when you least expected it. As I contacted the emergencies, giving our exact location, Angela and Jesus approached the boy who was frantically being attended to by an older one who was trying to administer CPR, although he had little idea what he was doing.

Angela eased the boy to one side so that she could assess the situation. First she tried to detect whether the boy was actually breathing. Her side-to-side head movement indicated that he wasn't. She then checked for a pulse. There was none. It appeared that the boy was already dead. Could he have had a heart attack, I wondered, following his period of exertion? Sudden Death Syndrome still occurred in young people even though a national screening programme had been introduced in 2015. Was this an example of a risk that had not been picked up, or of the boy's screening appointment having been missed?

At this point Jesus asked Angela if he could take a look at the boy. She moved to one side. He then crouched over and brought his own lips close to those of the boy. As he did so the other youngsters crowded round curious, to see if this complete stranger was going to make contact. They'd seen pictures of mouth-to-mouth resuscitation on their television screens, but not the real thing. The idea of boys kissing boys or girls kissing girls they still found amusing.

But Jesus did not make contact. Instead he forceably blasted his breath over the boy's face, then mumbled something. (Angela later told me that his words had been…Please Father, may it be thy will that this child is delivered back to me).

As if by magic, a terrible word to use in the circumstances, but nevertheless that was what appeared to have taken place, the boy's chest ever so slowly started to rise and fall. Angela was now able to detect a rapid pulse at the wrist. Seconds later the boy started to move his arms and legs, stretching them outwards as if to relieve stiffness. He then opened his eyes and uttered two words: "What happened?"

It was now important to keep the boy warm, his bare arms having taken on a bluish tint. I quickly extracted a thick woolly jumper from my rucksack and wrapped it round him. At the same time Jesus took off his padded anorak and placed it over the boy as one would a blanket. It took the air ambulance just twenty minutes to make the thirty mile journey from Leeds-Bradford airport. By sheer good luck we were positioned on the only flat piece of ground for some distance and this allowed the helicopter to safely land.

As one paramedic rushed across to us another extracted a lightweight stretcher from the helicopter. In no time at all the boy was wired up to some complicated looking equipment that included a screen displaying a series of wavy lines. After several minutes of observation the paramedic spoke: "It would appear that he's had a heart attack resulting in his heart stopping…It's now beating strongly, but irratically…We need to get him as quickly as possible to LGI." I whispered to Jesus: "Leeds General Infirmary." He nodded, not having heard the abbreviation before.

It was now a case of getting the boy onto the stretcher, into the helicopter and away and this was done in a matter of seconds. Obviously the boy had to be accompanied by an adult, and one of those in the party offered to go, as did one of the other boys, no doubt a close friend.

The leader had now to make a decision – to continue the walk or abandon it. There appeared to be little to be gained by doing the latter and the remaining youngsters were keen to continue. The decision was therefore made, a decision that I wholeheartedly agreed with even though it had nothing to do with me.

The now depleted group climbed the stile and headed for the long upward slope that would take them to the summit of Pen-y-Ghent. We had to make a slight detour because Tala was obviously unable to climb the ladder, and she was far too heavy to be lifted up and over. Fortunately a short distance along the wall the stonework had collapsed allowing her to leap over. We followed her, scrambling over the loose stones.

We were now some four hundred metres behind the group, and when we reached the summit they were already making their descent. During our ascent, apart the time we'd been involved with the group, Jesus, Angela and I had talked continuously. The topic of conversation had been the improvements that all three of us wanted for the Earth on which we lived, and had been promised by the wealthy nations and those that presented a risk to world peace.

As we stood there admiring the view it soon became clear that the weather was changing. Heavy cloud was rapidly approaching from the west and the summit of Ingleborough Hill had already disappeared in an advancing bank of rain. It was time for us to make a hasty retreat. But Jesus wouldn't move. When I asked him if anything was wrong his reply was Earth shattering: "I will not be returning with you…It is my intention to again join my Father in Heaven…From there I will be able to monitor the progress mankind is making to improve his planet…I will also be able to find out a little more about the approaching alien force…I will then return to Earth to reveal my findings to those who will be responsible for the defence of our planet."

My initial thought was to try and persuade him not to go through with his plan, but I knew that it would be a pointless exercise. He wanted to help his Father in his assessment of how mankind was progressing. But more important was the 'reporting back' procedure that he had decided to adopt.

What took place next I had witnessed before. A cylindrical column of thick mist about three metres across descended from the overhead cloud and enveloped Jesus making him invisible to us. The column slowly rose, taking him with it. He was ascending in order to join his Father in Heaven. Angela and I fully understood what had taken place, but poor old Tala couldn't make head or tail of it. She rushed to the spot where Jesus had stood, looked skywards and howled like a wolf.

The wind had now got up and it had started spotting with rain. We could already hear rumblings of thunder, indicating that lightning was in the air. In the interest of our personal safety we had to get off the summit, and as quickly as possible. We decided to follow the route we'd used to ascend the Hill. This enabled us to make rapid progress. As I strode along, my thoughts could not help but concentrate on the event I had just witnessed. Immediately some very familiar words came to mind, words that summed the life of Jesus Christ. The words were those of the Credo, one of the sections in the Grand Mass. Such was its importance that most of the greatest composers throughout history had written music for it...Palestrina in the 16th century (I hated Palestrina because vocally you couldn't give it a good 'go'), Mozart in the 17th, Verdi in the 19th and more recently Vaughan Williams in 1922. But without doubt my favourite was by the 20th century English composer Harold Darke who wrote his *Mass in F major* in 1926.

York Minster may still referred to the service as 'The Mass'. At Wakefield Cathedral, where I'd been a choirboy for some four years, it was known as the Solemn Eucharist, and at Ribbleswell Parish Church it was known simply as the Communion Service and not sung to any 'grand' version, mainly because it did not have the choir to sing it.

As I walked along I started to sing the Darke 'Credo', which in one short piece described the life of Jesus Christ, from his birth, through his death, resurrection and ascension, to his second coming. At first I sang almost in a whisper, feeling embarrassment, worried that Angela and Tala would think that I wsn't right in the head. But soon I was in full voice so that all the heavens could hear me. Angela simply smiled. Tala joined in, again howling like a wolf.

I believe in one God.
The Father Almighty, maker of Heaven and Earth.
And of all things visible and invisible.
And in one Lord Jesus Christ the only begotten Son of God.
Begotten of his Father before all worlds.
God of God. Light of Light. Very God of Very God.
Begotten not made, being of one substance with the Father.
By whom all things were made. ·
Who for us men and for our salvation came down from Heaven.
And was incarnate by the Holy Ghost of the Virgin Mary.
And was made man. And was crucified, also for us under Pontius Pilate.
He suffered and was buried.
And the third day he rose again according to the scriptures, and ascended
into Heaven. And sitteth on the right hand of the Father.
And he shall come again with glory to judge both the quick and the dead.
Whose kingdom shall have no end.
And I believe in the Holy Ghost, the Lord and giver of life.
Who proceedeth from the Father and the Son.
Who with the Father and the Son together is worshipped and glorified.
Who spake by the prophets.
And I believe in one Catholic and Apostolic church.
I acknowledge one baptism for the remission of sins.
And I look for the resurrection of the dead and the life of the World to come.
Amen...Amen

God, I did feel good after that.

Eventually we arrived back at the car park at Horton-in-Ribbledale where we'd left our car. Feeling cold we decided to call in the café close by for a warm drink. As we entered we were surprised to see the group that we had earlier helped during our walk. We decided to join them at their table. Tala, who was well known to the café owner, curled up on the floor at my feet. She knew that if I decided to get something to eat, if only a bag of crisps, one or two would fall to the floor.

I commenced the conversation: "I thought you were continuing the walk...I thought you'd be well on the way to Whernside by now,"

The leader explained: "When it started to rain the walk lost some of its attractiveness...Some of the youngsters only have light jackets...They'd have been soaked to the skin for most of the walk...But we still took a vote...No one voted to continue...So we're just having a warm drink before heading back to West Yorkshire."

My comment was short and to the point: "A wise decision in the circumstances."

One of the youngsters then spoke: "Where's the other man...Yer know, the one who helped Jimmy Briggs?"

The question put me well and truly on the spot. How was I to answer him? I could hardly tell him that Jesus had ascended into Heaven. Fortunately quick thinking Angela came to my aid: "Oh...He's gone to the pub down the road for a pint and a game of dominoes...We'll collect him when we've finished our drink here."

The young lad smiled, no doubt wondering why the two of us preferred a hot steaming cup of tea to a beer or a tot of whisky.

It was now time for the group to leave, but before they did so the leader put us in the picture regarding the boy who'd had the heart attack. The adult who had travelled with him to the LGI had phoned hoping that the walk had been abandoned and that the group were back at the minibus where all the phones were. He'd been right. The message was that they had arrived safely and at that moment Jimmy was wired up to lots of beeping 'fancy gear' to check him out. The leader said that he had already contacted the boy's parents who'd said that they'd get across to the LGI immediately.

We all left the café together. As I wished the group a safe journey home, Angela winked at the lad who'd asked where Jesus was: "We'll just pick our friend up."

"Bet yer call in for a pint missus."

"Maybe just the one," was her smiling response.

When the minibus had disappeared down the Skipton Road we doubled back and got in our car, Tala leaping in the back. It was strange returning home without Jesus. It would be stranger at home where we had got quite used to having him around. Poor Tala would certainly miss him. And how would we describe his absence to the congregation at Horton Church?

The following years seemed to pass at the speed of light. Angela and I were approaching eighty, not an exceptional age, many people in the United Kingdom already over a hundred years old. Of course we didn't have all our original 'parts'. I now had two new heart valves and Angela had had a kidney transplant. Both of us had new hip joints. We were in fact in remarkably good health, and still lived in our converted barn in the Yorkshire Dales.

We both walked regularly, if only short distances, just to keep our limbs and cardiovascular systems in order. We still drove into Skipton to do our shopping, refusing to have it delivered to our door step. Mentally we kept alert by the pursuance of our hobbies. Angela was still writing her children's stories and poems, and I was still painting, throwing pots and chiseling out the odd sculpture. .

Sadly we lost Tala five years ago. The circumstances of her death were bizarre, to say the least. She'd fallen asleep in the paddock one summer afternoon after we'd been for a long walk in the morning. Suddenly and without any warning the rickety barn door swung open, at the same time breaking away from its rusty hinges. Sadly the heavy door crashed down on her fracturing her skull. We managed to get her to our local vet but the internal bleeding had already done irreparable damage. She died shortly afterwards. Having had two wonderful pets, both black-as-coal Belgian Shepherds, and bearing in mind our advanced age, we decided not to get another dog. Besides, we couldn't go through all the heartache again. We had for the briefest moment wondered…if Jesus had still been with us would he have brought Tala back to life, or had it been the time for her spirit to pass into the care of his Father? We of course speculated at length on what exactly he was doing now.

***

Chapter Fifty

Narrator – God

Since the declarations of intent by some of the world's Leaders I and my Son Jesus have been looking down on the Earth in order to observe what was going on down there. What developments have taken place to improve the lot of not only mankind, but also the other animals that it shares the planet with, and also not forgetting the world's plant life? And equally important, what ground-breaking advances have been made in the field of military hardware? This would be required to enable man to put up a good show against the advancing invasion force from Alpha Centauri, and also to be victorious. I have always been against the development of weapons that will be used by man to kill his own kind, but in the situation that will soon face him that development will be essential.

As it has turned out, and showing great foresight on behalf of the three major powers America, Russia and China, with full support from almost all other nations, the two tasks of world improvement and weapon development had been brought together in one vast area of the world, namely the Sahara Desert.

But first let me describe where things have changed for the better for the three groups of living things – humans, animals and plants in all parts of the world. To make it easy for myself I decided to refresh my memory on the commitment speeches that were made by those world Leaders. How have things changed as a result of those speeches? For convenience I have listed the countries the Leaders represented and in the order they made their commitments.

America – Immediately after the speech had been made by the President his government consulted with other nations on setting up an international humanitarian task force. As a result of these consultations the force has been put together, much of the cost being borne by America itself, and based, for reasons I will described later, in mid-Sahara on the African continent. The force's most recent mission was only last year when it was able to move within twenty-four hours into a remote area of Kazakhstan that had been hit by a massive earthquake. The three thousand miles were covered by a hundred helicopters, all supplied by

America, refueling at various points along the route, carrying a force of some thousand rescuers, including engineers and medics. A makeshift runway was constructed allowing heavy lifting plant to be flown in. The whole mission wasdeemed an overwhelming success in what could only be described as tragic circumstances. Many lives were saved which definitely would not have been the case had the force not been in operation. I commend America for being the leading force here. There is a negative side however – On the domestic front the gas-guzzler is still king, the electric car not catching the American imagination. As a result carbon dioxide emissions are far too high. The country is still trying to sort out its gun laws. This is an area that concerns me greatly. How many more mass shootings will there have to be before action is taken? Unnecessary and unnatural deaths are abhorrent to me and always will be.

Australia *– Initially there was a hostile reaction by the indigenous population to their Leader's suggestion that his vast country could absorb many more immigrant people, possibly from the Indian subcontinent, thus relieving severe overcrowding and therefore poverty in that large area. I am pleased to see that the scheme nevertheless went ahead and already the nation as a whole is benefitting from the move. A vast electronic industry has been developed and is already being called Australia's Silicon Valley.*

On the negative side the nation seems to have waged war on the Great White shark, following several incidents where swimmers and surfers have lost their lives to the beast. Hunting expeditions are now common place and capturing and killing the animal is becoming a bit of a sport. I'm not at all happy with this situation. When all said and done, the sea is the natural habitat of this creature. It is not the natural habitat of man. It is simply a playground for him. It is an area that I'm keeping a watchful eye on.

Brazil *– Satellite photographs have revealed to humanity the huge amount of tree planting that has taken place within the Amazon Basin, although I personally do not need a satellite to see it. I simply look down from my elevated position. I am reliably informed that the replanting programme will continue for several years to come. Now a prosperous nation, the most successful in the southern hemisphere, I now want to see that success spread throughout the South American continent, especially to Colombia where the drug trade is still bringing misery to millions. Brazil is a neighbour and must exercise more influence there. On the*

546

international front I am pleased to see that the nation has used its increased wealth to play a major role in the setting up of the humanitarian force described above.

China – *Massive steps have been made in cutting down air pollution from heavy industry. Carbon-capture has been introduced and is now widespread, the carbon dioxide being deposited in the depths of the China Sea. The atmosphere over the major cities has improved out of all proportion. I am pleased to see that the country now comes down heavily on the import of animal parts, particularly ivory from Africa, with long prison sentences now the norm for convicted individuals. Regarding its neighbour North Korea agreements have been signed where the nation has stopped its nuclear ambitions in exchange for a security agreement, and massive food and industrial aid from its powerful neighbour. In cooperation with its neighbour Russia pressure has been applied to Iran to channel its enthusiasm for nuclear power into peaceful means. A security agreement has been implemented to protect that country from a pre-emptive strike from Israel. In this respect American support has been forthcoming.*

France – *This nation has succeeded in setting up its African working party, with representatives from the former French colonies now meeting on a regular basis in Paris. Many trade agreements have already been signed and massive aid and expertise have already poured into many areas. Once the initiative was seen to be genuine the African nations welcomed it with open arms. But this initiative cannot be one-sided. The African nations must put their own houses in order, and this means that all the tribalism and corruption must be eliminated for the common good. This is an area that I will be watching closely. I'm not prepared to see these petty squabbles hinder progress.*

Germany – *Being one of the world's wealthier countries the contribution to the international humanitarian task force has been great, with much of the heavy plant required such as diggers, bulldozers and cranes being donated by that country. The support for the African initiative of its neighbour, France, has also been considerable. As a result of German aid in the field of medicine, childhood mortality rates were now almost on a par with those of the European Community.*

Iran – *With both moral and technical support from Russia and China as part of the deal Iran has now dropped its nuclear ambitions, although it does have six nuclear power stations, built by the Russians. The nation has also signed a non-aggression pact with Turkey, a country it has a*

547

border with. *Regarding the country's old enemy Israel, monthly meetings are now taking place between the heads of the two countries in the neutral capital city of Turkey, Ankara. These initiatives have made the whole area of the Middle East and beyond a more military secure place. Since this was one of the world's potential 'hotspots' I am delighted at the progress that has been made.*

Israel *– As tension to the east of the nation has now been considerably reduced for the reasons I have stated above, a more relaxed attitude has been adopted in Israel itself. With America acting as both friend and 'big brother' the situation with the Palestinians has dramatically improved. The occasional missile launch from Gaza is now a thing of the past, and the sea blockade was lifted some time ago. One positive feature is the way Palestinian children are being educated in Israeli schools, with students going on to Israeli universities. It is hoped that this one initiative will create a better understanding between the young of the two nations.*

Japan *– This country, being one of the world's wealthiest, has contributed massively to the international humanitarian force, supplying all the large transport aircraft that were used in Kazahkstan. It is also active in Africa as part of the French intiative, supplying expertise in both oil and mineral exploration. As tension in the area has decreased, the result of China exercising some control over its neighbour North Korea, Japan has signed an agreement with that country whereby a car factory will be set up to produce a new range of electric cars. This will add considerable wealth to what is still a very poor country. On its domestic front Japan has introduced laws to stop the practice of whaling in Antarctica. This has been welcomed by all environmental groups throughout the world. It goes without staying that I am highly delighted with this decision.*

North Korea *– At long last this country has realised that there is little to be gained by antagonising the other nations of the world. Its nuclear ambitions had bankrupted the country and its people had been strickened with extreme poverty. Fearing that unrest could escalate into rioting on the streets of the capital Pyongyang the government decided to trade its nuclear ambitions for the massive aid that its neighbour China, and Russia were prepared to offer. The country has also realised at long last that the partition of the Korean peninsula has been of benefit to no one. Talks are now in progress to end this mad situation, with regular talks taking place in both Seoul in the south and Pyongyang in* the north. These I will watch very closely. As stated earlier the hand of friendship offered by Japan has been accepted, and the construction work on the new car plant has already started.

South Africa – Realising that the country itself should be playing a far greater role in the continent's future, but being limited as to what it could do on its own, it has welcomed wholeheartedly the offer by the European nations, and also China and Japan, to get things on the move on the continent. Accepting that it is not one of the more wealthy nations it has decided to concentrate its efforts on one particular area – that of peacemaker between the African nations, something that has hindered progress in so many areas. Much of this is still due to tribalism and South Africa has made a determine effort, with considerable success, to change attitudes. Once widespread peace is established the wealthier nations areable to move in with their considerable aid. Through these closer ties with the other nations, especially those in sub-Sahara Africa, the country has succeeded in drawing up a common policy that has led to the almost complete elimination of the trade in animal parts, especially ivory. In this quest China's cooperation has been essential and welcome. It also goes without saying that this is something I am thrilled about. Hopefully those majestic animals, my animals, will be seen roaming the grasslands of Africa again.

Finally **The United Kingdom** – Since my Son Jesus has spent some time in this country as a guest of the very man who collected together the thirteen pieces of pot that made up the Holy Square, he has been able to report back to me first hand on this country's contribution to world security and improvement. Without doubt the main thrust has been on the continent of Africa, where the UK has matched France's contribution both in aid and expertise in a whole range of areas. Initially it was looked upon with the utmost suspicion by the former colonies, but that barrier was soon broken down when the UK introduced a massive HIV programme using the latest retroviral drugs. This is already producing results, with the almost complete elimination of the disease being transferred from mother to the unborn child. The UK, with its domestic expertise in 'search and rescue' whether it be at sea, in the mountains or as a result of fire or explosion, has been one of the leading contributors of manpower to the new international humanitarian task force. Typically, there were more search-and-rescue dogs in Kazakhstan from the UK than from any other country, even Switzerland with its St Bernards. On the domestic front the UK is still wrestling with the *problem of energy supply. In its determination to show the rest of the world how 'green' it is, thus setting an example, it has placed too much reliance on wind energy. As its 'dirty' coal powered power stations have closed down the energy gap between supply and demand has closed to almost zero, leaving the country vulnerable to power cuts during cold spells of weather. To my disappointment Nuclear power has only been halfheartedly embraced, with just one station having been opened. Gas fired stations have had to be rapidy built, with little regard to the carbon dioxide emissions that are inevitable as a result, thus undermining the whole 'green' philosophy. Although governments of the day have insisted that the high taxes on petrol and diesel, amongst the highest in the world, have been to persuade people onto public transport or to purchase electric cars, they have not carried the people with them, who have seen their high taxes squandered away in areas such as wind farm subsidies and supporting failing banks that are still paying huge bonuses to their failed bankers. Finally, in the area of animal welfare the country has been at the forefront, supporting the world initiatives to stop the mindless slaughter of endangered species such as tigers in Asia for their body parts, and elephants and rhinos in Africa for their tusks and horns. Sadly this enthusiasm for animal welfare has not yet extended to the slaughter of animals by the 'Halal' method, still widely used in the UK much to the continued disgust of most non-muslim people. I look forward to the time when the government of the day 'grabs the nettle' and outlaws the practice, but I'm not optimistic. Perhaps my Son can get some sort of petition going when he next returns to the United Kingdom.*

One area of mankind's behaviour still worries me immensely. When I'd previously talked to my Son about it I had devoted a considerable amount of time to it, much to his surprise. It was mankind's attitude to sex. I remember going on at length about the six 'Ps', as I'd referred to them – procreation, parenthood, promiscuity, prostitution, paedophilia and the pill, later adding yet another – pornography. But these are areas in man's behaviour where there has been little or no change as far as I could see. In fact in some areas the situation appears to have deteriorated.

Procreation outside of wedlock is now common place, with many children throughout the world not even knowing who their father is, not what I intended when I gave men and women the power to procreate. Much to my disappointment the commitment made by a man and a women in a ceremony of marriage is becoming a thing of the past. This is a situation I am far from happy with.

Parenthood in most areas of the world appears to have weakened, with mothers, and fathers if they're still around, failing to act as good role models for their children. Most children now have the freedom to do their own 'thing', whether it be in their own interests,or not. They can say what they like, go where they like, do what they like, and it's all ok…and woe betide anybody who dares to say – no, you're not. The result of this of course has led to many children losing their way in the world. One extremely worrying effect of this is the increase in child suicides, especially young girls. If this was in any way due to a strong belief in me, with an equally strong belief that they were passing into my care I could understand, but of course not encourage it. This is a situation that parents, especially mothers, must get a grip of.

Promiscuity continues unabated, the age of involvement dropping year by year as children mature earlier. Girls are having babies at ten years of age, the fathers being of the same age. Is there any shame attached to the children's parents for allowing this undesirable situation to take place? No. In fact a report singing the praises of the event usually ends up on the various social media sites, with the grandparents proudly showing off their grandchildren. But this doesn't only apply to the young and naïve. Promiscuity is often the reason for the breakdown in relationships. And of course it applies to both men and women. It is my opinion that the strengthening of the institution of marriage could help reverse this trend.

Prostitution is as widespread as ever, with women still having little respect for their own bodies, and men quite willing to take advantage of this. It is still rife in poorer countries where the result is often yet another child being born into an unwelcoming environment. The suggestion, often made, that it should in some way be legalised within brothels is not what I want to see. Such a move would undoubtedly create an employment opportunity for young girls. Is that really what parents would want for their daughters?

Paedophilia has increased out of all proportion as communication on the various forms of social media have become more sophisticated, allowing paedophiles to be even more cunning. So-called 'grooming' of young girls is now widespread across the world, and this has undoubtedly been made easier by far too many parents adopting the attitude…I must allow my daughter to have her own space. This 'out of sight, out of mind' approach, where the child retired to her bedroom in order to seek out someone on line who will make them feel 'a million dollars', simply makes it easy for the paedophile. We're back to parenthood again.

The Pill is probably the only success story, in preventing children being brought into an unwanting, uncaring world. At long last those women in the poorer areas of the world are using it, no longer being prepared to rely on their menfolk to use protection. Sadly the attitude of many men is still 'nothing to do with me, mate'. In fact the 'riding bareback' attitude that my Son made me aware of in our earlier conversation, is still prevalent in many parts of the world. How this attitude can be changed I have not yet worked out...but I will.

Sadly, pornography, especially on the internet, is still an area where governments throughout the world are either not prepared to 'grasp the nettle' and take action to prevent it entering people's homes, or feel that they are incapable of doing so. It has become a bit of a nightmare for those parents who care about what their highly skillful and highly curious children are able to access on the internet. If pornography can be found on the internet by adults, it follows that it can be found by children. Those who disagree are simply being naïve.

So...on the issue of mans' attitude to sex the situation has continued to deteriorate. It is this one area where mankind has disappointed me most of all. But there is no point in harping on about it at this precise moment because there is a more pressing issue. But mankind can rest assured that I will come back with a vengeance on the whole area of his attitude to sex, in the not too distant future.

This now takes me onto that *pressing issue*...that of the Earth's security. How are things going? This is where the details get technical, not my strong point, so I have asked my Son to take over.

Narrator - Jesus

As the planet spins on its axis below my Father and I, I only need to concentrate on one of the five continents – that of Africa, and only the top third of it. The major nations of the world decided that all the research, development and construction work that would inevitably be required to produce a force capable of defeating the advancing army from Alpha Centauri would be concentrated on a purpose-built site in the middle of the Sahara Desert. The spot chosen was at Latitude 19°N,

Longitude 13°E, slightly north of the small oasis town of Bilma, in the country of Niger. The spot is roughly equidistant from the Atlantic coast to the west and the Red Sea to the east, the Mediterranean Sea to the north and the Gulf of Guinea to the south-west. Its vast flat area made it an ideal choice.

The first essentials to be constructed were the three runways. These were five thousand metres long and set in the shape of an equilateral triangle with the six ends of the runways slightly overlapping. This gave an internal area of just under eleven square kilometres. In the triangle's exact centre was the control tower, almost fifty metres in height, giving visibility to the extremities. This vast internal area was where the International Humanitarian Force was housed. It was used to store all the equipment that was required, along with a hundred fully maintained helicopters, both small search-and-rescue, and the larger transport ones that can lift a small bulldozer. Five large transport planes were permanently on standby, ready to go at an hour's notice.

There were voices raised when the idea was floated, that it was all a waste of money, but when disaster strikes speed is of the essence, and what price does one place on threatened lives, sometimes numbering in the thousands? Far too often in the past immediate help has been absent or late in coming, the Haiti earthquake in 2010 being an example. The Kazakhstan earthquake showed just how things could, and should be, done. Many people had been trapped under fallen masonry, but were themselves either uninjured, or slightly so. These were saved by the prompt action of the rescue force, arriving early with the necessary equipment.

Using the Centre of the triangle a circle was then drawn round it with a radius of some eight thousand metres. The perimeter of this circle now formed the outer boundary of the huge complex required to produce the Earth's defensive force against the Alpha Centauri invasion. This vast construction, almost completed, not only would provide the research and development facilities required, but also the construction facilities once the research had produced satisfactory results.

The requirements were well known. They were to produce a spacecraft technically capable of destroying the invading force. Using the knowledge gained from the crashed spacecraft in the Arizona desert a weapon of massive destructive force, using a beam of high energy particles producing atomic disintegration of any object it struck, has been successfully trialled. Good progress has also been made in the

553

technology required to make the craft undetectable by the most sophisticated detecting equipment.

It had been suggested sometime ago that the mode of attack should be in the form of an ambush using a line of many invisible craft stretching across many kilometres of empty space. The big uncertainty in the whole plan was the speed that the invasion force would be approaching at. It obviously had to slow down at some point otherwise not only would it overshoot the Earth, it would overshoot the whole Solar System. It was during this slowing down stage that the Earth's force would strike from its invisible positon.

Of course the whole site required huge amounts of special materials, particularly metals such as tungsten and tantalium, both with high melting points and considerable strength. Deposits of such metals were known to exist further south and were already being mined and transported northwards. Processing plants had already been constructed and these required huge amounts of energy. This was already being provided by the oil and gas deposits that were under the Sahara Desert. Vast quantities of water were also required and these were also being provided by wells descending deep under the desert.

And last but not least there was the workforce most of which had come from the poorer regions of the African continent. The men working on the site were required to send money back to any family they had and as a result the quality of life at home had improved out of all proportion. Health programmes were in full swing and many childen were attending achool for the first time. This has been the positive spin-off of the whole project taking place further north. Of course the massive workforce, now a huge community, required good accommodation and this was provided by flats in multistorey blocks. So that 'all work and no play didn't make Jack a dull boy', to misquote a well known English expression, there were a whole range of recreational facilities from gyms, swimming pools and cinemas, to restaurants and bars. And since on occasions drinking got out of hand there was also a civil police force. Sadly, and I suppose inevitably, a drug and prostitution scene had soon developed.

Finally, the perimeter of the whole vast complex was patrolled by a military force under the flag of the United Nations. Unfortunately the whole site could be clearly seen from space, as the over-passing satellites revealed on a daily basis, although the transmission of any pictures taken had been strictly forbidden. If a reconnaissance craft from the Alpha Centauri force, as we suspected the crashed craft could well have been, were to overfly the huge base it would soon be common knowledge to the it that something big and of a military nature has been constructed on Earth.Maybe 'two and two' would be added together to give four. But there was absolutely nothing that mankind on Earth could do about it. We would only know if some sort of pre-emptive strike were to take place on the site.

***

Chapter Fifty One

Narrator – Peter Robertshaw

It had been known for some time the year and approximate month that the Alpha Centauri invasion force would arrive in the vicinity of our Solar System. It could only be approximate because no one knew how quickly the speed of the force could be dropped from somewhere in the region of a quarter the speed of light to one that would allow it to move into orbit and invade the Earth. Could the drop in speed be done in a matter of seconds, or would it take considerably longer? The month and year were August 2034, give or take a month either way.

What was hoped was that we on Earth would be prepared. Since we did not have the knowledge to make an informed opinion about our preparedness we had to assume that we would be. There was little to be gained by 'the powers that be' allowing the world's population to believe that we were not ready. Uncertainty could easily lead to civil unrest, the very last thing that was required on Earth.

What we did know, because those in charge of the whole project had allowed snippets of information to be 'leaked' to the media, was that some sort of weapon had been developed that could stop anything in its tracks. There was little point explaining to 'Joe Public' (to coin a typical English phrase) that it consisted of a beam of particles exiting from some sort of gun at close to the speed of light. A sort of mini CERN, the particle accelerator built underground on the France/Swiss border. The gun would be mounted in the nose of a spacecraft that had the ability to make itself invisible by being able to absorb any probing beams that were looking for it. No technical details had been revealed, but none were necessary, the vast majority of the world's population not being able to understand them anyway. All that was required was reassurance, and that had been given. We now had to place our trust and our lives in mankind's ability to defend itself. We had no alternative.

But we were lucky, if 'lucky' was the appropriate word in the particular circumstances. We had God and his Son, Jesus Christ, or Jesus Nazarene as I had known him for many years now, on our side. Both had and still were playing a major role in our preparation.

Jesus had returned to Earth in a way that did not in the least surprise me. Angela and I had dropped into the habit of climbing Pen-y-Ghent once a month. The walk was enjoyable, the exercise good for us, but the main reason, although we never revealed our thoughts to each other, was that we hoped to meet Jesus Nazarene up there after he'd 'dropped in', so to speak.

Early January was no exception. With a layer of snow some ten centimetres thick on the hill tops we made our ascent. The sky was clear and there was no wind. Although one had to be well wrapped up the conditions were ideal for a steady walk. Tala would have loved it. Hopefully she was with us in spirit.

Following us, but some two hundred metres behind, was an lone walker also taking advantage of the ideal conditions. As we strolled up the gentle slope to the summit we detected on the western horizon beyond Ingleborough Hill a thin bank of cloud. We paid little attention, it being too far away. We would be home sat in front of our large log burning fire by the time it reached our neck of the woods.

But we were wrong. The build up of cloud was rapid and soon we were immersed in a thick wet mist that would have soaked us to the skin had we not been adequately clothed.

Then, both of us became aware that we were being approached by someone. At first we saw a fuzzy shape that rapidly developed into that of a person. We weren't in the slightest surprised, knowing that the lone walker would eventually catch us up. I shouted across: "Trust it to spoil itself after such a good start to the day…Have you travelled far?" Not knowing how experienced the walker was I added: "Shall we descend together, just to be on the safe side?"

The walker's reply bore no relationship to the two questions I'd asked, not surprising since it wasn't the walker at all. It was someone else, with a voice all too familiar to us. "As I was talking to my Father in Heaven I spotted both of you leaving your car in the car park at Horton-in-Ribbledale and I'd a good idea where you were heading…I decided there and then to join you…Besides, I need to return to UN Headquarters in New York, then travel to the complex in the Sahara Desert to report on what my Father has discovered about the invading force…I may need your help to do so, the complex I understand being harder to get into than Fort Knox."

My first reaction, being totally lost for words, was to simply smile. Angela, never ever lost for words, replied on both our behalves: "We'd a hunch that one day we'd meet you up here, and here you are…By the way, good morning…Now, I suggest that you accompany us back home where you can change, get warm and have a bite to eat…You can then tell us why you need our help, and what that help should consist of."

I nodded, wholeheartedly agreeing with Angela's choice of words.

We were about to commence our descent, when the lone walker did emerge out of the mist. His first words were: "Good morning…Typical Dales weather."

Before I could reply he added, or asked: "Er…Where did he come from?...Just before the mist enveloped you there were only you two on the summit."

I smiled, so tempted to reveal that there standing in front of him was Jesus Christ, the Son of God, who had not on this occasion ascended up toHeaven, but instead descended down to Earth, but obviously I couldn't. Instead I had to be a little economical with the truth: "Oh…He's climbed up to the summit from the south, intent on traversing the Hill, whereas we've approached it from the north…We may as well now join up and head down the way we came, just to be on the safe side…Ok?"

His enthusiastic nod told me that he was happy with both my explanation and suggestion.

Back at our smallholding Jesus changed into a clean T-shirt and a pair of jeans that had been hanging in one of the B&B wardrobes since the time he'd previously resided there. Angela quickly knocked together an omelette that appeared to have in it everything but the proverbial kitchen sink. I was prepared to bet my next month's pension that its recipe did not appear in the millions of e-books and hardbacks that had over the years been written. Had she been the sort to enter cookery competitions I was convinced that she would have won them all, such was her skill and originality.

There was only one area where she let herself down. She wasn't into carefully placing the food in fancy patterns on the plate then drizzling gravy or a sauce onto it, at the same time drawing fancy patterns. When our omelettes arrived they weren't perfect circles, looking instead like folded over pasties, but without the pastry. Needless to say, they tasted out of this world, washed down with an excellent Bordeaux Sauvignon Blanc.

It was now time to get down to business. How could we be of assistance to Jesus? There was only one way to find out…ask: "So…You earlier said you wanted our help…Why and in what way?"

The first part of his reply surprised us: "As I told you, I need to go toUN Headquarters in New York…I want to pick up my Holy Square… It is going to be required when the battle in space commences…Will you do the airline booking for me?"

I found it a strange request, and for two reasons. First - why did he need to take a plane to New York? Couldn't he simply 'fly' there, using the same method he'd just used to return to Earth from Heaven? And second - why did he want his Holy Square?

I decided not to ask him about the first, not wanting to give the impression that I considered his mode of transport to be a bit 'Startrekish', and Jesus definitely wasn't Captain Kirk. I did however quiz him about the second: "Why do you want your Holy Square?...I can't see what role it can possibly play in the coming conflict…And isn't there the danger that most or even all of it could become damaged, even lost?"

His reply revealed little: "As you are aware, Peter, the individual pieces of pot have remarkable properties, properties given them by my Father himself…It is these properties that will be fully utilised…I am not prepared to say any more at this stage."

But it was the second part of his reply, again in the form of a request that Angela and I found strange.

"Do you still have a 'hotline' to the Prime Minister of the UK?...I know that you used to…If so, can you tell him that Jesus Nazarene has valuable information about the advancing invasion force, and that he wishes to pass this on to the Officer-in-Charge at the base in the Sahara Desert?...The success of the whole mission could well depend on this information."

In my flippant way I was tempted to suggest that he should simply 'fly in', Pen-y-Ghent style, descending in a cloud, but decided against it. I did instead inform him that I did indeed have a hotline to the PM, and added: "In fact it had been used in reverse only a couple of months ago when the PM had asked me if there was any chance of me making contact with you…I informed him that maybe there was, and if I did I would immediately contact him…That was the main reason why Angela and I commenced our monthly walk up our favourite hill, one that we knew was familiar to you…We knew that if you intended to reveal yourself to us it would be on Pen-y-Ghent…And we were right."

Jesus smiled: "God…Am I so predictable?...Er, sorry for taking your name in vain, Father. "

Jesus Nazarene certainly had a sense of humour.

The following day I was on the Internet early, seeking out a flight from Manchester Airport to JFK, New York. Once this was arranged using the details on the credit card that Jesus gave me, the card that appeared to have an unlimited supply of funds on it, I phoned 10 Downing Street using my special hotline number.

The woman who answered immediately put me on 'hold', and I assumed that she was passing my name onto a higher authority who would in turn pass it on to the Prime Minister. The next voice I heard was his: "Good morning Mr Robertshaw...How's the weather in your neck of the woods?...The last time I was up there, just over twelve months ago, officially opening the new Dalesway Academy in Skipton, it was cold, wet and utterly miserable."

"You must have been unlucky, Prime Minister...We rarely have weather as bad as that...In fact today is glorious, as was yesterday when we climbed Pen-y-Ghent in near perfect conditions...It's one of the Three Peaks, you know."

"You've obviously forgotten, Mr Robertshaw...Being of the White Rose county like your good self I know all about your weather and your Three Peaks...Anyway, you've no doubt called me for a reason...Care to enlighten me?"

"I have Jesus Nazarene sitting beside me at this very moment...Don't ask me how my wife and I met up with him, you won't believe me anyway...He has asked me to contact you as a matter of urgency...He has strategic information that he considers essential to those planning the attack on the Alpha Centauri invasion force...It is most important that he has the opportunity to pass this information on, and this means him being transported to the Sahara Desert Base as soon as possible...Are you able to arrange transport for him and get him the necessary clearance to get into the Base?...Take my word for it, this is most urgent." I added the last sentence even though I hadn't the slightest idea what the information was and why it *was* so important.

There then followed a long silence and I was convinced that the line had gone dead. The PM then replied: "Can you get Mr Nazarene to RAF Linton-on-Ouse in the morning by ten-thirty?...A Typhoon will take him to the Sahara airbase where he will be picked up by our military representative there...He will be interviewed in order that an assessment can be made of the information he has…If it is deemed of sufficient importance he will be asked to appear before the full defence committee…Will he approve of that?"

"I'll ask him," and this is what I did.

He immediately responded loudly and positively, but pointed out an obvious problem: "Yes…I approve of the arrangements…But what about my trip to New York?…It's already arranged."

Indeed it was, but I was certain that those could be changed. To me, and I sensed that Jesus agreed with me, the appointment in the Sahara must take priority. I therefore relayed this to the PM: "Jesus approves the arrangements, and I will make sure he's at RAF Linton-on-Ouse in the morning at ten-thirty."

The PM thanked me and said goodbye. I and no doubt he were about to replace the handsets when he quickly asked: "By the way…Why does he want to go to New York?"

"To pick up his Holy Square."

"Why?"

"I have no idea…He won't tell me."

On that unhelpful note we both appeared to end the call at the same time.

My next job, one that had to be done immediately was to try and rearrange Jesus's flight to New York. This I managed to do although there was a hefty charge to do so. Fortunately I had not to pay for it.

The following morning, very early, the Robertshaw household was a hive of industry. Angela was in the kitchen area making scrambled egg on toast for three. I was getting shaved, and Jesus was in the B&B throwing a change of clothes into an overnight bag. I'd already worked out using an OS map (I love OS maps) that the journey to Linton-on-Ouse was about seventy miles and was going to take a good two hours, but if we left our home at eight o'clock we should arrive in good time, assuming of course that we didn't get stuck behind a tractor on the narrow road down to Horton, or worse still had a blow-out.

Once in the car, a new hybrid using both electrical power and an internal combustion engine running on hydrogen, I spoke the Linton-on-Ouse code into the voice activated onboard navigation computer. Once set, the car would now drive itself to its destination, and that is precisely what it did. I fully expected the internal combustion engine to click in early after the first part of the journey, all up-and-down, having drained much of the battery power, but no. As we pulled into the visitor carpark at the RAF Base the power indicator still showed ten percent availability.

As one of the two main gate guards strode across, rifle on his shoulder, I wound down the window. Before I'd time to say who we were he spoke to me in a coarse abrupt tone making a not-quite-right assumption: "Mr Nazarene?...Would you please accompany me, Sir?"

I quickly pointed out that Mr Nazarene was in fact the man sitting at the side of me. Jesus nodded verifying that fact and alighted from the car with his overnight bag. As he did so he turned and spoke to me: "Thank you, Peter...May I give you a ring tomorrow when I arrive back in the UK?"

"Of course...I will then come across and pick you up...Better still, see if you can phone from the Sahara to say that you are setting off...By the time you arrive at Linton we should be here...Okay?"

"Good idea...I'm sure it will be possible to do so."

Angela and I watched as Jesus passed through the gate and disappeared round the corner of a large building possibly a hangar. We then got out of the car and walked a short distance to a spot that allowed us to see the runway through the tall barbed wire topped security fence. Twenty minutes later we saw two individuals in full flying gear except their helmets, commence their walk toward a waiting aircraft, presumably the Typhoon.

One hesitantly and with assistance from the other climbed up and eased his body into the cockpit...obviously Jesus. The other expertly jumped up...obviously the pilot, who appeared to check that his passenger was correctly strapped in, presumably to the ejector seat. How strange it must have seemed to Jesus who would not have required the services of such a primitive contraption had the plane decided to drop out of the sky.

Both then put on their helmets after which the cockpit canopy was closed. Jesus was now ready for a flight in one of the fastest aircraft ever built. I wondered what he'd make of it all. Having said that, he had on more than one occasion travelled at speeds far in excess of what the Typhoon was capable of.

During the previous evening, utterly bored with television, I'd looked up some information about this particular aircraft. It was a twin engined fighter capable of Mach 2 at altitude and had a range of just short of 3000 kilometres. I'd then measured the as-the-crow-flies distance from Linton-on-Ouse to the Sahara Base and came up with a figure just over

4000 kilometres, way above the aircraft's range. It would therefore presumably have to re-fuel, but where...Gibraltar maybe?

As we watched the aircraft taxi to the end of the runway, turn, then accelerate at a frightening speed, quickly lifting into the air and eventually disappearing into the clouds, I couldn't help but smile.

Angela, spotted it: "What's so funny?"

"I was just thinking...One way of guaranteeing that the plane arrives safely is to have the Son of God on board."

"Very true," was her reply: "Very true."

Narrator – Jesus Nazarene

The acceleration was frightening as we sped down the runway. The strange feeling experienced when taking off in a modern commercial jet, as I had on my journeys to and from America, was bad enough, but here I was convinced that I had left my stomach behind on the ground. It only made matters worse when I was forced back into my seat by the pilot pointing the plane's nose to the heavens. The only plus point was that we were now in bright sunshine, way above the clouds. The fact that we appeared to be heading towards the sun told me that we were already on a southerly course. Seconds late the pilot confirmed through the intercom that I was correct: "We're now at an altitude of 50 000 feet, Sir, almost in heaven..."

I was so tempted to say: "Been there...Got the T-shirt," but obviously couldn't without causing confusion in my pilot's mind.

The pilot continued: "We're at the moment heading south, but as we fly over Birmingham we'll change to a south westerly course, that will take us over Land's End and into the Atlantic, not of course literally, Sir, unless something goes very wrong."

I was also tempted to say: "Oh...There's no danger of that while I'm on board."

"The southerly course will be again resumed taking us across the Bay of Biscay, until we reach the entrance to the Mediterranean where we will assume an easterly course that will take us into Gibraltar where we will re-fuel...May I suggest, Sir, that you sit back and enjoy the flight...Unfortunately at this altitude there is nothing to see, but I'm afraid that I cannot do anything about that...Time wise our journey time to Gibraltar will be just over the hour. "

As we flew south the cloud slowly thinned out and by the time we reached GIbraltar the sky was crystal clear. This enabled me to take in the amazing view of the Rock itself as we approached it. On the previous occasions I had passed over it I had been in Heaven, so it had appeared as a mere speck on the Earth's surface, which itself had appeared as a large disk. Now I was able to appreciate the Rock's sheer size and beauty.

Re-fuelling took place in a matter of minutes, the team having no doubt been made aware of our imminent arrival. We were soon airbourne and over the huge continent that was Africa. On a map the last lap of our journey looked a mere stone's throw away from Gibraltar, but the pilot put me wise: "We've still another seventeen hundred miles to go, all of it over desert apart from the Atlas Mountains that you can see down there on the right…Journey time should be an hour and a half…Again sit back and enjoy the flight."

And that was precisely what I did.

As we approached the Sahara Base I was amazed at the sheer size of the site. It was like a large town, with huge modern buildings in the centre and what looked like factories on the outskirts. A complex road network linked the two. The three runways, set in the shape of an equilateral triangle were clearly visible, as were the various aircraft, including helicopters that were part of the International Rescue Force

But what caught my eye the most was an array of what looked likemini versions of the Saturn rocket, all vertical, standing on one of the runways. I attempted to count them before they passed out of my field of view as we came into land, but stopped counting at twenty, and that appeared to be about a quarter of the total.

My pilot again put me wise: "That's the Force, Sir, that's hopefully going to defend us against the Alpha Centauri invaders…They're called *Gladiators* for obvious reasons and all are ready to go as soon as they get the word, all ninety-seven of them…Why not a straight one hundred?...Maybe they ran out of time building them…Anyway, a colleague of mine has test flown one of them out in space, including the armoury, and is confident that they can do the job, especially since they can be made invisible to any enemy."

It did seem a rather strange number to those not in the know, but there was another explanation, as I will reveal later. It was at that point that I realised just how important the information I had, was. Thank God (sorry Father for the blasphemy), that I would be able to pass it on before the Force took to the air, so to speak.

564

After landing and descending from the cockpit both my pilot and I were picked up by a jeep and taken to a close-by building where I extracted myself from my G suit and put on a T-shirt and a pair of chinos that had been provided for me. Both items fitted perfectly, why I had no idea, unless somewhere in some database my physical statistics were stored. Someone had looked them up and chosen the items accordingly. One thing was certain – I didn't care why they fitted. All I was interested in was the fact that they did and felt comfortable in the hot conditions.

At that point I left my pilot. As I did so he called across: "We leave for Linton at 0900 hours in the morning, Sir…I will meet you in this room half an hour before in order to get our flying gear on…Please be punctual."

I felt like pointing out that I was always punctual, but resisted, knowing full well that in the military things had to go like clockwork, and that included the time.

The same jeep took me to the entrance of some sort of conference room where I was first met by a man in military fatigues suited to the hot conditions, He introduced himself as Field Marshall Peter Norton, of the British Army, on secondment to the Sahara Desert Force. He spoke abruptly, which was probably his manner when addressing his subordinates: "It was our original plan, Mr Nazarene, to allow you to speak to a small group of military experts who would assess the value of your information before allowing you to address our full military assembly…But given the urgency of the situation you will address the full assembly only, and that will be in ten minutes' time if that's all right by you."

I initially gasped, at the same time feeling uneasy at how fast events were moving, but then remembered my United Nations addresses. I'd shown extreme confidence there. I'd show extreme confidence now: "That's fine by me…I know exactly what I intend to say."

With no further ado I was led into the conference room that was already full of seated people, both men and women, all in military fatigues. This was slightly intimidating because I, with very limited military knowledge, would be addressing the experts. But my confidence quickly returned, for I had information that they didn't have, but dearly wanted.

The Field Marshall first asked me to sit down on a seat at the front that had obviously been reserved for me. After silencing the audience with a wave of the hand he briefly introduced me: "Our guest speaker is

Mr Nazarene...I'll leave it to him to tell you a bit about himself and why he is here addressing us today...I'm sure that you will find his words both interesting and thought provoking...And I'm also sure that he will be happy to answer any questions at the end of his speech...Mr Nazarene."

I rose from my seat and took up my position behind a light wood lectern of simple construction. I had no notes to place on it. I did not need any.

"Thank you, Field Marshall...I am here today to inform you of what I know about the Alpha Centauri Invasion Force...I do not intend to go into details on how I come to have this information other than that my Father in Heaven has been monitoring its progress for several years and has passed details of its latest position onto me so that I can pass them directly on to you.

"At this precise moment the invasion force is stationary in space at a distance of seven million kilometres from the Earth and with the Sun directly behind it, where we feel it is preparing for the invasion...Maybe after its long journey of some sixteen years it needs some sort of re-energizing.

"Its plan is to approach the Earth at a velocity of thirty thousand kilometres per hour a mere snail's pace after its high speed journey through deep space...This will allow it to go into orbit in just seven days' time, from where it will shower thousands of missiles of devastating power on the heavily populated areas of many countries...Once this has been accomplished, with the Earth's population that has survived totally demoralised, the invasion proper will begin, with thousands of well armed mobile soldiers being landed on the five continents...This will take the form of a 'sweeping up' operation with the aim of taking people alive if possible who will become a giant slave force that will be used to prepare the Earth for the millions of Alpha Centaurians who at this very moment are on their sixteen year journey across space to our Solar System.

"So, what can be done to prevent this?...The only way is to attack the invasion force as it approaches the Earth, but is still a considerable distance away...I would suggest about forty thousand kilometres...I can tell you now that you will be defeated if you engage the enemy in open space combat...They will out-number and out-gun you...The attack must therefore be in the form of an ambush...I have it on good authority that the spacecrafts, with the name Gladiator, that I have seen on their launch pads outside this room are capable of making themselves undetectable.

"I would therefore strongly suggest that in this mode you form a line of equally spaced craft a kilometre apart, making a sort of inpenetrable wall in the region of a hundred kilometres long...I understand that one disadvantage that the Gladiators unfortunately possess is their inability to open fire when in the invisible mode, which has to be switched off first, thus immediately revealing their position...It is therefore essential that they open fire at exactly the same time as the order to switch off is given...Surprise is your friend...Delay, however slight, is your enemy.

"I will now tell you what the invasion force consists of so that you have some idea of the task that faces you...At its centre is the mothership that has been used to keep thousands of aliens in some form of cryogenic hibernation during the sixteen year journey...All have been revitalised and are now ready for their mission.

"The mothership is surrounded by a protective screen consisting of two types of spacecraft...I will describe them simply as Bombers, a hundred in number, whose role is to shower the Earth with missiles of unimaginable destructive power...These have only light weaponry, it not being thought necessary for them to be heavily armed...Then there are the Fighters, also a hundred in number, whose role is to provide a defensive shield for both the mothership and the bomber force...By the way, both types of craft have been remotely guided through space in a tight formation round the mothership...At this very moment pilots, if that's what they are, are transferring from the mothership to their bombers and fighters.

"Make no mistake, this is a well organised force, armed to the eye teeth with weapons of massive destructive power...But you will have two advantages that your enemy will not have – the element of surprise, and God on your side...The first is entirely in your hands and it is up to you not to 'mess it up'...The second is in my Father's hands, and he definitely will not do so.

"How the number of ninety-seven of your sophisticated spacecraft was arrived at is interesting...Maybe you only had time to build that number...But as you will see in a moment, maybe there has been some divine intervention there...I am now going to make a suggestion that you may find surprising, puzzling, even make you feel that I am entering into the realms of fantasy...It is this – please divide your force into twelve squadrons of eight Gladiators...Give the squadrons the following names, which are the names of all those who were present at my Last Supper all of two thousand years ago:

PeterMatthewAndrewJudasPhilipSimon
James Alphaeus Thomas John Labbaeus Bartholomew

...Then choose from your very best, thirteen squadron leaders and appoint one of them to be in over-all charge of your mission."

I could immediately detect a feeling of disbelief at my suggestion. How dare this preacher from way back have the audacity to tell us how to organise our Force? The nerve of the man!

Not put off in the slightest I continued: "After returning to the United Kingdom I intend to fly to New York and retrieve my Holy Square...To those of you who are not familiar with its story let me give you a brief resumé...At my Last Supper, just before my crucifixion, I gave each of my twelve disciples a small coloured piece of pot engraved with a Greek letter...These pieces when assembled in a special way around a central piece, fit exactly into a square to form a six pointed star, sometimes known as The Star of David ...This is my Holy Square...Each piece has a tiny hole in it allowing its owner to thread a thin leather thong through, tie it in a loop and place it round his neck...When my disciples left the Holy Land in order to spread my word abroad this small piece of pot protected them against many evils." On this last point I was in fact being a little economical with the truth, for several of the disciples had suffered horrific deaths. There was an explanation for this however. By that time each had in some way lost his piece of the Holy Square, and hence he did not have the protection it would have undoubtedly offered him.

More puzzled looks that asked: So they all had lucky charms that weren't lucky at all, then?

I pressed on, not prepared to be in any way intimidated: "It is my desire that the twelve squadron leaders wear the pieces round their necks, with the over-all leader wearing the central piece which is my personal piece...It all may sound a bit mumbo-jumbo, but I can assure you that this simple act will protect your Force and ensure victory, unless something unpredictable takes place.

"You now know as much as I do about the coming invasion...You also now know how victory can be assured...When it is, a message from the defeated Force will no doubt be hastily sent back to the those Alpha Centaurians who are hoping to build a new life on our Earth...Knowing that their invasion Force has been decisively defeated they will either return to the planet they left or seek another destination somewhere else in our galaxy…Our planet will be safe and secure, and we can get back to channelling all our resources into providing a better world for ourselves and all living things that share the planet with us."

At that point I nodded to the Field Marshall indicating that I had said all I wanted to.

He in turn returned the nod then spoke to the assembly: "I told you to expect an interesting and thought provoking speech and I'm sure that you have not been disappointed…I'm also sure that there are many questions that you would like to ask our guest, so who is going to get the ball rolling?"

I was staggered at the number of hands that went up. It was like a class of young children who had been asked to name their favourite food. What was I to do next? Who would I choose first? Fortunately the Field Marshall took the decision out of my hands: "Er…Harry, kick off please."

Harry was obviously a close colleague.

"Colonel Harry Jackson, British Army…You have given us some very useful information, but can we trust its authenticity?"

I expected a question along these lines: "All I can say is that my Father in Heaven is a see-all and hear-all God…He has in the interests of man on Earth closely observed the progress of this alien force…He has tuned into its communication systems, hence his knowledge of the force's strength and strategy…It all comes down to faith in the Almighty…But if you are a non-believer how will you plan *your* strategy?"

Colonel Jackson, probably not having an alternative strategy, nodded but preferred not to say anything. The Field Marshall then pointed to a woman, one of several in the room.

"Captain Irena Molotov, Russian Air Force…Surely the number of missiles will have to be huge in order to have the demoralising effect that the alien force hopes for?"

It was a good question. The earth was a big place: "Think what would have happened if during the Cold War between your country and the West hydrogen bombs had been dropped over all of Russia's major cities and over all those in Western Europe and North America…The expression used at the time to describe the result of such an act was - the end of civilisation as we know it…This is what we are talking about here, but it will also include attacks on China, Japan, Australia, the continents of Africa and South America…No area will come through unscathed."

After the first two questions several hands went down. Presumably their questions had been along the same lines as the two already asked.

The Field Marshall spotted another colleague: "Matt, your question?"

"Captain Matt Dawson, US Air Force…You mentioned that the alien force was stationary, directly in line with the Sun…Why have they done this, and won't their position change in relation to the Earth as both orbit the Sun?"

"Two very interesting questions…Let me answer the second one first…You are of course correct if the alien force is allowed to move freely in space…Being closer to the Sun than the Earth it will be travelling faster in its orbit, as do Venus and Mercury for example…But the alien's velocity is being intentionally slowed to keep the Sun directly behind it…You no doubt have flying experience, Captain…" He nodded in the affirmative.

"You therefore know how attacking out of the Sun gives the attacker a great advantage…The strategy was used extensively by fighters during World War II, although nowadays no doubt electronic rather than visual identification is used."

The next question had nothing to do with 'strategy' and came from the Field Marshall himself: "Do we know why the Alpha Centaurians have left their planet and are supposedly heading for Earth?"

My initial response was abrupt: "Not supposedly, Sir…They are definitely on their way…Now, why have they left their mother planet?…Their Sun is much older than ours and is in the process of expanding…It will eventually explode becoming what is known as a 'supernova', a super new star…Conditions on their planet have become intolerable with raging fires due to the high temperature and lack of rainfall…The atmosphere is heavily polluted and breathing has become impossible…Funnily enough this will also happen to the Earth, but not for many millions of years."

The Field Marshall, quickly wanting to move on after my mild rebuke, pointed to another raised hand.

"Commodore Francois Fouré, French Navy…You have said that the alien force have been in a state of cryogenic hibernation…Hasn't this method of prolonging life been tried, and hasn't it failed on Earth?"

Another good question: "You are of course right…Scientists on Earth have tried to perfect this method for three reasons – to give eternal life to the rich…to place a person with a terminal illness in cold storage until a method of successful treatment is found, and to allow space travellers to make huge journeys without ageing, as the aliens have succeeded in doing."

By this time there were only two hands up. The Field Marshall picked out one.

"General Xi Choi, Chinese Army…How do you know the strength of the alien force so accurately?"

As I gave my simple and very short answer I smiled: "Oh…My Father has counted them." Although no doubt still puzzled he decided not to ask a follow-up question.

Since only one hand was now up I pointed to its owner.

"Squadron Leader Ken Ridgeway, Royal Air Force…Won't the handing out of these strange bits of pot be like handing out lucky charms with dubious powers?...It's a bit like a crazy motorist blasting down the motorway expecting the *Saint Christopher* pendant around his neck to protect him."

It was a good question to round off the session. I hoped that my answer would satisfy the questioner: "When I gave out the pieces of pot during my Last Supper they were to protect those who had received them when they embarked on their journeys to far off places spreading my word, and by and large they did, although the evidence has been lost over time…More recently, following their re-discovery by an English professor of archaeology, there have been examples where the pieces have protected those who were in possession of them, on occasions probably saving their lives…I could go into detail, but I'm aware that we have run out of time."

The Field Marshall nodded to me, agreeing with my last comment. In his opinion time had definitely run out. But there was one extra thing I wanted to say, and did so before he closed the meeting: "As I have already told you, I fly back to the UK tomorrow…The following day I fly to the US to pick up my Holy Square from UN Headquarters…I will then return here to distribute all thirteen pieces to the squadron leaders who will, I hope, have already been chosen by you…The schedule is tight, but it has to be with the invasion due to commence in just seven days' time."

There were visible gasps at my last statement as the reality of the situation came home to them.

At that, I returned to my place. My mission at *Operation Sahara*, as it had now become known, now complete… at least for the moment.

***

Chapter Fifty Two

The following morning, after a hasty breakfast, I first rang Peter and Angela in the UK to let them know that I was about to take to the air. They could then set off on their journey to Linton-on-Ouse in order to pick me up. I then made my way to the changing room. Here I found my pilot who was already in his G suit. After quickly helping me on with mine, not an easy task, the two of us made our way to the Typhoon that was already fueled up and ready to go.

Remembering how to climb up and drop into the cockpit I was soon fastening myself to the ejector seat and plugging in my intercom lead. Before taking up his own position my pilot checked that I had got everything right. A 'thumbs up' indicated that I had.

The take-off wasn't as traumatic this time. Once experienced you knew what to expect. We were quickly through a thin layer of cirrus cloud, a rarity over the Sahara, and my pilot informed me that it would probably be with us all the way home. Since we were soon at an altitude of fifty thousand feet, whether there was cloud or not was of little consequence. It was impossible to see anything anyway, apart from being able to tell if one was over land or sea.

The return journey, including our refueling stop in Gibraltar, seemed much shorter. Why, I did't know, but I had noticed this on many occasions whilst travelling, especially over long distances. My pilot was soon informing me that although we couldn't see them we had just passed over the Isles of Scilly and would be soon passing over the Midands. What seemed only a few minutes later we were dropping rapidly in altitude eventually passing through the cloud that had rapidly thickened over the Bristol Channel.

I could now see the runway as it stretched out in front of us, almost reaching the horizon. I felt the plane shudder slightly as the undercarriage was lowered, and seconds later we touched down with a bump. As we descended from the plane my pilot apologised: "Sorry about the poor landing, Sir…At one point the runway's slightly dropped…Something to do with mining subsidence, so I've been told…Just my luck to land on the sunken bit."

I smiled at his apologetic attitude and replied: "No doubt something to do with Sod's Law…If there's a metre of uneven runway in five thousand metre of length, the law says you'll hit it...And you did."

He returned the smile, but his reply nevertheless had a serious note about it: "I hope that Sod's Law doesn't come into it out in space while our Force is in combat with the enemy."

I was able to give him some reassurance on that point: "Oh...I think the good Lord will keep an eye on things out there."

Typical of I and Angela, they were there waiting just outside the main gate of the airfield. After thanking the guard on duty, why, I didn't know other than it seemed the right thing to do, I jumped into the back of the car ready for my leisurely journey home. My mode of transport had gone from one of twice the speed of sound to one of thirty miles an hour in the space of just ten minutes. It was a wonder that my body was able to cope with the drastic change, but it did...such resilience.

This journey was also one of those where the return seemed shorter and therefore quicker than the outward one. We had soon crossed the A1, heading for Harrogate and in no time at all the Skipton sign appeared for the first time.

As we passed through Horton-in-Ribblesdale I glanced at my watch. The return journey, which had followed the same route, had taken twenty minutes less than the outward one. Maybe in one's brain time slightly shrinks on return journeys. I must quiz my Father about it. He will no doubt have an answer. What I did know was that during the time we'd been on the road the conversation, in the form of a question-and-answer session, I and Angela doing the questioning, me doing the answering, the theme had obviously been about my experiences at *Operation Sahara* the previous day. It only stopped when we pulled into the long drive leading up to the Robertshaw residence.

As we entered the front door Peter shouted across: "By the way...I didn't fancy making the journey across the Pennines to Manchester Airport tomorrow, so I've ordered you a taxi...The driver will also pick you up on your return and bring you home...All right?"

"Fine by me...I've heard others say it's a bit of a nightmare journey...Better to have someone who knows the route well."

"I hope you're not suggesting that I'm too old in the tooth to make it," replied Peter, a big grin on his face.

"Heaven forbid...Sorry Father," was my flippant response.

Peter then made a suggestion that I, quite frankly, had never thought of: "Why not take my copy of the Holy Square and asked them at the UN if you can exchange it for the real thing?...No one would know, and if they did, it wouldn't really matter…Many museums have copies of the real items…In the entrance to Doncaster Museum there's a model of a Roman soldier on horseback that I had specially made…It's obviously not the real thing, but who cares?...No one."

I thought for a second as an alternative solution briefly passed through my mind. Why not abandon the idea of going to New York in order to pick up the Holy Square and instead take Peter's copy with me to *Operation Sahara*? I could distribute its pieces to the thirteen squadron leaders that hopefully had been chosen? It all made sense…But it didn't. It would have been the height of deceitfulness and irresponsibility to lead those brave men into some sense of false security. They would think that by wearing the pieces round their necks they would in some way have my Father at their side protecting them, when all the time they were wearing useless copies. I certainly wouldn't accept it, and my Father would explode with rage at the very thought. No, all thirteen pieces had to be authentic, and if that meant a journey across the Atlantic, so be it.

With Peter's copy of my Holy Square in my overnight bag I left the Robertshaw residence by taxi at just after half past nine. The pickup time had been arranged by Peter for nine 'clock, but the taxi's state-of-the-art SAT-NAV had taken it down a never ending cart track just north of Horton.

Angela had earlier made me a cooked breakfast, English style, to send me on my way, and as I hurriedly passed through the door Peter handed me a children's toy, or part of one. It was an arrow with a sucker on the end, the type that was shot at a target, the sucker sticking to it. Smiling, he whispered: "You may need this," but refrained from explaining why.

Our seventy-five mile journey took us just two hours, the first half on country roads, the second on the motorway system where the driver over-rode the taxi's speed control system, thinking that the seventy speed limit did not apply to him.

Eventually we arrived at Manchester Airport. The driver dropped me off and as I paid him with cash that I had borrowed from Peter he assured me that he would be there to pick me up in twenty-four hours' time.

Although my 'aliens are coming' speech to the United Nations had been given worldwide coverage on all forms of media the population at large quite frankly didn't believe the story. It didn't help when astronomers throughout the world, using the most sophisticated equipment that was reputed to be able to pick up an object the size of a football at the distance of the moon, and one the size of a double-decker bus at the distance of Saturn, had failed to pick up the mothership that was of considerable size. Of course being in a position where the sun was directly behind it, it did not reflect any light, which the detecting equipment had been looking for.

As a result of this unconvinced attitude the activity at the airport was as normal as it could be with people going about their business. With my overnight bag of 'cabin luggage' dimensions I passed through the security check unhindered. I did get a suspicious look however when my passport was scanned, the scanner commenting: "Jesus Nazarene, eh?...Haven't seen that name before."

I was so tempted to say – no, there's only one of me – but thought better of it. He didn't seem the sort of person who you could have a joke with.

My flight to JFK was at 12:15 and the Boeing *Dreamliner* left on time. Peter had already contacted the UN Admin Section, informing them of my impending visit in order to pick up my Holy Square. Since the arrangement had always been expected no problem was anticipated. Before my departure Peter had informed me to the effect that all was ready for my arrival. When all said and done, it was *my* Holy Square.

The *Dreamliner* covered the 5600 kilometres in just over five hours, landing a few minutes late, the captain's explanation being that the plane had been flying into a slight head wind. It was my intention to go straight to UN Headquarters, exchange the Holy Squares, return to JFK and fly back home, home being a smallholding in the UK's Yorkshire Dales, at least for the time being.

The exchange should have been straight forward, but turned out not to be so. After reporting in at Reception, where I was fortunately expected, I was taken by an official who introduced himself as an aide to the Secretary General, to the Assembly Hall. Here the Holy Square display had been tastefully set up. It was the first time I'd seen it and I was very impressed.

The Square, although minute in relation to the over-all size of the display that was a good two metres across and a metre down, was prominently placed at the centre with pictures and panels of text in several different languages surrounding it.

At the top and in bold gold scripted letters was the title *Christ's Holy*

Square. Immediately below this was a good sized picture of Leonardo da Vinci's 'Last Supper' (although for obvious reasons my Holy Square wasn't there on the large table). And below this was my Holy Square, looking rather pathetic because of its size. Immediately below it was a length of Dead Sea Scroll a good half metre long, with the section of text that described my distribution of the coloured pieces of pot to my disciples set out below it translated into several languages.

Down both sides were six panels set out in the form of tablets showing information about all twelve individual pieces of pot – their shape, colour, the Greek letter engraved into them, which disciple they were given to, where they was found and by whom. Centrally and below the scroll's translations was a tablet showing my hexagonal piece of pot, with a description on how it had been found on a Roman Soldier excavated from an English bog. Finally, across the bottom of the display was the Greek anagram which when translated revealed the message 'rock from heaven', predicting that the World would come to an end by being struck by an asteroid of huge proportions unless man 'mended' his ways. I stood back and admired the display. There was not one thing that I would have changed.

The display was of course well protected, with what I guessed was armour plated glass, and the slow regular flashing of small red lights at the four corners indicated some form of alarm system was in operation, not surprising since the Holy Square itself was undoubtedly the most valuable object in the whole World. In fact it was priceless.

At a nod from the aide three hefty security guards who had been standing in the background moved forward. The four red lights went off presumably indicating that the alarm had been deactivated. How, I had no idea, nor did it matter. The huge glass panel was connected to the top of the substantial wood frame by six equally spaced chrome hinges. At the bottom of the panel were four equally spaced chrome locks that required their own individual key.

By the way the guards carried out the various stages that followed they were obviously implementing a well tried procedure. I noted the tiniest of flies dead on the inside of the glass that had somehow managed to get through the tiniest of gaps between frame and cover. Maybe the guards had to remove them at regular intervals.

First, two of the guards positioned themselves either side of the glass panel. The third one then proceeded to unlock all four locks. On the command 'go' all three carefully lifted the panel above their heads so that it was horizontal. This allowed access to the whole display.

At this point the aide moved in and carefully eased away the four clips that held the Holy Square in its fixed position. He then passed it to me. It felt good...really good. But I now had a problem. This Holy Square had had the protective transparent lid that Peter Robertshaw had made for it, removed. This undoubtely improved visibility, and within the display it wasn't required anyway. The replica in my bag had a lid. I therefore couldn't simply exchange one Square for the other. But what I could do was exchange the thirteen individual pieces of pot.

I knelt down, took the lidless Square and carefully inverted it as close to the carpeted floor as I could. I fully expected the pieces of pot to fall the couple of centimetres, coming to rest on the carpeted floor, but I was wrong. They stayed put. I tapped the top of the Square, but it did not release one single piece.

"Maybe the wood's expanded a little bit over time, tightening the pieces in," commented the aide.

I nodded. It seemed a distinct possibility. Then I remembered. Peter had given me a rubber sucker on the end of length of wood that resembled a pencil but without the lead. I now knew the reason why.

After turning the Square the right way up I licked the sucker and pushed it onto the central piece of pot, my piece. I then gently eased the sucker upwards. Sure enough, the piece came out. I quickly separated it from the sucker and repeated the procedure on another piece of pot. This I repeated until all thirteen pieces were on the floor in a straight line. It goes without saying that I blushed with mbarrassment when the aide clapped to show his appreciation of my 'skill'.

The pieces in the replica Square were not as tight and when I opened the lid and turned the Square over all thirteen dropped onto the carpet.

One of the guards shouted almost in panic: "Don't mix 'em up, Sir."

I smiled at him, at the same time making sure that I indeed did not 'mix 'em up'. Of course had I accidently done so, there was a tiny identifying 'm' on the back of each of the replica pieces. The potter friend of Peter Robertshaw who had made the pieces had done so for this very reason.

It was now simply a case of placing the genuine pieces in the Square with the glass lid that I would be taking back to the UK, and placing the replica pieces in the lidless Square that would then be returned to the UN display...Easy.

Once done, the three guards holding the glass panel slowly lowered it until it was vertical. The guard in the centre then locked the four locks. Immediately he had done this the four red lights commenced their flashing sequence. The alarm had been re-activated. This time I knew how, having observed the aide go to a small box on the wall, open it, revealing a keyboard and tapping in the necessary code. Any observer who had seen the display before and after the procedure would have been unable to spot any difference…except possibly that the tiny flies had been removed.

I thanked the aide for his cooperation, and the guards for their muscular help, then hastily left the UN building. My flight out of JFK to the UK was due to take off in just three hours and I intended to be on it.

As arranged by Peter and promised by the taxi driver my transport home was waiting when I exited the Arrivals building at Manchester Airport. We were soon heading north on the motorway system, before moving onto the winding country roads that would take me back to the Robertshaw residence. Just north of Horton-in-Ribbledale the driver slowed down and studied the road. As he did so he looked at me through his rear view mirror and spoke: "It was here where the SAT-NAV sent me down a cart track…I'm not going to make the same mistake twice."

As we approached a tight bend in the road, the driver going far too fast, the taxi's tyres lost their grip. The vehicle skidded, crashed through the boundary fence and careered down a banking into a deep dike filled with water.

Such an event concentrated the mind and I started to think quickly. I knew for example that as the vehicle slowly sank the electrics would soon short out. It was essential to lower the window nearest to me before it did so. I therefore firmly pressed the button controlling the mechanism. Fortunately for me it was still working. As I was doing this I became aware of two things - the driver's airbag had not inflated, and his seatbelt had failed to restrain him. Looking badly injured with the impact, though judging from his feeble movements still conscious, he appeared to be incapable of helping himself.

I hastily unclipped my seatbelt and tried to open my passenger door, but the water had already shorted out the central locking system. I therefore had no alternative but to ease my way through the open window. I thenhalf walked, half paddled round the car to the driver's door, but could not open that either. The water level was now up to the driver's chest. Soon his face would be below the surface and he would drown.

For some unexplainable reason my overnight bag, that had been on my lap, but I'd had to leave behind, came to the surface and floated through the gap between the two front seats and came to rest at the side of the driver's head. He grabbed it for a reason best known to himself. Maybe he thought that it would act as some sort of float. Seconds later the roof of the vehicle was under water.

In both desperation and anger I raised my eyes to the cloudless sky and yelled: "For God's sake, help him Father." Maybe in the circumstances a bit of blasphemy wasn't out of place…in fact it was justified.

As I stood on the bank feeling totally helpless I suddenly became aware that the water level in the dike was rapidly falling. Soon the top of the vehicle was visible and seconds later the driver's head was clearly visible above the water level. A slight movement of his head indicated that he was at least still alive. The water level continued to fall until the dike was completely empty and its muddy bottom could be clearly seen.

Still struggling, but unable to open the driver's door my acute hearing picked up the sound of some sort of vehicle, not a car, something much bigger and much more powerful. Round the bend trundled a huge tractor, the biggest I'd ever seen. The driver, quickly assessing the situation, stopped and jumped down. His first act was to call the emergency services on his mobile, his second was to extract a crowbar from some sort of toolbox at the back of the tractor.

He climbed down the bank, paddled through the mud and jammed the crowbar into the narrow gap between the door and frame. After several attempts he succeeded in prising it open. Working together we managed to free the driver and extract him from his vehicle. It was now simply a case of getting him up the banking. What his injuries were, were impossible to assess, but what was clear was the fact that he was having difficulty breathing. Maybe ribs were fractured. Maybe a lung was punctured.

A paramedic ambulance arrived ten minutes later. According to the driver he and his colleague had been in the vicinity at a nearby farm where one of the workers had fallen off a quadbike. Suspecting a fractured skull they had decided to take him to A&E for a check up.

The paramedics checked over the taxi driver, decided that he too should go to A&E and strapped him onto the other stretcher, alongside the farm worker. The Ambulance then sped off, blue lights flashing and siren sounding.

This left the tractor driver and me, staring down at the sorry sight of the taxi. What to do next and what to say, I had no idea. For one of the few instances in my life I was lost for words. Fortunately the driver was clear in hs own mind on both counts.

"First thing to do is to get you to where you want to be...You're soaked to the skin and will soon be suffering from hypothermia...Climb up beside me and let's get going...Just tell me where to."

As I was about to do so I realised that I hadn't retrieved my saturated overnight bag. This I immediately did for it contained my Holy Square, the very reason why I had made the round journey to the United States.

As I manoeuvred my wet body onto the large bench seat I gasped out: "Er...The Robertshaw smalholding just up the road there...You can't miss it."

"Ah...You're staying with Peter and Angela, are you?...I know them well...In fact Angela painted me a brilliant watercolour of my threesheepdogs...It's got pride of place in our lounge, just above the fireplace."

As we trundled along, the tractor's efficient heater starting to dry me out, I decided to check my Holy Square. As I carefully extracted it from my bag I could see through the glass cover that water had got inside. In fact when I inverted the Square, first making sure that the lid was firmly closed to prevent the pieces of pot from falling out, a considerable amount of water escaped from the Square.

My driver, concentrating on the road ahead, nevertheless stole a quick glance. I half expected that he had seen it before if only on his television. On my earlier appearances at the United Nations the Square had been prominently displayed. But no, his puzzled look told me that he hadn't seen it before. He did however make a good guess: "Looks like some sort of kiddie's game to me...Or a jigsaw puzzle, but the pieces don't interlock...Funny sort of letters though...Not English."

There was no way I could, or indeed wanted to give him a full explanation of what it was and its significance. It would take too long for a start. I therefore went along with his opinion of what the Square was: "You're right, except it's a word game for Greek children...The letters are Greek...You place the pieces in a line and make up words...It's old though...Very old." I failed to mention two thousand years old.

His response surprised me, although maybe it shouldn't have: "You mean like pi?...Pi's a Greek letter, you know."

"You're right...In fact pi's engraved into the centre piece...But how

581

do you know about pi?"

"It's to do with circles...If you divide the circumference by the diameter the answer's three and a bit...That's pi."

He was right, too: "So you were good at maths at school?"

"Not bad...I wanted to go to university, but my dad wanted me to work on the farm and eventually take it over, which I did when he died last year."

I wondered how familiar that story was in the Dales. I suspected a lot.

As our bumpy journey continued I got to thinking. There were several questions that needed answering. First, who was this good Samaritan? I knew that he was good at maths, but I did not know his name. Second, why did the dike suddenly empty? Third, why did the taxi driver grab my bag? And finally, a question that I felt should be asked even though it wasn't really important – what would happen to the taxi?

The tractor driver answered the first two for me: "By the way, I'm Tom...I have a farm up the valley, about a mile from where we're going...I'd passed the dike earlier during the day but did not think itunusually high...On my return from Horton, where I'd been to pick up a bottle of wine for my wife's birthday, I reached a junction in the road...A right turn would take me home and to the family get-together. The obvious choice...A left turn would take me up to the sluicegate...For some unexplainable reason I turned left...On seeing that the water level in the dike had increased considerably, the result of heavy overnight rain, I opened the gate in order to drop the level, otherwise the dike would have overflowed flooding the road...It was a good job I did, too."

I nodded, in total agreement. Had he not done so the taxi driver would have certainly drowned. I couldn't help saying what I knew to be true: "A bit of divine intervention, then?"

"You can say that again," was his terse reply.

What would happen to the taxi was preying on my mind. On our journey to Manchester the driver had told me that he was a 'one man band'. It was therefore essential that it was extracted from the dike as soon as possible so that the damage could be assessed and the repairs carried out. And its removal should be done as quickly as possible otherwise it would be soon stripped of everything that could be removed from it.

My new friend Tom would know the answer so I asked him. His reply was typical of those who lived in these remote areas: "I'll get you home first, ring the wife, telling her that I'll be a bit late and to put my dinner in the oven, then come back and pull the taxi out of the dike…At the same time I'll ring my mate Jim, down at Horton Garage…He'll come up with his breakdown truck and take the taxi back to his garage…It will be safe there."

I now felt a lot happier about the stranded taxi.

The remaining question I think I knew the answer to. The taxi driver had grabbed my bag because he somehow knew that it was something special, or rather it had something special inside it. That 'something', although he had no idea what it was, would keep him alive…And it did, too. Not only had he had the protection of one piece of my Holy Square, he'd had the protection of all thirteen. It didn't matter that they weren't attached to a loop of thin leather around his neck. He'd been remotely in contact with them and that had been sufficient.

As we approached the long drive going up to the Robertshaw residence there was one question that I was dying to ask Tom, so I did: "What do you make of this alien invasion threat…Worried?"

His reply was, I suspected, typical of most people both here in the UK and probably worldwide: "No…Don't believe it…There's no proof for a start…In fact only this morning on television they had one of them astronomers on who said that their equipment, that could pick up a golf ball at a million miles, hadn't been able to pick up any spaceships heading this way…And he should know."

I was so tempted to point out exactly what the position was and that if the invasion succeeded he and his family would either be killed or taken prisoner and used as slaves, but decided against it. He was better off not knowing. In this case 'ignorance was definitely bliss'. Besides, weren't we going defeat the enemy out in space? Of course we were.

Peter and Angela must have seen us coming, through the huge south facing window of the lounge. As I climbed down from the tractor, water still dripping from my trouser bottoms, both were waiting at the open door.

Peter greeted me in his usual flippant way: "What the hell happened to you? …Been swimming in the local beck?"

As it happened, his assessment wasn't far from the truth, apart from the swimming. I suppose I could have crawled the length of the dike, but did not have the time for a recreational swim. My reply therefore stated the bare facts: "The taxi left the road and ended up in a dike…I managed to get out, but the driver was trapped…Fortunately Tom came by and between us managed to open the door and free him, although he was injured."

Angela quickly chipped in: "How did *you* get out?"

"Oh…I managed to lower the window and climb through the gap."

"Good job you're slim…Peter wouldn't have made it…He'd have got stuck."

Peter nudged her playfully, propelling her across the yard, at the same time taking his life into his own hands by saying: "You've some need to talk."

He turned to Tom and me, and said: "Do you know…She's started wearing my jeans…Evidently they fit perfectly."

More nudging took place.

Tom wanted to get off. He had an important job to do down at the dike before going home. As he climbed into the cab he shouted, a big grin across his face: "I'll send you the bill, Pete."

In reply Peter shouted, matching Tom's grin with his own: "And pigs will fly, Tom."

I preferred to thank my good Samaritan in a more traditional way: "I'm most gateful for what you did, Tom…Had you not appeared on the scene when you did I'd have lost my driver."

"Just luck, I suppose," was his response as he started the tractor's engine and rammed it into gear.

But I knew different. My Father's hand was all over the rescue. Tom's decisions to turn left at the junction in order to go up to the sluicegate and open it, and then come down the road to where we were, wasn't luck. It was nothing less than divine intervention. I suppose that my Holy Square had also played its part.

It was now essential that I got out of my wet clothes and took a hot shower. I was intensely cold and the water in the dike had stunk to high heaven. (Sorry , Father, I really must stop speaking in a blasphemous way).

Once dried off I reached into my wardrobe and pulled out a clean pair of jeans and a T-shirt that I'd bought earlier in New York. I looked in the mirror and smiled, for on the front of the shirt it said 'I love God', with the word 'love' replaced by a large red heart. On the back it said 'And he loves me', with another heart replacing the word 'loves'. How appropriate, I thought. There had also been one with the words: 'I love

Jesus…And he loves me', but to have purchased it with the intention of wearing it would have been a bit pretentious, to say the least.

During the evening I described to Peter and Angela how my visit to the UN had gone, not that there was much to describe, for it had all gone smoothly. But I did go on at length about the 'taxi in the dike' incident because it was yet another example of my Father's intervention. If only more people in the world appreciated how much he loved the humans, animals and plants that inhabited their, my and his World.

As I lay in my bed that night I decided to communicate with my Father. It was time to get an update on what the alien force was doing, before I headed down to *Operation Sahara* in the morning.

***

Chapter Fifty Three

The following day mirrored exactly the same pattern as it had two days earlier – a hearty breakfast at an unearthly hour, a long winding journey to Linton-on-Ouse, a flight to North Africa in a Typhoon. The only difference was that I now had my Holy Square with me, still warm, Peter having placed it on top of the warm kiln to dry out over night.

As we came in to land I observed a hive of activity around the spacecrafts standing upright on one of the runways. It was obvious that the final preparations were being made to the Force before it launched into space to engage the enemy and defend planet Earth.

Our landing was smooth and the same jeep, driven by the same driver, picked us up. In no time at all I had changed into the casual clothes I had previously worn which, judging from their pleasant odour, had been washed, dried and ironed. Someone must have thought that it was essential that I did not look like 'a bag o' rags' when addressing those who would soon be defending our planet.

With my Holy Square in hand, safely inside a black leather tablet case that Peter had earlier given me, I entered the conference hall where I'd made my speech just a couple of days earlier. I was immediately impressed with what I saw. Typical of a military gathering those present were in some sort of formation, which I quickly worked out.

In front of me, spaced out equally across the hall, were twelve seated individuals of which four were women. In front of each one was a wooden stand supporting a piece of coloured card roughly half a metre in length and half that size in width. Written in large black letters on each card and arranged in alphabetical order were the names of my twelve disciples.

Alphaeus – Andrew – Bartholomew – James – John – Judas
Labbaeus – Matthew – Peter – Philip – Simon – Thomas
These were the twelve Squadron Leaders.

Behind each seated individual were eight others standing to attention in a perfect line extending backwards. Again there were several women, a sign how the sexes were being treated equally in the coming conflict. This made a total of ninety-six.

Finally, seated centrally a couple of metres in front of this assembly was a man with a sign in front of him with my name on it.

Jesus.

This seated man's position and the card displayed told me that he was in over-all charge of the whole Force. I also recognised him, for he had earlier asked me a question. He was Matt Dawson, a captain in the US Air force. This gave a grand total of ninety-seven pilots, the same as the number of *Gladiators*.

Of course Field Marshall Peter Norton, of the British Army, was there, preening himself as if to say – this is all my own work. I was impressed... Very impressed. In my wildest dreams I hadn't expected this military organisation to do precisely what I'd asked them to do. But they had. My task would now be easy.

The Field Marshall whispered to me: "Are you ready, Mr Nazarene?"

I nodded, indicating that I was, at least as ready as I ever would be.

He shouted, quelling what little conversation there was taking place within the hall: "At ease ladies and gentlemen, (how typically English public school, I thought)...As you can see, Mr Nazarene has again joined us, and he will be presenting each Squadron Leader with a piece of his Holy Square, as he said he would...Let's not forget that in the last twenty-four hours he has crossed the Atlantic twice in order to retrieve it from UN Headquarters."

With all eyes on me I slowly unzipped the top of the case and carefully extracted the Holy Square. As I did so I could sense a feeling of surprise, even disappointment, go round the hall, for the Square was so small – its side length being the distance between the tips of the thumb and little finger of a large spread out hand, barely twenty-two centimetres across.

At that point I panicked, not at the thought of addressing the assembly, but because I had forgotten all about the thin loops needed to secure the thirteen pieces of pot around the necks of the chosen Squadron Leaders. Hopefully the Field Marshall would be able to conjour up something that would do, even if only a ball of string from which pieces could be cut.

I removed the glass cover and immediately got a pleasant surprise. There, laid along the top edge, were what looked like several lengths of thin black cord. They had been obscured by the thick wooden frame that held the clear sheet in place, hence I hadn't spotted them. I suspected that

Angela, after raiding her huge haberdashery box, had put the lengths in place whilst the Holy Square had been drying out overnight...Good for her.

After removing the cords and putting them in my pocket I slightly tilted the Square so that at least those near the front could see the individual pieces of coloured pot. I could not assume that they'd been seen on television on the occasions they'd appeared at the UN.

It was now time to address the assembly, leading up to the distribution of the thirteen pieces of pot, but first I needed to pass on to them the information I had recently received from my Father about the alien invasion force: "Good afternoon ladies and gentlemen...Thank you for allowing me to address you." (To be honest I didn't really mean this because in the circumstances they should have been thanking me).

"I am here for two reasons, one you know already, the other is to inform you of the latest information on the alien force...How I know this is unimportant, sufficient to say that it comes from a reliable source."

I had no intentions of revealing my source at this stage, so I pressed on.

"Over the last two days the whole force – Mothership, Bombers and Fighters, has moved nearer the Earth...In fact at this moment it is stationary 400 000 kilometres away...That's roughly the same distance as the Moon is from the Earth...I am now in a position to tell you that the invasion will commence this coming Saturday...It is now Thursday."

At this news there were noticeable gasps, but there was no point in pussyfooting around. At least what I said next was intended to be of help.

"It is essential that your Force moves, undetected, into position within the next twenty-four hours...At a velocity of 30 000 kilometres per hour, which I understand your crafts are capable of, you can be in postion in just over thirteen hours...I have already told you that you will only be victorious if you use the element of surprise...A sort of ambush as the alien force approaches...Your first strike must wipe out at least eighty percent of the Fighter force, then you can concentrate on the Bombers, and finally the Mothership itself...Take my word for it the pieces of pot that your Squadron Leaders will be wearing will protect you, but only if you don't do something stupid...Your attack has to be carried out with military precision...There will be no place for heroics."

I was now ready to distribute the twelve pieces of pot to the Squadron Leaders, with my piece going to the over-all Leader who I hoped was the best man that the military could produce...a sort of Montgomery or

Eisenhower, even a Rommel. But before I got the chance to proceed, the Field Marshall spoke: Thank you Mr Nazarene…We expected some thought provoking words and we certainly got some …I'm sure that you'll have no objection to answering any questions."

Reluctantly I nodded in the affirmative, although I considered the time that would be spent on a question-and-answer session could be better spent in getting the Force ready for take-off.

When the Field Marshall asked for hands-up only two were raised. I breathed a sigh of relief. Thankfully the session would be short.

The first question came from a woman who I recognised from the previous session. She again introduced herself: "Captain Irena Molotov, Russian Air Force…How do you know that this alien force has moved towards the Earth, when my country's astronomers, using the best detecting equipment in the world, have been unable to even detect its presence, let alone its movements…Perhaps I am being disloyal to my colleagues on this base, but I do feel that you should be aware that there is a growing feeling that the threat, as portrayed by you, is non-existent." She glanced across at the Field Marshall, immediately dropped her eyes to the floor, possibly with guilt, and sat down.

All I could do was be honest with her, and all the others for that matter: "Thank you for your question…In answer, all I can say is that the record will show that all I have predicted in the past has come to pass…And can man really ignore my present warning?" I could add no more. It was all a question of faith. If she and others did not believe me, so be it.

The second question came from another woman, who I did not recognise. She stuttered asking it, maybe thinking that the others present would think it a silly question: "Er…C-Colonel Louise Lamaison, F-French Air Force…Er…According to you the aliens intend to attack on a particular day, that day being Saturday…D-Do you know if this day is in some way s-special?"

As it happened I did, my Father having told me during our evening chat. I decided to pass the information on to the Assembly: "Again, I ask you to believe me… One hundred years ago, the exact day falling on Saturday of this week, the Alpha Centaurians were attacked by a Force from another star system whose planet had also become uninhabitable…The Alpha Centaurians gained a glorious victory, one they have commemorated every year since that time…The hundredth one will therefore be very special…Unfortunately it will also be their last."

The assembly appeared stunned into silence by my answer – how the hell could he possibly know that? – written across many of their faces.

The Field Marshall took advantage in this lull: "Right…I will now ask Mr Nazarene to distribute the pieces of pot from his Square…He will give each recipient a small piece…Please don't drop it…He will also give you a length of black cord that you will thread through the tiny hole, tie the ends securely and place the loop over your head…Simple."

I thought so too, but we were both wrong. The first problem was mine, not theirs. During the hours after my Square had been immersed in the dike the wood sections making up the six pointed star within the Square had slightly swelled, tightening the pieces in. The drying process had helped, but had been far from complete. Fortunately I had anticipated the problem and had with me Peter's special 'extractor' – the rubber sucker.

I knew the order off by heart. It was as follows:

Alphaeus	Andrew	Bartholomew	James
υ	ν	ε	α
John	Judas	Labbaeus	Matthew
α	o	P	τ
Peter	Philip	Simon	Thomas
ν	ε	ρ	o

Jesus

θ-π

The second problem immediately became apparent when I gave the υ piece to the first recipient. He tried to thread the cord through the hole, but failed, the end fraying. The answer was however simple and well tried by all those who had tried to thread a needle.

Sitting directly behind the him was a young woman. Seeing his problem, and his embarrassment, she came to his aid, moistening the end of the cord in her mouth, squeezing it between her finger and thumb, and threading it through the hole. She then knotted the ends and place the loop over his head. Not surprising, she blushed with embarrassment when her colleagues clapped in appreciation.

As I proceeded along the line, distributing the pieces of pot, most recipients had no difficulty carrying out the threading process, and those who did, successfully carried out the solution as demonstrated earlier.

The final piece, my piece, the hexagonal piece that all the others had been in contact with, within the Square, had now to be passed on to a new owner. I presented it to the one who would be in over-all charge of the mission...Matt Dawson of the US Airforce. He was the one who would be responsible for issuing the order to switch off the Force's 'invisibility' mode and open fire on the alien force.

To make sure that he did not end up in an embarrassing position, struggling to thread the cord through the piece's tiny hole, the woman who had come to the aid of the first recipient also did the necessary with his piece. Skilfully, she threaded the cord, knotted it and placed it over his head. She even adjusted it so that it hung centrally on his chest.

At that point I remembered that at my earlier session at *Operation Sahara* I had expressed a personal view on how the Earth's Force should be arranged in space, ready for the attack. The formation I had suggested showed the crafts in a straight line stretching many kilometres across space, the assumption being that the alien force would take up a similar formation. But after speaking to my Father I realised that such a formation would be useless because the aliens had taken up an entirely different arrangement. I had to make the assembly aware of this.

"Following a word with my Father I can now reveal how the alien force is arranged in space...You will then be able to attack it with maximum effect...The Mothership is protected at the front by Fighters arranged in eight concentric circles, moving outwards, of twelve crafts, like the points on a clock face...Directly at the front of the Mothership are four Fighters...This makes a total of a hundred such crafts...Equally spaced along the full length of the Mothership and encircling it are eight circles of twelve Bombers...Directly behind the Mothership are a further four Bombers, making a total of a hundred such crafts...Quite a formidable formation...It is now up to your strategists to work out the best way to attack it."

My final words to the assembly were simple: "Don't forget, ladies and gentlemen, what I said earlier...You will have two advantages over your enemy...the element of surprise, and my Father will be with you every step of the way...But there will be no place for indiscipline on behalf of any individual."

The Field Marshall then rounded the meeting off: "Thanks to Mr Nazarene we now know what we have to do...Let's get out there and do it."

Those assembled rose to their feet and clapped enthusiastically. God (sorry, Father, yet again)…I hoped that it wouldn't all go pear-shaped.

***

Epilogue

Narrator – Peter Robertshaw

Immediately after Jesus's speech and presentation at *Operation Sahara* the world's media were allowed onto the huge base for the first time. Up to that point there had been a blanket of silence over all that had and was now taking place in the centre of the Sahara Desert. Even those who were in charge of the satellites that were passing overhead several times a day, had not been allowed to release the photographs that had been taken of what was going on below.

Of course speculation had been rife, with unauthorised reports and photographs being shown on the many and varied ways used to inform the public at large. But up to that final speech nothing official had been released.

Now the situation had changed, with information being released on a massive scale. It was as if a decision had been made at the highest level to do just that. It appeared that nothing was sacred. Details of the fighting Force were certainly released, even down to the timetable that would be precisely followed.

Of course all this media activity had two effects, one reassuring , one terrifying. Ever since the information that there was an alien invasion force heading for Earth from the Alpha Centauri star system had been revealed by Jesus at the UN the world's population had been split.

Some, mainly those with a religious belief, believed implicitly the message that the Son of God had sent to mankind. So, when photographs of the fleet of spacecraft, standing upright on one of the runways at the Sahara base all ready for take-off, appeared on their television screens, they first felt vindicated in their belief. They then felt reassured that since their God was involved victory would be forthcoming. How did I know this? The answer was simple. Angela and I were amongst the billions who believed. We had all our lives. We felt that we knew exactly how other believers were feeling at that precise moment... confident that all would go well. Victory would be forthcoming.

The non-believers were indeed terrified or at least feeling uneasy at what was now being revealed. Because of their lack of belief in a God and hence in him having a Son who was present amongst them, they never believed the 'alien invasion' message. Now its presence out in space ready to attack, had been revealed, the information coming directly from the high command at *Operation Sahara*, they had to accept the alien presence. Although the word 'terrified' was a bit strong the non-believers, their very existence now being threatened, with a strong possibility that defeat would be followed by slavery of the survivors, were now changing their view. There were now no vociferous outbursts ridiculing the various religions of the world as had been the case ever since Jesus had made his pronouncement. Many were now openly supporting their planet's response to the threat.

What surprised me the most was the level of information that was now being revealed through the media. The military hierarchy in America had never been able to establish if the alien who had crashed in the Arizona Desert had been on a spy mission or not. Had others of the same race succeeded in over-flying the Sahara base, photographing what they saw and listening into its communication systems, then reporting back to the invasion force? We had no idea. At that very moment it could be planning the demise of our defensive force, or was it now an attacking force?

Amazing though it may seem, during the two question-and-answer sessions that Jesus had recently been present at, not one of the questioners had asked him the most obvious of questions - was it just possible that the aliens were aware of the military force that was ready for take-off from Earth and would engage with them in deep space? There seemed to be an almost blind belief that the alien force was totally unaware of what had been taking place on Earth to protect it from invasion. All we could do was hope and pray that this assumption was correct, otherwise our pilots would be in for a very unpleasant surprise when they were within striking distance of the alien force.

Of all the information that had so far been released by *Operation Sahara's* high command the most revealing were details of the formation the *Gladiators* would take up in space. This was after details of how the aliens were protecting their mothership had been revealed.

Jesus had already described the alien force's formation to those present at his second Sahara meeting. It was all set round the mothership that had to be protected at all costs. On his return home I remembered asking him to describe it to me, which he willingly did, As he did so I sketched on a piece of paper how I though it would look. I now studied that sketch.

The view was almost but not quite from the front and showed the mothership at its centre with ninety-six *Fighters* surrounding it in eight concentric circles moving outwards, each circle having twelve *Fighters*. The remaining four *Fighters*, for there were a hundred in total, were at the centre of the first circle, directly in front of mothership.

The *Bombers* were also in circles of twelve, but of the same diameter, the eight circles spread equally along the full length of the Mothership and encircling it. The remaining four *Bombers* were in the same position as the four *Fighters*, but at the rear. The whole formation indicated that any attack, though not anticipated, would come from the front. There was no doubt about it, it was a formidable force.

The information then revealed how our *Gladiators* would be arranged in space as they approached, invisible of course, the alien force. It too would take up the 'concentric circle' formation of eight circles of twelve crafts, with one at the centre of the first circle, giving a total of ninety-seven.

The innermost circle of twelve, moving outwards, would be piloted by the twelve Squadron Leaders wearing their protective pieces of pot, having earlier been distributed by Jesus himself. The pilot in over-all charge of themission, Captain Matt Dawson of the US Air force, who would be wearing Jesus Christ's personal piece, would be in the single craft at the centre of the first circle. He would give the order to switch off the 'invisibility mode' of all ninety-seven crafts, followed immediately by the order to 'FIRE'.

The firing could not of course be random. It would be sheer folly for two to eliminate the same *Fighter* at the same time leaving another unscathed. There had to be a system, and there was, a simple one too.

Before the 'invisibility mode' was de-activated, immediately allowing the *Gladiators* to attack, but also to be seen, they would identify their opposite number in the concentric circle formation and fix it into their weapon's 'lock-on' computer. Once done, the alien *Fighter* wouldhopefully not be able to break free.

Of course all this had to be witnessed. The days were long gone when the public were 'kept in the dark' about what was going on, in case the battle wasn't going well and they became demoralised, something Ibelieve had happened during the First World War. Now all had to be witnessed, the public demanding it, and this meant a reporting team being in position to do exactly that.

As a result of this demand a special craft given the name *Communiqué* had been constructed. It would take up a position that would allow its team to observe the attack and report on it, those reports being instantly beamed back to Earth. There would be ten reporters in all, speaking in languages that would allow their reports to be heard and understood by the maximum number of people. They would view the attack through a large transparent 'window' in the nose of the spacecraft, along with a team of cameramen.

It had already been decided that *Communiqué* would take up a position beyond the outermost circle of *Gladators* and slightly behind it. This would allow those on board to look down and observe the attack on the alien force. Of course *Communiqué* had to be invisible in the same way as all the *Gladiators* were.

The preparation had been meticulously carried out, no stone being left unturned. No expense spared. The very survival of the human race was at stake.

In the final stages only one thing worried the strategists - did the alien force know anything about those preparations? Would they in fact be waiting to ambush our Force instead of the other way round? It was now simply a case of praying and hoping for the best. And just before take-off those prayers were indeed answered.

The evening before the grand take-off was due to take place at 12:00 hours the following day, the time well publicised to ensure that it would be witnessed by as many people as possible, Angela and I were seated in our lounge watching the final preparations at *Operation Sahara*. Jesus was in the kitchen filling up three wine glasses with an excellent red that Angela had purchased earlier in the day. Our intention was to 'toast' the mission and pray for its success, and that is exactly what we did, standing up to do so. Jesus led the toast: "To Operation Sahara."

"To Operation Sahara," were our replies. But one thing had plagued me in the days leading up to this grand event –

did the alien force in fact know that we were coming? They were obviously an advanced race, far more advanced than us. Surely they had the 'know how' to enable them to observe the preparations that had been going on in the middle of the Sahara Desert. Satellite photographs that had only recently been released showed the huge base sticking out like a sore thumb in the middle of nowhere.

As we sat there, eyes focussed on Field Marshall Peter Norton, who was giving a moral boosting speech to those who would soon be taking off on a journey that for some, maybe all, could well be their last, I floated my fears with Jesus: "Is there just a possibility that the alien force know we're coming?"

His reply should have been reassuring, but in a strange way it wasn't, seeming a bit vague, even uncertain: "Oh, I think my Father would have told me had that been the case, and he hasn't…I do however think that we, or rather I, am missing something important…Something that I should be anticipating, but I can't for the life of me think what it is."

It was now getting late and we retired to our beds. Tomorrow would be an eventful day. Life on Earth as we knew it would either continue or come to a shattering end. As I laid there looking at a beam of moonlight that had managed to find its way through a tiny gap in the closed curtains, having kissed Angela good night and wished her 'God Bless', I got to thinking. But only one thought was on my mind. If our force lost the battle in space and the *Bomber* force got through, would Leeds, our nearest large city, be a target, and if so were we sufficiently far away to survive relatively unscathed? Would there just be blast damage, a bit like being hit by a hurricane, or would there be radioactive fall out as well, Hiroshima and Nagasaki springing to mind? Quite honestly, no one knew.

The following morning at precisely seven o'clock Yorkshire Dales time, which just happened to be eight o'clock Mid Sahara time, the first of the *Gladiators* blasted off from its launch pad. The remaining ninety-six then did so at one minute intervals. At precisely twenty-four minutes to ten the runway was clear. The only evidence that they had been there at all was a straight line of scorch marks stretching along the runway's concrete surface.

The Earth's defensive force was on its way to defend the planet and its population, not only human, but also the animal and plant life, for they too would suffer if the bombing started. It was an 'all-or-nothing' mission with no room for any sort of compromise.

Communiqué had launched earlier with its full contingent of reporters, commentators and cameramen, and had already taken up its position in space. As each *Gladiator* rose off its launching pad the cameramen with their superzoom lenses soon picked it up. The pictures were immediately beamed down to selected points on Earth where they were transmitted to the population at large. Of course the commentators were hard at work, describing what they were witnessing in their own inimitable way. This ranged from a purely scientific description with a stream of information about gravitational pull and escape velocity, to flowery descriptions with references to vivid colours against a black background spotted with light from the distant stars that probably had their own planetary systems...even life.

It went without saying that the world's population were glued to their television screens, and Angela, Jesus and I were no exceptions.

"All seems to be going to plan," I said showing only a mild interest. I thought I would have been brimming with uncontrollable enthusiasm, but I felt a strange sadness, certainly a feeling of apprehension.

Angela simply commented about the bravery of the crews of the *Gladiators*, and wondered how their loved ones were feeling.

Jesus sat quietly preferring not to say anything. He looked worried and it was clear to me that something was on his mind. I decided to ask: "Penny for your thoughts, Jesus...You look as if the whole world is pressing down on your shoulders."

At first he remained silent, as if gathering his thoughts before he spoke. He then did so: "I still feel there's something I've overlooked...Something that I should have anticipated...Something that could jeopardise the whole mission...But for the life of me I cannot think what it is."

I knew that there was little I could say to point him in the right direction.

All ninety-seven *Gladiators* were now in position. The view was striking, all eight concentric circles with their twelve crafts perfectly shaped. It showed just how skillful the navigators had been. As the cameras zoomed in it became clear that someone had taken the decision to paint on each squadron the name that had been given to it - the name of one of the twelve disciples of Jesus. The alphabetical order, commencing at one o'clock and going clockwise had been maintained:

<pre>
                    Thomas
            Simon   Alphaeus
        Philip   Andrew
    Peter   Jesus   Bartholomew
        Matthew   James
            Labbaeus   John
                    Judas
</pre>

His own name could also be seen on the single craft in the centre of the innermost circle.

As one of the cameras moved round the inner circle showing the names one at a time, with a commentator saying a few words about each disciple, Jesus suddenly became agitated.

I asked him what was wrong. He simply nodded his head and snapped: "Nothing."

But there obviously was.

Then, without any sort of warning, the screen went black. The lines of communication had for some reason been cut. But they hadn't for when we looked closely we could still see the stars. All became clear when one of the commentators stated: "All ninety-seven Gladiators have now gone into invisibility mode, as has Communiqué...All will now start moving slowly forward, still keeping their tight formation...The alien force is out there somewhere...It's now just a case of finding it...And I can assure you that we, and you, will be there when they eventually meet...Hang onto your seats."

Now,where had I heard that expression before?

The cameras suddenly swung away from the now invisible *Gladiator* formation and pointed in the direction of the Sun. Presumably the necessary light filters had first been put in place for all we could see was an orange disk. One camera swung round to show the commentators putting on protective glasses as if they were about to observe a solar eclipse.

All eyes, both visually and through the cameras, were now focussed on the Sun's disk. At its centre could be seen a black dot, nothing unusual about this, sunspots being a very common feature of the Sun's surface.

One camera zoomed in showing more detail and it immediately became clear to all observers, both on *Communiqué* and on the

Gladiators that the sunspot was a perfect circle in shape – very unusual for a sunspot. They were usually irregular in shape. Increased zooming revealed more detail. The circular dot was in fact made up of many tiny dots arranged in circular patterns.

Everyone knew what they were looking at…It was undoubtedly the alien force. Understandably excitement broke out within *Communiqué*, the commentators getting carried away in much the same way as they did when a goal had been scored in an important game of football. What they and the world at large didn't know and therefore could only guess at, was the feeling of apprehension that must have been going through the minds of the pilots within the confines of all ninety-seven *Gladiators*.

Over the next hour the pattern of dots on the Sun's disk slowly expanded as the distance between the two forces diminished. Eventually a point was reached when the pattern covered the whole disk. It was now possible to see a larger central spot…the Mothership itself.

Once spotted, the man in over-all charge of our mission, Captain Matt Dawson was able to assess the alien force's speed of advancement. It had previously been decided that the optimum distance to engage the enemy was ten kilometres. It didn't sound a lot, but it had been chosen to ensure a maximum 'kill'. Tests previously made on the wreckage of the alien craft that had crashed in the Arizona desert had show that penetration of the fuselage could be achieved at that distance by the newly developed weapons. It had to be assumed that the alien crafts would be made of the same complex material or something very similar.

With the alien formation now rapidly approaching the eleven kilometre mark Captain Dawson shouted through the intercom linking him to all ninety-six *Gladiators* that made up his task force. The agreed countdown began:

"Ten – Nine – Eight – Seven – Six…"

Presumably on 'Zero' two actions would be made by the *Gladiators'* pilots, with only a fraction of a second between them. First the 'invisibility mode' had to be switched off, then the first salvo, which would hopefully wipe out the majority of the *Fighters*, assuming that the target lock-on procedure had been successfully carried out, would be released. The *Bombers* and finally the Mothership itself would then be destroyed.

As all those observing the scene, which of course included us down on Earth, waited for the number 'Five', followed by Four – Three – Two – One – Zero, to be shouted down the intercom by Captain Dawson, eight of the *Gladiators* suddenly became visible, revealing their exact positions. It was the Judas squadron. Why its Leader had 'gone early' was anybody's guess.

Jesus gasped and yelled out: "Betrayed again…Why, Judas…Why?"

It was as if Jesus thought that the Squadron Leader was Judas himself, and maybe he was, reincarnated by the Devil himself.

Immediately the alien *Fighters* opened fire, 'taking out' all eight *Gladiators*. And anticipating the presence of other enemy crafts, they commenced firing randomly into space. The close proximity of other crafts inevitably meant that some would be hit…and they were…ten of them being wiped out instantly. In such circumstances even the pieces of pot from Christ's Holy Square were unable to offer any protection.

But in true military style Captain Dawson held his nerve and continued his countdown – Four – Three – Two – One – Zero. Immediately the remaining *Gladiators* became visible and released their first salvo at the enemy…

THEN ALL HELL LET LOOSE

*****
***
*

www.ingramcontent.com/pod-product-compliance
Lightning Source LLC
Chambersburg PA
CBHW032252020726
47495CB00001B/68